The Castle of the Winds

THE CASTLE OF THE WINDS

Jeanne Montague

St. Martin's Press
New York

ACKNOWLEDGEMENTS
The author and publishers wish to thank
Harper & Row, Publishers Inc, for permission
to quote verses from *Lethe, Flowers of Evil*, by
Charles Baudelaire, translated by George Dillin, © 1962,
and *The Revenant, Flowers of Evil*, by
Charles Baudelaire, translated by George Dillon © 1962

Library of Congress Cataloging in Publication Data

Montague, Jeanne.
    The castle of the winds.

    I. Title.
PR6063.0499C3   1987   823'.914   86-24799
ISBN 0-312-00010-3

First published in Great Britain by Century Hutchinson Ltd.

First U.S. Edition

10 9 8 7 6 5 4 3 2 1

For Dora, with love: a friend is someone with whom you are not afraid to be yourself.

BOOK ONE

Mariana

Come to my arms, cruel and sullen thing;
Indolent beast, come to my arms again,
For I would plunge my fingers in your mane
And be a long time unremembering.

And bury myself in you, and breathe your wild
Perfume remorselessly for one more hour:
And breathe again, as of a ruined flower,
The fragrance of the love you have defiled.

'Lethe', Flowers of Evil
by Charles Baudelaire
translated by George Dillon

CHAPTER 1

Yorkshire, 1816

The small procession of black-clad figures trailed across the horizon towards the grey weatherbeaten church. Incongruous under the blue skies, they were a sombre group, like a flock of crows.

It was high summer, that glorious time of sunshine and abundance. The air hummed with faint, mingled sounds: bird-calls, the whisper of leaves, the rustle of fresh grass caressed by the breeze and, through all and over all, a low, mysterious tone as of a song coming from the heart of the earth itself.

This is not the season for death, thought Mariana Crosby as she walked behind the other mourners. Death is for the autumn, for the winter, not when the tide of summer is at full flood. The pathway led across the cliffs. A hush lay over everything, like a spell. Far below, the sea seemed caught and wrapped in a mantle of heat, its waters spun out to silvery thread, weeds roasting on the rocks. Mariana looked back towards the meadows. A pale reddish glow suffused the grass, buttercups scattered in stars of gold.

Ahead lay the church, set amidst that area of yellowish grass with its monuments and lopsided tombstones. The pall-bearers were already entering through the lychgate, sweating beneath their burden, strong, hard-working farmers who had offered to honour the dead. John Crosby had been gently but firmly dissuaded from doing so. He walked with bowed head, stumbling now and then. A stranger might have been moved, thinking him stupefied by grief, but Mariana's lips curled and she unconsciously held her head a shade higher. Grief? It was not grief that made him stagger. It was drink. The villagers were aware of it, those helpful neighbours who had gathered at the news of Henrietta Crosby's passing. Mariana's cheeks burned, feeling their eyes on her, sympathetic though somewhat uneasy eyes. She had never been truly accepted by them, though she had lived there since a baby.

The azure arch overhead was unbroken by a single cloud, and

the sun poured rays on the voluptuous earth, yet the churchyard seemed chilled by long-forgotten sorrows. The path of uneven flagstones wound towards the door, guarded by dark yews. There was a scar in the soil beneath a twisted cypress tree, a brown-red scar, opened up like a wound. The sexton stood beside it, leaning on his spade. Mariana faltered, then moved on. Soon her mother would lie in that hole, covered by heavy sods.

The breeze bore the heady scent of flowers, ancient stones scorched by the sun, the dry, dusty smell of chalky cliffs. Mariana took her place on the hard wooden pew, seeing yet not seeing the small, plain coffin, hearing but not hearing the rector's voice as he performed the burial service. She was thinking of summer which, outside, was investing everything with beauty and the glory of life. There was no restraint, no hoarding of this universal gift. Each bird that soared, the full-throated thrush, the melodious blackbird, the tireless swallows that dipped and swept above the church roof, each enjoyed the glad freedom of existence. From the stoutest tree to the slender-stemmed marigold, all shared that life. Not so her mother. She would never again lift her face to the sun, walk on the yellow sand, wade in the surf which surged over the pebbles.

Somehow, the service dragged to its mournful close and Mariana was standing at the edge of the newly-dug grave. The coffin had been lowered, and Reverend Grant was mouthing the last few words. A wave of annoyance swept over Mariana as she saw her two sisters clinging to one another and blubbering loudly. Could they not comport themselves with dignity? she thought angrily. Even Papa is quiet, though fidgeting. His eyes were glazed in his ruin of a face. She noted how his hand kept stealing to his coat pocket, then hesitating and dropping once more.

Let him wait till the dead are decently buried. Let the brandy bottle burn into his side. Let him be tortured by the feel and weight of it. Even he was not so debased as to raise it to his lips at the graveside. He had not drunk enough that morning to so far forget himself. Mariana had made quite certain of that. She had locked up every bottle she could find, but was sure that he would have a further, secret store. Though she had ransacked the barn, the piggery, stables and cellar, he was cunning, and that bottle bulging his jacket out of shape had slipped her net. She stared at him icily, daring him to misbehave. He shuffled his feet in the loosened soil, sending a tiny cloud puffing down on to the coffin lid.

He should be there, not her! The drunken sot! What use was he to man or beast? He can see only one thing, forgetting love, pride, duty and self-respect, craving liquor as a babe craves for the breast, thought Mariana. She stepped forward and threw her small bunch of wild flowers to rest with her mother for ever. It was wicked to be so filled with hatred, she who should be praying for her mother's soul, but Mariana could not pray. God was shaped as a man, and her father was a man too. God had not answered her when she had knelt at the sufferer's bedside for hours, watching her agony, unable to help her.

'Went off rather well, don't you think?' Papa was short of breath, shifty-eyed. She could not avoid walking home with him, encased in ice.

He was almost happy, she noticed, hand in his pocket now, fondling his treasure. His face was red, beaded with sweat under his black hat. He had shaved ineptly. There were several nicks on his unhealthy skin, the trace of greyish stubble where the blade had not reached. A pity it had not slipped and cut his throat, she thought savagely. He had been handsome once, but this had long since disappeared – mouth slack, nose veined, eyes bloodshot. His body should have been as well-muscled and hardy as his friends', but it was flabby, out of condition. He had thickened, his waist paunchy.

Mariana did not answer him, though his eyes were eager, filled with that expression of self-pity which sickened her. Like a whipped puppy or a naughty boy who fears a scolding. Mamma lay beneath the earth and he still walked upon it. Why don't you drop dead, surely your heart is pickled in alcohol? she thought, her face masklike.

Her sisters were dawdling in the rear. Their tears had quickly dried. Now they were looking back over their shoulders, smiling and whispering. Ernestine and Annabelle, aged eighteen and nineteen respectively. It was easy to see the reason for their change of mood. Dickon Braithwaite, broad-shouldered, strong as an ox, was a few paces behind them, accompanied by Jamie Robinson, a good-looking young fisherman. Did the girls really want to marry them? Could they set their sights no higher than an endless round of drudgery and childbearing? Mariana had decided long ago that she would break with the chains that bound her. Having witnessed the toll it had taken on her mother, she had vowed never to repeat this pattern. But it was quite useless to argue with Ernestine and Annabelle. They were blinded by the mating instinct, unable to see into the future as she did.

And her brothers? What of them? Mariana felt the responsibility of the family keenly, forced to shoulder it for years. Mamma had never been robust, and, from an early age,

Mariana had protected her. Looking back, it seemed that until the last two years, her mother had always been either pregnant or nursing a new infant. Yet only six children had survived, apart from Mariana. There had been repeated miscarriages and stillbirths. Mariana had dreaded the arrival of Mrs Dobs, the midwife, knowing that she would be forced to listen to her mother's groans from the bedroom, hush the little ones, wait and wait until either there came the squalling of a healthy infant or, even worse, the silence which denoted tragedy.

Whatever happened, whether the baby lived or died, her mother would emerge from the ordeal with her strength drained, an old woman by the time she reached her mid-thirties, gave up the struggle and her life. Two years before, she had been delivered of premature twins. She had never fully recovered. She had been so brave, Mariana recalled with that bitterness which was corroding her soul, still carrying on with the backbreaking work about the farm, but had become so ill that Dr Russell had been called. It had been in the autumn of the previous year, that poignant time of bonfires and first frosts, when the bronze trees submitted to the strong winds blowing from the north, their leaves spinning and whirling, dropping to the ground, covering it with a russet pall. A doctor was an important person in the community, a cut above the rest, almost one of the gentry. He had ridden to their old shabby house on a sturdy chestnut cob, dressed in black, carrying his gold-knobbed cane, symbol of his office. Margery, their only servant and one of the family, had spent the day attempting to tidy up. Certainly, their parents' bedroom had looked neat and clean. Papa had been so overawed that he had had to down several pints of strong ale to brace himself.

Mariana had wanted to die with shame as Dr Russell had been ushered into the room. Her father seemed a disreputable figure compared with the spruce medical man. She had hated the way in which he cringed and bowed, seeing how the doctor's nose had wrinkled at the beery breath blown into his face. She had been thankful that every available crock had been filled with flowers, brightening that stuffy sickroom where, in the canopied bed, her mother lay, small, pathetic, face grey with pain. The doctor had examined her, and then drawn Mariana and John Crosby to one side, his expression grave. In plain language he told them that the patient was suffering from a malignant tumour of the womb. She would not live for many months.

How many times over that gruelling span of time had Mariana prayed for her mother to be released? There was nothing that could be done for her, save increase the strong doses of opium. Mariana had coped somehow, aided by Margery. The additional work of the farm had been her lot, milking in the freezing dawns of winter, humping bales of dried grass for the cattle, going to market in all weathers to sell their meagre goods. Sometimes John roused himself enough to drive her, but she did the haggling, driving a harder bargain than he. For he was content to let the fruits of their labour go for the price of a bottle of gin, but not so Mariana. The farmers grew to respect her, admiring the forthright manner in which she guarded the money. Let John glower and grumble as he might, she would not see that hard-earned cash go into the pockets of inn-keepers. She needed every farthing to feed the family and the animals, to stem off the advances of the bailiffs.

'You're a hard woman, Mariana,' John would complain when, instead of allowing him to enter some cosy 'snug' and drink the profits away, she insisted on paying the bills and stocking up with necessities. 'A hard woman, by God! Not like your poor dear Mamma. A man needs a drink or two after rising at five and driving miles.' Mariana, in her cold anger, ignored him, whether he became violent or maudlin. In no way was she going to condone or support his addiction.

It was a half-mile walk along lanes thick with hawthorn hedges from the cliffs and the tiny port below them to Swinsty Farm. Mariana was so deep in thought that they reached it without her being aware. It was a sixteenth-century farmhouse, set on the side of a small hill, a lonely, inconvenient rambling place, awkward to get at and too far from the road. The garden in front was neglected and overgrown, a riot of flowers that had returned to the wild, consorting with bindweed and nettles. Try as she would to instil a sense of pride in their surroundings in the boys, they had inherited their father's feckless disposition and avoided work. When freed from the village school which they unwillingly attended, they would duck out of duties and go off bird-nesting with a gang of local lads.

Now the old house dozed under the hot sun, looking even shabbier than usual. Clumps of grass grew in the gutterings of the uneven grey slate roof. One or two panes were smashed in the gabled windows. Bees were busy among the endless jungle of foliage, and birds carolled in the gnarled tree, yet a miasma of depression emanated from it, speaking of dilapidation brought about by lack of money, of hardship accepted and endured, of a tenant who was supposed to till the land and keep the place in good repair, but who was powerless to do either,

7

seeking solace for all his problems at the bottom of a bottle.

The front door stood open, a very unusual occurrence, for everyone generally tramped round the back. Margery had hung a laurel wreath upon it, tied with a black ribbon bow. More and more people were trailing through the broken gate, wearing sombre black clothes and sober faces but drawn, as Mariana knew, by the kind of ghoulish curiosity which brings folk to a wake. She experienced a moment of panic. Would there be enough food? By scrimping and saving, she had collected money to ensure that there would be no cause for shame at her mother's funeral feast. The family would go short next week, but no matter. There would be ale, and spirits too. This could not be avoided. It was traditional. With any luck, Papa would imbibe a lot quickly and fall asleep somewhere, out of the way.

The parlour was cold, holding that secretive air of a room which is not used often. Mamma had been proud of her parlour, retreating there sometimes, before she was taken ill, putting aside her worn working clothes, wearing her one pretty dress which she had kept carefully wrapped between sheets of tissue paper in the bride-chest upstairs. Mariana stood on the threshold for a momoent, almost seeing her there, seated on the stool before the harpsichord, her roughened hands still long and tapering, playing the tunes she had loved. She had always looked different then, ladylike, delicate. Now the lid of the instrument was closed.

Margery had been busy. Mrs Dobs had come along to keep an eye on the children, stern with those scallywags, Bob and Tom, indulgent with the little girls, Susan and Margaret. Mamma had loved flowers, and the low-ceilinged room was filled with sweet-smelling blooms. There were two mirrors in wide white frames that made the parlour look bigger, and repeated the ormolu candlesticks under glass shades beside the cheerfully ticking clock. No matter how much debt John Crosby had incurred, Henrietta had never allowed him to sell her few possessions. There was a bookcase full of volumes in worn leather bindings, small tables holding the vases of flowers; a cabinet with a few pieces of fine china, and a tabby cat upon the hearthrug, worshipping a non-existent fire. She stirred as the room became filled with men and women in rustling black clothes, stretched as if she would dislocate every bone in her supple body and stalked out, tail in the air. Mariana knew that her destination would be Mamma's bedroom.

Margery, flustered by so large an assembly, was carrying a

8

tray round, helped by Ernestine and Annabelle who had
sprung to the task with alacrity, simpering and blushing as they
made sure that Dickon and Jamie had their fill of ham
sandwiches. People were conversing in those hushed tones
reserved for such occasions. John was filling mugs from the keg
on the trestle, the dark beer foaming out. It would not be long
before he entirely forgot the reason for the gathering.

'Mariana, my poor child – such a burden for so young a pair
of shoulders, but you're managing most admirably.' She was
being addressed by the rector's wife, a lady of middle years and
smug superiority, who was seated by the window on an upright
chair, a small plate in one beringed hand.

Mariana bridled at her patronizing tone. Mrs Grant was
arrayed in black bombazine and glittering jet, her small, thin-
lipped mouth pursed thoughtfully as she evaluated the contents
of the parlour and noted the poor quality of the china and the
patches in Mariana's mourning dress. Mamma had helped
her to make it five years before, from a remnant purchased at
the market – a dress for attending church on Sundays, a best
dress which had been let down, let out as growth and
development required. The words 'made over', 'make do', and
'hand-me-downs' had been the only sartorial instructions that
Henrietta had bequeathed to her daughters. In the summer,
they ran barefooted as young colts. In winter, stout boots and
clogs were the order of the day. Mrs Grant's manner suggested
that she knew all about this.

The other women were hanging on her every pronounce-
ment. She was 'somebody', married to the Reverend. A person
who occupied herself with 'good works', looking after the
deserving poor, ignoring those who fell from grace (judged by
her bigoted yardstick). Moved by sentiment, she had obviously
decided that the Crosby family were deserving, and she was
graciously prepared to give Mariana her advice. Her 'good
works' gave her the wonderful opportunity of dictating the lives
of those benefiting. Mariana started to move away, but
Mrs Grant refused to be cheated of her moment of pious
charity.

'You may call upon me at any time, my dear,' she said
loudly, aware of her audience. 'The rector and I will be only
too happy, should you need advice on the Christian welfare of
these motherless lambs.' She rolled her eyes theatrically
towards Ernestine and Annabelle, searching for the others, but
Bob and Tom were outside, playing on the swing, and the
younger ones were taking a nap.

'Thank you, Mrs Grant,' Mariana answered, wondering

9

what that lady would say if she dragged her father to the vicarage one night when he was far gone in drink.

'Your dear mother – a sweet person – one might almost have imagined she came from the nobility,' persisted Mrs Grant, encouraged by the murmured responses of the farmers' wives who sat on the edges of their chairs, awkwardly balancing their plates and glasses of sherry. 'Am I correct in thinking she was French?'

'Yes.' Mariana nodded, resenting that probing glance.

'A person of culture, was she not? I always thought her a trifle out of place in the farming community here.' Mrs Grant was digging, relishing this chance to wrest secrets from the bereaved. 'Not that she didn't carry out her duties to the letter – I'm casting no aspersions, but have sometimes wondered how she came to be amongst us. Do you know, Mariana?'

'No.' Mariana had never been told her mother's history, but had she known she would not have satisfied Mrs Grant's curiosity.

This unpleasant cross-questioning ceased abruptly. There was a bustle at the door and a murmur rippled round the room. Mariana, conscious of the heightened interest, turned to look. The rector appeared, and even his wife stopped talking, gazing upon him proudly. Everything about him was ample, from the waves of hair that rose in a crest on his broad brow, to the curve of his high nose and the fullness of his chin. His chest swelled under the snowy ruffles of his shirt to that fine display of black broadcloth where dangled the gold watch which methodically marked the flight of his self-satisfied moments. He smiled benignly, the bearer of important tidings.

'John Crosby,' he proclaimed in that rich, fruity voice which could as well have filled a theatre's auditorium as the nave of a church. 'You are honoured this day. Lord St Jules has come to offer his condolences on your great loss.'

A tall man walked through the door, and even in that first glimpse of him against the light, Mariana received an instant impression of dignity and an almost regal indifference. He was over six foot tall and slimly built, his face autocratic, with finely drawn features. His hair was flaxen, winged with silver at the temples, and he wore an impeccably tailored dark suit, the trousers strapped under shining black boots. Following the smirking churchman, and ignoring the gaping crowd, he came straight to John and Mariana with his hand outstretched cordially.

'Mr Crosby, I'm sorry to learn of your wife's passing,' he said.

John put down his mug of ale, wiped his hand on his trousers, and took that of his Lordship. 'Thank you, sir,' he said affably, confidence boosted by the beer. 'You've not met Mariana, have you?'

'No, but we must rectify that omission at once. Miss Crosby,' he bowed slightly from the waist and his lean ascetic face, sombre in repose, broke into a charming smile.

'Such a sad time – "Him who He loveth, He blasteth!"' Grant said stentoriously. '"Aye, even to the third and fourth generation!" You have my heartfelt sympathy, Mariana, and you, John.'

'You will appreciate their sorrow, my Lord,' put in Mrs Grant, who had already lumbered to her feet and dipped him a curtsey. 'Has not your life been blighted by the loss of a dear one?'

'It has indeed, Mrs Grant,' answered Christopher St Jules gravely. 'My wife died three years ago, as you no doubt know. I'm a lonely widower, like yourself, Mr Crosby, except that you're blessed with children.'

'Such a blessing they are, my Lord,' Mrs Grant enthused, feeling herself the cynosure of every eye as she conversed with the man who owned the port, the villages and farmlands for miles around.

'Oh, yes, my Mariana is a good girl – a fine girl. She'll care for us – has done so while my wife was ailing – don't know how I'd have fared without her.' John wiped a tear from his eye and reached for his tankard.

'May I offer you some refreshment, Lord St Jules?' Mariana was mindful of her manners even if her father had forgotten his.

'A small glass of wine, Miss Crosby, if you please.' His eyes held hers fixed and, for a moment, she could not drag them away. His face was pale and his eyes were of a peculiar vivid blue, startling in their intensity.

He is certainly handsome, she thought, bewildered by this development, frantically trying to gather her wits. She turned to the side-table where the wine bottles and glasses stood. Christopher watched her, noting the grace of her body under the dowdy clothes, the charm of her straight nose and pointed chin. He felt nothing but admiration for the lines of her throat, breasts and shoulders. Hers was a figure on the eve of perfection. It held all the beauty of the rose on the day before it should be plucked. Proud, oh yes, she was that, and this pleased him too.

Mariana came back with his wine, and he accepted it with

11

supreme politeness, talked with her father and the rector for a while longer, and then took his leave. The room seemed oddly empty after he had gone, though his tenants were relieved, restrained by his presence.

Mrs Grant sketched in details about him for the benefit of anyone interested. 'Mercy, but isn't he distinguished,' she breathed as the sandwiches were passed around again. 'He lives over in his great house called Thornfalcon, about ten miles from here. Haven't you seen him before, my dear?'

'No,' said Mariana, wondering when the guests intended departing. She was so very tired. It was as if the strain of the distressing sickbed nursing had come upon her with full, brutal force. Waves of weariness washed her, and she longed to be alone.

'Not to be wondered at,' sniffed Mrs Grant, accepting another glass of sherry. 'He leaves this part of his lands to his agent. Spends much time in London, so I hear – or abroad. He was married for several years, but his wife died in childbed. So tragic. He hasn't married again, as yet. Of course, he's very rich, but treats his farmers well, providing them with schools and chapels and bridges, anything they require, in fact. Mr Grant says that he is a devout man, and has given generously to the church funds.'

The shadows were lengthening and the world was bathed in the glow of sunset. Margery came in with a taper to light the candles, and everyone was mellowing, particularly John and his cronies, their voices rising as the ale went down. Their wives were giving them apprehensive glances and talking about going home. It was getting late and the children would be waiting for their suppers. Margery began to gather up the plates and glasses, and Mrs Grant took her husband's arm. Mariana walked with them to the front door, standing there saying goodbye as, couple by couple, her guests left the house, apart from that hard core of unattached males who were still drinking with her father. Ernestine and Annabelle, flushed and bright-eyed, asked if they might walk a little way with Dickon and Jamie. She nodded and watched them swinging down the path, their clear voices ringing through the twilight.

'I'll see to the washing-up, miss,' said Margery, her face swimming before Mariana's eyes in the flickering lamp-light of the kitchen. Margery was a tower of strength, hard-working, devoted. She had been with them for as long as Mariana could remember, scolding, instructing, with no family of her own to care for. 'You go and lie down for a bit. You look so tired.'

'The girls are out with Dickon and Jamie,' she warned,

12

pressing a hand to her aching temples. 'If they don't come back soon – '

'I'll go and drag 'em in,' Margery replied, taking up the big iron kettle from the crane over the fire and pouring from it into the stone sink. 'Don't you fret, miss. The boys are getting ready for bed, and Mrs Dobs has settled the little 'uns for the night. Off with you.'

Mariana did not go directly to her tiny room under the eaves. She had a pilgrimage to make. Her mother's bedchamber was almost dark. Mariana did not light a candle. She had spent so many hours there that she knew the precise positioning of every stick of furniture. The window was open and the scent of the herbs from the border below it was sweet. She gazed up at the great black chasm of the sky, her soul seized with trembling. Was Mamma out there somewhere? Did she now know the mysteries of the universe?

She shivered and drew back from the edge of the pit, that absolute and utter darkness into which her mother had vanished. Standing helplessly by the solid shape of the empty bed, she remembered so much. The long-drawn minutes dropped into the chasm of the past. To this house she had been brought at so early an age that any recollections of other hearth and roof were as vague as those of a dream-world. But vivid were the visions which now came crowding back – memories of childhood, of growing up, of Margery's kind face and wise rule. Of herself rolling on the grass and pulling at the tulip petals, of the child Mariana ranging and roaming in stable and farm, running wild on the cliffs and moorland. Of work too, for the farm was short-handed, Crosby could rarely afford hired help, and of seeing her lovely mother worn down by it till her beauty faded.

Mariana sank to her knees at the bedside, reaching out blindly as if seeking those wasted hands that she had held so often to console the sufferer's pain. The bed was a blank, the pillows laid aside, the blankets folded. It did not tell of those last terrible weeks, when her mother had lain on straw pallets which could be taken outside and burnt. The soft night air gave no hint of the stench of disease and death which had permeated the room, saturating Mariana's clothing so that she could still smell it even when she escaped into the garden. There was nothing left. It was as if Henrietta Crosby had never existed.

Something dark moved on the coverlet. It was Tibby, yawning widely, coming across on stealthy paws to rub her stripy muzzle against Mariana's face. She was sleek, warm, friendly, her deep purr thrumming. Mariana held her against her shoulder, pressed her face into the velvet fur and wept.

She stayed there for a long while, the cat asleep on her lap. She could hear the night-time noises of the house: the boys clattering up to bed, then Ernestine and Annabelle, giggling excitedly as they passed the door, too thrilled by stolen kisses under the dark trees to remember that their mother had been buried that day. Her father's voice rose from the parlour. He was singing, off-key, accompanied by the deeper rumbling of his companions. Later, she heard them staggering out, shouting farewells, and the crash as he slammed the door. He fumbled with the lock, then his heavy, lagging footsteps returned to the parlour. Silence fanned down. Practical issues impinged on Mariana's mind. Had he bolted the door securely? And what of the candles? More than once he had nearly set the house on fire when in his cups.

Outside, mists had risen from the ponds, a damp clammy moisture which would not pass away till dawn filled the eastern void with light. Mariana placed the cat on the bed, fetched a shawl, then went downstairs. A lamp still glowed in the hall and, with habitual thrift, she blew it out. The parlour door was ajar. Her father was slumped in a chair, head sunk on his chest, arms hanging limply, one hand clenched round the neck of a squat bottle. Mariana thought that he slept and went across to remove it. His eyes snapped open, startling her, a big, slack, repulsive-looking man, with grease down the front of his coat.

'Wha' you up to – trying to pinch m' booze, eh?' He was gazing at her, sly-eyed, having difficulty in forming the words, speech slurred. 'You ain't going to do it – not this time, you ain't. It's mine, Goddammit!' He struggled to sit up, clutching the bottle to his chest.

'Give it to me, Papa,' Mariana said firmly, holding out her hand. 'You'll only drop it and make a mess on the carpet.'

'Blast the bleeding carpet!' he snarled, glaring at her from under his thick brows. 'An' blast you too! Don't matter wha' I do in this damn parlour now, do it? She's gone. It's mine, see. I can piss all over the bloody carpet if I want to!'

'You probably will.' Mariana was losing patience. 'Mamma may be dead, but you've not got rid of me. I'll see that standards are maintained. There are the children to think about. D'you want to bring them up in a pig sty?'

'Don't give a toss 'bout nothing no more.' He sank back, screwing up his eyes in an effort to focus. 'She's dead – she's dead.' He was sinking into the morass of self-pity which followed hard on the heels of aggression, possessed of that lunacy brought about by the poison rotting his brain. Tears crawled down his cheeks, those slushy tears which she despised more than his violence.

'If you wish to revere her memory, Father, then I suggest that you go to bed, rise early tomorrow and resolve to look after your sons and daughters as she would have wished.' Mariana knew that he would think she was lecturing him, tormented by his own conscience, yet she had to go on. 'Stop drinking, Papa – please.'

'All men drink – all real men, that is. Would you turn me into some canting hypocrite who can't enjoy a drink wi' his friends?' he growled, staring at her from under his heavy lids. Wha' d'you want me to do? Start going to church? That's what she wanted – I told her when I married her I weren't going to change. I like drinking. Oblivion! Aye, 'tis a grand place to be – in oblivion!'

'You don't have to think then, do you?' Mariana could not keep the edge from her voice, showing him no mercy. 'Being drunk frees you from responsibility. You can behave as badly as you like and excuse it, blaming the drink! You can hurt people, wound them deeply, trample on their most sensitive feelings, and pretend that you only did it because you were drunk!' She stood over him, her face blazing with anger. 'You've brought this family close to ruin. You should have known better. Your father owned this house once. He was the squire. You had the same opportunity but you've squandered it. You lost the farm, the land, the stock. It belongs to someone else now. You made my mother's life a misery – made the children fear you. For what?' She stretched out her arm and pointed at the bottle. 'For *that*! Which means more to you than she did, more than any of us do. Enslaved by it, you've lost everything!'

John braced himself on the arms of the chair and hauled himself to his feet. The unreasoning anger was in him again. 'How dare you! You haughty bitch! I'm head of this family, no matter what you say. I'll do as I bloody please, an' no clever, wordy chit'll gainsay me. How do you think I've felt all these years, married to a woman who didn't love me? She'd stare at me wi' those damned great violet eyes of hers – just like you're doing now – and I'd know she was miles away, thinking of someone else. I'd hold her in my arms at night and, by God, I did hold her, damn her – but she wasn't wi' me – she was wi' him in her thoughts. Bloody stuck-up French whore! Who the hell did she think she was? I wasn't good enough for her, I suppose – but they was glad enough for me to marry her. Oh yes, they offered me money – wanted her settled in England – wanted a father for her brat!'

15

'What d'you mean?' Mariana was used to his ravings, but this was a new excuse he had latched upon.

'Didn't mean nothing – don't take no notice of me, lass – had a bit too much to drink tonight – understandable – just buried my wife,' he mumbled. His heavily-jowled face was red and shiny, and he was staring at her through bleary eyes, grinning fatuously, a dribble of saliva trickling over his stubbly chin.

'Go to bed, Father,' Mariana answered crisply, turning to leave.

His hand shot out, clamping on her arm. 'Ah, if it ain't my lovely little Mariana.' His speech was thicker, and he wavered uncertainly on his feet. 'Wha' a gal you are, to be sure – just like your mother. Don't leave me. I'm a lonely man. I need loving, be damned if I don't. Your Ma didn't love me – never loved me – I've been waiting m' chance to get back at her for years and years.' He stopped, losing track of his thoughts, gazing at her stupidly.

He looked unwholesome and ridiculous, his clothes awry, his hair plastered to his sweating forehead. There was no compassion in Mariana, only contempt for this corpulent man, a bully, a coward, only confident when he had been drinking, unable to face himself and what he had become.

'I'm tired, Papa,' she said, trying to push past him.

'No, don't go yet, precious – stay an' have a drink wi' me.' He thrust forward the brandy bottle which he had been swinging in one hand. 'You're a lovely lass – wi' that dark hair an' all.'

She shook her head, trying to wrest her arm free, but he held on tightly. There was a queer look on his face. He was grinning, his jowls quivering, and his eyes were hot and intense. 'I've got to go,' she repeated.

He dropped the bottle which rolled away into a corner. He pulled her closer. He was breathing hard, muttering hoarsely: 'Mariana – you'll be kind to me, an' not say nothing to nobody, won't you? A fellow gets lonely – needs a bit of female company, if you get my drift. I ain't had it from your mother, not for months.'

What was the matter with him? Mariana had never seen him like this. He seemed to be dissolving before her eyes, melting and dripping like a block of lard. He grovelled, almost hopping in his eagerness, like some bloated, poisonous toad. His rank, unwashed odour and sour breath disgusted her. And that horrible leer, like that of an idiot, but dangerous too.

'Let me be, Father,' she gasped, her hands against his chest, trying to push him away. 'We'll speak of it on the morrow.'

'Stay a minute – only a minute. Do you remember how you used to come into our bed sometimes, when you were little? Thunderstorms frightened you. An' sometimes, when she were asleep an' you cried out, I'd come to your room. D'you remember? I'd lie wi' you an' hold you tight – you didn't mind me then.'

Her mind was flashing back in time – yes, there had been something, but she could not or would not remember what it was. Darkness, thunder rolling, with her quivering in her little bed – then someone there – hands – soothing, then seeking – things happening that she had blanked from her mind. Disbelief flooded through her as she realized the truth, disbelief and a physical sickness that sent the bile into her mouth.

With a tremendous effort, she kept her control, her voice a low, terrible hiss: 'If you don't release me, I'll scream for Margery!'

He rumbled with laughter, his face distorted, almost unrecognizable. 'That slavey? An' what d'you think she'll do, eh? I'd like to step right up an' look her in the eye an' say to her: "Marg, you're a bloody old bitch!"' He had surrendered to his demon completely, holding her with one hand while he fumbled below his belt with the other. 'You'll stay, miss – an' do as I say, for a change. What I wants you to do won't take half a tick, nay, 'deed it won't – I'm good an' ready. Take a look!'

Mariana's eyes followed where he pointed, down past his paunch to where his trousers were unfastened. There she stopped and, in the confusion of the moment, thought that what she saw protruding was a part of his clothing. Then she knew her mistake, and the hot colour rushed up into her face. She averted her eyes with a gasp which pleased him hugely. He chuckled, his breath growing shorter as he passed the tip of his tongue over those wet, drooling lips.

'Father, for God's sake! Fasten up do!' she managed to splutter, dragging at her arm, but he would not let go, pushing her hand down to where he most wanted it. The thought of touching that swollen flesh made her want to gag.

'Come on, girlie, you don't really want me to do that. Not yet – not till we've finished, eh? Touch it – go on! Tell you what, I'll do anything for you if you will. I'll give up drink. I swear it!' His face was contorted as he jerked his body against her thigh.

Horror lent Mariana unexpected strength and she wrenched herself free. 'How dare you?' she cried. 'How can you suggest such a thing, you evil man? I'm your daughter, not some ale-house trollop – your daughter, your own flesh and blood. What you want is horrible – disgusting! You're a loathsome animal – worse than that – animals have dignity. Mother is hardly cold and you think that I'd – My God! You'd lie with your own daughter!'

He was hardly able to stand, sagging against the table, old, wretched, starting to sob, even the tool of his lust drooping. 'Mariana,' he whined. 'You don't understand. You're like her, you see. I've wanted you for years – so pretty – lithe – not worn out with childbearing, like her – '

'Monster!' Every word he uttered damned him even further, and Mariana's voice lashed him like a whip. 'You lusted after me – your child – your daughter!'

The tears were running down his face, and he was groping behind him on the table, searching blindly for the bottle. 'She never loved me – and I adored her. You ain't my daughter. She made me swear never to tell you, but I can't stand it – not you looking at me like that. She already had you when she came to me. My wife, my lovely bride! You was a twelve-month-old. I ain't your father. Oh God – God – she never loved me!' He was sobbing wildly, great tearing sobs that seemed to be dragged from his very guts.

Mariana saw before her a wreck, a shambles of a man, and she felt nothing but an enormous sense of relief. This cringing, weeping hulk had not fathered her. She owed him nothing. Her mother had paid in full for whatever sin she had once committed, some youthful folly which had driven her to take this creature as husband. Sweet Jesus, how she had paid!

She ran for the back door, not stopping till she was out in the starlit purity of the fresh air. She was free. Neither John Crosby nor the children were her kith and kin. His advances would continue to be a menace. There would be many times when they would be alone. Each night she would have to barricade her bedroom door. There was no one she could tell. Who would believe such a story? Everyone thought her to be his child. She would be called a wanton, wicked liar if she told it to Mrs Grant or the rector. She sat on the steps by the door, arms clasped round her body, bleakly accepting that, as she had long suspected, there was no justice or goodness anywhere in the world.

Next day Mariana felt quite different, as if she had been transformed by John Crosby's revelation. Yet nothing else had changed. Margery was the same, the children also, though now

18

Mariana found herself watching them closely. They were Crosbys all right. Except perhaps for Tom, who had a blond fairness that came from neither parent. Ernestine was like her father, stockily-built and sandy-haired, but Annabelle resembled Mariana who had her mother's looks. There was a waywardness about her which was irksome, a flighty longing for the attention of many suitors. She was cruel to them, particularly young Braithwaite who was besotted by her. Not so Ernestine, plain and faithful, adoring Jamie Robinson.

In the days following the funeral, both young men became regular callers at Swinsty Farm. As Mariana had expected, Crosby made no reference to what had taken place between them. He had probably forgotten or, if vague memories stirred, had dismissed them as a drunken dream. But Mariana had not forgotten. The incident was seared into her memory for ever. There was much for her to do now that Mamma was gone. The older girls looked to her for guidance. In many ways life was a little easier without sick-nursing. The fruit was ripe on the bushes and in the orchard. Margery and Mariana laboured in the hot kitchen, bottling and preserving against winter hardship. But one noon she straightened up, pushing her hair back from her face, and looking longingly out of the window towards the sea.

'Oh, I'm sick of being cooped up in here,' she sighed. 'Could you finish the jam? I'll take the little ones down to the beach for an hour or two.'

Margery willingly agreed, hindered by Susan who had her fingers in everything, her round face smeared with gooseberry juice, a danger to herself and everyone else when the preserving pan was bubbling with scalding, sticky liquid. 'You do that, miss. Get that young limb o' Satan out from under my feet.'

Annabelle was swinging across the yard, egg-basket on her hip, and Ernestine had just finished pegging clothes on the line. Mariana included them in the outing. Soon they were taking the cliff path which led to a small, sheltered cove. The adventurous Susan rushed on ahead, and timid Margaret clung to Mariana's hand. The snug little port of Fewston lay on their right, the cottages in its narrow streets packed tightly together, its prosperity dependent on the keel boats and cobles fidgeting at their moorings. Ernestine paused, shading her eyes with her hand, staring out to sea where Jamie might be trawling. The stretch of blue water was empty.

'Come along, Tina,' yelled Susan, jigging impatiently at the top of the worn, rough-hewn steps which led to the cove.

'You're a real slow-poke – slow as a snail. I want to catch some of those tiny green crabs!'

Ernestine frowned crossly, the breeze lifting her straight hair. 'That child's getting too big for her breeches!' she grumbled, then added, her eyes troubled: 'I wonder where Jamie is today. He said he'd be out with the boat.'

'Taken the catch to Thurley Market, I expect,' came the instant reply from Annabelle, who never lost the opportunity to goad her sister. 'Didn't tell you where he was going because he's after one of the serving-maids at the inn.'

'Who says so? You're a lair, Belle!' Ernestine gave her a shove.

'Pr'aps I'm not,' Annabelle retorted. 'You don't know what he gets up to when you're not around, do you?'

'And what of Dickon? How does he spend his free time?' Ernestine shot back.

'With me of course, stupid!'

'Shut up, you two.' Their constant bickering grated on Mariana.

She ran down the steps with the younger children shouting and laughing. This was her haven and, from earliest years, she had gone there when troubled, finding solace in the jagged frowning cliffs where the ocean beat an unending measure of mighty sound. As far as the eye could see, the rockbound coast stretched away, throwing out rugged, towering projections, with cruel fangs meeting the flowing tide. The waters came in under the smile of the summer skies. Mariana watched the dancing wave-crests, and thrilled to the ocean song. Yet she had stood there in winter too, hearing the heavy thunder of roaring surf, battered by the fierce winds that drove it onwards with an intensity of power which was both exciting and frightening.

She left the children by the rock-pools with their shrimping nets, while Ernestine and Annabelle sat on the sand, friends again, talking endlessly about their young men. Mariana did not need company in her discourse with the sea. The sun burned down, and she took off her brown skirt, tucking her white petticoat high above her knees, her bare arms and legs already tanned to honey-gold. She walked on, toes sinking in the dry sand, looking up wonderingly at the fantastic shapes wrought upon the summit of the giant heights, around huge amphitheatres of rock, rising sheer out of the pounding waves. Climbing over some boulders, she came to a cave, where the blue water turned to blackness under the gloom of the jumbled roof.

It was cold there, filled with uncanny dripping sounds which echoed in the emptiness. Mariana returned to her shore-wandering, worshipping the sun which drove away the grim despondency which haunted her. Gulls wheeled overhead, quarrelsome and noisy. The walls of chalk were seamed with ledges where kittiwakes occupied purselike nests, attached to the most unpromising-looking sites. There were guillemots too, perched precariously, and razorbills and puffins guarding their nests in crevices. The colony was rarely quiet and never still. For every bird on a ledge, there seemed to be two in the air, and on the sea were rafts of auks.

Mariana's spirits lifted. She was quite alone, shielded by a curving arc of rocks. A deep pool glinted and she pulled her skirt higher, wading in up to her thighs. The water was transparent, the sunshine rippling through the small molluscs clinging to the sides and pebbled floor. She ran her hand under the water, seeing how the droplets sparkled on her skin, and she was happy, sorrow slipping away. Then a shadow passed between her and the sun, and a voice said:

'Good afternoon, Miss Crosby.'

Sharply recalled from the world of underwater magic, she glanced round. Christopher St Jules stood behind her. He was the last person on earth she had expected to see, though she had thought of him often since their introduction. He was staring down at her with ice-blue eyes as cold as a winter sky. She was immediately conscious of her scruffy appearance, knee-deep in water, her chemise slipping from her shoulders, her hair blown by the salt wind. Whatever must he think of her? She struggled to step out of the pool. He extended a hand. She hesitated for a second, then took it, feeling those long, cool fingers close over hers.

'I'm spending a little time on the beach, with the children,' she blurted out. He gave her a strange sensation, half pleasurable, half shrinking and uncomfortable.

'How very thoughtful of you, but where are they? Playing with the fishes and crabs at the bottom of that pool?' He was smiling, but she found the irony in his tone daunting.

'I left them further off – near the steps.' She stood on the firm wet sand, conscious of his height, his elegance, the way in which his bleached-white hair shone. He was in his shirtsleeves and damask waistcoat, his jacket slung casually over one shoulder, hat under one arm.

'I know,' he said gently. 'I saw you from the cliff-top.'

The knowledge that he had been observing her unseen increased her embarrassment. What right had he to spy on her? Yet beneath her indignation lay a small seed of satisfaction that someone as important as he had considered her worthy of attention. She thanked her lucky stars that Mamma had been so careful to instil in her good manners and a correct mode of speech.

She carefully pulled her tucked-up skirt from the waistband so that it fell modestly to her ankles. 'Really, my Lord? I thought that you had returned to Thornfalcon.'

She began to walk back the way she had come, and Christopher fell into step with her, his black boots covered with grains of sand, the white trousers he wore displaying the slimness of his legs. He seemed perfectly at ease, as if escorting a farmer's daughter was the most natural of occupations.

'I've been staying at the Three Feathers, a pleasant enough hostelry down on the quay,' he informed her politely.

'You're a stranger in these parts, sir.' Mariana was mindful of her mother's words, having been taught to show an interest, though not too much, in the affairs of others. All the while, her mind was turning over the question: What can he want with me?

'Not a stranger, Miss Crosby.' He gave her a sidelong glance from those piercingly clear eyes. 'Admittedly, I've been absent over the past years, but as a boy I knew the place well. How else d'you imagine that I crept up on you? Did you hear me? Did you see me? No, you didn't, and this is because I used a pathway through a cave from the cliff. I'll wager that you didn't know of its existence.'

Her eyes challenged him. The proud tilt of her head delighted him. She was like a tawny-skinned water nymph. He liked the independent way in which she strode along, a strong, fearless girl.

'Indeed, I did know of it, sir, but had forgotten,' she said. 'There's hardly a corner of this beach that isn't familiar to me.'

She's every bit as lovely as I'd been led to believe, he thought. Aloud, he said, bringing his considerable charm into play: 'I gather that you run the farm, Miss Crosby. Word has reached me of your skill in marketing your produce. This is highly commendable in one so young and, if you'll forgive me, so beautiful.'

Mariana blushed. Praise was a most rare commodity in her life. She never expected it, doing what had to be done without thinking about it. In spite of a certain cynicism which warned her against flattery, his compliment pleased her. He was a gentleman, intelligent and cultured, and he was treating her in a frank fashion that appealed to her. She fell to discussing

22

livestock and arable products, delighted to find that he was as knowledgeable as his agent. Only when he mentioned John Crosby, with that slight hesitation which told her more plainly than words that he knew of his failing, did a cloud darken her eyes.

Her sisters were in the shade near a cave-mouth, the younger ones poking about between the rocks. Ernestine, propped up on her elbow, looked across, her face registering amazement when she saw who was with Mariana. With one accord, she and Christopher slowed pace, both reluctant to end their discussion.

He turned to her, the wind ruffling his hair, his lean face pale and fine-boned, his compelling eyes filled with admiration, as he said seriously: 'Miss Crosby, please send word to me should you need any help. You may think me a light-minded nobleman, but I can assure you that I take my duties very seriously indeed. True, I've not been at Thornfalcon as much as I would have liked. There's been business in London and abroad which has taken me from home, unfortunately.' He gave a sigh, accompanied by a rueful, intimate little smile. 'I hope to be there more often in the future. If you can make use of any advice, don't hesitate to ask me. I'd like to see the farm flourish.'

Mariana could not stop looking at his mobile, gently smiling lips. A shocking thought flamed through her, making her drop her eyes in confusion. Instead of listening fully to what he had been saying, she had been wondering what it would be like to be kissed by Lord St Jules. Flustered by such a notion, she stammered: 'Thank you, sir, but it isn't our farm.'

His fair brows expressed surprise. 'I was under the impression that it had been in the Crosby family for generations.'

Her voice was bitter as she answered, very low: 'It was. Oh, yes, indeed it was – once. We went through a bad time – the harvests were poor for several years – the cows yielded a low quantity of milk – we needed money desperately.'

'Ah, I see,' he said slowly, and she was ashamed, for she knew that he was aware that Crosby's drinking and gambling had caused their ruin, not crop failure or bad milch-cows. 'Your father sold it.'

'Yes.' To her dismay, Mariana found that she wanted to tell him everything, including the fact that John Crosby was not her father, but she kept silent.

Christopher was swishing his riding-whip against the side of his leg looking, not at her, but at the horizon where a small fleet of fishing-boats bobbed on the gentle swell. 'And who was the purchaser?' he enquired.

'Squire Middleton,' she replied, her tone unconsciously expressing a resentment years old.

'What a pity,' said Christopher musingly.

'I must return to the others.' Mariana looked up at him, wishing that she did not have to leave, but there were cows to be milked and a dozen small chores waiting for her completion before nightfall. A great reluctance possessed her, a discontentment with her lot. How wonderful it would be to turn her back on duty and ride off with Christopher St Jules. Perhaps her real father had been something like him, a man of standing whose horizons far exceeded anything she could even begin to picture. She felt in her bones that he could have been no ordinary, common man. She had broached the subject with Margery, but the old servant had hedged, obviously knowing something but holding her tongue. All that Mariana succeeded in worming out of her was that John Crosby had gone away suddenly, years ago, and had come home months later bringing with him a wife and a small child.

'I'll bid you good-day, Miss Crosby,' said Christopher. 'Perhaps I may be permitted to call on you and your father. Shall we say next Sunday afternoon?'

'We'll be honoured, sir,' she replied, hopes and fears warring within her as he lifted her bare brown hand and bowed over it, before raising it to his lips. Then he strode off the way they had come, leaving her staring after him in the greatest state of confusion she had ever known.

CHAPTER 2

The night was oppressively close and Mariana could not sleep. She rose from bed and knelt down by the low casement. Sheet lightning blasted the garden with blue flashes, and thunder rumbled far off. The land was baked hard and rain desperately needed, but she feared a deluge, lest it beat the corn into a soggy mess before they had finished harvesting. She had spent from dawn till dusk in the fields, working with the men, forming the ripe corn into stooks. Hardy though she was, every muscle in her body ached. That idle afternoon on the sand seemed an age away, but it had been under a week. Tomorrow was Sunday, and the fields would be empty of workers – Sunday, when Christopher St Jules had promised to call.

Would he come? And would she be disappointed if he didn't? She was tossed on a turbulent sea of emotions. He intrigued her, but she was aware of disquiet when she thought about him. Her sisters had been excited, teasing her about her noble suitor, but she had hushed them impatiently, saying nothing about his possible visit. Preoccupation with the harvest had given no one time for idle speculation. Tomorrow was nearly upon her, and it was this thought, more than the sticky heat, that had driven Mariana from her bed.

She was on edge, unable to concentrate on the stormy night with its atmosphere of impending violence. Instead, she kept seeing blue eyes and a gentle smile, and hearing a low, cultured voice. The field-hands had seemed remarkably cloddish in contrast, as dull-witted and resigned as cattle. She despised them nearly as much as she did Crosby. As usual, he had pretended to be as active as the rest, but not much was seen of him after noon, when he retired to the hedge with a cider-jar for company. Yet why, if Lord St Jules fascinated her so much, did she remember him with a sinking feeling, as if something deep inside her was sending out warning signals? she wondered.

Stop worrying, you fool! she told herself sharply, and was about to return and thump her pillow into a more restful shape, when she was arrested by a sound from the garden beneath her window. She held her breath the better to listen. The noise came again, a chilling sound in the darkness. Someone was weeping. A cold finger trailed down her spine as she remembered ghostly tales. Then she pulled herself together, dragged a shawl over her nightgown and went to investigate. The kitchen was even hotter than the upper rooms. Mariana had banked up the fire to prepare the bake-oven for bread dough at first light. She had planned sunday down to the last detail. If Lord St Jules came riding up, he would not find her tousled, up to her ears in chores and unprepared. And if he didn't arrive, she told herself sternly, then I'll be so well ahead that I can enjoy an hour or two of leisure.

In the dampness of the dim garden she found not an apparition but Ernestine, huddled on a wooden bench, crying disconsolately. Mariana sat down beside her and said: 'What's the matter? Why aren't you asleep?'

She had played mother so often to her siblings, used to their quirks of character, and now resigned herself to spending time soothing the distraught girl. 'I couldn't sleep,' sobbed Ernestine, wiping her tears with the hem of her nightdress. 'Belle spreads herself all over the bed – I've only got a miserable bit right on the edge.'

'Shove her over to her own side,' advised Mariana practically. 'Selfish little pig! Don't let her make you cry, she's not worth it. You'll make your eyes all red and puffy.'

Poor Ernestine, homely of features, dumpy of figure, lacking the annoying Annabelle's pert prettiness. Mariana wished she could wave a magic wand and turn her into a raving beauty. Only last Mayday, she had yielded to Ernestine's request that they go to the meadows at dawn so that she might wash her face in dew and cast a spell to make Jamie fall in love with her. She had set her heart on him, and the charm seemed to have worked for a while.

To cheer her, Mariana said something to this effect, but was rewarded with a fresh outbreak of tears. 'Oh, I don't think he really cares for me,' Ernestine wailed. 'The girls are saying that he is courting Milly Pearson.'

'But she's twenty-eight if she's a day, plain as a pike-staff and terribly fat!' declared Mariana, putting an arm about Ernestine's heaving shoulders and drawing her close. 'How can he possibly prefer her to you?'

'I've no dowry.' This sorrowful statement moved Mariana to pity, and anger against Crosby who had not provided his daughters with marriage settlements. 'Milly's father has promised her a handsome dot, and Jamie's ambitious. He's tired of working other men's nets, and wants his own boat.'

Mariana was silent, smoothing Ernestine's thick reddish hair, sadly recognizing that her sister's devotion, honesty and sincerity would be no match for Milly Pearson's money. Not with a go-ahead, cocksure young man like Jamie. He had bold ways and rough good looks, able to talk himself in and out of any situation, something of a rebel, quick to add his word to those of the hotheads who muttered against the landowners. He had wooed Ernestine through the spring and summer, flattered by her open-mouthed admiration, but was now swayed by practical issues.

Annabelle would get by without a dowry. Her lovely face and provocative body were sure passports to a good marriage. Dickon Braithwaite was putty in her hands, and she knew it. He did not need a wife of substance for he stood to inherit his father's farm. Mariana was certain that Annabelle did not love him, and she would lead him a merry dance once the ring was on her finger.

'I wish Mamma was here,' sniffed Ernestine.'

'So do I,' agreed Mariana.

She felt like going to Crosby where he snored on the floor of the parlour, kicking him awake and yelling at him to consider his sons, fair set to become vagabonds, to make provision for the girls. If he started saving now, there would be money for the youngest when they reached marrying age. The boys should be forced to attend school, they were always playing truant. Crosby took but spasmodic interest, sometimes beating them, then ignoring the situation for weeks on end.

'We'll think of something, dear,' she promised, and Ernestine, trusting her, stopped crying. 'You can sleep with me if you like. Things will seem brighter in the morning.'

She wished that she could believe it. It would be dreadful to stand by helplessly, watching Ernestine's disillusionment if she lost Jamie. Other men might present themselves, but Ernestine was a sensitive soul capable of loving only once, and that deeply. She was asleep long before Mariana, warm body curved against her back, while Mariana's mind chased round like a squirrel on a wheel, seeking a solution.

The rain came with daybreak, a torrential, almost tropical rain which fell straight down from iron-grey clouds. Crosby stamped about in a rage, cursing foully, shaking his fist at the sullen skies, but in an hour the wet fields, the tiles of the house, were steaming as the sun broke through. Mariana had not waited to complete her early duties, squelching through the downpour to feed the hens and pigs. The kitchen was fragrant with the smell of new, crusty bread and, after breakfast, Margery gathered up her flock to shepherd them to church. Ernestine was as red-eyed as Mariana had predicted. She wore a martyred look. Her black dress did nothing for her complexion, and Mariana sighed. Jamie would be at the service, Milly Pearson too, no doubt flaunting a fine silk gown and expensive bonnet.

The sermon dragged. There was no sign of Lord St Jules, though Mariana had half hoped he would attend. Vegetable stew had been left simmering on the trivet, and they ate on returning home. Annabelle departed to meet Dickon, and Ernestine was moping upstairs after seeing Jamie leaving the church with the Pearsons who had invited him to Sunday dinner. Mariana made her escape outside.

Under the arches of the stone bridge the river flowed in placid peacefulness. The waters moved so slowly that, apart from the low swish of idly drifting reeds, they hardly seemed to stir. Mariana stood on the centre of the bridge where it converged upwards to the highest point of its hump. It was so restful there. The river imparted a dreamy influence into her mind, dulling the edges of worry and dismay, so that she felt herself drifting down to its bed, where the shadow of the bridge fell darkly over it. Then her eye travelled further to where the surface of the water was no longer transparent but became a mirror, where the blue of the sky, the green reflection of the bulrushes, mingled in liquid beauty.

She willed herself to absorb the scene, not to gaze in the direction of the port from whence he might ride. Not necessarily so, she told herself; his sudden appearance on the beach showed him to be quixotic. He may be watching me at this very moment from some hiding place among the trees. The thought was rather chilling and not too pleasant. He won't come, she kept repeating, and I'll be glad. I shall go home and read to the children before supper. Tomorrow will be another working day and I'll think of him no more. Margery says he's a strange one. She refused to admit, even to herself, that she had steered the conversation in his direction as they worked together. Now she turned over in her head every word that Margery had uttered.

'I've heard tell, that if you're travelling on the stage-coach and look over the high walls of Thornfalcon from your perch on top, you'll be struck by its brooding air,' Margery had said, the wooden spoon scraping at the stew-pot so as not to waste a scrap. 'There's odd stories about the old place. Seems Lord St Jules spends much of his time looking at the stars through a great telescope he's got rigged up on the tower. Don't seem natural, do it? Don't seem right to go star-gazing. 'Tis like spying on God.'

'He lives there alone?' Mariana had been very casual.

'Apart from his foreign valet, and a housekeeper, and of course, a whole host of servants. He had a wife but she died.'

'And no children?' Mariana already knew this, but wanted to prolong the conversation.

'Never a one. I think Lady St Jules gave birth to several but none of them lived.'

The trilling calls of birds sounded in the woods. In the stream a trout poised momentarily, then suddenly darted into deeper water. Into this oasis of peace came Christopher, a black figure on a black steed, riding from the meadows where the cows moved in leisurely fashion. The hooves clattered against the rough paving of the bridge. He reined in when he reached Mariana, and doffed his tall hat. 'Miss Crosby, were you watching for me?' He gave an ironic bow from the saddle.

'No, sir,' she lied, wretchedly aware of her shabby dress, her bare head, her hands and face tanned like a plough-boy's. He'll think me frightful, she panicked.

'Good,' he answered blandly, but he did not believe her. The horse tossed its ebony mane impatiently. He gently calmed it, staring down at her.

She stood in a shaft of light. Her simple gown fluttered and turned to flame at the edges as it undulated round her limbs. The warm breeze stirred the white linen at her throat and lifted strands of dark hair away from her face – her beautiful hair, turned to sombre fire by the sun. She seemed hardly human, radiant, redolent with the promise of life and fertility, at one with the wind and the wildness of nature. Strong, vital, so much apart from Christopher's moods, his melancholy, the strange pathways down which his demon led him, as desirable as the stars which dazzled him during the night-watches. He laughed at himself for such romantic nonsense. She was not a disembodied sprite, but a real woman, made up of flesh and blood and passion, of greed and vanity and selfishness, like any other mortal.

'Shall we ride to the farm?' he said at length. 'Come, you shall sit before me.'

To have refused would have appeared churlish, but her heart was thumping and she wanted to run. She watched him dismount with fluid grace, then felt his hands at her waist as he lifted her effortlessly and placed her on the front of the saddle. For all his leanness, he was surprisingly strong. He swung up behind her, bobbed his heels against the animal's withers, his arms lightly clasping Mariana as he held the reins. The horse was tall, and the ground over which they travelled was a long way down. She sat with her knee over the pommel and it was most uncomfortable, the ridge pressing into her thigh, her position such that she had no option but to lean back against Christopher's chest. His breath brushed her cheek, his lips close to her ear, and she caught an elusive smell of scented soap, freshly laundered linen, and a sweet faint odour which she could not place.

She was achingly conscious of his hands on the reins, pale and shapely. A bloodstone flashed points of fire, set in gold on his little finger, a valuable ring which, if transformed into money, would have kept the Crosby family for years. Every feminine instinct in her knew that he was as much aware of her body as she was of his. It would be so easy to persuade him to be generous. Living so close to the earth had taught her the facts of life, and in this she was more fortunate than genteel young ladies who were kept uninformed until they were married. By observing the animals, she had put two and two together and come up with the right answer concerning human propagation.

She also knew that there were certain women in the village who, as Mrs Grant declared, had 'fallen from Grace'. They were unmarried mothers, and it was common gossip that they provided for their fatherless children by selling their bodies, not necessarily for money, but in exchange for bread, meat and fuel.

Mariana thought of Ernestine's much-needed marriage portion, of Crosby's gambling debts and the knife-edge of disaster on which they existed, but when she visualized trafficking her flesh in exchange for relief from these problems, a dark curtain descended over her mind.

As they rode through the gate and into the overgrown garden, she could hear the children shouting and quarrelling in the distance. She asked Christopher to wait for a moment, and ran round to the yard, to find Bob and Tom wrestling in the muck. She dragged them up by their collars and cuffed them soundly, sending them in to wash. To her annoyance, she caught sight of Margery, leaning on the wall and gossiping with Mrs Dobs. She signalled frantically and, with a puzzled expression, Margery answered her call. Mariana explained hurriedly, and Margery hastily retrieved Susan and Margaret from the apple-loft while Mariana went to open the front door to Christopher.

She took him into the parlour. He accurately surmised the reason for her heightened colour. Her innocence amused him, as did the way in which she pretended to be in control of the situation. She was bright, and it would be an interesting experiment to mould this immature mind. She had much to learn. Those hideous clothes would have to go, but her bearing was good, and she had delicate bone-structure and natural dignity. In no time at all she would be moving and acting like an aristocrat under his expert guidance.

'Pray do not put yourself out on my account, Miss Crosby,' he drawled, leaning elegantly against the couch.

'You must think me most unmannerly, but I was not certain that you would come,' she faltered, lowering her lids, but not before she had seen the smile on Christopher's face. Was he laughing at her and this rundown establishment? she wondered unhappily, feeling that she could not bear it if he mocked her, because already she wanted most desperately to impress him. Everything was going wrong, and she prayed for the floor to open and swallow her.

'My dear young lady, when you know me better, you'll realize that I always keep my word,' he replied softly.

She felt shame at doubting him. 'How kind you are,' she said. His gentleness steadied her. She stood motionless, bending forward a little, her face uplifted to his.

His fingers closed on hers in a firm grasp. A curious feeling as if of the realization of a beautiful dream took possession of his senses. The perfume of her hair, of her body, filled his nostrils. The touch of her hands, the subtle freshness of her presence in that cluttered, stuffy little parlour, struck chords in his being which he had thought long silenced. And her eyes! Never had he seen such eyes, long, tilted at the outer corners, veiled by curling black lashes.

'You have lovely eyes, Miss Crosby,' he murmured. 'They remind me of the stars I study at night.'

He had so much in his favour. She was impressed by his manners, the fit and texture of the clothing that clung to his spare, well-knit limbs; the contrast between his almost dandyish costume and his dreamer's countenance was perturbing. He gave the baffling impression of being apart from the world around him. His eyes, like crystals, what did they see as they looked at her so long, so straight? With all his charming courtesy, he had accepted her presence on the bridge, and shown not the smallest interest in her past or present circumstances. This stirred her imagination, and vexed her too. He had been more forthcoming that day on the sand,

and yet it seemed that he knew she would do as he willed, her feelings a matter of complete indifference to the ultimate outcome.

'Why did you come, my Lord?' she asked.

'You know the answer to that, Miss Crosby,' he replied, and the smile which warmed the austerity of his face changed its whole character into something gentle. It went to her heart and lingered there as a sweet memory.

He lifted her hands, and she thought he was about to press them to his lips, then realized his true intention, half-laughing, half-startled, as the kiss of this quiet yet alarming man was laid slowly on her mouth.

'Bravo!' shouted Crosby, leaning against the door-frame. 'She's a lass of rare merit, milord. Her mother was a lady – she won't disgrace you. Pure as gold, she is. A clean girl, a virgin. You'll not get the pox from her.'

Christopher released her hands, and his face was stern as he stared at the corpulent farmer. 'My intentions are honourable,' he said coldly.

Crosby gave him a leering wink. 'Oh, aye – to be sure! A kiss between a man and a maid, particularly a gentleman and a commoner, don't necessarily lead to fornication, do it, sir?' His attempt at sarcasm fell flat.

Christopher laid his hat and crop on the round rosewood table. Mariana liked the way he looked at Crosby as if he were some particularly unpleasant species of reptile. 'In my saddle-bag are several bottles of fine wine, Crosby. I'd like your opinion of them.'

'Wine, d'you say? From your own cellars? There's magnanimous of you, to be sure. You honour my humble house. Mariana, be a good lass and cut along and fetch them, will you? His Lordship and me'll enjoy a tot together, won't we, sir? I've always said, treat all men equal, whether they be dressed in velvet or sheepskin. Ain't that so, milord? Ain't that your policy to the very life? A liberal man! You won't find me putting up with any cheek from the labourers if they speak ill of the gentry. Oh, dear me, no! Someone has to lead, I always tell 'em. We can't all be born leaders, can we?'

Crosby was talking too much, falling over himself in his eagerness to please. Christopher watched him expressionlessly, seated in the wing chair, one leg crossed over the other. As he listened to him becoming even more incoherent, he wondered how anyone could have believed for a moment that this coarse animal had fathered Mariana.

When she returned with the contents of the saddle-bag,

Crosby's face glowed with a kind of frenzied eagerness, his hands trembling as they reached out for the dark green bottles. She took glasses from the cabinet. 'Give them to me, Father,' she said calmly, after he had exclaimed over the labels and fondled the slim dark shape of them.

She could see that he was incapable of pouring, though trying to cloak his drunkenness. 'Ah, what a colour! What a bouquet!' he cried, a foolish grin on his face.

'Don't fill the glasses quite to the top, Miss Crosby,' advised Christopher.

'Quite right. Do as his Lordship says, Mariana.' Crosby could hardly contain himself.

Christopher ignored the interruption. 'Wine should be sipped for the palate to savour its true quality,' he continued, addressing Mariana. 'Will you partake of a glass, Miss Crosby?'

She nodded, painfully embarrassed by Crosby's boorishness. 'Thank you, sir.'

Christopher was holding up his glass, eyeing the gorgeous ruby-red vintage against the light streaming in at the window. 'Drinkable sunshine,' he reflected, smiling faintly. 'It is quite possible that as the vine needs the sun's rays to give it this colour, so man may benefit from this distillation of sun-heat to liberate his potential. What say you, Crosby?'

There was a slur in the way in which he now spoke to him like an underling, but Crosby did not notice, crudely tossing his glass down in a single gulp. He held it out for more. 'Why, yes, milord,' he agreed without understanding the concept. 'How observant. A man after my own heart and inclinations. Mariana thinks that I'm too fond of liquor but, as you so rightly say, it does a power of good.'

He chuckled and threw her a defiant glance, and Mariana was disappointed, half expecting that Christopher might have dissuaded him, but he seemed determined to encourage his weakness. They were entering into some form of camaraderie from which she was excluded, yet not entirely so, for Christopher's eyes were on her, his smile deep, as if to say: I do this for you.

'If you consider this to be an excellent wine, then what would you make of the cellars of Thornfalcon, I wonder?' he asked in his smooth way. 'They stretch under the house, cool and vaulted, the temperature always consistent. There are rack upon rack of wines – some more than a hundred years old. Kegs of beer, casks of brandy, exotic beverages from foreign lands collected by my father and grandfather. Ouzo from

Greece, sherry from Spain, Tokay from Hungary – Riesling, Muscat, Pinot and Chardonnay from the sun-baked vineyards of Rumania and Germany.'

'A paradise, sir, a veritable paradise!' drooled Crosby, his glass empty once more. 'I'd give my eye-teeth simply to gaze on them!'

Something flickered in Christopher's eyes, too fleeting to pinpoint. 'That won't be necessary. A visit can easily be arranged,' he replied, placing his hand lightly over the rim of his glass and shaking his head when Mariana went to fill it again. He leaned forward, elbow resting on his knee. 'It would give me much pleasure to show your daughter my house. I think she'd appreciate some of the treasures in it – the paintings, perchance – the library. Would you like to accompany her? Would next Saturday evening be suitable? I'll send a carriage for you in time for dinner. You may stay the night and I'll have you driven back on Sunday.'

Crosby had given up the struggle of keeping to his feet, sagging on the couch, eyes fixed longingly on the unopened bottle on the table. He wanted to carry it off to a corner where he could drink it undisturbed, willing to agree to anything if only he could be alone with it. Visions of the Thornfalcon wine-vaults floated somewhere in his befuddled brain. He was actually being invited to go there, to taste and sample, to roll rare and potent brews around his mouth and swallow them to sink in pits of fire in his belly, the fumes rising in his blood to blanket thought.

'Happy to do so, milord – ' he mumbled. 'Greatly honoured – the girl and me'll come right gladly. What say you, Mariana? Thank his Lordship nicely, like a good girl. Vast acres of wine, you say? Unbelievable! We had wine-cellars here, long ago – when I was a lad. My father – he kept a goodly stock.'

'Then it is decided.' Christopher was standing, his hat in his hand, so close to Mariana that her heart started to pound.

The light was behind him, framing that handsome head with its curling hair, that upright figure and, above all, those eyes under the winged brows, singularly light and luminous in spite of their deep setting, gazing straight at her, through her, beyond her, the eyes of a seer, a visionary. 'I've requested that you come at night because I want to show you the heavens from my observatory,' he went on. 'D'you know anything about the planets?'

'Only that they're mysterious and wonderful,' she answered, wanting to move but unable to do so under his almost hypnotic stare.

'There's more, much more. I'll teach you, Miss Crosby.' His eyes burned with passionate enthusiasm. 'Life is so short, and we know so little about the secrets of the universe. So much beauty out there, but one is so limited. Science is advancing, yes – but it is frustrating to feel within oneself the intellect, the power to understand that vast creation, and to know the limitations forced upon one by the telescopes available. Yet I continue to try. Every night when I'm there, I gather a little more of that rich harvest.'

He is strange, she thought. A chill went through her – and a premonition. 'Are we meant to understand?' she questioned, moving back a pace, feeling almost smothered by his intensity. 'This is the work of God, isn't it?'

He smiled. The fire in his eyes had faded as they focused again on Mariana. They were less distant, less dreamily absorbed, more human. 'God? And what, my dear, is God?'

This shocked her. She had never met anyone before who dared ask such a question. She may have lost her faith, have doubted, but had never challenged the existence of the Almighty. She shook her head and could not meet his eyes, setting the glasses straight to give her hands something to do. Christopher did not pursue the argument, keeping his peace for the time being. He reassured her by turning the conversation adroitly into more ordinary channels, planning her visit, choosing the right words to fire her imagination. By the time he left, she was tingling with anticipation, willing the time away so that she might see this wonderful house, and be in his company again.

Mariana never forgot her first sight of Thornfalcon. From the shelter of the fine St Jules coach, she stared at the fantastic silhouette which loomed dark against the fiery sunset sky. From the road, it looked like a fortified city, with curious pinnacles and a hundred twisted chimney-pots adorning its turrets. The carriage left the highway, turning in between huge wrought-iron gates where stone griffons kept eternal guard, and along a tortuous drive.

Crosby, snoring in a corner, was jerked into bemused wakefulness by Mariana prodding him and hissing loudly: 'Wake up! We've arrived. Mercy on us, pull your cravat straight! Brush the snuff off your shirt-front! Try to find your manners, if you can.'

She was acutely nervous, though everyone at home had been excited, wishing her well. Margery had helped her to refurbish her black dress, but even so, she knew it looked shoddy and

35

down-at-heel. They had bullied Crosby into shaving carefully and putting on a clean shirt, had sponged and pressed his jacket and breeches, spent time and elbow-grease polishing his scuffed boots, and brushed his hat. As they were to stay, Margery looked out a nightgown which had belonged to Henrietta. It was old-fashioned but made of fine linen, with lace at the collar and cuffs. Crosby had been provided with a robe and tasselled night-cap, but Mariana doubted that he would ever reach a bedroom, falling asleep in the wine-vaults, if he had his way.

The coach stopped at the foot of a flight of stone steps which led to an imposing arched door. The house beetled over them, and Mariana felt a shock run through her. Despite the lights blazing in the many mullioned windows, the impression was one of overpowering gloom. Her eyes sought Christopher, but it was not he who welcomed them. He had left that to his housekeeper.

Mariana mounted the shallow steps, carrying a wicker basket which contained the few things needed. She stopped when she reached the silently observing figure of the woman in black. 'Lord St Jules is expecting us,' Mariana said in tones which would have done justice to a duchess.

'Yes, Miss Crosby,' she replied. 'I am Mrs Brockwell. His Lordship is detained at the moment. Pray come in.'

She had a meek, suave countenance under a spotless cap, well goffered and tied beneath her chin. Her cheeks were fresh and smooth, and her brown, greying hair was braided across her forehead. She was tall, big-boned and angular. Her hands were folded over her apron and near the bunch of keys which hung on a chain from her belt. Anyone more decent, repectable and attuned to her position it would have been impossible to find, yet Mariana was aware of a chill hostility.

Mrs Brockwell did not wait for a reply, but walked ahead into the hall. With a snap of her fingers, she summoned a footman who took Mariana's basket, his impassive face showing no criticism of such a tatty piece of luggage. She waited for Mrs Brockwell's next move, distrusting her purring voice, obsequious smile and flat eyes, thankful that Crosby was struck dumb by the magnificence of their surroundings. Mrs Brockwell suggested that she might like to see her room before dinner. Mariana nodded regally, managing to hide her discomfort. Another liveried lackey took Crosby in the opposite direction and, while glad to see him go, she felt terribly alone.

Up a great marble staircase, along a corridor of such grandeur that Mariana was spellbound, their feet silent on thick carpeting, the dying light augmented by shaded lamps hanging from the panelled walls. Then Mrs Brockwell paused before a door inlaid with marquetry. 'This is the Kingfisher Room,' she announced as she opened it and stood back for Mariana to enter.

With every step she took, Mariana felt herself moving more and more into some unbelievable fairytale. She had never dreamed of such glory, storing up each detail to recount to the children when she returned home. Swinsty Farm seemed very safe and desirable. She had the cowardly urge to scuttle back to it, not knowing how to behave or what would be expected of her.

'His Lordship left a letter for you, miss.' Mrs Brockwell moved easily through the charming room, going to the walnut desk and picking up an envelope which she handed to Mariana. 'I'll leave you now. Should you require anything, please ring the bell.' She indicated a heavy worsted cord hanging near the fireplace. 'Dinner is at half past seven. You will hear the gong.'

Mariana felt better when she had gone, her fingers closing round the letter, while she feasted on her surroundings. She was easing herself into this situation with as much caution as Tibby would have exercised, moving with catlike tread. Firstly, she must see what Christopher had to say. She did not wish to tear the thick, crisp envelope so found a paper-knife on the elegant writing-desk and slit it carefully. The letter bore the St Jules crest and was covered by a black, scrawling script.

'Dear Miss Crosby,' he had written. 'It would give me the greatest pleasure imaginable if you would be kind enough to select a gown from the wardrobe and wear it tonight. The Kingfisher Room belonged to my sister, who is much the same build as yourself. The garments were left by her, and I hope you will find something to your taste. Mrs Brockwell will advise you, should you need her. I look forward to dining with you this evening. I remain, your obedient servant, Christopher St Jules.'

This is a fantasy, surely? thought Mariana. I'll wake in a moment. But the room was very real and extremely beautiful. A young lady's bedchamber, decorated in the hues of the bird after which it was named. Though the evening was balmy, a fire roared in the chimney breast, a score of greedy tongues licking up the drops of sap that oozed, hissing, from the beech logs. Carpeted in blue, hung with blue drapes, the room contained delicate chairs, a large walnut dressing-table set with mirrors, and a bed with barley-sugar posts supporting a tester and blue silk curtains. How Ernestine and Annabelle would love it, Mariana thought, wishing they were there. Although so perfect, the atmosphere was cold, as if it had not been occupied for a long time.

Mariana looked around, from the large windows within a deep recess, to the ceiling representing the sky with large gold stars which had the curious effect of making it appear much higher than it really was. Then she saw the portrait. It was life-size, and of a young woman. She was immediately struck by the resemblance to Christopher. Her next thought was that there was a strange expression in the painted eyes. She could not place it for a moment, and then she realised that it was fear.

But this was the picture of a young and lovely girl. What could she possibly have known of fear? I must be mistaken, thought Mariana as she stood in the centre of the floor gazing earnestly up at the portrait. The rouged lips were smiling, and she was posed in a woodland setting with Thornfalcon in the background. Mariana went closer, on tiptoe so that she could read the small brass plate fixed at the bottom edge of the massive gilded frame. It said: 'Lady Agnes St Jules.' Presumably, this was Christopher's sister, the owner of the Kingfisher Room.

Mariana shivered. She had the eerie feeling that Agnes was watching her. She moved away, but those pale eyes followed her. The tall clock at the end of the room wheezed out seven beats and the strangled sound emphasized the silence. It roused her from the dreamy state which was smothering her mind. Dinner was in half an hour. She must not be late. She opened one of the two large wardrobes. A stale musky perfume spilled out, and Mariana paused in amazement at the multitude of garments hanging there: ball-gowns, morning and afternoon-dresses, cloaks and sumptuous furs, wraps and spencers and delicate night attire. A shelf held a variety of bonnets and hats, gauze-trimmed or feather-loaded, some wreathed with silk flowers. Below were row upon row of footwear: sandals, pumps, buttoned kid boots and those used for riding. The tallboy yielded up further treasures to delight the female heart: gloves, scarves, chemises, fans, bandeaus, reticules, beaded purses. Every article was of the finest quality.

Spoilt for choice, Mariana dithered, pulling out one gown after another. Finally she found the one worn by Agnes when she sat for the portrait. It was of white muslin, flowing to the ground from a high-waisted bodice, a thin, flimsy creation, worn over an equally diaphanous slip. It had a short over-dress of sky-blue satin, bordered by a Greek key pattern in silver. Christopher had been correct in his judgement and it fitted perfectly. She looked at her reflection in the mirror. No, it did not transform her into a second Agnes, her own personality was too strong for that. Agnes was blonde and pale, whereas Mariana glowed with warmth. The blue of the over-dress brought out the colour of her eyes. The whiteness of the gown stressed the honey-gold of her skin. Agnes's shoes pinched, but the sandals, open-toed and thonged round the ankles, were ideal for Mariana's bare feet.

With an eye on the clock whose hands seemed to be moving at an alarming rate, she swiftly swept up her long hair into a bunch of ringlets on the crown of her head, securing it with jewelled combs which she found in a trinket-box. The silver-backed brush bore the initials A. St J. There was no time for more preparation. The sonorous boom of the gong sounded from below. Mariana followed its echo, almost running, holding up the skirt which fell into a short train at the back, hooking the cunningly placed small loop round her little finger. When she reached the hall, a footman guided her to the dining-room.

Crosby was already there, a glass in his hand. He stared at her, goggle-eyed. 'Bloody hell!' he exclaimed, his hand shaking so much that he slopped the wine. 'Just for a minute I thought it was your mother walking in! Gave me quite a turn, damme if it didn't! Whew! If you ain't the spitting image of her, I'll go to sea in a sieve!'

Mariana was sure the manservants were laughing up their sleeves, though they stood at their posts as solemn as judges. The spilt wine was dribbling down Crosby's waistcoat like blood. She took a step nearer, glaring at him over the top of her spread fan.

'For heaven's sake! If you can't stop swearing, then keep your mouth shut!' Tears of mortification rose in her eyes.

'I was trying to be nice to you,' he growled, then he brightened as his eyes rolled around the vast, well-lit room where the long table was set with sparkling cutlery, china and glass. 'What d'you make of this, eh? Mighty fine, I call it!'

'I'm gratified that it's to your liking,' said Christopher from the doorway. He was dressed entirely in black, relieved only by the stock at his throat, and there was a light in his eyes which Mariana found almost overwhelming. 'Miss Crosby – how beautiful you look. That gown becomes you more than it did Agnes.'

She dropped a curtsey, the warm blood mounting to her face. 'The lady in the portrait. I guessed that she was your sister. She lives here no longer? Is married, perhaps?'

He led her to the table where a footman pulled out her chair. 'No, she isn't married,' he replied as he took his place at the head of the board. At a nod from him, another servant poured wine. 'She's of a delicate constitution, I fear, and is recovering from a lengthy illness, away from here in the care of doctors.'

His expression was shuttered and she asked no more questions. Her attention was fully occupied in trying to sort out the bewildering array of knives, forks and spoons ranged on either side of her plate, as course after course was served. She had never seen so much food at one sitting. It seemed wickedly wasteful. Fish dishes, game and poultry, meat and vegetables swimming in spicy, foreign-tasting sauces, followed by fresh fruit and cream, apple-tarts and syllabubs, each accompanied by a different wine. Much of it was taken away untouched. She was too nervous to eat, and Christopher's portions were small. Crosby stuffed himself greedily, then concentrated on drinking.

Christopher was an entertaining host, talking on many subjects, much travelled and well educated. He had spent some time in Greece, joining Lord Byron's party which visited there in 1809. They had been the guests of no less a personage than Ali Pasha, but had also roamed further afield than his palace, exploring ruined cities, seeking the roots of classical literature amidst the broken columns and temples. Relishing the opulent splendour of Ali Pasha's court, they had delighted in decking themselves in Albanian costume, bringing home souvenirs, not the least of which was the gifted, moody Byron's epic poem *Childe Harold*, which had made him the idol of London. Christopher's own memento was his swarthily handsome valet, Spyros.

He called him when dinner was finally finished, and Mariana was astonished at his attire for he had not conformed to English dress, neither did Christopher wish it, liking this reminder of his Greek adventures in the hectic company of Byron and John Cam Hobhouse.

'Our critics called us the "Levant Lunatics",' he told her with a smile. 'Turn round, Spyros. Let Miss Crosby see the full effect!'

The valet wore a white pleated skirt over highly decorated leggings, a striped sash, and heavily embroidered red wool jacket and waistcoat. On his dark curls was set a curious cap, like a loosely wound turban, one fringed end hanging down across his shoulder.

Crosby stared at him through slitted lids, unsure if he was real or an hallucination, but he got up quickly when

40

Christopher ordered Spyros to show him the cellars. 'You'll not wish to go, Miss Crosby,' he said, leaving his chair and taking her hand. 'Let me conduct you on a tour of Thornfalcon.'

Lights were lit in every main room, and they were full of sombre, magnificent grandeur. The servants were not in evidence and Mrs Brockwell did not appear, but Mariana had the impression that they were being watched as they progressed through the drawing-room and Grand Salon, each furnished with carved pieces, rich with gilt, damask and panelling, and unsuspected mirrors which threw back at them sudden, phantomlike images of their own passing countenances. He took her to the ballroom, where the silence and weighted air, the shrouded splendour and faded brilliance made doubly gloomy a space designed for laughter and music.

Christopher seemed oblivious to the atmosphere which was oppressing her. It was a part of him and he gloried in it. He was St Jules of Thornfalcon, a law unto himself and proud of it. They mounted the curving central staircase and paced down the Long Gallery, where the candlelight seemed to draw the pale faces of his ancestors from the gloom of their canvas backgrounds. He paused every now and again, to explain this or that. Here was the formidable founder of Thornfalcon, Roderick St Jules, who had gained his fortune by pandering to Henry VIII. Next to him was his son, Morris, one of Queen Elizabeth's privateers. His exploits on the Spanish Main had swelled the family coffers. As Christopher talked, he painted a vivid picture of waving banners and clashing steel, as well as scenes of wily diplomacy and shady dealings.

Not only the men, their wives too – pallid, stiff figures in far-thingales and ruffs, sly-eyed, plump, round-faced. 'That's Lady Agnes.' Christopher pointed one out. 'Don't be fooled by her simpering sweetness. She was known as "Agnes the Poisoner", owing to her habit of slipping a fatal draught into the wine glasses of St Jules enemies. Yes, my sister was named in her honour.'

To honour a murderess? Mariana found this unpleasant, but he was in such an expansive mood that she made no comment, listening as he continued. 'Over there is Lord Peregrine. He was a Restoration rake – slain in a duel in Hyde Park. Now this is an interesting fellow, his brother Joseph, who inherited on his death. Some said that he had had Peregrine killed, rigging the fight. He brought his ill-gotten gains from London during the Great Plague. Oh, yes, he had the good fortune to escape contamination, no doubt intending to squander his wealth on riotous living, but his villainy got winded abroad, and nobody would have anything to do with him. He had to spend the rest of his days alone, trying to wash away the germs of infection. It's said his ghost can be heard feverishly counting the tainted money.'

'How horrible!' Mariana shuddered. 'Have you heard him, sir?'

Christopher's face sobered. 'Perhaps. Who knows the cause of noises in the night?'

They had reached the end of the gallery where, on an easel, stood the last and most recent portrait of a stolid, dowdy woman, seated on a bench with a miniature spaniel on her lap. 'Who is this?' she asked, though something told her the answer.

'My late wife,' Christopher said curtly. 'Sarah Anne. The only thing she ever held in her arms was that damned dog. We had three children, but they died at birth.'

His mood had changed. He had withdrawn into himself. 'I'm sorry.' She laid a hand on his sleeve. He seemed so very lonely, despite his fine house, wealth and an army of servants.

He stared at her, the candles throwing harsh shadows across his face. 'I don't want pity,' he said coldly. 'I'm the last of my line. I had hoped to fill Thornfalcon with healthy sons.'

'You still may,' she soothed, wishing that the darkness would lift from his features. 'There must be many ladies only too willing to accept a proposal from you.'

He made no reply, drawing her into a dimly lit passage, through a low door at the end and up the winding stairs of a tower. When they reached the platform outside his observatory, she tripped and would have fallen had he not caught her in his arms. For a moment he held her close to his chest, strands of her hair blowing across his lips.

'It's cold up here, my dear,' he whispered, and picking up a fur-lined cloak which lay on the wall, he drew the folds together under her chin. With an arm about her shoulders, he led her in.

It was the strangest of places. With the unusual richness of sables wrapping her so snugly, she looked up at the dome with its triangular slit through which a slice of sky appeared, then down to the instruments gleaming with the brightness of brass and silver. She watched Christopher moving about, a shadow within a shadow, until the white flicker from a lamp shone on the pale, grave beauty of his face. She listened to the night's deep silence, to the dry beat of the astronomer's clock, to his voice as he spoke incomprehensible words.

'That chart over there is the mural circle, used for measuring the arcs of the meridian. The instrument below it is called an

42

altazimuth, invented for determining altitude and azimuth, but what I want to show you can only be seen through the equatorial.'

Under his manipulation the great telescope, mounted on an axis, moved smoothly, the domed roof turning with the roll of wheels to reveal a new aspect of the night. Mariana lay on the couch beneath it while he adjusted the pointing of the powerful lens, taking her on a journey into the mysteries of space.

She saw the blackness of an infinity so vast that she could not begin to grasp it, then several points of light, followed by more. Brilliant colours, red, flaming orange, diamond white, sailed slowly across the inky void. 'How wonderful!' she whispered. 'I never dreamed, just looking at the sky, that it contained so much.'

'This is but one of the many wonders I can teach you,' he answered, and she did not know which was the greater joy – the magnificent revelation of the heavens, or that tender tone in his voice. Later they stood on the open platform and still he talked. Some of his words had little meaning, too complicated by far, but as she listened she concentrated her attention upon his face.

'The night sky has become my mistress, Mariana,' he said intently, and she caught her breath at his first, unconscious use of her name. 'And what a mistress! Far more intriguing than most women. She's capricious – sometimes remote and virginal, at others passionate, full-mooned and crimson, pregnant with promise. She can be veiled and indifferent or a stormy, cloud-wracked harpy, screaming with the vengeance of the gods.'

His arm was around her, but his eyes were fixed on the indigo vault above. His passion was frightening, an obsession which filled his soul. In that all-absorbing tendency there lurked madness of a sort. 'Can we go down now, please?' she ventured. 'It really is cold.'

'Indulge me a moment more,' he said vaguely. Then he suddenly pointed. 'Look! The Heavenly Twins and Orion's Belt! And look – over there! Vega the Beautiful.' With the sefishness of the enthusiast, he was oblivious to the fact that the names he was reeling off made no sense to her. But, as he looked starwards, she looked at him.

The wind was blustering. The breath of the north-west had swept the heavens clear before bringing up its own phalanx of cloud. The great woods complained, far below their feet, the noises of moving leaves and branches swelling like the murmur of a mob into one giant sound. Whilst they had remained in the shelter of the observatory she had shared some of his excitement, but once in the open air that sense had died. The stars were chillingly remote. Christopher was remote too, their high priest and worshipper.

Was he a little mad? He was certainly unusual. She thought that he was gradually becoming oblivious of her presence, but feeling her move away, his grip suddenly tightened and those pale eyes glittering against the darkness stared down into her face. 'Mariana, no one comes here with me. I'm jealous of my stars, and will share them only with a precious companion. You are that one. I knew it the moment I saw you. I've brought you here, shown you my kingdom, shared the universe with you. I offer it as a wedding gift.'

'I don't understand,' she gasped, shocked by this arrogant assumption. Had he chosen his words more carefully, been a little less confident, she might have given him an unconditional 'yes'. As it was, her chief reaction was anger tinged with fear. He bewildered her, on the surface the answer to any woman's prayer – handsome, elegant, rich and powerful. She should have been on the heights of demented delight to be selected by such a man – but she wasn't.

'I'm asking you to be my wife.' There was the same alarming intensity about him as when he was speaking about the planets.

Her own strong feelings startled her. She was acting by instinct rather than reason. 'I can't,' she whispered.

A terrible expression hardened his features, and he withdrew his arm so that she stumbled against the parapet. 'No?' He gave a bark of laughter. 'You refuse me?'

'I don't know,' she said, almost pleaded. There was a tigerish ferocity about him, but he stood apart from her, cool and composed.

'You need time to consider, perhaps?' He spoke levelly, then he shrugged. 'Very well, have all the time you want. The end result will be the same.' He crossed his arms over his chest with the gesture of a man who is sufficient unto himself, and returned to contemplating the sky. His reserve was complete, austere.

Mariana stole away and sought the Kingfisher Room, hurrying through the quiet, empty corridors. She could not understand her refusal of Christopher's offer. She had everything to gain and nothing to lose. It was a golden opportunity, yet she could not shake off the feeling of deep sadness, almost of evil portent, as she wondered what would happen to her if she yielded and linked her life with his.

44

CHAPTER 3

Mariana and Christopher were married in the autumn. It was a morning of weeping skies. A delicate rain shroud enveloped the land. Thornfalcon looked desolate enough to be in mourning, the creepers clinging to its towers like sodden widows' weeds. The blurred panes resembled tear-dimmed eyes, and the dripping flag of the St Jules family hung limp and dark.

There had been no time to prepare. Once Mariana had agreed to be his bride, Christopher had taken her away from Swinsty Farm in his waiting carriage. Margery, Ernestine and Annabelle had stood in the drizzle, waving disconsolately, deprived of joyous celebrations. Two of Christopher's servants had dragged Crosby from bed, hustling him into the coach for he would be needed at the ceremony if, by the application of hot black coffee and a bucket of icy water, they could rouse him sufficiently to give his daughter away.

Given away. How apt a term, thought Mariana as she gazed out of the carriage window at the dreary landscape. But in all fairness, she could not lay blame on anyone else, not even Crosby. She wanted this marriage, was infatuated with Christopher, but the conclusion had come with breath-taking speed. She had left Thornfalcon on the Sunday evening after her visit there. He had not come to say goodbye. She had heard nothing from him during the following weeks. It was as if they had never met. Too proud to mention his name, she had become thin and wan, eyes huge in her pinched face, and Margery was alarmed by her lack of apetite.

She worked as never before, driving herself on with relentless nervous energy so that she might drop into her bed exhausted, and think of him no more. A futile hope. Over and over in her mind she relived every moment of their meetings, forgetting the uneasiness which his presence had provoked. Thornfalcon too became infinitely desirable, a fairytale palace which she, driven by pride and wilfulness, had refused. I must have been mad! she chided herself in her misery. She considered writing to him, started several letters but tore them up. She had missed her chance, offended that kind man, thrown his generosity back in his face. It was unforgivable.

Troubles rarely come singly, and Ernestine's unhappiness was added to her own. Jamie Robertson was conspicuous by his absence, and it was rumoured that he was spending his time with Milly Pearson. Crosby was drinking heavily, scowling at Mariana every time he saw her. He had been in his element in the Thornfalcon cellars, guessing that Christopher wanted her, visualising spending the rest of his days amidst fine vintages if she had only played her cards cannily. Give her away? Aye, he would have done so right gladly and without marriage vows, for that privilege.

There had come a further disaster in the bluff, beefy form of Squire Middleton, stumping into the yard one day, demanding the six months' rent owing. Mariana had been appalled, unaware that Crosby had defaulted on the payments. The squire had been adamant – they must either pay or get out. Crosby had made matters worse by becoming belligerent, instead of leaving Mariana to handle the matter tactfully. There had been raised voices, much cursing and an unseemly scuffle during which the squire had measured his length in the mud. He had stormed off in a towering fury, vowing that they would be kicked out by the end of the week.

Then, at the height of the panic, humiliation and despair, Christopher had bowled up in his coach, glittering with varnish, polished leather and brass housings. Like a saviour! An angel with a halo of golden hair. He had chivalrously offered to pay the debts and provide Ernestine and Annabelle with attractive dowries. He even went so far as to suggest that Tom and Bob went to boarding-school, the fees being sent to him for settlement. He had made no conditions, added no provisos, but he did go to Mariana and, before them all, had taken her hands and kissed them. His eyes had burned as they looked down into hers, and there had been no need to ask the question. It was already answered by the expression on her face.

'You'll come with me now,' he had said. 'Everything is in readiness at Thornfalcon.'

'Oh, yes, Christopher – yes. Anything you say,' she had breathed, eyes brimming with adoration.

No time to pack, no time to do more than kiss Margery, then into the coach and away. Crosby sagged in one corner, and Christopher hardly spoke, though his eyes sought her face repeatedly, feverishly bright. Then Thornfalcon loomed out of the greyness. Mrs Brockwell and Spyros were there, taking charge of Crosby, while Mariana waited in the library. She was

46

in a trancelike state, as numb as she had been during those awful weeks when one day followed another with dragging uneventfulness. It was incredible that she had awakened that morning and not realized that it was the day on which she would become Christopher's wife. She still felt that she walked in a dream, but it was a dream of drugged peace. All conflict, all violent emotion, all sense of having to decide her own future drained away. She was being guided, and went willingly.

Dreamy too was the simple ceremony in Thornfalcon's chapel, where a solemnly important Reverend Grant gave their union God's blessing. Rain spattered against the stained-glass windows. The light was dusky, apart from the altar candles. Mariana's heart jumped in sudden terror as she saw the recumbent wooden effigy of a knight lying beneath a carved oak canopy near the aisle. Under it, in stark, shocking whiteness, was the gruesome figure of a skeleton in a shroud. Her voice shook as she whispered the responses, and her hand was icy as Christopher slipped the heavy gold wedding ring on to her finger.

Walking towards the door on his arm, she saw Mrs Brockwell staring at her, a musing smile playing over her narrow lips. The dark-featured valet was there too, and Mrs Grant, puffed up like a pouter-pigeon, pleased beyond words at having been invited to attend this exclusive event. Crosby had performed his part reasonably well, and now stood exchanging platitudes with the rector.

Mrs Grant, satin-covered bosom heaving with emotion, was sheltering under the porch, hoping that there would be a wedding-breakfast, but Christopher had not planned on giving one. 'The coach will take you back to Fewston,' he said crisply. 'Will you see that Crosby is safely delivered to the farm?' The little party stood forlornly, sheltering from the rain, and Christopher was obviously impatient to have them gone. Very soon the carriage appeared through the downpour.

'Goodbye, my dear.' Mrs Grant swept Mariana into a clumsy embrace, already forming the hurried ceremony into a tasty story with which to regale the ladies of her sewing-party, quite carried away by such romantic impetuosity. 'You're a very lucky girl, very lucky indeed! Lord St Jules is a fine man. My goodness, I suppose that I must now address you as Lady St Jules! How very strange, well – so be it.' She lowered her voice, mouth in the region of Mariana's ear. 'Had we been given more warning, I could have spoken to you on the private aspect of marriage, if you know what I mean. My dear child, you mustn't be afraid. Do what your husband wants. We women have to endure. D'you understand me? He seems kind and considerate, and may not trouble you too much in that way. Be stoical, and God may bless you with offspring in due time.'

'Make haste, Mrs Grant.' The rector stood on the path, holding aloft a large black umbrella.

'My God, are they never going?' murmured Christopher. He had not once touched her, but his eyes were devouring. 'I want you to myself.'

The rain swept down in sheets, obliterating the coach as the door was shut. Mariana heard the crack of the whip, the crunching of wet gravel under the wheels, then silence, broken only by the hiss of rain, descended on the porch. Christopher hurried her inside, drew in a harsh breath and jerked her up against him. He kissed her savagely, bruising her lips. It was a crushing, plundering kiss, such as she had never experienced. She knew a moment's fear, then was engulfed in pleasurable sensations as his tongue explored her mouth. He felt her response and chuckled, low in his throat, releasing her suddenly, as if satisfied, for the moment.

'Would you have us consummate our nuptials in front of the altar – maybe, even on it?' he asked with a sardonic smile. 'We can, you know, if that's what you want.'

'Oh, no – ' she faltered, blushing.

'Perhaps you're right.' He shrugged, a tall slim figure in dark blue velvet. 'It's a sorry place for love-making. I know a better for our first mating, though there are many secret spots I'll show you later, stimulating places which will add to our enjoyment.'

She did not fully understand his meaning, so overawed and inexperienced as she was. He took her hand and led her through a door at the back of the chapel which connected with the house. She had assumed that they might eat together, though she had no desire for food. In her innocence, she had expected him to wait until nightfall, but this was not Christopher's intention. He had waited long enough.

Thornfalcon was utterly deserted, a place of hollow, empty corridors and vast echoing galleries. The rainy afternoon gave it a strange, watery light, greenish, translucent, as if they walked on the bottom of the ocean. The observatory tower was a part of Christopher's private apartment, and below it was situated the Master Chamber. It was candle-lit, the sumptuous purple drapes shutting out the day. A room which reminded Mariana of the interior of a church, with paintings and statues and the swirling smoke of incense rising to the fan-vaulted rafters.

'Our room, henceforth, beloved,' whispered Christopher, an intense note in his voice. 'Do you like your bridal-chamber?'

She nodded, but it was not true. She doubted that she would ever feel at home in such a place – not like church at all, on closer inspection, more of a temple. The air was sickly with perfume from the incense smouldering in gilded chafing dishes of strange device and from the flowers – masses of white flowers with trumpet-shaped blossoms, thick, fleshy leaves, and flamboyant orange stamens. She gazed around in chilled wonder. In an alcove with more candles placed before it was the statue of a goddess with bare breasts, from whose trunk sprang four arms which seemed to writhe and beckon.

'Is she not beautiful?' came Christopher's soft, sibilant voice against her ear. 'It is Kali, the Hindu goddess of destruction.'

'Beautiful?' Mariana exclaimed in bewilderment. 'She's hideous!'

'Ah, no. In time, you'll understand, Mariana,' he purred gently, and the candles were reflected as red stars in his eyes. 'Kali is the earth-mother, the harvest bride, but when armed with celestial weapons she becomes Durga, the demon-slayer.' He was caressing her as he talked, his hands moving silkily over her face and throat, but he was looking at Kali.

Mariana's head rested against his chest, eyes half-closed, melting under that sure touch, but: 'Why d'you have such an ugly thing in the bedroom?' she asked.

He laughed and smoothed her hair. 'You're such a child, that's part of your charm. Look at her, Mariana – really look. Let the pagan in you take charge. Forget the clap-trap you've learned in church. See how Kali stands on the prostrate body of Shiva, her husband, grinning with outstretched tongue. Like him, she has a flaming third eye on her forehead. She wears a girdle of severed heads and, like the Egyptian Isis, can hide herself in her long abundant hair. Don't you find her more exciting than pious Christian saints?'

His hand was on her breast. She could feel the heat of it through her bodice, and his lips had found the pulse at the pit of her throat, but his words cut off her response. She was not religious, but what he had just said amounted to blasphemy. She struggled away from him, turning her back on Kali.

'I was brought up in a simple faith, Christopher,' she said stiffly. 'I know nothing about the things of which you speak.'

'I intend to teach you, my little innocent.' There was a thread of mockery running through his voice. He let her escape him for a while, enjoying the game. 'Kali holds a weapon in one of her four hands. Ah, I wish I had that many with which to caress you! In another, she holds the dripping head of a giant, and her two empty ones are raised to bless her worshippers. She blesses us, my Mariana.'

'I'm not sure that I welcome such a blessing,' she replied, her voice low. Her every sense seemed painfully sharpened, and she knew that he was right behind her even before she felt his breath on her hair, his hands on her shoulders.

'Don't scoff, my dear. What does the church know of the mysteries of the ancients? How foolish and vain to dare send missionaries to countries in the east which are steeped in spiritual lore. Kali is another name for Hathor or Sekhet of Egypt – the "Eye of Ra".'

'You're so learned. I can't begin to understand.' She swung round to face him, spreading her hands in a helpless gesture. 'You'll find me stupid and ignorant, but I will try to learn and improve myself so that you'll have no cause to be ashamed of me.'

He was smiling at her indulgently. 'Don't worry, darling. I'll teach you everything I consider you should know. But you'll find me a hard taskmaster.'

'I'll obey you – I'll do anything for you, Christopher.' Even now the use of his name seemed an almost shocking familiarity. 'You've been so good, so kind, and I've so little to offer you.'

'Not so. You're lovely – you're strong and healthy and will give me lusty sons,' he declared.

'I couldn't come to you as a bride should,' she said, glancing down at the shabby black dress. 'I should've worn a wedding gown.'

His eyes were like blue fire. 'You'll never put that on again, and what does it matter for a ritual in the chapel, a rite without form or meaning. You came to me with nothing, but I'll give you everything. Wait here a moment,' he commanded.

He disappeared behind a carved screen and Mariana frowned, intrigued and mystified. She was afraid to move, her eyes darting from the candles, the idols, the strange Egyptian motifs which mingled with those of India, Greece and Turkey. In one corner stood a wooden mummy-case, shaped and painted to represent a female, the arms crossed over the breasts, hands holding a crook and flail, the huge eyes staring out obliquely from beneath an ornate head-dress. Close by, a bronze cobra reared up with an inflated hood, and its eyes were two glittering emeralds. On a carved ebony table, around which carved serpents writhed, was a black basalt figurine of a jackal-headed god.

I've no need to feel such dread, Mariana told herself. What do I know of aristocrats? Christopher collects foreign objects, that's all. He has travelled the world. What could be more natural than that he should bring home souvenirs?

Yet she had an irrational urge to press her back against the wall. Her eyes were drawn to the bed, a massive four-poster ornamented with beaten gold and hung with purple curtains. It reminded her of a catafalque. That was where she would sleep, henceforth. Sleep? With gods and demons guarding her? Would it be possible to sleep? But in the day, she promised herself, I'll draw back the drapes and let the light of the sun stream in here, banishing the gloom.

There was a movement near the screen, and Mariana stared in amazement as Christopher emerged. He was clad in a long white robe with a richly ornamented collar glittering with gems. Wide bracelets flashed on his arms, and his hair was banded by a gold circlet. His eyes were outlined in black, the lids shaded a deep turquoise blue. He carried garments which he spread over the leopard-skin quilt.

'Come, my love,' he said. 'Let me deck you for our bridal-night.'

His hands were upon her, slim white hands, each finger sparkling with a ring of enormous size and value. She stood, speechless, as he unbuttoned her dress, sliding it from her shoulders, letting it drop, a crumpled heap of rusty black, to the mosaic tiled floor. Beneath it she wore a chemise and petticoat. Christopher gravely untied the strings of both, his fingers cool against her warm skin, finding the buttons which closed the front of the cotton chemise, opening it wide. She mastered the urge to fold her arms over her naked breasts.

His luminous, painted eyes took their fill of her, and he sucked in a breath. His hands cupped each breast, his thumbs lightly revolving on the nipples. An exquisite feeling began to course through her, making her arch her spine and close her eyes. She felt his movement, felt his hands leave her, his arm pulling her closer, and then the brush of his hair and the scalding fire of his lips on her flesh. She moaned, writhing against him, but he raised his head and held her away a little.

'Not yet,' he said, his voice husky. She broke free from the whirling darkness of her closed lids, and his eyes came into her field of vision, gorgeously, dazzlingly blue.

Her petticoat followed the rest of her clothing to the floor, and Mariana was naked, no longer either fearing or ashamed, caught in a bewitching spell as he explored and caressed her. Then, with all the delicacy of an artist creating a masterpiece, he took up one of the articles from the bed. It was a skirt of the finest linen, which he draped around her hips, then fastened a wide, jewelled belt sat her waist, the triangular front panel falling almost to her knees. Gems came next. A wide collar like his own, bangles, earrings, necklaces, and on her head a striped cloth, banded by a silver serpent. He was trembling with an odd, suppressed excitement as he took pots of colour and fine brushes from a small gilt casket. After outlining her eyes with khol, he dusted the lids with violet powder and painted her mouth carmine. Satisfied with his creation, he stood her before a mirror.

'See, beloved. You're a goddess now – Hathor incarnate, and I am your high priest. Let us drink, and pray that tonight my seed shall be implanted in your womb. A son shall be born to us.'

A pair of shining goblets stood by the bed, and he lifted them with ritualistic solemnity, handing one to her. The liquid was sweet as honey, but with a slightly bitter undertone. Mariana did not want to drink it, though she dared not disobey. There was something the matter with her eyes. The room began to throb, or perhaps it was her head. She drowsed on her feet, and everything swam, changing sizes, shrinking and enlarging. Christopher's words bounced from the vaulted ceiling, loud and clearly enunciated:

'Many-throned, many-aspected daughter of the gods! To love me is better than all things. Come before me in a single robe, your hair bound by a jewelled head-dress. I who am all pleasure of the innermost senses, desire you. Put on wings, and arouse the coiled serpent flame of splendour within you. Come to me!'

Mariana saw his smiling eyes, his smiling lips, the teeth long – white. The dizzying sensation increased. She tried to take a step forward but felt herself falling. He shone like the sky at dawn, fire-opals flashing in his ears. His head was miles above her, disappearing up into the darkness, then his hand reached down. It seemed to be an hour advancing, growing phantasmally large.

His voice was a small, seductive thing within her head: 'You are the daughter of the sunset, the naked brilliance of the voluptuous night-sky. Sing love-songs to me. Burn sacred perfumes. Bedeck your body with jewels. Your eyes shall glow with desire as you stand, bare and rejoicing, in my secret temple.'

She wanted to say: I'm not an Egyptian goddess – I'm Mariana – but her tongue refused to work. Like her limbs, it was caught and cocooned in an invisible web woven cunningly around her, as in some nightmare when one needs to scream and struggle but is unable to move. Black mist engulfed her.

A tiny pinpoint of light appeared, growing brighter. It seemed to come from the sun, and this was odd because she knew that it was raining. Yes, she could clearly remember standing in the porch, could see Mrs Grant's eager moon-face as she hinted of marital duty and endurance. Then she realized that the glow was coming from an open doorway. She felt the play of cool air on her skin as someone divested her of her clothing. Light as a feather, she floated high, seeming to rise even higher, bumping softly against the ceiling which parted like water to let her through. She hovered over Thornfalcon, looking down on its maze of pinnacles and chimney-pots, thinking how nice it would be if she were a bird. The sky was the colour of sapphires. The earth below looked like black crêpe. Then she was sinking gently down to rest on a crimson cloth. She thought that she was in a church, lying on the altar, and did not know why. It hurt her head to think. No, not a church, a temple perhaps? Black and red predominated, the flaming hues of blood and darkness. Why were the altar boys naked, swinging censers and chanting? And herself? Though her lids were tight shut, she could see, and this convinced her that she was dreaming – she could see the outrageous shock of her bare breasts, coral-tipped, in the glow of the candles.

The priest wore a grotesque animal mask, and he was speaking in a vaguely familiar voice. Where had she heard it? Somewhere – somewhere – She was very hot, dry-mouthed, and the ceiling, with its peculiar designs of demon-heads and symbols, revolved slowly as she lay, flat on her back, unable to stir a muscle. She could not understand a word he was saying. Could it be a mass? Her mother had been a Catholic, but Crosby had forbidden her to follow her faith. She had died unshriven. Surely the angels would forgive and allow her to enter heaven? It would be horrible to spend eternity in limbo.

Ah, she could hear now. Her attention sharpened, faded, collected itself again as that rich, rolling voice spoke Christopher's name, and her own. The words rang out with each laboured beat of her heart.

'Hail, Ashtaroth and Asmodeus, Great Ones of Friendship, I conjure you to accept this sacrifice in return for the favours asked of you – that Christopher shall have and keep the love of Mariana – that she shall bear him a son – that her love for him shall wax and flourish – that she shall look upon no other man's face with desire!'

A mask floated out of nowhere, and Mariana had the absurd longing to laugh because it was such a wonderful imitation of Mrs Brockwell, though the long hair, loosened and flowing round it, made it look much younger, almost attractive. It materialized at the foot of the altar. Two hands came up, holding something out to the priest. Through the rhythmical singing which rose louder and louder, came the crow of a cock. Her mind did a backward flip. Was it morning already? Had dawn broken through the veils of that black night? She would wake in her attic, as a hundred times before. Milking – how weary she was of the daily milking. Sometimes the cows just would not stand still, and her fingers became so sore in cold weather.

The priest held the fluttering cockerel aloft, then with a downward stroke, plunged a knife into its throat. He held it, feebly jerking, head down over the chalice between Mariana's thighs, the bright blood gushing. Dipping in a finger, he trailed it around each of her breasts, with a straight line slicing through her navel, across her pubis and down. It felt warm, sticky, nauseating. Screaming, she was drawn into a vortex, spinning and reeling, dropping into unfathomable blackness.

'Dearest, how are you feeling now? You alarmed me, fainting away like that,' said a gentle, concerned voice.

Softness and warmth. A dim light. Mariana was in bed, but not in the attic as she had expected. She lay in the ostentatious marriage-chamber of Thornfalcon. Christopher was bending over her. His hair was ruffled across his brow, and he was smiling at her with infinite tenderness.

'I fainted? How strange. I can't remember a thing.' She stumbled over the words. Her tongue felt thick, furred. All the time, hammering away somewhere, was a bothersome memory which she could not pull to the surface. 'Poor Christopher. I'm a most disappointing bride.'

He held her hand, bent and kissed it and, with the clasp of his fingers going straight to her heart, she was able to focus on his face, his beautiful face, serene as a saint's. Waking more fully now, all her senses came to life. She knew fear, hesitation, an aching awareness of their closeness and of the hot, waiting sensation gathering like a knot in her loins. But when she moved, pain seared her, a deep smarting soreness accentuated when she struggled into a sitting position. She pulled back the coverlet, staring down. There was blood on the sheets, blood on her breasts, blood between her legs.

Christopher's hand came across, touching her cheek, her

hair. There was a half-apologetic expression in his eyes and he made a rueful grimace. 'I'm sorry, darling, I couldn't wait. You fainted, and I'd waited so long, wanting you most desperately.'

Mariana did not look at him. Instead she was gazing wonderingly at the long bloody scratches covering her arms, her shoulders, her stomach. There were livid bruises too. Slowly comprehension dawned. He had made love to her whilst she was unconscious. A strangely twisted glimmer of recollection made her heart thump – almost clear, then fading away tantalizingly. She tried to shrug off an apprehensive stab of grief. She had lost her virginity without even knowing.

'How can this be?' she whispered.

His lids were lowered. They were smudged with blue. The long lashes, black at the base, gold tipped, cast shadows on his angular cheekbones. 'Can you forgive a bridegroom's impetuosity?'

'There's so much blood,' she ventured, experiencing shame as if she had begun to menstruate, unprepared.

He chuckled, and it jarred her nerves. 'I was pleased. It proved that you came to me untouched. Virgins' blood has long been prized as a sovereign remedy for ills. I could have sold yours by the ounce.'

A cold hand closed round her heart, yet his smile belied the callousness of his words. She made excuses for him in her mind. He was a worldly man, an aristocrat. His ways were not those of the ignorant country-folk amongst whom she had been reared. She must learn his life-style, no matter how unorthodox. Above all, she longed to please him. His touch was consoling, seductive, and his attention shifted to her mouth. His pupils darkened to ebony, smouldering, intense.

A tiny sound, part protest, rose in her throat, but she was incapable of moving, not even turning her head to avoid his lips. His kiss opened her eyes to the passionate core of her being, a passion which she had suspected lay there, had rigorously held in check. But she had never before known a man so well-versed in the art of sensual arousal. She gave up the fight, sure that she was about to glory in defeat. He had cheated her the first time. It would not happen again.

That single kiss ignited the fire smouldering in her. The touch of his hands was so firm and sure that it seemed he had always been caressing her. A curling sensation went all the way through her as his hands roamed freely over her body. She inhaled the warm smell of him. It was like a drug to which she could so easily become addicted. His hands fastened on her waist and shoulders to pull her over him. His mouth sought the valley between her breasts and he was licking off the blood with a detached air of enjoyment, like a dog, an unpleasant action which, for a brief moment, jerked her out of the sensual dream in which she was drifting. Then his tongue was leisurely exploring her nipples, sending shivers down her spine, and her fingers dug into his neck. He lipped her ear-lobes, searching out each feature of her face and subjecting it to his magic.

Mariana forgot everything, trembling, eager, desire swamping her fears as he took his time with her, savouring each moment leading to gratification. 'It was as well, perhaps, that I did what I did, whilst you were unaware,' he murmured at one point. 'I may have hurt you, and I wouldn't like you to shrink from me, ever. This time, there will be but a small moment of discomfort. You'll learn how to enjoy, my sweet. It may take a while, but learn you will – from me.'

She did not fully understand, blind to her body's potential. He was right. Whatever soreness remained within her, was forgotten by the time he possessed her fully. Christopher was clever, knowing how to give her fulfilment before attempting penetration, so that she was still shaking from orgasm, too stunned to notice pain, receiving him willingly, passionately, wanting to give him as much pleasure as he had just lavished on her.

Afterwards, weak and exhausted, she lay in the crook of his arm. She closed her eyes, wanting no words to diminish this experience. Christopher gently wiped the tears from her face and pulled the covers over them. Mariana let herself drift away, on a rainbow cloud that avoided reality. But just before sleep finally claimed her, she was disturbed by a sound outside the windows – subdued voices – someone laughing, the laugh cut short as if warned to stop – wheels turning over cobbles and horses' hooves fading away into the distance.

'What was that?' she started up.

'Hush, darling,' he mumbled sleepily, pulling her down again.

'But I heard something. People – coaches,' she persisted, though now the room seemed to have sprung into a listening silence. There was no sound but the faint hiss of the fire. 'Who has been here?'

He yawned, looking up and smiling – smiling. 'Silly little goose, of course there's been no one here. We're quite alone. You're imagining it.'

She lay against his chest, hearing the steady beat of his heart, the fine texture of his skin beneath her cheek. She accepted that he was right. Christopher always was, her lord and master. Perhaps she had dozed and dreamed the noises, over-excited by the strangeness of it all, the awakening to bodily pleasure, the joy of being his wife. Yet something seemed to cleave through the soothing warmth, his understanding caress, like a chill breeze blowing between them.

As Mariana had hoped, the chamber seemed less awesome by day. Spyros was there promptly at eight o'clock, bearing a tray of tea, going over to the large windows and pulling back the drapes with the cheerful jangle of rings on wooden poles. Christopher was immediately alert, waking on the instant. He sat up, ruffling his hands through his hair, looking appealingly boyish and heart-warmingly normal. He rose when the valet had gone, walking to the window, pulling it open and, leaning on his elbows, looking out at the dewy garden. Then he said, over his shoulder:

'You must have a personal maid. I'll find a suitable girl, but meanwhile, call upon Mrs Brockwell. She'll be delighted to serve you.'

'I can manage, Christopher, truly I can. I'm used to looking after myself,' she answered practically, pulling on a brocade robe which lay over the back of a chair, and pattering across to join him.

He turned, still naked, strong and straight in the early light. His grave lips were lifted in a faint smile. 'You'll do as I say, Mariana. Lady St Jules does not "look after herself", as you put it.'

Mariana paused, a whole new world opening up at her feet. It was hard to think of herself as Lady of the Manor. Even now she was aware that it was shockingly late; she was usually up at five. She wondered if she should go down to the kitchen and supervise the preparation of breakfast. She had a vague notion that it would be her duty to oversee the stillroom, linen-press and marketing, even the welfare of the villagers. She knew so little about Christopher's expectations of her responsibilities. Though they had shared the deepest intimacy in bed, he remained an enigma.

With his uncanny knack of reading thoughts, he said in that mocking way that never quite lost touch with melancholy: 'I have a most efficient housekeeper. She'll not thank you for interfering.'

'I wouldn't dream of offending her,' she answered hastily, baffled by his remoteness, wondering uneasily if she had unwittingly upset him. Her eyes burned with tears. A hot tide of love, an inexplicable mixture of feelings rushed to her lips, and she gripped his bare arm fiercely. 'Oh, Christopher, I'm so uneducated. You must help me behave in the correct manner, as befits your wife.'

'Dearest child,' he murmured, drawing her to him. 'I'll spend my days instructing you. Remain simple and delightful. Just to gaze on your beauty is balm to my soul – unsullied – incorruptible. I'm far older than you – have seen much – experienced much. I had accepted that happiness was for other men, not for me.'

'But why? You were happy once, with your wife, weren't you? You can be happy again. I'll make you happy. I swear it, Christopher! This house should never have been empty for so long. Why did you go away from it? You could have married again ere this. There should have been children here. What have you done with your life?'

The tears brimmed over and ran down her cheeks. Then her strange passion fell from her, and she was ashamed at daring to speak to him so boldly. She did not know how she had come to the conclusion that, in some way, he had wasted his youth, despite his travels, despite his knowledge. He lived in a dream-world, divorced from reality, and she instinctively recognized it.

He frowned and put up a hand as if to thrust her words away. There was a long silence. When he broke it, he spoke with cold control, unwilling to admit to emotion. 'I had thought peace and love were denied me – until I met you.'

'Forget the lonely years,' she begged, reaching out blindly for his hand. 'I'm here now. I'll always be with you. I love you, Christopher. The house shall ring with light and laughter. We'll entertain if you wish, though I'd be quite content to be alone with you. And, if God wills, we'll have children.'

'Why d'you prattle on about God?' he said, and his voice was cutting. 'It shall be as I will, and we'll have sons – only sons.'

'Daughters too, perhaps.' She tried to smile, hoping that he jested, then halted as she read the seriousness in his lean face.

He shook his head, passing a hand across his eyes. 'I don't wish to talk of it now.'

There was that absorbed expression again, cutting her off. His pain, derived from something which did not concern her, something which had happened long ago, reached out to flay her mind. 'Ah, Christopher, let me help you.' The cry was forced from her, and she clasped her hands to her breasts. 'What could comfort you? Tell me!'

He seemed hardly aware of her presence. 'To be able to forget – perhaps,' he answered very low. He seemed to be enveloped in a great sadness, illimitable as mists rising dimly above vast seas and falling again. His gaze wandered from her, out through the window to the distant amethyst hills on the horizon.

The first weeks of Mariana's marriage were happy. Christopher was the perfect bridegroom, tender, loving and considerate. She thought herself the luckiest woman alive, and bloomed into more mature loveliness. The hollows in her cheeks filled out, her body became more rounded, and that beauty was emphasized by the magnificent wardrobe of clothes provided for her. Christopher did not take her shopping for them, giving her the run of the Kingfisher Room, and everything there, though rather out of date, was of superb quality. She hid her disappointment, merely demurring, saying that his sister might object to a stranger rifling through her possessions. He dismissed this with a wave of his hand. Agnes was in no need of them, he declared.

She began to become accustomed to Thornfalcon, though it could never be said that she was easy there. Its strict routine continued, in no way disturbed by a new mistress. She saw little of the servants. They were distant figures keeping the wheels of the estate running smoothly, almost invisible, like goblins who worked at night when the owners slept. During the honeymoon she and Christopher spent most of their time in the tower apartment. He wanted no intrusions and she was happy to comply with his every wish. She could look back and laugh now at Mrs Grant's tentative attempt to enlighten her on her wifely duty. What would the pompous dame think if she could see her not only accepting her husband's advances, but encouraging them and welcoming them? Was it sinful to revel in the sweet need which he aroused in her, and glory in his possession? If so, then she was an extremely sinful wanton indeed.

She had had no idea that so much bodily pleasure existed. Christopher was an ideal teacher and she a more than willing pupil. At first, he showed just the right amount of mastery and gentleness combined, bringing her to the peak of completion. There were occasions when some of the things he suggested shocked her, but slowly every inhibition was being removed. She was changing, not only outwardly, for he expected a great deal, demanding her cooperation in the task of preparing her for her new role. She had to study art, literature and history, and take an intelligent interest in his beloved astronomy, and she was eternally grateful to him as she began to realize the extent of her ignorance.

One day, shortly after the wedding, he took her to his laboratory, situated at the base of the tower, its outer door connecting with the herb garden where he grew many of the plants used in his experiments. It was a vault-like room where a black iron stove burned brightly, built into a recess and sheltered behind a glass screen under a black hood.

Mariana perched herself on a high wooden stool, watching him as he worked, his face absorbed, hair falling over his brow, clad in shirtsleeves and waistcoat with a protective linen apron fastened round his middle. The stove produced strange smells, sweet and aromatic. It also gave forth coloured vapours, and dancing flames of peculiar hues. There was a huge wooden press that cut off an angle of the room. It was constructed of heavily carved black oak, secured with sturdy iron locks, and had high double doors and small peeping keyholes which gave the impression of deep cunning. He told her that it was a place to receive and keep secrets, piquing her interest so that she came to stand behind him as he took a bunch of keys from his pocket, unable to tell by his manner whether he was serious.

'It doesn't look very sinister,' she said already learning to be wary of his sarcasm.

'Don't be deceived by its innocent appearance,' he replied with that irony which was habitual. 'Nothing is what it seems, my dear. You'd do well to remember that.' He threw open the doors. Nothing of a more formidable nature was displayed than rows of inner drawers, and shelves stacked with neatly labelled boxes, ranks of phials, and sealed tubes of crystals that gave off prismatic scintillations.

'What d'you do with these things, Christopher?'

He placed a set of glass vessels on a tray and carried them over to the work-bench. He smiled at her. 'Well, there're medicinal cures to be found amongst the herbs, as you, being a country woman, will be aware, but much more besides, if one knows what one's seeking.' He mixed several powders together, added a drop of coloured liquid, and went to the stove with a crucible in his hand, placing it carefully in its fireproof cradle and banking the glowing cinders around it.

'Such as?' she questioned, watching him as he bent forward, the paleness of his face coming under the radius of the light.

'Entrance to a magical world, my love,' he answered coolly, wiping his hands on the apron. Faint vapours, herb-scented, rose and circled to the groined ceiling. In the stillness, delicate bubblings and simmerings became audible. He shot her a sudden glance. 'If one seeks communion with the spirits or wishes to stretch the mind to new horizons, then the means to do this can be found in a wealth of narcotic plants. Some I grow myself. Others are brought from overseas. I expect you've used opium in the sickroom.'

'I gave it to my mother when she lay dying,' Mariana replied.

'And the soothing poppy-juice eased her passing, no doubt.' He hesitated for an instant, then went on. 'There are many more which open the doorways of experience. Hallucinogens – agents which in non-toxic doses produce changes in perception, thought and mood which are exhilarating.'

Mariana drew back. Something in his aspect sent fear tingling along her nerves. 'Can you be quite certain that they're harmless?'

He laughed so wildly that she began to wonder how often he experimented. Did she know the real Christopher or were his constant switches of mood dependent on herbs? 'Don't worry, I know what I'm doing,' he said, his eyes alight. 'I've tried them all – opium – cannabis – Erythroxylon cocoa from Peru. Then there are the fungi – *Amanita muscaria*, known as "fly agaric". I expect you've come across it in the woods, that pretty red toadstool with white spots. The strongest variety is found in Siberia, but it grows quite happily in the fields and forests of England, along with *Psilocybe* of the thin pale stalks and small cream caps.'

Mariana was becoming increasingly agitated. 'I was taught to leave toadstools alone as they're poisonous,' she said more primly than she intended.

He laughed again. 'Not if one knows how to use them,' he rejoined, and he was looking inwards, reliving fantastic dreams. 'How can I explain their effect? It's like forsaking the familiar world and, in full consciousness, embracing a sphere which operates under different rules, standards and dimensions.'

'Be careful, Christopher,' she pleaded. 'Supposing that you took too large a dose, by mistake. If you were to die, I don't know what I'd do.'

His eyes bored into hers. 'Do I mean so much to you? Are you sincere?' His grip on her fingers was painful.

'You're my husband. I love you.' As she made this simple affirmation, she shook her head helplessly. Whatever he did or said, no matter how controversial, nothing could slake her unquenchable passion for him.

'My beautiful darling,' he whispered. 'Perhaps at some time in the future, you may share these concoctions with me again.'

'Again?' She picked up on the word and froze, suddenly

recalling fragments of her wedding-night dreams.

'Why yes – in your wine – when I took you and you didn't know it. I had drugged your goblet.' His manner was casual, as if what he had done was perfectly acceptable.

'Why?' she asked flatly. She had never forgotten or entirely forgiven his cavalier action which had been tantamount to rape, a brutal, unfeeling invasion of privacy.

'To save you from pain.' He shrugged and turned back to the crucible, stirring it carefully. 'I was sure that you were a virgin and, truth to tell, other women who were not, have remarked on the size and force of my love-organ. I didn't wish to hurt or frighten you. Sarah Anne didn't stop complaining for a week after our first night together. She was also a virgin.'

He said this to impress Mariana with his thoughtful care but fell short of success. A small dark cloud began to gather on the serene blue skies of happiness.

At Christopher's order, Mrs Brockwell gave Mariana her unwelcome assistance. The housekeeper was an urbane, perfectly respectable-looking woman, but under that sleek exterior Mariana had instinctively recognized an extraordinary power of malice from which she recoiled with a repulsion nothing could conquer.

Mrs Brockwell seemed so much in tune with Thornfalcon, that massive echoing manor, encircled by a triple ring of silence – the towering walls, the still waters of the moat, the stately park with its mute army of trees. Mariana always had the feeling that Mrs Brockwell was watching her. She would pause at the bend of a passage, sure that she heard a stealthy footstep behind, and her heart would race for a moment with a sense of half-forgotten childhood terrors. Then her pride would reassert itself as she remembered that she was Lady St Jules. With a defiant toss of her head she would walk steadily on, feeling that she would rather die than own to fear.

Thornfalcon was a treasure-house of costly items, yet it never felt like home. Mariana appreciated its grandeur, admired its furnishings, but there was something about it which disturbed her, though she told herself bravely that she would come to terms with it in time. The days passed, however, and she waited patiently for the transformation to take place, the comfortable oneness with her husband's abode, the sense of belonging, of being its mistress. It did not happen. Shyly, she confided some but not all of her doubts to him.

'You'll feel differently when you've had a baby,' Christopher replied, smiling indulgently.

Mariana nodded, dropping the subject, dreading the coldness which swept down on him without warning sometimes – a cold, quiet anger which could presage mounting passion. At such moments he could be cruel, subjecting her body to his will and, by doing so, conquering her spirit, because she adored him.

The most stressful area was concentrated in the Kingfisher Room, and Mariana never crossed the threshold without recalling the one night she had spent there. She had kept the candle burning till dawn. Agnes's presence dominated the chamber. It was as if she might come in at any moment, challenging the interloper who had the temerity to wear her clothes, steal her jewels and view her own impudent reflection in the mirror. Fortunately Christopher had ordered most of the things to be moved to the Master Chamber, so it was rarely necessary for Mariana to make that shrinking journey to Agnes's room. Early on, she had toured the house resolutely, taking courage in both hands and daring Mrs Brockwell's domain below stairs. Her entrance had been unexpected, and she found the housekeeper and the valet taking their ease before the roaring kitchen fire, their plates heaped with delicacies, a bottle of vintage port at their elbows. Her stay had been a brief one. Mrs Brockwell had been most polite, but her deference had been delivered with a sneer and thinly veiled contempt. She had succeeded in making Mariana feel like an intruder. She had not gone there again.

Rebellion began to stir within her. 'Christopher, I'd like to go to town and buy some gowns of my own,' she said one morning.

They were breakfasting on the terrace. Mrs Brockwell, having duly examined the barometer, scanned the sky and tested the warmth of the air, had decided that perhaps for the last time that year, she might safely set the meal in the open. It was one of those days which a reluctant summer drops into the lap of autumn, a day of stillness and high vaulted skies, faintly but exquisitely blue. The leaves clung tenuously to the branches and, if stirred by the breeze, fell twirling, gentle as a sigh. Overnight the frost had laid a fine white tracery everywhere, and it added a tart purity which the warm sunshine failed to eliminate entirely.

Christopher chose to ignore Mariana's remark, absorbed in reading a letter. 'Did you hear what I said?' she demanded after a moment, amazed at her own daring.

He looked up, folded the sheet, laid it near his plate and reached for the bunch of purple grapes invitingly couched on their own dark foliage. 'Umm? Yes, I heard,' he answered calmly. 'Quite unnecessary, darling. You have all you need.' He changed the subject deftly. 'What delightful weather, isn't it? One might be cheated into thoughts of spring were it not for the falling leaves, the boughs that let in so much light between them, and the lonely eaves where swallow-broods no longer riot. Don't you agree?'

Mariana dug her heels in mulishly, glancing down at the taffeta gown with short green velvet spencer in which she was attired. A fine morning-dress to be sure, but it did not belong to her. 'I'm tired of wearing borrowed plumage,' she announced, waving away the white bread, the firm primrose roll of butter, the comb of heather-honey which he offered her. 'These things are your sister's.'

'And you look adorable in them. Sweetheart, you become them amazingly well. Far better than Agnes. I've told you, she would have no objections.'

'But I have!' Let him be angry, I don't care, she thought, adding: 'If you won't let me go shopping, then allow me to send for patterns and materials. I know of a competent seamstress in Fewston.'

'I'll take you to London soon.' His face was impassive and he threw one slim, booted leg over the other, wiping fastidious hands on a damask napkin. 'Till then, let the matter rest, Mariana. Good God, I should think that you have everything you could possibly desire. You've never struck me as being fashion conscious. I assure you that I am more than satisfied with your appearance at all times.' He added the rider with a reminiscent smile and a look that made her tingle.

He was referring, not to Agnes's garments, but to other, more fantastic articles of clothing. Thornfalcon was a positive warren of a place, and they had gone to the attics one rainy day. There under the rafters which hid a confusion of rooms, he had dragged out a large wooden trunk which contained a huge variety of theatrical costumes. In the watery light which filtered through the dormer windows, he had held up brass crowns, tarnished tinsel drapes, velvet cloaks and ruffles. He had had the manservants haul his find to the Master Chamber, smiling broadly as he told Mariana: 'Agnes and I loved dressing-up. We used to put on plays – quite good at it too. Some of these costumes are genuine, relics of our forebears – bits of armour, helmets, a sword or two, even perukes – look!'

So during the night hours or on wet afternoons when there was nothing else to do, he introduced her to the fantasy world of the stage, liking her to disguise herself, taking part in the game himself, transformed into a knight, a cavalier, a gypsy, even a priest if the fancy took him. He would become very dramatic, striding about and declaiming loudly. Sometimes he seemed possessed by the character he was portraying. One of his favourite roles was that of a corsair, whilst she had to be a captured Eastern slave, the make-believe degenerating into violence as he ravished her. Mariana did her best to enjoy these unreal episodes, wanting to please and entertain him. It was only sometimes, when she really stopped to consider what she was doing, that distaste soured her mouth.

She was gaining confidence as Christopher groomed her to be Lady St Jules. But always the ghost of Agnes hovered, and she wanted to lay it for good and all. She rose from the breakfast table and went to stand by him, braving his irritation as she persisted doggedly: 'I'm glad that I please you, but I'll be able to do so even more, if you'll only let me follow the plan I suggest. When is Agnes coming to visit? I'd like to be equipped with my own wardrobe by then. Can't you see that I would find it deeply humiliating to be wearing her cast-offs?'

The pale sun struck across him through the near-naked branches, forming an aureole round his head. He sat motionless, looking at her with that strange, quirky smile which never reached his eyes. 'Agnes? I'm not expecting her for a long while. You'll meet her one day, but not yet. Bear with me, my sweet – you shall have the best that money can buy, when I take you to London.' His arm slipped about her waist and he drew her to him, pressing his head against her breasts. She ran her fingers through his curls, resting her chin lightly on them, aching with love.

'I'll be patient, if that's what you want,' she sighed.

'Poor darling – it's not much fun for you here, is it? Cooped up with a crazy fellow like me.' There was a whimsical expression on his face, and like a kindly uncle who produces an unexpected treat for a child, he added: 'I've invited some friends for the weekend. We shall be very gay, and I'll be able to show you off.'

She wanted to be delighted, to please him with her pleasure. Instead she exclaimed in panic: 'I'm not ready! Who are they? Oh, dear, it's too soon – I'll make a fool of myself and shame you!'

'Nonsense, you'll behave perfectly or I'll want to know why. There'll be little for you to do, save be lovely and gracious. Mrs Brockwell will handle the arrangements.' He lounged to his feet, tall and golden as a god. In an instant, she was nestled against his chest, feeling the smooth stuff of his jacket beneath her cheek, inhaling the personal scent of him.

'Oh, Christopher, are you sure?' she sighed, looking beyond his shoulder to where the drawing-room doors opened out on to the terrace. The stone walls were tinged with pink and russet, and the old house looked calm and beautiful, wearing a pensive mysterious air. She almost liked it in that moment. 'I'll make you proud that you married me. You'll not regret it. But who are these people? Are they frightfully smart? Do they come from London? Tell me about them.'

She could feel him shaking with laughter, and then his hands came up to hold her firmly on each side of her head so that she could not escape his eyes. They were bright, the pupils small in the autumnal light. 'You know at least three of them – Reverend Grant, Dr Russell and Squire Middleton. As for the rest? Yes, they do reside in town, on occasions, but there's nothing about that to alarm you.' He released her abruptly, with that switch of mood which she had learned to accept, suddenly preoccupied. 'Run along now,' he dismissed her with a light slap on the backside. 'Find Mrs Brockwell. She'll tell you all you need to know.'

CHAPTER 4

Mariana entered the Kingfisher Room, driven to search the wardrobes for something really spectacular. The daylight made the chamber vivid and alive. The Agnes of the portrait watched her. As Mrs Brockwell had said on that first day, it was a beautiful place. The moulded mantelpiece, the starry ceiling, the furniture, the carpets and the drapes, were all items in which she would have taken great pride and pleasure, had they been her own.

She spread her hands wide in a gesture of apology, addressing the painting. 'I beg your pardon, Lady Agnes,' she said aloud. 'I hope you won't be offended, but your brother has especially requested that I wear a striking outfit tonight. We have guests, you see.'

'Please, madam,' came a low voice from behind her, making her jump. Mrs Brockwell was at her elbow, hands folded over her apron, droping a curtsey as their glances met, speaking in her purring, familiar tone.

'What do you want?' Mariana became very stiff and formal because the woman had frightened her.

'Lady St Jules, begging your pardon, but I made so bold as to follow you, thinking that you might need my assistance.'

'I'm perfectly capable of selecting my attire for tonight,' Mariana answered curtly, turning her back and going to one of the armoires, but the obnoxious presence was not so easily dismissed. It followed her. It breathed in her ear. After a minute of irritated endurance during which her mind refused to function, Mariana whirled round impatiently. 'Well?'

'The master has told me to help you, my Lady.' The woman stood there obstinately.

Mariana gave an exasperated sigh and turned to one of the wardrobes. It had a queer, stuffy smell, as if full of the powdery odour of dead moments. Mariana had been aware of it before, recoiling from it, that hint of perfume, stale and old, of wilting flowers.

'What I'd give to have just one gown of my own!' she burst out.

'I'm sure Lady Agnes wouldn't mind you borrowing hers, as

67

Lord St Jules says. She has a generous nature, and I know her well. I brought them up, you see.' Mrs Brockwell was being unusually communicative. 'In my care from the moment they were born, the pair of them. They were twins.'

Mariana could not hide her astonishment. 'I had no idea.' Why hasn't Christopher told me? she wondered, but then, there was no reason why he should have done so.

Mrs Brockwell nodded solemnly, those sly eyes in the round face expressing her evident relish in recounting this bit of family history. 'I came here as a young woman to help in the nursery. Lady Matilda and Lord Jonathan were expecting their first child. Such an exciting event, and all went well until the actual birth. Then, to everyone's surprise, a boy arrived, followed closely by a girl.'

Mariana had regained her control, but she was listening eagerly. Anything concerning Christopher was of intense interest. She longed to know his heart and mind, but these were often closed to her. More often than not, he wrapped reserve around him like a dark mantle. 'My mother had twins,' she said softly. 'They died, and she never fully recovered.'

Mrs Brockwell nodded her head with an air of deepest gravity and importance. 'A great strain on a mother, I agree, and the children are often lost, unless they go to full term. My little darlings were fortunate, strong and lusty, perfect babies, as fair and golden as cherubs. His lordship was as proud as a peacock, even welcoming the girl-child. He was confident that the legend was so much nonsense, an old wives' tale. He was a brave man, a sportsman, never happier than when riding to hounds. A hard-living, hard-drinking aristocrat, dismissing weird stories as poppycock, refusing to lose any sleep over something that happened so long ago.'

Mariana was aware of feeling very cold. Her heart was beating heavily, the housekeeper's words engendering the wildest speculations and direful forebodings. 'What are you talking about, Mrs Brockwell?' She brought this out with a mock steadiness which deceived neither of them. 'What is this legend?' She tried to laugh, adding lightly: 'In a house as old as Thornfalcon, there's bound to be a ghost or two, I shouldn't wonder. Christopher has already mentioned a fellow who counts his money,' but her laugh rang muffled, as if the air was too heavy to hold it.

Mrs Brockwell blinked like a cat and, like a cat with its claws retracted, she stood perfectly still. Her voice had a piously shocked note as she replied: 'Oh, dear, madam. Hasn't Lord

Christopher told you? Far be it for me to do so, if he's not thought it fitting.'

This was maddening and made Mariana furious. Having stirred her curiosity, Mrs Brockwell was now being deliberately evasive. 'I'm sure he'd have no objection. Speak, woman!'

'I'm sorry, Lady St Jules, but my lips are sealed,' the housekeeper replied primly. 'You must ask him yourself.'

'Oh, I shall!' Mariana shot back, thoroughly enraged by Mrs Brockwell's expression of servile, tight-lipped loyalty. 'You looked after the children, you say? Where were their parents?'

'Lady Matilda didn't make old bones,' she said, never taking her eyes from Mariana. 'She took sick and died after one particularly mild winter when the twins were but eighteen months old. As 'tis said in these parts: ''A green Christmas, a full churchyard before Easter.'' Lord Jonathan was not here often after that. He left me in charge.'

'And the children?' Mariana insisted, certain that this matter-of-fact statement hid far more.

'Dear little souls. They looked upon me as their second mother, if I may be so bold.' Mrs Brockwell's eyes shone with possessive pride. 'I lost him as they grew older, though he returned to me during school holidays, but Lady Agnes and I were very close, if you'll pardon my saying so, me being so humble and all. There were tutors, of course, but she came to me with her problems.' She pointed to the portrait. 'That was painted when she was twenty. Isn't she lovely? The pride of Thornfalcon.'

Nobody ever mentions Sarah Anne, thought Mariana, she's a forgotten nonentity. It's as if Agnes had been the real mistress here. Well, I'll vindicate you, poor pale thing, eclipsed by his brilliant, frightened sister. She turned away from Mrs Brockwell, no longer bothering to hide her dislike. 'How did Lady Agnes behave towards Lord Christopher's first wife?' she asked coldly.

The housekeeper's eyes were like glistening pebbles, though her smile was bland. 'Lady Sarah was of a retiring disposition, madam, totally unlike his twin,' she parried with the cunning of one expert at verbal fencing.

'Lady Agnes resented her?' Mariana continued relentlessly.

'I didn't say that, madam.'

'What of him? Did he love his wife?' Mariana had not realized until that moment just how much she needed answers to the questions that had been praying on the edges of her mind.

'The nobility don't marry for love.' Mrs Brockwell darted her a venomous glance which was instantly masked. 'He hoped for an heir. He still does. She produced nothing but stillborn females.'

Touché! thought Mariana wryly. Is she hinting that his love for me will wilt if I don't give him a son? This isn't true. He loves me for myself. I mustn't listen to her, must avoid distortions and exaggerations. You are Lady St Jules. Remember? You don't discuss personal matters with a menial.

'Thank you for your help, Mrs Brockwell,' she said with icy formality. 'Have this gown and its accessories sent to the Master Chamber. If I wish to know any more, I'll consult my husband.'

She swept to the door, head held high. Mrs Brockwell watched her with a thoughtful expression. 'Do so, madam,' she said quietly but clearly. 'Ask him to recount the story which concerns his sister's namesake – Agnes the Poisoner.'

The visitors arrived towards the falling hour of the day when the shadows grew long and the slanting light was amber. It struck across the deep emerald lawns, and Thornfalcon brooded, golden-grey in the light, purple in the shadows. They came with the clatter of hooves and the blasting of post-horns, followed by a retinue of valets and maids, to be welcomed by the chief servants and the master on the threshold of the manor.

Mariana, half hidden behind him, awaited her moment, observing them. The Reverend Grant climbed down from his gig and puffed up the steps, large, important, with the looks and stature which would one day make him an imressive bishop. He held out his hands towards her, a smile on his heavy features. 'My dear child, how well you're looking. Mrs Grant sends greetings.'

Mariana felt those smooth, well-tended hands on hers, and searched his face with an intensity which surprised her. Fleeting images from bad dreams flashed across her brain, but there was nothing about his stalwart integrity and calm authority which coincided with them. She felt a spasm of shame at doubting this fine man. Her soul must indeed harbour evil if she imagined for a moment that he was corrupt. She took comfort from his presence while he listened attentively as she asked about her family, learning that they were in good health and Ernestine and Annabelle preparing for their weddings. Dr Russell, riding in a little later from Fewston, added his assurance that Swinsty Farm had never been more flourishing.

70

'Left my practice in the care of my assistant for a couple of days,' he declared, bowing over Mariana's hand, a dapper figure in black, treating her with respect now. 'I expect he'll have broken heads to mend tonight. The villagers will be celebrating Allhallows Eve in the time-honoured way, addling their wits with cider.'

A lady appeared from the first of the two smart carriages which stood in the drive. She was wearing a rustling silk pelisse, her flushed, handsome face peering out from beneath her wide hat. She placed a small, neatly booted foot on the coach step, and rested her hand on Christopher's extended arm. He bent and brushed her gloved wrist with his lips.

'Mrs Wrixon – Thornfalcon greets you.'

'Good-afternoon, Christopher,' she replied in a languorous voice. 'And how are you enjoying wedded bliss?'

'We're agog to meet the bride,' put in one of her companions, jumping down after her. He was a foppish person, wearing the latest cut of trousers strapped over positively the latest mode in boots. The tightly corseted waist, the sprightliness of his manner, the macassared curls that hung luxuriantly over his collar, were cunningly contrived to convey an impression of youth.

'All in good time, Marvin, my dear chap,' Christopher replied with a smile as they shook hands.

'Thornfalcon's looking extremely noble,' Sir Timon Marvin remarked jauntily, his dark eyes assessing it. 'A grand time of the year, what? Mellow as rare old wine, or a mature woman.' He cocked an eyebrow at Mrs Wrixon, smiled sweetly and gave her an elaborate bow.

The greetings continued as an older lady, most grandly attired, alighted, followed by an impressive individual of military bearing, and a young man who did not quite fit in, though his clothing was equally expensive, if rather tasteless. Hardly had they reached the top of the flight of stone steps, before another, smaller vehicle rumbled to a standstill on the gravel. It contained a thin, worried-looking woman of middle years who insisted on taking sugar-lumps from her reticule and feeding them to the steaming, snorting team of horses. She was accompanied by a pale youth who carried her muff and various pieces of hand-luggage.

Mariana could make little sense out of the jumble of faces to whom she was presented. She was enveloped in feminine embraces: Mrs Wrixon with her vulpine smile and consumptive flush, Lady Somerville of the large round face and protruberant eyes, Miss Cora Blake, the vague anxious spinster. Then there were the gentlemen: Sir Timon with the close-set shallow eyes, Captain Wodehouse, frankly fifty, with a ruddy, handsome face under a sweep of greying hair, Mr Howard Blake dancing attendance on his aunt, a poetic young man with flowing locks, open collar and flying cravat, and Arthur Cartwright, moneyed, well turned-out, but unable to disguise a certain commonness of upbringing and outlook. Howard Blake seemed the most genuine and friendly, and Mariana liked him though he was at Cora Blake's beck and call. She was unusually possessive of her nephew.

The company were already seated at table when Mariana came into the dining-room that night. She stood for an instant, framed in the doorway. Despite its many candelabras, the great, oak-panelled chamber was essentially dark. The walls were almost black, polished by successive generations of servants to an inimitable gloss, and reflecting the flames of the candles like so many small yellow eyes. The perfect background for lovely women and fine clothes, for roses and silver and gold. Mariana appreciated this lovely setting, yet wondered why she felt so uneasily chilled by the sensation that she had seen her guests somewhere before, in a similar darkened room.

She had spent a long time preparing herself and, to her relief, had been left to accomplish this alone. Mrs Brockwell was far too busy overseeing the dinner arrangements. Mariana was determined not to shame Christopher before his sophisticated friends. As she dressed, she rehearsed her speech, her manners, little snippets of news which would make her appear bright and intelligent. There were a daunting number of things to remember, not the least of which was how to handle the confusing array of cutlery. He had already lectured her about this, explicitly stating exactly which knife, fork or spoon she must use and in what order. Perhaps, she had thought as she brushed her dark hair, if I don't say too much, be very quiet and unassuming, they'll think I'm shy and not press me into conversation.

The gown was lovely, and she had breathed silent thanks to the absent Agnes. It fitted her like an embroidered sheath. A narrow white satin train with a heavy border of golden scrolls swept from her shoulders in folds, adding to her height. The classic cut, laying bare her neck and arms, made her look almost regal. It complimented her warm colouring and sable hair. A pleased smile had curved her lips as she took a final look in the mirror before leaving the bedroom. Without conceit she had recognized that she was beautiful, had thought of

Christopher and been glad. The open admiration of the men when she had been introduced to them had stimulated her to make full use of her gifts to pleasure the eyes of the man she loved.

Mrs Wrixon was the first to see her. She put up her lorgnette and glared. Captain Wodehouse followed the direction of her eyes and started with delight. Then it seemed to Mariana that every eye was upon her, and her assurance wavered. Nervously, she shot a glance towards the head of the table. She met Christopher's eyes, saw the light which glowed in their depths and his small nod of approval. Her heart rose and, in the intense feeling of relief and happiness which swept over her, she gave the assembled company a dazzling smile.

She found it easier to entertain guests than she had dreamed possible. They were all very used to such gatherings, and Christopher was a most considerate host. It was a leisurely, elaborate repast, with a ceaseless round of dishes accompanied by much wine-taking. Mariana quickly discovered that they were so occupied with talking, mostly about themselves, that apart from the gentlemen subjecting her to glances of undisguised admiration, she was expected to do little more than add a comment here and there. As the evening progressed so the glass-clinking, jokes, laughter and exaggerated compliments gathered momentum. She had been seated on Christopher's right, with Grant on her left. Dr Russell was not far off, and it was comforting to see two familiar faces, reminding her of Fewston and home.

'Your father would appreciate this wine,' commented the rector, holding up his glass which whispered its fragrant secret.

'I doubt it, sir. The only virtue Mr Crosby looks for in a vintage is its potential for speedy intoxication,' she said acidly, wishing that he had not been mentioned. Squire Middleton was smiling across at her, nodding in agreement, and she could not help but remember that the last time she had seen him he had been spattered with muck and furious. She found that whenever she thought she had finished her wine, the glass was filled to the brim again, and began to feel hazy, unsure of whether she heard correctly when Middleton leaned towards Christopher and said, midst the general hubbub:

'Crosby's hellbent on self-destruction. A happy man now, permanently drunk.'

'And the farm?' Christopher was staring down into the goblet he held between both slender hands, a sardonic smile curving his lips.

'Going steadily downhill,' said Middleton with a shrug.

Arthur Cartwright was looking into Mariana's face with insolent intensity. 'Glad to meet you, Lady St Jules,' he said, none too sober and made over-bold. 'I've heard a lot about you. Oh, yes – they're saying that you're the loveliest woman in the whole of Yorkshire – maybe, even in England, come to that. I drink to you.'

She smiled mechanically, disliking his swaggering coarseness, wishing that he would be quiet for she was straining to hear what was being said about Swinsty Farm, but by the time he had taken the hint and withdrawn, Christopher and Middleton had stopped talking. She had not visited her old home. Christopher always managed to find a valid reason for preventing her from riding over.

I must go and see them, she thought, whilst Howard Blake tried to engage her in conversation. I'll insist that Christopher let me drive there tomorrow. I need to talk to Ernestine and Annabelle, look over their wedding-gowns, help Margery with the preparations, take Crosby to task and insist that I check the accounts.

'Have another glass of wine, Mariana,' said her husband.

A little later, he gave her the signal to take the ladies to the drawing-room, leaving the men to port and cigars. 'We must play faro again, Marvin,' declared Lady Somerville, resplendent in a crimson gauze turban and matching gown. 'I positively insist. You owe me money from last night.'

'You'll get it back, on my word as a gentleman,' Marvin snapped.

'Really? In my experience, you're not overconversant with the truth, sir,' sneered Mrs Wrixon, stopping the languidly pettish flap of her fan to shoot him a waspish glance over its edge.

'Why so, fairest lady?' Marvin looked pained while the others laughed. 'To my mind, truth is what one believes at the moment – and I believe, at this point in time, that Lady Somerville will be paid in full before tomorrow's dawn, though I can't guarantee the validity of this an hour hence.'

A shout of laughter went round the idle, half-drunken group. Christopher clapped his hands in mock reproval. 'Take the ladies away, Mariana,' he ordered. 'We'll join you shortly.'

She spent an uncomfortable hour with the women who seated themselves in the luxury of the drawing-room and proceeded to rip apart the reputations of several people whom they knew but she did not, and then started to talk about Lady Agnes, describing the parties which were held at Thornfalcon before she went away.

'That gown of yours, Lady St Jules,' said Mrs Wrixon in an irritatingly condescending manner. 'I could swear that I've seen Agnes wear one just like it. How very amusing and coincidental.'

Damn her! thought Mariana, unable to prevent a blush mounting to her cheeks. She stared back at her haughtily. 'It is her dress. I've had no time yet to order new clothes. Christopher said that she wouldn't mind me borrowing her things.'

Mrs Wrixon laughed, a brittle sound which suddenly ended in a paroxysm of coughing. Her eyes were burning over the folds of the handkerchief she pressed to her lips. 'I'm sure she wouldn't,' she gasped. 'Agnes would do anything to help her darling brother.'

Mariana was shocked at the sound of that cough, and by the sight of the scarlet stains on the white linen. 'Can I get you some water?' she offered.

'Ha! No. There's nothing can be done,' said Mrs Wrixon. 'It won't be long before I choke in my own blood.'

Her cheeks were flushed and her eyes shone with a feverish brilliance in their deep, dark-ringed sockets. She passed the back of her hand impatiently over her wet forehead and her lids closed. The blood-smeared cambric lay crushed in her hand against her silk skirt.

'You should go south, Beatrice,' advised Lady Somerville, fidgeting with the cards which she had already spread on the small, baize-covered table. 'Spend the winter in Italy.'

'And miss all the fun? Never!' panted Mrs Wrixon. 'I'll die in England, where I belong.' There was something awful in the contrast between her violent nature, the frailness of her body and the way in which they reacted upon one another. 'My only hope is that I'll be alive long enough to see Christopher's ambition fulfilled.'

She turned those terrible eyes to Mariana. 'It doesn't matter about the gown, child – concentrate on making him happy, if you can.'

'I pray that I do so,' she answered, thinking, is it the wine making me feel so frightened? I don't like these people. Why does he choose them as friends? That sick woman should be at home in bed, not struggling to be so gay, to hide her terror of death. And the fat one, obsessed by gambling – what can he possibly have in common with her?

'I'll prepare a posset for you, Beatrice,' offered Cora Blake, fluttering like a wounded sparrow at Mrs Wrixon's side.

'Bah! To hell with your possets! I'd rather have a strong

brandy,' expostulated the dying woman, with that peculiar kind of irony all her own.

Cora recoiled, her baby-soft, faded features puckered. 'I only wanted to help.'

'Save your energy for Howard,' snarled Mrs Wrixon. 'By God, Cora, but that boy's too young for you. I always knew you were a cradle-snatcher, but this is ridiculous!'

Cora withdrew to her corner of the couch with an indignant rustle of lilac skirts, and Lady Somerville looked up, hands still caressing the cards. 'Take no notice of her, Cora. La, shame on you, Beatrice, leave her alone. You're having your pleasure with Wodehouse, ain't you? Live and let live, I always say.'

There were odd ripples in the ether, and Mariana's uneasiness was mounting. These spiteful women knew one another intimately, of that there was not the slightest shadow of a doubt. A strange, ill-assorted group – Christopher's friends.

'You've known my husband long?' She directed her question to Mrs Wrixon, who lay back against the cushions.

She struggled to sit up, smoothed her curls, folded her handkerchief and slipped it into her beaded bag, then looked at Mariana, her nostrils fluttering with her quick breath, a singular expression of mocking cruelty on her face. 'Oh, yes – a long, long time. I accompanied him to Greece. Hasn't he told you?'

'No,' answered Mariana, realizing that there were a great number of things Christopher had neglected to tell her.

'Agnes came too. That was in the old, gay days before I became ill and she – '

'Went away,' put in Cora, directing a warning glance towards Mariana.

'Quite so.' That malicious, mocking smile deepened.

'The trip must have been so romantic, with dear Lord Byron there writing his wonderful poetry,' exclaimed Cora, starry-eyed.

Every line in Beatrice Wrixon's face softened, and she sighed heavily. 'Ah, but those were days indeed. Christopher is still handsome, but you should have seen him then! He was like Adonis – golden, radiantly beautiful, his skin kissed by the Mediterranean sun. We used to bathe mother-naked in the warm Adriatic. He's a superb swimmer, you know.'

Mariana did not know, and as she sat there, jealousy bit like a hideous serpent. She did not need to have it spelled out – Mrs Wrixon had been his mistress. She had loved him then, probably loved him still. The woman leaned towards her. She felt the clammy fingers stroke her hand. It was like being touched by a corpse. 'Don't look at me like that, my dear,' Mrs Wrixon said, speaking low. 'Fate has decreed that you are now his wife. You make a fitting mate for such a man. Sarah Anne was wrong for him, I told him so from the start. She was rich, of course, had a very large dowry and her build deceived him into thinking that she would breed like a rabbit, but I could tell that she'd never give him the son he desires so passionately. You're different. We approve of his choice of the second Lady St Jules.'

She had adopted an almost exaggerated gentleness under which lurked gathering danger. Mariana was appalled. They had known of his intention to marry her? It had met with their approval? What right had they to discuss it, possibly with Christopher himself? Mariana shuddered. Mrs Wrixon's hand seeming to hold contamination.

'How could you approve or disapprove?' she asked, her face pale. 'I've never met you before.'

'D'you think that such as he would marry on impulse?' Mrs Wrixon gave a mirthless laugh. 'If you do, then you're a bigger fool than I imagined!'

'I think you've said enough, madam!' A voice cracked across the room. Christopher had entered silently, ahead of the other men. He stood there watching them, leaning against the door-frame, a smile on his mouth but ice in his eyes.

Mariana's heart leapt and she was instantly grateful for the way in which he came straight to her, laying a hand on her shoulder, embarrassing her tormentor with his stern glance. She pressed her hands tightly together in her silken lap, and the taste of the tears she would not shed lay bitter on her tongue. The spell was broken by the entrance of the gentlemen, noisy and exuberant, having eaten well and now on the fine border line where sober enjoyment merges into the first elevation of slight intoxication. Christopher left Mariana then, and the lights, the flashes of colour, the babel of talk around her became a nightmare, an unreal world of mocking shadows, in which one thing only was horribly and intensely alive – the pain of her jealousy and confusion. After a moment, however, self-possession returned. She acted with an unguessed ability, the perfect hostess, seeing to their needs, answering the running fire of remarks that seemed to be levelled at her with diabolical persistency.

'What a capital party, Lady St Jules.' Arthur Cartwright's crudely carved features floated out of the haze. 'And you're the finest gem in the Thornfalcon crown. Stab me if you ain't!'

'Thank you, sir,' Mariana said from her place near the

court-cupboard where she was topping up glasses.

He was grinning, watching her graceful movements with hot eyes. 'My father owns a cotton-mill,' he announced with an edge of defiance. 'He's made a fortune out of the war. They'll elect him mayor of the town soon, I'll wager.'

'How interesting, Mr Cartwright,' she lied smoothly, speculating on Christopher's motive for allowing him to set foot in Thornfalcon. He was usually so scathing about this new strata of society, rich industrialists who were claiming the right to send their sons to the best schools and have their daughters reared as ladies. If Cartwright was an example of them, then Christopher's attitude was justified.

'I suppose you're curious about how I got to know your husband.' Arthur was persecuting her with his unwelcome attentions, thoroughly enjoying it. She was being cool and aloof towards him, but then so had many high-born women – until they found out about his father's wealth. Arthur sneered to himself. What was she after all? Nothing but the daughter of a drunken farmer who hadn't the wit to give up the booze and keep his holding together.

'No doubt he had his reasons.' She stepped past him with head erect and Arthur followed, just avoiding treading on her train as it dragged across the parquet flooring.

'Well, you see, he's got shares in my old man's business,' he continued stubbornly. 'I expect we'll be seeing a good deal of each other, Lady St Jules.'

This was a daunting prospect, and Mariana was relieved to see the seat next to Christopher vacant, The guests were gambling at the green tables, eyes relentless, teeth clenched, fingers clutching chips or coins, their banter replaced by ferocious jibes. Mariana glanced at the clock. It had just turned eleven. Following her eyes, Christopher smiled and said: 'I think you should retire, my dear. I'll have Mrs Brockwell bring you up a glass of hot milk. You look tired.'

She was glad to accept this decision, having had quite enough of his friends for one night. With a sigh, she remembered that they were staying till Sunday. A hunt had been arranged and a dance for the following evening. She did feel awfully weary, so she said goodnight to everyone and left the room on her husband's arm.

'I'm very pleased with you, my love,' he remarked as the door of their bedroom closed behind them. Kicking off her shoes, Mariana walked barefoot across the carpet to warm her hands at the crackling log fire. She had been cold all evening, as if the guests had brought a blast of freezing air with them.

'I'm glad,' she answered simply. 'I'll admit to being nervous. I've never met people like them before.'

'A rowdy, frivolous set, I agree.' He threw himself into the winged armchair, crossed one knee over the other, closed his eyes and laughed gently. 'Cartwright is deuced uncouth, but his father's a useful business contact.' He lifted his lids and subjected her to the intensity of his stare.

'Mrs Wrixon is ill.' Mariana was pulling the pins from her hair so that it began to uncoil across her shoulders.

'I know.' Christopher, watching her, answered casually, as if they were discussing the weather.

It was on the tip of her tongue to ask him about his relationship with her, but something in his eyes warned her to leave well alone. But: 'You don't sound unduly concerned,' she could not help saying.

He shrugged his velvet-covered shoulders, and his reflection joined hers in the mirror, hard, lean, with that thin sensitive face and the rather cruel line of the lips. She watched his fair head lower to the bare curve of her neck, and drew in a sharp breath. His hands slid down her arms, crossing them in front of her as he explored the pulsing vein in her throat. Turning her round, he lifted her in his arms and carried her across to the bed, vast and dim in the shadowy dusk of candle-glow. The statues of the ancient gods and goddesses watched, seeming to nod their approval.

'Darling, I'll have to leave you for a while,' he murmured, stretching beside her, still holding her. 'I've matters to discuss with the gentlemen. I'll not be long.'

His head moved down, his lips kissing the exposed hollows of her shoulders. Then he began to undress her, his hands skilled and gentle. When she lay naked, his hand cupped one breast, caressing it before lifting it to his mouth. A shiver went over her skin as his lips wandered down across her ribs, her pliant waist and taut, flat stomach. When he continued his downward descent, she became suddenly hesitant, though she yearned for him to go on.

'No, Christopher – no!' she whispered.

He laughed quietly, his breath warm on her flesh. 'I've told you, dearest, there are a host of fresh delights that I want to show you. You've been so good tonight – and I intend to give you a little treat. Don't be shocked – I'll enjoy this as much as you will.'

'Oh, Christopher.' She tried to push him away, yet would have been wildly disappointed if he had gone.

'Lie still,' he counselled, his hands and lips weaving strong magic. 'Later, you can do the same for me. The tongue can do more than speak or taste.'

A powerful, uninhibited force was taking over. Mariana's fingers were in his hair, holding his head between her thighs. She protested no more, as he roused her as never before, a tender, probing presence which sent searing fire roaring through her.

Christopher left her fully satisfied in this novel, exciting way, without taking his own fulfilment. He rose from the bed, smoothed his coat straight and twisted his cravat into position. Mariana lay watching him dreamily, complete as never before in her life. It seemed a wonderful thing he had just done, an undreamed-of delight, pleasure so acute that she had cried out at the peak of it. He bent to kiss her parted lips, admonished her to drink her milk and go to sleep, and then left her.

Mariana could feel a smile stretching across her face as she sat up and reached for the glass. He must love her very much to have pleasured her in such an intimate way. She was sure that he did. Why else would he take the trouble to teach her every amorous art he knew? It no longer mattered where or how he had learned such things. The past was dead, no concern of hers. She had the present and the glorious future – a future filled with Christopher, with Thornfalcon and their as yet unborn children. She longed for his baby, and had waited with bated breath for the month to pass, disappointed when at the end of it, her body behaved in its customary regular fashion, with blood and stomach cramps. Next time, she assured herself – next month perhaps I'll be pregnant.

She snuggled down into the feather mattress, firelight forming weird patterns over this strange room where Christopher had initiated her into the worship of their bodies. She almost liked it now, becoming familiar with his curios, fearing them less because he had carefully explained what they were. I mustn't be cowardly and superstitious, she thought. His friends are rich eccentrics, nothing more. My imagination plays tricks. Who could be more kindly than the Reverend Grant? Who more solicitous than Dr Russell? True, Arthur Cartwright is somewhat ill-bred, but there must be good in him for Christopher to offer an invitation. He's older, wiser than me. When I eventually meet Agnes, she'll be like a sister. I know it. I must learn to be more trusting. It's living with Crosby for so long that has warped my judgement of human beings.

Having lectured herself, she drank the milk prepared by Mrs Brockwell. It was warm and sweet and tasted of nutmeg. Before long, she was asleep, obeying Christopher's instructions. Some time later, she surfaced from dreams, an unnatural awakening for it seemed as if she still slept. The fire had died to a sullen glow. The candles had burned down. She did not know what had startled her into this half-dreaming waking state. The atmosphere of the room was charged with an expectant, waiting quality. The air seemed full of floating thoughts, of whispering voices and stealthy vapours, of those singular aromas from the laboratory that were like letters of a strange language which she had hardly learned to spell. She squinted into the darkness but could distinguish no figure or movement of any sort, yet from the floor up to the arched ceiling, the whole space was humming with mysterious activity. A thousand energies were in being around some secret project.

Not only in the room – through the whole of Thornfalcon, she sensed the same electric charge of force. She got out of bed, feeling for her dressing-robe, shrugging her shoulders into it. She went to the window and pulled back the curtains. Slanting moonlight fell from the great casement like a shower of ice. She recoiled from the ghastly face of the moon peering down into her eyes. There was a tingling along her spine, and the moonshine deepened the blackness in the outer reaches of the room where the guttering candles could not penetrate. It was alive with baffling apprehension, and now she was aware of something else. Somewhere, dim and far away, she could hear voices singing. No, not actually singing – they were chanting. My God, she thought, it's the same sound that haunted my dreams on my wedding-night! But Christopher said that he had taken me whilst I slept. Did I dream it? Am I dreaming at this moment?

The noise was coming from somewhere above her. A room in the tower, and she knew which one it was. Though Christopher had taken her all over Thornfalcon, there was one door that he kept locked. He had explained this by saying that the flooring was unsafe and that no one must enter there until he had had it repaired. That room was directly over the Master Chamber. Mariana found the brass candlestick on the dressing-table and lit a taper at the fire, then shielding it with her hand, touched it to the candle. The tiny light flared up, comforting and friendly. Holding it in her trembling fingers, she opened the door and looked out. The darkness was total, but the chanting did not stop and, crawling down to greet her, came a sweet, stagnant odour, familiar as an impression in a recurring dream.

Go on, you craven coward, she bullied herself, forcing her

reluctant feet to step out of the comparative security of the bedroom. The patterns of moonlight which fell across the corridor took on sinister shapes. She could see the turn of the stone staircase leading up and, haltingly, every footstep an agony of terror, she made her way aloft. The voices were louder now. Someone was beating on a drum and the thin reedy call of a flute wailed. She reached the forbidden door and it was ajar. Light streamed through the crack, a soft light, as of many candles, shadows crossing it as if the beings within were in motion, a drifting, dancing movement. The music swelled as she paused with her hand on the knob. Then she flung it wide and stepped inside.

She was met by inky blackness and absolute silence. Bewildered and afraid, she put out wide-spread fingers. The space rejected them, as if it was fashioned of thick glass – yet unlike glass in that the force which blocked the threshold had the weird resilience of flesh. Cold as the grave – cold as the air. It was the air – but somehow frozen. She tried here and there. Its density had no openings. Dear God, let me be dreaming, she prayed without hope, and then quietly closed the door, half expecting the hidden scene to erupt again, but it did not. I'm either going mad, she thought, or someone in the house is playing a horrible game, manipulating me like a puppet-master. I can almost feel the jerk of the strings. She wanted to fly from the haunted place. In her panic, she missed her footing on the stairs, felt herself falling, the candle arcing like a rocket, clattering and bouncing down, its feeble light extinguished. Then she knew no more.

Morning was streaming in at the windows, scattering gloomy nightmares like mist. Mariana woke to find Christopher at her side, stretched out on his stomach, innocent in slumber, his thick lashes screening those ice-blue eyes. Mariana's mind was a blank. She could remember nothing except drinking hot milk after he had left her last night. She coiled against him, pressing her body into his, needing comfort, reassurance, and she did not know against what. He stirred, muttering something in his sleep, then rolled over so that he could press her face into the moist hollow of his shoulder.

'Ouch!' she exclaimed, discovering that there was a tender spot on her temple.

This roused him. 'What is it, darling? Did I pull your hair?' he asked with a yawn.

Mariana was carefully touching the bruise. 'How did that get there? It hurts, and my head aches.'

Christopher was much more interested in running his hands over her waist and hips, as if to establish possession. 'I expect you knocked yourself when you fell. I came in about an hour after I'd left you tucked up in bed and very nearly tripped over you. You lay on the floor near the door. I couldn't wake you, owing to the sedative which had been added to your milk, so I just put you back to bed. What were you doing? Sleepwalking?'

Mariana sat up, elbows on her knees, chin resting on her hand. 'I've never heard tell that I walked in my sleep,' she replied thoughtfully, then she turned accusing eyes on him. 'Why was I given a sleeping-draught, Christopher?'

He smiled charmingly, always in a good mood on waking, like a child eager for the day's adventures. 'I wanted you to have a good long sleep, my love. It was a strain, meeting new people. I thought it best if nothing disturbed you.'

'What might have done so?' This suspicion was unpleasant, and she was ashamed of the instant doubt which flared up. Had he wanted her out of the way so that he might continue his affair with Mrs Wrixon? Her mind, voided of constructive thought, swam dizzily.

Christopher brushed this aside, eager to make love to her. She submitted but, for the first time ever, could not enjoy it, jealous thoughts buzzing like angry hornets in her brain. She hid her reluctance well, writhing and moaning at the right moment, pretending that she had reached ecstasy. If Christopher was aware that she was shamming, he gave no indication of it.

She pretended a great deal throughout the next hours. No one guessed that she was not entering with equal zest into her guests' revels. The men went hunting and hawking; the women passed the time playing faro and bezique or carpet-bowls in the Long Gallery. They wagered large sums of money on every game of skill and chance. They drank a great deal of tea. This was one of the delights of her new role in which Mariana rejoiced – tea served in delicate porcelain cups, poured from a silver pot. Reverend Grant was the first to depart, leaving on Saturday evening to prepare his sermon for the morrow. Dr Russell rode with him for company. Mariana gave him letters to deliver to her family: one for Margery, and two notes for Ernestine and Annabelle. Her heart ached as she saw Grant riding away.

After the last of their visitors had clattered off in their splendid conveyances, Christopher excused himself and left her to her own devices. She knew him well enough by now not to question him, thinking that he was eager to resume his studies in laboratory or observatory. At a loss in the sudden silence which now filled the house, she wandered aimlessly into the music-salon and tried out the ornate harpsichord. This brought little peace to her troubled spirit and her melancholy irritated her for, as far as she could see, it had no real foundation.

She had found the guests unpleasant, but Christopher had not marked out Mrs Wrixon for special attention, and she had been successful in keeping the odious Arthur firmly in his place. Although she was their hostess, with that art known only to females, the ladies had made her aware that they did not welcome her society, so she had been thrown upon the mercies of the gentlemen which they had extended to her with an all too ready charity. Captain Wodehouse was an opinionated bore, proud of his reputation as a roué; Sir Marvin a conceited, aging fop. Close examination in daylight had revealed lines on his rouged cheeks, and a wrinkled neck that even the highest stock could not hide. The only one among them with whom she had found the slightest rapport was Howard Blake, who seemed a guileless boy at heart, despite the fact that Cora, although his aunt, was also his mistress. He was, as Christopher bluntly put it, her 'fancy man'.

Music, embroidery or reading bringing no tranquility to the restlessness which tormented her, Mariana caught up her muslin skirts and ran, as if fleeing her own hesitation, up the curving staircase of the tower and across the threshold of the observatory. It was empty, so she sought her husband on the platform. The moon was full, the night deepening from pale sapphire to dark amethyst. The great woods of Thornfalcon whispered, and there was an edge of frost in the air.

Christopher stood, as she had known he would, with folded arms and face lifted to the sky. She laid her hand on his arm. He turned, looked at her for a second, then said: 'What do you want?'

She had meant to call him back to earth, but not like this. Here was the incomprehensible gaze which rested on her at times, but with an added fierceness which cut her like a knife. 'I came to be with you. Is that wrong? Christopher, what have I done?' she cried, weary of trying to gauge his moods.

His answer fell like ice on the heat of her pleading. 'Done?' he echoed, with that pale smile that seemed to mock itself. 'Done, my darling wife? Nothing that anyone – I least of all – could find fault with. One might as well chide the shifting winds as hold a woman responsible for her own nature.'

His flippant tone was in startling contrast to the flame in his eyes. She could find no clue to guide her, save that he and his friends had been smoking hashish and lacing their wine with laudanum throughout the visit. 'Christopher, what is it?' she asked again.

In her desire to break down the barrier between them, she stepped closer, noticing with pain that he drew away until his back was pressed against the parapet. When he could retreat no further, he threw out a hand in a forbidding gesture. She stopped, obedient but rebellious, like a child threatened without good reason. The wind played with tendrils of her hair and strained the soft fabric of her gown against her limbs. The moonlight flooded down, pouring over her arms, breasts and hands, glimpsed beneath her cloak as she moved. It glorified the smooth skin, scintillated on the burnished embroidery, and Christopher's eyes narrowed. She seemed to be enveloped with running silver fire.

Something – passion, mad desire, flickered across his face, succeeded by a look of contempt. Measuring her from head to foot, he murmured, with a slashing bitterness: 'You seek to disobey me, madam, and I'll not tolerate it.'

She rounded on him, arms clasped under the heavy swathe of velvet. 'I don't know what you mean.'

'Don't you?' He spoke over the shoulder which he now presented to her, remote, detached, elbows leaning on the rail, as his narcotic-glazed eyes fixed the stars. 'D'you take me for a fool? I heard you telling Grant that you planned to visit Swinsty Farm in the near future. I forbid it.'

'Explain yourself!' she shouted angrily. 'I've every right to see my family. The girls are getting married in a fortnight, a double wedding at which Reverend Grant will officiate. I want to be there!' She had never looked at him like that before, never used such a tone.

'I don't have to explain anything to you. You're my wife. You'll do as I say.' His voice was quiet, but held a steely quality. 'I feed you – house you – teach you. I allow you the privilege of my name. That should be more than enough for you. I've paid your father's debts – paid for your sisters' weddings, and in return I demand your undivided loyalty. You need no one but me.'

'How unjust! How monstrously ungenerous!' she raved, beside herself with indignation. 'D'you think that you own me? That you can buy my love and loyalty?'

The dark-shadowed eyes in that haggard face rested on her. 'I did precisely that, my dear. I bought you,' he said in a hoarse, whispering voice, then as if the pressure of pent-up feelings coupled with the confusion of drugs was too much for his already weakened defences, he shouted: 'Why d'you seek me? Can't you leave me in peace to contemplate the wonders of the universe? How can you possibly understand me, an ignorant peasant like you? What have we really in common, you and I, except the heat and rut of the bed?'

She could not believe that the man she loved could mouth such insults. They struck like a blade in her heart, a blade that would never be withdrawn. There it would remain, corroding and wounding until the day she died. Yet he looked ill, every one of his forty years weighing heavily on him. In spite of everything, she loved him with the all-forgiving love of woman that is kept tender by the mother instinct. Many cruel words sprang to her lips but she did not utter them. She could not bring herself to hurt him as he had hurt her.

'If I've offended you, then I'm truly sorry, Christopher,' she said quietly, battling with her welling bitterness. 'If you want me to renounce my family – so be it. As for buying me – I would've come to you had you been penniless, if you had told me that you loved me.'

'Love!' He took the word, twisted and tortured it, then flung it back at her. 'Love? And what, wife, is this magical ''love''? A weakness, a vulnerability. I was deceived once and once only, deceived by someone I trusted. My revenge was swift and bloody. I can't love, Mariana.' His voice sank, and he reassumed his old unnatural look of dazed self-absorption, staring inwards at the fantasies clouding his mind.

'If this is all you have to say to me, then I'll leave you here,' she replied gently. 'You need to rest. Come to bed soon, my love, and tomorrow we'll ride together, if you wish.' But as she moved to go, he put out a hand, hesitated, and did not touch her.

The frenzy of anger had left him with that sudden change of mood which betrayed his fevered brain. She sat down on the parapet without a word, unable to leave him if he needed her there. The night was tinged with frost, and under her thick cloak she was cold – cold to her soul. Even with his hand so close to hers, she felt that they were drifting apart, further and further across a dark waste of water.

CHAPTER 5

Spring came late in Yorkshire that year, as if winter was reluctant to loosen its grim hold. Yet pass it did, as it had done a thousand times before, and one morning when Mariana stood at the great windows of her bedchamber, she looked across the gardens towards the rolling moors and sniffed spring in the wind. She could feel it, taste it, smell it, giving a sigh of relief born from her harsh farmstead upbringing. It meant the cessation of bitter cold, of chapped fingers, and toes red and raw with chilblains, of struggling through snow drifts humping fodder for the cattle, of breaking the thick layer of ice in the well before water could be drawn up. These things still haunted her although she was a lady now, with others to perform the daily chores. Fires roared, warming the stately rooms; her bed was nightly heated with coals in a big brass warming-pan; hot water was brought to her in ornate china jugs for her toilet. There was a closet just off her dressing room, tiled, scrupulously clean and fragrant, no need to trudge across icy ruts to the privy in the yard, but hatred of the winter was ingrained, a part of her which she could never forget.

It had been a strange winter, incarcerated in the huge house with Christopher. He had become everything to her – father, brother, mentor and lover. She loved him obsessively, but was also learning to fear him. Sometimes he was a gay, delightful companion, each shared moment a perfect jewel of contentment. At others he was learned, serious, painstaking as he instructed her, making history live in a fascinating way, taking her on journeys through many lands as they followed the course of rivers, of mountain-ranges and continents on the large globe revolving on its ebony stand. Thornfalcon was in itself a schoolroom, steeped in stories of royalty, of wars and governmental strife. But there were days, made even more gloomy by the terrible weather, when he withdrew completely, locking himself away in the top of the tower.

They had not always been alone. The same group of friends who had been there in October came again just before Christmas on St Thomas' Day, and they had remained for the whole of the festive season. Their next visit coincided with Candlemas, in February, and on each successive visit, Mariana disliked them more.

On that spring morning, she was filled with the spirit of holiday. Christopher had been gone for three days, away on business in Lancashire. She had surprised herself by enjoying sleeping alone, reading late and sprawling over the bed without the fear of disturbing him. She could do as she pleased and rejoiced in her liberty. Of course, she missed him; it was lonely eating a solitary breakfast in the morning-room under the eyes of the footmen with their bland faces. Afterwards, Mrs Brockwell came to her, as usual, a broad, placid figure, white-capped and white-aproned, with folded hands. The very sight of her should have brought a feeling of comfort and confidence, but Mariana was inclined to give the woman her instructions with almost indecent speed. No, she would not be requiring luncheon, a snack in the library would suffice. Dinner? Well, the master was not expected home yet, so again, a meal on a tray would be satisfactory. Try as she might, Mariana could not shake off the unpleasant notion that she was a prisoner and Mrs Brockwell her gaoler.

What should she do with the remainder of the day? Mariana mused as she wandered round the house. Circling the great drawing-room, she was reminded of the hours her unwelcome guests had spent there. She could almost hear the rattle of the dice, and their loud laughter as they wrangled, added points and deducted loss and gain, could visualize Mrs Wrixon's harpy countenance, craning forward, greedy for revenge on a winning opponent, and Marvin's goatish face as he mouthed a scandal. Captain Wodehouse too, with his lustful glare. On that very couch over there, Lady Somerville had held court, staring with pallid eyes while Cora dithered, petulant and frantically worried every time Howard paid any other woman the slightest attention. What a sorry crew! Mariana thought, and Arthur Cartwright was the worst. She had felt compassion for Howard, aware that he still retained a measure of innocence amidst the corruption. The others knew it too, and went out of their way to involve him in their vices.

Memories crowded in, none of them uplifting and, after asserting her ownership by turning a pair of Etruscan vases around to show them that they belonged to the mistress of Thornfalcon, Mariana left, unable to endure the pressure of silence. With sudden resolution, she went to the bedchamber and collected her cloak. She was momentarily disconcerted by the stare of alabaster eyes. Kali had not moved from her alcove, but she was reflected over and over in the massive gilded mirrors. The room was still. One of the maids had opened a window and the air was tartly fresh, not over-hot and filled with cloying incense, as when Christopher was in residence.

The cobbled stableyard was deserted, the servants enjoying a break from the eagle-eyed scrutiny of their master. Even the mastiffs were not barking; probably one of the grooms had taken them for a walk. It was a relief to be able to enter that area without having to face their frantic snarls and ferociously glaring teeth as they lunged, pawing the air, at the ends of heavy iron chains. If Christopher had not been so insistent on keeping them at that point of rage, perhaps cats could have sunned themselves on the mossy walls, given birth to their litters in comfortable corners of the stable, even entered the house to enrich it with their elegance. Mariana missed Tibby, and happiness tingled through her at the thought of seeing her before the day was over.

She reached Swinsty Farm at noon. Margery was pegging out washing as the gig swung round to the back of the house. She immediately dumped the wicker basket on the straggling grass and ran to Mariana, holding out her arms, enveloping her in that embrace which she remembered so well and had missed so much. They hugged one another, laughing, nearly crying.

'My dear girl, what kept you so long?' asked Margery, wiping her eyes with a corner of her apron. She released her, scanning her face with growing anxiety. She did not notice the fine gown, the fur-edged cloak and fashionable bonnet. 'You've filled out a bit, but you're too pale. Aren't you sleeping properly? Eating too much fancy food, I'll warrant. Come you inside. I've just baked a batch of bread, and old Lizzie still yields milk every day. She had another calf back along, a fine little heifer. You can keep your bullocks. Give me a good old cow any day of the week.'

She was talking and talking to hide her worry. Mariana sat down in the wooden rocking-chair by the kitchen fire whilst Margery swung the kettle forward on its crane and tipped it over the tea-pot. 'How are Ernestine and Annabelle?' she wanted to know, relaxing in the homely atmosphere, but it seemed shrunken somehow, and woefully shabby. Tibby opened a golden eye, stretched, yawned, flexed her claws in the depths of the rag-rug, then humped her back and bristled, rubbing round Mariana's skirts. 'Up with you then, Puss,' she encouraged, and Tibby leapt agilely on to her lap, purring like the kettle, settling herself down to thrum and knead the luxuriant velvet, eyes ecstatic slits.

'Oh, they're fine and dandy.' Margery was busy spreading butter on a hunk of crusty bread and filling two earthenware mugs with strong hot tea. 'Those wedding-presents you sent over must've cost a mint. Don't know when they'll find a use for such beautiful linen and china, but still, I suppose they'll come in handy at some time or other. We'd have rather you'd come yourself. Why didn't you?' She gave Mariana a searching glance, still the same forthright Margery, unimpressed by the fact that she was entertaining a lady in her humble dwelling.

'Christopher was busy, and didn't want me to make the journey alone,' Mariana lied, but she could not meet Margery's eyes, and concentrated on the cat, smoothing the short silky fur.

'I see,' said Margery, who indeed did see much more than Mariana realized. She sipped her tea, waiting for her to speak.

'And how is life here?' Mariana brought out at last.

'Same as usual. The boys're away at school. Kind of your husband to offer to pay the fees. The little ones're getting as tall as bean-poles. Your father's still drinking.'

'Of course!' Mariana snapped bitterly.

They fell silent and Margery waited patiently, knowing that Mariana had not made the journey just to enquire about their health. I shouldn't have come, thought Mariana. I've moved so far from them. We can't speak the same language any more. If Christopher gets to hear of it he'll be furious, but I have an excuse – a grand excuse. He'll forgive me anything when I tell him. She put her mug down on the battered, well-scrubbed table and lifted her eyes to Margery.

'I wanted you to be the first to know. I think that I'm with child,' she said.

Margery's gaunt face lit up. She leaned over and took Mariana's hands in her rough ones. 'That's grand news! Are you well? When will it be? D'you want me to come over for the birthing?'

Mariana laughed shakily. It was so good to share this news with someone. For days she had been counting on her fingers and making half alarmed, half joyful calculations. 'I'm feeling very well – no sickness, nothing but a missed period and sore breasts,' she replied. 'I reckon I'll be delivered just after Christmas. I'd love you to be there but – ' she hesitated, and Margery did not need to be told.

'Your husband will secure the services of Dr Russell. They'll

90

not want an old country woman like me around the place,' she interjected. 'Don't you worry, lovey, I understand. The birth of Thornfalcon's heir is an important event. Nothing must go wrong.' She gave a short laugh. 'Merciful heavens, I'd not like to take the responsibility.'

'I haven't told Christopher yet. I wanted to be sure first, not to rouse his expectations and then disappoint him.'

'This is natural and wise.' Margery refilled their mugs. 'D'you wish me to hold my peace for the time being?'

'Please, Margery, don't tell anyone!' In Mariana's answer, her old friend caught a note of fear. There's something wrong, she thought. She was certain of it, though how or why she felt this so strongly was a mystery.

Mariana was fighting the urge to fling herself on that motherly figure and cry her heart out. It's a sign of early pregnancy, she told herself sternly, you must expect to feel weepy, and she hid her distress as Margery said quietly: 'Are you happy?'

'Of course I'm happy!' She was on the defensive at once, head high, chin up in that stubborn way which Margery knew all too well. 'Christopher's a marvellous husband. He's actually giving me lessons. I'm learning history and geography, literature and mathematics. Imagine that! A gentleman like him bothering to educate his wife! I'm not expected to do a thing about the house. We have a housekeeper, Mrs Brockwell, who looks to all that. She does positively everything. Her domain stretches to the duck-pond in the north, the dairy in the south, the stillroom in the east and the linen-cupboard in the west! She's most awfully efficient.'

'And you resent it,' said Margery calmly. 'You'd like to be mistress of your own home. You feel like an outsider.'

'I don't! Why in the name of heaven should I want to soil my hands and break my back? I've done enough of that in the past, thank you very much!' Mariana could not understand the anger which surged through her.

Margery smiled wisely, knowing Mariana better than she did herself. 'Send her packing, my dear. Find someone more biddable, someone who hasn't ruled the roost for as long as her,' she advised.

'I can't,' Mariana confessed, lips drooping, a cloud crossing her face. 'Christopher wouldn't hear of it. She was his nurse once, you see – nurse to him and his twin sister, Lady Agnes.'

'I know,' Margery nodded, automatically taking mending from her sewing-basket. She never sat idle if she could possibly help it. As she talked she poked a long darning-needle in and out of a sock. 'I've lived here all my life. Word has reached me about Lord Christopher and Lady Agnes and the all-powerful Mrs Brockwell.'

'Why didn't you warn me?' Mariana had dropped pretence. Her eyes were huge and questioning in her heart-shaped face, framed by ringlets and her shovel-brimmed straw bonnet.

Margery smiled, cocking an eyebrow at her as she bit off the thread. 'There wasn't much time. It was such a hasty marriage. Would you have listened to me? You were head over heels in love with him.'

'I still am,' said Mariana flatly.

Margery shrugged, taking up a torn shirt and threading a finer needle. 'Then why aren't you radiant? Oh, don't try to pull the wool over my eyes. You're talking with old Margery, my girl – Margery who changed your napkins when you were a babe – who comforted you when you skinned your knees. I'm a friend. A true friend. You can trust me.'

'It's purely a matter of settling down to marriage. That's what Christopher says,' Mariana replied, clinging desperately to hauteur lest she confessed too much. 'To go to Thornfalcon from this – !'

Her spread hands indicated the muddled room where washing hung over a length of rope stretched below the mantelshelf, muddy boots stood by the door, coats dangled from hooks against the flaking limewash of the walls, and water had to be drawn from the well, not pumped through taps. In the yard, the stinking privy squatted like an unhealthy fungus under a spidery canopy of ivy.

'I'm aware of that – I'm not daft, you know.' Margery's eyes followed as she pointed. ''Course 'tis bound to be different. Lord love you, living with a man is bad enough at the best of times if he's from your own class, leave alone trying to please someone who thinks he's God Almighty!'

Her vehemence stunned Mariana. 'You don't like him!' she gasped.

''Tisn't a case of liking or not liking. He's an odd one. I've heard tales – seems he's even odder than most of the local gentry.'

'I love Christopher,' Mariana repeated like a catechism. 'I'll not sit here and listen to you bad-mouthing him!'

'I'm speaking the truth,' said Margery, calmly packing away her mending. 'Now, if you'll excuse me, I've dinner to see to. The children'll be home from school directly. Will you stay and see them?'

Mariana felt that she was being dismissed. She no longer

belonged at Swinsty Farm. Where then did she belong? At Thornfalcon? She rose, a slim elegant figure in the dim kitchen. 'I'd love to see them, but I can't stay. Give them my love, and Ernestine and Annabelle too. I'll come again when I'm able. It isn't easy to get away.'

'And Crosby? D'you want him to know you've visited?' Margery asked as they walked across the muddy yard.

'I don't care if he knows or not. I've heard that he's drinking himself to death as fast as he can. It will be no loss to the world,' Mariana replied. Margery had never seen such hardness in her eyes before. She's changed, she thought. What's her husband been teaching her besides schoolbook lessons?

Mariana took her place on the single seat of the gig, the reins gathered in her gloved hands. Margery stood at the wheel. Her hair was greyer, Mariana noticed, her face more lined. 'I tend your mother's grave. Keep flowers on it when I can. The dear lady is not forgotten.'

Tears burned at the back of Mariana's eyes. 'Thank you, Margery. She's not forgotten by me either – never forgotten. As for Crosby! I'd like to see him crawling in the lowest pit of degradation!'

'If you need me, just send word,' Margery said.

She was very uneasy, reluctant to see this child whom she had raised with as much loving care as poverty and work had permitted, disappear from view with that bewildered unhappiness in her eyes. Oh, Mariana had covered it well, but gossip was rife in the district. Margery had heard of the parties at Thornfalcon, of his Lordship's interest in matters best left alone, his charting of the planets, his workshop where he brewed peculiar concoctions. Those guests who arrived periodically, a queer bunch, so it was said, turning night into day with their gambling, racketing around the moors in pursuit of game. The villagers whispered of other things too, of wickedness and ungodly vices and tampering with the Old Religion. Margery had dismissed the latter, knowing the peasants to be riddled with superstition, but now she wondered . . .

The moorland road wound among the brown hillsides where the breezy fell stretched for miles in rough undulations. There were still tenacious patches of snow on the higher slopes. Sheep grazed placidly, and the birds were returning from their sojourn in warmer climes, wheeling and dipping in search of nesting material. In the hazy distance rose the faint blue shimmer of far-off hills, dreaming under the peaceful skies, and the road meandered, falling gently into pleasant valleys dotted with homesteads and cottages. Primroses and violets were strewn along the banks, marigolds and campion brightened the meadows where the shadows of the newly-budding trees hung lazily across the flowing river.

Mariana gave the strong young cob little guidance, letting him take his own pace. She was in no hurry to return to the frowning walls of Thornfalcon. Here was reality, and she wanted to stay on the hillside with the free air and the majestic sky around and above her, and the moors bathed with the golden, gleaming sparkle of the afternoon.

'I must go now or I'll be late,' she told herself, thinking of Mrs Brockwell's inquisitive glance, of her pursed lips and that sanctimoniously servile attitude which cloaked a very different meaning. Of Christopher too – ah, but he was a complex person – moody, difficult and demanding.

Though knowing that she should hurry, she allowed the horse to stop. He lowered his head to munch the new, delicious grass-buds. She was telling herself to go, yet all she wanted just then was to stay, maybe for ever. This could not be and she gave a jerk on the reins, passing a ruined, roofless cottage around whose walls rank grass had grown. The track was wild and lovely, following an ancient Roman roadway. How glorious it would be, she mused, to be as lifeless as those stones. To lie there through the long, long years, feeling the spring awakening in the silent earth, basking under hot summer skies, and then to have the dead leaves of autumn falling down and burying me as the air grew cold and grey. Always at peace, subject to no one's moods and wilful fancies, unfettered by human thoughts and cares, yet aware of the meaning of everything.

She reached the outer wall surrounding Thornfalcon, passed between its high gates, and the drive wound away in front of her, twisting, turning, bordered by trees on either side. Pigeons were fluttering in the branches, giving their mournful, throaty love-calls. From the distance came the harsh weird cry of the peacock, strutting on the terrace, flaunting his gorgeous tail to entice his dowdy hens. As the gig approached, the dogs began to clamour. Mariana shivered. She still held the phantom warmth of Tibby on her lap, and wished the furry body of her old companion was with her, not back at the farm.

She had been dreaming, up there on the moors, deceiving herself into believing that it was reality. But no, this was reality – her life at Thornfalcon, the child growing in her body, the fact that she was Christopher's wife. There was no escaping it, and part of her did not want to escape. Three-quarters of her existence was happy, and it was selfish of her to long for more. No living being had the right to expect perfection.

She sensed at once that he had returned. There was a frantic bustle in the stableyard where only that morning had been an atmosphere of relaxation. Inside the house, the servants were earnestly going about their duties as if they had never known what it was like to loll in the kitchen, drinking small-beer and playing cards, gossiping about the goings on above stairs or courting their sweethearts. Yes, the master was back, all right. Mariana's throat tightened and her heart began to pound. She wished sadly that these symptoms were ones of joy at seeing her beloved. That element was present but buried beneath a bewildering assortment of other emotions, not the least of which was fear. Skirts swishing with the speed of her step, she walked towards the tower wing. I've committed no crime, she told herself bravely. Why should I cringe? Why can't I visit my relatives? Indignation steadied her and she felt anger rather than fear, as if her life force was aware that fear could not save it.

She did not see him for a moment when she entered the Master Chamber. The curtains were pulled across the windows and the strong odour of incense struck her forcibly. The fire leapt in the sudden draught as she opened the door, and the candle-flames slanted. Christopher was lying on the bed, arms clasped behind his head, and she forgot everything in joy, running to him, tugging at her bonnet strings, flinging it aside.

'Christopher!' she cried, bubbling over with her important news, longing to burst out with it, yet restraining herself. 'Oh, darling, I've missed you so much!'

He did not move, merely fixing her with those clear cool eyes. 'Have you, my dear? Such a warm welcome is most flattering.'

She was on the bed beside him, leaning over, her breasts pressed into his chest, hands in his hair, mouth close on his own. He did not need to invite her – she loved him, wanted him. He was no bogey-man, he was her lover, her handsome, cultured husband. 'Where've you been? What have you been doing?' she asked , smiling. 'Ah, this separation has taught me to miss you, dearest. It's been so lonely. I've tried to study, honestly I have, but I couldn't work without my master.'

His hands came up, holding her head, fingers smooth and strong. His eyes were slightly out of focus because they were so near. A shuddering sigh shook her and her lids closed languorously, parted lips hungry for his kiss. He did not give it. Instead his grip tightened painfully, dragging at her hair, and her eyes snapped open in shock, meeting the full blast of the rage contorting his features.

'Lying whore!' He snarled and flung her from him. 'Whilst I've been in Lancashire enduring the hospitality of that vile dullard, Cartwright the Elder, you've been gallivanting off to Swinsty Farm! Deliberately flouting my orders!'

Her delight and passion rushed back into her with brutal force. She crouched on the bed, watching him with wide violet eyes. 'Yes, I have. I don't deny it. I drove over there this morning. I hoped that you would not object – would understand when I told you my reason. I needed to see Margery.'

'That stupid crone! What possible need can you have of her? Perhaps you also longed to see your drunken slob of a father. Was that it? Or those idiot sisters of yours? Like calling to like, eh?' He shouted, throwing her into a state of terror by the ugly expression on his face. His contempt was directed not at the occupants of the farm, but with a nightmare sense of inevitableness towards herself.

'How dare you!' Her rising temper matched his own, though hers was a clean, healthy rage.

'Get out of my bed, you scheming bitch!' He made a threatening move towards her and Mariana moved like the wind, ducking out of his reach.

Shaking with fear and fury, she stood looking at him. Her pride was strong yet she would have reasoned with him, but could see that any words would be useless. It was not Christopher who had shouted at her, but a creature in a delirium. She was strong-willed and innocent and hated injustice, so: 'I'm not your slave!' she grated.

He lunged so quickly that she was unprepared. His blow caught her across the side of the face. She staggered back, arms raised, but he hit her again and she buckled, her ears ringing, stars dancing before her eyes. Then he grabbed her viciously by the arms, jerking her to her feet and dragging her back to the bed.

'You *are* my slave!' he mocked. 'Mine to do with as I will. Never forget it, madam, never forget it for a moment! I expect absolute obedience from you. Nothing less!'

'My God, Christopher! You're mad – mad!' she gasped, the breath knocked out of her.

He laughed and that laughter echoed through the room, a diabolical sound. Her control snapped. She raised her hand and slapped him across the face with all the strength at her command. She expected a return blow, uncaring in her outrage, but the target of his swift hands was not her head. Instead, he yanked her hard against his chest, holding her tightly. She struggled, but was pinned down on the tangled fur coverlet by the weight of his body. His groping hands fastened on her wrists, holding her arms above her head whilst he covered her with his length. He was hurting her, crushing her, and his eyes were intense above her, fire in their blue depths. He released an arm long enough to claw at one of the curtain cords. In an instant he had rolled her over on to her face and was lashing her wrists together behind her.

'Not my slave, eh?' he gloated. 'Oh, but you are. My slave to treat how I will.'

Half stifled by the pillow, her cries were muffled. She felt the air on her skin as her skirts were pushed up, felt her legs being spread and then his hand between her buttocks finding the place where she was still a virgin. Pain, horrible and intense, seared her when he penetrated her there, pushing into her with fierce thrusts so that she screamed. He roughly pressed her face deeper into the pillow, and she felt her body expanding agonizingly, opening to take him. Desperately she struggled to escape this man who was using her so selfishly, but in the grip of an uncontrollable lust, he could not be stopped. The violent assault went on and on until she longed to die and be released from such burning torment. At last, with a final frenzied burst of energy, Christopher found completion, slumping heavily on her.

Mariana turned her head so that she could breathe, gulping in air. She was sobbing, hurting, every delicate membrane in her loins on fire, but this subsided as he withdrew, lying flat on his back, his chest heaving, his laboured breathing gradually quieting. Her terror dissipated, but disgust remained. She was hampered by her tethered wrists, the cord drawn cruelly tight. She looked at the man beside her who lay there relaxed and peaceful, almost young and defenceless. He sighed as she moved, trapped by her long hair which was pinioned beneath his shoulder. His eyes opened and he stared at her. She tensed, expecting that change of mood which would make him heartless, but he gazed at her quietly, reading the fear and horror on her face.

'Mariana . . .' he whispered.

'Untie me.' Her voice was hard. He did so, and she sat there, chafing her numb wrists. She noticed, almost dispassionately, the bruises on her arms and shoulders. 'If you ever do that to me again, I'll kill you. I swear it!' she grated through clenched teeth.

He smiled, totally unrepentant, rather amused. 'You'll grow to like it. Spyros does.'

'What are you talking about?' she frowned, questions in her eyes.

'That's how men make love to other men, or didn't you know, my ignorant little peasant?' Christopher answered casually.

Mariana sucked in a breath of shocked understanding. Her husband and the Greek valet? It wasn't possible, was it? 'Christopher! What madness possesses you? How can you be so cruel to me?' Her voice broke on tears but she bit them back. She did not intend to add to his satisfaction by permitting herself to weep.

He swung his legs over the side of the bed. Mariana flinched, not knowing what to expect, but his words astounded her as he said: 'Tidy yourself, Mariana. It is time that you met my sister.' He stood for a moment, tall and straight and beautiful, before going to the mirror and adjusting his clothing.

As the sun sank a chill wind arose and whistled dusk up the valley. It was just after six in the evening when the coach halted outside a large, lonely house on a high plateau some miles from Thornfalcon. The hills glowed like hot coals where the dipping sun caught their rounded sides, and the hollows between were filled with luminous shadows.

Christopher slid down one of the carriage windows and gave an order to his armed postillions. They had driven into the eye of the declining sun and his face glowed with a pearly transparency. Mariana caught her breath. He looked so handsome in that queer light. It was hard to believe that she had not imagined the dreadful scene in the bedroom so short a time ago. Had it not been for the throbbing bruises and nail-marks, the ache between her thighs, she might have thought she had dreamed it. And now the suddenness of meeting Agnes. What was this place, and what would his sister think of her?

The coach rolled into motion again and she saw that they were passing between gates set in high walls. The tops glittered like blood, the sunset rays reflected on jagged broken glass cemented on the copings. The drive was edged by elms, and soon they came in sight of a large red brick house. Its shadow fell across the enclosed garden. Bats wheeled and swirled from its central clock tower as twilight passed into night. The windows glowed yellow, looking out over steeply sloping lawns where carefully tended cedar trees were permitted on their velvet surface. Beeches and walnut encircled them and hid the outer world with a shivering, rustling barrier.

They were met at the front door by a uniformed porter who conducted them down a flagged, damp-smelling passage. The place was very clean, the air overlaid by the odour of beeswax and cooking. They passed through a narrow closet with a barred door. The porter jangled a large bunch of keys, locking it behind them. Another corridor lay ahead, and at the end of it was a baize-covered door studded with brass nails. The man knocked and a voice bade them enter.

The room was sparsely furnished, but a fire glowed between the polished bars of the grate, and the woman who rose to greet them was spotlessly attired. In her severely plain dark grey dress with broad white collar and turned-back cuffs, she resembled a sister from a holy order. Her hair was modestly concealed beneath a starched white cap, and her face had the contemplative expression of one who spends much time on her knees in prayer, and the rest of her life in self-denial.

'Lord St Jules,' she said as she came towards them, her glance encompassing Mariana.

'Mistress Hollings,' he bowed over her hand. 'I've brought my wife to meet Lady Agnes.'

Mistress Hollings stood with her hands clasped at her waist, and a kindly smile warmed her face, the lines softening as she looked at Mariana. 'Lady St Jules. Thou art welcome. Pray be seated.'

She pointed to a hard-backed chair by the fire, and Christopher, taking another which was one of a row along the wall, gave her a piercing look as he asked, 'How is my sister?'

Mistress Hollings sighed, seated at her desk once more, back erect, her hands laid on the surface amongst account books and letters. 'Not well, I fear. Thou hast come on one of her bad days. Poor creature, one has to watch her constantly.'

Mariana's mind was whirling as she realized that this was a hospital. Perhaps Agnes suffered from diseased lungs, like Mrs Wrixon, and this quiet, calm woman must be a nurse. Her archaic mode of speech and dress suggested that she was a Quaker. Mariana had heard that this sect devoted themselves to the care of the sick and needy.

'It grieves me to hear this. Is there anything she wants?' Anxiety flared up in Christopher's eyes.

Mistress Hollings shook her head. 'Thou hast been most generous, my Lord. Thy gifts have provided many small comforts for my patients. I can never thank thee enough. Thou art remembered in our prayers.'

'I wish to see her.' Christopher was completely controlled, but his tension was betrayed by the set of his jaw.

Mistress Hollings bowed her head in acknowledgement. 'As thou wilt, sir.'

They followed her upright, angular form through the door and along several passages, coming at last to a large staircase that wound upwards. Lamps lit the gloom, and there was the sound of distant voices. Someone was singing out of tune. Sometimes a burst of laughter rang from a hidden room and once, as they passed a heavily bolted door, Mariana heard a woman crying, a piteous sobbing which Mistress Hollings ignored.

Every tile, every floorboard, each door and dark-painted dado was highly polished, but the shining windows were barred. It was more like a prison than a hospice for the sick. Another set of stairs led further up, spiralling with sharp turns and angles. At the top of these stood two tall, strappingly built nurses, their clothing similar to that of Mistress Hollings. They fell in behind Christopher and Mariana. A door yielded to Mistress Hollings's keys. She locked it carefully when they had gone through. A small, low-arched door stood in front of them. It was bolted as well as locked. Mistress Hollings slid back a panel and looked in. Then she nodded at Christopher, threw the bolts and conducted them inside. A strong smell choked Mariana's throat – the acrid, animal odour of urine and dung.

At first, she could see nothing. The only light was that of the night-sky filtering through a tiny aperture near the ceiling. One of the nurses hung her lantern on a hook, and its yellow, hesitant beam illuminated the bare, narrow apartment. There was no fire, no adornment of any kind. The only piece of furniture was a rough bed made of planks set against one wall. In the first flash of astonishment, Mariana thought that the cell was unoccupied, then she saw someone crouched in a corner, head bowed to the knees, arms folded protectively around itself, rocking backwards and forwards, oblivious to everything.

'Lady Agnes.' Mistress Hollings bent over her, speaking with the weary patience of one who knows that her words will not be heard or understood. 'Lady Agnes, thy brother hath come.'

The hunched form shook its head, tangled hair hanging forward over the face. She did not cease her rocking motion. Christopher sank on his knees beside her, his arms going round the wasted body. Mariana was flabbergasted by the horror of the scene and the expression on his face. Never once had he shown her such tender concern.

'Agnes. Sister, look at me,' he murmured. His hand cupped her chin, lifting her face from the mane of hair. The lamp shone on a waxen complexion and a countenance old beyond its years. Agnes's eyes focused on his, deep-sunk in dark circles and, for a second, comprehension drew her back from the weird world in which her spirit was imprisoned.

'Christopher?' The voice was so low it could hardly be heard. She gave a weary sigh and rested her head against him, whilst he soothed her and held her tightly. It was as if they were one person, the likeness strikingly apparent, the infinity between them deep, timeless, eternal. Agnes was not aware of the other persons in the room because she had moved so far from reality; Christopher was unaware because he was willing himself to share her fantastic realms.

Mariana stood as if frozen to the spot. Mistress Hollings, distressed for her, came to take her hand. 'Didst thou not know she was insane?' she asked.

'No.' Mariana replied helplessly, the shock so great that a merciful numbness held the horror at bay.

Mistress Hollings cast a stern look at Christopher. 'Thou shouldst have prepared thy wife, my Lord,' then she added, to Mariana: 'She is not always thus. At times thou wouldst find her so ladylike. Why, only last sennight we apparelled her and she walked in the garden, as quiet as a lamb. There is naught to fear, Lady St Jules. Nurse Forbes and Nurse Bearcroft are nigh.'

Those two great women, built like prize-fighters, brawny-armed as stevedors! They were employed to restrain the ravings of the mad! 'I didn't know – never dreamed – ' Mariana faltered, stabbed with guilt. She should have known. She was Christopher's wife. His pain was hers also. Bewildered feelings jostled for supremacy; she rejoiced that he had brought her to the asylum, taking her into his confidence, yet was angry because he had not told her what to expect. A fog of dread swayed her mind as further realization came. Others had known of it. Mrs Brockwell for sure, Mrs Wrixon too, and those terrible friends of his that visited with awful regularity. 'How long has she been here?' she whispered at last.

'Five years.' Though Mistress Hollings gave nothing away, Mariana caught a flash of sympathy in those steady eyes. 'There have been occasions when she hath returned to Thornfalcon, but not for long, I fear.'

Mariana wanted to tear the dress from her back, throw away

the sable muff, the soft leather gloves, the feathered hat, the velvet cloak. It was as if insanity was contagious and she could catch it wearing Agnes's garments. He should have told me! He should have told me! This was the only thing that stood out crystal clear. How cruel! How deceitful!

Christopher had ignored Mistress Hollings's remark, but now he looked up, seeing Mariana's chalk-white face, her accusing eyes. He caressed Agnes's hair, saying softly: 'See, my love, I've married again. Her name is Mariana. She's strong and healthy. There will be a son for the St Jules soon.'

He held out a hand to Mariana and she went to him with the greatest reluctance, feeling the innate repugnance of the mentally stable towards those who are considered abnormal. Agnes's disturbed psyche seemed to shoot tentacles towards her – tentacles of fear and confusion, of darkness and despair. The balance between sanity and insanity was but a hair's breadth, and Mariana knew only too well how dreams could impinge on reality. She had been subjected to bad dreams since living at Thornfalcon, dreams so horrible and obscene that they might well have sprung from a disordered mind.

Christopher's fingers closed tightly on hers and he drew her nearer, till he had one arm round her and one holding his sister. Mariana's wide-spaced violet eyes looked into Agnes's vacant blue ones. Rationality returned for a split second and something glowed in the blackly-dilated pupils. It was a plea for compassion, then it changed to a malevolent glare, evil incarnate staring out from that terrible face.

Because she knew that Christopher was expecting her to make some gesture, Mariana steeled herself and laid her hand gently on Agnes's matted hair. She stayed passive under her touch. 'Agnes, I've been wanting to meet you for so long,' Mariana began, then turned to Christopher indignantly. 'She must be frozen! She'll take a chill! This is monstrous, Christopher. Do something about it at once! Order a fire to be lit here – find some blankets for her bed.'

'We can allow her nothing, Lady St Jules.' Mistress Hollings stood behind, her long shadow falling over the mad woman. 'Had she sheets, underclothing, laces, she might do herself an injury. Naught with a sharp edge, my Lady, lest she cut her throat or slash her wrists – no ligature for strangulation. We guard her well, thou may'st believe. ''Do unto others'' is the watchword here. These sad creatures in our care are managed almost entirely by reason and kindness, though at times restraint is a vile necessity. We're not called upon to use it often, thanks be to God.'

Neither Christopher nor Agnes was listening, totally wrapped up in each other. Mariana felt superfluous. Apart from dutifully introducing her to Agnes, an act which she was suddenly convinced would not have taken place had they been alone, he was blind to her existence. No one existed for him but his sister.

'Agnes, dear Agnes.' Her ears caught his words. 'My sweet – there, don't cry, your tears wound me. I've not abandoned you, neither have the others. We work for your recovery and restoration to us.'

Agnes nodded, her eyes wandering his face, mouth working as she mumbled meaningless phrases, but she trembled as she wound her arms about him, and tears crawled slowly down her cheeks. Soon her sobs increased, awful sobs moaning like the icy winds blowing over the cold blue wastes of hell.

Mistress Hollings alerted. 'My Lord, methinks thou shouldst leave. She becomes distressed. Go now, before the storm breaks.'

The nurses had moved closer, flexing their big hands. Christopher shot Mistress Hollings an uncertain glance, then seized Agnes's wrists, struggling to prise her arms open. Her cries rose, hysteria buffeting her before the deluge of insane fury took command. He had to use all his considerable strength to break free. She backed against the wall, moving inch by inch, glaring at him, at Mariana and the nurses. Her lips writhed open and a stream of filthy oaths roared round the room with the voice of dementia – a torrent of words, abusive, insulting, mingled with screams and laughter. The nurses were waiting their chance. Agnes knew it, groping for a weapon. Her hands clawed along the walls, seeking for something with which to maim or kill.

With a shriek of triumph, she pounced on the heavy metal pail which had been left there in the hope that she might use it for the relief of nature – a vain hope by the state of the floor. Raising it high, she hurled it at Mistress Hollings. The nurses launched themselves upon her. She kicked, bit and scratched until they pinioned her arms in a strong canvas jacket, binding them to her sides. It was the work of seconds to fling her on the bed and tether her like a rabid beast.

'Come away, Lady St Jules,' Mistress Hollings advised calmly. 'Accept my humble apologies. She is over-excited – a visit from her brother always affects her thus.'

'I wish that he had warned me,' said Mariana.

In the pale, scant flicker of the carriage lamp, she watched her husband sitting with his chin sunk in the tight folds of his cravat. His blond curls brushed his velvet collar, his low-crowned topper was pulled down over his eyes. He huddled in his great-coat, hands thrust deeply into the pockets. His legs in tight breeches and top-boots were stretched straight before him. He had not said a word since they left the asylum. Mariana felt drained, too tired to think coherently. He was quite likely to brush the incident aside and never speak of it, not even obliquely. At one time this capacity for ignoring the unpleasant baffled her, but she was learning to accept it, along with so many other of his peculiar traits.

She wanted desperately to communicate with him. Perhaps he was feeling as badly about the situation as herself, but his pride, masculine as well as pure St Jules, was preventing him from voicing his distress. She had a gift for him, one which would solace his sorrow, and now was the time to lay it at his feet. The coach swung round a corner, the momentum throwing them close. Her shoulder pressed into his, her hand clutched his arm to steady her. She took a deep breath and said: 'I think that I'm pregnant.'

The change in his face was frightening. He came to life, seizing her hands, almost shaking her. 'Are you sure?'

She nodded, petrified lest she had been mistaken. 'Yes, reasonably sure. That's why I visited the farm today – to consult with Margery. She knows about these matters.'

There was wild exaltation in his eyes. 'Why didn't you tell me?'

'I feared to raise your hopes, and then disappoint you,' she said angrily. 'Then may I go again? You won't mind, and hit me like today?'

'My dear, you may do what the hell you like, if you give me a son.' His arms were round her, his face contrite, lips brushing her cheek as if she was a vessel containing something infinitely precious.

'Supposing the baby is a little girl? What then?' Her hands folded themselves defensively over her flat stomach.

His smile faded, and that icy glint she had learned to dread crept into his eyes. 'It won't be.'

'No one can be sure of that,' she protested.

'I can. I've made myself master of my destiny. Would you be here as my wife, if I hadn't?'

She looked at him in dismay. What he said was true, but his words seemed to carry a certain dark, secretive emphasis. She knew his stubborn pride which would never accept defeat on any issue. He found it untenable to be thwarted of his will. Oh, he might pretend to do so, but it usually concealed a strong virulent purpose which he kept hidden until he was ready to strike.

'What of Agnes?' she asked, made cruel by apprehension. 'Even you could not prevent your beloved sister from falling ill.'

He folded his arms across his chest and leaned against the padded seat. 'Agnes, my dear Mariana, is the reason why we must never have daughters.'

The coach bounced and rocked on its leather springs. The night flashed past the windows. Mariana was aware of the length of her husband's thigh pressing into hers, saw his profile etched against the glass panes. Within her brain came a faint, sinister sound, like bells tolling a warning of dangerous rocks muffled by dank, grey fog.

CHAPTER 6

From that day forward, Christopher's manner towards Mariana changed dramatically. He was as she had first known him, soft-spoken, warmly loving. His every action seemed now to be centred on insuring her well-being and tranquility. She revelled in being the object of so much cossetting and attention. He cherished her as one cherishes a fragile plant, about to produce a rare blossom. He expressed being profoundly annoyed with himself for subjecting her to the horrific revelation at the asylum, and did his best to reassure her. Agnes was as comfortable as wealth and the devoted Quakers could make her. The doctors had said that she might recover in time. Mariana was not to worry – she must not worry about anything.

He drove her to Swinsty Farm himself soon after and, to please her, ordered the stone-masons to erect a monument over Henrietta Crosby's grave. At a later date, they took tea with the Grants. He was charm itself, beguiling Margery, flattering Mrs Grant, and if he and the rector took themselves off to the study for a while, it was perfectly fitting that the secular and spiritual welfare of the villagers should be discussed at length. Dr Russell was appointed to supervise her pregnancy and to be there at the accouchement. Mariana was permitted to visit her married sisters and, on one memorable day, they were invited to Thornfalcon.

'You've changed so much, Mariana,' exclaimed Ernestine in breathless awe after she had conducted them through the magnificent rooms. 'And taken to the grand life like a duck to water!'

Mariana had been uneasily conscious of just how different she was, as they sat in the silk-hung drawing-room, full of gilded chairs and high mirrors and porcelain vases from which rose leaves spilled on to inlaid chests. 'I've not changed inside,' she murmured with a smile, but she knew that this was not true.

Her sisters wore their best dresses, but even these showed glaring discrepancies, of poor cut and cheap material. Their bonnets were outmoded, their gloves and shoes of inferior leather. They both vigorously affirmed that they were happy, married to such fine men as Dickon and Jamie, but as they spoke their eyes wandered across the soft-toned rugs spread over the polished floor, then up to the chandeliers with hundreds of lustres, hanging like ice stalactites from the ceiling. Mariana poured tea from a silver pot into Wedgewood cups set on a buhl table, and it was hard to make conversation once everyone's health had been examined and proved to be admirable. They did not stay long, and neither made plans for return visits.

The days turned from spring to summer and, towards the end of June, the house rang with bustle and noise. Christopher had invited his friends to stay again. On the morning that they were expected to arrive, Mariana slipped away to the garden, determined to enjoy her last moments of solitude. With the house full once more, there would be so many claims on her time. Mrs Brockwell shouldered the extra work, but she knew that even her condition would not save her from the persecuting admiration of the gentlemen. There had been many occasions when Captain Wodehouse's and Arthur Cartwright's shadowing attendance had become so embarrassing that she had been glad to turn to Howard Blake for protection. Sir Timon Marvin remained a puzzle, his only concern that of winning at cards and maintaining his dandyish appearance. He did not pursue the women and, since Christopher's behaviour on that never-to-be-forgotten day when he took her to the asylum, she wondered if Spyros might be more to his taste.

Now she was steeling herself for the long hot days ahead, when there would be picnics in the woods, drives to the beaches, drinking and gambling to the small hours. Would she be sent to bed early on the first evening, following the pattern of their former visits? She had long ceased speculating as to why Christopher insisted on this.

She walked slowly down the gravelled path to the herb-garden, with its iron railings and small gate to which she had a key. There was a basket over her arm and scissors in the pocket of her pinafore. She let herself in and idled along, absently fingering a sprig of balsam, wondering if its fresh dark green foliage would complement the great drooping tea-roses which she intended to gather and place in one of the Chinese vases in the music-salon. The sun was already high, gathering its late morning ferocity. She breathed in the fragrance of the plants, and the child stirred within her. Those tiny, thrusting kicks of which she had become lately aware, soothed the soreness in her soul – constantly there, despite Christopher's pampering.

She heard rapid steps behind her, a burst of laughter and, as she turned, the triumphant face of Wodehouse loomed before her. Her heart sank. Peace was shattered. He strode along with his military bearing, clad in a befrogged coat and smart hessian boots, accompanied by the silent, fair Howard. A short way behind them dawdled Marvin, fanning himself with a languid hand, dressed in the extreme of fashion, with an eye-glass on a black ribbon, tight trousers, a silk waistcoat embroidered with silver flowers, and a chain dangling with seals, fobs and a large gold watch.

''Pon my honour, we've been looking everywhere for you, Lady Mariana. Ain't that so, Howard?' began Wodehouse, flinging a quizzical glance at the young man.

'To offer our congratulations, don't you know,' Howard said earnestly, his smile frank and friendly.

'A happy event! Christopher's a lucky dog!' Marvin added, bowing and kissing her extended fingers. 'I wish you and your infant well.'

'And I.' Howard was not to be outdone, taking the basket from her, saying that she must not tax her strength.

All three fell into step beside her, walking between the flower-beds where bees dodged in and out of blossoms. Wodehouse swung his cane and looked at her from the tail of his eye, as he remarked: 'Christopher tells me that he took you to see his sister.'

His loud, hearty voice cut through the drowsy summer stillness of the garden, jarring unpleasantly. Mariana stooped to pick maidenhair ferns. 'That is so, sir.'

'Poor lady, such a tragedy.' Wodehouse rested his weight on his cane and crossed his ankles.

'You know her?' Mariana concentrated on laying the ferns in the basket, wondering what excuse she could make to escape them.

'Lord, yes! There was no one quite like Agnes in the old days. Thornfalcon was the very hub of activity then. You've never seen such balls and dinner-parties! Go on for a week, sometimes.'

'Deuced hard on the purse, what?' added Marvin, flicking open his snuff-box and proffering it. 'Lost a thousand guineas in one night's play, if my memory serves me correctly.'

Wodehouse was staring at Mariana, smoothing his moustache and laughing on that carefree note on which so much of his popularity rested. Most people found it impossible not to respond to his breezy manner, but there was no change in Mariana's serious expression. She was thinking of Agnes, finding it difficult to associate the demented woman in the asylum with anything gay, beautiful and light-hearted.

'Howard! Where are you?' They were interrupted by Cora's querulous call from the distance.

'Dammit!' he snapped, looking angrily in the direction from which it had come. 'She can't bear me out of her sight!'

'You *are* her lap-dog, remember?' Marvin said spitefully.

'Yes, run along, there's a good boy,' Wodehouse commented with his usual commanding urbanity. 'I expect she wants you to hold the skein while she winds wool. The confounded woman's always knitting.'

Howard was furious, kicking the toe of his boot against the gravel. 'Go and see what she wants, will you, Wodehouse?' he implored.

'Lord, I'm damned if I'd let a female get me under her thumb, even one as charming as yourself, Lady Mariana,' answered Wodehouse with a shrug of his broad shoulders. 'Right, Howard, I'll do you this favour but in return, you must promise to let me have your dances with our hostess tomorrow night. Is it a deal?'

Sulkily, Howard shook hands on the bargain, and Wodehouse strolled off, swinging his cane and whistling. With a supercilious smile and a nod, Marvin went after him in the direction of the shrilly agitated voice of Cora.

'That's really not very nice of you, Howard.' Mariana glanced at him from beneath her thick lashes. The brim of her hat cast cool mauve shadows over her face. 'D'you feel no pity for her? She loves you with all her heart.'

'I know, and I don't care! She's a bore – a fussy demanding bore! She acts as if she owns me, body and soul.' His lower lip was rolled out petulantly, brown eyes stormy. 'I wanted to stay here with you, Lady Mariana. There'll be little chance for us to talk later. The whole damned bunch are gathering at the house!'

He broke off suddenly and a flush spread over his face. Mariana sensed that he had not came there to air his grievances about his aging mistress, so she waited quietly, fingers busy culling flowers. 'Don't you enjoy their company?' she encouraged.

They had reached a small stone bench in a clematis-covered alcove. Mariana sank down on it, resting her trug on the paved surround. Howard sat at her side, eyes heavy-lidded and brooding. 'Sometimes – it depends,' he answered cagily.

'You spend a great deal of time with them,' Mariana said softly.

He looked at her in confusion, though a trace of irrepressible humour still lurked in his face. 'What else is there to do? Cora fancies herself as a socialite. I tag along. I've no money of my own.'

'Why don't you work?' she asked innocently.

'Work!' It was as if she had mouthed an obscenity. 'My dear Lady Mariana, I can turn my hand to nothing. I've no head for learning, and am certainly not trained for anything manual. I'm a gentleman, albeit a poor one. You see before you an impoverished orphan. Cora has taken me under her wing, until such time as I can marry a wealthy heiress, though I'm beginning to doubt if she'll ever let me go. My role is to be entertaining. I'm a dancing partner, an escort, a companion – '

'And lover?' she added, half laughing. It was impossible not to like him. There was something infectious in his honest nature that lay open for all to read. It was a relief to be with him, to jest and tease, like meeting a breeze from some lost land of youth.

He flushed again, playing with the fobs at his waist. 'If she wants me,' he admitted. 'One of my duties, to make love to her.'

'In exchange for which she pays your debts and buys you gifts.' Mariana tried to keep her tone light, but could not hide her distaste.

'Maybe she does,' he replied. 'But no one would look on this askance if the position was reversed. Men have mistresses and keep them in high style, so why shouldn't women do the same?'

'I hadn't thought of it like that,' she answered, realizing that what he had said was perfectly true. If an older man seduced a young girl, then his status amongst his male friends went up a notch. He was considered to be a gay dog. But if an older woman took a young lover, then society frowned. Mariana had decided a long time ago that there was a lot of injustice in the world.

Howard was fidgety, glancing round him with furtive eyes, and she thought it was because he feared the captain would not divert Cora, then: 'I want to warn you, Lady Mariana,' he said suddenly.

Mariana felt her every muscle tense. 'Against whom?'

Again, that darting of the eyes, the nervous twitching of his hands. 'Then you don't know?'

'What are you talking about, Howard?'

110

'If Christopher hasn't told you, then I'd better keep my mouth shut.' He was sweating, jerking his cravat loose. 'Just be careful, that's all. There's danger when we're gathered together. Haven't you noticed the dates on which we come? Allhallows Eve – St Thomas' Day – Candlemas. Tonight is the Eve of St John.'

Her brows winged down in a puzzled frown. 'These are country festivals, always celebrated in the villages.'

'Oh, yes, so they are, and they stretch back to pre-Christian times. They're also celebrated by others and for a very different reason,' he said seriously and paused, wondering whether to go on, before adding in a rush, 'We knew before it happened that Christopher was going to marry you. It had been planned down to the last detail. You had been chosen with great care. Now you're carrying his child and, for both your sakes, I hope and pray that it's a boy.'

Her heart seemed to wither. The smile was paralysed on her lips. 'Mrs Wrixon said something about his choice meeting with their approval, but I thought she was motivated by spite and jealousy.'

'She most probably was, amongst other things,' he said warily.

'I wish you'd speak plainly, Howard. Tell me what you mean!' Her voice rang louder and harder than usual in her effort to control the rush of blood that was making her feel faint.

He glanced round again, fingers twisting together as he battled with himself. 'I can't – don't ask me – but be on your guard.'

'Ah, there you are, Howard!' Cora came round the corner, giving Mariana a caustic glare. 'Didn't you hear me calling?'

Behind her walked Wodehouse and the Reverend Grant, that benign pillar of the church, in his long clerical coat and unmistakable neckband. They loomed over Mariana, their shadows blotting out the sun. Even Cora seemed ghastly in that moment, with her aging, anxious face and small eyes almost mad with jealousy. It was a fleeting impression, for when they next spoke, it was with laughter and jollity as they gathered her and the discomfited Howard up and bore them back to Thornfalcon.

Howard's words reverberated through Mariana's head throughout the day. She watched her guests keenly, whilst appearing not to. Was there a false note in their gaiety, their childish romping, the hectic boisterousness which possessed

111

them? Their use of drugs was habitual, she knew that, but sensed something more. A hundred unconsidered pointers came back to her with remorseless persistence. She wrestled with each one, trying to convince herself that all was in order. It was possible that Howard was expressing concern with some purpose of his own in view. He had never disguised his admiration for her. Jealousy and envy work in mysterious ways, and she tried to believe that he was trying to poison her mind against her husband.

That evening they dined, drank and played cards, but the house held a strange anticipation, so strong as to be almost tangible. Christopher, in his beautifully tailored suit, was in an expansive mood. No host could have been more charmingly attentive, more witty, more entertaining. And he was so very proud of Mariana, drawing her into every area of conversation, saying again and again 'My wife – '

On every side she met smiling glances, except from Cora whose eyes were vindictive, and Mariana was lulled by Christopher's loving smile, by his adoration, and his praise. People addressed her and she answered, but even while answering, forgot the speaker's presence, mesmerised by Christopher, thinking as she sat under his spell: Love is the crown of Life. A life without love is a life wasted. I've been so fortunate. Howard must have been intoxicated or drugged to speak to me as he did. My husband loves me. He will protect me always.

The time came for him to conduct her to the Master Chamber. 'I'd like to stay up a little longer tonight, Christopher,' she protested, as he held her in his arms in the seclusion of that fantastic room.

He laughed down into her face, a gentle, tender laugh. 'You mustn't get overtired. It may prejudice the child. Really, darling, nothing exciting will happen. You know that gaming bores you. I'll not delay long for there's nothing more important in my life than being with you. To lie with you in our marriage-bed, to hold you and to know that in doing so I also cradle my heir – this is joy beyond compare. So drink the waters of Lethe which will give you sweet oblivion.'

It was true that she was weary. Whenever they entertained this motley crew, she always felt drained, as if their very presence in the house sucked the energy out of her. She obeyed him, reluctantly undressing when he left her, and putting on her nightgown. The warm milk stood on a silver salver at the bedside but, instead of drinking it, she carried it to the water-closet and flushed it away. I don't need a sleeping-draught tonight, she thought, though feeling guilty at not carrying out Christopher's orders and unwilling to admit that her action was prompted by the fear which Howard had engendered. She told herself that she wished to sleep undisturbed by drugged dreams – dreams of chanting – of occupied rooms which yawned black and silent when she opened the doors – blacker than night and thick with despair. She would sleep naturally, healthily, dreaming of her child.

Sleep she did, but fitfully, sleep coming and going like a wind. At last she roused, hearing herself saying aloud: 'I should have taken the draught.'

It was a hot breathless night. The flame of the candle hardly dipped, sending its straight smoke up into the darkness. Mariana recognized that a storm was in the offing. Her country upbringing whispered of the violence to come. In the stables the horses would be aware, stamping in the straw, eyes rolling, snuffing distant thunder to which the human ear was deaf. The house was silent, as if it held its breath. Then, at the far end of the room, the longcase clock struck twelve, a muffled portentous sound. Its striking seemed to go on endlessly, hammering into her skull but the silence, when it ceased, was painfully acute. Where were her noisy guests? Were they in bed, alone or with congenial partners? Why hadn't Christopher come?

In that moment a breeze began to stir, rushing in with the thunder-clouds from the sea. Her silk scarf, hanging on the back of a chair, billowed and clung, then slipped to the floor. Mariana rested against her frilled pillow and closed her eyes, hoping that she was falling asleep, leaving Thornfalcon, leaving her body, but she was deceiving herself. Though everything else became blurred, her ears remained perversely alert, waiting for stealthly movements, for sounds of singing – longing even for that rather than this tomblike quiet.

The wind gathered strength, howling in the corridor outside. There were other noises too, eddies in the ether. Mariana sat up, her eyes wide. The candle flame stretched out flat and quenched itself in a little pool of wax. The darkness was stifling. Mariana felt her breath run back into her mouth as if for shelter. The house shook as a tremendous clap of thunder sounded right overhead, accompanied by the glare of lightning which pierced the windows. Mariana heard another sound. The crash of splintering glass. She sprang from the bed and ran in its direction, out into the pitch-black passage, expecting to bump into servants, roused by the noise. No one was there. She reached the door at the end

113

which led to the garden, and was nearly flung from her feet by the wind which hurled itself on her as she dragged it open. There was another particularly sharp and explosive clap of thunder, followed by a gigantic jag of lightning which lit up the entire sky and the terrace which lay beneath the windows of the Master Chamber.

Mariana froze, one foot over the threshold. The force of the storm flattened her robe against her, the wind whipping her hair with cruel fingers. The blue glare sparked on shards of glass scattered like diamonds on the paving-stones and on the dark form spread-eagled there. Walking in a trance, Mariana approached it. Splinters cut her bare feet so that she left behind small, scarlet trails, but she was unaware.

Darkness swooped down, then another lurid blast and the rumble of thunder. She was bending over the body. The blood on her feet was no longer her own. A great, dark, ever-increasing pool spread across the terrace. She glanced up. The topmost window of the tower glared blankly, its glass shattered. Something wetted her upturned face. A bloody gout mingled with the first big raindrop that heralded the torrent which now rained down as the skies opened. In a second she was soaked, the weeping clouds pouring their contents on her, and upon the twisted, motionless body at her feet. In the next flash of light, she fell to her knees, and found herself gazing into the bloody face of Howard who lay with his glazed eyes fixed upon her from what remained of his smashed head.

They said it was suicide. Dr Russell came in his dressing-gown after Christopher had answered Mariana's screams. Servants brought flares. People gathered. Lady Somerville in flowing night-attire, the Reverend Grant, all of them shivering in the doorway or gazing from windows as strong menservants carried the broken corpse within. A note was produced, found, so Christopher said, in Cora's bedroom. In it Howard had declared his intention to throw himself from the tower. He was weary of life and could see no happy future.

Christopher would not permit Mariana to become involved, apart from a very brief interview with the local constable who seemed satisfied that the unfortunate young man had, indeed, killed himself. Later, she recalled fragments of that dreadful night: Cora's hysterical weeping; Christopher lifting her and carrying her back to their bedchamber; Mrs Brockwell bathing the blood from her hands and feet, getting her out of her stained nightdress and into a clean one, then Dr Russell standing over her, insisting that she drink some medicine he had prepared, and after that – nothing.

She was treated like an invalid and drowsed the days away until after the funeral. When she came to herself at last, Christopher took her to Whitby for a holiday and, in the quiet of the select hotel in which they stayed, she began to wonder if it had happened at all. He would not let her ask questions, smiling into her eyes, laying a finger on her lips, and saying: 'No, my dear. You must forget – think of our child.'

They spent six weeks in Whitby, just the two of them attended by Spyros and a maid whom Christopher had hired for her, a bright, jolly girl named Sadie. 'May I keep her?' Mariana asked as the peaceful interlude was drawing to its close.

'Of course you may. You can have anything you want,' he replied with that charming smile which melted doubts and fears.

She dreaded returning to Thornfalcon, but on an evening in the middle of August when she looked at it as the carriage drew near, she tried to be rational. Christopher, all solicitude, hurried her to their bedroom, and they spent the first night entirely alone. No one could have been more loving. They did not speak of anything unpleasant and she was satisfied, though never again entering that area where Howard had died. Christopher also avoided any reference to Agnes. It was as if the visit to the asylum had never happened.

As her body became heavier, she entered that dreamy stage of almost animal complacency, her mind turned inwards, communing with the developing embryo, filled with wonder and awe when she felt its strong, kicking movements in her womb. Christopher did not arrange any more visits from his friends, though he twice left her for a night and she guessed that he had gone to meet them somewhere. Thornfalcon's woods turned yellow, and rain set in with wind and storm. The country donned its autumn livery. Mariana made several calls at Swinsty Farm, but there was a gulf between her and the Crosbys now; she recognized and accepted it. She belonged to Thornfalcon and Christopher, the child had cemented the bond and, like Sleeping Beauty in an enchanted palace, she was content to let outside influences slip away. They were no longer real or significant.

November brought driving sleet and gales that turned to heavy snow, making the barrier against the world complete. Winter pressed a blank face at every window, and Christopher closed the shutters at dusk, pulled the curtains tight, and built his castles of sorcery in the nights. Dr Russell was virtually a resident, for Christopher was frantically worried lest the doctor should be prevented from being present at the birth. The hour of Mariana's delivery was approaching. She had wanted Margery there, but Ernestine was also expecting her first child and there would be no expensive consultant at her lying-in. The weather was so bad that it was impossible for Margery to divide her time between the two of them. Blizzards raged on the moors and the snow made the roads impassable.

They enjoyed a quiet, peaceful Christmas and the New Year was almost upon them. One evening, towards the end of the month, they were dining together, Mariana, Christopher and Dr Russell. Outside the storm howled, but within the elegant room all was tranquil. Her eyes sought Christopher's where he sat at the head of the long table. She basked in his approbation, remembering that although she was heavy with child, he still found her beautiful. In bed that very morning, he had been sweetly tender, his hand coming to rest on her swollen belly, chuckling to feel the child stirring within her.

'He's a big, healthy boy, darling,' he had said, hugging her.

She had wound her fingers in his fair curls, staring up into his laughing blue eyes. 'How d'you know it's a boy? It might be a pretty little girl.'

'Nonsense. Of course it's a boy,' he had announced confidently. 'Even my groom is sure of it, and he's worked among mares for long enough to be an expert.'

Mariana had indulged him, agreeing that he was probably right. Frankly, she did not care, just as long as the baby was perfectly formed. Boy or girl, she would adore it, the fruit of their love, living proof of their union. But she had learned to hold her tongue for Christopher became quite angry if she as much as mentioned the choice of girls' names. The child was to be called 'Roland Jonathan Christopher Matthew St Jules', and that was that! She concealed the list of female names which she had spent secret hours compiling.

She was feeling particularly well that night and had eaten a hearty meal and drunk several glasses of wine. Contentment wrapped her like a sable cloak, and Christopher's singular charm made her catch her breath as she looked across at him. He was an aristocrat to his very marrow, so proud and handsome, wearing that air of unquestioned authority. Mariana was of a nature designed for the heights and depths of love, faithful until death, but also capable of an equal hatred if the object of her desire should betray her. But now it seemed that the greatest moment of her life was about to strike.

Christopher's continuing love would be assured when she gave him his heir.

Full of gay confidence, she turned her lovely smile on Dr Russell. 'And what is your prognostication, sir?' she asked, patting her stomach. 'Is it a boy?'

The doctor glanced at her, then at Christopher, and raised the brandy goblet in both hands. 'It would seem so, Lady Mariana,' he replied suavely. 'I drink to this happy outcome. Soon we shall know beyond doubt, for your abundant energy over the past days tells me that the birth is imminent.'

She had been unaccountably restless it was true, conscious of time rushing by, yet feeling it dragging too. The old carved rocking-cradle was in readiness in the Master Chamber, and the tallboy in the nursery contained a dozen minute garments. There was the baby-gown on which she had been working for weeks in a desultory fashion. She had fished it out of her sewing-cabinet, finished it hurriedly, then remade the cradle for the umpteenth time, happy fingers fondling the crested sheets and fine woollen blankets which would soon cover her infant. Mrs Grant had sent a hand-knitted shawl, and she had draped it over her arm, trying to imagine what it would feel like to hold the baby. Lord, but you're being silly, she had scolded herself mildly, you've looked after enough babies in your time. But this was different – it would be her own to love and rear. Sometimes she forgot that it would also have a father – a dominating, possessive father who would expect to take over once it had left the toddler stage.

That night, in the dim grandeur of the bedroom, Christopher insisted on disrobing her. More than ever now, he liked to see her nude, kneeling before her, his hands cupping her full breasts, caressing the melon-shaped lump of her belly. 'My darling Mariana,' he whispered huskily. 'Mother of my son – my goddess – Moon-Mother of Fertility!'

Mariana smoothed the hair back from his forehead, over-whelmed with tenderness. 'You mustn't kneel to me, Christopher,' she whispered. 'It isn't right.'

'I kneel to my goddess,' he exclaimed, throwing back his head and looking up at her with frightening intensity. 'I worship my goddess!' His grip on her bulging stomach tightened and the child kicked as if in protest. 'There! Feel it? My son answers me! He knows what his father has sacrificed to bring him into being. My son – my son – ' and he laid his face against her.

The dull ache in her back which Mariana had been experiencing on and off all day was becoming more insistent, and she longed to lie down. Very gently, she disengaged herself from Chrstopher's arms and sought the comfort of the bed. Christopher joined her, wide awake and annoying, still talking wildly, full of plans for the child. He was drinking, and adding drops of laudanum from a small green phial to his wine. Soon he became still, sleeping with that innocent expression which erased the harsh lines from his features.

An hour passed, lit by the dancing flames of the fire and the quality of Mariana's discomfort changed, pain fanning out over her belly, hardening it into a tight ball, then fading away. Oh God, she thought, fighting panic, I'm in labour.

She waited with held breath. It came again, rising to a peak, then dying back. She leaned over Christopher, shaking him awake. She did not have to speak. He knew at once and was out of bed in an instant, rousing the house. Lights sprang into being everywhere. Dr Russell came, clothing flung on anyhow.

'Do something, man!' Christopher shouted, striding the chamber in his brocade robe as Mrs Brockwell entered with clean towels, sheets and medical paraphernalia. 'It's my son's life you're playing with!'

'Easy, my friend,' Dr Russell answered calmly. 'One can't hurry nature. She's a strong woman. All will be well.'

Christopher's fingers bit into his arm. 'Nothing must happen to the child,' he hissed, and their eyes met in a long, meaningful look. 'If it comes to a choice between them, you know which to take.'

Mariana's mind was clouded by pain which gathered and receded with miserable, grinding persistency. Mrs Brockwell brought her a drink, laced with opium. She swallowed it greedily, not caring had it contained hemlock in that time of direful agony. The housekeeper was muttering to herself, going round the room, making sure that every knot was untied, following tradition.

'What are you doing?' Mariana surfaced enough to ask at one point, feeling the woman's hands on her.

'I'm fastening this amulet round your thigh, my Lady, to insure a speedy delivery,' Mrs Brockwell replied.

The hours crawled by on leaden feet. Time had lost all meaning. People came and went, their faces hanging mistily above her as she writhed and sweated on the bed. She knew that Christopher was there, awaiting the emergence of his heir. Mrs Brockwell was on her knees at the bedside, rubbing round and round the small of Mariana's back every time a pain began to grow to an agonizing crescendo.

'I know it's a bad pain,' she said, face expressionless. 'But you won't remember it afterwards.'

118

'What?' Mariana gasped unbelievingly. It seemed incredible that she could ever remember anything but this torture.

'No,' Mrs Brockwell assured her briskly. 'You'll find that no mother can describe it to you.'

She's so hard, thought Mariana. Has she ever had a baby herself? Oh, I wish Margery was here! She was on the verge of breaking down and howling, but panic would not help. Mrs Brockwell had said that it would not last for ever and the memory would be dim. She was grateful for that, clinging to it desperately. She had been promised no aftermath of this cruel grovelling and squirming. How could she have hated the kind housekeeper? How could she have been afraid of the competent Dr Russell? They were giving her the strength to go on.

Christopher was anything but calm, however. His face was very white and pinched about the nostrils. Mariana wanted to say something to him, but thought was wiped out in agony. She felt that she was about to be torn asunder. Oh, God, I'm going to die! she thought. I want to die! Let me die! Mother! I want my mother! She was lying in a pool of fluid, but it wasn't blood. She had not been disembowelled. Mrs Brockwell was knotting a towel to the footpost of the bed, then she thrust it into Mariana's clenched hands.

'Hold that!' said Dr Russell, sternly. 'Take a deep breath and push when you get the next pain.'

She opened her eyes, saw the flickering light of the candles, saw Kali illuminated by a ring of them, her jewel-eyes glittering. I don't want to give birth here! she wanted to yell, but the words were locked inside her. I don't like this room! I've never liked it!

Like distant, rolling thunder the pain began, gathering speed, terrifying in its power, but this time it was better. Now Mariana was a fighter and she grappled with it, using it to the full so that it, not she, was used to the limit. A different pain. A warrior pain. She had a fleeting sense of triumph, a fierce, storm-ridden feeling, a primordial urge impossible to control. It washed over her and she strained on the towel, eyes screwed shut, teeth clenched, hearing her own throaty, expulsive grunts. The pain was huge, indomitable. It roared and thundered, turning into light – as bright as spun-gold – growing, growing till it broke off into space like a shooting-star. Mariana felt a splitting sensation. She heard herself screaming – heard a squalling cry – felt the child leave her.

Mariana was aware of nothing but enormous relief then,

into the sudden silence, she heard the doctor exclaim with horror in his voice: 'It's a girl!'

Her eyelids flew open. She saw Mrs Brockwell holding the naked baby. 'Give her to me!' Mariana cried, her voice demanding and fierce, and the housekeeper placed the child, warm, wriggling and wet, on her flat bare stomach.

Mariana was quite unprepared for the rush of overpowering love that poured through her. She had done it! Oh, wonderful little life! What a beautiful child! Frowning, puckered and chubby, the baby's mottled limbs shuddered with the tremendous effort of drawing breath, and her little chest expanded as the room resounded with her shrill yells. Lusty. Strong. Mariana had never seen anything more perfect, and her hand went to the tiny, gripping fist and then to the stirring toes that had kicked so impudently within her over the past months.

She felt transformed, vital, almost holy. She was a mother at last, feeling that she understood all the secrets of the universe in that magic moment. She looked at Christopher, eyes shining with rapturous tears, expecting him to share her wonder.

The savage fury on his face was like a freezing blast. He stood staring at the child with menace in his poised body. Then without a word or gesture, he turned on his heel and left the room.

Mariana floated in the drowsy peace that follows childbirth. In this state of confused joy, nothing seemed real except the child at her breasts, and it was only later that she began to feel hurt and worried because Christopher had not come to see them. She was much alone. Dr Russell dropped in from time to time, and Mrs Brockwell brought her food, did what was necessary for her and the baby. Her face was shuttered and she was disinclined to talk. The child was very content, sleeping for long stretches, suckling as if she knew just what to do, and Mariana feasted her eyes on that funny, old-young face under the shock of black fluff, talking to her softly when she opened her large blue eyes, seeming to stare at her with recognition.

'Elaine, my little Elaine,' Mariana would say, holding her up, such a sweet-smelling bundle. 'That's what I'm going to call you, my love. When your Papa comes, I'll tell him so. Oh, I know he's cross because you weren't a boy, but you'll have a little brother next time, I promise you.'

Then she would cradle Elaine against her shoulder, rocking her blissfully, convincing herself that Christopher would get over the disappointment, given time. 'Where is Lord St Jules?'

she asked Mrs Brockwell one morning when the baby was almost a week old.

She was sitting by the fire in her dressing-robe while the housekeeper changed the sheets. Mariana would have preferred Sadie to have attended her, but had been told that the girl's mother had fallen sick and that she had gone home to nurse her.

'He's in his observatory, madam.' Mrs Brockwell did not look at her, thumping the pillows into shape. 'Been there since the birth. I've had meals sent up, but he sends them back, untouched.'

Tears of weakness rose in Mariana's eyes. She was feeling depressed that day, her breasts engorged with milk, and above all things she longed for Christopher to come to her and forgive her for presenting him with a daughter. 'Oh, dear,' she sighed, wishing that she felt strong enough to mount the stairs and beard him in his lair. 'Is he terribly upset?'

'That he is, my Lady.' Work done, Mrs Brockwell came to stand by her, hands folded neatly over her apron. 'Girl children are bad news for the St Jules family.'

The day was dull, the skies pewter, and snow beat a remorseless tattoo on the window-glass. Mariana shivered, though her cheeks burned and the sweat was running down between her heavy breasts. 'But why? Why?' she burst out, hand going instinctively to the cradle. The baby lay within, staring about her with the wide, unblinking eyes of the newly born.

Mrs Brockwell's plain, round face was guarded, but she drew in her breath and then said: 'It began two hundred years ago, when Lady Agnes, whom they called the Poisoner, lived here. The tale goes that she gave one of her deadly mixtures to a rival, and as the victim lay dying in awful agony, she cursed the family, saying that every female child who bore Agnes's blood would be as mad as she was.'

The room sprang into listening stillness. There was no sound but the hiss of the logs and the insistent snowy fingers tapping on the casement. 'Go on,' said Mariana.

'From that day to this, every daughter has been stricken with insanity when she reaches maturity. Even my own dear Lady Agnes.'

With a swift movement, Mariana snatched up Elaine, holding her tightly, eyes wild as a cat's as she glared at the woman over the top of the tiny dark head. 'I don't believe you!' she shouted. 'My baby is perfect. It will not happen to her!'

Mrs Brockwell folded her arms, and her eyes were as bleak as the storm outside. 'I thought the same about Agnes. I prayed that it would never happen, but you've seen her, madam – you've visited the asylum. She's now a poor, filthy, disordered creature.'

'It's this dreadful house and the St Jules men who drive their women to madness, not some invented curse!' Mariana cried, wanting to escape, to fling a few things into a bag for herself and Elaine and leave Thornfalcon for ever. Her helplessness appalled her.

'When you've lived here as long as I have, madam, you'll grow to realize that there are many things which can't be explained,' replied Mrs Brockwell with fatalistic calm. Her lips parted in a bland and terrifying little smile.

'Lady Sarah Anne's children died,' Mariana whispered, and coiling, twisting serpents nipped at her heart. Then there came another thought, lashing her with unknown horror. 'And she died too!'

'She was delicate, madam. The air didn't suit her.'

'I want to see Lord St Jules.' Mariana swayed as she struggled to her feet, clutching Elaine.

'That you shall do presently, my Lady. The Reverend Grant will be here this afternoon for the child's christening.'

The memory of this steadied Mariana. As was customary, the ceremony must take place a few days after the birth, far too soon for her to attend. She would speak to the rector. He was a good man and would allay her fears. Perhaps he would talk to Christopher. Hugging this comforting thought to her, Mariana permitted Mrs Brockwell to replace the child in the cradle and conduct her back to bed. But she wished with all her heart that she was not to be parted from Elaine, even for an hour. Alone again in the great room filled with pagan deities, she tried to console herself by thinking: Elaine will be protected once she's christened. It has to be done soon, for the villagers say that an unbaptized infant isn't guarded against evil. She might be 'overlooked' by a witch and changed into a Gabble Hound to hunt for ever the devil who prevented her from being christened.

Christopher could not avoid being present at the ceremony, and he arrived in the early afternoon, accompanied by Dr Russell and the sedate Reverend. He looked terrible. Mariana stared at him, stupefied. His face was thin and drawn, with a sallow, unhealthy tinge. His suit was crumpled, as if he had slept in it, and his linen was dirty. The sweet smell of opium clung about him.

Mariana leaned across the fur coverlet, holding out her hands imploringly. 'Christopher – darling! I've been so worried about you.'

'No need, my dear,' he answered coolly, then he smiled, but behind the smile lay something dire. 'I'm perfectly well, and you seem to be recovering. What a pity the child is anything but robust.'

The words struck her like a stone. 'What d'you mean?' she cried. 'She's very strong. A fine baby.'

'That's not what the doctor tells me,' he replied, still smiling. 'No matter. Let us to the christening. It will be as well if it's carried out with all speed.'

Mrs Brockwell was waiting, Elaine in her arms, wrapped in a long piece of gold silk lined with white satin and elaborately trimmed – the christening pall. Mariana watched them leave the room, Mrs Brockwell in the lead, followed by Christopher, Dr Russell and Reverend Grant. Inexplicable terror assailed her.

The baptism took place in the chapel where they had been married, and the housekeeper soon brought Elaine back to Mariana's eager arms. Beneath the magnificent covering, the child wore a length of white linen called the Chrism-cloth, denoting that she was now a Christian. She clutched her child in panic as the housekeeper explained that if the baby lived, Mariana was to take the cloth with her when she went to be churched, but if Elaine died, then she would be buried in it, and remembered as a 'Chrism-child'.

No such custom had been carried out at Swinsty Farm, but Mariana knew only too well that the shadow of the coffin hung over every cradle. Pregnancy was commonplace, a yearly occurrence, and though a mother might give birth to a dozen children, she would be lucky if half that number reached adulthood. In her weakened state, morbid thoughts could not be stemmed, and she cried herself to sleep on the night of her daughter's baptism.

The days dragged past, each one bereft of Christopher. Mariana was allowed up now, permitted to dress but not to leave her room. She stared from the high windows, across the barren wastes of the snow-covered lawns. The sun swam up briefly. A rosy fire illumined the hill-tops, long shadows and colour slid across the distant fields. Steel sheen came to the sunward side of the beeches, warmth glowed on the edges of the bare boughs, the walls of Thornfalcon shone with a myriad spears of frost that caught the rays and were transformed into gems. The hills beyond the valley were violet and grey and black, as if they were smouldering into wood-smoke without visible flames. Mariana fetched the baby so that she might look at the view, saying: 'See, darling, this is your land. This is Thornfalcon which will be yours one day, for it seems that the brother I promised you will never be born. Your father doesn't love me any more.' Her eyes closed and slow tears slid down into the baby's soft hair where her head nestled against Mariana's cheek.

He came to her at the footpad hour of dusk, and she could not believe the evidence of her own senses. He was in such a pleasant mood, elegantly dressed in a claret velvet jacket and cream trousers, his linen dazzling in the candlelight, his hair curling about his fine head. His eyes were feverishly bright, but this was no cause for concern. If the drugs he took had brought about this change of mood then she could only bless them. He watched her with those strange blue eyes while they dined, for he had ordered Mrs Brockwell to serve the meal in the bedchamber. It was like the old days, and Mariana was spellbound, for he toasted her, admired her, even stood for a while by the cradle, staring down at the sleeping infant.

'Isn't she pretty, Christopher?' Mariana ventured, hoping against all hope that parental love and pride were stirring in him as they did in her. 'And so lusty! You should see how eager she is to suckle. There's not a thing wrong with her.'

He did not answer, changing the subject, embracing her affectionately but making no sexual overtures. Mariana was glad of this. It was too soon. 'We must have a party before long,' he said, filling her glass with dark rich wine. 'When the weather breaks and travelling is possible.' His friends? she wondered with a pang. Then he drew an envelope from his pocket, giving it to her. 'The post boy brought it today. The poor lad was nearly frozen to his pony. We had to have him in to thaw.'

She took it, broke the seal, and held the letter towards the shaded candelabrum. 'Dear Lady St Jules,' she read, the light reflected upwards on her face, making a warm cavern in the surrounding darkness. 'My husband has brought me your sad news. He says that your daughter is not long for this world. Please accept my heartfelt sympathy. Try to see that it will be a blessing if the angels take her soon. You are young, my dear, and the good Lord may see fit to bless you with further children, ere long. Do not grieve too much. You must regain your strength. It is your sacred duty to care for Lord St Jules. Remember what Jesus Christ said: "Suffer little children to come unto Me." Your obedient servant, Judith Grant.'

'What does she mean?' Mariana cried, made violent by fear. She dropped the letter as if it were a live coal. 'There's nothing the matter with Elaine.'

'Dr Russell thinks that there is,' he said, his hand coming to rest on her clenched fist on the damask table-cloth. 'You must be brave, darling. I'm here to support you in your hour of need.'

Mariana broke from him, for the baby had begun to stir and whimper, a protest that would soon turn into a hungry bawl. Picking her up, she sat on the low, nursing chair, unbuttoned her bodice and put the child to her breast. The tiny rosebud lips closed over the nipple, the jaws working vigorously. Mariana touched the petal-soft cheek. feeling the life-giving nourishment swelling her breasts and the child's appreciation of it. She had never seen a more healthy specimen of babyhood. What Christopher was suggesting was absurd.

He was standing before Kali, taking a spill and lighting the candles and incense. 'You've been neglecting the goddess, my dear,' he said, gently chiding. 'She doesn't like to be forgotten.'

'This child is whole and hearty,' Mariana repeated stubbornly, eyes slitted as she stared at his uncaring back. 'I don't believe Dr Russell.'

He would not look at her, and she could tell by the set of his shoulders that the thought of her giving suck to Elaine displeased him. 'So, you consider yourself more knowledgeable than the most skilled doctor in the district, do you?' he replied mildly.

'If you're so convinced that he speaks the truth, then why aren't you sending to London for eminent physicians? You'd do so had Elaine been a boy!' she accused, her voice hard.

Dormant as chrysalids, a thousand thoughts lay thick in the shadows, pulsing imperceptibly. Memories rose, hovered and soared, seizing Mariana's soul and thrusting it towards the verge. What did she really know of Christopher? He was strange at times, strange and cruel. Yet she loved him still, drawn to his darkness, aching for him, yearning to touch him, yet fearful with a horrible, compulsive fear.

He did not speak, absorbed in placating his deity. It was only when she had tucked the satiated, sleeping babe in the cradle that he turned those slumbrous eyes to her again.

'Come, sit with me, Mariana.' His voice was soothing, hypnotic. He moved towards the daybed, drawing up a small round table and placing the decanter and two glasses on it.

She hovered over the cradle, a slender figure in a dress of

burgundy wool. She was even more beautiful, with that added maturity and depth which motherhood had given her. Her hair, dark and lustrous, hung in heavy waves about her shoulders. Her gown was simple, falling in straight lines to her feet. She wanted to refuse him, to ask him to leave, but it was impossible to refuse Christopher anything.

When she had seated herself on the soft cushions of the couch, he stretched out his long limbs and lay with his head in her lap, smiling up into her face. 'That's better,' he said with a contented sigh. 'Now you're mine again, not fussing over a brat. I'll not share you with anyone, darling. You are mine. Never forget that.'

She brooded over him, tracing his features with her fingertips, letting his crisp curls spring around her hand. He was like a bright, wild-eyed angel, regarding her steadily from beneath his golden lashes. A silence like eternity prevailed, then she said: 'Tell me about Agnes, and that other Agnes, the one who poisoned people.'

Something flashed across his face, but he went on smiling. 'Old Brocky has been speaking out of turn, I think.'

'You can't believe that legend, surely?' she asked, still caressing his hair.

'You consider me far too rational? Wrong. I'm a dreamer, my dear. Perhaps I do believe in the supernatural. How can I answer that when I don't know myself?' He sat up suddenly, reaching for the decanter. 'No more gloom tonight. We'll embark on a second honeymoon, you and I, when your lying-in is over. Let us drink to the future.' He placed the wine glass in her hand. Mariana acquiesced, wishing to lengthen his pleasant mood. His eyes were shining, azure, beautiful – smiling at her. That was the last thing she saw.

She felt herself to be swimming beneath some sort of dark, translucent waters. Her eyes were heavy, her limbs drifting, and there was the sound of a fountain. She surfaced, as dreamers will, as formless as smoke. Yes, there was a fountain, leaping up and flowering in many roses. Bright moonlight flared on them. Their crystal petals changed, broke for ever, became falling tears.

She was awake, a taste like fire in her mouth, coming to herself in blackness, disorientated. She stretched out a hand, encountering the plush of the daybed. The fire was powdery, ashy, sullen red. No other light glimmered. A strange cold held her. Christopher had gone. The silence was vast, complete. No sound at all entered her straining ears. How long have I been asleep? she wondered. Even the clock no longer ticks away life by the second. She started up, reaching for the cradle, feeling for that reassuring warm little bundle. Her hands encountered blankets, flatness, nothing. With a strangled cry, she leapt for the fire, poking a taper into the embers, trembling so much that it took time to ignite a candle. She bent over the cradle again. It was empty.

She searched the room, frantic, hurried. The fourposter was chastely neat, its coverlet unwrinkled, the pillows lying side by side in virgin purity. Shuddering with cold and horror, Mariana snatched a cloak from the armoire and ran to the door, pulling it open, shouting as she did so: 'Mrs Brockwell! Where is the baby!'

Only the shadows answered her. At the bottom of the tower stairs she stood, staring up into the gloom, crying Christopher's name repeatedly. He did not reply. Then she knew that the house was deserted. No one came to her aid and, as she hesitated, listening to that awful silence, long shudders shook her from head to foot. Someone had stolen her child. She tried to think, her reason flickering this way and that. Very carefully, so as not to stumble over rugs and stairs, she began systematically searching the house. In the passages and rooms beyond the tower candles burned brightly, displaying the mute emptiness, the long silent corridors. Even the kitchen was deserted, though the kettle steamed on the hob, and the remains of supper lay on the table.

Back to the Master Chamber to check that she had not been mistaken. The cradle stood there like a reproach. So be it; she must look further afield. She let herself out, averting her eyes from the spot where Howard's body had lain, oozing, abject and vile. The snow was thick there, obliterating telltale traces which soap and water had not been entirely successful in washing away. A trail of footprints stood out starkly against the crisp whiteness. There had been no attempt to cover them. Had they been deliberately left for her to follow? The storm had abated and the moonlight was almost blinding, fire-white, blasting wood and stone, branch and bush. Mariana crept in the wake of the footprints, as they wound to the back of the house, disappearing into the stables. There they reappeared, but unclear, mingled with those of horse's hooves. Deep prints now, weighted by a determined rider and his animal. Out through the gates they led, and Mariana followed, placing her feet in those churned snow-holes.

Thornfalcon lay behind her, crouching like a slumbering beast and, as she ascended the slopes, so the wind sprang up. The air was full of its noise as it shattered itself against the hills.

The trees creaked and groaned in torment, bough and hedges whispered and chattered, and the trail beckoned. Mariana was not aware of cold at first, but slowly its deadly grip penetrated. Her thin slippers proved no protection, her cloak no barrier against the spiteful blast which whipped it from her hands and flung back her hood. No sign of the house now. She had reached the desolation of the moors, but still the prints continued inexorably. There was something on the skyline, pointing gaunt fingers to the moon. The regular marks led straight past it. She had traversed several miles to the place where malefactors leapt into eternity wearing a hempen necklace. Mariana whimpered, holding her numb hands to her face, but still her eyes sought the horror of its burden swinging in the gale, with the creak and rattle of chains.

The gibbet stood against the sky like a black tree, sharp and clear. The crows had done their work. In the moonlight the eyes were holes. Bloody entrails were frozen to the thighs where they had fallen from the blackened gash of the decayed belly. Something moved at the foot of the hanging-tree. Mariana screamed as the thing came towards her. She was enveloped in the stink of gin and filth, and a harsh, guttural female voice said:

''ee were my man – they scragged 'im afore Christmas. Sheep-stealin' 'ee were – fer we was starvin', an' 'ee couldn't abear to 'ear the little 'uns cry.'

'Who are you?' Mariana whispered, staring at this nightmare.

The woman was drunk, half-mad, a wretched bundle of rags, inhuman with misery and desperation. ''Don't make no mind. I be nothin' – nobody! They 'anged my man. I saw 'em do it. I comes 'ere by day, an' stays wi' 'im at night. 'Ee were a good man – '

Clouds were scudding across the moon as they fled before the ice-barbed whips of the wind. The low sullen skies seemed to rain pure horror. 'You'll freeze to death up here,' said Mariana, dragging at her flying cloak, battling with the storm-demons.

'I might 'ave done, if you 'adn't come along.' The hag lifted the bottle to her lips and took a deep swig. 'You've saved m'life, lady dear. Gi' us yer clothes! I could do wi' a thick cloak like that.'

Mariana turned to escape, but the woman had her rag-bound foot on the hem of her dress. In the dim light, something glittered in her hand. She lunged and Mariana cried out as she felt the knife bite through her garments and into her skin. 'You'd leave me here naked, to die!' she gasped.

The beggar-woman chuckled. 'You can 'ave my duds.' Then the knife pricked again savagely. 'Get 'em off, lady.'

Still Mariana resisted. 'Have you seen a rider pass this way?'

The ugly face swivelled towards her and a sly demon peeped forth from the sunken eyes. ''Appen I 'ave. So what?'

'What was he like? Was he carrying something?' An extra jab of the knife caused Mariana to tear off her cloak and gown. The wind bit through her thin underclothes with cruel fangs.

'Couldn't see much. 'Ee were a tall feller – fair too. Gi' us yer rings! Get a move on!' The woman was only concerned with her loot.

When Mariana left the gallows to follow the trail which was rapidly becoming indistinct, she was clad in the beggar's disgusting rags. She did not look back, every ounce of energy concentrated on trying to see through the buffeting, whirling whiteness. She thought she had lost the prints – but no, upwards they led, up and up into that icy hell, till she came to a craggy mound of rocks. Panting and exhausted, she sank down in the lee, tiredness sweeping over her in waves so that she crouched there for what seemed eternity, her breath rasping in her lungs. But she must go on or lose those guiding prints.

She dragged herself up a winding track between the boulders, coming out on a small plateau, sheltered by an enormous crag. The wind howled as she peered about her, knowing in her bones what this place was. The locals called it the 'Devil's Tor', and no one ventured there after dark. Mariana staggered on, searching, searching. The marks were no more. Time had gone. Sense had deserted her. She knew that she was sobbing, could feel the tears freezing on her face, groping blindly. Then her hands encountered that which they sought. On a ledge, naked as when born, lay her baby.

'No! No!' Her cries rang and rang, taken by the storm, tossed on high. She touched the little dead thing, then recoiled in horror. She ran to the top of the tor, standing there facing the moor and Thornfalcon, arms upraised as the wind nearly swept her from her feet. 'Christopher! Christopher!' she screamed, but her voice was lost in the wild tumult of nature, merciless yet covering her child with a soft blanket of snow.

Stumbling, sometimes crawling, Mariana left that fearful place. She staggered for miles, demented and unaware. Something loomed out of the storm and she fell to her knees, looking up. It was a massive gate, reaching up to the snow-filled skies. It glittered like crystal. Perhaps I'm dead and it is the gate of hell, she thought, and was glad. She clung to the freezing iron, feeling it burning her palms. The snow was beginning to pile up around her, and the instinct for survival stirred her limbs. Her lashes were thick with ice. She rubbed a hand over them, and then saw the plaque on the gate. Slowly, meaning penetrated her mind. It read 'Kenrick Old Court'.

She felt the warmth of her mother's presence, heard her gentle accented voice saying: 'There is a house many miles from Fewston – Kenrick Old Court. A lady lives there, Mariana, an old, old lady whom the villagers call "The French Woman". You must never go there, *ma petite* – they say she is a witch but they lie. She's not a witch but she's as evil as one. She hates me, and she hates you too.'

'Mamma!' Mariana sobbed, more alone than ever before. 'Mamma! Help me! Come back! Don't leave me here. He's killed my baby!'

The words were torn from her lips by the blizzard. She could feel herself sliding down the gate, unable to stand any longer, welcoming the surrender to the insistent snow. Then her fingers fastened on a great iron ring and, as she clung to it, so the deep sonorous clang of a bell resonated above the storm.

BOOK TWO

Maria

Love seeketh not itself to please,
Nor of itself hath any care,
But for another gives its ease,
And builds a Heaven in Hell's despair.

> *'The Clod and the Pebble',*
> *by William Blake*

Soon as she was gone from me,
A traveller came by,
Silently, invisibly:
He took her with a sigh.

> *'Never seek to tell thy Love',*
> *by William Blake*

CHAPTER 1

Sleep. No, she must take back the word. It was too exact. Rest, perhaps? How much sleep did a woman of eighty need? Precious little – and it was precious, that brief oblivion from aching limbs and feebleness of body, a state calculated to make one fractious, when one's mind was still alert. Fools! thought Madame la Duchesse irritably. I'm surrounded by fools and blundering idiots!

She shifted uncomfortably in the massive bed which, more and more these nights, reminded her of an ornate gloomy sepulchre. She extended an arm tentatively, the purple velvet of her fur-edged wrapper sliding back. The flesh was that of a stranger's; scrawny, with skin blotched by brown pigmentation, her hand like a chicken's claw, the nails curved, brittle, each carrying a dirty half-moon at the tip, the knuckles distorted by age and rheumatism. Is this really my own arm? she wondered, gazing at it, puzzled. She avoided mirrors now, unable to stand the sight of the ugly crone's face staring back at her, plastered with a thick layer of dead-white cosmetic, a badly applied dab of rouge on either withered cheek. It was the face of a clown, ridiculous, obscene. Madame had always hated ugliness, and had managed very successfully to have no contact with it, until the time when her world had tottered and reality had been remorsely forced upon her. So many years ago, another life, almost another world.

With incredible slowness, her hands closed on a book which lay on the bedside table. She drew it towards her, then fumbled in her beaded reticule and found her glasses. With these perched on her thin, aristocratic nose which had miraculously kept its shape while the rest of her features disintegrated into pouches and lines, she opened it, the last of six thick journals, painstakingly kept throughout the years, each page covered in copper-plate script. Tonight, she could not raise the energy to add more, having no patience with the quill, inkhorn and sander. What was there to enter, save a boring repetition of what she had written yesterday and the day before that? Nothing happened any more. The weekly visit from her

133

physician was the most exciting event, relieving the monotony. If he deemed it necessary to try cupping instead of leeches to stir her sluggish blood, it was something of a red-letter day. Her lips, painted in an absurd cupid's-bow, curved into a grim smile. Perhaps the very fact that she clung to life so tenaciously was worthy of record.

She turned the pages for a while, noting the deterioration of her writing, eyes troublesome, hand shaky. Mercer had settled her into bed some time earlier and, since then, she had drunk two glasses of brandy poured from the decanter into her favourite pink crystal goblet. Now she needed the commode. With fierce stubbornness, she refused to tug at the bell-pull hanging beside the tapestry bed-curtains. Dammit! She'd manage herself! Thank God she still had control over her functions, not yet reduced to the humiliation of being washed and changed like a baby. She wanted to die before reaching that stage of utter dependency. Slowly, painfully, she swung her legs over the side of the mattress and eased her thin frame down the two wide, shallow steps which flanked the four-poster.

Hell, this unwieldy body of hers! How she loathed it! Could it be the same one which had danced with such grace, ridden the finest bloodstock, run lightly as a gazelle, lusted after handsome men and known ecstacy in their arms? Though she despised it, she yet felt an unwilling tenderness towards it, such as one might feel towards an aging, crotchety friend. Aye, we've been through much together, haven't we? she addressed it from the plush-covered throne of the commode. You've served me well on the whole, given me pleasure and my children, not that they proved much of a blessing, all of 'em dead whilst we linger on. 'Tis not your fault that you're wearing out. I mustn't blame you, but curse Dame Nature, eh?

She chuckled at the absurdity of talking to herself, then pleased with the small triumph of getting out of bed unaided, she commenced the task of returning. It took a long time, but what did this matter? There was nothing for which to hurry. No impatient husband or ardent lover awaited her with burning loins beneath the sheets. Not now, though there had been a time – God, what times! Men – good looking, virile – elegant courtiers, swashbuckling military men, fanciful poets, wily politicians. They passed before her inner vision, though dry bones for ages, most of them. Yes, she'd had her pick of the bunch. Gentlemen? Aye, in the main, though she'd not been too pernickerty as she grew older. If a fellow had that certain appeal, she'd not enquired too closely into his background, but in her youth the cream of the beaux had been hers at the snap of her fingers.

With half a dozen grubby pillows stuffed at her back, she settled down. Her lids began to droop, the book to sink, and she thought with satisfaction: Now I'm asleep. But she remained suspended with half-dreams smothering her mind. Old events, old situations: she seemed to be back in Paris before the Revolution, dancing at a ball in the Palace of Versailles, rivalling Queen Marie Antoinette with her loveliness. The musicians played like mad, the candles shone, the wide hooped skirts eddied and billowed, the naked arms and shoulders gleamed, jewels flashed, gentlemen bowed and preened, and the soft, tinkling music rocked – rocked –

She spoke aloud to someone who did not exist, startling herself into wakefulness, back in her huge, dim bedchamber at Kenrick Old Court, England, seeing a corner of the enormous fireplace with its great carved central shield bearing a coat-of-arms which were not hers, and the flames licking hungrily at the logs below. Seeing, but not wanting to see the border of fruit and flowers which surmounted the oak panelled walls, and the dancing shadows between the footposts of the bed. Tangled there, between sleeping and waking, she saw the pictures on the wall – too far away to give more than a hint of their subjects – cloudy landscapes, hunting scenes – except for one, positioned where she could look at it at all times, though why she wanted to do so was beyond answer.

It was the life-size portrait of a young woman wearing a formal, wide-panniered white satin gown, thirty years out of date. Her dark hair was piled high, unpowdered but arranged in sculptured curls. She held a painted fan in the tapering fingers of one hand. A beautiful girl with arresting eyes of an unusual shade of violet-blue. Madame was apt to stare at it for minutes on end, sometimes imagining that it depicted herself at the height of her glory, sometimes sourly remembering that it was that other who had inherited her once striking looks. Then rage would filter through her veins and sinews, till she pushed the memory away, slipping back into the pretence that it really was herself. A tear crawled down her cheek, making a runnel in the rouge. She wiped it away with one shrunken hand. How foolish to weep. She had not cried for years. Lonely? Yes, she was lonely tonight, touched by the chill of age, haunted by approaching death. Soon she would follow the rest into the night that had no morning.

It was as if she was the only living being in the world, the room very still, though outside the blizzard shrieked, hurling bloated white blobs against the window-panes. Ah, this wretched cold, damp country to which she had been exiled. She had never learned to tolerate it. Even before she became infirm, she had rarely ventured beyond the gates of the manor. She chose to forget that once she had been only too thankful to hide within its walls, hounded like a beast from her native shore. Gradually those walls had closed in, becoming both sanctuary and prison. Rooms had been shuttered and locked. No visitor ever rang the bell at the bolted front door. Madame had remained there with a few faithful servants under the command of Mercer, her housekeeper and nurse. This suited the Duchesse. She wanted no one, content to immerse herself in dreams of the halycon days of her girlhood, and the triumphant reign of her married life before –

The hammering at the bedroom door made her jump. Mercer's homely face appeared, disembodied, floating above the candle she held. She was in her dressing-gown, grey hair in two thin plaits hanging down beneath her nightcap. 'Madame! Madame!' she hissed through crooked teeth, trying to keep the excitement and alarm from her voice. 'A person is here!'

Madame la Duchesse stared straight at her, head up. 'Control yourself, woman!' she rapped out, loudly, firmly. 'What's the matter? Stop dithering!' Her accent was strong. She had never lost it, feared by the villagers, known by them as 'The French Woman'.

Mercer advanced, shaken from her half servile, half bullying attitude to her mistress. 'At the gates, Madame – a young female – nearly dead from the cold. Benedict brought her in.'

Madame was wide awake now. Here would be a tasty morsel for her journal, but she was as wary as a wounded vixen in her den. Strangers were not welcomed. Even the doctor did not prolong his visits. The locals hinted at dark doings in the secluded confines of Kenrick. The French Woman was a witch, one of Boney's spies! They continued with this though the war with Napoleon had been over for years. The goodwives used her name to frighten naughty children into obedience.

'Then Benedict must deal with it,' she replied crisply. 'How dare you disturb me in the middle of the night? Don't stand there gawking! Away with you!'

Mercer held her ground doggedly, mouth opening and shutting in a ludicrous manner. 'Madame, you must see her. She insists.'

For an instant, Madame felt young again, the blood surging

136

through her veins. It was like the old days. There was something in the air. She could smell it. A heady whiff of danger. 'Does she indeed?' She hesitated for a second, then: 'Show her in,' she commanded imperiously.

Mercer bobbed a frightened curtsey and hurried to the door. Madame could hear her outside in the corridor, mumuring with Benedict. The sounds of the storm were clearer, beating, howling, tearing round the house, as if the stranger had let it in. Then Mercer and Benedict entered, supporting someone between them, bringing her nearer to the bed. Madame, bolt upright, looked at the wet, tattered cloak, the streaming hair, the white face with large eyes staring back into hers. She gasped. By some devilry beyond human control, she was being confronted by the creature of the portrait, yet changed, brought low – only the face, the eyes were the same.

'Who are you?' she breathed, her words dropping into the silence.

Mariana did not reply at once, confused by the sudden warmth, the light, the sight of this monstrous vision seated like some heathen idol in the bed, a continuation of the nightmare in which she had been living for hours. She saw the thing's lips move, heard the cracked voice, saw the caricature of faded beauty etched on those terrible features beneath the towering, dirty powdered wig. An osprey crest juddered amongst the stiff curls, jewels sparkled in the false hair, on the nobbly fingers, around the skeletal wrists.

Mercer prodded her in the ribs. 'Give answer to Madame la Duchesse! Speak! She's waiting!'

The room was whirling, colours, impressions rushing together. The fugitive was chilled to the marrow, but heat laved her, sending the sweat to her brow. With a supreme effort she kept to her feet, outfacing that awful old woman.

'You *know* who I am,' she said.

The glittering eyes in that travesty of a face never left hers.

'Indeed I do,' answered the Duchesse, 'and that knowledge brings me no joy.' Without looking at them, she dismissed her servants. 'Leave us.'

'It's not safe, Madame.' Mercer was flustered by this disruption.

'Get out!' thundered Madame, the feathers in her wig shaking. 'Stay within call, if you must, but go away.' When they were alone, she said to Mariana: 'Why are you here? What is it you seek?'

'Sanctuary.' The single word echoed through the room.

The crimson-smeared mouth opened on decaying teeth as Madame cackled. 'You dare to come here, begging sanctuary?'

Mariana's head lifted. She straightened her spine, drawing her rags about her with a regal gesture. 'I don't beg. I demand it.'

This pleased Madame and her grin widened. 'You've spirit, I'll grant you that, wench. So, you've braved the lair of the evil *sorcière* of Kenrick, have you? You must be in dire straits.'

'I don't fear you,' Mariana retorted. Nothing here compared with the terror that had driven her from Thornfalcon.

'Weren't you warned never to see me?' The ancient eyes were hooded, veiled by pink, transparent lids – watching – gloating.

'Yes,' came the prompt response. From a child she had been told not to venture near the rusty gates of the forbidding house. It was only when her mother lay dying that she had beckoned her close and whispered the secret. So easy to promise then, throat swollen with tears, seeing that agonized face against the linen pillow, the feverish eyes imploring her to keep her word. How could she have foreseen that one day she would be forced to break that vow?

'Why are you dressed in those disgusting rags?' Madame sneered.

'There was a drunken beggar-woman on the moors. She wanted my gown, my cloak, my rings.'

'Ha! And you gave them? More fool you!'

Mariana shrugged. 'She had a knife, and murder in her eyes. I took her rags in exchange, so that I wouldn't freeze.'

Madame glared fiercely. 'How dare she? Those damned peasants! *Canaille! Dieu!* My father would never have permitted such insolence. He'd have ordered them flogged till the blood ran – hanged 'em high – turned their whelps out into the street! The world has gone mad when such filth can threaten their betters and get away with it!'

'The old order has changed, or hadn't you noticed?' There was sarcasm in the tired voice, a contemptuous curl to her lip.

'For the worse,' snarled Madame. 'Those apes, those reformers who preach that all men are born equal! What do they know? Give a peasant the upper hand and he turns on his master like a wild beast. We cared for our vassals at the chateau, and what happened? How were we repaid, eh? By death and destruction! By a savage mob howling for blood!' Her eyes were glazed as she looked inwards, reliving horrors.

She looked so much a corpse that when she spoke, it was shocking, like the dead coming to life. She seemed no longer human, a puppet in a wig of dirty-white ringlets, animated by invisible strings. Mariana forced herself to appear unmoved, calling on deep reserves which she had not known she possessed until that awful day.

'I know nothing of these events,' she said. 'They happened long before I was born. You asked me to explain my clothing. I've told you how I came by them. And that's all you'll learn about me.'

Madame's face contorted into the semblance of a smile. 'So proud! I too was proud, but pride can be broken, you know. Why should I shelter you? Answer me that.'

'For the sake of blood.'

'What impudence! Blood, say you?' Madame crouched in the bed, toying with her prey like a cat. 'And what makes you assume that I recognize any such obligation? I made it quite plain, long ago, that I never would.' The wig shook, slipped askew as she jerked her head at the portrait. It glowed against the darkness. 'You hope, perchance, to arouse pity for her sake?'

Mariana's dark brows winged down as she looked at the painting. 'I don't understand. What has she to do with me?'

'You don't recognize your own mother? Call yourself a dutiful daughter? Hell and damnation! You're almost as dutiful as she was!'

'My mother!' There was a catch in Mariana's voice. She pressed her hands against the sodden shawl. 'That is my mother? You lie!'

'Look at yourself,' Madame said mockingly. 'Look in that mirror. Bedraggled slut that you are, the likeness is marked. Why d'you suppose I've gone so far as to admit you? You could've been an assassin, hired to murder me. Come to think of it, as her child, you probably have come to kill me.'

This was madness. A scene enacted in an asylum. Mariana stared into the pier-glass, tilted on its carved stand. Her reflection stared back, pale as death, gaunt and haggard. What a contrast to the portrait sitter! Yet it was impossible to deny the resemblance. She shook her head, wondering, denying. 'That's not my mother. She never owned a dress like that, her husband is a poor man.'

Madame's tongue crept out to lick over her lips. She was delighted. 'I made quite certain that he was. She had to be punished.'

Hatred for this vindictive hag flared up in Mariana. 'How

cruel you are! How heartless! But you've been punished too. You're alone and unloved. You'll die alone and unloved. I pray God that in your hour of dying you'll regret your actions most bitterly.'

Their eyes locked and something sparked between them. 'If I do, then I shan't cringe and whine,' said Madame levelly. 'I did what I considered to be right. Nothing will shake me from that conviction, neither man, woman, god nor devil. The Eastern world calls it karma – the Christians – Divine Judgement.'

'And you? What do you believe?'

'I believe in myself. I've learned to rely on no other. I trust no one. Suspect everyone. Thus, I'm never disappointed, because I expect nothing.'

Her voice was cold, ruthless, rising and falling in time to the dizzy swaying of the warm, gloomy chamber. Mariana felt sick, the words beating into her brain. Trust no one. Suspect all. It was a doctrine close to her heart. To trust was to suffer. To love was to weaken. Suspicion was a stout buckler against life's cruel caprices. It was a hard concept, but one which she accepted. Pain seeped through her as the numbness abated. Her body ached, her breasts throbbed with the milk which Elaine would never again suckle. Her mind screamed in torment, the terror, the heartbreak too black to dwell on.

'No one must suspect that I'm here,' she said.

'Secrets? Deception? Duplicity?' Madame replied with a relish. 'Ah, you'll be well trained in those virtues. Your mother's daughter. Don't fret, Mercer and Benedict have their orders. They speak of nothing that happens within these walls. As for the others? They never come to this part of the house.'

'I need shelter only till the weather clears.' Mariana walked across to the fireplace, holding her hands out to the flames, sighing as she felt the warmth penetrate her wrists. 'You'll help me to get away.' It was a statement, not a question.

'Gladly. I don't want you under my roof a second longer than necessary.' Madame's tone was as icy as hers, but she was enjoying this battle of wills. Here was a worthy adversary on whom she could sharpen her claws. The days ahead promised rare sport. It was not much fun being unkind to Mercer or that doddering old fool, Benedict. By giving vent to her spleen she would be hitting at the woman who had once hurt her so much. Lust had gone, love departed, vanity was no more, but vengeance still ran hot, giving form and substance to her existence.

Mariana knew this, as sensitive as if flayed. Tears burned

behind her eyes, but she was unable to shed them. She had wanted to die, out there on the desolate moors, thrashed by the storm, bereft of hope. Her body was thawing now, but ice encased her soul. She would live. She would escape her thralldom and carve a new life. Her mind was functioning again and, like an animal tortured in a snare, she knew but three driving emotions – hatred of Christopher and the determination to survive and be avenged.

She heard Madame giving orders to Mercer. 'Prepare a room,' she was saying. 'See that it is properly aired. Put hot bricks between the sheets. Make sure that she has everything she requires.'

'We should have departed for London weeks ago, before this appalling weather took hold,' complained Georgiana to her husband when he strolled into their chamber from the adjoining dressing-room. 'Heaven only knows when we'll arrive there now.'

David Cunyngham smiled indulgently, looking at his lovely wife with quiet pleasure. She was seated before the triple-framed adjustable mirror on the shiny surface of the toilet-table, putting the finishing touches to her appearance. Going over to her, he bent his tall head, brushed aside the little fronds of pale curls at the nape of her neck, and placed his lips there caressingly.

'Don't worry, my angel,' he murmured. 'There are signs that a thaw is in the offing. It won't be long before you can swan around town again.'

Georgiana half closed her eyes, purring with contentment under his tender touch, resting her head back against his frilled shirt-front. 'I don't really mind, David. I just miss it a trifle sometimes.' A smile curved her generous mouth. 'What do I want with society and the Winter Season? I have you.'

His lips trailed softly from her throat to her mouth, and he kissed her warmly, affectionately. His kisses were always supremely satisfying. This was one of the reasons why she had been so determined to marry him. She prided herself on being an expert on the subject of kisses, having had plenty of opportunity to sample a variety in her rather giddy youth. She had been a gadabout, a fashionable belle, one of the raffish Devonshire House set. Lady Caroline Lamb had been a close friend, until she had caused a scandal by her wild affair with Lord Byron. Georgiana had had quite a reputation herself by the time she met David. He had proved to be the man strong enough to curb her, and she had fallen in love with him deeply and forever. His first kiss had wiped any doubt from her mind. She had never been kissed in such a way before. Not the sort of kisses that left her feeling cheap, as if the man concerned was out for everything he could get as soon as maybe. Not silly, timid kisses either, that made one think he was not really interested and might as well have been kissing his sister. No, David was a wise, experienced lover, an instinctive judge of a woman's moods, using his kisses accordingly.

She nestled into him, having just spoken the truth. She did not care if they were imprisoned in the depths of snowy Yorkshire for months – not really, though she liked to tease him. They were that rare thing, a happily married couple, annoying less fortunate friends by their total absorption in one another. It was most unfashionable, but neither cared a jot for the opinion of the rather jaded circle which constituted smart society. Both had found peace at last after a series of hectic affairs, appreciating their secure haven. Not that Georgiana had turned overnight into a boringly domesticated hausfrau, with nothing of greater importance than the setting of her jam or the whiteness of her laundry. Far from it. She had been reared a lady, adored and indulged, and could well have followed in the footsteps of Caro Lamb had not David swept her into his arms, that broad, quiet man with the humorous eyes and innate streak of common sense.

Acquaintances expressed amazement at the way he had tamed her. She was witty, lovely and spirited still, a sought-after guest, an entertaining hostess, radiating a gentle happiness. David too had mellowed. He still did his fair share of gambling, a patron of 'the fancy', encouraging up-and-coming boxers, proud owner of several Newmarket winners, but concentrating more on business these days, accepting the responsibility of his title and commitments.

They were ready to go down to breakfast, yet lingered in the intimacy of their bedroom – rendered even more pleasant in contrast to the gale gusting outside. Brilliant daylight streamed in at the tall, narrow windows, accentuated by the snow blanketing lawns, bushes and bare trees. David took up a cashmere shawl, draping it carefully about her shoulders.

'Keep warm,' he advised, ''tis like the North Pole out there.'

She rose, a tiny, elfin woman, slender as a boy, her baby-fine hair cut short, forming crisp, cherubic curls around her shapely head. Such small bones, thought David, she wears a deceptive air of fragility, yet she's strong as a horse beneath. A twinge of anxiety shot through him for, robust though she was, her hips were narrow. How would it be for her in childbirth? Would she be able to produce the children they both desired so much?

No such forebodings seemed to cloud her serenity, her smile so piercing and so beautiful that he wanted to hold her close, enfold her in the armour of his love. Gay, provocative, green eyes dancing, she ran a light finger along the hard line of his jaw. 'Why did I have to fall for a man whose estate is situated in this inhospitable corner of England?' she asked.

'Because that same man is one of the richest in the kingdom, and you like luxury, my little minx,' he replied, his leanly handsome face amused. 'Jove, we don't visit here often. What of my villa in Greece? My *schloss* in Austria? Don't they suit your Ladyship?'

'They'll suffice, till I find something better,' she replied airily, her heart flipping over as she looked up at him. Even after two years of matrimony, she still found him devastatingly attractive. He was a big man, wide-shouldered, long-limbed, elegantly attired, almost as fair-haired as herself, with eyes too expressive to be blue, too lively to be grey, a delightful combination of the two shades.

Many men of his class were thick-witted fops, wasting their time and fortunes on cards or loose women, often drinking too much. David was intelligent, well-educated and cultured, shrewd as well, handling his Yorkshire investments with considerable acumen, not only owning wool-producing sheep-farms, but mines, steel works and cotton mills. Yet, when in town, he contrived to appear a dilettante, if it suited him to do so.

Georgiana responded to the fresh, clean smell of him – newly laundered linen, shaving soap, a hint of tobacco, that personal scent which was all his own. She was easily aroused in the mornings, and liked him to make love to her at unusual moments or in circumstances when she least expected it. The thought of doing so now, when breakfast was ready and their rather starchy butler poised to serve, was most exciting. She glanced over to the unmade bed, and David followed her eyes. He grinned and nodded, then went to turn the key in the lock. In seconds she was lying on the bed, skirts riding up, slim legs in white stockings exposed for his inspection, waiting for him in eager anticipation. She adored the way he came to her, eager, needful, tugging at the fastenings of his clothes. Her hands were finding his skin beneath his shirt, lovely skin, hard, smooth, warm, her body fitting against his hungrily, wantonly. David, my beloved husband, she thought, whilst she made tiny, indefinite moans of pleasure, how lucky I am to be married to such a wonderful lover.

A little later, Georgiana slipped her arm through David's as they walked through the corridors of their home, Coleshill Abbey, on the way to the breakfast-room. The house had retained its original name, although fifty years before, David's uncle had constructed a splendid new mansion on the site of the monastic building. Like most noblemen of his day, he had gone on the Grand Tour of Europe, returning after eighteen months fired by the baroque architecture of France, Italy and Germany. From that moment on, he had been obsessed with rebuilding Coleshill, incorporating Ionic arches, obelisks and Corinthian pillars. The grounds had taken even longer to landscape. The local gentry had looked askance at his ground plans, shaking their heads over the folly of copying the schemes of hare-brained foreign draughtsmen, whose designs were only suitable for warm climates. He had obstinately continued against all opposition and, in the end, many others had followed suit.

The new Coleshill Abbey had arisen, its façade ornamented with columns, niches holding larger-than-life statues, and long pleasant terraces on either side. The gardens were set out with symmetrical lawns, artistically positioned trees and shrubs, a lake where once the monks had fished for carp, a folly representing a ruined temple placed where it could be viewed from the drawing-room windows, a grotto and several fountains. Across the years its white stone had mellowed, blending in with the background. It was no longer a talking-point among the squires and gentlemen farmers. Most people had forgotten that Coleshill had ever been different. Tucked into a tree-sheltered hollow, it had settled down comfortably, and now David owned it.

He felt family pride stirring strongly as he and Georgiana passed through the passages, their footsteps muffled by Aubusson carpets decorated with flowered garlands. Mirrors in huge gilt frames alternated with portraits on the white-painted walls, and the atmosphere was one of light and space. He glanced down at his wife, the warm blood of recollection in him from their love-making. She was cool and perfectly groomed again, and he approved of her fair complexion, her beautifully tended hands. Always exquisitely gowned, she wore a dress of fine green wool, cut high in the waist, the skirt ankle-length and full, the sleeves ruched, the collar upstanding and frilled. She graced his home delightfully, though still keeping that faintly childish air which had captivated him when he first saw her, running barefoot in the gardens of Devonshire House.

They reached the staircase which swept down in a curve to the hall where a footman, clad in black and gold Cunyngham livery, stood like a pawn on a red and ochre marble chessboard. In a few moments they entered the breakfast-room. David's uncle, Phineas Cunyngham, had not counted the cost when it was being designed. Not quite as grand as the reception rooms, it had a pleasant, informal feel, the ideal place to start the day. The colours were muted, beige and cream covering walls and ceiling. Fawn damask curtains flanked the curving bay windows, and the same material upholstered the Chippendale chairs. On the marble mantelpiece an ornate bronze and tortoise-shell clock gave the time as fifteen minutes past nine.

The aroma of fresh coffee greeted them. Covered silver entree dishes lay in readiness on the walnut sideboard. The odour of liver and bacon joined that of the coffee. The oval table was spread with lace place-mats, and set with gilt-rimmed, exotically patterned Spode ware and glittering cutlery. Footmen were in attendance, wearing plush breeches, their calves bulging in white cotton stockings. Edwin was already seated, napkin across the knees of his tight-fitting trousers. He rose to peck his sister-in-law's cheek, while a lackey pulled out her chair punctiliously.

'Good morning, Georgiana,' he said brightly. 'Radiant as ever, I see. And you, David,' he turned to his brother. 'Lord, I wish that I could sit up late, drink as you do, and still rise spruce next day. How the deuce d'you do it?'

'Take more water with your wine, Edwin,' David advised, assuming his place and nodding to the butler who hovered in readiness with the coffee-pot. 'That's the secret. Let the others tope on, and keep your head clear if you want to win at cards. You were in a monstrous sad way by the time we'd finished play last night. Can't think for the life of me how you let old Bridely beat you. Most careless.'

His normally good-natured face wore a frown as he eyed Edwin. He was a problem. David had invited him to spend Christmas at Coleshill for two reasons, one of which was to stem the rising tide of his debts, the other to remove him from London for a while in order that a rather sordid scandal concerning a married lady might die down. Edwin had a knack for attracting trouble, yet seemed to sail through life with an exasperating insouciance. David felt the responsibility for him keenly, for he was not yet twenty-one, and their parents were dead. Their sisters had made admirable marriages, but Edwin showed no inclination to settle down. He had not done well at Eton or Cambridge, and had flitted from one interest to the next. At the present time he fancied his chances as a poet, fired by the notoriety acquired by Lord Byron, and had surrounded himself with a bawdy, talented, malicious clique. A kind of defiant, spendthrift jauntiness was one of his less endearing characteristics.

Edwin sipped his coffee, waving away the offer of fried food with a grimace. 'I had a run of back luck,' he grumbled, seeing that David was in the mood to lecture. 'In my opinion, Bridely's a sharp.'

'Poppycock,' David grunted, disturbed by a sense of annoyance. He wished that he and Georgiana were alone. Edwin was ten years his junior, and he did not relish this role of surrogate father. The truth was that their mother had spoilt her last-born.

'I'm certain that you're mistaken, Edwin. He's an honourable man,' soothed Georgiana, watching out for storm signals. David, usually so understanding, had a blind spot where Edwin was concerned.

'You always see the best in everyone, so sweet yourself that you make angels of us all.' Edwin's hazel eyes twinkled at her, knowing precisely how to exaggerate that boyish, rather lost look which most women found irresistible. He had perfected it at his mother's knee. Somehow, he succeeded in making it appear that Georgiana was his ally.

'Flattery is all very well, providing one doesn't inhale it,' David said in cold displeasure.

Georgiana laughed, her hand coming to rest on his where it lay, fist clenched, on the inlaid wood of the table. She had never given him cause for jealousy and did not propose to start. 'Edwin jests, my love. You know that he never takes anything seriously.'

Tactfully, she turned the conversation to less personal topics, amusing them with her mimicry of several nosy neighbours who lost no opportunity to leave their calling-cards. But as she talked, her thoughts were running on the two brothers, so dissimilar in temperament. They shared the family good looks, both tall men, both fair, but Edwin's face was of a softer mould not entirely due to youth. He had been doted on by a middle-aged mother and both his sisters. This had left its mark. At times it seemed that he lived in a dream-world, incapable of distinguishing fact from fantasy. She had mentioned this to David but he, rather harshly, had dismissed this as nonsense, saying that Edwin was a born liar.

David was forthright in speech, masculine in outlook, yet retaining a certain refinement and sensitivity. Edwin was very much the ladies' man – casual, fun-loving, debonair. He was well aware of his appearance, rather dandified in his high cravat, silk waistcoat, mauve broadcloth jacket with the fitted waist and tails, cream trousers and glossy black shoes. His light brown hair was thick and curling, deliberately ruffled as if he had run a careless hand through it while composing his latest ode. Georgiana sighed inwardly, having made up her mind that he needed a steadying influence in his rumbustious life. She turned the talk round to include mention of several daughters of the nobility who were seeking husbands.

Edwin caught the inference and his smile became taut. 'You want to see me take on the snaffle,' he accused, half joking, half piqued.

David put down his cup, steepled his fingers together and nodded. 'If you like to put it that way, yes. Why shouldn't you marry? There are any number of suitable ladies who wouldn't be averse to taking your name. Let's face it, Edwin, you could do with a bride who has a substantial dowry.'

Edwin did not answer, keeping his eyes sulkily on his plate as he spread butter and quince preserve on a hot muffin. He had no intention of marrying yet, though he could see the sense of David's suggestion. The majority of younger sons in his position courted heiresses, with an eye on the main chance. He felt a prickle of resentment and envy. David had inherited Coleshill Abbey and everything it entailed. He had married for love, capturing one of the most delightful beauties of the day. It wasn't fair.

The butler entered the room, correct and stately, bearing a silver salver on which reposed a letter. He presented it to David with a bow. David frowned. 'What is this, Melville?'

Melville's face was calm and unmoved. 'A groom brought it to the door, my Lord. He said it was to be delivered to you without delay.'

David was already passing a knife under the flap of the stiff envelope, slitting it open. He read the enclosed note, then exclaimed: 'Good God! Here's a rum go! It's from the Duchesse.'

'Darling, explain yourself.' Georgiana gave him a smile. 'Which duchesse? We know several.'

'The one who lives at Kenrick Old Court.' David was staring down at the letter, none too pleased. 'She requests that I go to see her at once. What the devil can she want with me?'

147

'There's only one way to find out,' commented Edwin dryly, welcoming this diversion. 'D'you want me to come?'

David shook his head, tucked the message into his pocket and pushed back his chair. 'She's a recluse, and may take offence if her instructions aren't followed.'

He was already dressed for outdoors, in a serviceable brown double-breasted coat, buckskin breeches and leather top-boots. He dropped a kiss on Georgiana's head and went through to the hall, where Melville helped him into his caped greatcoat. He picked up his gloves and curly-brimmed hat on the way out, running down the flight of wide stone steps which led between fluted columns from the canopied front door. A stable-lad stood at the bottom, gentling David's horse, a magnificent bay of Irish extraction whose breath trailed like smoke on the frosty air. David put a foot in the stirrup and swung himself up, then shook the reins. The animal moved forward eagerly, his hooves soundless on the fall of snow which carpeted the long, straight drive.

There was a stiff wind blowing down from the moors, so that wisps and tails of snow curled along the skyline behind which hurrying clouds disappeared. When David cantered up to the lodge, the keeper was already swinging open the gates. The road lay ahead, rutted, icy, treacherous. He guided his horse carefully, turning his head away from the village, taking the opposite direction. The track climbed steadily, trees thinning, wind increasing as he breasted a rise. The hills dropped away to the steep valley in which his manor lay, the ring of hills, cuplike, enclosing it. From that height, he could breathe salt in the air, blown from the North Sea. On every side lay moors, a vast expanse of smarting white, hurting his eyes as the sunlight struck it.

He knew this land, visiting there many times when a lad, intrigued by it, fighting it at first, then coming to terms with its harsh beauty, learning to love and respect it. It was a bleak, merciless country, far removed from the colourful softness of Sussex where he had been born. It had never crossed his mind that one day a substantial part of it would belong to him. A quirk of fate had decreed that, on Uncle Phineas's death, he had become the eccentric old man's heir, he and Edwin being the only remaining male Cunynghams. The revenues from the coal, cattle and arable lands were his, as was a fine house in London, and Coleshill Abbey. There had been one peculiar clause in the will. David scowled as he thought about it, a solitary figure against the whiteness, collar turned up, hat rammed down. It was the reason why he was making this damned cold journey.

The moor rolled endlessly before him, heather and gorse bushes heavy with the snow gusting from them in dizzying swirls. The force of the wind was such that the horse leaned into it, struggling along, up to his fetlocks in drifts. David rode easier when he found the stony path, noting a break in the distance, heading for it, then traversing a steep, slippery slope. Jugger Tor loomed like a white giant above him, but there was shelter at the base of the gorge. A waterfall crashed from the heights, too fast to freeze, tumbling into Hell's Beck at the bottom. The way widened into a secret valley. He could see the thick screen of pines that partially hid the house, and the high, iron-spiked walls which enclosed it. From that distance, the gabled roof shone in a pattern of grey slate and snow, smoke coiling up from its chimney-pots.

The main gate was fastened by a rusty chain and padlock. Ivy and creepers hung tenaciously to it, defying the winter. David went round to the back, dismounting and leading his horse to an arched wooden doorway, half hidden by bushes. It creaked open and he entered the yard. An air of neglect hung everywhere. There was no sign of life, but after he had shouted several times an ugly man, bent and twisted as a yew tree, shuffled out from the kitchen. David could see several round-eyed servants peering at him through a steamy lower window.

'Where's your mistress?' David asked the old retainer sternly. 'I'm expected. Lord Cunyngham of Coleshill Abbey.'

'Yes, sir.' Benedict nodded his balding grey head, wringing gnarled hands together, a shabby figure in a suit of rusty black. 'Please come this way, my Lord.'

A surly groom had slouched from the stable to take the horse, whilst David glanced round at the decayed appearance of Kenrick Old Court. The cobbled yard was a sea of frozen slush. A thatched well with moss-covered wall occupied its centre. A slatternly maid was lowering the bucket with forcible bangs to break the ice-crust. Wanton neglect and bad management. It made David's blood boil. Why hadn't the old bitch spent some money on it? he raged internally, his stare of blistering scorn making the groom jump to attention.

This was satisfying and David felt better, but not for long. Though the Cunynghams laid claim to have sprung from the loins of Danish kings, a healthy injection of common blood, by way of marriage into Saxon farming-stock, had given them keen business brains. At bottom, they had always been astute bargainers. Even when an odd trait or two came out, as in Uncle Phineas, it inevitably took the form of somehow adding to their wealth and possessions. It hurt David to see this building, once the semi-fortified family home, ruined by the whim of a woman who was not even a member of their brood.

Benedict did not take him to the grand entrance nor through the servants' quarters, but into a dark passage to one side. He opened a heavily timbered door which led to the Great Hall. It was huge, panelled from floor to ceiling in dark oak. From the rafters of the arched roof hung an enormous bell. A carved black staircase, with balustrades in the shape of monsters, curved upwards at the far end where it linked with a gallery. Latticed windows cast a dim light over the uneven flooring. The leads of a couple bore the date '1627' and the initials 'I.C.' David wondered if these had been scratched there by the legendary Isabella Cunyngham, another eccentric who, so the story went, had carried her winding-sheet about with her.

It was a strange, gloomy house, its windows filthy and obscured by ivy which had been allowed to sprawl, unchecked, about most of the lower ones. The light filtering through was greenish grey, giving the distinct impression of walking in a succession of caves beneath the sea. Statues gleamed like phantoms, in the corners of corridors hung with mouldy tapestries or at the foot of dark stairs. The dull patina decorating the fronts of ebony dower chests and massive mahogany pieces, the blotched surfaces of ancient mirrors, threw back faint reflections of that grey-drenched light creeping in from outside.

Benedict conducted David to a drawing-room on the south side. By that time he was thoroughly chilled and it was a relief to step over the threshold into warmth. Logs blazed between fantastic brass dogs in the wide central hearth. The curtains were closely drawn, and the room was illuminated by candles in branching holders. Light glinted on the furniture, which was old-fashioned, dating from the Tudors, the chairs padded in stamped Spanish leather, nailed and fringed. The long narrow table had grotesque projecting feet. Teak cabinets, swarming with gilt and lacquer, displayed a wealth of silver ornaments and valuable Dresden china. Paintings jostled for place on the dark panelled walls; here an Italian landscape where shepherds and sylphs frolicked, there a Madonna and Child. The saturnine features of King Charles II sneered down from one side of the ponderous fireplace, and near at hand was his mistress, Nell Gwynn, plump and bulging-eyed, an unflattering likeness. But the most remarkable sight in the whole cluttered, colourful apartment, was the figure occupying a chair drawn close to the fire.

It was almost a throne, and the person seated in it was tiny but regal. The chair was armless, and her enormous hooped skirt jutted out each side, its gaudy scarlet folds spilling to the floor, scintillating with gems, its flounces heavily embroidered with gold thread. Such garish colour was horrific in contrast to the parchment-like, painted skin of its wearer. The thin, wrinkled neck seemed weighed down by the gross high wig, beneath the matted curls of which two eyes regarded him malevolently.

Pulling himself together, David ventured nearer to this wax effigy. A hand was extended towards him and he bowed low, placing his lips to the back of it, sickened by the touch of old, unwashed flesh. 'Madame la Duchesse,' he said, straightening. 'I understand that you desire to see me.'

Madame shook her head, the gash of a mouth grimacing. 'You're wrong there, young man. I've no desire at all to see you. This is a matter of sheer necessity.'

Jove, but she's as dictatorial and tiresome as ever, he thought. He had not seen her for five years, and she had hardly changed, save to become even more mummified. He stepped back a pace. The room was airless and she stank. David had a strong stomach; he had served in the army, and was used to hot, sweaty ballrooms where even the highest in the land were not noted for personal hygiene, yet this odour smacked of disease, nauseatingly foetid. He hoped that she would say what had to be said and end the interview. As when the lawyer had told him the contents of Uncle Phineas's will, he again cursed that perverse man who had left him so wealthy. That damned codicil! It had been impishly added by that odd, clever individual who had delighted in amassing antiquities, in investing cannily, and gaining a fortune on the stock-market. David had been given no option but to agree, or forfeit everything.

He smiled grimly, hat beneath his arm, crop and gloves in one hand. 'Be that as it may, Madame, if it is business, then we must discuss it. I've no more liking for this than yourself.'

Madame grinned in her skull face, and nodded towards the portrait which seemed to mock them from the opposite wall. 'My faithful friend, Phineas Cunyngham. Even when he lay adying he didn't forget me. How it must have galled you to learn that I was to stay here. You'd like to own Kenrick, wouldn't you? But it belongs to me, mine to bequeath to whomever I wish, or I can leave instructions for it to be pulled down, brick by brick.' She lifted her brandy goblet high. 'Phineas, I drink to you! We'll meet in hell, ere long.' She took a sip. Some of the liquid dribbled down her whiskery chin.

David's face hardened. 'It was his wish and I honour it. The house is yours, Madame, but if you don't spend money on it soon, it'll fall about your ears. The roof is in a shocking condition. Damp must be seeping in to the upper rooms.'

Madame's eerie witch's laughter rocked the room. 'Ah, bravo! There speaks a true Cunyngham, an aristocrat with the instincts of a peasant, never slow to sell his own soul for a handsome profit. Your family know only one sin or dishonour, that of being cheated out of their full dues in the shape of beef, mutton or coal!'

Cantankerous old piss-pot! David muttered savagely under his breath. She's glorying in this! Why the hell did Uncle Phineas harbour and protect her? Aloud, he grated: 'There's no shame in conserving one's property. No dishonour in keeping one's accounts in order and running one's estate efficiently.'

'There are ways and means,' she said mysteriously, replacing her glass on a small table beside her chair. 'My forebears were also rich, but they never lowered themselves to the level of husbandmen and shopkeepers. Your progenitors were bandits. Mine were kings.'

She's quite mad, David decided, senile and wandering. 'What is it you require of me?' he asked coldly.

'All in good time. You people are in such a hurry these days – no respect.' Madame prevaricated. Let him wait. Arrogant lordling, forceful, energetic, so sure of himself. Let him stew a little longer. She smiled slyly. 'Surely you can spend a few moments of your time with me? Let your bailiff earn his keep and see that your tenants don't cheat you. You've never visited me before.'

'You have never invited me,' he snapped.

'Neither have I bothered you with complaints,' she shot back. 'But now I'm about to order you to fulfil Phineas's condition that you assist me if I request it. Be seated, sir. It's quite unnerving to have you towering over me like one of those bloody crags on that benighted moor out there.'

David kept his temper with difficulty, seating himself on a joint-stool, hat dangling between his knees, uneasy in that stuffy room. It was unnatural to light candles when the blessing of daylight abounded. He was highly suspicious of Madame. She was a baffling enigma. None of the Cunynghams had been able to understand Uncle Phineas's interest in her for he was a confirmed batchelor. It had caused an uproar when she had arrived in England in 1794, fleeing from the revolutionaries. Phineas had never discussed the subject, installing her at

Kenrick and, as far as anyone could ascertain, continuing to reside at Coleshill Abbey. Had she been his mistress? David doubted it.

Madame thoughtfully fingered the magnificent diamond necklace that adorned her throat and ran an expert eye over the irritated man, appreciating his fine body and handsome face. He did not resemble Phineas in the slightest degree, but then Phineas had been the runt of the litter, making up for his crippled leg that gave him an ungainly limp, thin hair and the features of a mischievous imp, by his sharp wits. She missed him. How long had he been dead? Could it really be five years? He too, had shunned company, yet he had habitually ridden over to play backgammon and gossip. His wit had been razor-keen, even towards the end. No, this nephew was not a patch on him, for all his swagger.

A minute ticked by, and she was amused to see David shifting impatiently whilst trying to appear indifferent. 'I suppose you're eager to know why I sent for you?' she said at last.

Her tone was deliberately insulting, as if he was an underling hired to do her bidding. David glared. 'I'd be obliged if you told me. I'm a busy man, Madame.'

'Very well.' She leaned forward, bird-bright eyes fixed on his face. 'I'm about to place a young lady in your care.'

His head went up. 'The devil you are! Explain yourself!'

'I know I have trouble with this uncouth English tongue, but should have thought my meaning clear – even to you.' Her sarcasm coiled out from those thin red lips. She spoke again, enunciating the phrase, as if addressing an idiot. 'You are to take charge of a girl.'

Exasperation drove David to his feet. 'You rave, Madame!'

She reached for a silver hand-bell and shook it. Mercer appeared so swiftly that she must have been within earshot. 'Bring her in,' the Duchesse commanded.

The morning had been full of surprises, but none was so great as that which shocked through him when Mercer returned, accompanied by a thin, pale young woman. She was dressed in drab brown, her dark hair falling across her shoulders and halfway down her back. It waved and curled like a gypsy's, and her face gleamed in the midst of that dusky frame. Her movements were graceful, dignified, head held proudly on a slim neck. She was beautiful. Perhaps the most beautiful woman he had even seen. As she came closer, staring straight at him, he saw that her eyes were of a blue so intense as to border on violet, fringed by long black lashes.

'This is Lord David Cunyngham, who is to be your guardian,' said Madame, as delighted as an evil child by the havoc she was causing. 'My Lord, permit me to present Maria Malton, a quiet, though not over-obedient female, who will become a member of your household.'

'Nothing has been settled, Madame,' said David firmly, feet wide-spread on the carpet, hands locked behind his back. 'This needs careful consideration. I must discuss it with my wife.'

Wicked glee lit up in the old woman's eyes. 'Sir, am I to understand that you're hen-pecked? La, in my day, a husband's word was law. I have heard that your lady is somewhat wilful and hot-headed.'

David took the bait, despite himself. 'Georgiana obeys me, Madame, have no doubt of that.'

'Then there's no problem,' she replied conclusively. That grotesque mask under the even more horrible wig turned to the girl. 'Maria, you're to go with this gentleman. Put on your cloak.'

David's face flushed, a vein throbbing at his temple. 'This is ridiculous! I can't take her.'

'You can. You will.' Madame was implacable. 'If you refuse, I'll inform my lawyer. I'll drag the matter through every court in London. Phineas was adamant. It's all there, plain as a pike-staff, in his will. Whatever I want, you will perform, without let or hindrance.'

It was on the tip of David's tongue to tell her to sue and be damned, then sense prevailed as he visualized the scandal, the unpleasant publicity. The newspapers would pounce on it, painting him as a black-hearted villain denying the simple request of an aged lady. Also, he was becoming intrigued by the girl's aloof stance which belied the agony in those compelling eyes.

'What d'you make of this, Maria?' He spoke to her gently. It was unfair of them to decide her future without asking her opinion. 'Would you like to come and live with me, a total stranger?'

Mariana's eyes met his, full of questions and fears. 'I've no say in the matter.' Her voice was low but clear. There was no hint of a country accent, no foreign intonation.

She was holding herself in check with agonizing effort. The humiliations she had suffered over the past week made her want to cry out: Oh, take me away from this dreadful old monster!

Control. How painfully she had learned to exercise it through the years. It had been her standby in this present crisis. Only when alone could she surrender to grief, beating her fists against the pillow at night, stuffing her handkerchief into her mouth to stifle her sobs. She refused to give the Duchesse the satisfaction of seeing her broken; she remained cool, unmoved, no matter what cruel taunt was flung at her. Madame had been utterly merciless, treating her as a debased slave, never allowing her to forget for one second that she had done her a great favour by hiding her at Kenrick.

She had accepted the name 'Maria Malton'. As such she might be able to shelter under a cloak of anonymity. The price had been exorbitant, but the way to freedom was opening. David had a kind face, honest eyes. Whatever menial tasks he set her or however humble her role, nothing could be worse than living with the Duchesse.

'Well, what d'you say?' Madame had not enjoyed herself so much for ages. This was more entertaining than a play.

'Who is she?' Compassion moved in David. He could feel his opposition weakening under the girl's steady regard.

'That's nothing to do with you,' Madame rapped testily. 'Suffice to say that she's from the finest stock, on her mother's side at least. I'll tell you no more. Take her and keep the bargain you made wth him.' She pointed a bony claw towards Phineas's portrait, then grinned banefully. 'You've no choice, have you, my Lord Cunyngham?'

David fastened his top-coat, then clapped on his hat, hatred of the Duchesse like a poison in his breast. He began to stride towards the door, knowing that he must go before he struck that harridan who behaved as if she still resided in her chateau, grinding the unfortunate peasants beneath her heel. He paused as he passed Mariana. Her face was white and she was trembling. Such pathetic helplessness moved him deeply. Mercer was close by, holding a cloak over her arm. He took it, placing it around Mariana's shoulders. She did not move or speak, looking up at him with those tragic eyes, shadowed by the hood which covered her cloudy hair.

A smile curved his pleasant mouth, and he touched her cheek gently. 'Cheer up, Maria. I'll take you to meet my wife.'

'Thank you, sir,' she whispered and followed him, her mantle brushing the floor. The door stood open and as she reached it, light streamed in on her, clean, crisp daylight, making the theatrical candles seem wan. She did not look back, but David did.

'You've had your way, Madame,' he thundered. 'I trust that you'll trouble me no more.'

The door thudded behind them, and Madame remained motionless in her great chair, looking at it. Silence fanned

155

down, a silence which seemed thick after the ringing tones of the angry man. She was alone again, alone with her thoughts, her memories. She had rid herself of the girl for good. What happened to her now lay in the lap of the gods. The Cunynghams lived in high style, so she had heard, their connections many and varied. Her granddaughter might sink or swim, according to which way the wind blew.

What do I care? Madame grunted, whilst that chill emptiness enfolded her. I hope she gets seduced by some debauched roué. I hope he gives her a dose of the pox! I hope she ends up in Newgate Gaol!

Yet, all the time persistent visions passed before her eyes – of evenings which had become almost enjoyable with Mariana playing chess with her, turning a deaf ear to her barbs, keeping her secrets, expecting no favours, hiding her emotions behind a blank countenance in which not even her eyes had mirrored the state of her inner being.

Madame gave herself a shake. To hell with it! She was getting maudlin. The chit meant nothing to her, less than nothing! She hugged her revenge like a beloved child, watching it grow, feeding on it, but suddenly it no longer held sweetness, bitter as grave-dust in her mouth.

CHAPTER 2

Transylvania. Spring, 1818

The horns rang clearly through the forest. Hounds were baying excitedly in the distance. The dark horseman galloped through the trees, following the sounds. The wind sweeping the Carpathian Mountains tossed the branches of the tall firs. They creaked and soughed as he rode beneath them, taking a winding path alongside the gorge, with green-white waters tumbling far below him to the left, and sheer cliffs rearing upwards towards the blue vault of the sky on the right. The sun was hot, the air sharp, and the horns brayed urgently.

As he drew closer, shouts, frantic yelping, the whickering of terrified horses made him him spur on his black stallion who hurtled out into a glade where huntsmen were circling a wild boar at bay against a thorn-thicket. It was a large, savage, scarred veteran of many a vicious skirmish. Its red, mad, blazing eyes told of a seasoned ferocity. Blood dripped from its murderous tusks, and two of the hounds were slinking off, badly gored. Just as the newcomer arrived, the enraged beast lunged again and a third dog went flying, viscera dangling in pink ropes. Further away, a man lay on the grass while a comrade applied a makeshift tourniquet to the gash in his thigh.

A crowd hovered, gesticulating, arguing, uncertain what to do next. Some were on horseback, very showily dressed for the hunt. Those in more perilous position on foot were attired in coarse woollen clothing and sheepskins. They kept glancing anxiously at their superiors, awaiting orders. The scene was sharply etched against the vivid green of the woods, backed by huge, limestone mountains with gold peaks. The beaters on the pine-needled carpet, the hounds cringing, tails between legs, and that engine of destruction, the squat, hideous boar, were caught in time. It could have been a crude cave-painting daubed by a primitive tribesman to propitiate the gods, or a sophisticated sporting canvas executed by a Court artist. The tall, dark man leapt from his horse, breaking the spell. His hunting knife flashed once as he plunged it into the boar's heart.

157

Amidst the cheers which startled the birds, one of the watching riders turned in his beautifully tooled saddle and remarked to his female companion: 'Trust Radu to arrive in the nick of time and dispatch that brute so elegantly. Always so tediously brave and skilful. What say you, my dear?' He was a large man in a black uniform laced with silver. His intent face was full of power, his ungloved hands clenched so tightly on the reins that his knuckles shone white.

The woman at his side gave him a glance from slanting amber eyes. 'His timing is perfect, I'll grant you, and what a fine figure he cuts on that horse.' She laughed and shrugged her shoulders under the green velvet riding-jacket, adding: 'Or off it, come to that.'

'Dearest Countess Elizabeth,' he answered smoothly. His left cheek was seamed by the pale, thin scar of an old sword cut. It drew his lip up at one side in a perpetual sneer. 'So susceptible to the male form. What a pity you were born an aristocrat when you'd have made a first-class whore.'

'D'you really think that my blue blood has stopped me?' she retorted gaily. 'I'm rich, but I can never have too many diamonds.'

Grigore Petresco permitted himself a tight smile. He edged his mount a shade nearer so that his knee bumped against hers. She was a fascinating woman, to all appearances as innocent and guileless as a convent novice. There she sat, sideways in the saddle, her skirt flowing over the chestnut's shining flanks, the personification of gentility. No way did her modest demeanour hint at the unbridled lust which burned through every fibre of her being. One would never guess unless, like Grigore, one had been numbered amongst her many lovers.

Softly spoken, invariably sweet, with harmonious features and a gorgeous body, she seemed hesitant, virginal, cleverly concealing the deepest depravity and knowledge of refined vices. They had each other's measure, a well-matched pair of dissemblers, neither trusting the other an inch. Grigore amused himself with her, whilst she used the relationship to her advantage. At the present time it suited him to convince the world that he had nothing in mind but idling with his new mistress. She was more than just useful; everyone who was anyone angled for invitations to her parties where she entertained on a lavish scale. She was adept at wheedling secrets out of her guests. Little happened in and around the wide-spread Habsburg Empire without it reaching his ears almost immediately.

'Remember what I've told you about Radu. He's a hard

158

man, but has a weakness for lovely women.' Grigore was staring across to where his half-brother was receiving the congratulations of the hunters. His head rose above those of the clustering nobility. He was smiling and listening attentively, keeping that delicate balance between authority and fraternization which was a gift he had, a gift to be envied.

Hatred ate into Grigore's soul. He concealed it through long practice, leaning easily on the pommel of his saddle, smiling as if nothing gave him greater pleasure than to see Radu acclaimed. Their likeness marked them as brothers. Grigore was ten years Radu's senior, almost as tall, handsome in a harsh, dark way, perhaps even more arrogant. He had inherited the aquiline Varna nose, prominent high cheekbones and square jaw, but his colouring was different. From his Turkish mother had come wiry black hair, dark eyes and olive skin.

Grigore brooded on this under the warm spring sunshine. Though traditional enemies of the Turks, the Varnas had never been able to resist Turkish women. Their mutual ancestor, Mathias Varna, had hurled a challenge at no less a person than the conqueror of Constantinople, Sultan Mohammed, back in1461. His courage and ferocity had become a legend, and his support of the local Voevod, the war-lord, had put the family on the map. He had acquired the title of Prince because of his warrior exploits, not through heredity. Prior to this, the Varnas had been robber barons, carrying out their lawless operations from the forests between Rumania and Wallacia.

The grateful Voevod had given Mathias a tiny duchy as reward for bloody services rendered. It was called Montezena and, like many other states in this war-torn area, had changed hands repeatedly during three hundred and fifty years. The Turks had taken it, then the Austrians, it had been overrun by boyars from Russia and magyars from Hungary. Using cunning, resourcefulness and a kind of lunatic bravery, the Varnas had won through, keeping a toehold on their property. Prince Alecsandri, the father of Grigore and Radu, had negotiated with the powerful Habsburgs and it was now under Austrian rule. The Varnas were a stiff-necked, haughty race, marrying where policy dictated, and here was the rub. Grigore Petresco was not Prince Alecsandri's legitimate son. There was a story of a morganatic marriage between the Prince and Zoe Manissa Petresco, a lady from the Turkish nobility. She had always fiercely maintained that papers existed to prove her claim. These had never come to light and, after her death, Grigore had forged a set.

Alecsandri had publicly married Arta Filotti, a Hungarian Princess, and Radu had been the sole offspring of this later union. His birth had been announced to a delighted Montezenian people, and his popularity had increased over the years. Grigore's position was awkward, to say the least. His father had given him a title, but invisible fences separated him from the European aristocracy. His feeling of injustice, his simmering resentment of Radu had come to a head six months before when, on the death of the Prince, Radu became ruler.

It was noon. The hunters were handing round bottles of wine while servants produced a cold luncheon from picnic hampers. Grigore could hear them laughing and joking. Radu made a remark which sent them off into fresh gales of merriment. Even the beaters were grinning at him with admiration and respect. Stung by this fresh reminder of his precarious claim, Grigore dug his heels into his bay's sleek sides and headed for the group under the trees. Elizabeth cantered after him.

'Congratulations, sir.' He addressed Radu crisply. A hush fell. Heads turned in his direction. 'That was a masterly stroke.'

Radu was leaning against the bole of a pine, long legs crossed at the ankles, arms folded lightly over his chest, relaxed but watchful. He was simply dressed, but the quality of both cloth and tailoring was superlative. His jacket was dark blue, his tight beige breeches revealed the muscular strength of his thighs, his black boots were highly polished. A military cloak with a sable collar hung from his shoulders, adding to their impressive width. He was bare-headed, and the light slanting through the pines touched his curling black hair, his nose, his chin, the rest of his face shadowed. His eyes glittered as they stared at Grigore, arresting grey eyes, piercing as steel.

'Thank you, Baron.' He inclined his head slightly. 'The beast was too knowing. There was nothing to be gained by delay. I'm surprised that you hadn't tackled him yourself.'

'I was contemplating doing so.' Grigore lied without thinking. Lying was second nature to him. 'Just as well I didn't. It would have been a pity to steal your thunder, dear boy.' He changed the subject – Radu had been praised too much already. 'Are you alone? Where are your attendants? We waited for you. I was rather worried when you didn't arrive last night.'

'I came shortly after your hunting party had set out this morning. My servants are settling in, I imagine. Yes, I came to the meet alone, considering myself perfectly safe in these mountains. I have no enemies on your estate, have I?' The hint of a smile played about Radu's lips.

Games, he was thinking, what games we play, Grigore and I. He hates me and I know it, but pretend that I don't. I suspect his every move, yet hide the fact. We had the same father, but for all the love we bear each other we might as well have sprung from warring camps.

That silent rivalry had always been there. When a child, Radu had been unable to understand why this person, seen only occasionally, was accorded favour by the Prince. The relationship was explained when he grew up. That secret marriage, vigorously denied by their father and scornfully dismissed by Princess Arta. Radu remembered the occasion well. He had been received by that handsome, autocratic lady in the floridly baroque royal apartments. Her voice had been icy as she told him about Grigore and 'that woman' who had borne him.

'Your father's concubine!' she had called her. 'A Turkish houri, who had the temerity to say that he married her! Probably some Moslem gibberish that wouldn't stand up for five minutes in a court of law! The whole thing's preposterous! I am his wife! Ha! He's had mistresses by the score. What man doesn't? But marriage! Never! Don't forget this, my son. Never forget it. Grigore is a bastard! You, and you alone, are your father's heir.'

One thing was for sure – he and Grigore would never be friends. Radu thought this a pity, for Grigore was shrewd and could have been of inestimable help in governing Montezena. When he had received the invitation to join him at Castle Horia for a few days' hunting, Radu had accepted, wondering if his half-brother had experienced a change of heart. It did seem that he was offering the olive branch, though Radu's cynicism warned him to beware.

'You've not yet been introduced to Countess Elizabeth, I believe.' Grigore swung down from his saddle, and assisted her to dismount. 'My charming guest, a compatriot of your esteemed mother, also a Hungarian – Countess Elizabeth Rogalski.'

Radu drew himself up to his full height and extended a hand as she curtsied. He bowed as he raised her. 'Countess – I'm delighted.'

Elizabeth noted his brief greeting, devoid of fulsome flattery. This was challenging, for generally her attractions provoked an ardent response. She would have been piqued, had it not been for something in his eyes which hinted at more than casual

161

awareness. Excitement thrilled through her. Grigore's order that she make herself agreeable to the Prince was not going to be a hard task, she decided. He certainly was handsome, and Elizabeth was a connoisseur. She liked the way in which his white stock contrasted with the healthy tan of his skin and, with a little contemplative smile lifting her red lips, admired his strong legs displayed in the form-hugging breeches.

'I'm honoured, your Highness,' she murmured, glancing at him in a way which rendered most men tongue-tied. 'I've heard so much about you.'

Radu laughed. 'Favourable reports, I trust.' While his brain told him to be alert, his body was responding to her charms.

He was experienced with women. His student days at Leipzig University, his service in the army, his own high-powered magnetism had provided him with plenty of opportunity since he was fourteen. His splendid presence, that dark sombre quality, made him irresistible. He had rarely met a girl able to say no to him and, perversely, this had lowered the sex in his estimation. He thought women gullible, too easily conquered. His mother was a prime example. Oh, she was proud, full of righteous indignation about her husband's illegitimate offspring, but her weakness for fops half her age was an open scandal.

Elizabeth succeeded in blushing delicately, wide eyes promising delights, as pink and gold and artless as a child. 'The things people say about you are so complimentary, sir, that I was quite certain I'd be disappointed, but I'm not,' she breathed.

'Indeed,' he answered sceptically, with a lift of one curving black brow. 'Then I hope you'll be staying at the castle for a while, Countess. We can get to know one another better.'

For an instant, his glance swept over her, and she felt her heart miss a beat. Even without Grigore's prompting, she would have been drawn to Radu, and not only because of his title. She suddenly longed to be alone with him, with that beautiful mouth claiming hers, those strong, well-shaped hands caressing her flesh. His faintly mocking smile told her he knew what she was thinking.

Grigore watched the interplay between them, having no qualms about using his mistress for his own purpose. There was nothing he could do as yet. Radu would be treated with the utmost respect as a guest at Castle Horia, Grigore's fortress in the mountains, a gift from Prince Alecsandri. Grigore was content to mark time. He had had years of practice – biting his tongue, controlling his resentment, but such constraint had warped his nature. When he did give vent to his rage, every pent-up emotion burst forth like a dammed torrent, savage, violent and murderous.

The huntsmen, fortified by liquor, were waiting for Radu's signal to mount. The servants had slung the boar by its feet to a long pole and hoisted it to their shoulders, ready to hump it back to the castle for roasting. Radu nodded to Grigore who barked an order. The brothers rode at the head of the cavalcade as it left the forest by a defile gouged from the cliff-face. It was a bright, lovely morning, the sun pouring into the valley, glittering on the river, highlighting the distant castle on its lofty perch. It stood on a rock, the summit crowned with walls and bastions situated in a nigh unassailable spot, commanding the countryside. Radu scanned his brother's stronghold as he guided his stallion over the slippery, pebble-strewn ground.

'My God, what a place,' he remarked to him.

'Mighty fine, I agree.' Grigore followed his eyes with evident satisfaction. 'Even in these days of modern warfare, it would be a hopeless task to attempt to take it, other than by starving out the occupants.'

'Or by treachery from within.' Radu gave him a sideways glance.

Grigore's scarred face darkened, and there was a cold glint in his black pupils. 'None would dare. I've a reputation for being neither merciful nor even just where traitors are concerned.'

'Word has reached me of your somewhat severe methods of dealing with miscreants,' Radu said levelly.

'Order must be enforced. You should know this.' Grigore did not look at him, his hands ungentle on the reins.

'I do know it, but I follow my father's example. He was renowned for justice.' Radu was finding it hard to remain composed as Grigore's character became more plain with every word he uttered.

'You'll soon see my methods in action.' Grigore had not missed Radu's reference to 'my' father, not 'ours'. 'There'll be a hanging in the morning.'

Radu turned in the saddle and stared at him. 'What d'you mean?'

Grigore smiled, secure in his supremacy in that district. 'My men brought in Stefan Danesti. You've heard of him?'

'The champion of the peasants.'

'Some champion!' Grigore bit off the words. 'He's nothing more than a *haiduc*! Stealing where he can, robbing, raiding – usually from me! He'll swing high at dawn, and I'll tie the knot myself so that he strangles slowly. Jesus! I've a good mind to impale him on a stake! That's what my ancestors would've done!'

'He should be moved to the capital for trial. You can't take the law into your own hands.' Radu had drawn his animal to a standstill.

'Can't I? We shall see,' Grigore grated, and Radu was aware of the men behind him, huntsmen maybe, but also Grigore's private army.

He regretted neglecting to bring more troops with him, but had not yet adjusted to rulership, used to travelling light and going where he willed. The habit was dying hard, and he had only ordered a handful of guards. No doubt Grigore had arranged for the execution to take place whilst he was there, to test his reaction or score a point.

Elizabeth, riding just behind them, was listening whilst appearing to be absorbed in light chatter with a bewitched subaltern. Her eyes were quick to catch the anger in their discourse, her mischief-making mind storing it away. To her intense disappointment they rode the rest of the way in frigid silence, ascending slowly to a step in the rock, beneath the crag dominated by Castle Horia. Elizabeth gave the young soldier her most radiant smile, and commented breathlessly on the wonders of the view, whilst he went as red as his uniform, stammered, grinned and hung on her every utterance.

Down below swept an ocean of green, covering the slopes, then thinning further off to verdant meadows and the swiftly flowing river. It was a spectacular sight with hills and vales and waterfalls, the rocks tossed in wild confusion from some prehistoric eruption. The air was like wine and sounds travelled clearly on it; the whistle of a labourer, the lowing of sturdy cattle, the distant tinkling of sheep-bells. The hollows were shadow-filled, while the mountains glistened, blinding white, snow-capped.

The horses knew that it was time for their mid-day meal. Above the slither of hooves on shale and the jingle of harness, their restlessness could be sensed. Some of them pressed against the bit, squealing in protest as they increased their pace. The valley fell back and soon an entrance gate frowned upon them. A drawbridge spanned the dizzying drop into the ravine. Hooves thundered on wooden planks as they passed over it. A number of uniformed men were collected under a second arched gateway, and several horses stood saddled close by. The courtyard was large, gloomy and awesome. Little had changed since the fourteenth century. Everyone started to dismount, and grooms came running from the stable block. Radu cocked a foot out of the stirrup and stood by his horse in an instant. There was general bustle and confusion, then a blue-clad figure uncoiled itself from a lounging position against the steps of the main building and strolled across.

'Was the hunting good, your Highness?' he asked as he saluted.

Radu grinned at him. 'Pretty fair, Cornel. Let's go inside. What are my quarters like?'

His aide grimaced. 'Deuced draughty, sir. I've left Axos sorting things out. He's grumbling like the very devil. Says your suits'll get damp and you'll catch your death, the braid on your uniform'll tarnish and your sword'll go rusty. Apart from that, he's content!'

'He worries too much, seems to forget that I'm a grown man, well able to withstand mouldy lodgings.' Radu slapped his friend on the shoulder, laughing at the apprehensions of his batman.

He nodded towards Grigore, bowed to Elizabeth, turned on his heel and followed Lieutenant Cornel Cazacu up the stone steps and under the gigantic portal of the castle. Cornel swaggered past Grigore's guards, a dashing sight in his short blue jacket rich with gold trimming, his fur-edged dolman slung carelessly over one shoulder. His matching blue trousers were thick with braid down the outer seams, and as tight as if moulded on him. The high sheen on his short boots spoke of the diligence of his valet. A long sabre knocked against his left thigh as he walked. The chain strap of his tall fur *kalpac* fitted under his jaw, giving a fierce aspect to his face which was open and boyish. Even the twirled and waxed brown moustache failed to give an impression of age and dignity, for Cornel smiled a lot, finding a source of comedy in almost every situation.

'What a dump!' He commented as they crossed the echoing hall. 'That staircase looks as if it needs a scaling-ladder, by God! But the maidservants aren't half bad. Pretty little things, these peasant girls.' He smiled at Radu as they climbed the grey stone steps, set against the grey stone walls. Curious eyes watched them, Grigore's minions. 'Henchmen, more like,' added Cornel as they reached the gallery, pausing to look back into the massive hall where logs flared in a huge hearth. Its hood reared up a good fifteen feet, supported by granite pillars. A couple of wolf-hounds were sprawled before it, but scrambled up when Grigore shouted. Elizabeth was with him.

'Now that's what I call a fine bit of skirt,' Cornel remarked, smoothing his moustache reflectively.

Radu did not comment and, when Cornel pushed open the iron-studded door of the bedchamber, he asked him to stay awhile. Axos was fussing, a little, wizened man, who immediately began to voice his disapproval. 'A sorry place, your Highness. And those surly brutes of servants! The difficulty I had in obtaining hot water!'

Tossing his cloak over the back of a chair, Radu glanced around the gloomy room. Its walls were hung with red and brown gilded leather. The floor was bare, the surface broken by oriental rugs. A fire crackled in the carved fireplace, but draughts whistled under the doors, lifting the heavy tapestry curtains. Every piece of furniture was heavy and ancient, and the canopied four-poster fully six feet wide.

'I'd hate to winter here,' shuddered Cornel. 'Imagine being snowed in, with wolves howling round the place and that strange fellow, Baron Grigore, as one's sole companion. Give me Vienna any day.'

Radu was changing out of his riding-gear, braced in one of the armchairs while Axos hauled off his boots, then rising to divest himself of breeches and hose, throwing off his soiled shirt and stalking naked to the window. Undaunted by the chill, he flung open the casement, staring out at the landscape. The untamed beauty of it clutched his heart. Montezena, the country willed to him by his father. He loved it more than any place on earth. Below him spread the escarpment, the forests, the silvery snake of the river. He had never visited this part before, and had been surprised by Grigore's invitation. Princess Arta had urged him to refuse, distrusting everyone except those least deserving of trust – the effete youths who fawned on her.

There was such an intent set to his profile that Cornel, one leg thrown over the arm of the chair in which he lolled, watched him warily. He had lived with him during campaigns, ridden with him, fought at his side, and knew him to be a creature of moods. As a military leader, he had earned the respect of rank and file. Quick of thought, decisive in action, his boldness and resolution had distinguished him in the war against Napoleon. He had no patience with incompetence which might endanger lives, was sometimes brutally frank and, as with army officers, so he behaved towards the statesmen who now attempted to advise him. He had told Cornel that he wanted to see Grigore's domain, sound him out, and get an idea of his strength.

Standing in a patch of sunshine, Radu made an impressive study in gold and deep shadow. He was superbly built, his body tough and muscular. There was not an ounce of surplus fat about him, every sinew, each bicep honed by the rigours of campaigning. His shoulders were broad, tapering to a narrow waist and lithe hips, long, strong legs planted firmly on the floor. His corded arms hung at his sides as, head up, he gazed across the land which belonged to him. Even the proud *mosneni*, the free peasants who had never accepted serfdom, had given him their allegiance.

Oh, yes, he's the people's Prince, mused Cornel, but I'm not so sure about the nobles. There had been ominous rumblings at Court against Radu's intention of removing the traditional manorial rents and changing the law which decreed that if the owner of a demesne found it profitable, he could add land to it by abolishing the peasant holdings. Obviously Radu was feeling his way through a tricky situation, seeking a peaceful solution. The last thing he wanted was a repetition of the violent *jacquerie* which had happened in Rumania ten years before the French Revolution. Then hundreds of serfs, marching under tattered banners, armed with scythes and hatchets, had rebelled against the taxes and extortions.

Radu's thoughts were similar to Cornel's as he felt the crisp air refreshing his skin, filling his lungs with it. One thing he was learning fast – it was a lonely business being at the top. One had to be so careful. His army career had pointed the way, for colonels were lonely people too. Yet soldiers had been easy to deal with compared to slippery courtiers. Once he had been clear in his motives and intentions, but six months of power had taught him that in everything, moral and physical, there were twisted paths. Nine times out of ten, when a man seemed to be telling the truth or acting sincerely, the opposite was the case. It was a dark, bitter reality. There were nearly as many crooked roads and circuitous ways in every aspect of human life as there were in those deep woods that cloaked the sides of the hills outside the window.

He roused himself, swinging round and startling Cornel by his sudden burst of energy as he said briskly: 'Grigore intends to hang Stefan Danesti. Tell me what you've found out about this man.'

No one could complain about Grigore's ability as a host. That night a banquet was held beneath the arches of the hall, lavishly prepared with traditional as well as local dishes. The twenty-foot-long oak table was bright with candles in gilt stands, flower-holding épergnes, monumental salt-cellars shaped liked mosques, the finest china, and glassware from the Varna-owned factory in Neuhaus. There was a predominance of military men, a great deal of gold braid and epaulettes, orders and medals. Several ladies had been invited, drifting like jewelled butterflies in silks and muslins. Gems gleamed on naked arms, on part-concealed breasts, in dark, gold and red hair. None was more dazzling than Elizabeth with her grace, wit and amusing conversation. Grigore placed her next to Radu at table.

Well after midnight, the Prince went back to his apartment. The echoing castle consisted of a bewildering assortment of staircases, towering doors and galleries, all spacious and sombre, abounding with guards and servants. Cornel had had too much to drink, and been carted off to bed by his valet quite early in the evening. Radu entered the bedroom, dismissed the grumbling, yawning Axos, and changed from his uniform into a voluminous East India robe, lavishly finished with silver fox at collar and cuffs. He filled a glass with Moselle, sat down in the winged chair by the glowing embers, and waited.

Before long there came a discreet tap at the door. He called to enter and Elizabeth appeared, tiptoeing in with over-elaborate caution, turning the key in the lock. Radu did not move, his eyes glinting as he surveyed her. Her hand was still on the lock. She leaned back against the wood, her tawny hair flaming against its darkness. A feline smile lifted her lips.

She wore her evening gown, a high-waisted skimpy garment of white muslin over a satin slip, low-necked and sleeveless. A sumptuous mantle of sapphire velvet flowed from her shoulders. Diamonds flashed in the candle-glow, at her throat, in her ears, on her wrists. Her hair was arranged to appear casually tousled, further diamonds winking among the curls. She was like a fairy, drifting in a gossamer world. What an act! thought Radu, as he admired her breasts and limbs glimpsed through the soft material. She's no virgin!

'So, you managed to give Grigore the slip.' He was smiling, lazily watching, not bothering to stand. Let her come to him, if that was what she wanted.

'He's not my keeper,' she replied, beginning to glide towards him, hips swaying seductively.

'I rather gathered that he was.' He shot her an amused glance. 'Aren't you his mistress?'

She gave a small pout, at his side now. He could smell her tantalizing perfume, see the flush that touched the delicate cameo of her cheeks, the eagerness in her topaz eyes. 'What an antiquated concept. How very quaint. I owe no man favours.

I'm free to follow my own inclinations, quite independent.'

She was leaning over him, an arm braced each side of his chair. Any other man would have been unable to resist drawing her on to his knee. Radu did not move. He kept her waiting deliberately. 'Not one of those radical blue-stockings, surely, Countess? You've not been reading that English-woman's book, have you? What's her name? Mary Wollstonecraft. She called it *Vindication of the Rights of Women.'*

Elizabeth's puzzled expression told him that she had no idea what he was talking about. She was disappointed. He had been flirting with her all evening, they had arranged this tryst, and there he sat, cool as you please, making no attempt to grab her. Throughout dinner she had been keenly aware of his stunning appearance in his blue hussar's uniform, feasting her eyes on his face, greedily noting the play of his hands as he gestured, aching to go to bed wth him. And with Grigore's blessing too! It seemed almost too good to be true.

'I've never heard of her, or her book. I only read novelettes,' she answered sulkily.

'I doubted that you had,' he replied. 'The opinions you express are your own, I take it, gleaned from experience.'

She changed tactics, demure again. 'I'm sure I don't know what you mean. I like to enjoy myself. What's wrong with that? I love dancing, especially the waltz. Do you waltz? I should imagine that you're a superb dancer. Will you dance with me sometime?'

'Dancing wasn't exactly what I had in mind,' he replied wickedly. 'Nor in yours, I'll wager.'

His smile tightening, he reached out and pulled her against his body, between his thighs. One hand buried in her fiery curls, he brought her mouth nearer to his own. Elizabeth knew a thrill of something allied to terror before his lips met hers. It was so exciting that it diverted her from scheming, even from thought. She settled across his lap, winding her arms about his neck. Radu allowed himself to sink into the sensuality of her embrace, the uninhibited caressing of her soft fingers, using her for his pleasure. In a few moments they were lying on the bearskin rug before the flames, and her pale skin was turned to pure gold in that dancing light. He freed himself from her arms and shrugged off the robe.

'Highness,' she whispered, staring at him, almost in awe. 'Don't think that I'm used to doing this. You're a very special person whom I greatly admire.'

Radu was not really listening, stretching himself at her side, saying: 'I knew you weren't wearing any underclothes – guessed it when you walked into the hall tonight.'

She giggled nervously, marvelling at his power to make her feel like a raw girl. 'Is that what you were thinking about whilst in such deeply serious discussion about the vineyards of Kecskemet?'

'Maybe,' he murmured, his mouth sliding gently across her throat, then travelling down to her breasts.

While her body responded, her mind was working again, busy with a plan of her own. Despite her bold assertions, she did hold a rather precarious position with Grigore. An advantageous match was exactly what she needed. Power was like a drug to her and, as Princess Varna, she would have it in abundance. Of course, marriage was the last thing in Radu's head at that moment. He had never married, but now pressure would be brought to bear on him to do so and produce an heir. In Elizabeth's veins ran the ardent blood of the magyars, the ruling nobility of Hungary. She would be a most suitable bride.

If only she could make him fall in love with her! What a triumph! He would be generous, she could tell, showering her with gifts and money, raising her to the highest peak. By sharing his bed, she stood a better chance of sharing his duchy. Other clever women had manoeuvred themselves from the position of mistress to that of wife. Let him sample her wares first. Practised in love, she had no doubt that she could offer him manifold delights on their journey down the secret pathways of pleasure.

For a while she forgot her conniving as Radu made love to her. They both surrendered to sheer physical enjoyment. They were equals, two expert contenders in the savagely primordial battle of the senses. It was the mating of a pair of healthy animals, devoid of affection. He took her without tenderness, but this very streak of selfish brutality excited her. He was across her, into her, pressing her against the rug, bruising her breasts, her thighs. He completed the act hurriedly, as if by doing so he need not allow himself to think.

Afterwards they rested in silence. She rubbed her tangled head on his shoulder, running light fingers over his chest, playing with the crisp dark hair which matted it. 'Well, Highness, if I'm not careful, I'll be falling in love with you.'

He had one arm flung over his eyes. Now he lifted it, smiling crookedly as he looked at her. 'There's no need to say that. Don't pretend. We know precisely where we stand, you and I.'

It was like a dash of cold water. 'That isn't very nice.' Her voice was sharp and she stopped fondling him.

Radu propped himself up on one elbow, staring into her

lovely, dishonest face. 'I'm not a very nice person.'

Hiding her nervousness and plunging sense of disappointment, she said coolly: 'I can't believe that.'

He was grave, aloof, putting a thousand miles between them though their bodies were still entwined. 'You should. It's true.'

The dusky chamber was quiet, save for the purr and crackle of the logs. The wind keened against the grim walls outside, and somewhere on the ramparts a sentry called to a comrade. Elizabeth repressed a shiver. It was as if someone had trailed a cold finger down her spine. These Varna brothers were men of power, as ruthless as their forebears. This element thrilled her more than good looks, even more than wealth. She had bedded them both and, of the two, Radu was the most thrilling, though Grigore showed an interesting penchant for perversions. Early days yet, she mused, who knows what sexual quirks Radu may later display? This won't be my last night in his arms.

His hand clenched on her bare shoulder, hurting her. 'How well do you know my brother?' he asked abruptly. The cold look on his face was alarming.

Startled, her big eyes met his and excitement bit deep into her loins. 'As well as anyone can. He's not an easy person to know. Why? Are you jealous?'

'He's going out of his way to be friendly.'

'Perhaps he's merely trying to heal old wounds.' She was rubbing her foot up and down his leg soothingly, wondering how much he knew and if his spy system was as competent as Grigore's. 'You're his Prince now, and I'm sure he wishes to see the country prosper.' Her mouth was against his chest, the black hair tickling her face as she lipped over his skin. 'He's in an especially good mood, having lately captured an enemy. We'll be treated to a hanging in the morning.'

'You'll enjoy that?' Radu was stirred by her caress, but shocked at the callousness in her voice.

Her hand wandered to his groin. 'I've seen men die before. This rebel deserves to swing, rousing the peasants with his wild words.'

'And this condemns him to be hanged without trial?' He nuzzled her ears and neck. Tingling anticipation began to course through her body as she started to moan and stir restlessly.

'Oh, damn him! What has this to do with us?' she gasped urgently. 'Love me quickly, darling – now!'

He was chuckling, and he suddenly released her, pushing her away, rising and jerking on his robe. Elizabeth sat up, furiously angry, cursing Grigore and his intrigues. 'Where are you going?' she demanded, tossing the tangled hair back from her face.

He shot her a stern glance. 'I'm not going anywhere. You are.' He was fastening the girdle firmly about his waist, his shadow thrown against the wall, a great black, grotesque shadow with the fur collar framing the head.

Anger burned in Elizabeth's breast as she got up. 'You don't want me to stay the night?' She glanced at the carved bed where he stood leaning easily against one of the posts. There was a controlled power about him which gave the lie to his relaxed pose.

'Supposing Grigore hungers for you? He'll come seeking you in your room. I've no desire to quarrel with him – yet.' Then his mouth hardened with suspicion. 'I presume that he doesn't know about us.'

Elizabeth was putting on her gown, head bent. 'Certainly not. He'd be furious. I've risked much to come to you.' She peered up at him from beneath her lashes. This was a dangerous game she was playing and the nature of it made her shake with excitement.

'What of your talk of freedom?' he said quietly. Had she known him better, she would have realized that when Radu was still and quiet he was at his most deadly.

She bit her lip, face shadowed as she drew on her pink silk stockings. She must be careful. He was no fool. 'That still applies, but your brother fancies himself in love with me.'

'Then we must keep him sweet,' he answered unemotionally. 'You'll sleep in your chamber, and I in mine. Goodnight, Countess.'

He walked with her to the door. Her cloak was draped loosely around her, the dress beneath in disarray. She stopped, looking at him expectantly, reaching up to link her arms about his neck. 'I'll see you tomorrow,' she murmured, hoping for his kiss.

With an unreadable expression, he disengaged her arms. 'Yes. Aren't we to attend a public execution?'

She tapped him lightly on the chest with her fingertips. 'Don't be provoking. You know what I mean.'

He opened the door without answering and she slipped out. Radu turned the key, then went swiftly to the armoire, pulling out clothing. In a few moments he was ready, transformed into a peasant in baggy trousers tucked into rough leather boots, a woollen shirt, a felt embroidered jacket tightly girded by a black cummerbund and a shaggy wolfskin coat topped by a fur hat. After fastening a knife at his waist, he slipped a pistol,

172

powder-horn and shot into the two pockets of his outer garment. He let himself out of the room, locking the door behind him. High in one of the towers, a clock boomed the hour. It was two in the morning. From the direction of the hall came the sounds of carousing, drunken laughter, women's high voices, the dip and swell of sweet, sad gypsy music.

The corridor was lit by flares set in sconces. Silent as a cat, Radu edged his way towards Cornel's room. My God, he thought grimly, Grigore has some sloppy guards. Were this my castle, I'd have them at their posts, the idle wretches! They're down in the mess, I suppose, getting drunk and fumbling the local harlots. He must think himself pretty damned invincible up here in his eyrie.

He kept to the shadows, flat against the wall by the door, tapping once, twice, thrice, very softly. It was opened immediately by Cornel. He was ready, fully armed and wrapped in a long cloak. There was no need to talk. Cornel had done the groundwork earlier, when everyone thought he was far gone in drink. He led the way, Radu close at his heels. Soon they left the inhabited part of the fortress, descending by steep wooden stairs with nothing but a rope between them and the inky drop of the well, reaching a long passage below, flanked by tall windows and numerous small doors. Cornel produced a lantern, but the darkness was so profound that it served only to dissipate the obscurity directly around them. The rest of the corridor yawned like a vault, filled with gloom and shadows.

'Is this the way to the dungeons?' Radu pitched his voice low.

'So your spy informed me.' Cornel raised the lantern, squinting into the blackness ahead.

'He's reliable. I pay him well.'

They reached a larger staircase and, after going carefully down, found themselves in a vestibule containing two exits. Cornel tried the lock of one. It was studded with nails and banded with iron, and groaned as he opened it. They held their breath, listening. The only sound was the wind sighing through the black aperture. They stepped through into a vast, disused hall. There were mouldy stains on the paved floor. A number of torn, dusty pennons, still attached to the lances that had carried them to the battlefields, waved overhead in the breeze which gusted through broken windows. They rustled, whispering of past glories.

'Christ! It's bloody eerie,' muttered Cornel.

'Let's get on,' growled Radu.

A further door yielded to the force of his shoulder. A chill

173

dampness coiled out, with rotting undertones. They strained their eyes against the solid-looking darkness. It was a low winding passage cut into the stonework. The walls glistened with an unwholesome slime. The floor was slippery. There was the drip, drip of water. Crops of pale, sickly fungi covered with noxious dew festered in corners, spreading a faint, unpleasant odour in the air. Another flight of steps led down into the bowels of the castle. The lamp burned dim, its flam diminished by the impure vapours.

'Sweet Mary's arse!' gasped Cornel. His face was beaded with sweat. 'I'd rather face a battery of gunfire than this!'

Radu went down first. The square-cut stones formed a shaft in which the steps turned in the roughly hewn rock, well below the foundations. They could see nothing but cavelike walls and low arches which spread out interminable. With nerve-tingling shock, a bat swept past their faces on leathery wings, nearly extinguishing the lantern.

'God!' shouted Cornel.

'God! God!' the echoes mocked.

Radu recovered and started to laugh. His laughter rebounded among the arches. 'Pull yourself together, man. It's only a bat.'

Cornel was thoroughly shaken. 'Only a bat!' he grumbled. 'You know what they mean in this part of the country. Vampires!'

'Horse-shit!' snarled Radu, striding forward.

But even his courage quailed as he saw that they were passing through a crypt. On the monuments lay banners, swords and ragged surcoats, the colours faded, blotched with deep stains and mildew.

'Highness, this is a very strange and horrible place,' muttered Cornel, crossing himself, keeping close to his leader, glancing over his shoulder repeatedly.

'Nothing of the kind!' replied Radu edgily. 'The dead can't harm you. Worry more about rousing Grigore's hellions.'

They came to a tunnel which ran in opposite directions. Cornel, fighting his superstitious terror, was trying to recall the spy's instructions. They decided on the right-hand passage which linked with the dungeons. The other would take the prisoner to freedom. They were confronted by another door, low and spider-webbed. The bolts were corroded. Radu scraped away the rust with his dagger, straining to shift them. There was a grating sound which tortured their taut nerves as first one, then the next gave way.

'Be careful, sir,' warned Cornel, as, inch by inch, the door started to move inwards. 'If your spy is right, we should come out in the gaoler's room.'

'You've fixed him, I hope.'

'I drugged the flagon of wine sent down from the kitchen.' Cornel's teeth flashed in a grin. 'All it cost me was half an hour in the hay with one of the maids. She was more than willing to help by the time I'd done with her.'

'Trust you to involve a woman.' There was a thread of humour in Radu's voice. 'They'll be your downfall, my friend – that's if the guards don't get us first.'

A crack of light appeared at the edge of the door, blurred, pale. Cornel doused the lamp and drew a pistol. There was no sound from the gaoler's room beyond. He was slumped at the table, head down on his folded arms. Radu gave him a swift glance, then strode across to where iron bars and a heavy gate contained the prisoner. Cornel took a bunch of keys from the unconscious gaoler's belt.

A rustle of straw from the far side of the cell, and a fierce-eyed, bearded face at the bars. 'Who the hell are you?' demanded Stefan Danesti.

'Friends.' Radu wasted no time, inserting one of the keys in the lock. The door swung back. The prisoner was free.

He was a giant, filling the small, damp place with bulk. Red hair flamed round battered broad features, running into, and mingling with long drooping moustaches and a full beard. A pair of shrewd greenish eyes, set in a scribble of wrinkles, scrutinized Radu and Cornel. He was as ferocious and wary as the boar dispatched earlier. He crouched, muscles bunched, knotted fists ready to punch. He was filthy, clothing torn, sweaty, blood-stained – peasant's clothing, like Radu's. A dirty shirt, trousers criss-crossed by the laces of his leather *opinci*, a wide belt, and waistcoat thonged across a massive chest and belly.

'Friends?' he grunted. 'This is a trick.'

'No trick.' Radu threw him one of his pistols. 'Can't stop to explain. We've come to get you out.'

Danesti narrowed his eyes. 'That's all I want to know.'

After spitting on the gaoler in passing, he followed where they led. They carefully erased tell-tale footprints and closed the door. With any luck it would remain a secret escape route. The tunnel twisted and turned, sloping upwards. They did not talk but their laboured breathing broke the silence. At the end of the passage the way was blocked by another door.

'Stand back,' said Danesti and leaned his heavy shoulder against the rotting wood. A heave, a tremendous snap, a blast of night air and the sting of pattering rain. They were on a small, tree-shrouded platform at the base of the hill. The brigand stretched his great arms till the joints cracked, shaking his mane at the sky, careless of the rain washing into his eyes. 'By the Saints, it's good to be out of that bloody hell-hole!' He looked at Radu and Cornel, shadowy in the dim lantern light. 'I don't know who you are, but thanks anyway.'

He turned, about to plunge into the darkness. Radu stopped him. 'Wait. We got word to your men. There should be a horse for you.'

Something moved in the hedge of trees. It was a rider, leading another mount. Danesti grunted. With a foot in the stirrup, the reins gathered about the animal's withers, he threw them a few words. 'I'd like to know who saved my life. I pay my debts.'

'You've friends in high places.' Radu was looking up at that black, shapeless figure outlined against the stormy night-sky.

'I? Danesti? The rebel leader who spits on tyrannical masters?' He forgot to be quiet. His deep-bellied mirth boomed among the rocks. 'You jest, my friend.'

'I don't.' Radu's voice and manner arrested him. 'Have you forgotten that Montezena has a new ruler?'

'So I understand. They say he's a fine soldier. If it's the Prince who's helped me, then tell him that I'm at his service.' Danesti leaned over to slap a hand on his horse's neck, quieting him.

'I will,' Radu answered gravely.

Danesti swung round once, hesitated, then added: 'There's treachery afoot. Warn him. He needs all the men he can muster. I'll answer for my own. Our swords are his to command.' He saluted, then vanished into the wet darkness. Radu and Cornel turned into the tunnel entrance.

'He's a good man,' said Radu.

'A robber? A rebel? Can he be trusted?'

The lantern planed harsh shadows over Radu's face. 'He spoke of treachery. He's right. I feel it in my gut. I want brave men with me, and I don't care where they come from.' His hard voice echoed in the rocky passage connecting with Grigore's dungeons.

CHAPTER 3

'I'm sure I don't know what to do with her,' Georgiana sighed, lying in the circle of David's arm as the afternoon faded into evening. 'Oh, she behaves correctly. I've no complaints on that score but, try as I will, I can't persuade her to come shopping or take tea with my friends. She flits away like a startled ghost when I receive callers. You've asked me to make sure that she has everything she requires, but how can I do this if she refuses to visit my dressmaker? Answer me that, you exasperating man!'

David grunted sleepily, wanting nothing more than to doze after love-making, but his wife had selected that moment to hound him. He pulled her close, enjoying the feel of her pliant body, attempting to stop her mouth with kisses, but she would have none of this. Seeing that she was quite determined to air her grievances, he sat up, took a cheroot from the casket on the side-table, and glanced down at her.

'Damn it, Georgiana, you give a chap no quarter.' He lit the small cigar, inhaling the smoke, then blowing it reflectively upwards into the tester. 'She's of a retiring nature, I suppose. Not all are as bold and confident as yourself.' He grinned and added: 'You've an enormous advantage, married to me.'

'Conceited bully!' she shouted, displaying a flash of that famous temper which had once been her bane. She bounced up, reminding him of a cross fairy, fluffy curls sticking out, small breasts as bare as the rest of her. 'You think it isn't your problem. You've now handed Maria over to me to deal with. Ha! How very convenient! What can I do? I've lent her copies of *La Belle Assemblée* and *The Ladies' Magazine* to improve her dress sense. To no avail. She isn't interested in clothes or balls or parties. She won't come with us to Carlton House tonight, says she's nothing to wear. Of course she hasn't, the silly jade! She hides from Madame de Ropp, the best modiste in London. I offered to loan her one of my own gowns, much as I hate anyone borrowing my things, but she's too tall. Nothing of mine fits.'

'Not every woman is a midget,' he teased.

'Brute!' she retorted, touchy about her lack of inches. When a girl at Warrington Close, her parents' mansion in Kent, she had spent hours trying to stretch herself on exercising machines, to no good purpose. Her lower lip rolled out. 'I think you admire her, David, that thin waif drifting wanly about our home. Is that it? Are you in love with her? Edwin is.'

'Oh, Edwin.' David dismissed his brother with a scowl. 'He falls in love with every girl he meets.' He slid an arm about her, ignoring her protests. 'I love no one but you, my shrew. I'm sorry for Maria. I've promised to help her, but how the deuce am I to do so if she won't appear in public? Speaking of Edwin, can't he talk her round?'

'I'm sure he's dying to, but I don't think she'll listen. He's mightily smitten, over the moon about her. Writes poems in her praise, would you believe?' She was sitting with her elbows on her humped knees, chin cupped in her hand, a brooding expression on her face.

David yawned, stubbed out his cigar and eased down under the sheet. 'Does this unrequited passion keep him out of the gambling-houses, I wonder? That would be a miracle. However, even if she were to return his ardour, I'd hesitate to give my consent. She has no dowry, and I don't intend supporting him and a wife for the rest of their lives. He's a lazy young cub.'

Her eyes slitted thoughtfully. 'It's impossible to discover what goes on in her mind. She's deep. Are you quite sure that the Duchesse didn't tell you more about her, things which I should know?'

'Nothing, you inquisitive witch.' David ruffled her hair affectionately. 'I've no idea who she is or where she comes from. I meant to make a few enquiries in the district, but you were in such a tear to leave, giving me no chance once the roads were passable.'

'It's nice to be back,' she murmured, her eyes wandering their beautiful bedchamber where silk hangings and furniture echoed the Egyptian motifs which had taken France by storm when Napoleon invaded that country. Marble sphinxes, lotus flowers and exotic birds, a long low couch with a wedge-shaped bolster, a writing desk decorated with brass pharaoh masks, these stylish objects adorned Georgiana's boudoir. The bed in which they lay was redolent of Eastern opulence, with turquoise curtains suspended from an enormous scarab near the ceiling.

The house was in Berkeley Square. London hummed a background chorus. This was Georgiana's world, the west end of the capital. She knew nothing of the slums or the business centres where David consulted with bankers, merchants and brokers. For her the city consisted of mansions whose occupants wore fashionable clothes, owned bloodstock, had liveried servants, and drove out in glittering barouches and landaus. She existed among gorgeous crescents and railed squares, with bow-windowed shops, classical assembly rooms, theatres and fine ancestral residences. Not for her the dark, sordid closes, crooked alleys and cellar-dwellings of the under-privileged. Now, as dusk fell, her London was made up of the sound of well-sprung carriages rolling homeward, bearing wealthy businessmen, or conveying ladies and gentlemen from an afternoon's entertainment. Restful hearths awaited them, good food served by respectful lackeys, and the pleasant anticipation of further gaiety in the evening. Town-bred, she took comfort in these noises, much more to her taste than the howling gales of bleak Yorkshire. How contented I should be, she thought, if it were not for Maria Malton.

She would never forget how David had brought the girl to Coleshill on that stormy day. He had stalked straight into the drawing-room where she was passing an idle hour with her crewel-work and Edwin. He had been seated on a low stool by the fire, sharing it with her feet, reciting poetry, devoted and attentive. She remembered looking up, but her delight in seeing David had changed to puzzled alarm when she noticed the girl with him. He had quickly explained, and she had done her best to make Maria welcome.

The situation was proving awkward. David had suggested that Maria might be her companion. She did not need one – she had him. A bright jolly girl called Fanny was her personal maid. As yet they had no children, and were not seeking a governess. He had confided the tantalizing information that Maria was well-born, so there was no question of putting her into service. It was most infuriating. Georgiana did not want an unattached female forever in evidence, particularly one as mysteriously lovely as Maria.

'If something isn't done soon, the summer will be quite ruined,' she announce gloomily. David lay half listening, half following his own thoughts which were occupied with the thoroughbred he was about to purchase. 'I was planning on spending part of the season at Brighton, but how can I plunge into the social whirl with that odd creature lurking about our seaside cottage?'

She usually revelled in Brighton, planning her wardrobe with the greatest care. It was an annual source of delight,

179

rivalling Bath, the favourite resort of the Prince Regent, a flourishing watering place, with villas, a pier, dancing-rooms, libraries and his Highness's own fantastic, Eastern-styled palace. Really, it was all too annoying! David seemed not in the least perturbed, hands laced behind his head, muscular torso and long legs stretched out under the turquoise brocade coverlet. Usually compliant with Georgiana's wishes, he was being stubborn on this issue. She did not understand his link with the Duchesse de Labisse. Till now, she had never bothered to enquire. David did not approve of her meddling in what he termed 'man's work'.

'I think that she may be ill,' he answered thoughtfully. 'I've tried to communicate with her myself, but without results. I might ask Lance to examine her.'

Georgiana bridled. 'She's getting far too much attention, and seems perfectly healthy to me. A touch scrawny, perhaps,' she added waspishly, 'but that's her nature. Pale too, but we can't all possess peaches and cream complexions.'

'Meow! We do have our claws out, don't we?' he mocked, but his face was anxious. 'I wasn't speaking of her physical state. It's as if she's suffered some terrible shock. There's a blankness in her eyes which baffles me. You know that Lance is an admirer of Franz Mesmer.'

Georgiana flicked him impudently on the nose. 'Tush! Are we to allow our doctor to practise the preachings of a charlatan on her? Really, darling, what nonsense!'

'Don't jeer at something which is beyond your comprehension,' he replied sharply. 'Lance isn't a fool. He's often spoken of the time he saw Mesmer demonstrate his remarkable powers. It was in Paris, when he was a student.'

'Before the revolution?' She stifled a yawn. In her opinion, David had some peculiar friends, and she was quickly out of her depth when they sat in earnest conflab after dinner.

'Long before.' David sometimes found himself wishing that she was a seeker after knowledge. There were many subjects that he would have enjoyed sharing. 'Mesmer took Paris by storm with his work on animal magnetism, as he called it. He could cure patients by putting them in a trance, just by looking at them.'

'What flam!' She was not impressed. 'Pure imagination, I expect. I've seen fairground tricksters do the same.'

'Look who's talking!' he expostulated. 'You, my love, are the most easily gulled person alive! Fortune-telling, astrology, palmistry – you believe in them all, lock, stock and barrel!'

'Naturally,' she nodded vigorously. 'That's different.'

He flung back his head and roared with laughter. 'My angel! Lord save me from the logic of women!' He sobered, looking at her seriously. 'Then you don't want me to introduce her to Lance?'

The subject was boring her. She wanted his full attention. 'Do whatever you think best, dearest,' she said softly, mouth pressed to his smooth-shaven cheek.

She was captivating, and he wanted to dwell no further on Maria's future at that moment. 'Darling, it's time we concentrated on our own concerns. We must beget an heir.'

'Haven't we been trying?' A shadow darkened her happiness. Every month brought its cruel disappointment. 'Maybe I should be mesmerized, so that I may conceive.'

'I can think of nicer ways of bringing this about,' he whispered. 'We've time to attempt it again before we dress for the party.'

The room became quiet. The glow of sunset sent scarlet fingers between the blue drapes at the tall casements as the thunder of traffic died away. Affairs of the day completed, Londoners prepared for the affairs of the night.

Sleep evaded Mariana as it so often did. Rigid, she lay in her room, a pretty place with madder-printed curtains and light, delicate furniture, yet the muslin-hung bed seemed stifling. How could she pass the leaden-footed hours till dawn? Reading was impossible, the words making no sense. Thoughts for which she could find no expression came between her and the page, and against those formless clouds her hatred shone like a lurid comet. She drew it into herself – into body, brain and soul – overwhelming hatred. A hard core of intransigent anger ran in her blood, the incarnation of anguish and despair. Her flesh was inhabited by a spirit that cursed God.

Earlier she had visited the music-room, but the butler had been hovering and she had not played. Music had always been her comfort. Mamma had taught her on the battered old harpsichord at home. She remembered her family, her bedroom under the eaves with the apple tree's branches tapping at the tiny window, and wondered if perhaps everything that had happened to her was no more than a nightmare and, in reality, she was back at Swinsty Farm. Certainly, her life with Christopher had defied everything normal. Oh God, she prayed, though no longer believing in Him, let me wake and find it was a dreaming fantasy!

Her eyes burned with tears. Her throat was sore with them. She pressed the heels of her palms against her lids, her temples, but could not ease the pain. She rose, pulling on a thin white peignoir over her nightgown. David was a kind man. He would not object to her soothing her troubled mind with music at so late an hour. He had often repeated over the weeks, concerned, perplexed: 'You must do whatever makes you feel at home here, Maria.'

It comforted the raw ache inside her to think about David, that considerate, good-humoured man. She was not so certain of Georgiana. They stalked around each other like huffy, suspicious cats. I would have done the same if a strange woman had been brought into my house without so much as a by-your-leave. Georgiana was continually pressing her to go out, but she could not. There was a remote chance that someone, somewhere might recognize her. It was unlikely, for Christopher had not honoured his promise to take her to London and she had resented this, kept hidden away, as if unworthy of public view. Now she blessed the fact, but dreaded mingling. Fate had played so many cruel tricks on her. Supposing she chanced upon a native of Yorkshire who might remember and, unwittingly or maliciously, betray her?

Earlier she had heard David and Georgiana come in from the party. Their voices had risen, complacent, happy, as they passed her door. With sudden resolution, she made her cautious way down to the music-room. The fire was still smouldering but the butler had snuffed the candles. She, who had once feared nothing, now hated the dark, and she lit every one she could find, then settled herself on the circular stool, having found some sheet-music in the cabinet. She had chosen unfamiliar works which carried no associations. Most of them were gay popular airs. Georgiana was accomplished, performing prettily at soirees, so the choice was a random collection of carefree melodies, waltzes and sentimental ballads.

Mariana's fingers were stiff from lack of practice. She was intrigued by this modern instrument, with its brass inlay of Greek scrolls and the maker's name, 'Thomas Tomkinson', set in a small plaque just above the keys. The sound was excellent, felted hammers hitting the taut strings, unlike the harpsichord where quills plucked them. Rummaging to the bottom of the pile, she found an aria from Gluck's opera *Orphée et Eurydice*. The words were haunting, the tune melancholy – 'What is life to me without you – what is life if thou art dead?'

She bit back her grief which had nothing to do with the lost love between man and woman. Oh, she lost someone who had been dearer to her than life itself. Would I, like Orphée of the legend, venture into Hades searching for Elaine? she thought. Oh, I would! I would!

The manuscript was blurred, but she concentrated every effort on its challenging fingering,. Don't look back on the past, think only of the music – go over the difficult passages again and again. The sad sounds rang through the room in great golden rings. She could feel the chords vibrating through her hands, into her arms, making her head swim. 'What is life without my love – without my love – without my love?'

Edwin came in late, long after his brother and sister-in-law had left the Prince Regent's magnificent house. He swayed a little as he entered the drawing-room. Good old Melville, he thought vaguely, he's left the candles burning and banked up the fire. I'll have to tip him in the morning. Must've known I'd be cold. Damned chilly outside. Lord, what a climate! Why can't we go to Italy soon? Must tackle David about it. He's getting bloody miserly! Had a face like an undertaker's when I wouldn't come home with 'em tonight. He knew I'd go on playing. Couldn't refuse Prinny, could I?

One could not refuse the Prince Regent anything. He was omnipotent. Edwin was one of the young men of his circle who slavishly followed fashion, seeing the dandy as the acme of perfection and style. Beau Brummel had once been the leader of the *haut ton*, before offending Prinny and having to leave England in a hurry, but his influence still held sway. Edwin mixed with those who dominated the scene from their vantage point in one of the clubs – White's or Brook's, occasionally sharing their power with the great dames at whose nod one was or was not admitted to Almack's assembly rooms.

The gathering at Carlton House had been typical of the events to which the Cunynghams were automatically invited. Their coach had joined the endless stream which had wound towards Carlton House. It had been lit from top to bottom, and powdered, gold-laced flunkeys had lined the steps. There ahd been no room to sit inside, the gentlemen standing about, passing snuff-boxes, exchanging witty comments, affecting a bored, condescending air. It was not the done thing to laugh or appear to enjoy oneself. One preserved curled lips and contemptuous eyes as one measured any newcomer from top to toe.

The ladies took their tone from the men, gossiping spitefully and flirting outrageously. The coversation had consisted of the latest modes, who had been seen where and with whom, of concerts where Rossini had performed, of the new opera at the

Haymarket Theatre where Catalini had sung. Edwin had spent much time talking, elbowing, drifting from one imposing room to the next, seeking companions of a like ilk, raffish men, reckless and showy, whose crowning interest was gambling. He was a member of Crockford's Club and the Roxborough, with their green hazard tables and croupiers in white neckcloths, princely establishments, magnificently furnished, offering free delicacies to patrons. Edwin knew perfectly well that within their walls more than one great estate had been lost and unfortunate gentlemen driven to courses damaging to their honour, but he could not resist them.

He had drunk too much champagne with the stout, aging Regent, still the leader of the dandies, still lolling with his fat mistresses and fortifying his wine with laudanum. It had gone to Edwin's head. He had defiantly squandered a large percentage of his monthly allowance losing at faro, drunk more to forget, then eventually excused himself and left.

On the way out, one of the bucks had placed a hand on his arm, drawling languidly: 'Where're you off to, sport? Lost your deuced nerve, have you? You'll offend Lady Jersey if you go – I know she's vulgar and bloody haughty, but one can't afford to upset the bitch. What of the other beauties, eh? You may be somewhat toped, but you look in prime and plummy order to me – dem fit to please 'em, dem fit – ain't seen anyone so dem fit for rogering 'em, be demmed if I have!'

Edwin had shaken himself free, snarling, 'Piss off, Davenport.'

The beau, a brittle young man whose cravat had been so high and tight that he could hardly turn his head, had tittered and collapsed in the arms of his companions. Pursued by their drunken jibes, Edwin had made good his escape. It was a crisp night, and he had turned over in his mind whether to go to the Roxborough where meals were served from midnight till five in the morning, to sample more champagne, turbot and plovers' eggs, or visit Mrs Wilkin's bagnio in Balingham Street, but in the gloom of the hired hackney-carriage, he had suddenly thought of Maria. Rapping on the roof with his amber-headed whitethorn cane, he had ordered the driver to take him home.

Maria – visions of that elusive girl plagued him. He had thrown off his cloak in the hall, left his gloves and hat on the table. In the drawing-room he went to the chiffonier and poured a large brandy. His reflection started back at him from the mirror behind it. He pressed his hands flat on the polished surface and leaned forward, subjecting himself to close, alcoholic inspection.

His curling fair hair was thick and wavy, and his features,

though flushed, were clean-cut and pleasing. With his cultured speech, debonair manner and fastidious attention to dress, he had never before been refused. It was galling. The Regent's overblown harem had been giving him the eye all night, behind the royal back. He was elegance itself in his sleek trousers which strapped beneath his shoes, fine cambric linen, rose waistcoat dangling with gold fobs, cut-away jacket which showed him to full advantage. Yet Maria persisted in giving him the cold-shoulder. He gazed into his brandy and brooded.

Damn her, the stuck-up little nobody! Baffled lust knotted in his gut. He cursed the impulse which had stopped him carrying out his original plan. By now he could have been humping some willing whore, instead of mooning here alone. Damn David for bringing her to live with them! He had taken one look at those violet eyes and had been lost in their tragic depths.

There was something about her. He could not tell what it was, but old ambitions, yearnings buried beneath selfish indulgence, had driven him to seek solitude on the moors, searching for inspiration in the snowy wastes, the hills, the clouds. He had found himself quoting from his favourite poets as he strode along, Shelley, Keats and Byron, contemporary radicals who were making their literary mark. He longed to be famous, having seen how the women in particular flocked to adore them. The words had been torn from his lips, scattered like dead leaves around the craggy peaks, yet the cobwebs had been cleared from his brain on the spartan moorland. He had taken up his pen again, though his poor efforts had only increased his discontent, leaving him steeped in wistful nostalgia, harking back constantly to something lost, and he did not know what it was.

He had thought, till that night, that London had cured him, exerting its powerful charm when he arrived. He had fallen in with old comrades, younger sons of titled men who had nothing to do but waste their allowances, drink, gamble and indulge in illicit love-affairs. Edwin was ripe for any spree, which generally meant frolics which involved himself and others in trouble; he racketed round the clubs, sought the company of harlots, but could not fill the void in his existence. A shoal of amusing friends and the charms of obliging women could not prevent him from feeling lonely and depressed.

He chewed his nails, scowled and took another drink. Why did Maria hold herself so aloof? She was like a phantom in the house of the living, a sad wraith appearing when summoned to meals, then gliding away as silently as she had come, avoiding conversation, avoiding *him*. Beautiful – God, he'd never seen anyone so beautiful! Lovely as the reflection of a crystal mountain in a silver lake.

Edwin repeated the phrase, rather pleased with it. Not bad, not at all bad. His hand dived into his pocket, searching for a pencil. He scribbled the words on the back of an envelope, noting dispassionately that it was a *billet doux* slipped to him by a bold-eyed brunette during the course of the evening. She'd be easy meat. No frustration there. Her thighs would fall apart at his first touch. He gave a deep sigh. Bloody Yorkshire, why the hell had he gone? It was too remote, too earthy, almost pagan. One could not avoid looking into one's soul. Damned disconcerting, and Maria was a part of it. There were plenty of women in London, eager to take him to their beds, married or single, it didn't matter. He seethed with baffled anger and desire, enraged that he should be so affected by a penniless chit who denied him satisfaction.

The servants had gone to their quarters. The huge house was still. Then a sound reached him, penetrating the fog of drink and introspection. Someone was playing the pianoforte. Without giving himself time to consider, Edwin staggered in pursuit of that thin trail. He went across the tiled hall and along a passage panelled in leaf-green, down several carpeted steps hung with large paintings, and pushed open the high cedar-wood doors of the music-room.

The glow hurt his blood-shot eyes. There were candles everywhere: on the overmantel, on the serpentine-fronted bureau, on top of a rococo cabinet, shining from a many-branched candelabrum on the piano lid. The yellow points of flame shone on rows of calf-bound volumes behind the glass fronts of a tall wall-case. Edwin blinked owlishly, clinging to the carved architrave for support.

Mariana heard him and stopped playing, hands resting on the ivory keys. She turned like a tigress, her pale face startled, almost disembodied in Edwin's hazy sight. Her heart was thumping. Fright made her angry. 'Edwin! Why d'you creep up on me?' she demanded.

He left the door, advancing towards her, sheepish, apologetic. 'Sorry, Maria, didn't mean to alarm you – heard the music – wanted to see who was playing. By Jove, didn't know you were so clever. Don't stop. I'll just sit here and watch you.'

'You're drunk!' she accused contemptuously. She had seen enough of drink and its effects to last her a lifetime. In a way, her present affliction could be traced to it. Had Crosby not urged her marriage, had their circumstances not been so reduced by his habit, perhaps she might never have become involved with Christopher.

She shut the lid with a bang, her hard-won tranquility shattered. She half rose, but Edwin's hand closed on her arm. His face was red. He breathed out brandy fumes. Memories crowded in on her, thick and fast. Her eyes scanned his features, and there was that in her white face which made him quail.

'Maria, dearest Maria,' he said thickly, struggling to make sense. His pulse was racing, awed by her scorn yet terribly aware that she wore nothing but a light wrap over her lawn nightdress. There was lace at her wrists, and her bare feet were thrust into slippers of swansdown. Her long dark hair cascaded over her breasts. He wanted to say so much to her, but his tongue seemed too big for his mouth. 'Why d'you avoid me? Why torment me? Damn it, you must know how I feel about you,' he managed to mumble.

She froze under his grasp, lashes sweeping down as she stared at his hand, remembering the night of her mother's funeral, and Crosby's disgusting proposition. When she looked at Edwin again it was with a level coolness which checked him. 'You're hurting me. Let me pass.'

The touch of her, the perfume which seemed to breathe out of her body, was too much for him. Sober, he would not quite have dared, but now: 'I won't,' he muttered, brain on fire. 'Not till you've promised to go out with me. Why this silly refusal? There's so much we can do. Water-parties on boats with bands, fetes in the park – you'll love it. I'll look after you. Come to the Ranelagh Rotunda tomorrow night. Say that you will.'

He felt a tremor pass through her. 'I can't. Don't ask me. Leave me alone,' she whispered.

The vulnerability of her trembling made him bold. He felt no pity, only a blazing lust. He wanted to go on hurting her, to crush her, bend her to his will. His whole body was aflame, leaning into her, aching for her. 'Too proud to be seen with me, eh? Bloody little tramp! What's wrong with me? Scores of other women want me to roger 'em! Well, you won't get away. There's no time like the present, that couch will serve us.' He was mouthing words, sick words, evil words from which she could not escape and she shuddered. She'd heard them before – from Crosby – from Christopher. He tugged her towards the chaise-longue. 'No one will know. Every bloody soul's asleep. Let's stop pretending, Maria. I want you. Don't act the simpering virgin. You're no innocent, not a girl like you!'

Mariana struggled in his grasp, and her revulsion saddened her. Would she ever be able to allow a man to touch her again? He was young, personable, yet his ardour made her feel sick. In his hurried breathing, in his eyes and the tension of his body, she read passion, and passion was allied with violence. Desire was destructive, torturing, humiliating. She did not want it ever again – that physical act devoid of love and dignity.

She tore free and fled for the door. Edwin, crazed with drink and longing, caught her gown and jerked her back, pressing her against the hardness of his groin. 'Whether you like it or not, I'm going to have you,' he grated.

'Edwin, don't be a fool!' She was furious at his superior strength and that masculine ego which demanded subjection. Her hands came up, wide spread, claws reaching for his face.

He grabbed her wrists, holding them apart. 'I don't care what happens – I've got to have you,' he insisted, and his mouth came down on hers with the remembered brutality with which Christopher had sometimes used her.

Her knee was captured between his legs. She jerked it upwards sharply, forcibly. He yelped in agony and let her go, doubling up, starting to vomit. Without looking back, Mariana ran for her room, slamming the door, throwing the bolt. She leaned against it, giving choking sobs. Men! They were all alike! Disgusting animals! Even Edwin who had lulled her fears, seeming kind and gentle. Lies, all lies! He was like the rest, wanting to abuse her, control and master her.

She groped her way towards the bed, seeking its security, sinking into the billowing feather-mattress, covers up to her chin. Why had she not died that night on the moor? Better far to have gone into eternal oblivion than face this continual misery. I'm going mad, she thought, reason tottering as she shook with rage and sorrow. There was no way in which she would venture into the world. She would stay in her room. Let David coax till he was blue in the face. Let Georgiana scold till doomsday. Here, at least, was a modicum of safety, and here she would remain – for ever if need be.

The windows were wide open and the chintz curtains stirred in the early-morning breeze. From the small railed balcony outside, the river could be seen, with a sailing boat swinging easily at her mooring-post. A bridge spanned the water below, and several urchins were hanging over its stone parapet, dropping sticks into the Thames. A beech tree stooped over the flow near the barge stairs, its leaves rustling. The day promised to be fine, and everything wore a sparkle.

Lancelot Gilmour, an impressive, discontented figure in a shabby dressing-gown, leaned back on his elbows against the florid marble fireplace, and spoke his mind bitterly to his guest on the subject of servants. 'God knows I pay 'em well! Idle lot of bastards! Just because I'm unmarried, they think to take advantage. I'll sack 'em! Take this lousy coffee for example. It's muck! Smells like a sewer. I swear they've served up the grouts and kept the fresh beans to swig in the kitchen. One good thing about soldiering on the Continent – we got bloody good coffee.'

He heaved his shoulders away from their support, seized a brass bell and rang it violently. A servant popped an enquiring head round the door. His big, solid, ruddy-faced master glared at him, and pointed an accusing finger at the squat silver coffee-pot on the round table. 'Remove that object at once, Fred, even a self-respecting savage wouldn't drink it. Tell the maids to wash up in it. Clean the privy with it. I don't care what you do with it, just get it out of my confounded sight! Send down the road to the inn, if you must, but bring me a fresh pot of good, strong coffee. I'm entertaining Lord Cunyngham, and this swill offends both our palates.'

David smiled from his seat by the fire, his legs in tightly strapped pale blue trousers stretched straight before him. 'Don't fret about it, Lance, there's a good chap. It really doesn't matter.'

His burly friend exploded in a fresh paroxysm of indignation. 'Of course it bloody matters! 'Tis enough that you've arrived at an ungodly hour, rousing me from my bed. I was up half the night delivering an obstinate infant who insisted on coming into the world arse-first. Devil knows, I'm a crusty old beggar, till I've had my breakfast. What brings you here?' He stared at David from beneath bushy brows. 'Is Georgiana pregnant at last? Has Edwin a dose of the clap? Has he got some servant-girl in the family way?'

The doctor was an imposing figure, even in his robe and tasselled night-cap. What he lacked in height, he made up for in sheer bulk, well able to defend himself in the slums of St Giles, Tothill or Seven Dials, criminal areas where even the Bow Street Runners did not care to venture. Lancelot had set up free clinics in their midst. One look at his stern face and bulging muscles was enough to prevent any pickpocket plying his trade. A single glance from his bright blue eyes brought gin-sodden mothers to their senses, as he upbraided them for neglecting their children. Vain young blades, seeking a cure for venereal disease or wounds inflicted during law-breaking duels, found their braggadocio wilting after five minutes in his consulting-room. Hysterical highborn maidens were rid of their fanciful symptoms when he ignored their vapourings, telling them bluntly that they needed to get away from dominating mothers and find themselves vigorous studs. Sickly, genteel wives were asked, point-blank, if their husbands were impotent, and given earthy advice.

He was in his fifties, but still a vital attractive person, mature, cynical, prone to coarse language, even with well-heeled clients, disliking bigots and telling them so, tolerant of advanced ideas, not religious in the accepted sense but with a sincere belief in his calling. He had once told David that he had been born to serve his fellow creatures and would do so to the last drop of his blood, but that he could not abide humbugs! He was a mass of contradictions, outwardly a philistine, inwardly a philosopher.

They had met during the war when David had served under the Duke of Wellington and Lancelot had been a camp surgeon. Their liking for one another had been instantaneous. After the defeat of Napoleon and the establishment of peace, that friendship had remained. Lancelot had bought a neat house west of the river and set up in practice, quickly gaining popularity. The nobility might grumble about his fees and brusque manner, but they continued to send for him, wearied of other physicians with their quack remedies, abysmal lack of knowledge, and their fanatical cure-all of cupping and leeches.

'Neither of these things are my reason for calling.' David accepted a glass of claret whilst they awaited the return of Fred. 'I've a problem, in the comely shape of a young woman.'

The penetrating eyes in the heavily-jowled face bored into his. 'What's this, David? Taken a mistress, you dirty old pig? I thought you were devoted to your pocket-Venus. Beware of the pox, my lad. Don't blight your chances of producing a healthy son. Look at the royal brothers. Seven of 'em, all dissipated, given to God knows what vices, and what have they got to show for it? A stable full of bastards, but no one to inherit the throne of England.'

'This has nothing to do with my love-life,' David answered calmly. 'I'm more than happy with Georgiana. Something happened while I was in Yorkshire. Stop pacing about like a

190

caged bear and listen.' He launched into the story of the Duchesse and Maria.

Lancelot flung himself into an armchair which creaked in protest. 'I fail to appreciate your concern', he said when David paused. 'The girl's refined, so you say – quiet and obedient. Consider yourself lucky, my friend. You could have been foisted off with some giddy hedonist, like so many of that motley crew who pose as delicate young ladies. Harpies, most of 'em.'

'Hell, I know that,' David exclaimed, running a hand through his hair. 'Truth to tell, Georgiana's mighty put out.'

'Ah,' said Lancelot.

'And Edwin wants to bed her.'

'Ah ha!' said Lancelot. A broad grin spread over his face, deepening the laughter lines at the corners of his eyes. 'So the breeze of disquiet is rippling the tranquility of hearth and home, eh, David? The fair Georgiana objects to sharing you, be it in never so innocent a fashion, and Edwin's been pierced by Cupid's darts. Does he want to marry her? Why don't you agree to this? You're not related to her, I suppose.'

'Not at all,' David replied, looking puzzled.

'Good. Don't hold with in-breeding.' Lancelot settled back in his chair, hands clasped over his stomach. 'Not in humans. Weakens the strain, marrying too close. Apart from the pox, booze and opium, that's what ails the Princes. Half the crowned heads in Europe are dotty through near-incest.'

David nodded for his cup to be filled when Fred appeared at the door with breakfast dishes and coffee-pot. 'King George and Queen Charlotte had a huge family. I fail to follow your logic.'

Lancelot moved to the table, tucking into his favourite morning repast – grilled sausages garnished with apple sauce. 'I'll not deny that they've been well blessed – quiver full to bursting, so to speak. Fifteen children, neatly arranged in alternating sexes.'

'Which proves my point,' nodded David.

'Not quite.' The doctor spiked a roll with his fork so firmly that the dish skidded on the polished table. 'The last ones were sickly, dying young. Virtue seemed to have gone out of the stock.'

'Even so, thirteen healthy offspring is a considerable achievement. I'll be more than content if Georgiana and I manage half that number,' David commented, declining breakfast, watching his friend with amusement, knowing it was pointless hurrying him.

191

Lancelot spread butter on the bread with a lavish hand, bit a deep crescent into it and chewed vigorously. 'An odd couple, potty old George and his Consort. Unpopular with the British, of course. Who wants damned foreigners on the throne? But Queen Anne's babies were all stillborn, so there was nothing for it but to invite the Germans to fill the post. Sad really, when you come to think about it. Couldn't have the Stuarts back, because they're Papists, so it had to be the distantly related Hanoverians, in the early seventeen hundreds. George I wouldn't even bother to learn English and looked upon Hanover as his home. Poor old Prinny's been waiting for years for his father to kick the bucket so that he can be George IV. The King's completely barmy now, shut up in his gilded mad-house at Windsor. Prinny's Regent, but he don't stand a hope in hell of his descendants ruling. That was knocked on the head last year when his only legitimate child, a daughter at that, died.'

David pulled a wry face, listening patiently, for the state of the English monarchy was one of Lancelot's hobby-horses. 'You're right, Lance, you clever devil. You always are, God damn it! Twelve middle-aged Princes and Princesses are all that's left.'

'The females are spinsters or childless, and the males can't boast of a single brat who ain't either a bastard or otherwise debarred. Inbreeding! That's what's done it.' Lancelot grunted knowledgeably, wiping his lips on a napkin, sitting back and belching his appreciation of the excellent sausages. 'The palace is in an uproar. The Princes are being bullied into giving up their mistresses and marrying suitable ladies. They're thin on the ground. France is out, what with the revolution and the war. Narrows the field when it comes to eligible women of the Blood Royal who're still of child-bearing age. Take heed, dear chap. Don't mess with whores, don't marry your cousins, and see to it that Georgiana presents you with a boy before too long.'

Having put the Crowned Heads of Europe under scrutiny and found them wanting, Lancelot re-filled his cup, topped it with cream, ladled in sugar and sipped it, eyeing David over the rim.

'That's my intention, never fear,' David replied, lighting up a cheroot. 'And with this in view, I don't want to distress her further. Maria's a thorn in her flesh at the moment. I'm committed to helping the wretched girl. You know the reason.'

Lancelot nodded, having seen David inherit his uncle's wealth, guiding him through the early years as a land-owner, offering the benefits of his considerable experience. 'This is an unexpected turn-up for the books, and no mistake. How can I help?'

David did not answer at once, drawing the smoke back into his lungs, savouring it. The sunshine flooded onto the cream walls through the square-paned sash windows, showing up the richness of the bronze brocade drapes and thick-pile amber carpet. It glanced off the sleek rosewood tallboy and high chest, and made a shiny lake of the mirror. The bed, domed like a temple, the curtains flung up above the ceil, was unmade, covers tossed anyhow. David had dragged Lancelot from its depths. Outside, traffic was beginning to gather momentum as London stirred into life. The cries of passing street-hawkers floated on the clear air.

'She's most distraught. Oh, not hysterically so – she's too quiet, if anything. She's resisted our efforts to introduce her into society.' David frowned down at his smouldering cigar, pondering on Maria. It was so difficult to explain. She seemed to lead a life remote from outer contact, although once ar twice he had found her looking at him strangely, as if gauging him, but she always lowered her eyes when caught. Yet there was something about her which suggested the wisdom and knowledge of one far older.

Lancelot was busily engaged in balancing a tiny dune of snuff at the base of his thumb. He raised the back of his hand to his nostrils and sniffed deeply. 'Still can't understand why you're in such a wax. She could be costing you money, what with gowns, bonnets and all those hundred and one fripperies which women demand to make life bearable.'

'I wish she was more light-hearted. She seems terrified and won't say why.' David's eyes hardened angrily. 'That stupid ass, Edwin, has made things worse.'

'What's he done now?' Lancelot sighed, wiping his nose with a large silk handkerchief.

'He found her alone the other night, and was rather more forceful in his attentions than he should've been.'

'He raped her?' Lancelot did not doubt Edwin capable of it.

'He tried. Maria kneed him in the cods and got away.'

Lancelot rumbled with laughter. 'Good for her. Serve him right, silly young fool.'

David stood up, tossing his cigar butt into the fire. There was a tension about him which Lancelot had not seen since the war days. 'He came to see me about it next morning. Afraid she'd tell on him, I suppose. He'd been drinking too much at the Regent's party, came home late and found Maria playing the pianoforte. She was in her night-attire apparently.'

'A scantily-clad Muse,' Lancelot grinned up at him. 'Too much for his self-control. Why the devil didn't he pick up a whore? He usually does.' His mouth drew into a sardonic line. He did not have much time for David's brother. 'Wouldn't it be wise to get him married? He's been serving his apprenticeship among the ladies for years, idling along the primrose path – far too fond of the flesh-pots.'

David paced the carpet, hands locked under his coat-tails. 'We had a row about it, for he's really upset her. She wouldn't leave the house before, and since that night we can't get her to come out of her room. Will you see her?'

The doctor was taking a little resuscitation in the form of another glass of claret. He held the wine glass up to the light as if his attention was focused solely on its ruby glow. 'Certainly, if you think it'll do any good. You've roused my curiosity, I'll admit. The female mind is extraordinarily convoluted. They're most complex creatures, worthy of scientific study. When would you like me to call?'

David sprang into life, relief in every line of his body. 'Come now. Get dressed, you sluggard. I'll wait, and we'll ride together.'

Lancelot grimaced, sighed, heaved himself from the table, and rang for his long-suffering manservant, Fred.

CHAPTER 4

'Go away!' Mariana shouted, pressing against the bedroom door.

'Maria! This is foolishness,' David protested, his voice muffled by the screening wood. 'No one's going to hurt you. Please come out. Edwin isn't here. I'm so sorry about what happened the other night. So is he, I assure you. He was drunk.'

'So that excuses him? How often have I heard that – "I was drunk. I didn't know what I was doing!" Leave me alone, David. I don't want to see anyone.' Her voice broke and she sank down to the floor, head in her hands.

He had tried to make contact every day, but she would not let him in, refusing the trays of tempting delicacies brought up at his orders, sending them back untouched. She was light-headed through hunger, confinement and the loneliness of the long days and black nights. She had spent much time staring out of the window, seeing the new green carpeting the lawns, the nodding daffodils, the bright gems of yellow, purple and white crocuses. Spring filled the air. In the trees the birds were frantically nesting. Just beneath her casement, a pair of quarrelsome tits were constructing their cunning nest, flitting in and out, raising their first brood of the season. Life was swinging upwards, leaving the gloom of winter, stretching towards summer. Mariana felt all the more isolated, cut off from love, gaiety and hope, but she had no choice.

She prayed that David had given up, but could hear murmured tones from the corridor, his own and another, deeper one. Then someone rapped firmly and that voice addressed her. It held a note of authority difficult to deny.

'Miss Malton? Are you there? I'd deem it an honour if you'd be so kind as to open the door and speak with me.'

The quality of that briskly confident request cut through the fog of misery. She was so tired. It swept over her in waves, a weariness beyond endurance. The voice was mature, fatherly. It made her want to meet its owner, to be warmed by his unseen smile, patted on the head and told that she'd been a good girl – she couldn't be blamed for what had happened – it wasn't her fault.

'Who are you?' she faltered.

'I'm a friend of David's. I may be able to help you, but I can't do anything if you won't let me in.' There was a trace of humour there, the promise of strength, but she did not answer, letting the breath slide slowly between her lips, fearing that its sound might somehow betray her. She was shivering, though the sweat trickled down her back. He rapped again, beating out a brisk tattoo. 'Come along, Miss Malton. Open up. I won't eat you,' he said. Her hand crept to the lock, almost of its own volition.

'D'you promise to leave at once, if I ask you?' she quavered, the brass fitting beneath her hand.

'I give my wood as a gentleman.'

'A gentleman's word means nothing to me,' she said bitterly, but the key turned, the lock clicked and a foot was thrust through the narrow aperture. It was then pushed full open. David was framed there, and another man too. He stood square and large, in brown double-breasted jacket and chequered trousers, incongruous midst the feminine décor of the room. Raw terror flared through her. She backed away, turned to run, her goal the haven of the bed. She reached it, stood at bay like a hunted doe, shaking, staring at him.

Lancelot looked at her ashen face and huge, burning eyes. Pity welled in him for the blind panic which was making her suspicious. Her thin hands were clenched, dark hair loosened, making her face a pallid, sick mask. He took a step towards her, then stopped dead as she shrank against the bed-curtains.

'Don't touch me! Don't come any closer!'

'My dear Miss Malton, be calm.' Lancelot brought all the skill at his command into play, and this was considerable. 'I want to be your friend. Trust me.'

'Trust you? If I do, you'll hurt me beyond belief!'

'That's not true. My name is Lancelot Gilmour. I'm David's physician. He's asked me to talk to you.'

He held out his hand but she refused to take it. 'I've nothing to say.' Her eyes glittered with an intense, feverish brightness. 'If he's sent you to spy on me, then I must ask you to go.' With that she retreated into the solitary grief which emanated from her.

So sad a creature, so defenceless in spite of her brave show of defiance. He mentally saluted her, his medical experience telling him that someone had used her mercilessly, bruising her mind. Not Edwin. This had happened long before she met him. He spoke over his shoulder to the quietly waiting David. 'It'll be best if we're alone.'

When the door closed softly, he relaxed his vigil. Mariana was still stiff, but he sensed a slight change, as if she was longing to give up the fight. Very gently, as if schooling a high-strung mare, he took another step. This time she did not cringe, but her lips shaped the word 'no' and she shook her head.

'Miss Malton, or may I call you Maria? David hopes – I hope, that you'll stop shutting yourself away. He has great plans for the summer. He's off to Vienna and wants to take you with him.'

A light sprang into her eyes. 'Vienna?'

'Yes. He and Georgiana have been invited to spend time with friends there. Would you like that?'

To leave England, to go to a country where she would be completely unknown. Hope struck a timid root in her heart. She was so tired of these four walls, this prison of her own making. To be free! Able to walk in the streets with her head high – to forget. 'Oh, yes, I'd like that very much,' she whispered.

Lancelot went into action, sweeping towards her, big, dominating, his black cape swinging behind him. 'Capital! That's more like it! We'll soon have you putting on weight, not too much of course, you ladies like to look willowy, I know. First, I'd better examine you, just to ensure that there's no bodily cause for this melancholy.'

In the next second, he was cursing himself for over-confidence. Mariana had taken flight, running to the window as if she would fling it wide and jump. This was in her mind, some crazy, disjointed idea of escape. Although to Lancelot she moved like lightning, she found her progress agonizingly slow, every straining muscle in her exhausted body screaming in protest. She reached the casement, fumbling with the catch, hands trembling so much that she could not lift it.

A shape loomed up behind her. She knew it was the doctor, yet for a nightmare second, her imagination saw Christopher – Christopher who haunted her nights and turned her days into a dream-world hell. She screamed, and Lancelot was in time to catch her as she collapsed. With an angry mutter at the cruelty of humans, he held her tightly against his broad chest, then swung her up as if she was made of thistledown and laid her on the bed. She was moaning, rolling her head from side to side, tears streaking across her temples.

'Hush, dear child. There, lie quietly.' Lancelot leaned over her, his hands as gentle as a woman's as he took her face between his broad palms, looking deeply into her half-closed eyes.

He fished in his waistcoat pocket. Light flashed on a gold coin, dangling from a length of chain. He held it suspended, set it swinging like a pendulum. Mariana began to struggle again, shielding her eyes with her arm, desperately confused.

'Take it away,' she begged. 'I don't want your help.'

Lancelot would have none of this. With his free hand he firmly pushed her arm down. She could not fight his stronger will. 'Watch the bauble, girl. That's right. Now, see it swing – watch the movement – it glints in the sun. It's like a little sun, isn't it? Round and gold and beautiful. Feel the warmth of it – relax in its rays. You're feeling tired – warm and tired – your eyelids are becoming heavy. Now they're closing – closing. That's my girl. Rest, Maria, and while you rest, tell me what troubles you. Let me take you back – back into your past. I'll be with you every step of the way, so don't be afraid. When you've emptied your heart of its burden, you'll sleep – a deep refreshing sleep. When you wake, you'll barely remember that we've faced these old, sad things. Come, Maria – come with me. Let the poison run out – let it go—'

A while later, Lancelot let himself out of the bedchamber, deep in thought. He whistled up a passing servant and instructed her that Miss Malton was not to be disturbed on any account, then found his way down to the library. Melville, solemnly patrolling the hall, was dispatched to find his master. Lancelot tossed his cloak over a chair, helped himself to a tot of brandy and, when David came in, was stationed on the hearth rug, tails flipped back, warming the seat of his check pantaloons.

'Well?' David's eyes met his across the cosy, book-lined room.

'Not too well, but better than before,' growled Lancelot, head bent, chin resting among the frills of his cravat.

'Don't be tiresomely evasive, Lance.' David had been thrown into an increased state of agitation by Maria's woeful appearance. 'Is she ill? By God, she looked it! Can you help her? What did she say?'

Lancelot held up a hand, blowing out his cheeks in comic alarm. 'Questions! Questions! One at a time, if you please. I'll answer you with one of my own.'

'What's that?' David regarded him with impatient respect, taking a seat near the fireplace, glad that Georgiana had left the house early to attend to some urgent shopping, thus being spared this further upheaval.

Blue eyes twinkled down at him, and Lancelot rocked slightly on his stocky, spread legs. 'Are you inviting me to luncheon?'

David gave an exasperated sigh, then grinned. 'That goes without saying, but I wish you'd tell me what happened. I really can't afford to spend more time and energy on the matter. I've much to do if we're to leave for Europe by the end of the month.'

The doctor sipped his brandy, his eyes fixed on the strip of blue sky visible through the bay windows. Summer was coming. He could snuff it in the air, and he ached to leave grimy London with its poverty, its miseries, its overwhelming contrasts between the very rich and the disgustingly poor. There were times when even his expansive, optimistic nature was affected by the hopelessness of those who visited his dispensary.

Over-crowding, ignorance, dirt and disease were the ills with which he battled daily. The poor lived in squalor, seeking relief in gin and opium, exploited by factory-owners, used and abused by their own kind. His clinic was in a thieves' sanctuary called the 'Rookery', where they in turn were robbed by greedy fences. It was the children who pierced Lancelot's armour. He could cope with the adults, be angry, even contemptuous – but the children with their huge eyes, pinched faces, thin bodies in skimpy rags – uncomplaining, resigned, knowing no existence but that of harsh masters and brutalized parents. He was starting a fund to buy a house as a shelter for the homeless waifs who hung around his door, begging for scraps.

He knew that David was waiting impatiently for his diagnosis on Maria. He glanced over at him. David crossed one elegantly clad leg over the other and held out a letter. It bore an impressive red seal. 'This awaited me on my return this morning. It's from Prince Radu. You remember him, don't you?'

'Ah, the call to Vienna which you mentioned upstairs.' Memories warmed Lancelot. Those days during the war when friendships had been forged from bloodshed and danger. The sufferings of the wounded had been tragic, but the sense of comradeship was like nothing else on earth. 'Of course I remember him. A brave man and a first-class rider. No side to him either – had a lot of *bottom*. His troopers would've followed him to hell if he'd asked 'em. What's he up to these days?'

'Read it.' David pointed to the letter. 'He doesn't say a lot, but there's more in it than meets the eye. His father died last year and Radu was recalled from the regiment. He's responsible for his country now – Margrave – Landgrave or whatever the damned title is in that remote corner of Europe. Seems he wants to see me, has fixed up a visit where we'll be the guests of Baron Carl von Gundling. I think Radu plans to stay for a while, then take us to Montezena.'

'Ah, yes, one of those little states which the Turks and Germans fight about like dogs over a bone,' Lancelot answered, holding a pinch of snuff between forefinger and thumb. He offered the silver box but David declined with a shake of his head. Taking the letter in his free hand, Lancelot scanned it then passed it back. 'You lucky devil. What does Georgiana say?'

'Why d'you suppose she's rushed off shopping?' David smiled. 'Vienna's gay, and its inhabitants terribly stylish. She feels the need to outdo every pretty woman there. It'll cost me a packet.'

'Are you taking Edwin?' Lancelot's eyes were slitted under the thick brows.

'I must. Can't leave him to shift for himself.' David flung the letter down on the table. 'His morals are deplorable, and he'd turn the house into a gambling den, filling it with rakes and painted ladybirds. I'm afraid he'll have to come.'

'And Maria?'

David's eyes switched to his face, filled with uncertainty. 'I want to take her, but you still haven't told me what happened.'

Lancelot stroked his chin musingly. 'She's suffering from lack of food and overwrought nerves. What the hell was she trying to do? Starve herself to death?' He did not wait for David's answer, continuing: 'The girl has suffered, you may depend on that.'

'Did she tell you anything about her past?' David leaned forward eagerly.

Lancelot shook his leonine head, one broad hand resting on the mantelshelf. The coals in the ornamental grate fell with a crash, and the fire burned up with an increased glow. 'Indirectly, but doctors are like priests, you know that. We don't divulge confessions.'

'But – ' David broke in.

'No buts, David.' His friend looked at him sternly. 'I'll not betray my Hippocratic oath, even to ease your mind, old lad. There appears to be no physical illness that a few square meals and a dose of fresh air won't cure. I think you'll find her more receptive to kindly overtures from now on.' His expression indicated that no amount of persuasion would make him change his mind. Then he smiled, rubbed his hands together and added: 'What's for lunch?'

David eyed the longcase clock. 'It's only half past eleven. Georgiana won't be in yet. You'll have to wait. Jove, you had a monumental breakfast.'

Lancelot groaned. 'That was hours ago. How that girl refused food for several days beats me.' He paced to the window, staring out as if willing Georgiana's chaise to come swinging round the corner. 'I advise you to take Maria away with you. The first spark of interest I managed to get from her was when I mentioned Vienna.'

David's brows swooped down and the lines of his mouth were serious. 'I wish I'd never become involved with her. Supposing she's ill abroad? Supposing she refuses to come? Am I to drag her along by force? Georgiana'll have strong words to say on the subject.' He struck himself on the forehead with his fist as the possibilities rushed in. 'Hell and damnation! Imagine the expense if she consents! It's bad enough with my wife buying up the contents of every milliner's shop in town.'

'Harrumph!' snorted Lancelot, patience wearing thin as they waited for the extravagant Georgiana. Once launched on a spending-spree she would lose all account of time. 'Women have minds like corkscrews! Your wife will probably make Maria her bosom-friend if she suddenly develops an interest in frills and furbelows. Bless my soul, how'll you fare when you've a parcel of daughters to rear? Look here, I'll wager ten guineas that Maria will jump at the chance.'

David stabbed him an annoyed glance. 'I decided long ago not to bet with you, Lance. You always win. I wish I had your capacity for turning every situation into a joke.'

'Believe me, my friend, it isn't easy,' Lancelot said heavily, thumbs hooked in his watchchain. 'I'll admit, I find it hard to take your troubles seriously, after what I see on my daily rounds. There's *real* trouble for you – children like walking skeletons, fighting in the gutters for onion skins and bits of gristle, bones sticking out of their brittle skins, teeth rotting in their gums – infants screaming because their mothers' tits are dry – others who've been lulled with so much opium that they've entered that quiet from which there's no awakening. Life's a bad joke, David. One either laughs or cries about it, and I'm not given to tears.'

'Now will you come shopping with me?' begged Georgiana of Mariana when they met for breakfast in the Hotel Meurice on the morning after arriving in Paris.

'Yes,' Mariana replied, smiling widely.

She had wakened to the noise of traffic, seeing the sunshine pouring in at the windows of the small balcony which faced the wide, busy thoroughfare beyond. Linking her hands behind her head against the lace-frilled pillows, she had lain there in the luxurious bed, hardly able to believe her good fortune. Once they had left the shores of England, deep wells of vitality and energy had opened within her, flooding her being. What had taken place between herself and Lancelot was a nebulous, misty memory. All she knew was that she had come to herself hours later feeling that an intolerable burden had been lifted from her. There had been doubts, of course. Had she revealed too much? Would he betray her? But a further meeting with the doctor had convinced her that he was her friend, and she believed his assertion that he had told the Cunynghams nothing.

She had been cautious none the less, and although, as Lancelot had predicted, she and Georgiana had become friends, she had still refused to make public appearances, visit shops or have anything to do with the dressmakers and tradesmen who flocked to the London residence as Georgiana prepared her wardrobe for Europe. Keeping very much to herself, she had accepted a few necessary items, several plain dresses and cloaks suitable for the journey. She had been impatient, longing to leave, and at last the day had dawned when they embarked on a packet-boat at Dover, bound for Calais.

Now they had reached their first major stopping-point – Paris. After eating with Georgiana and David in their well-appointed apartment, an open carriage was ordered. Tingling with anticipation, Mariana followed Georgiana along the carpeted corridors and down a sweeping staircase to the foyer, a central, circular area which rose to the full height of the building and was lit by stained-glass windows in the great dome. The stiffly correct concierge in his bottle-green uniform greeted them politely from behind a shining mahogany desk. Everywhere there was a lively bustle as guests arrived or departed, porters humped luggage, servants organized the loading or off-loading of the vehicles drawn up outside. Elegant men and gracious women with retinues of children, nursemaids, valets and ladies' maids paraded through the lobby and were either ushered to their suites or bowed on their way.

'Where are we going?' Mariana asked Georgiana as they settled themselves in the pretty, brightly varnished coach, its hood folded back so that they might see and be seen as they bowled along the tree-bordered boulevards.

'Since you've decided to come out of your shell, my pet, I intend to make it my mission in life to turn you into a raving beauty,' chuckled a delighted Georgiana. 'Leave everything to me. This is my speciality.'

Mariana was entranced, staring in wonder at the passing scene – magnificent buildings to stun the eye, decorated with huge marble bas-reliefs depicting Napoleon's triumphs, carved with eagles and laurelled cyphers, with everywhere trees and parks and long straight busy roads lined with cafés and large imposing emporiums. Georgiana did not pause at any of these, however, ordering the coachman to turn into a small, select side-street near the Rue de Rivoli and stop outside an attractive frontage with bow-windows on either side of the white-painted door. Hanging-baskets filled with cascading flowers swung from its canopy. Tubs of tulips and syringa stood in the tiny cobbled courtyard. Just below the upper windows was a sign, its scrolled lettering proclaiming the single word *Printemps*.

As the two women opened the door and stepped inside, a bell tinkled to announce their presence. Mariana glanced round the gilded showroom which was filled with a multitude of delights. There were samples of garments on display, reduced to half size to fit the mannequins, realistic dolls who stood stiffly in arched, white-painted alcoves, surveying the customers haughtily from painted eyes. There were shelves behind a long, carved counter, holding bales of silks, satins, damask and subtle shades of velvet. Neat curtained recesses offered privacy to clients and, as at many other similar modistes', there were on offer not only clothes and ensembles but also perfume and accessories.

With a rustle of taffeta skirts and an excited little squeal, the *couturière*, Madame Polette, appeared from the back of the shop. 'Lady Georgiana! How delightful! When did you reach Paris?'

'Last night.' Georgiana was drawing off her cream kid gloves, and taking the hands of her old friend warmly. 'So, my dear, the first thing I had to do was to come and see you. You simply must show me the very latest designs, and I want you to meet Miss Malton. She needs to be provided with everything essential to a young lady journeying to the European resorts at the height of the season. Will you help us?'

'Need you ask, Lady Georgiana? *Absolument!* It will be my pleasure!' Madame Polette was a small, birdlike lady with silvery ringlets, speaking eyes and a tripping gaiety of manner. She turned to Mariana, assessing her, measuring her mentally, knowing Georgiana from way back in the past, when Madame Polette had a shop in Bond Street. Like many another aristocrat driven from France during the Revolution, she had arrived in England penniless and, a resourceful woman, had applied her knowledge of fine materials, her chic and dress-sense, to making a living with her needle. Not until the cessation of hostilities between her country and the land of her adoption had she been able to return to her native shore, wealthy again by this time and ready to set up an establishment in Paris.

Feeling awkward under that steady, speculative stare, Mariana held her head up, determined to take full advantage of this situation. Madame Polette smiled kindly. 'You have a lovely figure, Mademoiselle Malton, but that dress is far too sombre. We must choose shades that will enhance your complexion. Of course, colours are still tender rather than violent, especially for formal attire – lavender grey, pale yellow, mignonette-green, and rose – although scarlet ball-dresses are not unknown amongst the *demi-monde*.' She gave a flashing smile, arching one pencilled brow at Georgiana then glancing back at Mariana. 'Not for you, Mademoiselle. You're too fresh and innocent.'

I'm a fraud, thought Mariana guiltily, wishing that she had not come. Yet, after a few moments, she began to forget her problems as Madame Polette spread out yard after yard of striped crêpe, flock gauze, rainbow gauze, plain *barège*, silk and tulle. They perused large folders stuffed full of patterns and beautifully executed drawings, discussed cut and fit and examined the miniature replicas of ball-gowns, morning-dresses, afternoon wear and promenade garments which clothed the mannequins.

'She needs things at once!' insisted Georgiana, when they drew breath over cups of coffee and *pâtisserie* served by a pert maid.

'Don't be alarmed, Lady Georgiana,' the *couturière* soothed. 'Let me see – I've measured her for six evening gowns and we've decided on the fabric and trim. Also several for day-wear. These will be ready within the week. Underclothing has been selected, and a dozen pairs of white stockings, a further six in pink. I do suggest you take at least two pairs of flesh-coloured pantaloons for riding.'

'But there's a ball at the Embassy tonight!' wailed Georgiana. 'She has nothing suitable! What are we going to do?'

Madame Polette smiled impishly and led them into a large airy room where the *grisettes* stitched busily, chattering as their needles flashed in and out of costly cloths. Some did plain stitching, others specialized in embroidery or arranging gold threads, sequins and beads into intricate designs. A couple did the pressing, goffering pleats and ruffles, sweating over heavy, charcoal-heated irons. Each girl knew her job but, if she failed to reach Madame Polette's high standards, she did not remain in employment for long.

'Here we are. What about this gown for Mademoiselle? I think it will fit her. And I have several ready-made dresses suitable for strolling in the Bois or driving through the Tuileries. Would you like to try them for size, Mademoiselle Malton?'

Mariana retired to one of the secluded cubicles, glad to be alone for a few moments, overwhelmed by all she had seen and heard that morning, fearful that by inspecting her figure Madame Polette would guess that she had had a baby. She realized that she was ill-prepared for the startling change in the pace of life which had been thrust upon her. She looked at herself in the long mirror hanging on one wall, seeing her dull dress, her unfashionable bonnet, holding out the creation which Madame had considered correct for daylight hours.

It incorporated the latest points of high fashion, bringing home just how out-dated Agnes's clothing had been, and how dowdy the articles selected in London. Waistlines were still high, but they were slowly descending to a more natural position. Shoulders were wider, skirts gored, not draped like Greek robes – shorter too, the hems stiffened and padded, reaching no lower than the ankles. Mariana stripped to her chemise and petticoat, pulling on a somewhat daring innovation – a lilac velvet bodice with a white muslin skirt. The sleeves were puffed, and slashed with pink, in pseudo-Elizabethan style, the neck finished with a small ruff. She called in Madame to fasten the row of tiny buttons which fastened it at the back.

The modiste gave a pleased cry when she saw her. 'I knew this would be perfect for you! It is charming! Now we must find a hat to complement it.'

She swept Mariana out to show her off to Georgiana, who had been busy adding purchases of her own to the bill, knowing full well that David, with Jove-like patience, would pay up without a murmur. Next Madame produced a gown for that evening's event, promising that everything else should be ready *tout suite*. A porter was called, staggering out to the coach laden with a large ribbon-tied dress-box and further parcels, while Madame Polette waved farewell to her delighted customers. Mariana was wearing her new ensemble, and Georgiana kept exclaiming in wonder, overjoyed by the transformation, rushing her back to the hotel so that they might present this stunning image to David. It was the beginning. From the chrysalis was emerging a gorgeous butterfly.

'Oh, how I love travelling!' said Mariana as they rolled along the highway. 'I think it's perfectly wonderful! I'd like to be a gypsy and live in a wagon, continually on the move.'

Georgiana laughed across at her from the opposite seat of the big, comfortable carriage. 'What a splendid gypsy queen you'd make. I can just picture you decked in beads, hooped earrings and a shawl. My dear, why don't we have such a costume designed for you? You could wear it at the next masked ball.'

'Will Vienna be as exciting as Paris?'

'Every bit as exciting,' Georgiana assured her. She gave a little yawn behind her gloved hand. 'And every bit as exhausting. I wish I had but a quarter of your energy, Maria. I've never seen anyone so mad about waltzing. You'd dance all night, given the chance.'

It was true, and Georgiana gazed at her with pride. The change was astonishing. Both she and David had agreed that Lancelot and Paris combined had wrought a miracle, though he still refused to discuss what had transpired in the bedroom on that fateful day.

She looked radiant in the light filtering through the glazed windows of the Cunyngham coach. Georgiana felt not the slightest twinge of envy. She was proud of her protégée who was such a credit to her. A healthy flush warmed Mariana's cheeks, animation and life lit up her eyes. Her hair was dressed in ringlets beneath her new Paris bonnet, with its flaring brim and curling red feathers. She wore a costume of crimson *barège*, with puffed shoulders and slightly raised waist, its skirt finishing at the ankles with a quilted rouleau to give that highly-prized, extremely fashionable weighted appearance. It was too warm to wear a mantle. This lay, a spread of sumptuous velvet, on the empty seat beside her, along with kid gloves, a fringed reticule and a lace-edged fan.

Mariana's confidence was growing with each passing day. It was as if she had left a dank, dark prison, though it was still hard to accept that the human beings with whom she now came in contact were truly kind and sincere, not hiding devious purposes behind a mask of friendship. Europe in late spring was intoxicating. To walk in the pleasant squares, visit the shops and sit at a roadside café with the carefree abandonment of a boulevardier, was sheer bliss. Crammed into a few short days was every aspect of girlhood which had been denied her. Feverishly, she embraced each new sensation, beginning to enjoy the heady awareness that she was worthy of the admiring glances which encompassed her on every side. Georgiana cheerfully instructed her in the art of enjoying the attention she commanded when entering a ballroom. It was something to glory in and exploit to the full.

'I never dreamed you'd comport yourself so well. How could I have done, when you were as close as a clam, my love?' Georgiana remarked, gently probing. No matter how intimate they had become, Mariana had not divulged anything concerning herself. 'For one thing, you speak French like a native – such a surprise.'

A guarded look crept over Maria's face. 'My mother taught me.'

'She must be a clever lady,' Georgiana went on. 'You play the pianoforte with professional skill worthy of the concert platform, were it not *infra dignitatem* for the aristocracy to appear on the stage, and your mastery of the French tongue's above reproach, yet you don't mention her. Why is this?'

'She's dead.' Mariana shut Georgiana out curtly. It was the only way she could protect herself. Many a time she had longed to confide in this gay, open-hearted woman, particularly in Paris where, despite the excitement, every step of the way had been overshadowed by her mother's gentle shade. Had she been a Parisienne? Mariana had found herself wondering. Had she too gone to some *fête champêtre* or strolled in the gardens of Versailles with her lover – the man who had fathered Mariana? She felt in her marrow that he had been a Frenchman but had no way of knowing for sure. The Duchesse de Labisse had given no hint, deliberately keeping from her any information about the daughter she had despised.

Aware that she had touched a sensitive spot, Georgiana turned the conversation, gossiping of the notables they had met in Munich and Salzburg en route. They had chosen the best time for such a lengthy trek. France had been bedecked for spring, recovering from the war, with the Bourbon régime gaining ascendancy. They had been on the road for a fortnight since leaving Paris, treated with all the formal deference due to a cavalcade of vehicles containing servants and luggage, led by the huge black carriage with coroneted panels embellished with gilt, guarded by armed out-riders. Mariana was charmed by the grey towns with steep roofs and towers like candle-snuffers, scattered throughout the fertile valleys. Sometimes they drove alongside blue lakes in the hollows of wooded hills where orchards drowsed on the outskirts of hamlets, and solitary fairytale castles commanded the heights.

Horses had to be frequently changed, and there was a well-organized network of posting-houses, where weary travellers could pass the night. These inns were picturesque, with painted flower-friezes and hand-carved pillars to support overhanging roofs. David, that experienced tourist, explained that the pitch of these tiles was a necessary precaution against the heavy snowfalls of the dreadfully cold winters.

He did not ride in the coach, insisting on taking horse with Edwin who fancied himself on a high-spirited prancer. Lancelot, however, had declared that he was not a spartan. Mock him though they might, he was travelling in the comfort of the carriage, with the ladies. 'After all, you talked me into coming on this damn-fool trip,' he had grumbled at the onset, 'so I'll please myself how I go.'

David and he had had a conflab before leaving London. Listening to him, Lancelot had agreed that maybe he was right and Radu's message contained more than appeared on the surface. To clinch the deal, David had offered to donate a substantial sum to aid Lancelot's plans for an orphanage. So the doctor had left both clinic and wealthy clientele in the care of his two young, enthusiastic assitants, and ordered Fred to prepare himself and pack the old, worn leather valises. Much of his time in the foreign cities had been spent in backstreets given up to dusty book-shops, where he had pored over volumes and pocketed rare editions, after the obligatory haggling.

He appeared to while away the journey in sleep, propped in a corner of the vehicle, a handkerchief spread over his face, but this was a ruse by which he avoided being drawn into idle chatter. Also, it gave him the chance to observe Mariana, while he mused on what he had learned about her whilst practising the teachings of Mesmer. He had noted the improvement, but also sensed something disturbing. There was a hectic determination in her gaiety. She was plunging into life full-tilt, yet sometimes, when she thought no one was watching, her face held a lingering sadness, her thoughts a million miles away, dwelling in dark, forbidden places of the mind.

They paused at an inn for lunch, eating Austrian goulash, and salad tossed in oil, seated at little round tables in the garden. The maid, flaxen hair strained back from her forehead

208

and a spotless apron girding her waist, brought them bottles of Riesling, and set pale green twisted glasses on the red and white checked cloth. Mariana picked up hers and the sun seemed to be imprisoned in the yellow wine. The inn was situated on high ground, above the clustered pastel-washed houses which formed the nucleus of the hamlet. Against the azure sky, small transparent cumulus clouds were poised over the mountains. The air was pure and pink. The bud-laden branches of the apple trees stirred overhead. It was so peaceful, and she blanketed her mind against those thoughts which always hovered, striving to get in.

'You should address the serving-wench, Maria. Order coffee for us. Doubtless your German will prove as fluent as your French.' A sarcastic voice broke across her reverie. Edwin was staring at her, a spiteful smile twisting his lips.

He had never forgiven her for getting him into trouble with David. Thwarted desire and the blow to both body and self-esteem had gone sour within him. He never lost an opportunity to goad her. In the towns where they had stayed, he had hinted to the rakes whom he always succeeded in finding, be they French, English or German, that she was a woman of loose morals.

Lancelot came to her rescue. 'I'd prefer a large glass of schnapps, myself,' he said, his eyes challenging Edwin, till he was forced to drop his gaze.

Mariana was annoyed because she allowed Edwin to rile her. 'I'm afraid I've not yet mastered that language,' she answered quietly.

'Really? How astonishing.' He flicked her a disdainful glance. 'I was under the impression that you could do anything. I've found the constant recitation of your virtues most monstrously boring.'

'You unpleasant little cannibal!' flared Georgiana, covering Mariana's hand with hers and smiling at her. 'Don't take any notice of him. He's jealous because you're prettier than he. Thank heaven he's not sharing the coach, that's all I can say!'

It was afternoon before the increasing traffic indicated that they were approaching Vienna. The road became wider, edged with linden trees, and large houses could be glimpsed behind shrubs and walls, set back in lovely gardens. Vehicles bowled along the highway, dashing calashes, heavy berliners, beautiful equipages harnessed in the full glory of the lorimer's art, with postillions in brilliant liveries. Overtaking these slower conveyances trotted exceedingly smartly turned-out young men in highflyer phaetons. Several gaudily uniformed dragoons, straight-backed and high-nosed, pranced by on grey horses.

Georgiana had her face pressed to the window. 'Oh, just look at those officers! Did you ever see anything so fine? How handsome! How bold! That one with the pigtails and dark moustache is making eyes at me! The wicked creature! It makes me glad that I'm a respectable married lady or I might be sorely tempted to encourage him.'

'Pish!' grunted Lancelot from his corner. 'Toy soldiers who've never seen action. Parvenu officers whose only military occupation is designing their own uniforms!'

'Lance, you tetchy old bear,' she laughed back at him. 'What d'you know about it?'

'Ha!' he barked, giving her a hard stare between hat brim and handkerchief. 'I've served in army hospitals, trying to put right the damage done to human flesh by your so-called paladins. You'd not be so impressed by their swagger if you'd seen gaping wounds and inhaled the rotting stink of gangrene.'

Georgiana gave a toss of her head, and turned back to admire the passing scene. At last the carriage swung round a final bend and they saw Vienna lying in a jumble of roofs, spires, gardens and parks below them. It shone in the sunshine with dramatic unreality, in purple shadows and golden glow, a legendary city.

The palace of their host, Baron Carl von Gundling, was situated in the most select residential area. The cortège rumbled between giant gates and crunched over a curved gravel drive to the main entrance. Great steps led up to a huge double door, beneath an arch upheld by Ionic pillars. The alighting party were dwarfed by its baroque grandeur. The splendid façade was richly swagged with wreaths, acorns and cartouches. Statues stood like Titans between tall, balconied windows. Footmen in mulberry jackets, satin breeches and white wigs, came in solemn procession to take the luggage. An army of grooms led the carriages and horses away. Baroness Hildegarde von Gundling ran down the steps, hands outstretched to greet her guests.

'David, my dear David – and Georgiana too! Welcome to my house!' she cried. Her command of English was good. She had been a Lady of the Bedchamber to Princess Caroline of Brunswick, the estranged wife of the Prince Regent, and had spent time in London.

Mariana was presented to her, and Lancelot bowed over her hand with rusty gallantry, then she kissed Edwin impulsively on both cheeks, chattering the while. She swept them into the house, eager to hear every detail of the journey, promising that their stay in Vienna would overflow with joyous occasions.

Everything within was on an equally gigantic scale. Huge reception rooms, monumental staircases, galleries of enormous height and width, the architecture of that style beloved of the Empress Maria Theresa in the eighteenth century, when so much of Vienna had been rebuilt. Having ensured that Edwin, Lancelot and their valets were escorted to their rooms, Hildegarde accompanied David and Georgiana to the apartment which she had prepared for them, saying, her arm around Mariana's waist:

'And you, my dear, shall be placed in a chamber not too far away from them, so that you won't feel lonely. David tells me that you're his ward. He's such a sweet man.'

She snapped her fingers at a footman who leapt to attention, thrusting open the doors at which they had paused. They were led by her into the drawing-room of this guest-suite. Gilt ornamented every piece of furniture. The fabrics were of embossed damask, the carpets woven in France, the statues imported from Greece, the paintings, representing scenes from Venice, hung in florid goldleaf frames.

'I trust you'll be comfortable.' Hildegarde rushed to the glass doors which gave access to the balcony. 'There's a fine view of the gardens.' She dimpled at David. 'You had slightly less grand quarters in the army days, when Carl used to bring you here on leave, but now you're a married man, and your wife must enjoy every convenience. Is this not so, Georgiana?'

Georgiana, for once, had hardly been able to get in a word edgeways. Their hostess was a woman of strong character and considerable determination. When she decided that something should happen, it usually did. She was of sound country stock, though as well-born as anyone could desire, and showed an unnerving interest in domestic arrangements, laughingly referring to herself as 'Frau Gundling'. Yet she kept abreast of current vogues, an apple-cheeked matron, glowing with health, patting her stomach and telling them frankly that she was pregnant with her sixth child. She had a firm mouth, melting brown eyes, blonde hair and a rounded figure of which she was fully conscious. There was nothing negative about Hildegarde.

When David had excused himself, wandering off to find Lancelot, she swung round to Georgiana and Mariana. 'Now we can have a cosy chat. Tell me the latest London scandals. Have you visited Brighton this year? What has that villain, Prinny, been up to? I'm dying to know. Is he as promiscuous as ever? God, he led my poor Princess Caroline a dance! And you, Maria? Goodness, such beauty! You'll set every young guardsman in Vienna by the ears. I'll be mortally offended if you're not betrothed to royalty by the time you leave.'

Georgiana removed her hat, swinging it by the ribbons before tossing it to a chair and herself on the day-bed, happy to oblige Hildegarde. She had the gossip of the English palaces, clubs and dance-rooms at her fingertips, and the knack of imparting it so that it lost nothing in the telling. Hildegarde's eyes grew round as she listened, lips open in shocked delight. At length, reaching saturation point, she recalled her duty and rang a bell. A footman appeared and she ordered tea to be served. Whilst they waited, Georgiana asked: 'And how is Baron Carl?'

Hildegarde raised her eyes and hands towards the naked cherubs who sported with bosomy goddesses on the painted ceiling. '*Liebling*, he's so changeable, that one, just like an English barometer. I think he's only happy when absenting himself on army courses, back with the regiment again. He comes home noisy, boisterous and given to vulgar jokes. In my opinion men enjoy the company of their fellows – they only need us for bed. Even there, I'm not convinced that they wouldn't find greater satisfaction with these oh-so jolly comrades.'

'Some of them do, don't they?' Georgiana smiled, playing with the fringes of her long gauze scarf.

'*Ach, ja!* To be sure.' Hildegarde was matter-of-factly pouring tea from a gilt pot into flowered porcelain cups. Her bright eyes went to Mariana who had hardly said anything since arrival. 'And you, sweetheart? You find men charming and fascinating, I expect.'

If you only knew! thought Mariana, but aloud she made a noncommittal answer, lowering her gaze to her cup. The Baroness was overpowering, and she needed to be alone to assimilate the impressions crowding in, but first they must visit the nursery. Hildegarde was insistent, bustling them off to the south wing, where the tiny scions of the House of von Gundling were cosseted by an army of attendants.

Vienna had been the seat of the Habsburg dynasty for decades, a centre for art and architecture, music and culture. Lawyers seeking employment, writers attracted by a big city, musicians seeking patrons, businessmen interested in governmental incentives, had come from everywhere to reside in its precincts. Its banks were the richest in the world.

David mulled this over as he took a stroll through its squares that evening. The Danube drank in the gold of sunset, church spires stabbed a red sky, the spaces between pine and linden glowed with colour like cathedral windows. He knew his way around, having visited it several times already, particularly during the Congress. What a circus that had been, he thought. While the Heads of State had struggled to sort out the turmoil of war-torn Europe, Vienna had become a huge market-place teeming with soldiers and merchants, princes and knaves, great ladies and harlots, all scheming, spending and dancing.

Yet even as the Viennese had feasted and celebrated, back in 1815, so Napoleon had been laying his plans. David had been present at the ball when the news of his escape from prison had dropped like a bombshell. He remembered the consernation and the final great battle, fought at Waterloo, when the wily, brilliant little Corsican had been finally defeated by Wellington.

Evening was falling, the air heavy with the scent of flowers. The shopkeepers were putting up their shutters, the theatres, concert-halls and salons were opening. Music drifted over the plazas from brightly lit buildings – the lilt of the waltz. David smiled as he walked, swinging his cane to the rhythm. Ah, the waltz! He hummed the tune under his breath, trying to recall what that sardonic, low-moraled fellow, Byron, had said about this craze: 'The waltz is the only dance which teaches girls to think!'

He passed the Lindenallee in the Augarten, a tree-shaded park where restaurants served food and drink in the open air. This was not his destination. He found instead a café in an alley off the Neue Markt, a shabby place with bare tables and wooden benches. The floor was strewn with sand. In one corner stood a great brick stove, and several men were sitting near it, smoking pipes and talking loudly. He glanced around, then took a stool at a table between stove and door. He ordered beer which was promptly brought by a buxom girl who flashed him a smile that must have been a trade asset.

Two men were shuffling cards at the next table. One was stout, dark-complexioned, the other small and ferret-faced, flashily dressed. He had sly black eyes that met David's as he played. After a few moments, he paused to stuff tobacco into the bowl of his pipe, then he rose and came across to light it at the candle near David's stein.

'Mr Clark?' he asked, keeping his voice low as he puffed.

David nodded, eyes keen over the pointed flame, not surprised to be addressed by this name he sometimes assumed. 'That's correct.'

'I'm Gautier,' the man replied and took a seat beside him.

'I was expecting you.' David was curt, instinctively distrusting him. An oily individual, typical spy material, so his army training warned. A note, slipped by one of the von Gundling footmen and supposedly signed by Radu, had told him of this assignation, but David could not fathom the reason. Looking round at the grubby hostelry and its seedy occupants, he regretted not bringing Lancelot. The place reeked of treachery.

'Good – very good.' Gautier was rubbing his hands together, eyes glinting at him. 'No one followed you, sir?'

'Not that I'm aware.' David was speaking in French, doubting that Gautier would have mastered English. His fist was clenched on the dirty boards. A hard fist. Gautier glanced at it. David's eyes were equally hard as he added: 'You have something for me?'

His tone was contemptuous and Gautier did not like it. He prided himself on his skills and this arrogant Englishman was addressing him as a menial. 'I understood that you'd pay me first,' he said. He had received his commission but was wondering if it would be possible to wangle a further sum.

David called his bluff: 'I was told that you'd already been paid.' He was enjoying this. Too long restrained by dull business enterprises, he found it brought back a whiff of the adventures he had known in the war. Testing men was challenging, pitting his wits against double agents much more exhilarating than the stock-market.

Gautier changed direction. He gave a philosophic shrug. 'You're no fool,' he admitted grudgingly. 'I was merely trying you out. One can't be too careful.'

'Too true,' David agreed meaningfully. His hands were resting on the knob of his cane. It was not simply a fashion accoutrement. He never ventured far without his sword-stick. 'Give me the message.'

Gautier leaned closer, bringing with him a strong wave of garlic. 'A certain party – we both know his name – is having trouble with an ambitious relative.' The black eyes darted from side to side, but the other patrons were engrossed in cards, in arguing, in excursions into heavy gallantry with the serving-girl. She was giving sharp retorts which convulsed them with glee.

'I see.' David touched the cane thoughtfully to his chin. His mind drifted back – he was in a tent close to the Belgian battlefield during that last, bloody struggle with Napoleon. They were awaiting Wellington's orders and Radu, uniform torn and blackened by gun-powder, had eased off his crested helmet, wiping the sweat from his grimy face, grey eyes steely as he had said to David: 'My God, I pray that such strife never again comes to Montezena.'

'Why should it, once this is settled?' David had asked, bone-weary yet knowing that he must up-saddle before long, forcing his aching right arm to wield a sabre once more.

'I've a half-brother, Baron Grigore Petresco.' The Prince's face had been like carved granite in the flickering lamp-light. 'When my father dies, he'll do his damnedest to oust me from my rightful place.'

The letter which had been delivered to David in London had been little more than a request that they should meet in Vienna but, putting two and two together, he guessed that the anticipated crisis was at hand.

Gautier settled back and, flicking his fingers at the giggling maid, ordered another mug of beer. He was decidedly restless, and kept glancing towards the door. Catching David watching him, he tried a confidential grin, saying: 'There's something further, Mr Clark. This person will be at the ball which the von Gundlings are holding tomorrow night.'

David was about to question him when the door swung violently inwards and several soldiers swaggered over the threshold. Their leader was a short man with a bronzed face beneath his shako, cold eyes, and a heavy moustache brushed back over irregular white teeth. He paused for a second, leering around with the air of a man who has already visited two or three beer-cellars. He stumped across the room to the stove, his companions following, rattling their swords. As he passed the table where David and Gautier sat, he lurched against it. Ale slopped on the boards.

David looked up sharply, for this was more a deliberate stagger than a drunken one. 'If you can't take your liquor, you should leave it alone,' he barked in German, slipping back easily into the role of an officer reprimanding a ranker.

A titter went round the room. The other customers pricked up their ears and turned in their seats to watch. The soldier glared belligerently. 'D'you want the whole bloody café to yourself? You sound like an English swine to me! Bah! Vienna stinks of goddamn foreigners! Son-of-a-bitch! Why don't you stay on your rat-infested island, and leave Austria to us Austrians? Who the hell d'you think you are? Sitting there as if you own the bloody place!'

'Ignore him, sir,' whispered Gautier, anxious to keep in with everybody. 'He's one of Petresco's men.'

David cursed himself for falling into an ambush. Under

orders to provoke him, the soldier leaned across and knocked his hat off. David was on his feet in one bound and flung himself on the man, giving him no time to draw his sword. Everyone leapt to their feet. The maid screamed up the stairs for the proprietor. David closed a hand on the soldier's thick red neck, and with the other forced his sword-arm behind his back. Twisting him round, he frog-marched him through the room. The soldier clutched at a table. It fell with a crash of breaking glass. A pool of beer flowed in a brown stream then soaked into the sawdust. Boots ploughed it into mud.

'Gentlemen! Gentlemen!' The café-owner puffed his way into the mêlée, aghast at the damage.

David ignored him, forcing the soldier down until his face was almost against the floor. He was a hefty man, but he struggled in vain. 'I'll break your bloody arm if you don't take back your words! I swear it!' David snarled through clenched teeth.

'I won't!' gasped the soldier. 'English bastard!' His arm creaked in its socket and he groaned. David exerted more pressure. The soldier yelled. David's knee was boring into his kidneys. He was being smothered by sawdust and beer slicks. 'All right!' he shouted in agony. 'I apologize, damn you!' David dragged him up and slammed him against the wall, where he sagged, breath and brag knocked out of him.

'Well done, milord,' drawled a voice from the doorway. 'You've beaten him fair and square. Schoene, you're a dolt – a mutton-headed idiot! Thick as two short planks! I suggest you take a leaf out of the Englishman's book. Remove yourself to a gymnasium and practise the art of fisticuffs.'

The owner of this laughing, languid voice was an exceedingly debonair young man, dressed in the last extreme of fashion. He strolled in, and David did a double-take when he saw Edwin bringing up the rear. The host was bowing, explaining, making excuses for the shambles. The dandy brushed him aside, continuing his progress, though stepping with great care lest his highly polished black boots should be smeared. David, watching him come on but alert for renewed attack from Schoene, stood flexing his hands and judging the distance between himself and his cane, propped against the table-leg. He did not want to shed blood at this juncture, but was quite prepared to do so if necessary.

The exquisite reached him and regarded him with eyes of an unholy blue beneath long, straight sandy lashes. He bowed deeply. 'Let me introduce myself,' he said in near-perfect English. 'Count Dimitrie Baranga, at your service. I'm Prince

216

Radu's cousin.' He nodded towards the spluttering Schoene who had not moved since his sudden entrance, staring at him from a bloodied face with the expression of a whipped cur awaiting his master's orders. 'If you have any more trouble with this misbegotten spawn of a crippled camel, let me know.'

Mariana ran down the long corridors and past the ranks of footmen, heedless of their raised eyebrows. She reached ground level, went out through a side door, and did not stop until some distance away from the grandeur of the von Gundling palace. Only then did she feel able to breathe.

The gardens were wide-spread, a symmetrical design of green lawns, pleached alleys, sundials and topiary. The light was azure on the silvery expanse of a lake; scarlet canna lilies glowed like fire, reflecting the dying sun, their foliage blue-green, their scent cloying – a scene in no way horrible, yet to her it was an image of terror and sadness. Groundsmen were walking homewards, tools over their shoulders, and she turned from them, taking a random path, screened by high walls swarming with wisteria, coming at last to a quiet spot, away from prying eyes.

The flowers grew wilder there, and the aroma of herbs was poignantly reminiscent of the garden at Thornfalcon. In the centre of a paved area, a fountain cascaded over a plump Venus supported by dolphins with knotted tails. Birds were wheeling above the lime trees before settling to roost. Water splashed into the marble basin. Mariana sank down on its rim, buried her face in her hands, and surrendered to her grief.

The tears trickled between her fingers, and sobs racked her – deep, hoarse sobs, dragged from the depths of her soul. She had been so certain she had gained control. Since arriving in Europe it had been much easier to keep memories at bay. She had filled her days with frenzied activity, even when travelling, shortening the nights by staying up late, throwing herself into every entertainment offered. As luck would have it, her peace of mind had been secure in the other great houses which had fêted them. Either the couples playing host were childless or had kept their offspring in the background. Not so Hildegarde von Gundling. There had been no way in which Mariana could avoid inspecting her brood.

I should never have gone to the nursery, she thought despairingly – better to have feigned illness, fainted – anything! She had not been spared. Fate had deliberately contrived to make her drink the bitter cup to the dregs. The sunny, toy-cluttered rooms set aside for the young von Gundlings had become more cruel than a torture-chamber. Two head-nurses had been present and a gaggle of nursery-maids, each crisply starched and uniformed, smiles wreathing their round, Germanic countenances. Hildegarde had proudly introduced the heir, Frederick, a plump seven-year-old, and his two sisters, fair and blue-eyed. A toddler sat in a high-chair, dimpled fists clenched round a silver and ivory teething-ring. This had been torment enough, but then Hildegarde, on tiptoe and whispering, had led them across to the net-draped rocking-cradle, face as radiant as a Raphael Madonna as she peeped in at her youngest.

Mariana's heart had seemed to stop, then race on madly. Unwilling but fascinated, her eyes had been drawn to the sleeping infant. Happy, welcomed child, lying amidst satin and lace, its breathing gentle, silky lashes making semi-circular fans on the pink, healthy cheeks, thumb tucked in its rosy, baby mouth.

'Oh, how perfectly divine,' Georgiana had cooed, while the other women murmured, smiling beatifically into the cot.

'Another son,' Hildegarde had announced merrily, her hands resting on her rounded stomach. 'And this little "Hans-in-the-cellar" will be a daughter, I hope.'

Mariana had stood transfixed for a second, then with some mumbled excuse, had fled as if the hounds of hell were after her. Perhaps they were. She fancied she heard them baying triumphantly. That baby. Dear God, she did not know how she had stopped from snatching it up and straining it to the raw wound within her.

'My dear girl, what's wrong?'

The deep, kindly masculine voice made her start up, poised to run again. Lancelot stood under the rose arch, a concerned frown sobering his face. Caught out, unable to think of a nimble lie, Mariana hung her head and turned away. He was dangerous – too gentle, too understanding. She fought to recall just how much she had told him, but couldn't. If she wasn't very careful he could be her undoing. She gulped and shook her head, drooping at the fountain's edge, the long shadows of evening engulfing the bower, one or two scarlet fingers picking out fiery tints in her hair. Her hands were nervously plucking at a fold of her skirt.

The sight of those distressed, restless hands went through Lancelot like a knife. Life was incomprehensible, a sick joke devised by some grotesque prankster. The innocent suffered while the wicked prospered. Recollections twisted in his brain, and there was guilt too, squeezing his heart. But why? He had done nothing to harm the woman he had adored so many years ago. He stood there, ferreting back half-forgotten things. He saw, not Mariana and the dusky garden, but the pale face and sorrowful eyes of one he had loved and planned to marry. She had kissed him in an arbour, very like this one, when romance and dreams were possible. He could never smell roses without feeling rather sick. In the heavy, perfumed atmosphere of summer roses, his beloved had told him what he already suspected. She was dying. Consumption had burned out her young life. Lancelot, a student then, had watched her waste and fade – held her through the terrible paroxysms of coughing which had left her sweat-drenched – seen the red blood frothing from her lips – been with her when she died in agony.

Most people thought him a sarcastic old bachelor. None knew that he still made a monthly pilgrimage to her grave in a quiet corner of Highgate Cemetery, to stand, head bowed amidst the hush of loss and forlorn stone angels, seeing her frail hands, so like Mariana's, plucking at the quilt which covered her deathbed – searching hands seeking an anchor-sheet, one which he had been unable to give her.

Without hesitation, he sat beside Mariana and took her hands in his strong, capable ones, steadying her. 'You can't go on running, my dear. You should return to England and face your past.'

'I can't.' Her breath caught on a sob, face still averted.

'It would be for the best,' he counselled gently. 'If you don't, you'll always remember and suffer the torments of the damned.'

A shuddering sigh escaped her. Again that denial, that unspoken dread to which he was now party. 'Please don't make me – not yet,' she whispered, almost pleaded, dark lashes matted with tears. 'You won't tell David or Georgiana, will you? They think I'm happy.'

He stared into her eyes, refusing to release her hands. 'They may, but I know different. Emotions can't get through closed doors, child. It would help if you'd talk to me about it again, in the full light of consciousness. Perhaps I could aid you in practical matters concerning your tragedy. I fear for you. You may do something foolish. Supposing you were to fall in love. What then?'

Words trembled on her lips. She wanted so much to confide in this large, untidy, lovesome man. Just for a second, he thought he had won her over. He felt her leaning towards him, losing her rigidity. In her eyes, in the parted mouth, he read her yearning to truly free herself. Then she took fright, sharply pulling away her hands, her body, her mind. She rose, brushed back the hair from her face and held herself upright, dignified in her anguish, unwilling to share it.

'I must go.' She was calmer now, veiling her emotions. 'It's time to change for dinner. Please excuse me.'

The delicate moment had slipped away and he sighed. 'So be it, but remember that I'm here if you need me.' He gave her a lop-sided grin and heaved to his feet. 'I'll stroll back with you. The charade must go on.' He offered her his arm and, as they walked, he continued to talk, attempting to coax a smile from her. 'Tonight your introduction to Viennese society will be at a small dinner-party given by the Baron and his lady. I say small – probably no more than two dozen people! No doubt, we'll hear all about the genius of their children. Give me a nudge if I happen to nod off!'

CHAPTER 5

'You must tell your brother that it isn't wise to brawl in backstreet beer-houses,' advised Dimitrie as he hailed a hiring carriage outside the café.

'Unusual for him to do so.' Edwin was puzzled by David's behaviour. 'Can't understand what he was doing there, rot me if I can. I thought he'd be with the von Gundlings this evening.'

'Out for a constitutional, perhaps?' murmured the Count as they climbed into the vehicle and he gave the driver an address. 'He's a devoted husband, the good milord? Had I not thought him to be, I'd have asked him to accompany us.'

'Where are you taking me?' The skies were lit by a myriad stars, the scent of flowers as heady as the wine Edwin had already consumed.

'Wait and see,' chuckled Dimitrie, settling back against the brown leather and crossing one slim leg over the other.

Edwin asked no further, congratulating himself on falling in with such an agreeable companion almost as soon as he set foot in Vienna. He had been rather wondering how he was going to endure the domesticated scene with the Baron and Baroness. That pompous medic, Lancelot, would have scorned seeking out the low-life. David was far too wrapped up in his wife and, in any case, he felt distinctly uncomfortable in his brother's presence. That left only Maria, and there was such bad blood between them that she did not count. Edwin had succeeded in finding convivial company in Paris, and Munich and Salzburg had not been without adventure, but he knew no one in Vienna.

He had taken a walk earlier and come across Dimitrie in the first gambling-house he entered. They had taken to one another at once, or so it seemed to Edwin. Dimitrie had announced his intention of showing him the town. Edwin was dazzled by the Count's charm and panache, his air of knowing his way around. He had just that touch of bored, ironic wit so essential in a dandy, was well-travelled and, moreover, appeared to have an inexhaustible fund of money, judging by

221

the casual manner in which he risked it at the card-tables.

Vienna by night was almost as busy as in daylight. Its street-lamps glowed on the idle pleasure-seekers. The broad promenades were thronged with people, sauntering about, sitting at cafés, or entering the entertainment centres. Anticipation coursed through Edwin. He forgot the questioning glance which David had given him in the beer-house. No doubt he was in for another lecture in the morning, but to hell with that.

The driver weaved the carriage skilfully through the traffic and presently drew up before a stylish mansion. 'We're about to enter Paradise,' said Dimitrie as he paid the fare. 'I'll wager you've seen nothing like it in London or even Paris. You're in for a pleasant surprise, my friend.'

They went up a flight of stone steps, were greeted at the door by a dignified major-domo, and entered a well-lit, spacious hall, brightened by a mass of flowers which perfumed the air. A beautiful woman with a statuesque figure swept down on them.

'Ah, my dear Count, how good to see you back in Vienna!' she exclaimed, enveloping him in a warm embrace. She turned lustrous, heavily-painted eyes to Edwin. 'You've brought a companion with you? How splendid!'

Dimitrie slipped an arm about her waist, smiling into her rouged face. 'An Englishman, Madame Feodora. His first visit to your lovely, wicked city.'

'I like Englishmen,' she gushed, carmined lips smiling as she took Edwin's hand. 'My ladies like them too, especially very young Englishmen. They'll be overjoyed.'

She was wearing dove-grey silk of so fine a weight that her limbs were clearly defined beneath the gown. She had an abundance of dark red hair enticingly curled but disordered, to suggest that she had just risen from bed. It fell loosely over her broad, bare shoulders. The whiteness of her skin contrasted with her vivid, bold colouring. Her strong arms were naked too, and her bodice was cut very low, displaying superb breasts. Edwin could not keep his eyes off them. If there was one thing on earth he worshipped, it was breasts: small ones, opulent ones, breasts neat and pert or swinging like ripe melons – he didn't care. Madame Feodora's body may have been substantial but it looked amorously flexible, with those shoulders and limbs suggestive of a Greek goddess. Her combination of energy and grace promised fierce delights.

As she moved closer to him under the glittering lamps, he could see that she was older than at first sight. A mature woman, probably in her late thirties. This did not deter him

222

one jot. He liked older women, enjoyed having them dominate him. Several of his mistresses had been old enough to have been his mother. This added a faintly incestuous element which was exciting. The first woman to arouse him sexually had been his nurse, a big woman too, who had enjoyed handling his childish body when she bathed him. Often, when he reached adulthood and began to take women, he would pretend that he was having intercourse with his middle-aged nurse. Now, standing in the hallway of Madame Feodora's brothel, desire was spoiling the cut of his tight pantaloons. Before he could turn away, she glanced down. There was something terrifying in her eyes and in her smile, a predatory look which roused him almost beyond control. When she spoke, her words made him delirious with delight.

'What a randy lad, to be sure! My girls will adore you!'

She held his arm in her broad, soft fingers and led him into a salon, bright with gilt, red plush drapes, and a thick crimson carpet. The walls were hung with yellow silk, the ornate chandeliers bringing out the full glory of the erotic paintings and bronze statues, the rich shades of the furnishings. Dimitrie and Edwin were not the only clients. Several gentlemen reclined on couches, drinking wine and enjoying the bevy of beauties who sat with them or strolled about, the better to show off their charms. They wound silky arms round their necks, whispered in their ears or conducted them up the broad staircase. There was much to whet the most jaded appetite in Feodora's exotic garden, rare blooms from every nation, smiling, willing and welcoming. The setting was decidedly oriental. Flutes wailed sensuously in the background, hookahs stood on low tables with their burnished bowls and long snaky tubes, smoke rising dreamily from the hashish smouldering in their brass burners. The rose-water within them bubbled like little kettles as the drugged fumes were drawn into appreciative lungs.

Wearing racy underclothing or diaphanous scarves, the women were like sirens, with ardent eyes and pouting lips ripe for kissing. Edwin's heart beat like a drum at the sight of their tossing heads and provocative postures. Jewels encircled slender necks, gossamer drapes floated like clouds. Some wore hats, cocked at a saucy angle; some were costumed as demure school-girls in plain white, high-buttoned frocks; a couple paraded in nuns' robes, complete with wimples. There were aristocratic women with haughty stares, and plump, lazy ones with a certain earthy coarseness. Several black women, holding their heads high with challenging dignity, wore leather loincloths and carried whips, while almond-eyed Chinese pattered daintily about. A Persian was swaying in time to the music, dropping a scarf every so often, till she was naked. Her nipples were gilded. Every hair had been plucked from her body, and the palms of her hands, her feet and pubis were traced with henna patterns. The audience howled their appreciation.

'Better than the cafés – more stimulating than the faro-tables, what?' Dimitrie shouted, from his place on a divan where he lay in the arms of a smouldering Italian and a tiny geisha. The Italian had unfastened the front flap of his trousers, hand inside. 'Choose yourself a couple of priestesses from Feodora's Temple of Joy. Have no fear. The doctor inspects them regularly. Any found to have the pox are slung out into the street.'

'Why not me, love?' murmured a substantial bleached blonde, her tongue working gently round the rim of Edwin's ear. She pressed heavily against him, breasts bulging over the top of her fancy corset, eyes veiled, her low, surprisingly London accent holding a very marketable imitation of raging desire. He thought of his nurse, seeing the faint shadow of down on her upper lip. Yes, she would do.

He glanced over at a girl seated on a satin cushion at floor level, a sloe-eyed Arabian whore, smoking a hookah. 'Her too,' he commanded, feeling suddenly omnipotent.

'Ooh, fancy two at once, do you?' The blonde's china-blue eyes widened in admiration. 'What a stallion! Come along, Yasmin.' Aside she added to the dusky wench: 'Let's do him quick and get it over with. It's been a sod of a day and I want an early night.'

Yasmin took the amber mouthpiece from between moist red lips, handing it to Edwin. The sweet, cool blue smoke carried him to euphoria. The scene became unreal, hazy. He found himself transported to a large room, decorated with grilles and latticework, like a mosque. It seemed that he was looking at a golden sphere, wondering if it was the sun and what it was doing there, then he knew it to be a circle of yellow light coming from a great crystal lamp hanging on chains from the cupola. Red and silver glass sent forth stabbing rainbow points of colour, hurting his eyes. He was floating over a carpet, perhaps travelling on it. It glowed in browns and reds, with a dazzling border of pale turquoise, gliding towards a large bath of pale green marble veined in white, sunken and square. Water gushed from a fountain – it sounded like thunder – falling incredibly slowly. He saw each scintillating droplet before it hit the water.

Women sported in the scented warmth, laughing, chattering. Deft fingers removed his clothing. The water parted, then its rich velvet folded over his skin. The blonde was even bigger when naked. Her hands were soapy. She was rubbing them all over him. Yasmin perched on the tiled edge of the bath. Is it a bath? He wondered dreamily. Or is it a lake? It seems to go on for ever, but how did they get a lake in here? He took the hookah from her. Even his name was slipping away. He was drifting somewhere on a bejewelled raft on the gentle swell of a fabulous sea. Dimitrie appeared out of the clouds. Perhaps he was a god. He looked like a god, robes flowing around him – a *caftan* of purple silk, gold flashing at the neck, sleeves going on endlessly, merging with the water. It was open all the way, displaying his erection. He was laughing down at Edwin, a striped *kaffiyeh* covering his hair, a braided *agal* round his forehead.

'Tonight I'm a Bedouin chief,' he cried, his voice echoing loudly, eyes glittering like stars spangling the cupola which was now milkily transparent, 'and these are my concubines. Share my harem.'

Edwin was lying on the silken cushions of a vast divan. Silver drapes formed a canopy and clouded the walls. The fantastic rising and falling ocean became a sea of sinuous limbs, curtains of perfumed hair, of breasts and arms, mouths and loins. Dimitrie was there and, in mindless ecstasy, Edwin was lifted high to the peaks of exquisite sensation, unable to know or care what was being done to him or by whom. Male – female – it didn't matter. Pleasure, sublime and prolonged, was his only goal.

Edwin found his way to Dimitrie's hotel when the morning was already advanced. He had awakened in his room at the von Gundling palace. He could not remember how he got there. His head ached as if he had been pole-axed. His valet, cool and bland of face, had not enlightened him much, merely saying imperturbably: 'You were brought home in a cabriolet, sir. At dawn, sir.'

The concierge at the hotel's entrance directed him to the Count's suite, and he found him already up, looking so fresh and wholesome that Edwin began to fancy that he had dreamed the unorthodox happenings of the night before. Everything about him was spruce. His high-collared violet coat fitted without flaw, his stock looked as if it had been untouched by human hand, the black satin fobs that swung from his waistcoat pockets were of precise length, the polish of his boots was like glass, and his breeches were a second skin.

He was propped elegantly, indifferently, against the balcony rail outside the window, amusing himself by watching the women pass below and ogling the girls serving in the shops opposite, for his hotel fronted the Marktplatz. 'Good morning, Edwin,' he called gaily, half turning. 'Come and take a look. Did you ever see anything so perfect as that little darling arranging flowers over there? I'd like to get between her thighs.'

'Christ, didn't you have your fill of thighs last night?' Edwin laughed ruefully through the pounding in his temples. But he had to agree that the brunette, busying herself with the bouquets and wreaths in the florist's window, was quite remarkable.

'Can one ever have enough of gorgeous legs and that which lies amidst them?' Dimitrie succeeded in catching the girl's eye, pantomiming with expressive hands and blowing kisses. 'I like to wallow in flesh, personally, never happier than when drowning in a voluptuous sea.'

'So I've noticed,' said Edwin.

They exchanged a memory-charged grin. Dimitrie pummelled him on the shoulder. 'You braced up bravely to the assault. I was proud of you. Madame Feodora expressed the fervent hope that you'd patronize her establishment again, ere long.'

Edwin struck himself on the brow. 'Lord! Who paid? I can't remember a bloody thing!'

Dimitrie bowed, a faintly mocking, intimate smile curving his full lips. 'It was my pleasure to foot the bill.'

They lingered a moment more, watching the passing street cavalcade. The square was filling up with townspeople: solemn merchants walking out with their neat, stout wives and hordes of children; nursemaids with attendant guardsmen; students in short jackets and peaked, tasselled caps, swinging leather-strapped books; housewives, servants, citizens, everyone bustling midst the endless stream of traffic. Two nuns shepherded a flock of convent-girls.

'Thunderation! Just look at those prissy young chits,' said Dimitrie, gilt snuff-box poised in mid-air. 'How very chaste! They simper along as if butter wouldn't melt in their mouths, yet I'll wager they think of nothing but rogering. The sisters too, with their holier-than-thou expressions, waddling in the rear, keeping them in line. I'll bet that school throbs with repressed lust. I'll bet you anything that they dream about cock! What it looks like. What it feels like. Jesus Christ, it makes me want to stand up here stark naked and horny, just to show 'em what they're missing.'

226

Edwin was rather embarrassed. 'I say, Dimitrie, isn't that going it a bit strong? Well, I mean – nuns and all that. Brides of Christ and whatever – dedicated women.'

Dimitrie gave him a sideways glance. 'I piss on their false modesty. In my experience women are as obsessed with fornication as we chaps, for all their pretence. I was brought up with four sisters, and know the games girls play with each other at bedtime.'

A change came over Edwin. He scowled, the headache making him feel sick. Bile rose in his mouth and he swallowed quickly. 'There's one who isn't in the least interested. The bitch!'

Dimitrie's eyebrows shot up questioningly as they strolled to the door, picking up their hats as they went. 'Oh? And who might that be?'

'Maria Malton,' growled Edwin sullenly.

'Rejected you, did she?' Those devilishly blue eyes were shrewd as he looked into Edwin's sulky face. 'Tell me about it.'

Hildegarde was a most conscientious hostess, genuinely concerned that her guests enjoy their stay. So, after a relatively simple breakfast, she ordered her open carriage and took Georgiana and Mariana on a tour of the city. Paris had been intriguing – the Bourse, the Palais Royal, the Tuileries Gardens, but Vienna excelled it.

One of the most important aspects of the outing was shopping. They spent a happy time browsing in the small, extremely modish, fiercely expensive haberdasher's, situated in the Michaelerplatz. After which Hildegarde instructed her coachman to take a route past the portico of the Karlskirche, the Palace Trautson, the University and the Academy of Military Surgery, every building a baroque work of art, bludgeoning both eye and senses. Exhausted by sight-seeing, they had lunch in the peace of the Prater, with its wooden, open-fronted cafés where, beneath the trees, customers could eat alfresco.

The waiter had only just taken their order when they were joined by David and Baron Carl who, though now a civilian, managed to maintain a rather martial air. He twirled the fobs at his waist, sat on the edge of his chair with his hat in his hand, raised his eyeglass and stared, a habit which Mariana found disconcerting. His vocabulary seemed limited to sporting-terms and army matters, and he addressed David in the main. Through a canopy of leaves, the sun made a pattern of greenish-grey on the grass and gravel paths. An alpine-filled rockery bordered a raised platform where several violinists and a flautist played selections from popular operas.

Luncheon passed pleasantly enough, but then Hildegarde shaded her eyes with her hand and gazed across the crowded park. Two men were coming towards their table, wending their way between the sprinkling of officers and their ladies, the well-dressed civilians and sparks, each group placidly drinking wine and talking.

'Here come Edwin and Count Baranga. How very nice!' she exclaimed, a smile deepening the dimples each side of her mouth.

Mariana's eyes narrowed and she became aloof. There was something about Edwin that made her skin crawl. The young man with him looked insufferably conceited, though he was as handsome as Apollo. There was a knowing expression in his eyes as he bent over her hand when they were introduced. She wondered what Edwin had been saying about her.

Hildegarde was bubbling with excitement. 'Dimitrie, you rogue! You've not been to visit me for ages. What have you been doing? Breaking hearts all over the place, I'll warrant, but I forgive you – you're such a pretty fellow, and I simply adore that suit!'

Dimitrie sat beside her, lilac gloves on the tablecloth, lilac topper tipped casually to the back of his head. He nestled his shoulder into hers, cocked an eye at her stomach and smiled into her eyes. 'I see that someone's been busy again. Could it be the Baron?'

'Of course it's the Baron!' She giggled in scandalized delight. 'Oh, you're the naughtiest person I know, but I do like you! You still haven't said why you've been neglecting me.'

'Dearest Baroness.' He kissed his fingertips to her. 'A thousand apologies, but I've so many calls on my time these days. However, I'd not miss your ball tonight for all the tea in China. Did you know that Radu has arrived?'

'What wonderful news! I was expecting him, but wasn't certain when. How perfectly thrilling!' She turned to Georgiana, curls bouncing beneath her ribbon-crowned bonnet. 'You haven't met our Prince yet, have you? He's most wickedly attractive.'

'Damn fine shot too,' put in the Baron, breaking off from singing the praises of his hawks.

His wife ignored him. She often did. 'Radu sets every female heart aflutter wherever he goes,' she continued, then sighed. 'But he's had a worrying time lately, poor lamb, with his father dying and the care of Montezena falling on his shoulders. Then there's his mother and her young men. Such a scandal! She's Hungarian, of course,' she added, as if this explained everything.

'So am I,' reminded Dimitrie.

Hildegarde beamed at him. 'Only on your Mamma's side. In any case, one accepts such behaviour in gentlemen but not in elderly princesses. I'm quite sure that you're discreet.'

'How wise you are, Baroness, one doesn't openly defy convention – one merely ignores it in private.' Dimitrie stretched languidly and accepted a cup of black coffee spiked with cognac. 'Are you aware that Baron Petresco has also taken up residence here?'

This caused the consternation he had expected. Hildegarde became flustered and her cheeks turned a deeper shade of pink. 'Oh dear, I was hoping he wouldn't accept my invitation. I couldn't avoid asking him. Is Countess Elizabeth with him?'

Dimitrie was watching the group from under lazy lids. 'Yes, indeed. Another Hungarian, Baroness, and an exceedingly lovely one.'

Hildegarde did not want to dwell on Countess Elizabeth. She was a simple woman, and could not fathom devious people like Grigore and his mistress. Unfortunately, they never stepped beyond the mark, giving her no excuse to ostracize them. She changed the subject and gathered up the ladies, saying that they must hurry if they were to have at least two hours' rest in preparation for the rigours of the evening.

David had insisted that Mariana should be provided with a lady's maid. He had selected a plain, earnest girl called Sophie to fill the post. At first, Mariana felt this to be quite unnecessary, but had grown to appreciate the wisdom of his suggestion. Travelling would have been awkward, to say the least, without the services of the admirable Sophie. She performed her tasks cheerfully, laundering, ironing, packing and unpacking, carrying out small sewing repairs, running errands. In addition, she was a clever hairdresser, spending much time off-duty studying magazines in search of the latest styles. A capable, optimistic person, she was obedient without being servile, forthright but never rude. Mariana began to rely on her.

On her return to the palace, she took off her walking-dress, lying on the bed in her curtained room, drowsily listening to the sounds of the von Gundling children playing in the garden. Edwin's spoilt, angry face swam behind her closed lids, and that of his friend, Count Baranga. Neither of them inspired confidence. She seemed to hear Margery saying, from

somewhere in the past: 'He's too handsome for his own good.'
'Oh, Margery, I wish you were here,' she whispered.

She slept, roused into the headachy heat of late afternoon by
Sophie, bringing in a tray of tea things. Mariana sat up,
yawning, stupefied, sipping the refreshing brew. Sophie was
full of the impending ball. 'You'll outshine them all, miss,' she
enthused. 'That new gown's so becoming.'

Mariana smiled, duty-bound to uphold the honour of the
British for Sophie's sake. She was a Londoner and did not
approve of foreigners. 'Is my bath ready?' she asked, wishing
that she could spend the evening alone. There was always this
sneaking fear that, though unlikely, she might meet someone
from her past.

The Baron had spent a fortune having bathrooms installed in
each of his six residences. A large, cast-iron tub squatted on
lion's feet in the centre of the adjoining room. Sophie tossed a
liberal handful of perfumed crystals into the warm water, and
Mariana sang as she bathed. Her mood had shifted and she
now felt oddly light-hearted. Sophie watched her fondly,
relieved to see her gay. The sadness which so often darkened
her mistress's face made her depressed too.

Ablutions over, Sophie set to work on Mariana's hair,
producing a professional rendering of a fashionable coiffuer,
then she whisked about the chamber, flinging open the doors of
the armoire, attacking the tallboy and looting its drawers,
returning with garments draped over her arm. Mariana had
noticed with amusement that whenever they arrived at a new
venue, she took over with the thoroughness of a quartermaster-
sergeant. When at length Mariana was dressed, her maid ran a
critical eye over her.

'You look like a queen, miss,' she nodded, satisfied. 'You'll
knock 'em into a cocked hat, if you'll pardon the expression.'

'Thanks to you, Sophie dear,' Mariana replied, but as she
stared at the image flung back by the mirror, her awareness
was flickering, time and space overlapping in a frightening
way. Another bedroom, not so long ago, another mirror and a
portrait. Dear God, I look just like Mamma, she thought, with
a queer stab in her heart. She could almost hear the Duchesse's
mocking cackle, and see those eyes hooded by lids like grainy
parchment.

She repressed the shiver which ran down her spine. What
would she think of me now, I wonder? Would a spark of pride
lighten her withered soul? Or would she continue to taunt me?
I've been so well groomed. Does David hope to find a bidder on
the marriage-market? That would free him from a bothersome

230

responsibility. She conjectured on how long she would be able to stave off the advances of the men to whom they hopefully introduced her. They meant it for the best, she knew. It was the general view that every woman wished to be married. How could they guess that this was impossible for her?

The cheval-glass reflected the room behind her. It spoke of wealth, security and gracious living. Like every other chamber there it was enormous, the ceiling vaulted, the walls decorated with paintings in the manner of Watteau. Earlier on, a cat-footed manservant had come to light the lamps. They glowed behind frosted glass globes. Mariana knew that she was not out of place in such surroundings, yet could not shake off the feeling that she had no right to be there. She looked the part in oyster satin, a gown designed by Madame Polette. The skirt had a hem stiffened and looped with moiré ruching and the sleeves were full, complementing the hemline which swirled about her ankles. The low oval neck displayed her shoulders and the curve of her breasts. Yet still she wondered: Who is this stranger?

It was a lady who stood there, someone used to refinement and luxury with expectations of a happy future. There were no lines of sorrow on that subtly painted face, no horror lurked in the long-lashed eyes. Yet it was herself, hiding behind a masquerade costume. Carmine outlined her mouth, making it inviting. A lie. She invited no man's kisses. Her eyes sparkled, unnaturally bright, thanks to the khol which outlined them. Alluring eyes. Another lie. She did not wish to allure anyone. Unless – those eyes narrowed thoughtfully – unless by doing so she could be revenged.

She took up a glass perfume bottle, touching the crystal stopper to her lobes, her wrists, the cleft between her breasts. Why not? whispered something small and dark within her head. You're lovely. Torment the vain fools.

Taking up her gold-fringed scarf, she draped it about her and, fan and bag in one hand, was ready when Georgiana called for her. They spent some moments exclaiming over and admiring one another's gown. Georgiana was bubbling with an excitement that had nothing to do with the ball. As they left the room and passed through the corridors, she suddenly stopped, hand on Mariana's arm.

'It's no use. I must tell someone or I'll explode,' she whispered breathlessly. Her face wore an astonished but deeply contented expression as she added: 'I'm not quite certain yet. I've not spoken of it to Lance, though I must. Maria, I think I'm with child.'

'Oh.' Mariana could find nothing else to say, her heart sinking like a stone while she chided herself for being so selfish.

'Isn't it divine?' Georgiana was rhapsodic. 'We've been longing for this to happen. Just think – a lovely baby – like Hildegarde's little treasure. My dear, you'll be able to help me. I don't know one end of an infant from the other. Have you any experience with them?'

'No,' said Mariana as they continued their progress.

'I've dropped a hint to David and he's as proud as can be. I've not had my female complaint since before we left London.' Georgiana was already different, holding herself carefully.

'The change of air, perhaps – the journey,' Mariana suggested hopefully. The future stretched like a desert before her. She would have to watch Georgiana swelling into motherhood, be with her during labour, have charge of her nurseling. I can't bear it, she thought.

'That wouldn't have upset me. I'm always so regular,' Georgiana answered complacently. They stopped at the head of the Grand Staircase. The hall was humming as the coaches disgorged themselves of passengers at the front door. She turned to Mariana, her small face suddenly anxious. 'It means so much to me – to us. Pray for me, dear.' She attempted a light laugh, but was close to tears. 'This must seem like nonsense. I'm not religious, but I want a child so desperately. Perhaps a prayer or two won't go amiss.'

'I'll pray,' Mariana promised. Georgiana gave her a grateful hug, then linked arms and they went down to the ballroom.

It was like stepping into a garden. Sweet aromas came from rare blossoms cascading from jardinieres, on bamboo stands, in priceless vases on tables, in alcoves, everywhere. The illustrious and powerful were gathered there, with jewels and orders blazing under the light of a thousand candles. Enormous mirrors reflected the scene over and over. The two dozen musicians stationed in the gallery were playing tunes which set feet tapping. Flunkeys stalked about, offering glasses of strong wines from the Rhone, blood-warming Tokay from Hungary and heady Roussillon from French vineyards. Everyone was served with a glass of the finest champagne as they entered.

Gowns of palest pastels, uniforms and evening suits, tiaras and medals flashed under the glittering droplets of the chandeliers. The laughter and music seemed to buoy up Mariana as she advanced. As each person arrived, their names were announced by a Master of Ceremonies with rouged cheeks and a high white wig of classical curls. The Baron and Baroness stood beside him to receive their guests.

'Miss Maria Malton!' The stentorian accents rang above the din.

Good God, that's me! she thought and dropped a curtsy. The Baron raised her hand to his lips, staring at her briefly through his monocle, a polite, meaningless smile hovering round his lips. She was hemmed in, with David on one side and Georgiana on the other. A long string of foreign titles was being presented to her: ladies nodding, gentlemen bowing, several youngish men appearing like genies from bottles, champagne corks popping like a barrage of miniature artillery. A boyish guardsman with a red face and weedy moustache secured a glass for her, and attempted to draw her into the privacy of a large potted palm. She was rescued by watchful Georgiana.

Baron Carl and Hildegarde opened the ball, leading a quadrille. David came over to claim his wife. Mariana's dance-card was filled with names to which she could not put a face. She had scribbled them in hurriedly, using the tiny pink pencil attached to it by a ribbon. An elderly roué, dripping perfume, took her hand, guiding her to the floor. She smiled and pretended to enjoy the touch of his flabby hand. The quadrille ended. He bowed, gave her an arch glance and extricated himself. A tall, foppish person with chestnut hair came up to her.

'Miss Malton. I'm on your card, I believe. Yes, there it is. Dance Number Two – Count Dimitrie Baranga.'

'I don't recall writing it in.'

'You didn't. I made it up.' His cocksure smile was annoying. 'We met this morning over lunch in the Prater.'

She had forgotten who he was momentarily. There had been so many strangers: ladies eyeing her with veiled suspicion, heelsnapping soldiers, dashing beaux, all clacking away in a variety of tongues. But now she remembered those impudent eyes, and Edwin's sarcastic introduction. She felt the pressure of his thumb against her palm. It burned through her kid glove. He was stripping her with his eyes. To her chagrin, she knew that she was blushing.

The band struck up a waltz and he put an arm lightly about her waist. The wine was doing its work, the pace quickening. No one wanted the minuet or stately gavotte, demanding the licence of the waltz. She was in Dimitrie's arms, her hand resting on his velvet-covered shoulder, the white ruffles of his shirt brushing her breasts. Catching the eye of several other women as they whirled by, she realized that she was envied. Dimitrie was handsome enough to make most ladies mad with desire, but not her. His lazy, insolent glance ran over her face, her lips, coming to rest on her bare shoulders. He smiled, and his arm tightened.

'By Jove, but you're ravishing,' he murmured, his mouth close to the curls hiding her ear. 'How can I stop Grigore stealing you?'

Round and round, the room spinning until he skilfully reversed. Mariana was a good dancer. The pain of memory was lancing – the parlour of the farmhouse with Mamma at the harpsichord, saying: 'You must learn to dance, my love. That's right – one, two, three – one, two, three!' Now her feet followed the measure without conscious thought.

'Who is Grigore?' she asked, turning and turning, in waltz time.

'He's just come in,' said Dimitrie. 'We'll dance in the opposite direction.'

Looking across his shoulder towards the main door, she saw a dark, strikingly handsome man, but there was something sinister about him. Perhaps it was his black uniform, bare of trimming. He looked like a priest. His cold eyes raked the crowd, gleaming with a malice which was disturbing. A woman with honey-hued hair was on his arm.

'Baron Grigore Petresco.' Dimitrie smiled because her curiosity showed. 'Hildegarde was apprehensive about him appearing tonight. When you get to know him, you'll understand why. That innocent-looking charmer is Countess Elizabeth. She's Grigore's mistress, and not only his, if rumour's to be heeded. They're saying that he shares her with his half-brother, Prince Radu.' He raised a quizzical eyebrow, staring down into her face. 'Do I shock you, little English miss?'

She returned his stare levelly. 'I'm not easily shocked, Count.'

'Aren't you?' he rejoined, adding smoothly: 'Edwin told me otherwise. He said you were mighty prim and proper. An ice-maiden, no less. I find this intriguing, Miss Malton, and suspect you've hidden fires which might warm a fellow, if he could find his way to them. How old are you, may I be permitted to ask?'

'You may not!' She gave him a freezing glance, but far from deterring him, it only served to double his interest.

'Oh, come,' he teased, succeeding in holding her so close that his lips touched her cheek. 'What are you? Sixteen? Nineteen?'

She strained back as far as his grip and the waltz would allow. Sixteen! How ridiculous! She wanted to tell him the

234

truth about herself, to shock *him* for once. It was hard to resist the impulse. The dance seemed to go on for ever. She had the unpleasant notion that she had died, condemned to purgatory where she danced through eternity with this man. Lancelot's furrowed features swam hazily. He was leaning against a pillar, exuding boredom. It was unusual for a doctor to be invited to such a blue-blooded event. Then she remembered him telling her that his father had been a lord, and that he had the right to add 'viscount' to his name. If ever this waltz ended, she was determined to escape from the Count and ask Lancelot to hide her away somewhere.

The trouble-making Dimitrie had changed his mind as well as direction, now guiding their dancing feet towards Grigore. 'Good evening, Baron,' he shouted as they waltzed past.

Black eyes considered her bleakly, though the lips smiled. His features should have been noble, but were marred by a certain coarseness. A scar puckered his left cheek. The woman at his side gave her a sweeping glance. She was beautiful, tawny hair tumbling about a shapely head, her pale, pure countenance ethereal, as if she knew nothing of passion or the seamy side of life, although her gown was daring to the point of indecency.

'That'll get him going,' grinned Dimitrie, waltzing her back into the crowd. 'I'll bet he'll be over as soon as this finishes, angling for an introduction.'

'I don't want to meet him or his friend.' She had lost sight of Lancelot. It was terribly hot, the perfume of flowers all-pervading. In Petresco and Elizabeth she had recognized characteristics which were all too familiar. She felt the breath of fear tingling her spine.

'You don't have to. It'll be my pleasure to escort you to the supper-room.' Dimitrie did not give up easily. This cold girl was a challenge. He was thoroughly enjoying the furore which his attention to her was causing among several ladies to whom he had made love in the past. Even Elizabeth was signalling with her fan. He revelled in this situation, cruel beneath his charm, using women, despising them.

Mariana recognized that she could not refuse without being downright rude. The buffet-tables had been set up in a room on the left. Dimitrie edged through the crowd surrounding them, drawing her along with him. There were salads and cold meats, little cakes, flavoursome dainties, the most tempting trifles, colourfully arranged on fine china, midst foliage as light and frothy as ocean foam. Pyramids of fruit were piled into Sèvres dishes, pineapples, grapes, peaches, everything that money could buy. Everyone was talking at once, jostling round the tables. Mariana felt isolated among them, attention focused on a golden épergne given pride of place. Upon its ornamental base reclined a miniature camel with turbanned Arab driver leaning against the trunk of an eighteen-inch palm tree. Its jewelled leaves spread out, cupping a crystal bowl from which trailed roses, ferns, jasmine, cascading down over this costly oasis. Oh, for a magic spell, she thought, so that I might shrink in size, mount that camel and gallop away into the night. I don't like it here.

Dimitrie snatched up two dishes of scarlet strawberries, topped with whipped cream and castor sugar. He found a small couch in a corner and urged her to sit with him. She refused, wanting nothing but to flee the heat, the chatter, the eternal music.

'Not hungry?' Dimitrie remarked as he chose the largest strawberry from the bowl, dipped it in cream, popped it in his mouth and ate it with delicate appreciation. He wiped his lips with a lilac silk handerchief. 'Have a glass of champagne. It's a capital vintage.'

She did not reply, standing by the couch, one hand resting on the carved frame. Where was Lancelot? She needed him. Dimitrie was so pressing in his pursuit of her. She was at a loss how to handle him. Frankness seemed the only course, so she said: 'I don't want to drink with you. I wish you'd leave me alone.'

An unpleasant spark leapt into his eyes. 'How foolish. I'm one of the most popular men in town.'

'Not with me!' Though her voice was low, every word stood out distinctly. Those nearest to them turned their heads, anticipating an interesting scene.

'Didn't I warn you that she was a hard nut to crack?' Edwin appeared from the other side of a tubbed orange tree. His eyes were heavy-lidded and, though controlled, it was apparent that the fire of the dessert wines, coupled with what he had been drinking all day, had muddled his brain.

'Go away,' Dimitrie drawled. 'Leave this to an expert.'

'What unmannerly beasts you are!' Mariana lost her temper, layer upon layer of memories swimming in her head. They were too like Christopher's cronies who had tormented her. She flung round and left the room.

It was at that moment, when her opinion of men was at its lowest ebb, that she saw him. He was striding towards her, weaving through the press of drinkers and dancers, not pausing if any tried to engage him in conversation. Elizabeth was on tiptoe, trying to catch his eye. He ignored her. He was the tallest man present, towering over every head. But it was his eyes which captured her, vividly compelling. They met hers – held them. Something seemed to pass from them right into her heart. The ballroom faded. Sounds were suddenly muffled. She was aware of no one but this dark, vital stranger.

He reached her, took the dance-card and tore it into little bits, scattering them over his shoulder like confetti. They fluttered to the polished floor. 'This is our dance,' he said, his accent strong, his voice deep, 'and all the others for the rest of the evening.'

She caught her breath, the significance of the moment holding her still. From each side men and women were watching, eager to note the slightest irregularity, striving to catch a single word. Had it been any other treating her in so cavalier a fashion, she would have turned on her heel, but now she did not argue. He took her hand, bare of its glove. When they moved to the floor, people stood back for them.

'My name is Radu,' he said. 'David is my friend.'

Nothing could have been more simple. She was aware of the looks, the whispers, recalling what Hildegarde had said about him. He was reputed to be arrogantly head-strong, a destroyer of women's hearts. She smiled up into his slate-grey eyes, and still said nothing. There was no need for words. This was a precious, preordained moment. He was challenging her to join him in a wild, exciting adventure, and she had the conviction that this was nothing new. She already belonged to him – had always been his. The way he looked at her showed only too clearly that he shared the shadowy memory. Then the music began and she went into his arms gladly, like a tired child coming home at last. He understood, drawing her close.

It was as if they danced alone on a bare mountain-top. She fitted perfectly against his body and their feet moved as one. He was an ideal partner, with superb grace for so large a man. Mariana was cloud-high, the music swelling in sweet harmony. When it stopped, they walked through the conservatory. Other couples were there, some starry-eyed, some fencing verbally, nearly all were drinking. Radu pushed open an outer door and took Mariana into the garden.

They stood, hand in hand, looking up at the indigo sky with its sparkling dusting of stars, breathing in the scent of the ensorcelled night, neither questioning this mutual, over-whelming attraction. The lawns were as lifeless as dark velvet. The moon was high, sailing serenely. Music coiled out from the ballroom, tinged with sadness. Mariana had the impression of some extraordinary happiness just within her grasp, yet it was so shy, so elusive, likely to melt at a touch.

I don't want to fall in love again, she pleaded with the moon. But it was already too late. She turned her eyes to Radu. Her head did not reach the black silk stock wound round his throat. He was so beautiful and frightening, with that suggestion of power in his stance. His uniform was that of a hussar; frogged and braided short jacket, tight trousers, a loose dolman, lined with brown fur, slung across one shoulder, a sword at his hip. How did we dance whilst he was wearing a sword? she wondered, but it did not matter.

Gravely her eyes wandered over his face, recognizing and memorizing it. His nose was thin and slightly hooked, his cheekbones high, hollowed with shadows beneath, and his lips were firm, the upper finely chiselled, the lower full. It was a serious mouth, but she knew it could curve in humour too. His hair, steel-blue in the shadows, had a natural curl, but it was his eyes which held her attention, slightly tilted at the outer corners, suggesting an infusion of Tartar blood somewhere in his line. They seemed hard eyes, but in them she read a certain unhappiness and questing. He was not so sure of himself as he liked people to think.

So this was Prince Radu. 'Why did you destroy my dance-card?' she asked at last, testing her own ability to speak.

'You're the most beautiful woman here.' He said the first thing that came into his head, unable to explain that which he did not understand himself. In a blinding flash he had seen her and recognized her as his mate – his mirror-image – his twin-soul.

'That isn't true.' She shook her head slowly.

'Hush, don't ask the whys and wherefores.' He laid a finger on her lips with infinite gentleness. 'There's no turning back. We shall be lovers, you and I.'

'It doesn't happen like that – in a moment,' she protested.

'In a second, sometimes, if one is very fortunate.'

His arms reached out to enfold her, but carefully, as if she was made of spun-glass. 'You want me to be your mistress,' she murmured, not asking, accepting it as a fact.

He stiffened, then relaxed, and there was a thread of laughter in his voice. 'No.'

She threw back her head the better to see him in the moonlight. His eyes and teeth glimmered. 'What then?'

'You'll be my wife.'

She had not expected that. His wife? Bit by bit, the dream started to crumble. 'I can't,' she said.

He gave her a little, teasing shake, laughingly confident. He was accustomed to having his way. 'You will. No one shall stop us.'

'I can stop us,' she whispered bleakly.

'No.' He lowered his head and kissed her and the die was cast.

Mariana gave a helpless moan, moving her lips under his, emotions she had prayed never to feel again springing to life. The strength went out of her. She lay limp and unresisting in his arms, surrendering to his kiss as he had known she would. Her lips were soft and warm, generously receiving him with a candour and honesty which convinced him that his impulse had been right.

He had not wanted to go to the ball, would have much preferred meeting David after it was over, yet had been determined to confuse Grigore's spies. Elizabeth had not been clever enough to deceive him, and had unwittingly divulged many of Grigore's secrets during pillow-talk. Stepping into the ballroom, arriving late, his eyes had swept the customary crowd of sycophants and idlers, mentally yawning at the prospect of a tedious evening, then he had seen her. Rage had flooded him as he watched her dancing with his rascally cousin. Proud but so helpless. It had seemed that she cried out to him across the packed room. He had fired a single question at David, standing with him. Who was she? David had given him her name.

He could have had his pick of the eager females there, but they wearied him, bashful or bold, buzzing like a swarm of hopeful bees. She had not looked in his direction, her smile fixed as she waltzed with Dimitrie, but the strain in her eyes touched that soft core within Radu which few knew he possessed. He had lost sight of her for a while when she entered the supper-room. He had not followed. Somehow, he had known that she would come to him. When she did, he had unhesitatingly taken her hands in his.

Now, embracing her in the garden, he could smell the perfume of her hair. It aroused memories he had thought lost for ever: the scent of lavender in the sun, of cherry-blossom, of meadowsweet among new-mown hay. Her mouth tasted like honey and he feasted on it, then lifted his head, smiling at her. 'They'll try to stop us – my advisers – my mother.'

'This will be wise, perhaps,' she ventured, voice husky. 'You're a Prince, whereas I! Who knows where I come from?'

He laughed with a sound as wild and free as the winds on his native plains. 'By some trickery or other, my ancestors succeeded in obtaining a title, though they were *haiducs*, robber barons who fought for whichever Voevod happened to be in power. There are many princes in this part of the world.'

'You live far from Vienna?' She was making herself talk, better that than dare to think of the consequences.

'I'm in charge of a small state in Transylvania,' he said, his hand tenderly smoothing the curls back from her brow. 'It's difficult to reach. The roads are bad, and the people poor. It's a rugged, savage country, sometimes merciless, but I love it. It's called Montezena, and I don't suppose you've ever heard of it. I want to take you to my home in the mountains – *Szelnek a Kastelya* – The Castle of the Winds.'

The Castle of the Winds! It was as if voicing that name was a secret spell, evoking the power of love. A safe place where she and Radu could live in peace and no one from the outside could reach them. She wanted to leave at once, before the arm of fate could stretch out over the miles and stop her from tasting this forbidden joy.

'When can we go?' she asked, trembling.

'My little one, don't cry.' He was distressed, moved by her tears. 'You're shaking like a frightened kitten. Who has hurt you? Tell me. Your pain is in me too.' His hands on her shoulders were rough with concern. 'You must tell me that I may avenge you.'

'Radu, don't ask me. The past is dead. I'm yours now. Take me away with you.'

His hold slackened. 'Forgive me, I didn't mean to be so severe. I'll not force you to speak. Keep your secret. In time, you'll learn to confide in me. We'll go tonight, when the ball is ended.'

It was her turn to grip him. Her fingers dug into his forearms. She could feel the hard muscles beneath the smooth cloth of his uniform. 'You mean it? If you're amusing yourself with me to pass an idle hour, I swear that I'll die by my own hand.'

His face was grave. 'I give you my solemn oath on it. I love you, Maria, and you'll be my bride, come hell or high water.'

She shuddered. 'Don't speak of hell. It may be closer than you imagine.'

A little later, they returned to the ballroom to find David in conversation with Grigore and Elizabeth. Her brilliant eyes pinned Radu's. They've been lovers, thought Mariana. He would have walked straight past but David detained him, wishing to introduce him to Georgiana. It was an uneasy meeting. Though Radu was extremely civil to his half-brother,

240

he hated the way he fawned over Mariana's hand. She was able to examine this man who exuded that same air of danger which she had known at Thornfalcon. His face was handsome, yet famished with ambition, and his eyes were like flat black stones.

'Phew! Get me a drink someone,' panted Lancelot, flushed and sweating as he joined them. 'I've just disentangled myself from that well-corseted widow over there. She's decided that she wants to be a doctor's wife! Heaven help me, I'm getting too old for this lark!'

'One's never too old for amour,' threw in Dimitrie, leaning on a lazy elbow against an ornamental plinth. 'What about one of Count Bronski's daughters, Herr Doctor?'

'God forbid!' Lancelot took a glass from a passing footman. 'They're built like warships.'

'Dimitrie would overlook that,' growled Radu, face like iron. 'He'd do anything to get his hands on a dowry worth fifty thousand pounds a year.'

'Hold hard, dear cousin,' Dimitrie expostulated, wearing an air of injured innocence. 'I draw the line somewhere.'

'Do you?' Grigore's lips were raised slightly from their usual downward curve, almost forming a smile. 'Can a man who runs up such exceedingly high bills with his tailor afford to be fussy?'

'I keep on the move. That's the secret of my success,' Dimitrie answere flippantly.

'Damned sensible – a singularly wise policy,' Edwin put in. He was rocking unsteadily and his eyes were glazed. 'You're a good fellow, Dimitrie. What we chaps in England call a real out and outer. Down as a nail! A trump! A Trojan! Must come to London – I'll show you a time. I've a spanking new highflyer. I'll teach you how to "fan the daylights", we'll ride down the high streets like the very devil, smashing windows with our whips. Rare sport that!'

'Edwin, you're foxed! Go to bed,' said David sternly.

Edwin swung round, fists raised truculently. 'Go to bed? Go to hell!' he shouted. 'The party's only just getting going. Come on, Dimitrie, let's grab a couple of girls and dance. I feel like waltzing round and round – round and round.' He knocked over a table, sending glasses crashing. He teetered dangerously for a second, then suddenly fell to the floor and lay there in a drunken stupor.

David flushed with embarrassment, but Baron Carl merely laughed, saying that such behaviour was a compliment, proving the party to be a success. Most of the guests were intoxicated. Foreheads were beginning to sweat, faces going red, eyes lighting up, the revelry swelling to a crescendo, von Gundling's expensive poisons doing their work.

'How boring of him to have collapsed so soon,' complained Dimitrie as Edwin was lifted and borne away by several flunkeys. 'I refrain from too much wine. It makes a man such a dashed poor lover – the spirit's willing but the flesh, alas, refuses to rise to the occasion. I dislike my virility being impeded, don't you, Radu?'

Radu controlled the desire to knock him down. Dimitrie was a nasty piece of work, an unprincipled blackguard, but he possessed a certain rakish charm, whereas Grigore was a villain with no mitigating qualities. He wished that Maria had not had to meet these unwelcome relatives, and he kept a hand at her elbow, exerting a light, reassuring pressure. He met Elizabeth's questioning eyes with their obvious message. She seemed tawdry in comparison with Maria. One of his brows lifted and his upper lip curled. Elizabeth's fingers gripped her fan as if she longed to strike him across the face with it.

'May I have the pleasure of the next dance, Miss Malton?' Grigore leaned nearer to her. There was something unpleasantly reptilian about his eyes, the lids heavy, faint blue stains beneath them.

'She has promised it to me.' Radu did not move a muscle.

Grigore straightened. 'Far be it from me to deprive you of the privilege, your Highness,' he said in his sauve way. He gave her a fleeting glance. 'Another time, maybe. I'm sure we'll meet again.'

As they danced, Radu murmured: 'Go to your room soon. This rabble's getting out of hand. I don't like you mixing with them. Put a few things in a valise, only a very few. I'll buy what you need later. Meet me at the stable entrance at three-thirty.'

'The guards,' she demurred, seeing Grigore's ravaged face as they passed. He was dancing with Elizabeth, who shot her a blistering glare of jealousy and hatred.

'Leave the guards to me.'

When the music ceased, Mariana said goodnight to Hildegarde and Baron Carl. Headaches were capital excuses, she had discovered. Everyone believed her, or if they did not, pretended to. There had been so much champagne. Too much, she smilingly agreed.

CHAPTER 6

When some of the guests had summoned their servants and left, while more hardy ones still danced, Radu met David in a deserted gaming-room. The quiet was pleasant after the noisy merry-making, and they were soon joined by Lancelot and Cornel Cazacu. The decanters were brandy-filled, and the doctor poured for them.

'You're having trouble with Petresco?' David asked as he seated himself, coat-tails whipped back out of the way. 'How can I assist?'

'I haven't made up my mind yet.' Radu's lips were compressed into a hard line, and David mused on the dark fire of the man. He knew that he could be ruthless.

'He's got your measure,' he said. 'I fell into a neat trap last night, organized by him. You didn't send a note telling me to meet a certain Gautier, did you?'

'No.' Radu flashed him a glance.

'Someone did, and I'll stake my life it was your brother. He'd ordered one of his bullies to pick a quarrel with me. I left him regretting that he'd agreed.'

Lancelot had found a box of cigars and was handing them round. 'I think I've missed my vocation – should've been a butler. Better perks by far than my present profession,' he grumbled, then sat down, tilted his chair back as far as it would go, and planted his feet on the table. 'My goddamn corns are giving me stick! All that prancing about. Felt like a bloody circus ape.'

'Dear old Lance,' grinned Radu, tension easing as Lancelot had intended it should. 'As crabby as ever. We may have changed, but you go soldiering on.'

'Moderation in all things. That's what does it, my boy,' Lancelot grunted. 'Fresh air and a frugal diet are the hallmarks of a healthy constitution. "Nothing in excess" is my motto. The Greeks knew a thing or two – had it carved over the gate of the oracle at Delphi.'

'You should tell this to Grigore.' The Prince's face darkened again ominously.

'He's plotting against you, as you suspected he might?'
David was holding a brandy goblet in both hands, inhaling the
bouquet.

'I've every reason to think so.' Radu was scowling, not at his
friends but at a mental picture of his brother's face. 'He's
always envied me, and is now spreading a rumour that my
father married that Turkish bitch who spawned him. He says
he has papers to prove a morganatic marriage.'

'Morganatic pig-crap! That's one of the oldest tricks in the
bastard's book.' Lancelot dismissed it with heavy scorn.

'Nothing will make his claim legal and he knows it,' said
David emphatically. 'He's talking out of his backside.'

'I'm well aware of that, but there are those who'll uphold
him, nobles who don't agree with my reforms and who'd like to
see the Turks in power again. My father freed the country and
it's now under Habsburg protection.'

'Ha! You've changed one tyrannical government for
another.' Lancelot was not impressed.

'The lesser of two evils, I believe,' Radu shot back.

'You have my support, that goes without saying.' David set
down his glass.

'Thank you. I can trust no one, except Cornel.' Radu
nodded to where his lieutenant sat, playing with the trim of his
kalpac. 'The peasants are for me, so is Colonel Alnoch, but the
other counsellors are dotards whom my mother will not permit
me to retire.'

'You've the army behind you to a man,' Cornel averred
stoutly, his face alight with loyalty.

'What's left of it,' Radu answered grimly. 'We've never
recouped our losses at Waterloo. I've asked the Emperor to
send me a company of his own troops, but you know how tardy
he is.'

'So, what's to do?' asked Lancelot bluntly, planting his
large, square-nailed hands on his thick knees.

'I'd appreciate it if you could stay in Vienna for a while,
keeping your ears to the ground. I employ spies, but can't be
certain if they're trustworthy. Grigore's wealthier than me.
Don't forget his mother was a Turk and he's probably in their
employ. He can afford to pay his ferrets handsomely.' Radu's
hands were pressed flat on the table's surface, and he leaned
his weight on them with such ferocity that David was glad to be
his friend, not his enemy. 'I suspect that Grigore plans to
assassinate me. This would be the simplest way out. In the
ensuing uproar, he could stake his claim, produce his forged
documents – and I'm bloody sure they are forgeries. He'd have

the Turks behind him, squashing opposition.'

'You can rely on me.' David was more disturbed than his calm, almost phlegmatic appearance betrayed. 'But what about you? Christ, you'd be well advised to get out of Europe for a bit, if what you suspect is a fact.'

Radu's head went up, his features holding all the fine pride of his race. 'Run from that imposter? Never! I'll outwit him. Heir to Montezena be damned! He doesn't stand a chance – while I live!'

'That's just what David means. He wants you to go on living,' Lancelot said as he took a meerschaum pipe from his pocket and proceeded to fill it with Bristol tobacco from a waterproof pouch. He stuffed the bowl lightly and struck a match. 'Why don't you have the blighter killed? Turn the tables. Make sure that your assassin's bullet gets him first,' he suggested, between puffs.

'I'll not sink to his level.' The Prince's eyes were like honed steel. 'I'd prefer to meet him, as gentlemen should, to shoot it out or fight to the death with sabres.'

Lancelot shook a dubious head. 'You're too honourable, sir. With rattlesnakes like him, one shoots first and asks questions after.'

'This is different. I've a responsibility towards the peasants. They're simple, pious people who look upon their Prince as their father. Easily influenced, as excitable as children. I must do nothing to discredit my House,' Radu explained with quiet dignity.

Lancelot sat back, cursing the folly of princes, though impressed by Radu's high standards. He took no further part in the discussion, forced to knock out his pipe and go about his duties when a servant appeared, saying that Lady Cunyngham was unwell.

'Too much wine, I'll warrant,' said the doctor grumpily.

David shook his head and grinned, hugely pleased wth himself. 'Too much rogering, more like. She's not seen a flux for two months.'

'Ah, good news at last!' Lancelot's bright eyes twinkled under his shaggy brows. 'We may soon be seeing a fine young sprig for the House of Cunyngham. I'll go to her at once. She must rest, but not too much, gentle exercise is good for expectant mothers.'

'Congratulations, David.' Radu shook him by the hand. 'I envy you. I'd like a son to follow after me.'

'Plenty of time, Highness.' David was feeling warm and contented. 'First, you must find a suitable wife.'

Radu looked him straight in the eyes. 'I've found one. I wish to marry your ward.'

David's jaw dropped. 'You *what*?'

Radu smiled, seating himself on a corner of the table, one booted leg resting on the carpet, the other swinging. 'Don't look so astonished. As you so rightly observed, I need a wife, but not simply anyone. I want Maria.'

'You've only just met her.'

'I know,' the Prince said softly, seriously. 'But that doesn't matter. I love her and she returns that love. Say what you like, call it madness. I don't care. Love never comes as an invited guest. Who needs its chains? But who, on the other hand, can live happily without it? Don't you believe in love at first sight, David?'

'"She never loves at all who loved not at first sight!" The poets are wise old birds,' said David, his mind winging back to the day he had seen Georgiana, a wild young thing romping in a summer garden. He had fallen in love with her then and there, knowing without the slightest shadow of doubt that she was the one for him.

He believed Radu's sincerity, but Maria as Princess Varna? Oh, she had the appearance to carry it off, but she was rather unstable. Then, thinking it over, David concluded – why not? If his restless friend and that lonely girl would find joy together, who was he to stand in their way? There was not enough love in the world.

'Have I your consent?' Radu was eager as a young boy.

'Would it make that much difference if you hadn't?' David laughed. 'My quixotic Prince, you'd simply elope with her.'

'You're right, but I'd rather you gave your approval before I carry her off. We intend to leave at dawn. Will you do me a favour and pretend to be outraged? This'll put Grigore off the scent. I don't want him to suspect that you and I are such close friends.'

David rested a hand on his shoulder. 'What lady wouldn't be completely bowled over by a proposal from you? I don't need to stress Maria's virtues, I can see that, but I assure you that even your haughty Mamma'll have nothing to complain about regarding her blood, which is even more royal than your own.'

Radu shrugged, his dolman swinging. 'I don't care if she's the child of a mountebank.'

'You don't but others will,' David said seriously. 'Frankly, I know little about her. I was forced into the position of accepting her as my ward, but I was given a sealed envelope holding

246

documents pertaining to her birth. I took them to my lawyer and, whilst not divulging their contents, he hinted that she's a very high-born young lady. He has them in safe-keeping.'

Mariana walked quickly across the vaulted hall. At the top of the staircases she stopped to look back. Radu was down there somewhere. Radu. His name was magical, yet he had been a stranger till an hour ago – a stranger who had stormed the citadel of her heart. Her footfalls seemed to beat time to his name as she sped along the lofty corridors and arrived at her bedchamber door. It was only then, when quite alone, that she suddenly realized how much she had healed. Had anyone told her, even a day ago, that she who had sworn never again to take on love's yoke, would be stirred in that old, sweet way by the touch of a man's lips, she would have laughed them to scorn. Welcome? Oh, no, this feeling was not welcome. As one awakes from a fevered dream, so she felt as if she was waking into a kind of madness. Delirious, uncontrolled, wildly happy. It must be insanity! Dare I become involved? she thought. I've bolted the door against it, desired nothing but to sit by a lonely hearth, sleep in a lonely bed, deny love with all my strength.

Sophie had gone to her quarters, so Mariana was able to slip into her room undisturbed. She stood in the centre of the floor, wondering what to pack and if she should go at all. It was folly. Worse than folly. How could she hope to get away with it? But England's so far from here, she told herself, surely I can grasp the happiness which is every human being's right? It may be possible to convince Radu that marriage is unnecessary. Then remembering the determination in his eyes, she knew this to be a foolish hope. Oh, why couldn't he have been a little less chivalrous!

She pulled open drawers, and stuffed a few essentials in a bag. Her lovely gowns hung reproachfully in the armoire, and it saddened her to abandon them. Radu had promised to replace them. Could she trust him? She had placed her trust in Christopher, loving him, believing in him and it had cost her dear.

Taking off her ball-gown, she put on a dress of fine cotton, printed with flower sprigs. Over this went a velvet pelisse, and she added a shovel-bonnet, gay with pink silk roses. She hesitated at the escritoire, wondering if she should leave a note for the Cunynghams. No, Radu would take care of this. From now on he would be in charge of her life, not seeking to dominate or control, but to smooth out difficulties with loving care. Exhilaration thrilled through her, though her bruised inner being kept hinting darkly that she must not make the same mistake again and collapse herself into this union. By nature she was warm, passionate, never truly whole unless sharing life with someone on every level. To be so filled with suspicion and destructive anger was alien to the bright force burning in her. It blighted her soul, brought winter to her spirit and would slowly but surely have killed her, had she not discovered the core, the fibre of her existence in Radu.

She opened the windows to let in the night. Below lay the scented garden, above lay a purple sky. The heavens seemed to sing the glory of the universe. From a full heart, she gave thanks for this newly-created world. She and Radu were about to steal the night. An owl hooted in the pines, saluting the moon-goddess. Standing there, entranced, Mariana's eyes were blinded by stars.

In some distant belfry, a clock struck three. She began to move swiftly, gathering up her few belongings. As had happened once before, she was being carried along by powers too strong to fight. Picking up her valise, she said goodbye to the room. It held no memories, as impersonal as an hotel. She closed the door quietly on it. No sounds wafted up from the darkness below as she hurried down the staircase where moonlight pierced the high windows. The Grand Salon was as tidy as if the ball had never been. She found one of the glass double-doors to the terrace had been left unfastened. How careless of the servants. It would never have been tolerated at Thornfalcon. She shivered, despite her warm coat. Kenrick Old Court too had been barred and bolted like a prison. It *had* been her prison for a while, her own grandmother her gaoler, with her ill-tempered pinches, her cane which slashed without warning or mercy, her sarcasm and demands. Don't think of it – and don't dare dwell on Thornfalcon, she whispered to herself. The past is gone, dead and buried. Happiness awaits you out there in the darkness.

A few steps took her across the paved terrace, down a short flight of stairs, across a dewy lawn and into the stableyard. The gate to freedom lay ahead. The heavy bolt screeched and she pulled it open in terror, expecting a horde of guards to come bursting out, armed with muskets. Nobody came. Not even a dog barked. The road was beyond, black, frightening in that still hour which heralds day. Supposing Radu had not been serious? The thought went through her like an icicle. He had told her to be there at half past three. She could not read her fob-watch, staring down angrily at its dim enamelled face, cursing the obscurity. It could not have taken her long to reach the gate. She settled down to wait, starting at every sound. Her heart leapt in her chest when something black and stealthy began to circle round her skirts, tipping them with a hardly tangible brush, while a vague, spinning-wheel whirring rose up. She stepped back. The thing followed, seeming to swell larger, while the noise multiplied, punctuated by an occasional catch, like the click of a clockwork toy.

Mariana lectured herself on her cowardice, bending to stroke the cat who permitted this caress, his great tail sweeping to and fro, stretching up to rub her cheek with whiskers like a butterfly's wing, his enigmatic eyes glowing green in the faint light. Mariana laughed aloud, suddenly gay. Radu would let her have a kitten, she was sure. She had missed feline company so much. There had always been Tibby at home, stretching before the hearth, crouched on sunny walls with neatly folded paws, stalking small furry creatures through the bushes.

Then she forgot her newfound friend, hearing the jingle of harness and the rumble of wheels on the road. She could make out the shape of a hooded britska coming towards her, drawn by a pair of sprightly horses, shining like ghosts. Radu was driving, immensely tall in his high fur hat. He hauled on the reins and waved as she ran to meet him. The horses were breathing hard, snorting at being made to stop when they had been getting up a brisk trot. He reached down for her, and pulled her on to the single seat, laughing at her glimmering pale face. He tucked the valise in the back, put a rug over her knees, then touched the horses with the whip.

'That was bravely done, darling,' he said, his profile turned to her as he watched the swiftly passing road fly beneath their wheels.

'I thought you'd never come,' she sighed, resting her head on his shoulder. She was out of breath, fear, excitement and nervousness gnawing at her.

He grunted in response, and brought his free arm about her, holding her hard against his side. 'No fear of that. I've told David about it. He's given us his blessing.'

'Where are we going?' It was cold now, that chill which was coming with the dawn flushing the east.

'Leave that to me,' he replied. 'I've arranged everything.'

There comes at least one moment in every life, so compellingly powerful that it cannot be denied. The usual logical process is held in abeyance, rationality suspended. One acts by instinct. Thus it was with Mariana. A tightly coiled spring had suddenly been released, and the joy of it struck her dumb. At first glance she had known Radu, had been unconsciously awaiting his coming since her birth. She had found the other half of herself – a self that had been pining for its twin. When she had married Christopher, she had thought, for a while, that it was he, but had quickly learned her mistake.

As the britska gathered speed and they drove through sleeping Vienna, she was living entirely for the moment. What had gone before was unimportant. What lay in store had yet to be. She existed – her arm linked with Radu's, the warmth of his body penetrating her wrap, journeying with him as if she had done so for countless centuries. There was no smallest trace of doubt. She knew. And this man, as silent with wonder as she, knew it too. It was a magical moment of unity, a touching of souls more significant than if their bodies had been locked in a sexual embrace. They had found one another again, filled with awe, this awakening almost a religious experience.

They were following the Danube, that wide, splendid river which wound its way across so much of Europe, linking countries, linking cities, a vast waterway for trade and pleasure. The houses had thinned, and the straight road was bordered by trees. The earth seemed newborn, as fresh and innocent as when created. Mariana's spirits soared as the sky brightened, washed with pale lemon, delicate apricot and fiery pink. They left the highway, taking a poplar-fringed track, broken occasionally by cross-timbered farmhouses, solid stone barns, and windmills with lazily stirring wings. The fields began to fill with peasants working in the early sunshine. Rosy-cheeked children watched fat cattle on the roadside verges. Several oxcarts lurched by, stirring up the dust which hung in the air before drifting slowly across cultivated vegetable gardens and vineyards.

Late in the morning they came to a large village where the older women sat outside their houses in the shade of the trees, carved distaffs in their hands. Radu turned the britska into the courtyard of an inn, ducks and hens rushing, squawking, from the wheels. It was a posting-house, its stone walls hung with carved wooden balconies under shallow-hipped roofs of uneven curved tiles, the red faded and lichened with age. On one corner of the building, a bronze weather-cock twirled slowly. Radu reined in and the vehicle braked. They turned simultaneously and smiled into each other's eyes. Till that moment, they had not uttered a word, speech a crude intrusion into that eternal space of timeless recognition which enwrapped them.

At last, she said: 'Where are we?'

250

'Near the Hungarian border.'

He let the reins trail idly, touching her cheek, almost fearing her to be a dream-woman who might disappear in broad daylight. Her beauty moved him. Such a slim creature in her red coat, the white fur collar about her throat, that frivolous little bonnet shading her face. Within its depths, he could see her broad brow and pointed chin, the violet eyes, fringed by long lashes, meeting his openly.

'Are you taking me to Hungary?' She was asking ordinary questions, yet he knew that what she really meant was: 'I've found you. I love you.'

He nodded, still stroking her face, and her lids closed under his fingers, tranquillity soothing her heart. 'We go to Budapest, then on to Montezena. I've an escort meeting us here.'

With her eyes tight shut, she swayed towards him and his arms claimed her. Her head fell back as his mouth opened hers in a series of deep, searching kisses. That painful desire which she had hoped never to feel again, tingled to her nerve ends. She was melting in exquisite delight which culminated in a sense of emptiness, as if he had drawn her soul from between her lips, but there was fullness too as she somehow became a part of him.

When he lifted his head, she caught her breath at the intensity of his expression. Her awareness was acute, everything diamond-sharp – the black hair which curled on his brow, the sideburns which marked his jaw, the fineness of his bronzed skin.

'Am I dreaming?' he whispered. 'All my days have been a path to this one morning.'

Mariana nestled into him, the pressure of his chest balm to the ever-present wound within her own. 'It was meant to happen. One can't swim against the tide.' She was concentrating on the protective wings of his shadow that fell across her, and that lovely feeling of beatitude, close to tears.

Their moment of intimacy was invaded by the clatter of hooves as half a dozen men in blue uniforms tittuped into the yard, followed by a green-varnished coach with a coat-of-arms blazoned on its doors. Radu looked across and, with one arm still holding Mariana, shouted to their leader: 'Good morning, Cornel.'

The lieutenant saluted smartly, smiling above his high, braided collar. He swung round to issue a command and the horsemen formed a line. People appeared on the balconies and at windows, attracted by the commotion. A swag-bellied host wearing a striped apron came from the inn and trundled over to the britska.

'Daily life already intrudes into Eden,' murmured Radu.

'I'll be always beside you.'

'For ever?' There was a shadow in his eyes and she knew that he had been wronged and betrayed, like herself.

'For ever,' she repeated, praying that the gods would be kind.

With a foot on the carriage step, he leapt down. He held up his arms to help her alight, and Cornel stood stiffly to attention, snapping his heels together as they were introduced. 'Everything's in order, your Highness,' he reported, speaking in halting English so that she would not be excluded. 'Axos has your luggage in the carriage.' He was admiring Mariana as he talked, smart and good to look upon, every inch the mettlesome soldier.

'Poor Axos, no doubt he cursed me, having to pack up again just after we'd arrived in Vienna,' Radu chuckled. 'He loathes any disruption of routine, so you must be prepared for his disapproval, Maria. He's my devoted valet, and once you can convince him that you haven't the slightest intention of cleaning my boots or brushing my uniform, he'll take to you.'

Axos was standing by the coach, exchanging brisk insults with a man struggling to unload the baggage. Radu called out to him and he stumped over, looking Mariana up and down with a critical eye. Radu gave him instructions and Axos, muttering beneath his breath, took himself off to the inn, venting his spleen on the servants. Radu accepted the bowing homage of the landlord who led them into the parlour where his jolly, beaming wife conducted Mariana to the best bedroom. She was obviously curious, but they could only communicate by sign language. Smiles went a long way, Mariana discovered, and she nodded her thanks for the hot water in the flowered china basin on the wash-stand, with soap and clean towels to hand.

Alone again, she removed her bonnet, brushed her hair, and washed away the fatigue of the journey. Taking some cosmetic jars from the valise, she powdered her face and touched rouge to her lips. Later she could not recall performing these mundane actions, moving in a daze, fumbling over her toilet, already missing Radu.

He was in the parlour with his élite bodyguard who bowed solemnly when she entered, swords jangling. The windows of the clean, panelled room were open, and she could see the garden with apple-trees thick with blossom, brilliant beds of larkspur, stocks and tulips, and the corner of a crumbling ivy-clad wall. The table was spread with a cloth, and the crockery had a deep purple border, the landlady's best. Mariana slipped into the vacant seat next to Radu, and his smile was like heaven to her. He was so splendid, and although she could not understand what was being said, it was impossible not to pick up on the genuine affection which his officers showed towards him. He had changed out of his uniform, and was plainly dressed in black with a white frill in his pleated shirt, a white stock under his chin. A travelling cloak hung over the back of his chair.

Mariana had not been conscious of hunger, but now found that she was ravenous. The food was unusual but delicious: caviar from the Danube estuary, thick soup made with sour cream, which Radu said was *ciorba*, and a dish of paprikas stuffed with rice and minced meat covered in a rich sauce. Baskets of white bread were flanked by platters heaped with golden butter. There were a number of bottles standing in ice-buckets or warming in the sun, and plenty of dark, aromatic coffee.

The soldiers rose to a man at one point, toasting the Prince's lady. *'Noroc!'* they shouted, before tossing back their drinks.

She thanked them in English and then in French, appreciating their welcome. Had they not been so overwhelmingly genial, they would have been alarming, with their waxed moustaches, pig-tails, high headgear and glittering weapons. They became louder as the wine circulated, and she guessed that their brand of humour was probably embarrassingly broad, glad that she could not understand them. Radu seemed more relaxed in their company than he had been at the ball, leaving the banter to Cornel, who was proving an engaging table-companion, attentively charming to Mariana.

No one was in a hurry to leave but at length Radu gave the order to depart. He had decided to ride in the coach with her, and she was glad to be alone with him again. To see him with his men was a constant reminder of his position, and the rash step she was taking. The carriage was another pointer to his status, luxurious and well-sprung. The tan leather upholstery was button-studded, and the window fitments of brass and ivory. There were shallow lockers under the seats for hand-luggage, and a shelf which could be pulled down to form a table. She ran her hands over the silky leather, and knew that she was slightly drunk because her thoughts were so clear. The Chadony had been cool and deliciously fruity. Yes, this seat was comfortingly solid. She wasn't dreaming. Radu too was real. He knocked on the panel with his knuckles and the coach

253

swayed into motion. She could see the flash of blue and gold as his men trotted on either side.

Then he was kissing her lips, her throat, and his hands were on her breasts, pushing aside her gown, eager for the flesh beneath, but he did not attempt to seduce her. This thing that had happened to them was too precious to be rendered sordid by a hasty coupling on a carriage-seat. He wanted much more – companionship and understanding. Though her beauty delighted him, it was her personality which held him captive. Oh, yes, she would bring him to ecstasy when the moment was right, and then give him tranquillity of mind. She was offering her inner self as well as her body. Control was an effort for he was used to gratifying his desires without restraint, but he swore not to lose it till their wedding-night.

Mariana was more impatient. Why not snatch at satisfaction now? Life had a nasty habit of preparing shocks just around the corner. He wanted to marry her, was being so sweetly gallant, but dared she do it? Unhappy thoughts cooled the heat of passion. She fought them desperately, seeking comfort in the fact that she was so far removed from old ties, soon to be lost in the mountains. When winter came the snow would lock them in and intruders out. No one would ever know, and yet: 'I'll be yours now, Radu,' she cried. 'You don't have to marry me. I don't ask that.'

'I want to marry you.' He spoke very low, his lips near hers. 'Nothing else will content me. You must belong to me – my Princess – the mother of my children. I've sent messengers to Montezena. A priest will be waiting for us. Don't make it harder for me, darling.'

He carefully buttoned her bodice and folded her mantle around her. She knew disappointment, yet was flattered by his concern, making up her mind to go through with the ceremony. She would leap into the void, trusting in the power of love to overcome all obstacles. The coach rocked like a boat on a peaceful sea, and she fell asleep, cradled in Radu's arms, giving her destiny into his keeping.

'Are you mad?' thundered Lancelot, glaring at an astonished David. 'How could you give your permission for those two to marry?'

Everyone had slept late after the ball, and Lancelot had found David on the terrace, finishing a solitary breakfast. Georgiana was in bed, warding off morning-sickness, and their host and hostess not yet in evidence. It was then that David had dropped the bombshell.

'What's the matter, Lance?' He frowned up at the doctor who was standing over him like an outraged Jupiter. 'I would've thought you'd be delighted. Georgiana is, in as much as she can be pleased at anything just now. The poor darling can't even keep a glass of water down. How long will this wretched sickness continue?'

'No more than a few weeks.' Lancelot was not concerned about his friend's pregnant wife at that moment. 'You must stop the wedding, David. Send a post-boy after 'em.'

'I can't do that. I don't know their route.' Bewilderment was mingled with David's annoyance. 'Why're you in such a sweat? I thought you liked Maria.'

'Merciful heavens! I do! That's the bloody trouble!' Lancelot took to an agitated prowling over the tessellated paving.

David misunderstood, even more amazed. 'Don't tell me that you're in love with her yourself?'

Lancelot's face turned puce and he pulled up short, cracking his fist down on the round table under the striped awning. The china rattled violently. 'What a damn-fool idea! Hell, why is it that everyone immediately assumes that one's motives are guided by passion, if one shows the smallest interest in a girl? I like her. I feel affection for her. I'll not see disaster overtake her.'

David set his cup back in its saucer and filled it with black coffee. 'There's nothing disastrous about marrying a prince. You think she's not worthy of him? Can foresee trouble with Princess Arta? As I told him last night, to the best of my knowledge her blood is as blue as can be.'

'Is it, indeed?' Lancelot said gloomily. Then he lowered himself into a wicker chair and stared into the cup which David handed him. 'You think this ends the matter? You're quite happy about it?'

'Positively delighted.' David was relieved to see that he was calmer, yet Lancelot had managed to upset him. Before his arrival, David had been sitting there quietly enjoying the sunshine and the view, congratulating himself that he had done rather well by his ward. Lancelot had sown the seeds of doubt. 'You never did tell me what she confessed to you in London,' he added, making Lancelot squirm with discomfort. 'Can't you bend your sacred oath a trifle, if there's really something I should know?'

Lancelot tugged at his mop of hair, exasperated. 'Can't be done. You've put me in a devilish awkward predicament, David. I'll tell you that for free.'

The speed with which the news spread was remarkable. In

no time Vienna was buzzing with the exciting story of how Prince Radu had run off with Lord Cunyngham's ward. Dimitrie carried the tale to Grigore who was staying at Madame Feodora's brothel. He owned the establishment, though few knew this. He had a large number of similar interests with various mesdames fronting his whore-house investments all over Europe. Others in his pay worked the prosperous gambling-clubs, while those lower down the scale kept opium-dens. Prince Alecsandri had provided generously for his bastard. The title of Baron Petresco had given him revenues from the countryside around Castle Horia. His mother had been exceedingly rich, both from her royal Turkish connections and her nefarious activities. But Grigore was a greedy man. He could never have enough of money and power. They were a drug more essential to his well-being than wine, hashish or the embraces of a thousand beautiful women.

Dimitrie was taken to Grigore's private apartment by Feodora herself. It was his influence which had dictated the eastern décor, and nowhere was this more evident than in his own reception room. Islamic tiles covered the walls, citron and blue, umber and pale green, with rich arabesque borders. The furniture was of delicately carved filigree, gilded and inlaid with semi-precious stones. The chimney-piece was striking, having a pointed brass canopy twelve feet high. There were recesses on either side, lined with cushioned divans, and every door was worked with patterns of ivory and mother-of-pearl. Traceried windows filled the bay at one end, looking out over a patio, beyond which could be seen the glittering blue of the Danube.

Grigore was seated, cross-legged, on one of the sofas, and Elizabeth lounged amongst a pile of silk cushions, wearing a provocative *djallaba*. Yasmin stirred the air with a peacock-feather fan. Grigore did not look pleased to see Dimitrie.

'What d'you want? I don't recall sending for you.'

Dimitrie took one of the other divans without being invited, and told Yasmin to fetch him a glass of wine. 'I thought you'd be interested to hear what's been happening among our English visitors,' he drawled, stretching out his well-tailored legs, and folding his arms behind his head. 'It concerns Prince Radu.'

Elizabeth uncoiled her limbs, leaning on one elbow and plucking at the bluish-purple grapes in a golden bowl. Grigore scowled, the scar a livid line against his olive skin. 'Come to the point, and then get out. I hope no one saw you entering my rooms.'

Dimitrie smiled his feline smile, and chucked Yasmin under the chin. 'I'm discretion itself, as you well know, dear boy.' He sipped his wine, taking his time. Grigore was a black, moody devil and Dimitrie detested him but was always in need of money. Grigore struck a hard bargain and expected one's soul in return, but his devious machinations amused Dimitrie who was reckless enough to defy him, though not beyond the point of personal safety.

'Get on with it.' Any mention of Radu's name was calculated to stir the evil fires smouldering in Grigore. His half-brother had become an obsession with him. He could not know for certain, but suspected that the Prince had been instrumental in the escape of Danesti, who now roamed free in the forest of Castle Horia, giving Grigore no respite from harassment.

Dimitrie was watching the light sparkle on his snuff-box, a smile on his lips. He looked at Grigore through screening gold-tipped lashes. 'Edwin Cunyngham's a useful fellow, though rather too fond of the bottle. Even this failing can be advantageous, for in his cups his tongue runs away with him. I've learned much regarding the admirable David Cunyngham, facts which I'm sure will be of interest to you. For example, did you know that he and Radu served in the army together, fighting Boney? Did you also know that Maria Malton is his ward?'

Grigore shifted impatiently, staring at Dimitrie with distaste. 'So, you insufferable puppy? Is this worth disturbing me to report? You're too late. Don't expect payment for something I already know. I sent Schoene to teach him a lesson the other night. He's under constant surveillance. If Radu thinks to enlist his aid against me, he's in for a disappointment.'

Dimitrie examined his carefully manicured nails. 'I knew Schoene was one of your bullies. A waste of money, my dear Baron, he's a thick-witted dolt. He came off badly. Cunyngham's handy with his fists,' he observed, then he looked up again, blue eyes sharp. 'Something's taken place which even you didn't anticipate. Radu has eloped with Maria. He intends to wed her.'

Even he was shaken by the spasm of diabolical rage which contorted Grigore's face. 'When did this happen?' He sprang up, his broad shadow lowering over the Count.

'In the early hours of this morning.' Dimitrie did not lack courage. He out-stared the Baron, refusing to be brow-beaten.

'Where are they?' An iron hand shot out, seizing him by the cravat. 'Tell me, damn you!'

'I don't know, and that's the truth,' Dimitrie spluttered. Grigore let him go, and he smoothed his creased shirt-front, mortally offended. 'They're gone – scarpered – and Cunyngham's going around pretending to be furious, but Edwin thinks he was party to it.'

'Give Edwin anything he wants – drink, opium, women, money.' Grigore was glaring out across the Danube as if he would swim down its length in pursuit of his enemy. He had laid elaborate and costly plans that Radu should be slain during a hunt which Baron von Gundling had arranged for his visitors. 'Does he love his brother?' he asked slowly. 'Would he be willing to work for me?'

'Cunyngham's strict and baulks at paying his bills. He dislikes Maria heartily. He was too free with her and she repulsed him. He hasn't forgiven this insult, though I think it showed remarkably good taste on her part, what?' Dimitrie's flippant tone aggravated Grigore's inflammable temper.

He said nothing for a moment, but in that silence his terrible anger grew till he felt unable to contain it. It was like a demonic possession, shaking his whole being, bringing the dark blood to his sallow face, murder peering out through his eyes. Radu had nimbly taken horse from Vienna, and Maria was to be his bride. Soon there would be a child. Grigore had looked her over last night. Yes, she was a breeder without doubt. Once a son lay in the great State cradle in Neograd, his own chances would fade. He must strike. His assassins had been prepared, the hunt rigged to make Radu's death appear a tragic accident. Money wasted, time and opportunity lost, and all because some haughty English bitch had caught Radu's fancy.

Someone had to bear the brunt of his frustration. He sneered at Elizabeth. 'That's foiled your ambitions, my dear.'

'I don't know what you mean.' She had quickly recovered from the first shock of Dimitrie's news, though equally infuriated. One look at Maria last night had convinced her that she was a dangerous rival, but she had not realized how dangerous. Elizabeth was not the kind to give up easily. Radu would tire of matrimony, all men did, then she would renew her attack. Also there were other subtle ways by which Maria could be destroyed. Elizabeth favoured a particularly undetectable brand of poison which she had adopted as her own weapon for removing undesirable obstacles.

'You're so transparent, Elizabeth.' Grigore was staring at her with that look of erotic evil which excited her. 'I know that you wished to be Princess Varna.'

'Perhaps I did,' she admitted lightly, raising her arms above her head with languid grace, so that her robe fell open. 'But only when you were Prince, darling.'

'How easily you lie, bitch,' he said, half admiring, half hating her. Having abandoned the ruined plan, he was busy constructing another. 'Radu's new love may prove his downfall. If we can get our hands on her, he'll do anything to have her returned, even abdicate in my favour.' He took his place on the divan again, darkly brooding, the embodiment of malevolence. 'Cultivate Edwin. This is an order, Dimitrie. I want to know everything that happens in von Gundling's circle. Meanwhile, I'll send a man to Montezena to keep a close watch on the lovebirds. Radu will rue the day he decided to marry.'

The coach party had penetrated deeply into Hungary by the time night fell. They rested in another small village and, after dinner, Radu and Mariana wandered in the garden beneath a yellow moon, and he told her about his life as a child in the palace at Neograd, as a student in Leipzig and Heidelberg, and as an officer in the army. He was frank about his love-affairs, including the liaison with Elizabeth.

Mariana remembered her, that lovely creature with the fiery hair, who had smiled with hatred in her eyes. Images of Radu embracing her rose tormentingly. She felt sick with jealousy. 'You loved her?'

'No.' He was leaning against a low wall, his arm round her waist. 'I've never been in love till now.' He sighed, face troubled. 'How can I expect someone like you to understand the indulgence of the senses, the mindless lusts which have driven me, without once touching my ideal? I thought the perfect woman a mirage, never to be attained, so I used the others for my selfish pleasure. Can you possibly comprehend such cynicism?'

'Yes,' she replied, knowing it only too well. She had been taught by a master.

He thought that she was humouring him, as he struggled to be honest. 'Elizabeth amused me for a while, but I was never deceived by her. She's one of Grigore's spies, yet is prepared to betray him. Watch her, Maria, should you meet her again. She's clever and will try to gain your confidence.'

A cloud crossed between herself and happiness. 'I'll be careful,' she promised, thinking: My God, I must beware, if she found out about me she could ruin everything. Why does it have to be like this? Radu wants no secrets, and he's waiting for me to open my heart to him. And I can't – I can't –

259

He did not insist, telling himself that she would bare her soul when they were man and wife. He sensed that she had been badly hurt, and would not add to her pain or resurrect sad memories. For the moment, it was sufficient that she loved him. Time is a great healer, he thought, content to be enthralled by her beauty, enjoying the novelty of being a prospective bridegroom.

He kissed her gently at the door of her bedroom and did not ask to come in. She wanted him with her, conflicting emotions pulling her this way and that. It was wonderful that he was willing to wait. It made her feel truly loved, yet it would have been so much simpler to have become his mistress. She lay awake for hours, watching the logs sift through the iron bars of the grate, and the glowing mass crumble into fawn and grey dust. Would her hopes crumble in a like manner?

Radu owned a house in Budapest, but insisted that they press on. Two more days of travelling before they finally came to the mountains, following a haphazard, zigzag path, twisting and writhing upwards. Wild flowers bloomed on the slopes and hung from steep rock-faces, turning them into fantastic gardens. The road was rough, down through valleys and mountain passes, then up again. Urged by the driver, the coach team struggled up a further rise and came to a grassy plateau which gave a breath-taking view of great plains, ancient forests, a swift river and sorrel-coloured mountains with snow-capped peaks away on the horizon. Nestling at the base of a nearby escarpment lay a most unusual building.

It appeared to be half monastery, half castle, as if its architects had been warrior-priests. Built of the rock itself, it was a dirty grey colour, as were the surrounding high walls. There was a guard at the gate, leaning on his musket. He leapt to attention as the cortège came closer and, very soon, the large wooden doors opened and they passed beneath an arch, coming out in a cobbled square. People came running, men, women and children, greeting them with shouts and wide smiles. Several large hounds were barking frenziedly until a few dexterous blows with a heavy whip-handle sent them off howling. A gigantic man came to the door of the coach as it stopped.

'Welcome to my home, your Highness,' he bellowed, throwing back his mane of tangled red hair and roaring with laughter.

'Good to see you, Danesti,' Radu smiled, as the brigand clasped him in a bear-hug, crushing him to the cracked surface of his sheepskin waistcoat, nearly choking him with the mingled smells of sweat, garlic and tobacco. 'Has the priest come? Is all ready?'

'Ah, ready and waiting.' Danesti treated him to a knowing wink. 'The villagers have gathered from miles around to see you married.'

'There's been no word from Neograd?' Radu asked as he gave Mariana his hand, helping her down.

'Not so far.' Danesti was regarding her from his great height, smiling kindly. 'And this is the lucky little lady?' She could not understand a word, but was unafraid. Danesti had about him the air of a genial, tail-wagging mastiff.

'Yes, this is Miss Malton, shortly to be your Princess. Honour her, my friend. I put her in your care, should I ever be absent.'

'Anything you command, I'll obey.' Danesti set his legs wide on the cobbles, his sword, point-raised, in his right hand in one of those dramatic gestures that he loved. He thrust his red beard forward. 'You saved my life, and I'll never forget it.'

It had soon leaked out that the person responsible for his escape from Castle Horia had been none other than the Prince. They had met several times since, and Radu found that this large scarecrow of a man possessed qualities which made him a born leader. Though preferring out and out attack, he was not above adopting all manner of disguises to spy on Grigore's supporters, prepared to risk life and limb for the Prince, longing to see the traitor brought low. Now, sweeping off his shaggy hat, he offered Mariana his obedience, then pushed through his smiling followers, striding to the entrance of his castle, tossing his cloak to a ragged lad to whom he administered a vigorous pummelling by way of showing his affection.

The old, shabby fortress resounded to the tramp of booted feet as Radu's bodyguard made themselves at home, the air humming with greetings in various dialects. One of the gaily-attired serving women took Mariana to a bedchamber. In sudden panic, she realized that this was her wedding-day and she was still wearing the dress in which she had eloped. She had hoped to go shopping in Budapest but Radu had given her no time. The peasant girl smiled and, in dumb-show, indicated that the gown spread out on the bed was for her. It was sumptuous, a masterpiece of silk and embroidery, and the thought that Radu had remembered to order its preparation moved her deeply.

'It's beautiful,' she said, though knowing that the girl would not understand her. 'I've never seen a dress quite like it.' She touched the fine linen and handmade lace, the silk overskirt dyed a vibrant crimson, its surface covered in patterns of gold thread and sparkling beads.

The girl smiled and nodded vigorously. She was clad in her best, ready for the celebrations, a striking young woman with sun-kissed features, fair hair, a finely-shaped mouth and white teeth. With gestures of encouragement, she expressed her admiration of the lady soon to be her Princess.

'What's your name?' Mariana had to ask her several times before the light of comprehension dawned in her blue eyes.

'Ah, *ma numesc? Ma numesc – Lucia.*'

'Well, Lucia, you must help me get ready,' Mariana smiled.

Lucia poured warm water from a ewer into an earthenware basin, then hauled over a tapestry-covered screen so that Mariana might have a strip-wash in privacy. She had almost finished when a soft white chemisette was draped over the screen, its ballooning, tight-cuffed sleeves worked with scarlet and gold flowers. It fastened at the front with little ball-buttons, finishing in a deep V between her breasts. A flounced petticoat came next and when she had put it on, she stepped out into the room and Lucia helped her into a rustling, ankle-length white skirt, again lavishly embroidered. The red overskirt was added, slit up the front, calf-reaching, its border stiff with gold threadwork. A parti-coloured token apron completed the outfit, tightly girded by a striped sash.

Mariana had clean white stockings in her valise. These and a pair of flat black pumps seemed perfectly suitable, and she viewed herself in the mirror with a shock of pleased surprise. When her willing helper had fixed a net veil, sparkling with sequins, over her loose dark hair, she did indeed look a Rumanian bride. A necklace comprised of gold coins was fastened around her throat, crescent-shaped earrings hung each side of her face, and the illusion was complete.

Lucia clapped her hands. *'Frumos! Frumos!'* she cried.

Laughing, more secure in this disguise, loving the world and Lucia in particular, Mariana spun round and hugged the astonished peasant. She was ready to be married and there was Cornel knocking on the door to fetch her down. When he offered her his arm, she felt herself to be moving in a jewelled haze and floated out, fingers clutching his sleeve. Danesti had ordered that the castle should be gay with flowers. People were arriving, peasants in a blaze of finery, red and green and yellow. There was the sound of excited voices, the distant notes of fiddlers tuning up.

'You're trembling, my lady,' said Cornel, with his kind, shy smile. 'Don't be nervous. It'll be quite painless, you know.'

She returned his smile, feeling the smooth stuff of his blue uniform under her hand, fighting to check the memory of a building, grey and sunless, not dazzling with the white glare of a hot summer afternoon. Don't think about that! It never happened! She fixed her mind on Radu. The past was something she had dreamed. He was her reality. But if she shut her lids, she saw Christopher – not in her eyes, but somewhere behind, in a sort of dark mirror. For a fraction of a second, he was as solid as if he stood before her, with his remote smile and accusing, mocking stare. I don't want to think of you, she cried silently. I don't belong to you now. I'm not your wife. You killed our child and forfeited my love. Oh God, would that the ceremony was over! I need to be alone with Radu. He'll make me forget.

'Not long now,' comforted Cornel as they crossed the courtyard and entered the cool purple shadows of a chapel.

It was incense-filled, a remotely-foreign place of worship, and its very strangeness, its smell, made the memories difficult to control. Faded frescos portraying martyrs and saints decorated the white-washed walls. Priests gathered like blackbirds. They made Mariana increasingly uneasy. A bearded young monk led in the procession, beating a gong. Another followed him, resplendent in red and gold, carrying a jewelled icon. Smoke from thick white candles curled blue into the still air. The altar lay ahead, glittering with gold and gems, dominated by a tortured Byzantine Christ. She looked away from its face, so hollow-eyed and haggard – like Christopher's on that grey day in Thornfalcon's dim grey chapel. But it was Radu who awaited her at this altar.

If only I didn't feel so guilty, she mourned. The priests moved with slow, measured paces. A woman broke from the crowded stone benches, kneeling with bowed head on the flagstones to kiss the shining icon before resuming her place. Mariana had the urge to fling herself down and do the same, begging forgiveness for what she was about to do. Somewhere, unseen, boyish voices were chanting. Oh, I wish they wouldn't, she thought, horribly apprehensive. There was so much hidden chanting in that place I'm trying to forget, though Christopher denied it, said I imagined it. I mustn't cry – not at my wedding – it's a bad omen!

She drew level with Radu, not daring to look at him. A large, black-bearded priest faced them, in white and purple robes, with a flowing black headcloth. He raised his hands and the ceremony began. She was lost in a wilderness of strange phrases, unrehearsed for this almost pagan ritual. It dragged on interminably – the incense, the tinkling bells of the altar-boys, the blurred candles, the sunlight diffused by blue smoke, striking through an arched stone window. A theatrical atmophere, as if they were actors in a play. The priest delivered the final lines. Radu lifted Mariana's veil and kissed her lips. A sigh rippled through the emotion-charged audience, and the curtain came down.

Mariana went under the arch with her arm through her husband's. He was smiling, waving to the waiting crowd outside. Peasants and gypsies in gala costumes rushed at them, throwing handfuls of rice and petals. Everyone was shouting, cheering, laughing. The couple made slow progress against the incoming tide of well-wishers. Danesti, who had been quietly devout during the service, was now bawling instructions, taking his responsibilities seriously. He ushered the bridal pair up some steps and into a big hall. He had done his best to put it to rights, but the armour hanging on the walls was rusty, faded curtains were askew at the windows and chairs sagged sadly with their stuffing poking out. At one end stood a fine screen but it was smashed in places as if victim of some drunken brawl. Fortunately the swarming guests hid these disasters. Rituals over, they were now settling down to the serious business of feasting.

Radu had spared no expense, and the long oaken tables groaned beneath the weight of laden dishes. Danesti's men had been posted to guard the ramparts, but they were taking these duties in shifts, clumping into the hall, smelling strongly of sheepskins and *rakiya*, fierce, bearded ruffians, bristling with weapons, fur hats tipped forward over wild eyes, filled with boisterous high spirits.

'They're great fighters,' said Radu from his chair at the head of the main table. He commanded the assembly in his magnificent crimson uniform, with shimmering epaulettes widening his shoulders. He had seen how Mariana flinched every time one of them staggered to his feet, stood there swaying as he shouted a toast to his Prince, and then to his *condottiere*, not forgetting the new Princess, before hurling his glass to shatter on the stone hearth. 'Loyal to me, my love. Don't be alarmed by their barbaric manners.'

None of it was real, only the pride she felt in being his wife. 'It's all rather strange, Radu. Teach me the language so that I can talk to your people.'

'Our people,' he corrected gently. 'You're Princess Varna now.'

264

What would be expected of her? she wondered, sipping the strong wine of the country. She wished that he had been an ordinary man, a farmer or a shepherd. He had warned her that he might sometimes be called away. She would be left in Neograd, surrounded by strangers with whom she could not even communicate. I don't really believe it's happening, she thought.

The feasting looked fair set to last throughout the night. Gypsy violins throbbed sweetly, mingling with the rippling notes of the cimbalom and the high-pitched bird-call of a flute. As the wine flowed, the dancing became more abandoned, the young men taking the floor amidst cheers, each showing off, stamping his way through the intricate steps of the *hora* or the *calusari*.

'This is the music that sings in the hearts of the peasants and gypsies.' Radu's hand closed over hers as he spoke and everything was perfect again. 'It's their guiding light through sorrow and joy, persecution or triumph. It runs in their veins with their lifeblood.'

Mariana responded to the beat, applauding the grace of the pretty girls in their embroidered blouses, skirts spinning out, showing slender brown legs amidst the frothing petticoats. The tambourines vibrated in their hands, and the handsome lads clapped in time to the exciting rhythms.

Radu led her amongst his guests, approaching one of the gypsy chieftains, a dignified man, his features carved with that same fierce independence which was reflected in Radu's. He wore his finery like an emperor, black velvet trimmed with silver, nutbrown fingers flaming with gems, hooped golden earrings gleaming against the black tightly curling hair.

'May God shower you with blessings, my Prince,' he said.

'I pray that you'll be happy here, my child.' His wife laid her slim hands on Mariana's head. She was a handsome woman, dressed in emerald silk with many gold chains and rings, swarthy-skinned, sable-haired, with eyes as deep as night and as wise as the mountains on which she roamed.

'You speak English.' Mariana had not expected that.

'I've travelled far. My name is Sylka, and I'm a true Romany,' she replied graciously, a queen in her own right. Mariana had the sudden desire to confess everything to her.

'Ask her to read the stones for you.' Radu's voice recalled her.

'The stones?' Mariana looked at him, puzzled.

'The Runes,' he smiled, though part serious. 'She'll tell you what the future holds. Will our firstborn be a son, Sylka?' His tone was gay, but the gypsy's face was serious.

'She has her future here, your Highness.'

Radu was insistent, so Sylka drew Mariana into a recess near one of the windows. The dusky trees and flaming sky, all the deepening shadows in the bronze and gold of encroaching night, swam around them in circles of darkness and light. Sylka was bathed in scarlet, in emerald and brown, with black braids shining, and silver earrings glistening in the fading sunset.

'You're unwilling that I do this, aren't you?' she said, but as she spoke she took a small leather pouch from a pocket in her skirt.

'I know nothing of such things.' Mariana attempted a laugh which choked in her throat. 'What are the Runes?'

'Some call them the Runes of Destiny.' Sylka was spreading a white scarf on the window embrasure. She closed her eyes, face lifted to the sky, lips moving as if in prayer or talking to invisible beings. When she opened them again, they were misty. 'These are ancient, powerful stones, used by the Northlanders time out of mind. Sometimes, I consult them – sometimes the Tarot cards or the crystal. All are gateways to the unknown.' She held out the bag to Mariana. 'Shake it well, think of an issue, then draw out six. Lay them face down on the scarf.'

Maria hesitated, then plunged in her hand. Her fingers were chilled by the smooth, flat pebbles. Soon the selected Runes lay on the cloth, glistening milkily in the twilight. They were small, varying in contour. Sylka arranged them into the shape of a cross, then turned them over. Each was deeply indented with a different symbol. Sylka bent to study them, then she gasped.

There was something wrong. Mariana felt it in her bones, and a trembling sensation grew within her. 'What d'you see?' she asked.

Sylka started, roused from her trance. She gave Mariana one blank, appalled glance, then hurriedly gathered up the sacred stones and hid them in the bag. 'I can tell you nothing – nothing,' she mumbled.

Mariana gripped her hand, detaining her. 'You saw something. What was it?'

'No, Princess. The power wasn't with me tonight,' Sylka lied, looking across to where Cornel and her husband stood laughing with Radu. Her face was pale, and her voice dropped to a low, urgent whisper. 'My dear, enjoy this day – live for it, and for your wedding-night. Grasp this tiny piece of happiness. Be greedy for it. It may be all you'll ever have.'

Mariana listened with a strange sound like rushing water beating at her brain. She did not understand, and yet the reddish light on the wall beyond, the silver sheen on the earrings of Sylka's bowed head, the colourful blaze of the dancers, eddied round her in a dizzy maze. I don't believe it, she tried to tell herself, it's nothing but superstitious nonsense. From that moment on, she was extremely gay, charming everyone she met, drinking more than usual. When she next looked for her, Sylka had vanished, and she was glad.

Supplanting the sun, night had resumed its interrupted power. The celebrations were at their noisy height, and Radu said to her: 'We can go now. No one will notice.' He took her hand and led her through long passages and up staircases to the bridal-chamber.

He did not light the candles, his form and face in silhouette. They became as one when his arms enfolded her and she went silently to his embrace. She could feel the thump of his heart beneath the stiff, military jacket. Hers was beating in time with it. Radu did not hurry her, cherishing every moment, yet she was soon naked, her flesh indented by his buttons, hair flowing free, the cool night air on her skin. He lifted her, carried her over and laid her on the bed. The sheets smelt of herbs and homespun linen. A new bed is always strange, taking its time to become friendly, and this couch, very wide and thickly carved, held strangeness indeed, and magical enchantment. Mariana's head was spinning. She had drunk a lot of wine, feeling drowsy and desirous. It was so long since she had been loved by a man.

Radu took off his clothes and slipped under the covers. He was strange too, quite alien, though by now she recognized the pleasant, personal odour of him. He drew her against his naked body. He was more hairy than she had imagined, and muscular. She ran her hands over his arms, his chest, his face, tracing the peaked brows in the darkness, the deep eye-sockets, the strong nose, resting her fingertips on his lips. Then there was nothing but silken blackness and bodily sensations. She gave herself without reservation. Loving him, wanting him, longing to blend with him, and letting him know that she did.

'You're not new to this,' he said at one point, and she was afraid, thinking: I've been too bold.

'Neither are you,' she reminded gently, before being swallowed up in the heat and passion of surrender.

It was a cleansing fire. She allowed it to consume her, pour through every corner of her body and soul, accepting its purification. He was everything to her as they lay hidden in the night – lover, friend, child. She ached with tenderness, holding his head to her breast, feeling his mouth on her nipple, his body fused with hers, offering him ecstasy as an open-handed gift, a tribute to his manhood. His joy was hers, his fulfilment also. She would have died for him. Never, when lying with Christopher, had she felt wanted for anything but her body. This was different. It was as if she came to him a virgin – an equal in spiritual and physical expectations.

She slept at last, empty, satiated, her face pillowed on his shoulder, and as she slept, she dreamed. She was running down a dark alley. Houses reared like huge cliffs on each side – weird, jumbled houses, the like of which she had never seen in waking life. She was being pursued by formless terrors, wraithlike beings who spiralled in the air behind, around and before her. Slimy tentacles reached out from these shapeless entities. One caught her hand. It slobbered, and sucked at her fingers. Unable to free herself from the loathsome thing, she hammered at the door of a tumbledown house. It opened, and a woman stood there, framed against the deeper darkness beyond. A gaunt face with mad eyes peered into hers. A sick, starved child was hanging on the woman's skirt. It was sobbing piteously. The whirling blackness of insanity hit Mariana with psychic force as strong as a backhanded blow. Madness! Horrible! Grotesque! There was no escape. A lunatic blocked her way, and behind her were the writhing, bellowing, sucking nightmare things.

She woke with a gasp of relief, yet could not shake off the dream. It clung to her like a clammy mist. She got up, dragging a quilt round her bare body. The moon was blanketed by clouds and, as darkness pressed through the windows to the sighing of the trees, the room lost shape and she felt very frightened and alone. She half turned to wake Radu, but he lay on his stomach, face buried in his arms, lost to her in a dream-world of his own. She was sober now, no longer able to drown in passion. Sylka's warning rang in her head, voiding her mind of consecutive thought. Deny it though she might, primitive dread haunted her. She had been reared in a village where the countryfolk believed implicitly in ghosts and pixies, in being 'overlooked' by witches, so that crops failed, cows aborted, milk turned sour and children sickened.

Her meeting with Radu had been a miracle. She had found love again. Shivering, she sat on a stool near the window. Try as she might to recapture the joy of their marriage-bed, now she saw no fairytale future, no fantasies, only the memory of old terrors and a darkness peopled with eerie shapes.

Foreboding filled her, and the certainty of shame and disaster.

It was the hour of the wolf – that dead time before the dawn when worries and deep-seated fears rise up to haunt the insomniac, stalking across the tired brain, exaggerating problems till the throat constricts and the longing for daybreak becomes almost unendurable. Mariana was very familiar with it, that strange, cold space when a breathless hush holds all in suspension – a time when babies are often born into the long, grim struggle of life, and the dying leave it, slipping away on the tide.

CHAPTER 7

'Are you quite certain of this?' Grigore said, staring hard at the unprepossessing young man whom Dimitrie had brought to Madame Feodora's house. Edwin had come in with them, and this afforded Grigore scant consolation.

'D'you doubt my word, damn you? I'd know her anywhere.' The fellow glared at him from rather prominent eyes in a bony, mobile face under lank brown hair slicked back with macassar-oil.

He was English and a sharp dresser, his low-crowned topper set at a tilt, hands buried in the pockets of his loud check trousers. His collar and stock were over-high, his gold watch-chain and fobs just that much too big. Edwin had run across him in a beer-cellar, delighted to discover that he was a free-spender. It was perfectly clear that he was what the Corinthian Toms called a 'cad', heartless, deceitful and conceited, the flashy son of an upstart factory-owner who had made a quick fortune from the sweat and misery of the underpaid cotton-mill workers. Standards had lowered since the war, the once-rigid class distinctions becoming blurred, and Edwin was one of the younger generation who tended to mix with such men, ripe for trouble. What he did not realize was that whereas he was arrogant, wilful and capricious, Arthur Cartwright was cunning and out for everything he could get.

He was in Vienna on account of his father's booming business, dispatched to sell cotton to the textile manufacturers. He made no secret of the fact that he hated foreigners, and much preferred to hang around the dog-pits and public houses of Manchester and London, consorting with bookies and loose women.

It was not by chance that he had been present in the beer-cellar which Edwin was in the habit of frequenting. He had a piece of interesting information which his nimble brain told him might be profitable. Edwin, for all his grand airs, had fallen for it, hook, line and sinker. Arthur despised him, hating not only anyone born outside England, but also the upper classes into whose ranks, for all his father's wealth and fine new house, he would never be truly accepted. Arthur was used to spying and deceiving, as canny as a fox, which he rather resembled. He had even gone so far as to learn a smattering of German, which he spoke with a vile accent, in order to be in the know. It had not taken him long to pick up on the gossip concerning the von Gundlings' guests, and it was child's play to meet Edwin and wangle his way into the brothel. Foreign whores were as good as English ones when it came to appeasing his low-grade, brutal lusts, but more than this, he wanted an introduction to Baron Petresco. He had gathered from various sources that here was a powerful individual very well worth cultivating.

'Where did you see Maria Malton – now Princess Varna?' There was a sarcastic bite to Grigore's clipped words. He snapped his fingers at a half-naked girl who dropped to her knees as she gave him a glass of wine. He permitted her to hand one to each of his visitors. Arthur leered at her.

'Having lunch in the Prater, a few days ago,' he replied, flinging himself into a chair, hat on the back of his head, propping his legs up on a low table and staring into the serving-girl's bodice. 'She didn't see me – would've had a bloody fit if she had. Talk about surprised! You could've knocked me down with a feather!'

Grigore was detesting this ill-mannered lout more with every passing second, but he showed no emotion. 'What d'you know about her? She was Lord Cunyngham's ward.'

'Ward my arse!' Arthur swung his feet to the floor with a bang and sat up. He tapped the side of his pointed nose mysteriously. 'I know everything about her, never you fear. She ain't what she seems, not by a long chalk, and Maria Malton ain't her name.'

'You could be lying.' Grigore's lip curled, and he was planning by what painful and unpleasant manner this nasty person should meet his end, when he had finished with him.

'Oh, I could, blast my liver! I could indeed, but I'm not.' Arthur's accent was obscure. Though reared in the North, he nipped down to London whenever he could, where the young bloods aped the talk of the lower classes and vice versa. 'Be buggered if I am!' he added, with a sneer.

'That may very well happen.' Dimitrie wore a pained expression, as if a bad smell lingered under his aristocratic nose. 'It's a common practice in these parts.' He tapped the ash from his cigar to the floor, taking care to avoid the shining perfection of his boots.

'Bloody filthy foreigners!' muttered Arthur.

Grigore silenced Dimitrie with a glance, then stretched his legs out and contemplated his slim black trousers and neat ankles set off by black silk hose. 'May I ask who she is, if not Maria Malton?' he enquired blandly.

Enormously satisfied in capturing so much attention, Arthur rose to his feet. I've got 'em on the hook, all right, he thought. With the same defiance with which he faced the whole world, he now took up a stance in the centre of the group, legs astride, feet planted firmly, thumbs hooked in his waistcoat pockets. Small of stature though he was, ruthlessness was stamped all over him.

'It'll cost!' he barked.

'I didn't think that you had come here from altruistic motives,' Grigore observed coolly. 'I'm accustomed to paying highly for information.'

Arthur's brain was working furiously. Though his father supported him, he was tight-fisted, and Arthur had expensive tastes. Along with foreigners and people of the upper echelon whom he labelled 'snobs', he also hated his father. He was plotting his downfall. It was his ambition to make money fast, a considerable amount of money to enable him to set up a factory of his own to rival the family concern.

At this stage of the game he did not intend to play his ace. 'What about another drink?' he prevaricated, lips drawn back in a wolfish grin. 'My mouth's as dry as an old maid's tit. I fancy a bumper of champagne. Let's drink to a successful partnership, eh, Baron?'

Grigore gave an order. When the bottles had been brought and glasses filled, they started to haggle. Grigore named a sum which was received with withering scorn, Arthur's slashing rejection larded with oaths. Edwin, listening, almost wished that he was not his fellow-countryman. Even he was horrified by the man's brash coarseness. Dimitrie had withdrawn from the lists, lolling on one of the divans, putting as much space as possible between himself and the objectionable Arthur.

'You'll have to offer a bloody sight more than that!' Arthur had not enjoyed himself so much since a time in Lancashire when he had blackmailed and bankrupt another mill-owner, driving him to suicide. 'I'm not prepared to tell you anything, but I'll make sure that she's removed from Europe for ever, if you make it worth my while.'

Grigore decided that it was high time to bring up the reserves. He rang a hand-bell and Elizabeth drifted in. Arthur's eyes nearly popped from his head. His tongue crept out like a small, disagreeable animal from the dark cavern of his mouth, licking over his lips.

'May I present Countess Elizabeth Rogalski?' Grigore rose to his full, impressive height. He led her towards Arthur, offering this tempting prize.

Arthur was what he liked to term 'fly'. He knew exactly what Grigore was about, yet what a woman! He longed to have her at his mercy. He'd make the bitch yelp! His heart wobbled as she looked at him from under her curling lashes, as demure as a school-girl. This stirred Arthur's loins. The sight of innocence, even if it was a charade, made him yearn to smirch it in the vilest manner.

Because she roused him, it made him doubly cautious. They wouldn't get him that way. 'D'you take me for some stupid country bumpkin?' he asked nastily.

'Oh, but Mr Cartwright, I know you'll help us,' Elizabeth cooed like a turtle-dove. 'I couldn't help overhearing what you've been saying. If Maria is an imposter, then she can't possibly be allowed to occupy such an important position, can she?'

'I'll see that she don't hold it for long, darling,' said Arthur familiarly. 'If your friend and me come to a suitable financial arrangement, and you agree to show me the town, then we'll cook her goose, once and for all, you may depend on that.'

Elizabeth dimpled at him, an angel in a gown of purest white, a gauze scarf draped over her alabaster shoulders. 'I never intrude in business affairs,' she lisped. 'My poor brain can't comprehend such matters. I leave them to my superiors.'

When Arthur eventually left with Elizabeth on his arm, Grigore turned to Dimitrie, furious at having to pay so highly for Arthur's services. In fact, he had not inveigled much out of him, other than his promise that Maria would be gone within a short time.

'My God, but the air smells sweeter after the departure of that pestilential dog!' he shouted, his contained rage reminding Dimitrie of a caged tiger lashing its tail.

'He's one of the nastiest pieces of work Satan ever made,' Dimitrie agreed, cleansing his nostrils of Arthur's odious presence with a gracefully applied pinch of snuff. He gave Edwin a sneering glance. 'Trust you to introduce him into the fold.'

Edwin glowered at him drunkenly. He was almost always drunk lately, or taking opium, his moods shifting and changing. 'Thought he'd be a useful sort of cove, and so he will be, if he can get rid of Maria.'

'He's crafty, I'll grant you.' Grigore was staring into space. 'What the hell's he playing at? When Elizabeth walked in, I thought I had him in the palm of my hand.'

Dimitrie yawned, bored with the subject. He uncoiled his limbs and stood up, fiddling with his coat-tails to ensure that he had not creased them. 'He's keeping his cards very close to the chest,' he remarked airily. 'He could be bluffing, or have a pair of twos.'

The cold reptilian eyes sharpened under the hooded lids. 'He'd be wise not to cheat me, or he'll end up in the Danube with his throat cut, turning it from blue to crimson. Actually, he may not fit too badly into the scheme of things. I'm about to make sure that word reaches Cunyngham that I plan to have Radu shot in Montezena. This will flush him back to Vienna, Maria with him. Make certain that Gautier thinks he's uncovered a plot. That should suffice.'

By the time they rode into Neograd, the whole country was aflame with the news of the Prince's marriage. Entering by the West Gate, the bridal pair were greeted by rapturous crowds and the pealing of bells. A military escort came to meet them, falling into jogging line behind the bodyguards. Radu was astride his black stallion in the lead, a resplendent figure in glittering helmet and cuirass. It was a sight calculated to engender loyalty in the most rebellious heart. He was long-legged, stiff-backed, arrogantly at home in the saddle, moving like a conqueror. The cheers rose to a deafening roar which made Mariana duck her head back through the window of the coach.

When Radu had awakened to call her to bed on the morning after the wedding, she had gone to him gladly, and with a kind of mental frenzy had locked her fears away. An idyllic fortnight had passed, during which they had explored the wonder of their love. Physically they were perfectly matched, yet Radu was curious as to why she had not come to him a virgin, annoyed because this hurt him, telling himself that he was being unreasonable. She was his now. What had happened before they met was not his business, but it continued to rankle. As the first rapture lessened, he became conscious of other barriers too. She was secretive, and this perplexed him though, once again, he trusted in time's healing process.

Then a letter had come from Neograd. In it Princess Arta complained of a disquieting rumour which had reached her ears: 'Some talk about you taking part in a secret marriage. Come home at once, my son, and explain,' she had written, along with a good deal more in the same vein.

He had been expecting it and, whilst not a man to be mother-dominated, had realized that he could no longer delay in presenting his wife at the Montezenian Court. They had set out next day. The weather continued hot and dry, and the journey took them from the mountains to the plains, filled with fields of ripening corn, vineyards heavy with dusty, purple grapes, and limpid streams. Chamois bounded on the low hillsides, and Radu told her of other wild life: the boars which he hunted; the wolves which ravaged the area in winter; and the brown bears, much prized by a caste of gypsies called *ursari*, bear-leaders who made a living by exhibiting them at fairs. They captured them cunningly, placing a jar filled with brandy and honey near their dens. As soon as the bears became helplessly intoxicated, they clapped chains on them.

Mariana enjoyed hearing about this wild land and its people, spending evenings with him, drinking plum-brandy, while he regaled her with stories of the long-ago wars with the Turks. There were more horrible legends too, ones which she did not like: of vampires, the terrible Nosferatu or undead, who rose from their graves at night to drink the blood of their victims, and of the werewolves who, at full moon, were changed into animals to wander the darkness seeking human prey. Joking, Radu would imitate one of these monsters, roaring and rolling his eyes, while she fled from him. It was too near the truth of her own experiences to be lightly dismissed. She knew that it was only Radu playing the fool, but hovered on the edge of belief, reality and myth becoming mixed until he turned into himself again, laughing, catching her up in his arms and taking her to bed.

Neograd was a small town of spires and domes, much influenced by its Turkish past, with crooked streets, red roofs and white walls sliced by black shadows under the glaring sun. Its citizens were a conglomerate of Armenians, Russians, Tsigani, Tartars and Magyars. Much of the ornamentation, particularly on the churches, was in the Moslem style. Mariana employed Lucia as her maid, and the girl was mastering English and in return teaching her to speak and understand the liquid, almost Latin tongue of Radu's country.

Lucia had never visited Neograd before, and she was perched on the edge of the carriage seat, agape with excitement. 'Madame, it is *frumos* – beautiful!' she announced.

Everything was *frumos* to her, for she had a rose-coloured view of life. She admired Radu tremendously, and would have performed small tasks for him as well as her mistress, had it not been for the possessive Axos. They waged a running battle, for the cross-grained valet did not approve of his Prince's marriage. His long features, of a naturally sour cast, became longer every time he set eyes on Mariana. This distressed her, but Lucia dismissed it with a shrug, pulling faces behind his back.

''Ee weel give you 'ees – ah – friend?' Lucia faltered and she struck her hand against her forehead, lost for the right English word.

'Friendship?' suggested Mariana.

The lively face brightened. 'Yes, Madame – friendship. Not soon – but – but – '

'One day?' Mariana smiled at her earnestness.

'Yes, one day.'

'You don't like him? You prefer Danesti or Lieutenant Cazacu?' Mariana was amused by Lucia's adoration of the young soldier.

She blushed, smiled and shook her head. 'Not Danesti,' and she succeeded in conveying that red-haired people were thought to be children of the devil.

The Castle of the Winds was built in a hill outside the town, its conical towers and twirled chimney-pots standing proud against the cloudless sky. Mariana wished that she was an artist, able to capture her first impression on canvas. Her delight increased when Radu took her inside. Though securely girded by thick walls, it was a comfortable home in every sense. Radu's personality was imprinted on each room. He had gathered the most unusual and rare treasures over the years: tapestries, carpets, paintings, curios and fine examples of native art. The library was full of books, and not only for show. He had read most of them, a scholar who could have made his mark in academic circles. He was interested in matters military, and his armoury held a collection of weapons, ranging from the archaic to the most modern, along with maps, books and charts pertaining to tactics and strategy.

'But, Radu,' Mariana exclaimed when they were in their bedroom after a whirlwind tour. 'I didn't know that you were so clever.'

He was pleased but made light of her praise, yawning and wearied. When they had arrived at the castle his servants and officials had been lined up in the Great Hall. There had been a deal of hand-shaking and hand-kissing. He had managed to avoid a confrontation with Colonel Alnoch, knowing that his elderly adviser was waiting the chance to interrogate him. The marriage of a prince was no ordinary affair. Radu had flouted centuries of protocol by his action. The Colonel would want to know why.

He eased off his helmet and uniform, soon standing in

276

creased linen shirt and trousers. He ran a hand through his sweat-drenched hair, grinning at Mariana. 'I'm going for a swim. Are you coming?'

Axos was hanging his master's clothing in one of the massive wardrobes. 'There are several dignitaries expected for dinner, your Highness,' he reminded with a disapproving sniff.

'There's plenty of time till then, you tyrant.' Radu pretended annoyance. 'I'll be back, never fear. Come along, Maria.'

He took her arm and they escaped together, using the backstairs and fleeing into the garden like fugitives from justice. A broad flagged terrace faced them, covered by a loggia of open stone arches with a raftered roof. Further on was an arbour where roses rampaged over trellises and low walls. The air was full of dreamy fragrance. Pigeons paced the tiles with pretty pride. A cat slept on the flags. Cool, moist, deep-veined creepers clambered about the stones. There was a peach-tree in the full beauty of its blossom, and everywhere grew close-set olive trees, the ground between scarlet with wild-rose bushes. Steps led into a secluded dell in the pinewoods. The grass was springy, the sunlight falling through the leaves in a dappled skein of light and shade. Mariana heard the rush of water as they approached a blue pool, walking as if through paradise, her husband's fingers linked with hers, the warm breeze rustling among the trees, birds calling in the boughs.

'What a lovely spot,' she said.

'We'll spend many happy hours here,' he promised, beginning to tug his shirt from his belt. 'I'm looking forward to the day when I can teach our son to swim.'

The scene darkened. She wished he had not said that. 'Supposing we only have daughters. Would you mind?'

He was undressing, sitting on the bank, tugging off his boots. 'Of course I wouldn't mind. Women make excellent leaders. Look at the late-lamented Empress Maria Theresa of Austria for example. The country flourished under her long régime.' He grinned up at her. 'I can teach girls to swim just as well as boys.'

How wonderfully normal he was. She felt that she had never loved him quite so deeply as in that moment. He was so large, so vital a man, yet kind and gentle. There were old scars on his sun-browned skin. Some were crooked as if from deep, ugly wounds. She wondered if Lancelot had sutured them as army doctor. Radu stood on the edge of the pool, then dived. His arms cleaved the surface without a ripple, and he reappeared further out, tossing back his dripping hair.

'Are you coming in?' he shouted.

'I can't take my clothes off here. Someone may see me.'

'This is my private watering-hole,' he answered, lazily kicking the water. 'Even grumpy old Alnoch knows better than to disturb me.'

Mariana had not swum naked since bathing in the sea as a child. She had visited Brighton with the Cunynghams, had entered the water there, but from the modest seclusion of a bathing-machine, clad in a chaste grey robe. Now reckless with the mid-summer heat, she began to remove her clothes, soon wearing only a flimsy chemise which reached her knees. Radu was watching her, and this made her unaccountably shy.

'Don't look,' she said primly, sending him into spasms of mirth.

'Take that damn thing off,' he ordered, adding practically: 'You'll get it wet. No one has more right to gaze on you than me.'

She was completely at ease when nude in their bedroom, but here? In broad daylight? He was almost daring her to do it, so she pulled it over her head, grumbling: 'I hope you're right, Radu, and no stray servant will act the peeping-Tom.'

The water was icy, carried straight down from the mountains. She gasped at the shock of it. It was not deep near the edge and, at the noise they were making, a dappled fawn who had been drinking on the far side, pricked up its ears and leapt for the sheltering undergrowth. Radu pulled her towards the waterfall. The deluge cascaded over her, though his shoulders took the full force. His hands were on her, touching her back, her buttocks, as she clung to the hard flesh of his upper arms for support. The fall ran over their faces, and his lean, bronzed body was god-like, every sinew rippling.

'Oh! It's so cold!' she cried, stumbling away from the downpour. The chilling numbness was too much for her, and she stood in the shallows, shivering and gulping air.

Radu smoothed back his hair with both hands, waist-deep in the pool, the sunlight pouring across his glinting grey eyes and wet, spiky lashes. There was a second's pause before he gathered her into his arms, guiding her to the bank, lifting her and depositing her beneath an enclosing willow. He held her tightly, kissing her eyelids, the damp, fresh smell of him mingling with that of the wild garlic crushed beneath them. There were leaves all about them and the light was on his face – alone under the sapphire sky, the burning wild roses. The door to heaven was entered by a touch, a glance, a breath. He drew her arms up about his neck.

Mariana needed nothing but the joy of that moment. Whatever darkness lay in the future, all was light in the present. His body was hers, naked flesh to naked flesh. He lay over her, supporting his weight on both elbows, taking her face between his palms, looking down into her eyes, her dark hair spread out, tangled, wet, on the grass under her head. He drank in every detail, every line and contour, murmuring: 'My darling, I love you so very much.'

This is enough, she thought, while thought was still possible – enough, here and hereafter. Our love is greater than death, as great as eternity itself, a love that shall leave earth with us when our souls quit our bodies. It will reach its uttermost perfection in other lives, other worlds. A love that time cannot chill, nor trouble destroy, nor God sever.

Mariana met Princess Arta that night. This stately, promiscuous Hungarian dame swept into the castle with her coterie of men. They fawned around her, an artist, a poet, a musician – all exceptionally handsome, apparently utterly devoted but, in Radu's jaundiced view, totally insincere. Mariana, dressed in a gown which had been made for her by a skilled peasant seamstress, stood up bravely to her mother-in-law's scrutiny. Princess Arta was not amused by her son's action. She should have been consulted, and had taken this omission as a personal insult.

Radu met her at the entrance, annoying her even further by wearing local costume. 'My God!' she was sharply condemnatory. 'Must you wander around like a common farmhand? Either that or a swaggering brute of a soldier. I rarely see you attired as befits your station.'

'You rarely see me, Mamma.' He had difficulty in controlling his resentment. How dare she criticize him when the stories of her amours were so uninhibited and sensational? She was a woman of wit and intelligence, and her refusal to recognize that she was getting on and her beauty fading, infuriated him. It was in poor taste and lacking in dignity. He had expected better of his mother. Her sycophants did not help, for though her magnificence of proportions was now tending to overweight, to listen to them one would have thought her as slim and fresh-faced as a milkmaid of sixteen.

'So this is your common-law bride.' Princess Arta's eyes were as grey as his own, and as cold with indignation, but her hair was of greying gold. Radu had got his dark colouring from his father, as well as his tendency to hobnob with inferiors.

'We were married in church by a priest.' Their eyes locked in a battle for supremacy. 'There was nothing underhand

279

about it. Our union is as solid and irrevocable as it can possibly be, so don't meddle.'

Princess Arta took a step forward, her gold tissue gown swishing, an ermine-trimmed mantle flowing to the floor from her shoulders. The evening was too warm to merit it, but it was undoubtedly impressive. A priceless necklace of rubies and diamonds flashed about her throat, their glow repeated on her wrists and fingers. She wore a spiked tiara on her elaborately dressed hair. It made her look taller, and she was of an imperial height as it was, always a fine woman. Mariana felt dwarfed, both by her size and her autocratic manner.

Princess Arta brooded down on her chillingly. 'Hum – well, I suppose it could have been worse,' she admitted grudgingly.

'Mamma, will you have the goodness to converse in English or French,' Radu snapped, goaded beyond endurance by her insistence on the Rumanian tongue. 'Maria can't understand a word we're saying.'

'She'll have to apply herself to learning, won't she?' came back the instant retort. 'She must forget that she's English. In your Court, and in mine, she'll address us in our own language.'

'Shall we go in to dinner?' Radu answered grittily, glad when Alnoch came to the rescue, offering the Princess his arm.

This upright, aging statesman was like a kindly uncle, with his iron-grey hair and drooping moustache. Mariana had taken to him straight away. He at least approved of her. Thought by some to be a crusty old soldier with his limp and barrack-square bluntness, he was as devoted to Radu as he had been to Prince Alecsandri, keeping a watchful eye on his interests. He had hoped that the Prince would marry, had even put forward several likely ladies, rather alarmed when word came of the wedding, but greatly relieved when he was introduced to the bride. His honest nature recognized a kindred spirit.

Faced with little alternative, Princess Arta decided to be amiable, and Mariana's life fell into a routine during which she studied languages, went hunting with Radu, entertained at the castle and visited her mother-in-law in her own smaller establishment a short distance away. Lucia was a lively companion, and Radu spent every available moment at home. It began to seem that she had always been a princess, respected, almost revered, spending much time being decked for her rôle. Princess Arta had raised her plump hands in horror when she learned that no proper trousseau had been prepared, taking command so that Mariana spent hours in the company of milliners, mantua-makers and an endless

280

procession of foreign noblewomen calling out of curiosity. The strain of it began to tell, making her cross and weepy, but even Radu agreed that it was a necessary evil. She now owned so many beautiful things. He loved to give her presents – an emerald cross, a necklace of pearls with a moonstone drop, a set of diamonds, an amethyst coronet. He said they were family heirlooms.

'You spoil me,' she protested one morning after she had been there a month. She had awakened to find a small red plush box on her pillow. Inside was a cameo, set in a delicate brooch of gold filigree and rubies.

'You're worth it, darling. The peasants are saying that you've brought good weather. They predict a bumper harvest.' He lifted his eyes from the newspaper he was reading at the breakfast table. He thought her more beautiful than ever. She had come to full bloom, her skin as smooth and scented as the roses in the silver vase placed among the dishes. 'They offer prayers for you in the churches, and the village women will be performing fertility rites on your behalf.'

Her sun-touched cheeks turned pink and her eyes shone. 'They really like me? That's wonderful. Everyone is so kind.'

'Even Mamma?' He cocked a quizzical eyebrow.

'Especially Mamma. I thought you told me she was an absolute dragon.' She took up the coffee-pot and primed his cup.

'She can be, when it suits her.' Radu was running a paper-knife under the flap of a large envelope. He opened it and perused the contents of the letter. 'This is from David,' he said after a moment. 'He wants us to return to Vienna at once – says he has some urgent business to discuss with me, and that Georgiana is missing you.'

Mariana froze into stillness. He noticed that only her fingers were moving, nervously pleating a fold of the damask napkin near her plate. Her head was bent, hair falling forward to hide her face. 'Must we go?' she whispered at last.

'Don't you want to see them, and Lance too?' He knew what she was thinking. They were so content here, needing no big, noisy city, no frivolous social whirl. But he understood the message behind David's cautious words. Grigore was up to something.

She shook her head, raising her eyes to meet his across the table. 'I'm afraid,' she said.

'Afraid?' His black brows quirked downwards, and he reached out to press her hand. 'Foolish one, what is there to fear?'

She dared not tell him – could not put into words her dread of leaving. She loved Neograd, felt safe in the Castle of the Winds, even enjoyed the quaint, rather eccentric Court of Princess Arta. Vienna was fraught with peril. It represented the world – cruel and insensitive. Guilt grinned at her like a spectre. Radu rose, worried by her expression, coming round to drop on his heels beside her, covering her hands with kisses, pressing her against his body.

'I want to stay here always,' she murmured, face buried in his shirt-front. 'Radu, nothing must come between us.'

'Nothing will, my sweet.' He held her a little away, smiling reassuringly. 'Just think, you'll be able to talk about babies with Georgiana, and I'll have the chance to show you off in Vienna. I'm very proud of you, my dearest.'

Lucia adored Vienna. It did Mariana's heart good to witness her servant's excitement. When they arrived at the von Gundling palace, one of her first tasks was to reconcile her with a rather sullen Sophie, who had been mortified when her mistress eloped without making her party to the secret. Mariana adroitly enlisted her aid in instructing Lucia, and left them together while Sophie organized a smart costume for the peasant girl, something suitable for her post as assistant lady's maid.

Radu and David retired to the library, closing the door firmly, and Mariana went to see Georgiana, who was still in bed though it was late morning. She was propped up amidst silken pillows, wearing a cream lace peignoir and matching frilled cap. She seemed in robust health but said, after they had kissed: 'Lance orders me to rest, though to tell the truth, I've never felt better, now that awful sickness has gone. But, my dear, I'm getting so fat! I'll be like a tub of lard by the time baby comes in December.'

She wore that smug look of the expectant mother and Mariana, so happy now, could be glad for her. One day, very soon she hoped, she would be carrying Radu's child. Elaine would never be forgotten, holding a sacred place in her heart, but there would be others to fill that empty ache in her arms which even Radu failed to satisfy.

When she went back to their apartment to await his return, Sophie was there, bursting with a mysterious message. There was a person in the garden who wished to see the Princess urgently. Mariana was puzzled, wondering if it concerned Radu. Princess Arta had alarmed her, hot in her criticism of Grigore, making no bones of the fact that he wanted to rule

Montezena, adding darkly that he would stop at nothing to attain this end.

Apprehension sent her speeding down to the arbour where she had once met Lancelot. Then she had been a miserable wretch bereft of hope, now she was quite a different woman, blooming under Radu's tender love. She had talked herself into acceptance of the Vienna visit, chiding her cowardice and selfish desire to keep him in their enchanted castle. She must learn to share him. He had his duties and she should not grudge this. He belonged to Montezena too.

The perfume of roses was heady and the sun scorching hot. It burnt into her back, although her head was shaded by a straw hat. She paused for a moment, sensing an alien presence, her hand coming to rest on the stiff curls of a little stone satyr. Then she saw him, and clutched at the pagan creature's hair with fingers suddenly colder than the stone. That one glance killed her faith in God and man.

He was staring at her from below a cluster of roses which stirred lazily in the faint breeze. The chirp of a bird seemed shrill in the silence. There was a soft splash of water in the fountain's basin. These things were disturbing and horrible to her.

'Good morning, Lady Mariana,' said Arthur Cartwright.

Outrage broke the spell that held her paralysed. 'What are you doing here?' The words seemed to suffocate her as she spoke, a hundred horrible possibilities chasing across her mind.

He grinned, that ignorant, coarse-grained young man. 'Oh, deary me, that's not a very warm welcome for an old friend. Ain't you pleased to see me, Lady Mariana?' His eyes were going over her, assessing her fine clothes, her jewels.

Terror rose around her, like poisonous fumes of baleful fire, stifling the life in her. She loathed herself as much as she loathed him. God, how much she hated him! 'Pleased? To see *you*?' she cried.

Arthur laughed as he came close, his eyes feeding on her. 'Don't look so shocked. I'm not a ghost. I'm real. Here, feel me.' He grabbed her hand and thrust it against his groin, grinning as she flinched back in horror. 'Still shrinking away from me, are you? Always was a hoity madam, even in the old days.'

'What d'you want?' The blood in her burned like flame. She snatched her hand from his with unutterable revulsion and passion, lifting it as if to strike him.

'That's more the ticket.' Arthur accepted this rebuff, perching himself on the basin's edge, one foot braced on the gravel, the other lightly swaying. He did not take his eyes from her. 'I've come so as we can have a cosy little chat – Princess Varna.' He put mocking emphasis on the title.

'I've nothing to say to you.' She did not cry. Her eyes were hot and dry. His coming had shrivelled every emotion in her.

He grimaced, looked down at his ragged fingernails, then up at her again from under his lids. 'In that case, I'd best go and see your Prince. I'm sure he'll be interested.'

'No!' The word was dragged from her lips.

'You don't want him to know about you? Tut, tut! Keeping secrets from your – er – husband already? Fie, Mariana,' Arthur gloated, savouring every moment, physically roused by her agony.

He was like a basilisk, turning her to stone, the golden garden reeling, the beauty of her life struck dead at one glance. Her mind was working slowly, stultified by the arrival of that treacherous, base born fool who had no simple, natural virtues of kindliness and honour. 'Did Christopher send you?' she asked dully.

'He thinks you're dead. Everyone does. They've had your funeral and all. A grand, sorrowful affair, I can tell you. No, it was business brought me here – father's business, God rot him! But it's turned out bloody lucky for yours truly. Who'd have thought it? Little Mariana a princess!'

Her death? A funeral? What did he mean? She was too appalled to ask, her present danger too pressing. 'You intend to betray me.' There was no doubt in her mind. Why else had he come so stealthily?

'Ah, that depends.' He teased her by seeming to give the matter consideration. 'I've heard that Prince Radu's rich. He's generous towards you? Pays well to hump you?'

'I'm his wife. I love him and he loves me. There's no talk of payment.' Shame tortured her, roused by the words of this brutish person. At a stroke, he succeeded in dragging her love down from its heights, levelling it to all that was poor, base and mean.

'Bollocks!' Arthur spat on the gravel. 'Love! Marriage! What the hell! It's nothing more than legalized whoredom! You're not his wife, and you know it. He gives you presents, doesn't he? Forks out on your dress-bills? He pays to roger you, just as I pay in the brothels. Don't give me any of your high-flung notions of pure, perfect love!'

'I have no money,' she answered.

'I've seen plenty of Jews in Vienna, and where they are

284

you'll always find pawn-shops. Hock your costly baubles, they'll fetch a pretty penny.'

'Name your price,' Mariana said coldly. Beyond everything, she was proud. This man should not degrade her further. Beneath the sting of his lash, her pride rose up in tenfold strength.

'Now you're talking,' Arthur replied, but he was disappointed. He had hoped to see her weep, cringe, throw herself at his feet, begging for mercy. But her head was up and her face, though white, held an expression that made him feel uncomfortable. He defied it. There was no way in which he intended to back down. 'For starters, I want five hundred guineas.'

'You shall have it. Come here tonight at eight o'clock, and I'll send my maid with the money.' She turned and left him without a backward glance.

Going straight to her room, she locked the door and flung herself on the bed in a stupor of despair. Her eyes were dry, no cry escaped her where she lay, face down, but like a wild animal in a trap, she bit and tore at the silk coverlet of the couch she shared with Radu.

She was both blind and deaf in that horrible time. Her nightmare had become reality. She obtained the money for Arthur, sending Sophie to the silversmith with a minor item of jewellery, lying to her – it was easy to lie – convincing her that the man in the garden had been a horse-dealer who was helping her to buy a steed for Radu. A secret, she said. She wanted to give him a belated wedding-gift.

Despair and deadly woe swamped her senses, her trouble slow to dawn on her, so terrible, so blasphemous, making her resort to falsehoods so that she could go on living with Radu, with him unsuspecting, in the tainted sunshine, in the plague-smitten beauty, in a paradise of lies. This was only the first of Arthur's visits; he came again and again. Mariana met his demands. If Radu asked, where was her pearl necklace? she smilingly replied that the catch had broken. Her diamond bracelet? Oh, how silly of her – she must have mislaid it.

Two weeks dragged by and Radu, worried by her pallor, thinking her homesick for Neograd, did his best to please her. She was gay, desperately so, learning to live with the constant dread of seeing Arthur's face somewhere among the crowds in the Prater, at the theatre, in the concert-halls, watching her with his knowing smirk. One evening, when she was in Baron Carl's box at the opera, he came to her during the interval, when Radu and the others had gone to the refreshment-room.

He wanted to talk with her, he said. She arranged to meet him next day in the park.

There, seated with him in a secluded gazebo to which he had insisted on taking her, the summer skies seemed to darken as he made the ultimate demand which she had known was coming. 'Money ain't enough, darling,' he said, his voice thickening, eyes hot. 'I want you. I've fancied you, since the first time I clapped peepers on you at Thornfalcon, shining like a star amongst those damned members of your husband's zoo!'

Mariana shifted to the far end of the iron bench, her icy hauteur putting space between them. 'Never!' she hissed, clutching the handle of her parasol, ready to hit him with it if he attempted to touch her. 'I'd rather die!'

Arthur's lip curled, cruelty stamped in every line. 'No doubt you would but I can't allow that. You're too good a money-spinner. I'm telling you straight, if you don't have me as your lover, I'll write to St Jules – let him know that it weren't you he put in the family vault. God only knows who it was – that don't matter. Can't you just picture how delighted he'd be to get his hands on you again? 'Course, he'll not be too pleased when he learns you've been whoring with someone else. He can get quite nasty when annoyed, can't he? Shouldn't like to be in your shoes, if he gets wind of this. But he won't, I promise, if you do what I want.'

'You'd have me, knowing that I hate you?' Her heart was thumping as she tried to recall what course she had decided to take when this situation arose. The moment had come, and her mind was numb.

Arthur sprawled back against the seat, one leg flung over the other, an arm snaking along behind her. 'Makes it all the sweeter,' he replied with an evil grin. 'Adds a bit of spice, you might say.'

Mariana could hear the band in the distance, could just glimpse people strolling about, enjoying themselves, their lives continuing normally, while hers was in ruins. She gripped the parasol till her knuckles were chalky. Time. She needed time – time to think, to plan, maybe even to pray. 'But how could we do this and when? Prince Radu's nearly always with me.'

Arthur gave an unpleasantly gleeful chuckle, jubilantly certain that he would soon be poaching on the preserves of his betters. To his warped mind, this redressed the balance somewhat. 'Oh, don't you worry about that, my beauty. We'll find ways and means, never fret.' There was a patina of sweat dewing his upper lip, and he edged closer. 'This is as good a place as any to begin with. Come on, up with your skirts. I can't wait. Warm weather always makes me randy.'

His hand was stroking her silk-covered thigh. To her disgust, she could see desire misshaping his trousers. She cast a hurried glance at the people promenading not many yards away, but if she screamed it would start a blazing scandal. Despair gave birth to inspiration. 'I can't. It's the wrong time of the month!' She blurted out the embarrassing lie.

'Hell!' Arthur snapped, baulked of fulfilment. 'All right, but next week you oblige me or I post that letter. Meanwhile, I'll need a little something to be going on with, to pay for a whore. You've got me going and it's either that or my hand'll have to be my mistress.'

There was a ball that evening and, while Mariana was dancing with Cornel, Elizabeth appeared at Radu's side. He turned away, unwilling to exchange words with her, but she placed her hand on his arm in the cool dimness of the terrace.

'And how are you finding marriage, Radu?' Her amber eyes shone up at him from beneath her cloth-of-gold turban.

'Thank you for your concern, Elizabeth,' he answered levelly. 'Maria and I are very happy.'

'You've found your ideal mate at last?' She was toying with the ostrich plumes of her fan, eyes downcast. 'A woman who loves you – and forsakes all others?'

Radu frowned. 'What are you driving at?'

She moved a shade closer. He caught the aroma of frangipani, and it stirred his senses, reminding him of hours spent in her arms. 'I wish only for your happiness, Radu,' she breathed, lips glistening like ripe strawberries where her tongue had moistened them. 'I'd not see anyone put the horns on you.'

He drew on his cigar. A thin wisp of smoke trickled from the corners of his unsmiling mouth. The strains of a waltz came from the ballroom. 'Maria will never turn me into a cuckold,' he answered confidently.

'How can you be so sure?' The paper Chinese lanterns cast an orange glow on her seductive face. 'D'you really know what goes on in her mind? You want an heir, but be mindful of the old adage! "It's a wise child who knows his own father."'

The taunt stung like a lash, and Radu lost his temper. 'You bitch! How dare you even hint at such a thing?'

The rage in his face was exciting, and when his fingers closed painfully on her arm, a thrill raced through her. 'You should've stayed with me, Radu. I'm a lady, for all my faults. Is she a lady? Or did she spring from the gutter?' She was pouting, eyes half closed, begging for his kiss, blood stirred by the heat and passion of him. He did not yield and this angered her. 'There was a man speaking to her in the box last night,' she added viperishly. 'And today, whilst driving in the park, I saw them together in most earnest conversation, hidden in a corner. He's a common fellow – English, I'm told. Maria appeared to be agitated.'

Radu struggled to control the impulse to hit her across her lovely, treacherous face. Instead, he grated: 'I won't stay here and listen to such a pack of lies.'

Elizabeth watched him stride away, his fine proud head, straight back and narrow hips making her burn with desire. She smiled. A man on the rebound was most vulnerable. Get rid of Maria and he might come back to her. It would not be the first time such a thing had happened. She was an old hand at causing rifts between couples.

Part of Radu's anger was because she had succeeded in making a tight spasm of jealousy knot within him. His wife was in the supper-room with Cornel, and he found himself watching her closely. Was she flirting with the lieutenant? There was no doubt that Cornel admired her tremendously, always most attentive, but Radu had thought this due to his loyalty to them both. Was she hoodwinking him? The worries which he had subdued roared up in a wild storm. She had not been a virgin. She never spoke of her former life. Who was she? What had she been before they met?

He held his peace until they retired to their room for the night. He was conscious of tension, and not only in him. Mariana chattered brightly whilst she undressed but, mind honed by Elizabeth's malicious insinuations, he caught a false note in her gaiety. At last, able to bear no more, he strode towards her where she sat at the dressing-table, busy with the ritual brushing of her hair. The candlelight turned it to tumbling silk and pain stabbed him. At any other time he would have buried his hands in that fragrant mass, but now: 'What's wrong, Maria?' he asked.

The silver-backed brush was arrested in its sweep. So it had come, the question she had been dreading. She felt as if she had aged ten years over the past weeks. 'Nothing is wrong.' A meaningless smile lifted her stiff lips.

'There is. Don't lie. I've been aware of it for days. Why won't you tell me?' His face bore mingled pain, anger and bewilderment.

The brush fell from her fingers, clattering on to the walnut veneer. 'I tell you there's nothing – '

'Oh, Maria,' he groaned. 'You're part of me. How can you believe that I wouldn't know if you were in trouble?'

He caught her to him, holding her tightly, as desperate as if she had just died. The seconds passed and she lost count of them. As there are years when one does not live a moment, so there are moments which last a lifetime. The dark shadows swam round her like eddying water, the floor seemed to shake, and her eyes closed beneath his kisses. In that sweet, hot darkness of a summer night, she prayed for death.

The trance of hopeless passion faded. She strained backwards, away from his hold, and shivered where she sat. She had seen him with Elizabeth. What had she been saying, poisoning his mind? Swiftly she turned defence into attack. 'The Countess! She was flirting with you! So that's it. You accuse me of being troubled. It's your own conscience which is troubling *you*!'

There was quick anger in his eyes. 'Why d'you look at me like that? I've nothing to hide,' he shouted, and then was still.

'That woman was your mistress once,' she continued with a cruelty of which she had not known herself capable. 'Perhaps you plan to resume the relationship. Maybe this is the real reason why we came back to Vienna.'

He was quiet. All the eagerness and glow, even the anger had faded from his face. It grew cold and colourless, with an impenetrable stillness that masked his anguish, then: 'In your heart you know that isn't true. But you, Maria, are you faithful? Elizabeth told me that she'd seen you in the park with a man.'

This is how it must feel to receive a deathblow straight through flesh and bone, she thought, and live a little space to look death in the eye. She rested a hand on the table to steady herself. 'I did meet a man, an Englishman. Is it a sin to converse with a compatriot?'

'Why don't you introduce us?'

'It's not important. You must trust me,' she faltered. He was being so generous, never once lifting his voice, curbing his temper.

'If it's of no moment, then why aren't you happy?'

'I am!' she shouted, rising to her feet, small and fragile against his height and bulk. 'Heavens! Do I have to dance around all day, laughing like a silly child to prove to you that I'm in a state of blissful delight?'

His face flushed, then paled under the tan. He looked at her with no anger in his eyes, only confused despair so great that it chilled her into speechless terror. Her love welled up and she longed to throw herself into his arms and cling to him, fighting her way back to their old understanding. But she did not move, standing there silent and unyielding, with burning, tearless eyes.

Something in her attitude, her look and her silence, stung him like an insult. He drew himself up. 'Even you have no right to talk to me in that tone,' he said icily. 'You're being deliberately wayward, and I think that you're lying. I'll not sleep here tonight.'

He was gone before she could fully measure the force of what he had said. A single step, a single cry would have brought him back. But Mariana let him go.

Lancelot was aware of the rift between Radu and Mariana. He had kept his oath and her secret, answering the appeal in her eyes when she returned from her honeymoon, giving her the chance of happiness. But he was not easy, sensing a kind of desperation in the way she flung herself into every enjoyment, seeing the blind adoration on her face whenever she looked at her husband. She was like a patient with a terminal illness, grabbing at life with a kind of frenzy, as if each second was her last. Georgiana kept him busy, making the most of the attention provoked by her pregnancy. David was totally preoccupied with her, giving scant heed to anything else. He had warned Radu of Grigore's plot to kill him, satisfied that they had successfully foiled him, with the help of Gautier, but Lancelot was suspicious.

It was as if a storm was in the offing, clouds gathering ominously on the horizon of the carefree summer days, the atmosphere heavy with it. Experienced campaigner that he was, Lancelot knew that the crisis was coming. Instinct shouted it, and he almost pawed the ground as a war-horse will before battle.

To all intents and purposes, the von Gundlings and their guests were as jolly as could be and, one beautiful afternoon shortly after the ball, the doctor took his ease in a hammock, slung beneath the branches of a great oak, watching the others playing croquet. Hildegarde was noisily exuberant, shrieking triumphantly every time she succeeded in driving the wooden ball under the hoops with her mallet. The women were garbed in dazzling white gowns, though Georgiana was not joining in. She lay on a chaise-longue, parasol aloft, a glass of iced lemonade to hand. Radu, David and Baron Carl paced solemnly through the ritual, wielding their mallets with skill, indulgently allowing Hildegarde and Mariana to win sometimes. A footman was just coming across the emerald lawn towards the summer-house, bearing refreshments, when suddenly two figures appeared on the terrace.

Mariana, poised to take a swing at the ball, looked up and saw them. In that moment her soul shrivelled and died. Arthur Cartwright was swaggering over the grass as if he owned the place. Beside him walked the man whom she had prayed never to see again on earth or in hell. A tall, thin man, wearing a dark suit and long black travelling cloak. He was bare-headed, the sunlight giving his fair head an undeserved halo; a man who bore himself with such cool dignity that he could have been an emperor. His features were those of an ascetic and burned with fanatical fire. It was Christopher.

So Cartwright had betrayed her after all. Her first thought was: Thank God I didn't give myself to him. He was disgusting, the lowest thing that crawled. He must have already sent to Christopher long before making his foul proposition.

The Baron frowned, lifted his eye-glass, then left the game and went up to the strangers. 'Sirs?' he addressed them in German. 'Are you lost? Do you seek me, perhaps?'

Christopher stopped, staring directly at the group on the grass. His chin lifted and he gazed down at the Baron with his icy blue eyes. 'I'm English, sir. Oblige me by speaking in that tongue. I've been told that Lord Cunyngham's staying with you.'

David's hackles rose at that peremptory tone. He pressed his wife's hand as he passed her, and went over to join the Baron. 'I'm David Cunyngham,' he said briskly. 'What can I do for you?'

That crystalline stare switched to him. 'You, sir, have been misguided, meddling in matters which had nothing to do with you.' He flung his cloak back over his shoulders, lifted an arm and pointed at Mariana. 'I've come for her.'

Radu leapt forward, his face dark with rage. 'Where are your manners, sir? That lady is Princess Varna.'

'Stand aside.' Christopher's voice rang with contempt. 'I'm Lord St Jules. She's no concern of yours.'

The two men glared at one another, one as fair as an archangel, the other as dark as the devil. A hush had fallen, and the moment seemed endless. 'You're wrong there,' said Radu at last. 'She's very much my concern. The lady is my wife.'

Christopher's mocking laughter rang through the glory of the summer garden, making the trees, the flowers, the vine-dappled walls shake as if by a wintry blast. 'Your wife? Oh, no – her name is Mariana St Jules, and she's married to me. The woman is a bigamist!'

BOOK THREE

Lady St Jules

Like angels with bright savage eyes
I will come treading phantom-wise
Here where you usually sleep,
When shadows of the night are
deep.

And I will give you, my dark one,
Kisses as icy as the moon,
Caresses as of snakes that crawl
In circles round a cistern's wall.

When morning shows its livid face
There will be no-one in my place,
And a strange cold will settle there.

Others by some more tender art
May think to reign upon your heart.
As for myself, I trust to fear.

'The Revenant'. Flowers of Evil
by Charles Baudelaire.
Translated by George Dillon

CHAPTER 1

To ride, driving the animal to its limits, without pause or rest, as if by so doing, a man might leave the torments of his soul behind him, this was Radu's aim. He was more merciless to himself than to his sweating, foam-flecked beast, gaunt, black-visaged, tall in the saddle, a grim figure from whom the peasants in the villages through which he thundered drew aside and crossed themselves. But with every beat of those hooves that carried him away from Vienna, he could feel himself disintegrating inside, cracking open, splitting apart.

The hamlets thinned as the road climbed steeply, rising out of sight between the granite cliffs that seemed to touch the sky. Radu turned and looked back towards the promontory that rose at the mouth of the gorge. He had crossed the border into Montezena. He was home, but even this brought no comfort. Only a moment ago, bright beams of fiery sunset had danced on fields and running streams, farms and vineyards, but here the narrow cleft was plunged in shadow, holding nothing but loneliness and time without end. He guided his horse down the rugged defile, the bleakness suiting his mood. Here he might find solace from the pain which was like a thick, inflamed wound rotting in the depths of his heart.

'Maria! Mariana!' To ease the burden he shouted those names aloud, and the echo repeated them mournfully. They seemed to pass above him, through him, crushing all the nerves in his body. Maria. Mariana. The memory of her cut like swords, and bitterness held him as in the coils of a terrible serpent.

Before him lay a plateau, bordered by thick trees, rimmed with mountains. The light was dying. A young moon, chasing the sun, glimmered overhead. Radu went very quietly in the hush of evening, past the trees against the outer wall of his hunting-lodge. The building had, in the closing dusk, lost form and substance, becoming a rampart of unidentifiable blackness that loomed up into the darkening shield of the sky. There was a silver sheen on the roof-top, and the ground sparkled as if with powdered glass.

The lodge was deserted. Radu had often used it as a retreat from the world, and never had he needed such sanctuary as now. He unlocked a small solid wooden door set in the thickness of one of the walls and entered the courtyard. The house was completely dark and silent, a pleasant-enough place, with stone walls and a steeply pitched wooden roof, built over a century before by one of his ancestors. Radu lit a lantern in the stable, and unharnessed his exhausted stallion, finding oats from the storeroom and settling the animal for the night. He had food and clothing for himself in his saddle-bags and went into the building by way of the kitchen. Lamp in hand, he continued through the shrouded rooms to the one in which he always felt most at home: a large apartment on the ground floor, filled with books, paintings and hunting trophies. There were a deep couch, armchairs and an open fireplace. Kindling and logs were stacked to hand, and in a short while the lamplight was supplemented by hungry flames consuming the dry tinder.

Radu leaned his forehead on his folded arms against the overmantel, gazing down into the fire, seeing her face in the smouldering peaks and caverns. Her beloved face, etched indelibly on the screen of his brain. Maria, laughing, loving! Mariana, white-faced and terrified! The terrible scene on that summer afternoon which had destroyed everything. He would never forget the austere, handsome face of Christopher St Jules as his cultured English voice claimed her as his wife. Oh, he hadn't been violent, not even impolite, explaining it clearly. Mariana had been distraught at the death of their new-born daughter. The family doctor had diagnosed post-natal insanity, brought on by child bed fever, a common enough occurrence, accentuated if the infant had not survived. He had watched her with the greatest possible care but, one night, she had escaped his vigilance and run away. It was winter with continual blizzards and, though he had sent out search-parties, she could not be found. He had feared for her life and, sure enough, when the thaw set in, a body had been hauled from one of the lakes. Though disfigured beyond recognition, it was that of a female and it had been wearing Mariana's clothing and jewellery.

Radu's hands clenched against the carved wood till the knuckles shone white, and he groaned aloud. St Jules had told his story so convincingly, speaking of his sorrow at the premature death of his young bride. The corpse had been placed in the family vault beside the coffin of baby Elaine, and he had shut himself up in Thornfalcon, grieving for both of them. Several months had passed and then, to his joy and amazement, he had received a letter from a friend, Arthur Cartwright, saying that he had seen a lady in Vienna who resembled Mariana to the life. On enquiry, he had learned that she had recently come from England with Lord and Lady Cunyngham, but that she was now married to Prince Varna. St Jules had lost no time in making his way to Europe, hoping against all hope that this was not a wild-goose chase. Then he had expressed his happiness at being reunited with Mariana, and announced his intention of forgiving her for marrying again, convinced that she was suffering from amnesia.

And throughout the telling of this incredible story, Mariana had stood there under the blue Viennese skies, saying nothing, her face waxen, those beautiful violet eyes dead. The rest of them, David, Georgiana and Lance, had been struck dumb whilst he, when St Jules had finally fallen silent, had gone to Mariana and taken her cold, lifeless hands, staring into her eyes and saying:

'Is this true?'

Then she had looked at him, and he prayed never to see again such anguish in a human face. 'Yes,' she had whispered at last, and added on a heart-tearing sigh: 'But I had not lost my memory, Radu. I knew what I was doing. I deceived you, did you a mortal injury, but oh, if you can only forgive me! I did it because I love you so desperately!'

St Jules had come between them, an arm clasping her waist possessively. She had shrunk from him with such fear that Radu had almost flung himself upon the man. 'What nonsense is this, my dear?' His voice had been smooth, but his eyes deadly. 'You were very ill, are still very ill. You didn't know what you were doing. You must cling to this thought, for if I believed otherwise, then I might have to start legal proceedings against you and Prince Radu. This would be most unpleasant and cause much scandal. We don't want this, do we? You will come with me at once, and nothing more shall be mentioned of the unfortunate matter. I'm sure that you'll see the wisdom of this course, won't you, Mariana?'

Shudders had shaken her slim body, and she had drooped in his grasp like a flower denied light and nourishment. 'I can't come back to you. Don't ask it of me, Christopher!' she had pleaded. 'It is over between us! How could I live with a murderer?'

'Good God, Maria – I mean Mariana – what are you talking about?' Cunyngham had recovered his power of speech and leapt forward as if to protect her.

St Jules had answered for her. 'This is part of her sickness, my Lord. She's under the illusion that I killed the child.' He had given a sad smile. 'As if I would've done such a terrible deed! We longed for the baby to complete our happiness. I was dreadfully distressed when the poor little thing was too weak to live. Our medical adviser, Dr Russell, warned me that Elaine's heart was deformed, but my wife wouldn't listen to reason. It's obvious that she will have to continue treatment. I pray God that she recovers.'

'Liar! Christopher, you are wicked. Evil!' Mariana had screamed, tearing herself away from the man who claimed to be her husband. Her eyes had raked the horrified group, the Cunynghams, the von Gundlings, and alighted on Lancelot. She had run to him, gripping that solid, experienced man who had been watching her closely with those deep, penetrating eyes. 'Lance!' she had cried, shaking him in anguish. 'Lance! You know! You understand! I told you all this when first we met. Convince them that I'm not the one who is mad. He is! It's he who's deranged. He murdered my baby because she was not the boy he had determined we were to have. More than that – I think he killed his first wife and her infant girls too!'

'You knew about this, Lance? Why the devil didn't you tell me?' Radu had shouted.

His old comrade-at-arms had shaken his greying mane, face deeply troubled. 'How could I, your Highness? Yes, Mariana did tell me what had happened to her. The tale was so wild that I scarce credited it, but I had to believe it because it came from her innermost consciousness. What could I do? I took an oath never to reveal my patients' secrets. Perhaps I might have been forced to betray her had I known you two were about to marry. But I was given no chance. The ceremony had been performed before I could reach you.'

'She's out of her mind,' Christopher had broken in, at Mariana's side again, forcing the doctor to step back.

'I am perfectly sane.' Her head had gone up, and the quiet tragic dignity of her had been almost awesome. 'I did Radu a great wrong. Foolishly I'd hoped that fate would be kind and allow me to live in peace with him. In that, I was irrational, I'll admit, blinded by my love for him.'

Radu believed her, unable to doubt the sincerity which had shone in those lovely eyes as she looked at him. 'What proof have you, sir?' he had demanded coldly of St Jules.

He had subjected him to an icy smile and produced documents. Marriage-lines, signed by Mariana Crosby and her father, John Crosby, a note of a child's christening, witnessed by Reverend Grant; a paper giving the cause of death of the baby, signed by Dr Russell. Damning proof against which he was helpless.

'Divorce her!' Radu had declared. 'You have the grounds. I'll confess to adultery, if you'll set her free.'

'No, Radu!' Mariana had stopped him, tortured but unshakable. 'You can't be involved. Think of your country – your people. Can't you see that Grigore would take advantage of such a scandal to oust you? There's nothing we can do, my love.'

At this small endearment, delivered with so much tenderness, Christopher's face had lost its calm, becoming a vengeful mask. 'Much as it would satisfy me to see you dragged through the law courts, Prince, I'll never let Mariana come to you. She is mine. My wife until the day I die! No other man shall have her!'

He had refused to discuss it further, refused to allow Mariana to say goodbye to Radu or even to pack, saying that she must bring nothing with her which he had provided, then with Cartwright in tow had bundled her into his carriage and taken her away.

Radu left the fire and paced the room, up and down like a caged tiger. He was not by nature a patient man and frustration ate at him. He had found the woman who could make him happy and she had been torn from his arms. Oh, she had lied to him, had practised a cruel kind of deception, yet he knew that she had spoken the truth when she told him that she loved him. He hated to think of her sufferings if her husband was the villain she had painted, longing to throw himself on his horse and pound through Germany and France, taking a packet-boat across the English Channel and not resting until he had caught up with that devil, St Jules, and brought him to justice.

On that fatal day, he had not wanted to speak with anyone, brushing aside the sympathy of David and Georgiana, and returning to his house on the outskirts of Vienna. He had not stayed there long. A deeply concerned Cornel brought word that St Jules had left the city and, without enlightening him or giving his staff any instructions, Radu had mounted his horse, uncertain of which direction he would take, but finding himself on the road to Montezena. He knew that Vienna would be agog and the thought of facing those curious eyes and mocking smiles was abhorrent. The gossip-mongers would have a field-day! And Grigore? Radu had the gut feeling that his brother had something to do with St Jules's sudden arrival. There was nothing he could put a finger on, but the whole business stank of duplicity and double-dealing, Grigore's natural element.

It was impossible to accept the fact that he would never see Mariana again, his life, his star. Even more difficult to think of her as Lady St Jules, the wife of another man, who must bow to that man's commands, share his bed, give birth to his children. Radu stopped pacing, driving his fist into the palm of his hand and, in the blackness of the night and the blackness of his own despair, his mind was filled with obscene images and terrible doubts. She had said she loved him, but didn't he know all too well that women were born deceivers? Why should he be fool enough to think her any different? Mariana, so soft and warm and deliciously scented. On their last morning together she had been a silken thing in his bed, glimmering in the half-light like a pearl in a deep lagoon. She had held his head between her hands, smiling into his eyes and kissing him.

'Hold me close, Radu, never let me go,' she had whispered, and now he could see that there had been a kind of fierce desperation in this plea, as if she had known she had reached the end of the road.

He had embraced her, and she had lain for a while with her head against his, her face pressed down on the pillows. Would she be doing the same thing with St Jules? Perhaps they were even now locked in sexual congress, laughing at him. The thought was so terrible that Radu cursed and took long swigs at the brandy bottle he had brought with him for company, his mind eddying with memories of vampire and succubus, demon-women who come from hell in the dead of night, to lie with men and drain them of strength. Was Mariana such a one, and did her loving arms hold death?

What am I going to do? he thought, slumped on the couch, drinking like a man possessed. Oh God, let me sleep. Let me forget. The thread of the dark years ahead unwound slowly, and he longed for oblivion, that precious gift of being without thought, without emotions, totally blind. The brandy settled like fire in his stomach and ran through his veins. His brain became cloudy, dull eyes fixed on the flames which danced in purple and green patterns against the glowing logs. His eyelids began to droop, fantasies ran in his mind. He thought he saw Countess Elizabeth and heard her lisping voice begging for his embraces. He grinned sardonically into the darkness behind his eyes, saying, 'Ah, you're another of the treacherous female crew! But I'm wise to your game. It's quite useless to slide your hand along my chest, it has already been plundered by the soft paw of another woman that clawed as it caressed. It's no good hunting my heart, Elizabeth, someone else has eaten it.'

A sound struck through this alcoholic contemplation. His military training sobered him immediately and also held him in the same pose, lying on the couch with closed eyes. That same instinct for danger told him that he was no longer alone. For a split second he regretted being drunk and his right hand shot to his pocket. As it did so, a strong grip closed on the wrist. Cursing his slowed reaction, he tried to jerk himself free, at the same time rising to his feet. He thrust his shoulder into his assailant's chest, striking a thudding blow with his left fist into a red, heavily-moustached face.

The soldier's teeth clashed under the force. He flung his free arm round Radu's throat, and a second man came quickly round the couch. Radu bent his knees to spring, and suddenly hurled himself backwards. He fell violently to the floor with his captor, but before he could take advantage, the other bully was upon him. The three of them rolled along the parquet, aiming wild blows in the confusion. As he struck at the snarling face of his first attacker, Radu was conscious of a voice behind them.

'Go easy, Schoene,' said Grigore. 'I don't want him killed yet.'

Radu smashed his fist into the face again, feeling the nose pulp. The shako came off and the shaven head of Schoene cracked dryly against the floor. Blood streamed from a gash in the brow. The other henchman flung himself squarely on top of Radu, pressing steel fingers into this throat, tearing at it with the ferocity of a savage beast.

'Well done!' Grigore shouted. 'I'm enjoying this spectacle immensely! Go to it, lads!'

Radu rose to his knees upon the squirming body beneath him. He drove a fist against the open mouth below, felt teeth breaking under the blow, and wrenched himself round upon Schoene's mate. The man roared and launched himself recklessly. Radu went over, and they slid along the highly polished floor, hitting the carved pedestal which held the bronzed statue of a boar. The second soldier had lost his hat too but Radu, trapped beneath his sweating bulk, was unable to draw his arm back for a knock-out punch. The pedestal juddered and the boar toppled over. Its full weight crashed on to the man's unprotected head with a resounding crack. The point of one of its tusks struck Radu on the temple and into unconsciousness.

When he recovered his senses, he found himself facing Grigore. The reptilian eyes viewed him with the unwinking stare of a blind man. The white thread of his scar was livid against the flush staining his cheekbones. Nothing broke the threatening silence but the crumbling and settling of the logs on the hearth.

'What's the meaning of this outrage?' Radu snarled, unable to move for the cords binding him tightly to a chair.

'Time we had a little talk, brother,' Grigore answered. 'I've come to offer my condolences on your recent sad loss. How trying to find that your beautiful bride was, after all, nothing but your whore! T'ch-t'ch! What a crafty little baggage! A move worthy of our own dear Countess Elizabeth, what?' He chuckled as he spoke, and folded his arms, hugging them against his chest in a gesture of barely controlled violence.

'I suspected that you were at the bottom of all this,' grated Radu, glaring at him with naked hatred.

'Not so. I merely provided the wherewithal to set the wheels in motion. You can thank Edwin Cunyngham and Arthur Cartwright for freeing you from the machinations of an adventuress,' replied Grigore calmly. 'And none too soon either. How very calamitous had the lovely Mariana produced an heir for Montezena, and then it came to light that the child was illegitimate. You should be grateful to me for saving you that embarrassment.'

'What d'you want?' Radu asked frigidly. His eyes travelled to the ruffians who were grouped behind his half-brother, eyeing him balefully, villainous-looking and armed to the teeth. 'I can't believe that this is a social call.'

'Want, my dear Prince? There's nothing new I require, simply my rights.' Grigore was as restrained and still as a poised snake. 'What could be more natural than such close relatives as ourselves meeting in this pleasantly remote spot? Most convenient for many purposes.'

'Assassination, for example!' growled Radu.

'Assassination?' repeated Grigore slowly on a questioning note. 'What a nasty idea, brother. Oh, come, come!' He paused with his head slightly tilted, and a smile lifted his lips sideways like a snarling beast's. 'That would be most uncivilized and we are, if nothing else, civilized gentlemen. Is that not so?' He swung round and turned his gaze to his bodyguards. They grinned and nodded, watching his face, wary of his swift, unpredictable changes of mood.

'You? A gentleman? God rot your evil soul!' Radu's contemptuous voice slashed across the room.

'Ah, brother, how uncharitable.' Grigore took malicious joy in claiming the relationship. Then he rose suddenly to his feet and loomed over his prisoner. There was the faint smell of musk about him, and his clasped hands were level with Radu's eyes. 'You're wrong about that, as you're wrong about so many things, not the least of which was the virtue of that slut you took to wife. But you've played into my hands, dear brother. I guessed that your damnable pride wouldn't allow you to stay in Vienna. You thought yourself safe, eh? You're not as clever as you think. It was easy to figure out where you'd go to lick your wounds. As I've already said, this is a capital place for my purpose. Oh, yes, little Maria – darling Mariana – has played her part to perfection. It would take a bloody army to turn me from my course, and my rights!'

A sneer lifted Radu's mouth. Bound though he was, he exuded an air of authority which made Grigore's hellions fidget uncomfortably. 'Rights! Bullshit! You have no rights!'

Grigore's flat-handed blow jerked Radu's head back. Rage mastered Grigore and words poured from his lips, so fast that only one in three was comprehensible. He cursed Radu, cursed their father and Princess Arta. Head thrust forward, eyes glaring madly, he threatened, ranted and blasphemed. Then, suddenly aware that his men were listening, he pulled himself together.

'Have you finished?' Radu asked coldly. Blood was trickling from the corner of his lips.

'I've not yet begun,' Grigore muttered, face working, his huge distorted shadow flung against the panelled wall behind him. 'But, by God, when I do, heads are going to roll! There'll be some changes in the government of Montezena.'

While Grigore meditated on bloodthirsty revenge, Radu was planning his next move, very aware of that small pistol which lay secretly within the pocket of his coat. Grigore and his men were careless fools. Had he been in their position, the prisoner would have been thoroughly searched. He was trussed like a capon, arms roped behind the chair, and though he had been stealthily attempting to free his hands whilst Grigore was talking, the bonds refused to yield. He knew that death was very near, waiting for him with remorseless inevitability, as certain as dusk following day. Grigore would not let this ideal opportunity slip away. Why do I care? he thought, and was cynically amused to find that he minded dying – he who had convinced himself that life was meaningless without Mariana. Keep Grigore talking. Angle for time. Something may yet happen, he advised himself, saying aloud:

'And why d'you suppose that you'll have any part in governing my country? Neither I, Princess Arta nor Colonel Alnoch will agree to this.' He used a deliberately insulting tone, pushing Grigore to the point of this confrontation.

Grigore's head went up, a spark in those eyes which were as flat and black as basalt. 'They'll obey my orders or face the consequences. As for you – you'll not be alive. I intend to kill you, brother.'

'And how exactly? My murder will not be easy to disguise.'

A smile deepened the grooves of Grigore's cadaverous face. 'Simple, my dear Prince. In a moment I shall free your hands and you will write a suicide note. As I said before, Mariana did me a great service. You'll state that you can't live without her, can't face the shame of her betrayal. A perfect reason for ending it all.'

'And if I refuse?'

Grigore nodded to one of his minions. 'Muller, have the goodness to plunge that poker into the fire, will you? That's right, it won't take long to become red-hot. I've found that few men remain stubborn when their flesh begins to sizzle. Even you, Prince, will eventually yield, so why not save yourself unnecessary suffering?' He spoke with slow relish, savouring the emotions his words would awaken.

Even more than the desperate urge to save his own skin, Radu was driven by the thought of what would happen to the people of Montezena if this monster came to power. He stared up grimly into Grigore's face. 'Very well,' he said. 'Untie me.'

'You agree? How wise, though I'll admit to being a trifle disappointed. I was rather looking forward to branding you here and there, seeing you squirm, hearing you scream for mercy. However, I'll keep to the bargain.' The triumph on Grigore's face was sickening, but Radu held his temper in check, nerves tingling as Muller, with a regretful glance at the glowing iron poker, obeyed his leader and loosened the ropes.

Cautiously, knowing that every eye was on him, the atmosphere charged with an intense and murderous excitement, Radu stretched his cramped limbs. Grigore watched him from his place against the mantelpiece, one black-clad arm lying along the shelf, a double-barrelled pistol held lightly in the other hand. 'Muller, provide his Highness with writing materials,' he said.

Men guarded the door, others stood with their backs against the walls, alert for the slightest sign of resistance. Muller spread a sheet of note-paper on the table and laid a pencil beside it, then beckoned Radu over. A single candle had been lit there, and he stood, hands pressed flat on the surface, looking across at Grigore. 'Well?' he rapped out. 'And what d'you wish me to write?'

His features were accentuated by the upward glow, the chin, nose and cheekbones reminding Grigore of Prince Alecsandri, the father who, by his refusal to bend tradition, had denied him his birthright. His fingers played with the pistol, almost negligently. He dictated the words, and Radu scribbled them down, signing his name with a flourish. With an ironic bow, he handed the letter to his brother who perused it, folded it and had Muller replace it on the table.

'That seems to be in order,' said Grigore, idly weighing the long pistol in the palm of his hand. The firelight caught the muzzle so that it shone like a white-hot coal. 'When the news of your disappearance reaches Neograd, I'm sure that the worthy Colonel will organize a search. No doubt, you'll eventually be found, dead in this room. Your note will explain everything. Meanwhile, I'll wait, keeping myself discreetly quiet, but as soon as your death is publicly announced, I'll stake my claim. I've an army in readiness, and any resistance will be easily dealt with. Later, I intend to marry a suitable princess and establish my line. You may rest in peace, dear brother, knowing that Montezena is in my loving hands.'

'You think that you can trust this rabble to keep silent?' Radu jerked a thumb at Grigore's followers.

The pistol swung up, slowly, almost languidly. Then it exploded with a deafening concussion. The bullet whined past Radu's ear. There was a sound like breaking ice as the window behind him shattered. 'No man here will betray me,' said Grigore's contemplative voice.

Radu kept his eyes fixed on his half-brother and the smoking pistol that was aimed casually in his direction. Grigore was revelling in this war of nerves, confident of his victory, delaying the moment of truth, and Radu was aware of a strange bond between them. They had hated each other for so long that it had given a peculiar meaning to their lives. In Grigore's eyes he caught a hint of regret. Oh, he would kill him, there was no doubt of that, but once he was dead, the sport would be gone. Grigore would hunt others, but never again be goaded by such a fierce, obsessional spur.

While this thought was running through his mind, Radu slipped his hand into his pocket. 'The first blow is half the battle, bastard!' he shouted and as he spoke, his forefinger closed on the trigger of the concealed pistol. The burst of its firing shocked like a thunder-clap.

Grigore staggered. A spreading crimson stain marred the whiteness of his shirt. His own gun clattered to the floor. His mouth opened in astonishment, and blood not words gushed out, then he crashed heavily to the floor, like a tree uprooted by a gale. A gasp went up from his men, and in that split-second pause, the scene was imprinted for ever in Radu's memory – Grigore lying face downwards on the hearth – the ruffians stirring into life. He leapt into action before they had time to recover their wits, and the scene vanished as he hurled himself through the broken window, out into the pitch-black night.

'I doubt you'll have further trouble with those roughnecks,'said Danesti, standing in the courtyard of his stronghold. The first rays of the rising sun shot sparks from his hair. 'Leave everything to me, Highness. Those trusty fellows yonder will accompany you back to Vienna.' He nodded to where a dozen armed, wild-eyed brigands sat their spirited mounts, impatiently awaiting his orders. 'They'll welcome the chance to crack open a few heads on the way. As for me, as soon as you're gone, I'll lead another bunch to the lodge and flush out any remaining rats! They won't stand a hope in hell's chance. They'll be keeping a rendezvous with death!'

Radu was already up-saddled. His horse's breath smoked in the chilly air. The mountains were pink-tipped, glowing, and in his state of exhaustion which had passed mere weariness and now left him light-headed, his consciousness was honed almost unbearably. He could smell the icy streams, the snow from the highest peaks, could scent bark and pines and rocks. His eyes followed an eagle, poised far aloft, gliding on the thermals, its wings hardly stirring, as it searched for prey far below. The sky was faint blue, like an ocean on which coral craft drifted. He raised his face to that huge, splendid depth and felt that he had no more weight or substance than a shadow.

He had arrived at Danesti's hideout in the small hours, having made good his escape from the hunting-lodge. There had been an altercation at the gates until he was recognized. Danesti's guards were nothing if not zealous. Then their leader had been roused from his bed, stamping down, a smelly wolfskin cloak pulled over his battle-scarred frame, in a bad temper at having to leave the arms of his new, fifteen-year-old mistress. As soon as he clapped eyes on Radu he had stopped being disgruntled, bearing him to the fire in the echoing hall, plying him with cognac and listening grimly to his story. Radu had at last rested for an hour or two, wrapped in a borrowed riding-cloak, though sleep was out of the question. Dawn had found him up, engaged in writing letters, which he now handed down to Danesti.

'These are to go to Montezena. One for my mother, the

other for Colonel Alnoch.' He spoke precisely, his orders clear, and when he had finished, he said: 'You understand?'

'I do indeed, Highness,' Danesti answered, that blunt-spoken old rogue whom Radu had found admirably trustworthy and loyal. 'Now that Black Grigore's been sent to Hades, your troubles should be over.'

'I'll despatch Cazacu to aid you.' Radu leaned over to pat the thick, perfectly groomed mane of the chestnut who had replaced the tired stallion. Danesti and his men were expert judges of horseflesh – this one, and those of his escort, were of a dazzling, powerful beauty. Their coats had the gleam of wild silk; their deep shoulders, broad chests and muscular arching necks spoke of tireless strength, endurance and spirit. They had to be that way. The bandits' lives depended on them.

'Don't you worry, sir. The country will be in safe keeping while you're away, or I'll want to know why.' Danesti stood, foursquare on the flagstones, his legs planted wide. A sabre dangled at his left hip, a yard-long knife was stuck through his leather belt. As he talked, he flourished a whip, its short handle fitted with a metal joint to allow the lash full play. It was a heavy rawhide plait, razor-edged and iron-tipped, his companion over the years in raids and battles. There was no trace of its original colour. It had ripped open so much flesh that it was darkly lacquered with blood.

A taut smile played over Radu's lips. 'I've absolute faith in you, my friend,' he replied, as the sun climbed higher, its beams shifting across the grey walls of the keep. 'When I return, you must remain with me and help me to govern wisely. I'll promote you to a high office, with a place in the council chamber.'

Danesti took off his shaggy fur hat, frowned down at the lining and put it on again. 'No, my Prince. I'll give my heart, blood and guts in your service, but I prefer the hollow of a saddle to all other seats.'

'We'll see,' Radu conceded, then he straightened his back and tightened his hands on the reins. 'But first, I've a formidable task before me.'

'God go with your Highness!' shouted Danesti, giving the signal for the great gates to be rolled open. 'Bring back that beautiful woman who was born to be Princess Varna!' And suddenly his whip lashed out with a hiss as it cut through empty air. In an instant the cortège was charging under the arch and down the mountain track.

More than anything, Radu needed to see David and Lance, but there was something he had to do first, and on reaching

Vienna he sought out Cornel. His aide had been holding the fort, stemming off the stream of callers who had come to gloat over the disaster which had struck the House of Varna. There had been a more pleasant task, in the delectable shape of Mariana's erstwhile maid, Lucia. Both she and a distraught Sophie had been worrying about their mistress. The English girl had a great deal to say about the situation, never for a moment doubting that Christopher St Jules was a brute and her beloved Princess an innocent victim of terrible circumstances. She had been offered a post in the Cunyngham household and had gladly accepted it, if only for the sake of returning home with them and being there should Mariana need her. Lucia, however, had been encouraging Cornel's attentions, her blushes at the mere mention of his name, her sighs and abstracted air speaking volumes. For the moment, David was paying her wages and finding her employment, but she had no intention of leaving Europe and the dashing Lieutenant.

Radu's abrupt return threw his staff into a state of confusion. His unkempt appearance was enough to give Axos apoplexy. He strode into his residence looking like a Tartar tribesman, dirty, unshaven, his clothing crumpled, his boots filthy, the voluminous fur-lined cloak adding to his height and power, an untamed light in his fierce grey eyes. He found Cornel in the study, and he was not alone.

Radu stood in the doorway, and his aide looked up, registering a comical, mouth-dropping astonishment, before tumbling Lucia from his knee. He got to his feet awkwardly, clad in breeches and shirt, very embarrassed to have his chief catch him in such disarray. Lucia was wearing his hussar's jacket, and not much beneath it. Radu took in her bare brown legs, and the full bosom which flashed momentarily before she dragged the front of the coat together.

'Your Highness! Good God! I mean – I wasn't expecting you!' gulped Cornel, adding a flustered aside to his mistress: 'Get your clothes on, don't just stand there!'

'I can see that,' commented Radu dryly, then he grinned for the first time in days. 'I'll turn my back, Lucia, while you dress.' And he walked to the window, his broad, fur-clad shoulders towards the disconcerted lovers, staring out until he heard the door close behind her. He swung round, facing Cornel, who was now uniformed and standing stiffly to attention.

In a few brief sentences, Radu told him all that had taken place since he left Vienna. 'So, Baron Grigore is dead,' Cornel said when he had finished speaking. 'And how are you going to explain that away, your Highness?'

There was a look in Radu's eyes which made the young man glad that they were on the same side. 'Should the body be still in the lodge when Danesti gets there, he has orders to stage an accident. If it's dropped down a ravine no one will know that he was shot first. By the time it's found, no doubt the wolves and eagles will have had a fine feast. There won't be much left, certainly not enough to engender awkward questions.'

'And his followers?'

'Danesti knows how to deal with them.' Radu had come to rest against a corner of the table, one booted leg braced on the floor. His rough clothing may have denied his royal birth, but the hauteur of his features could leave no one in doubt. Cornel stood up straight, hand on his sword hilt, sensing that there was more to come. 'I want you to go to Neograd and help Colonel Alnoch keep order till I get back from England,' continued Radu. There was a cynical twist to his lips as he looked the young soldier over. 'You shouldn't have too much trouble with my mother. She can't resist good-looking boys.'

'Please, sir, can I take Lucia?' Cornel plucked up the courage to ask, his eyes fixed on some point just above his Prince's dark head.

Radu regarded him sternly, on his feet again, intimidating in his outlandish costume. 'You may, if it doesn't take your mind from your duties. You'll have much responsibility now, *Captain* Cazacu.'

Cornel flushed to the roots of his fair curly hair, and his eyes shot to meet Radu's smiling ones. 'Yes, sir. Thank you, sir. Lord, I'll have to get kitted out with a new uniform! Captain! I wasn't expecting to rise in the ranks so quickly.'

'Your loyalty deserves it.' Radu clapped him on the shoulder, then his face darkened. 'I don't know how long I'll be away – have no idea of the outcome of my mission. All I want is to prise Maria away from that man somehow. I may not succeed, may be forced to leave her with him, but by God, I'll not give up without a struggle.'

His face expressed the terrible torment within him and Cornel, deeply in love himself, was unable to offer consolation. He waited quietly for the spasm to pass, then said: 'Sir, will you give me your permission to marry?'

Radu came back to the present and the eager man hanging on his answer. He sighed deeply, new lines etched on his features, his eyes world-weary. 'Lucia? The lady's maid? Hardly a suitable choice for a captain, surely?'

'We love each other.' This simple statement cut Radu to the quick, and an ignoble envy twisted in his gut. The captain and his sweetheart were free to find joy in each other's arms, whilst such bliss was denied him. This base feeling lasted but a moment.

'Well, my friend, then I suppose this will suffice,' he said slowly, his voice filled with infinite sorrow. 'Not long ago, I too believed that love would be enough to vanquish the world.'

'She's not nobly-born, I agree,' put in Cornel clumsily, almost insensitive in his desire to receive the Prince's blessing. 'But her father owns his own farm, and she's vaguely related to Danesti.'

Radu's eyes were remote as they returned to Cornel's face. That sombre austerity which the youth had known when they fought together on the battlefield held him in thrall. 'Marry the girl, if that's what you want. But now, you must accompany me. I've work to finish before I can feel free to leave.'

Madame Feodora waylaid them in the hall of the brothel with a grotesque parody of coquetry which failed to mask her terror. Radu brushed her aside and, with Cornel staunchly bringing up the rear, mounted the staircase and pushed his way into Grigore's private apartment. He paused at the edge of what appeared to be a huge mother-of-pearl shell draped in rose curtains, and stared icily down at Dimitrie and Elizabeth who lay within it.

'What the hell?' Dimitrie began, a hookah tube dropping from between his lips.

'Don't try to call in your bullies,' Radu barked. 'It'll do you no good. Give me any trouble and the cur will follow his master through the gates of hell!'

Dimitrie recovered himself, easing back against the black satin pillows, his skin golden-brown amidst that gloomy luxury. He ran a hand through his tousled hair and smiled up at the furious Prince, the laughter-lines creasing about his bright blue eyes. 'What an unexpected pleasure, cousin,' he remarked lightly, his hand exerting a gently warning pressure on Elizabeth's bare shoulder. 'I'd no idea that you frequented Feodora's Temple of Love. But then, I suppose you've come here seeking consolation. Can't understand your deuced reference to "curs" and "hell" though, damme if I can. Explain yourself, my dear chap.'

Radu towered above them both, his head bent forward so that his hooded eyes missed nothing of their wanton sprawling in that decadent bed. Elizabeth was wide-eyed, her flesh like milk, a petulant look playing about her crimson, inviting lips.

Yes, she *should* lie in a black satin shroud, he thought grimly, the treacherous bitch! But even as the thought crossed his mind, she moved voluptuously, so that the sheet slid down exposing her white breasts, tipped with coral, perfect in contour. A formidable enchantress. So pretty, so dainty, so gentle! Who would believe that she could watch men go to the gallows without so much as a tremor? And Dimitrie, his kinsman, that good-looking fop who did not know the meaning of the word honesty. Radu's fingers itched to draw his pistol and shoot them both where they lay, spattering that evil couch with their blood.

He controlled the dark urge, the hard lines in his bleak face accentuated by an enigmatic smile as he answered: 'You'll need another protector now, Dimitrie, and you, Elizabeth. Grigore is dead.'

The shattering effect of his words was almost as satisfying as that of a bullet. Dimitrie forgot to be nonchalant, for once in his lifetime paying attention to someone else. 'Dead? I don't believe you!' he exclaimed, his cheeks draining of colour.

'You'd better believe me and do exactly as I tell you, if you don't want to follow him to the grave.' The pair sickened him, and Radu wanted to get the unpleasant business over and done with. 'I know that you've both been deeply implicated in his treachery, don't bother to lie. If I had any sense, I'd kill you, and if you ever cross me again, I will. Now, I strongly advise you to pack up and get out, away from Vienna, away from Germany. I don't care where the hell you go, but I never want to clap eyes on either of you again.' His voice was low, ominous as the distant rumble of thunder.

Elizabeth was made of sterner stuff than Dimitrie. She was still under the illusion that she could sway Radu with her body. Quickly recovering from her stunned anger, she hollowed her shoulders to emphasize the curves of her throat and breasts, dimpled at him, and said in honey-sweet tones: 'I'm not surprised that you managed to beat him. You were always the better man by far – in every respect.' She gave him a meaningful stare from beneath her curling lashes.

'Don't try it on, Elizabeth. I'd rather lie with the scabbiest hag in the world than you!' Radu cut off her attempts at seduction.

A remarkable transformation took place in the Countess. From a delicately fragile lady, she became a raging harpy, leaping up at this insult, not caring that she was naked, flinging herself towards Radu with snarling lips and raking nails. He caught her by her wrists and threw her to the floor, where she lay spitting venom. Cornel had drawn his pistol, keeping it trained on Dimitrie, but he had no intention of offering resistance. He valued his hide too much.

'Hold your fire!' he protested, with a cynical smile. 'I'm not arguing. I find this military attitude frightfully disturbing. La, I shall either have to faint or call my seconds, and I've no stomach for duelling with you two! Give a chap time to get his breeches on! Elizabeth dear, do stop that caterwauling – such a terrible row! Makes my head ache, and it won't do you a bit of good. Can't you see that the game's up?' Under Cornel's wary eye, he swung his legs over the side of the bed and reached for his trousers.

'You're being unusually sensible, Dimitrie.' Radu had no faith in this genial compliance, suspecting trickery. As it was, his ears were alert for sounds of Madame Feodora and a gang of thugs.

'I'm not a warlike being.' Dimitrie tucked his full-sleeved shirt into his belt, thrust his arms into his damask waistcoat and searched under the bed for his boots. 'We are but travellers on the road of life, and as such, we must feel our way and speculate as to our journey's end.'

Elizabeth had scrambled to her feet and was also hurriedly dressing. 'You won't get away with this,' she cried vengefully. 'Even *you* can be charged with murder!'

Radu, watching her face made ugly with baulked ambition and frustrated greed, wondered how he could ever have found her remotely attractive. 'Who said anything about murder?' he asked coldly. 'I was defending myself. He was going to kill me!'

'I shall say something about it!' she vowed, fully dressed now, rushing about the room, collecting clothing, jewellery, every valuable object on which she could lay her hands. 'I'll go to Paris, and you won't be able to intimidate me there! The authorities shall hear what I have to say, and it will be plenty! I'll see your name dragged through the muck – High and Illustrious Prince Radu!'

There was something frenzied about the way in which she was collecting loot. She had pulled several small trunks from a cupboard, flung back the lids and was now piling goods into them with the mindless avidity of a mercenary bent on pillage. There had been no moment of grief for her dead lover, only a determination to salvage everything she could from the fall of his empire. Dimitrie aided her, spreading a large shawl on the carpet and heaping candlesticks, ornaments, even brocaded cushions and silk drapes on to it.

Radu turned away in disgust, saying over his shoulder: 'A

carriage has been ordered. You'll leave Vienna at once.'

He was aware of quick footsteps behind him and swung round to find Dimitrie looking at him, jaunty once more, a casually elegant figure. 'I say, old man, any chance of a loan?' he drawled, totally without shame, almost as if he was bestowing a favour, offering him the opportunity to be generous. 'Must say I'm a bit pushed for cash. It'll be all right once I'm in the gaming-rooms of Paris, don't you know – but on the journey – a gentleman must travel in style, what?'

Cornel had never heard Radu swear with such violence and fluency, not even when they had been in the midst of the heaviest, most bloody battle. His ears were still ringing when he followed as Radu stormed from the room and out of the house.

Their next call was to the von Gundling palace, and on the way Cornel did not dare address the furious Prince who rode his horse in grim silence. The Baron and Baroness were not at home but David was, and Radu quickly told him about Grigore. Lance was called, listening quietly to the news. David begged Radu to say nothing in Georgiana's hearing, hushing him when she appeared in the doorway of the Grand Salon. She guessed by Radu's looks that something momentous had happened, but held her peace, confident that David would tell her in his own good time.

'When are you returning to England?' Radu asked, his haggard face expressing his chaos of mind.

'Almost at once,' answered David, his conscience troubling him because it was he who had introduced Radu to Mariana and been the unwitting source of his anguish. 'Must get Georgiana home soon. I want the baby to be born on our native soil.'

He gave his wife an affectionate glance. She seated herself on a couch, her eyes going from one stern masculine face to the other, deeply concerned for both Radu and the unfortunate woman whom she had befriended. She had been very upset by the arrival of Lord St Jules, and angry with Mariana for her deception. But later when she had talked it over with David and Lancelot, who had told them everything he had learned from Mariana under hypnosis, she had wept for her.

'I shall come with you,' Radu said firmly, and the look in his eyes told David that argument was pointless.

'As you wish, my friend,' he replied slowly, his hand closing reassuringly over Georgiana's. The last thing he wanted was any distressing scene which might alarm her. He glanced over at Lancelot, seeking his support, but that annoying individual was lounging in an armchair, eyelids drooping under those

313

bushy brows, seemingly half asleep. 'You're welcome to stay with us for as long as you like.'

Radu was too restless to remain still for long, and he suddenly got up, travel-stained and untidy in that spaciously elegant chamber, pacing the floor, huge, angry, rather frightening. 'I can't let her go. You see that, don't you, David?' he shouted. 'I must be with her again – talk to her – talk to St Jules, damn him!'

'Won't do you a scrap of good,' growled Lancelot, coming awake and watching him. 'Lord, man, stop fretting your bowels to fiddle-strings! He's a tough customer, and won't yield an inch, no matter what anyone says.'

'Talk to Lance, Radu,' said Georgiana, leaning forward and using every bit of tact at her command. 'He'll tell you exactly what you're up against. Maria – oh dear, I find it so hard to think of her as Mariana – well, anyway, she did confide in him. You know you're amongst friends here, who'll do everything in their power to help.'

'Thank you, Georgiana.' A tired smile lifted Radu's mouth, and he bowed to her, lifting her hand and kissing it. Then he took the seat beside her and tried to control his impatience. 'Well, Lance, what have you to tell me?'

The doctor lit his pipe and launched into the story. He spoke slowly, letting each word tell. Radu grew still as he listened, and the lines in his face deepened with the set of his jaw. The evening shadows were growing long, bathing the room in an orange glow, yet he was not aware of anything but that voice droning on, exposing secrets which Lance's oath had bound him to keep till all else failed. Gradually Radu understood Mariana's reserve. How could she have confessed to him, her new, illegal husband, even though she loved him more than life itself? It had been many years since he had cried, but now he felt the choke of tears at the back of his throat, consumed with pity for her as he heard that tale of murder and madness.

When at last Lancelot paused, Radu could no longer contain his fury, bursting out: 'That devil! Then what she said was true! He killed her child! My God, surely he can be charged with the crime?'

'Not so easy, my friend,' Lancelot replied gloomily. 'What proof has she? St Jules is a clever man, and most plausible. Furthermore, he's exceedingly rich and powerful.'

'But this Dr Russell, and the Reverend Grant? Couldn't they be convinced that the man's insane?' Radu's hands were clenched together between his spread knees and he was scowling blackly, not yet fully comprehending the extent of Christopher's villainy.

Lance stared into the bowl of his pipe as if seeking a solution there, then his mouth turned down at the corners. 'It was this doctor, apparently, who said that the child had a malformed heart. You've seen the death-certificate, and so have I.'

'But why? Why, if what Mariana told you was true?' Radu groaned, sinking his head in his hands, shoulders bowed in despair.

Into that atmosphere of luxurious normality, Lancelot dropped a single, highly evocative word. 'Witchcraft!' he said.

His audience stared at him aghast. 'You're crazy!' David exploded, then he tried to laugh. 'Great Heavens, Lance, we're living in the nineteenth century, not the middle-ages! You can't be serious!'

His war-time comrade and closest friend looked back at him gravely. 'Oh, but I am. Deadly serious. I'm not saying that the black arts work, though there're many strange aspects of it which can't be explained rationally, but if the followers of Satan believe that they do, anything can happen.' With his wide strong hands resting on his brawny knees, he addressed them earnestly. 'Look at it this way. Just supposing that St Jules is so determined to get his way in all things that he's prepared to adopt any creed likely to make him even more powerful. He probably believes in what he's doing. He'll need others to back him up and he'll get 'em by any means, fair or foul. Blackmail – extortion – I'll wager he's quite ruthless. So, he gathers his coven and, once they've committed themselves to God knows what evil deeds, there's no way they can break free from him.'

No one spoke for a moment. Georgiana's face was pale and she sat with her arms folded over the rounded bulge of her stomach, protecting it. Then: 'Did Mariana say that he practised black magic?' asked Radu.

'Not in so many words.' Lancelot shook his head solemnly, and those intelligent eyes held the Prince's. 'I don't think she understood what he was about, but from the things she told me, I formed the opinion that his preoccupation with the occult bore the hallmarks of a Satanist. I've studied the subject, you know. The workings of the mind interest me.'

'D'you think he's mad?'

Lancelot pondered for an instant before he replied. 'I would guess that he suffers from delusions, and that these are accentuated by drugs. His sister's confined in an asylum and she's his twin. Perhaps heredity is at fault. The whole damned

315

St Jules line may be tainted. Who knows?'

'Oh, God! And Maria's chained to him!' Radu was on his feet again, as if he would leave for England at once. He rounded on the doctor, menacing in his fear for her. 'She's in danger, isn't she?'

'Yes, very grave danger, I imagine. But bear in mind, Radu, that she's his wife and the law will be biased in his favour. Wives stand precious little chance of winning a case against their husbands.'

With a curse, Radu tore himself away, and ran without a word into the twilight of the garden. David had his arm round Georgiana's shoulders, and she leaned against him, tears wetting her cheeks. 'Oh, we must help them, David! We must!' she sobbed.

'My dear, don't cry,' he begged, patting and soothing her, proffering his large white handkerchief. 'You mustn't upset yourself. We'll do all we can. Lance will offer his valuable advice, won't you, Lance?' He was filled with fear, for his wife, for Radu, and for the girl for whom he had developed a strong affection.

Lancelot tapped out his pipe in the brass basket of the pink marble fireplace. 'All the advice in the whole universe won't get her out of that mess!' he barked, then squared his broad shoulders and looked down at the Cunynghams. 'You know that I'll help, of course I will. St Jules thinks he's won. He may be in for a nasty shock!'

CHAPTER 2

Hell must surely be cold and damp, not hot and fiery. The thought came to Mariana as she stood on the deck of the dingy little ferry-boat. It was late afternoon, but fog smothered everything in a shroud of darkness that resembled midnight. The sun had gone, seemingly for ever. She could not remember seeing it since they left Vienna, but then, steeped in misery, she had not noticed much.

She gathered her cloak more closely around her. Tendrils of mist, like the ghostly fingers of dead children, left drops of moisture in her hair. The wind had died and the vessel was almost stationary. It rocked slightly on the swell, as if the fog had solidified round it, like a trapped mammoth encased in ice during a cataclysm which had plunged the world into frozen night. Her eyes strained against the greyness, and the dripping, shifting mass thinned, giving a glimpse of Whitby. The muffled, disembodied voices of sailors, the mournful wail of fog-horns broke the silence. Ah, God, would that they might never reach their destination! Rather this chill which ate into her bones, rather anything than that. Will I ever be warm again? she wondered. It was more than a physical chill. For a short space of time, fate had given her all that she asked for, then callously taken it away. This was what the gypsy, Sylka, had foreseen on her wedding-day – this emptiness and horror.

The ship groaned and complained, and she rested a hand on the rail to balance herself. The fog was lifting and there came the jarring screech of ropes as the wind flapped at the wet sails. They were moving forward, gradually gaining speed. She could see the harbour, the gaunt bare masts of the anchored boats rising from the murky water into the grey air. They looked like gallows. The cliffs were dominated by the abbey, its ruins jagged against the skyline. Memories hammered at her brain. Last time she had visited Whitby, Elaine had been curled safely in her womb. Oh, don't, she pleaded, don't let me remember! I mustn't think of her, nor of Radu – never dwell on what I've lost, lest I go mad!

Christopher would not delay. There was more travelling

ahead, by coach over bad roads, driving ever deeper into the sullen moorland. Pale hope timidly suggested that they might never reach Thornfalcon. Perhaps there would be an accident. The carriage might overturn on some desolate stretch, killing them. She prayed for this, but without conviction. Why should God heed her? She was a sinner. She had broken sacred vows, knowingly, wilfully, thinking to escape Nemesis in a far country. How mistaken she had been! Retribution had followed hard on her heels.

There were lights springing up along the wharves, the boats speeding home to warm fires, buxom wives and rosy-cheeked children. Ernestine was married to a fisherman. She had been expecting her first baby when Mariana fled from Thornfalcon, and she wondered, not for the first time, how Ernestine had fared. She would be living in a cosy cottage in Fewston, cooking Jamie's supper, eagerly waiting for him. Fortunate sister, whose happiness had been secured by Mariana marrying Christopher. No such warm welcome awaited her. No children, no peaceful hearth, only gloom and endless regrets.

Dry-eyed, she stared at the bobbing, glow-worm lights. At first she had cried so much that it seemed every tear due to her through the milleniums had been exhausted. No more tears then, but never acceptance. A rebellious fire seethed inside her. Life was unjust. She had sinned, yes, but had been driven to it by desperation. Don't try to justify yourself, said the nagging voice of guilt. You vowed that you'd pay any price to have Radu. Now comes the reckoning.

She had not turned her head, still gazing at the rapidly nearing shore, but she knew that Christopher was close by, aware of his eyes boring into her back. He was always watching her. He would have entered her dreams as she slept if he could. Whenever she woke from fitful slumber, it was to find him staring at her with an intensity which seemed to go right through her. But he had not touched her, never once during that awful journey across Europe, when they had driven at breakneck speed, pausing only to change horses and snatch a meal. He was obsessed with reaching Thornfalcon, and she dreaded their arrival, aware of the wealth of passion lying within him devoid of ordinary human emotions. The fire that burned in his soul was an icy one. What was he planning to do to her once the massive door of his domain had closed upon them?

He had drawn nearer. She did not hear him, but she knew. She glanced round and saw him crossing the deck towards her, tall, graceful, wrapped in a boat-cloak, hatless, the wind tossing his linten curls. She wanted to run but there was nowhere to go. The time for running was long past. Closer he came, till she had the feeling that he was enveloping her in the sable wings of his cloak, folding her into him, stifling her. His eyes were like hypnotic pools. They seemed to absorb her, sapping her strength. A long shudder shook her from crown to feet as she felt her personality slipping away. He was sucking out her spirit, her life-blood. His presence filled her with loathing, fear and an inexplicable compassion. He smiled down at her with that chill, questioning smile that did not warm his eyes. Before she could move, his hand came out to rest on hers, cold as death.

'You should go below,' he said, his voice smooth as silk but menacing. 'I'd not have you inflicted with ague. I want you at the peak of health, so that you may fulfil your duty. You take my meaning, dear wife? You're too pale, and dreams cloud your eyes. All will be well when we reach Thornfalcon. A surprise awaits you there. One which I'm sure you'll find pleasing.'

His grip tightened painfully on her hand. He was strong. Only too well did she know the power of the muscles in his whiplash lean body. Thornfalcon, the place she detested more than anywhere on earth. Thornfalcon, her prison for the rest of her days!

Mariana had been right in her assumption that Christopher intended to reach there without further delay. The journey was even more fraught than she had anticipated, alone in the great crested St Jules carriage with him. With Spyros and the baggage installed in a second coach, Christopher had taken a brusque farewell of their other travelling-companion, Arthur Cartwright, that unprincipled man, who had scuttled away from Vienna and Radu's wrath. He had been so pleased with himself, fawning on Christopher, expecting favours in return for the service he had performed. Mariana had been relieved when he left but knew, with sinking certainty, that she had not seen the last of him.

It was terrible to be so frightened, to feel so threatened. She huddled in a corner of the carriage, as far away from Christopher as possible. He said nothing as the road rolled under the wheels, his collar turned up about his ears, hat low. She felt his concentrated gaze, and the great silence which weighed the atmosphere. It was as if he were trying to burrow beneath her skin, to reach the deep essential fibres, the hidden springs of her innermost being.

At last she could bear the tension no longer, crying: 'Why don't you let me go? Can't you see that I hate you? Why take me back to that dreadful house? Have you no pity? No shame for what you've done? Our baby, left to die in the blizzard! What an act of despicable cruelty!' The words were hardly out before she instinctively raised her hands to protect her face from the blow that such boldness would surely provoke.

The only thing that showed his rage was the tension of his lips – an expression like the grin of a wolf. He stroked the handle of his silver-mounted cane with his beautiful, well-cared-for hands, and said: 'You speak from the coils of delirium, my dear. Elaine died in her cradle. Dr Russell will corroborate my story, Mrs Brockwell too. You were so feverish that you knew nothing of what was taking place. From the moment the baby was born, Russell had warned me to expect this. Everyone was aware of it. Don't you remember receiving a letter of sympathy from Mrs Grant?'

'You lie! You lie!' Her voice was harsh with held-in fury. 'I don't know your motives, Christopher, and can't begin to understand why you are saying these things or why you made up your mind that she had to die. But I know that I didn't imagine it! I had recovered from my lying-in. I was as healthy as she. Nothing you can say or do will ever make me believe differently.'

He sighed, leaning on his cane with both hands, as motionless as stone. 'You'll keep your opinions to yourself, for if you don't, I may have no option but to have you committed to an asylum. If you deliberately gainsay myself, the doctor and the good housekeeper, it will prove that you've not yet recovered your wits. Strict treatment in close confinement may be necessary.'

She glared at him through narrowed eyes. 'Like Agnes?'

He nodded. 'Precisely.'

'You beast! Cold, heartless beast! Did you treat her in a similar way, so that she ended up completely insane? I'll wager that even your sister suffered in your hands. I wouldn't put any devilry past you!' She leaned forward, the rocking of the coach making her sway from side to side, and voiced a suspicion which had tormented her for months. 'Howard Blake. You said it was suicide. What really happened?'

'My dear girl, d'you expect me to discuss such a matter with someone as sick as yourself?' he drawled. 'Why don't you ask Dr Russell or Grant? They were both present.'

Mariana felt herself being sucked into a morass. No matter how often she protested her sanity, the seeds of doubt were beginning to take root. 'Why are you doing this to me?' She cried, her voice breaking with desperation.

'I? I'm not doing anything. It is you who are torturing yourself,' came his bland reply. 'My actions have been blameless. I came to find you in Europe, was overjoyed to know that you were still alive. I've even forgiven you for your unfaithfulness, excusing it on the ground of your diminished responsibility. I've brought you home, expecting you to play your part humbly, as befits a wife who has transgressed and been pardoned. I'm amazed at your ingratitude. This strident, hostile behaviour is most unseemly.'

'You damned hypocrite!' Her indignation could not be controlled, no matter how he punished her. And he would punish her, that was for sure. 'You lied to the Cunynghams. Lied to Radu. Lied to me! D'you know the difference between truth and falsehood, or are they one to you, any means justifying the end?'

He moved with the swiftness of a snake, his fingers bruising her arm. 'Be quiet!' His voice was low but deadly. 'I'll hear no more of these ravings. You'll never speak of it again, d'you hear? Or it will be the worse for you. And you'll tell no one that you married Prince Radu under false pretences. I've brought you back, but I don't intend to be made the laughing-stock of the district. No one must know that you were another man's shameless concubine.'

Mariana sank back, her face stony. Christopher released her and the carriage moved like a juggernaut, crushing her hopes beneath its wheels. Even her considerable courage quailed before the prospect of living with him. It was total domination Christopher sought, not love. A hundred unconsidered pointers came back to her. This had always been his aim. The great gates of Thornfalcon reared out of the gloom. She had never felt more alone and threatened by this towered place through whose high corridors and stately rooms the menace of chill evil swept. She must get away!

There was a moment's comfort when the first person she saw in the Great Hall was Mrs Grant, never guessing that she would be so pleased to see that cheerful, interfering busy-body. She wanted to fling herself on to her broad bosom and implore her aid. But she held herself rigid, Christopher's hand closing warningly on hers.

'Lady St Jules! Oh, my dear child, how wonderful to see you. We came as soon as we received his Lordship's message! What an answer to prayer!' Mrs Grant was upon her, taffeta gown rustling, jet beads clicking like agitated bats. Her face was puckered, and it looked as if she was about to burst into tears.

'The prodigal has returned,' boomed the Reverend, standing in the background with Dr Russell. 'Heaven be praised!'

'We had given you up for lost!' His wife was thrilled by the drama of it. It was very nearly the most exciting thing that had ever happened to her. Puffed up with importance, she felt herself to be Lord St Jules's confidante, for he had particularly asked her to keep the matter to herself, his grave demeanour convincing her that he looked on her as a trusted friend. For days she had been going around the village with a mysteriously important air, dropping hints all over the place.

'My wife is tired.' He was full of charmingly solicitous concern. 'Would you be good enough to accompany her to the bedchamber, doctor? A brief examination, perhaps, to assure us that she is on the road to recovery?'

'I am not ill!' Mariana burst out, then swung to the medical man. 'You must have been mistaken. Elaine wasn't a delicate child. I don't understand.'

Russell's clean-cut features were solemn. He exchanged a warning glance with Christopher. 'Lady St Jules, such a tragic occurrence, but not unusual. You weren't in a fit state to comprehend how weak she was. I did everything I could for the wee mite. Try to forget it. We're so happy to have you back. There will be more children – '

'Not if I can prevent it!' Her eyes shone with a fierce light as she backed away. Though they had not moved, it was as if Christopher and the rest of them had stepped closer, encircling her. Her glance switched to the rector, and she held out her hands piteously. 'You must help me, sir. You're a man of God, a pillar of the church. When you hear what I have to tell you, surely you'll protect me?'

Mrs Grant rolled her eyes towards her husband helplessly. The last thing she wanted was to offend Christopher, and she decided to believe Mariana to be unhinged. This embarrassed her and she did not know what to do or say. The Reverend was her oracle, and to him she always looked for guidance. He knew best, and her heart swelled with pride in the knowledge that she was his lady. Dear Horace, so commendable and solidly handsome, his features those which might have graced a Roman coin.

He gave Mariana a serious though not unsympathetic stare. 'Bless you, my dear lady, your wish is my command, but alas, I'm not a doctor. My advice is, therefore, that you should listen to him who is qualified. Layman though I am, I feared for Elaine. When I held her in my arms at the baptism service, I prayed for her soul, recognizing that she was not long for this world. The happier for it, perhaps. She is now with Our Blessed Lord.'

'Untrue – untrue,' Mariana cried, then with a certainty which seemed to grip her very marrow with icy fingers, she knew that they were in league against her. Not Mrs Grant, Mariana was convinced that she was an innocent dupe – but the others! She did not know why, could not begin to fathom their reasons, but they were presenting a solid, united front. In that same instant it came to her that protestations were useless – more than that, downright dangerous. If she acted hysterically, it would but give credence to the tale of her insanity. Her voice trailed off in defeat.

'Never mind, my dear.' Mrs Grant kept a nervous eye on her husband. 'You'll feel better now that you're with Lord St Jules again. And you won't be alone any more.' Her broad, rather stupid face brightened.

'Quite right, Mrs Grant. How perceptive of you. Of course, a companion of her own sex will be of great comfort,' Christopher said smoothly, throwing Grant a silencing look as he went to the door and called into the passageway beyond: 'Mrs Brockwell. You may come in.'

It is almost complete, thought Mariana wildly. Will he finish the matter, surround me entirely with enemies by summoning Mrs Wrixon and the rest of his cronies? And her heart dropped like a stone when the housekeeper answered his command. With her walked the slim, wiry Spyros, and between them someone else, someone vaguely familiar.

Christopher relaxed. A smile softened his features and he went towards them eagerly, seeing neither his valet nor Mrs Brockwell, his attention riveted on the woman in their midst. She was dressed in pearly-grey silk stippled with a faint small pattern of leaves, the waist shaped by a lavender sash, the full skirts rustling to the floor. In the dim pale-gold light, Mariana saw arched eyebrows, curved lips, slender hands, a remote, fragile elegance. Christopher took her in his arms, folded her to his heart, and Mariana knew who it was. That great panelled room, its high fireplace, its stags' heads, banners and armoured ornaments seemed to rush towards her, crushing her spirit with an awful sense of defeat and terror.

'Agnes,' she heard her husband say tenderly, 'I told you I wouldn't be away long, and I've kept my word.'

Mariana shook her head in denial of what her eyes beheld. She drew in a shuddering breath, then hissed it out between her teeth. 'What is she doing here?' she demanded of Mrs Grant.

'She's so much better, quite recovered from her illness, so I understand,' Mrs Grant fluttered, eyes darting frantically from her husband and Dr Russell to the group by the door.

'You mean to tell me that they've released her from the mad-house?' Mariana's voice was harsh with horror.

Mrs Grant was a woman of broad simple principles, not too intelligent and completely lacking in imagination. She gave Mariana a shocked glance. 'Mad-house? Oh, no, Lady St Jules, I beg your pardon but you're mistaken. Lady Agnes has been in a hospital, and treated for congestion of the lungs. I heard nothing about a mad-house. Dear me, what a dreadful thing to say.'

'How long has she been here?' Mariana could not tear her eyes from the picture of Christopher holding Agnes in a tight embrace. He was laughing down into her faded, lovely face and she was smiling up, worshipping him.

'She came back shortly after the funeral, when they buried someone, thinking it was yourself.' Mrs Grant's face was puce, most distressed by Mariana's attitude. The home-coming which she had visualized sentimentally as being one of unalloyed joy was not going well. Even she could not but be aware of the stormy undercurrents in the atmosphere.

At last Christopher became conscious of Mariana's intent gaze. He lifted his eyes from Agnes's face, turned and with an arm about her, walked with her towards his wife. 'This is the surprise I promised you, Mariana,' he said with a queer look in which were mingled triumphant mockery and arrogance. 'You can have no idea of the happiness this gives me. I'll have my beloved sister, my beloved wife, living in harmony with me under the roof of Thornfalcon for ever.'

The falling dusk of that miserable day found Mariana seated at the long table in the dining-room. It was a lofty room, its walls hung with tapestries. Opposite her, she could see, in exquisitely worked needlepoint, a goddess elegantly reclining midst a Grecian temple, eternally smiling in calm delight upon a romantic world of trees, blue skies and handsome shepherds. Her wider field of vision brought in the row of flunkeys who were waiting at table, the silver candle-sconce directly before her, and a painting, all rose and olive-green, depicting a naked lady poised immodestly on the bank of a river.

No sound disturbed the silence, not even the tick of a clock. The footmen were soft-footed and dexterous, moving like mechanical figures under the eye of the butler. Three huge chandeliers caught stray gleams on the myriad facets of their cut-glass drops. Agnes sat near Christopher, and it was as if the lady from the portrait in the Kingfisher Room had stepped down from the canvas for she wore the same gown. Her hair was dressed the same, her figure had not changed, but her face had aged, imprinted with lines of suffering, and dark hollows marred the once-perfect curves of her throat.

She was quiet, toying with her food, lashes lowered and Mariana was glad of this. Only once had Agnes looked at her, and she had found herself staring into a pair of blue ice-cold eyes, just like Christopher's yet different in that they held no emotion of interest, curiosity or anger. Mrs Brockwell had brought Agnes down to dinner, and she stood at the far end of the room, watchful of her charge. It appeared that Agnes occupied her old room, wore the clothes stored there for her, was withdrawn and apparently harmless, guarded by her one-time nurse and personal maid.

Christopher said not a word, eating sparingly, drinking deeply, adding drops from his tiny pocket-phial to his glass. Both he and his sister seemed lost in worlds of their own, but every now and again, when Mariana glanced up, it was to find him watching her with brooding intensity. When the meal could be no longer protracted, Mrs Brockwell stepped forward, her dull grey face and beady black eyes resting on Agnes.

'Time for bed, my Lady.' Her voice was soft as ever.

Like an obedient child Agnes rose, dipped a little curtsy to her brother, bent those expressionless eyes on Mariana for a second and then preceded the housekeeper out of the door. The servants too had retired and the darkness and silence folded thickly over the room. Mariana laid down her napkin, pushed back her chair and rose. Christopher was slumped at the head of the table, his eyes glazed, his attitude suggesting that he had entered the euphoria of drug-induced dreams. She held her breath, wondering if it might be possible to slip away unnoticed, but as she moved, the satin of her gown slithered softly and his eyes alerted. She stopped, hands clasped against her breasts, poised like a wild animal ready for flight.

Christopher's lips curved in a blood-chilling smile. 'Time for bed, my Lady.' He repeated Mrs Brockwell's words in a voice of drawling mockery, the unnatural cruelty and lust of his intonation turning her cold. 'We shall be taking up residence in the Master Chamber tonight. Doesn't this thought bring you joy? Kali will watch us making love. Kali will ensure that you conceive a boy this time, not some puling girl.' He got to his feet, swaying unsteadily, coming over to her.

'How can you speak so, when my flesh shrinks from you?' She side-stepped out of his reach, head flung up, gold-striped shawl clasped about her.

He laughed, shrugging her protest aside, his hand snaking out, grabbing at the shoulder of her gown. She felt the material rip, felt the air on her naked skin. 'What do you know of love?' he jeered, forcing her back, back till she could go no further, the panelling biting into her hips. 'You know nothing – nothing. You think you loved your soldier-prince in his pretty uniform? Bah! Calf-love! Sickly romance fit only for adolescents! Don't you remember how I used to take you? That was the true dark side of loving. Remember how I feasted on your body, using my tongue for more than words, bringing you to ecstasy? Now we're alone, my child, my love. Fight me if you must. I want this more than meek, sickly submission. Kick, scratch, bite – tear at me with your nails! Do what you will but you'll be mastered by me! By the end of this night you'll have forgotten that your fairy prince ever took you. You are mine! Mine!'

Mariana twisted in his arms, wrenching herself free. She ran for the door, but Christopher caught up with her, the blood running in his veins, full and lively, the drugs giving him added strength. He seized her, lifted her in his arms and began to run with her towards the Master Chamber. A moment later she was lying on the bed, her gown in rags. Christopher fell upon her, impaling her with the violence of a killer driving his stake deep into the belly of his prey. She screamed with outrage and pain. The grin widened on his face.

'That's right! Scream!' he said, between tight lips. 'This is only the start of your torment!'

And now he became an executioner intoxicated with the agonies he inflicted. His loins, his hands, his mouth were the instruments of torture with which he pleasured a dark, forbidden yearning that he could at last assuage. He was her husband, granted licence to defile modesty, decency and humanity, to crush and trample her as he willed. His was the right to compel her to every form of pain and dishonour, in order to stimulate his desire. With an insane ferocity, he strove for an ecstasy beyond human limitations.

He opened his eyes, feeding on the sight of her humiliation, gasping with the joy of it. Tears ran from her eyes, and her mouth, smeared with blood, torn, stretched wide by her screaming, was the acme of perfection, the fulfilment of his dreams. Teeth bared in a snarl, he searched for the most sensitive places of her body. His nails became vulture's talons, ripping at her shoulders, her nipples, the insides of her thighs. He champed at the delicate skin of her neck, her face. He seized a fistful of hair with one hand, her throat with the other, beating her head against the carved bed-post.

'Does that convince you?' he shouted. 'What price Prince Radu now, bitch?'

He felt himself master of the universe in that moment of savage hunger, possessed of a godlike virility, equipped to serve a hundred women, prepared to take the world to bed with him, a drinker of virgin blood, the embodiment of Pan. He needed no innocent eden-paradise of young love, the singing, the sighing, the wooing, kisses and flowers. It was violence that aroused him. Mariana's cries were the most exciting music and he abandoned himself to a fathomless orgy of pleasure, redoubling his barbarity, inflaming his flesh.

He was riding the serpent-fire roaring along his spine with its burning spell, through the black and crimson haze of his hellish Nirvana. The great beast reared, vast head twisting round on its long scaly neck. Its slavering jaws widened to a scarlet pit, blood dripping from its fangs. Its tongue protruded, becoming a mighty spear transfixing his loins with an agonizing ecstasy which forced a single cry from his lips. His body, absolved, replete and softened, broke away from Mariana's, and he lay there without thought or feeling.

She folded her arms about her stripped, ravaged form, past noticing pain, tearless, held in an arid misery the desolation of which no well-spring could relieve. After those months of full life, after her gorgeous dreams of happiness, this was all that was left her. The road had opened before her, alluring, fantastic in its promise, but it had been a trick, a crazy labyrinth, leading her back to this madman.

Mariana went out into the dewy morning world, down through the long stone corridors that still held night and silence, seeking the freshness, the awakening, the light. The trees were turning yellow. There was the scent of fallen leaves in the air, and the ground beneath her feet was spongy. It was a sad and cloudy morning, but there was a brief respite from the gusty wind and rain, a streak of blue in the watery sky above the soaking land.

Wrapped in a dark, hooded cloak, she passed between the formal flower-beds, their late blossoms weather-beaten and drooping, and through the avenues of cypress and box, their grotesque, fantastic shapes duskily cut out against the sky at one moment and, in the next, seeming to be fringed with green flame as the level rays leaped at them. She walked slowly, drinking in the peace of that hour, a peace which was so rare these days. Her life had settled into a strange routine, and she had learned the salutary lesson that no matter how horrible, humiliating or heart-breaking, one gets acclimatized to almost any existence. Thus she moved through Thornfalcon like an automaton, slept in Christopher's bed, saving her skin from bruising, her soul from shrivelling by being compliant. She despised herself for her cowardice, but had reached rock-bottom where nothing seemed to matter any more. It was fatal to permit her thoughts to stray to Radu. She would never forget him, always dream of him and pray that they might meet again in another life. But this was all she could hope for. Christopher owned her now, possessive, obsessive, hardly allowing her out of his sight for an instant. And if he was not there, Mrs Brockwell prowled around, or the shifty-eyed Greek.

Then there was Agnes, that crazy female who floated about like a phantom. She was constantly changing her gowns, appearing in first one outfit, then another. It was quite usual for her to wear six costumes a day, like a child discovering the glories of a dressing-up box. Most of the time she seemed to inhabit a play-time world of fantasy, but at others, the dark, dark days, Mariana would hear her screaming from the Kingfisher Room. Then Mrs Brockwell would bustle, order Spyros to help her, send for Dr Russell and advise that Christopher keep out of his sister's sight. When the abyss yawned before her, his presence aggravated her dangerous violence.

As Mariana stood, musing, near the herb-garden, she heard a rapid step invading this sanctuary reserved for herself and the wild things. A darker shadow detached itself from the heavy shade of a yew tree. She turned quickly to face it. Christopher was beside her.

'The purity of the morning,' he said sardonically, 'and the dawn lingering in your eyes.'

Always that flashing message from brain to legs when he appeared – the urge to run. But she did not move, quietly watching him. He had not been in the bed when she rose from it. He was a nocturnal creature, often leaving her side to perambulate through the house, to watch the stars from his platform in the high tower, or spend the black hours working in his laboratory. She glanced up at the frowning grey stone mass that was beginning to cast its long, sharp shadows on the garden, then looked back at his pallid, drawn face. And if he had seen the dawn in her eyes, she saw in his the mysteries of the night-watch. He had pushed through the wild luxuriance of herbs and shrubs to reach her, and the crushed plants gave forth their spicy ghosts.

'What do you want?' she asked coldly.

He gave a smile, watching her face the while. 'Why d'you ask? Isn't it natural that I should come seeking you, wishing to share this corner of the garden?' He answered her question with one of his own, a disconcerting trick of which he was past master.

'I'm like a prisoner in this house!' she cried, forgetting caution. 'You watch me as you watch Agnes!'

'You too have been sick, as sick as she,' he replied evenly. 'My care of you both is nothing more than tender concern.'

'Ha! You show this in an odd manner, Christopher,' she shot back at him. 'Does she too carry the welts of your passionate cruelty?'

He shook his head sorrowfully. 'These are, alas, self-inflicted. At times you aren't aware of what you're doing.'

'You lie!' she shouted, bereft of clarity of thought. 'You say that you love me. If you did you'd let me go!'

'I do love you, Mariana, but what you ask is impossible. My love is deep as the ocean and as relentless. What I have, I hold.' Others who did not know him well would never have thought it possible that those dreamy eyes could give so cold and angry a flash. His brows were hardly knitted, and his voice, though raised to extra clarity, was singularly controlled, yet she was dreadfully aware of his present anger, of his enjoyment of it, and his terrible appetite for weird, abnormal sensations.

'You've a peculiar way of demonstrating it,' she said, pausing to pull a dead rose from its stem, lifting the powdering flower to her lips, inhaling its faint, nostalgic fragrance.

'Maybe I have. To love is indeed a strange, selfish process,' he rejoined. 'Happiness in love is an illusion, found only in fairytales. Love hurts, aches, disappoints, tortures.'

He was standing quite still, eyes cast down, absorbed in those deep waters of his soul that for so many years had lain black and stagnant. Mariana had stirred them, and they had risen in waves to dash against his laboriously built dykes of cynicism and renunciation. He had thought that he could control her, had been so certain that her infatuation would accept his every word and desire. This had proved to be false, and he could not forgive her. She had questioned his wisdom – her lord and master. How dared she? She had run away from him, but it must never happen again. He loved her, in so far as he knew love, but would kill her rather than lose her.

For all his quietude, Mariana knew that if she dared walk away, he would pounce like a stalking panther. Menace was in him and dark melancholy. It coiled out towards her, touching her heart. She pitied him, as she pitied Agnes. No one would ever believe her, neither the villagers, Mrs Grant nor the Reverend, but she knew him to be as mad as his sister. Her love for him had once been overwhelming, and an echo of it lingered on, but the other side of the coin was fear and hatred. She recalled that once before she had stood on that spot, and then a child had been growing in her body. Her daughter whom, despite his assertions to the contrary, she knew that he had killed. Pity him? Permit the slightest stirring of an emotion which had once swept her away? She shuddered and, as one wakes from a fevered dream, so she woke from her brief madness.

She turned and looked him up and down, recognizing that he was unrepentant and remorseless. Nothing she could say would sway him. All muscle and bone, his face was like a falcon's trained for the kill. Above all, clearly expressed in his every attitude, from the way he stared about him to the way he walked, was a haughty off-hand certainty of his supreme status.

'I want to visit my sisters and Swinsty Farm.' She said it quickly, expecting a rebuff and prepared to argue.

As she had guessed, he shook his head. 'You need no contact with them. Agnes and I are your family now.'

She drew in a deep breath and tried again. 'The farm – '

'Crosby is dead. He was staggering home from the inn one night and a farm-cart knocked him down.'

'Why didn't you tell me?'

'Oh, come, let us have no false filial tears.' His voice was bitingly sarcastic. 'You loathed the man. He wasn't your father.'

Shocked, she took a step forward. 'How d'you know that?' Thinking about it, she decided that Crosby must have blurted out the truth when in his cups.

A taunting smile flickered across his face. 'My dear wife, I've known for months. There's a great deal I know about you, probably more than you know yourself. You don't imagine I married you by chance, do you? Ah, no, you were chosen very carefully. I learned every detail, and when I finally met you there was no longer any hesitation.'

Mariana swallowed the lump which seemed to be lodged in

her throat. It was horribly unpleasant to realize that she had been spied on, a kind of dossier prepared weighing and assessing her suitability in a calculationg manner, but she still did not understand. 'Why me?'

He smiled again, and his hand reached out to lift a curling tress from where it lay across her breast. Her emerald gown was girded at the waist, falling loosely open at the throat. He saw how the peach-like tone of her face and breasts faded into creamy whiteness where the skin had been protected from the sun. His own flesh prickled with desire at the sight of such physical perfection. 'Why not you?' he murmured. 'This beauty ravishes my senses, has done so since the very first moment I saw you, and that, coupled with your expectations, is all that any man could want.'

She laughed without mirth. 'You must be moonstruck, Christopher! My expectations, quotha! A broken-down farm, up to its roof in debt, some inheritance to be sure!' Then she paused, anxiety for Margery and the younger children running through her like fire. 'What has happened to the farm? Has Middleton taken over?'

One thin fair brow shot up. 'Middleton? What the devil is it to do with him?'

'He owns Swinsty Farm.' Something in his manner sent apprehension tingling along her nerves.

There was a faint, supercilious lift to his lips. 'Oh, no, he doesn't. It has always belonged to me. Now I've rented it out to more profitable tenants.'

'But you said – you paid our debts –' Her voice faded as everything became crystal clear. For some reason best known to himself Christopher had allowed her to think him chivalrous, had made her his dupe, softening her so that she would rush into marriage with him. And this was just one layer of mystery, others more sinister would gradually be peeled away when the time was ripe.

'And the children, and Margery? What has become of them?' she asked in a whisper.

'The boys are still at school. Oh, yes, I'm a man of honour, my dear. I keep my side of the bargain.' A ray of sunshine danced over his bare head forming a golden halo, but beneath it his cruel face belied this angelic touch. 'The little girls and Margery have gone to live with Ernestine. She had a boy, you know, and is expecting again – Annabelle too. It seems that your family breed like the proverbial rabbit – with the exception of yourself. Why is this, Mariana? All you could produce was a weakly girl. No doubt gallant Prince Radu did his damnedest to get you with child but to no avail. You've been back with me for almost two months, and still you're not pregnant. Alas, my dear, if this is not rectified shortly, I may be forced to start looking for the third Lady St Jules. It would be most foolish of you to try to prevent conception by artificial methods.'

Mariana was ignorant of his meaning, but the threat was very clear, and a shiver coursed through her. What price his love if she did not give him what he wanted? Her life would not be worth a twopenny damn! He had spoken of an inheritance. If this were true then she was in even greater danger. Any inheritance due to her would automatically become his, were she to die.

'You know about Crosby. You know that I have nothing. How can you imagine that I'm worth a farthing?'

He mused for a moment without replying, playing with the lace at his cuff, then: 'The Duchesse who lives at Kenrick Old Court is your maternal grandmother, is she not?'

'Yes,' said Mariana sullenly.

'And you are her sole surviving relative?'

Again, she answered in the affirmative, shuddering at the memory of that tyrannical woman. Christopher lifted his shoulders in a dismissive shrug. 'There you are then. It'll be yours when she dies, and the old witch can't last much longer. I've heard that she has treasures galore stored in Coutts's Bank in London. Jewels beyond compare, smuggled out of France, including diamonds that once belonged to Queen Marie Antoinette.'

The expression of greed which flooded his face stunned Mariana. 'But you're rich!' she gasped. 'You don't need more!'

'I serve an expensive Master.' Fanatical fire blazed in his eyes. 'I can't be hampered in any way, or deny Him whatever He demands. You'll not be allowed your sisters, but you shall visit the Duchesse. I command it. You'll be a most devoted granddaughter. She'll leave you everything she possesses.'

With a cry of horror, Mariana tore away from him, running through the little iron gate of the garden and making for the house. She heard his swift footsteps following, and he caught up with her at the door of the tower. 'I won't do it!' she shouted, glaring at him.

'You will, my dear. You'll do exactly as I tell you.' His lips were drawn tightly over his teeth in a grim smile. 'By the by, I'm expecting a visitor. No, don't shrink away, it's not Mrs Wrixon. She's no longer with us, coughed up the remains of her lungs in the summer. And I've decided that I'll give no more parties. I like a quiet life with you and Agnes. It's our old friend, Arthur Cartwright, whom I'll be entertaining. We've a little business transaction to complete. You'll be nice to him, Mariana, not too nice of course, but a perfect hostess. He'll be arriving at any moment.'

Angry with her he would most certainly be, but Mariana could bear no more, escaping from him, her feet taking her almost unconsciously to the little chapel, a place of memories too. There was nowhere she could go at Thornfalcon which was free of them. She could not have said why she went; perhaps to pray, perhaps to try to commune with her mother, with her dead baby. Her mind was so confused, her state so desperate that she had reached the brink, groping blindly for any lifeline.

The door was not locked and she let herself into the cool dimness, sinking down before the altar, head in her hands. This was the place where she had exchanged marriage vows with Christopher, vows that she had subsequently broken, deceiving a fine, good man – Radu, who had believed in her. Christopher deserved to be betrayed, yet even so, her conscience troubled her. There was no comfort from the crucifix on the wall, no peace in the thick grey walls, the hard wooden pews. The atmosphere was claustrophobic, the ghosts of St Juleses appearing from the shadows to threaten her. She started up, seeing a movement in a dark corner. Her knees turned to water and a scream rose in her throat. But it was not an apparition. Agnes drifted towards her, incongruously clad in a white ball-gown.

'Agnes! Where's Mrs Brockwell?' Mariana knew that she was never far away, half expecting to see her lurking in the gloom.

Agnes came closer, leaning towards her confidentially, a ghastly, playful smile on her rouged, unhealthy face. 'She's busy welcoming Mr Cartwright. I haven't met him yet. Christopher says I'll like him, but that I'm not to be too familiar.' Her face creased and tears swam up in her blue eyes. 'He never lets me have gentleman friends. But I must obey him. He's my twin brother, you know. Don't you think it odd, being carried in the womb with another person? I don't like to dwell on it – gives me a funny feeling in here.' She pressed her hands to her stomach.

Mariana had never heard Agnes so verbal, but she had never been alone with her before. She knew a stab of fear, remembering Agnes's violence, but there was something childishly pathetic in the lined face beneath the piled-up faded blonde curls, threaded with ribbons and beads. She seemed desperately eager to be friendly, slipping her cold hand into Mariana's.

'You like the chapel?' Mariana repressed a shudder at her touch.

'Not the chapel.' The look of scorn was reminiscent of her brother. 'I don't come here to pray to *him*.' She jerked a contemptuous shoulder towards the Christ above the altar. 'I visit those in the crypt. They like me to talk with them. All our ancestors lie there. Why don't you come down and be introduced? You're one of us now – Christopher's wife.'

Her grip tightened, her smile fixed, eyes vague and dreamy. Mariana was too frightened to refuse, and she allowed Agnes to draw her through a low doorway and down a flight of stone steps. She had expected the crypt to be dark, but light radiated from a dozen sconces set in the walls, streaking across the stone tombs. Her guide was extremely knowledgeable, pointing out this one and that, then pausing before a particularly ornate edifice.

'Here lies Lady Sarah Anne,' said Agnes, running a caressing hand over the satiny surface of the marble. 'She rests in peace with her three babes. All girls, alas, so they had to die. Poor little things. I begged him not to do it, but he said they would become mad, like me. It was our Master's will that their blood be shed, so I helped. Your child is over there. He told me about her. Such a pity she wasn't a boy. He wants a son – promised the Master blood if only an heir might be born to him.' A puzzled frown creased her pencilled brows. 'I wonder why He hasn't granted his prayer? D'you know, Mariana? Certainly we've given Him a glut of sacrifices, yet He still doesn't listen to dear Christopher.'

'I can't tell you why, Agnes,' Mariana whispered through a mouth dry with horror.

Agnes was dancing round the crypt, her elaborate gown suggesting that she moved to a macabre waltz. 'This coffin is very important but rather a joke really.' She stood by it, giggling inanely. 'It's empty now. There was a body in it. Christopher thought it was yours, until he learned that you were still alive. Of course a common, unknown woman could not rest here amongst the St Juleses, so he had it taken out and buried in the churchyard. But look, your name's still on it!' She seized the candle and held it over the lid which had been pushed back. The casket yawned hungrily, and Mariana read the brass plate. It said: 'Lady Mariana St Jules, beloved wife of Lord Christopher, 1795 – 1818.'

Dear God, she breathed in stark terror, how long will it be before this is reality? How long before I take the beggar-woman's place and lie here in dank darkness with the rest?

'It was always Christopher and I,' Agnes was crooning, seated on the top of a tomb, chin in her cupped hand resting on her knee. 'I was his help-mate. There were a group of us eventually, all working for the Master. You'd never guess who they are – so respectable!'

Blackness swam before Mariana's eyes. Her fingers gripped the cold stone until the dizziness passed. She tried to remember that Agnes was insane, deluded. What was she hinting? Who had been involved? When she spoke, her voice echoed in the underground chamber. 'Do you know Miss Blake? She had a nephew. His name was Howard.'

'He came after I had gone away. Christopher has told me about him. He fell from the tower. He was trying to fly, you see. It's possible to fly when one's been eating magic mushrooms. I often fly.' The candle-flames were points of light in Agnes's eyes, her pupils glowing red. Her teeth were bared as she smiled widely, long white teeth. 'It wasn't suicide, but it sounded tidier that way. Christopher wrote the note. Christopher is very, very clever,' she added proudly.

'I'm sure he is,' said Mariana grimly.

Agnes hunched her knees and locked her arms around them, at her ease atop an earlier St Jules. 'I love Christopher,' she announced, nodding solemnly. 'And he loves me. I was his goddess, his sister, his bride.' Her voice changed, sudden tears strangling it. 'But they wouldn't let me have the baby. Mrs Brockwell and Dr Russell did something to me. They laid me on the table with my legs spread and pushed sharp instruments into me! It hurt so much! There was blood everywhere, and after that – I can't remember! There's a long time that I can't remember – a strange house – women in grey looking after me. Then he came one day and brought me home. You won't let them hurt me again, will you, Mariana?'

Numb with the horror of what she had just learned, Mariana put her arms round Agnes and drew her down from that night-marish perch. 'No, I won't let anyone hurt you,' she promised, and together they went up into the light, and fresh air.

As they neared the house, Mariana looked through the great glass windows which faced the terrace. She could see her husband within, and Arthur Cartwright was standing before the fireplace, legs planted wide, thumbs hooked in his gold watch-chain. She could not hear what they were saying, but their laughter rang out, making her ears throb and her brain spin.

CHAPTER 3

The sullen, stormy day aptly matched Mariana's thoughts. The grey sheet of the sky canopied a wet world, silent but for the hiss of rain and the squelch of mud at wheels and hooves. The carriage was traversing the moors, but she could see little of it from the windows, everything curtained by the steady deluge. Only Christopher's determination on obedience had forced her out on such a morning, his stubborn insistence that she must cultivate her grandmother.

She had expected him to accompany her. Last night he had been in an excitable mood, and had loudly asserted his intention of doing so, becoming ever more rambling in his speech as the evening wore on, cogitating huge plans, needing her as an audience, feeling himself to be powerful, wise, superior to ordinary dull mortals.

'Yes, my darling wife, you'll be most pleasant to the Duchesse,' he had nodded at her across the bedroom. 'We'll visit her tomorrow. Perhaps I'll even tell her about the temple I'm going to build in Thornfalcon's grounds.'

He had continued in this vein for hours, while Mariana ached with fatigue but was glad that he did not want to go to bed, too intent on gazing inwardly at the distorted mirrors of his mind. She had slept at last and, on waking into the dawn-light, had seen him still seated in his armchair by the fire, though now torpid, lost in a reverie from which he had refused to rouse, solitary and remote from human contact. He would not have noticed had she countermanded his orders for the carriage to be ready at nine o'clock, but later, when he came to himself, he would have been violently angry, so she had dressed herself with care and set out on the journey to Kenrick Old Court.

She was greeted by Mercer, who eyed her up and down with blatant curiosity before conducting her inside. 'How is Madame la Duchesse?' Mariana asked as the heavy oak door thudded behind her, imprisoning her in that neglected ruin of a manor house which she had hoped never to set foot in again.

'The same.' Mercer gave a shrug as they went upstairs.

The same. Unpleasant memories flooded up, every step forging them into present reality. But it won't be the same, she tried to assure herself. I was a fugitive then. Oh, God, I'm still a fugitive! In heaven's name, what's happening to me? I'm nothing more than a marionette in a grim show, moved by the whim of a brooding puppet-master. She was not mentally abnormal, did not experiment with drugs, and yet she was gradually deteriorating, becoming as disoriented as the twins, as if their sickness was insidiously infecting her.

'She's in her room,' Mercer announced, leading the way along the corridor. Mariana and she had never found any common meeting ground during the days which she had spent there. The woman had done what was strictly necessary for her, acting under Madame's orders.

It was the smell that first hit Mariana when they entered the chamber – the smell of dirt, old-age and approaching death. 'Good God, Mercer, don't you ever open the windows?' she said angrily, through the handkerchief clapped to her nostrils.

She pushed past the companion-cum-nurse, and went straight to the casements, careless of the wind and rain, letting the sweet moorland air pour in. Force was needed for the frames were glued fast through years of disuse, but she enjoyed pitting her strength against something real, rather than nebulous thought-forms and threats. The wind thrashed the fusty drapes, flapped at her skirts, tore at her hair, blew out the candles and slammed the door shut.

'Are you trying to kill me, slut? Think to finish me off with a fatal dose of pneumonia, do you?' That well-remembered, much hated querulous voice addressed her in French from the towering four-poster.

Mariana flung round, seeing the room springing into light and wholesomeness as the charcoal veils of rain parted momentarily and the watery sun flowed between the diamond-panes, enabling her to discern colours, softening the layers of dust which covered all and disguised the ravages of time and neglect.

'Good morning, Grandam,' she answered her in her native tongue, walking towards the bed.

'What's good about it?'

Mariana came to rest beside that rank-smelling heap of old bones and musty quilts, and an extraordinary thing happened. She took one look down, seeing the tiny, humped form, the wrinkled painted face twisted into a malignant expression, the grim eyes beneath dirty ringlets of false hair, and felt a sudden surge of power She was no longer afraid, awed or even respectful. She was in command.

'A deal of good, for you.' Her tone was brisk, forceful. 'I've come to look after you, and none too soon it seems! Mercer, I want hot water – lots of it. Clean towels, clean linen and a whole heap of clean blankets. These look as if they haven't been changed in centuries! Jump to it!'

'How dare you come storming in here throwing your weight around!' The light of battle flared in Madame's rheumy eyes but Mariana ignored her. With a swift movement, she bent and twitched the wig from the old lady's head. Holding it at arm's length she tossed it on to the fire which roared in the chimney-breast.

'That's going right away! It's crawling, Grandmother. Why, you've a lot of your own hair left – curly too, I wouldn't be surprised, if it had a good wash. When Mercer brings up the water, I'm going to give you a bath.'

'You are not, miss! I'm not prepared to break the habit of thirty years! Bath indeed! And where's that husband of yours? What's his name? St Jules? Why the hell did you marry him? His eyes are set too close together! Never trust a man unless his eyes are wide-spaced! I know. I've seen men come and go. None of 'em are worth a fig! Keep their brains between their legs, those of 'em that have any brains, that is.' Madame glared at her fiercely, like a baleful vulture. She reached for her cane which lay on the coverlet, flourishing it.

'You've met Christopher?' Mariana paused, surprised, wondering exactly what he had been plotting.

'He came barging in, shortly after you'd left with Cunyngham, without a by-your-leave, demanding if I'd seen anything of you.' The eyes narrowed and she smiled for the first time. 'I pretended to be senile, talking a lot of twaddle, confusing him entirely, and that's not difficult. He has the look of one too fond of opiates. Oh, I've met his sort before! I sent him away with a flea in his ear!'

'Why didn't you tell him?' This was a most formidable lady, Mariana decided, warming to her. Anyone shrewd enough to deceive Christopher was worthy of admiration.

'Didn't like his attitude. None of his damn business!'

'But he is my husband.'

Madame chuckled, an ancient imp who adored meddling. 'Husbands were made to be tricked! If you chose to run away from him and put yourself at my mercy, then you must have had a bloody good reason.'

'Oh, I did, Grandam. In a while I'l tell you the whole story, but first – your bath.' Mariana felt happy for the first time since leaving Radu.

This was a most cantankerous, self-opinionated, dictatorial woman, but blood will out, and Mariana's stirred in her veins in response. Back in January, she had been in a fearful state of shock, terrified, weak from childbirth, her breasts throbbing with milk for her dead baby, unable to withstand Madame's bullying. But the various efforts, anxieties and rewards of her life in Europe had made her strong. Anything her grandmother might do, no matter how unpleasant, was a mere bagatelle compared to her present conflict with Christopher.

This was put to the test at once. Madame had made up her mind that she was not going to wash. 'God curse you!' she rasped, her eyes flaring into red, spiteful embers. 'Get your hands off me! How dare you!' Her body shook on the bed, becoming more coiled than slouched.

'Stop making such a fuss. It has to be done.' Mariana insisted with steely patience.

'Get out of my house! Leave me alone!' Madame seized her cane and it hissed through the air, but Mariana had experienced its sting in the past and jumped out of the way. Madame became tangled in the sheets, curses pouring out of her in a raucous, venomous screech.

Mariana made a leap for the lashing cane, wresting it away. Then she enlisted Mercer's aid to half-lift, half-drag her from the bed, strip off the disgusting gown and get her into the hip-bath set before the fire. She was as stubborn as Madame, ignoring the flow of insults, soaping the layers of dirt from the wasted frame, washing and de-lousing the long white hair, then bundling her into warm towels and taking the scissors to it. Madame screamed, complained and blasphemed, but Mariana took no more notice of her than a troublesome toddler.

While she attended to Madame's toilet, Mercer and Benedict ran in and out, obeying her commands. 'Light a fire in the garden, Benedict,' she said. 'Those stinking sheets and blankets can join the mattress on its pyre. Fetch in another one immediately!'

'You bossy bitch! Think you own the place already, I suppose. Well, I'm not dead yet!' yelled Madame, twisting and squirming under her hands, then she suddenly subsided and her rasping voice became a whimper. 'I want my medicine. I'm aching all over. That damned water's got into my joints! You're trying to get rid of me! I know your game, Satan scorch your hide! Bring me my medicine – stoke up the fire – I'm so cold – '

Mariana had no intention of relenting till she was thoroughly satisfied that her work was completed. She dusted Madame with perfumed powder, found a snowy lawn nightgown, frilled and lacy, a pink wrapper of wool so light that it resembled a spider's web, and ensconced her once more in the massive bed. She permitted a sprinkling of orris-root gently patted across the wrinkled cheeks, a hint of rose-colouring to the lips, then stood back and surveyed her handiwork.

The Duchesse looked years younger, eyes sparkling at so much attention, though barbed spite continued to punctuate her remarks. Without the garish paint, traces of the beauty which had once fascinated the whole of Paris were revealed – a delicacy of bone-structure that had also belonged to Mariana's mother, that was hers too, and which should have been bequeathed to Elaine. The fluffy silver hair curled closely about her finely-shaped head like a cherub's.

Naturally, she did not approve, saying when Mariana gave her the hand-mirror: 'You trollop! You've ruined my hair!'

'Nonsense!' she retorted disrespectfully. 'It suits you. That wig made you look like a gargoyle. It's time you acted your age.'

'Harrumph!' snarled the Duchesse, but she was prinking in the looking-glass, unable to suppress a pleased smirk.

'D'you still require your medicine?' Mariana straightened the quilt and tweaked the pillows, amazed at the glow which was softly filling her, easing the ache in her heart. She realized that this simple act of kindness towards a lonely, proud old woman was fulfilling a need within her, a longing to serve which would have been satisfied by caring for her infant, in the normal course of events.

'Stuff the medicine!' Madame sounded almost jolly. She patted the side of the bed. 'Sit there and talk to me. I want to hear everything about you, Granddaughter. Hang on a minute.' Her voice rose to an imperious yell: 'Mercer! Bring some tea, you lazy cow! What the blazes do I pay you for? Worthless good-for-nothing! Is there any food in the damned house? Lady St Jules and I want something to eat. I'm bloody starving! *Mon Dieu!* These pigs of English servants!'

When Mercer had huffed off, extremely offended, Madame grinned puckishly and lapsed back into French and they talked all through luncheon and deep into the afternoon. Mariana found that the floodgates of her emotions, once opened, poured forth a torrent. She held nothing back, and Madame listened, her face growing stern when she heard of Christopher's practices.

'Sweet Mother of God, he should be burnt at the stake!' she hissed, crossing herself. 'He would have been, a hundred years ago in my beloved France.'

'He is ill – mad – ' Mariana was shaking, unable to control herself as she relived the shocking scenes of her bizarre marriage. Then she dragged out the most damning truth of all. 'He murdered my baby.' In halting, disjointed sentences she spoke of that never-to-be-forgotten day of blizzard and grief.

At this, a remarkable change came over the Duchesse. It was easy to see how once she must have terrified the peasants on her estate, awesome in her rage and indignation. In clear, precise terms, she vilified Christopher for daring to harm one of her own. 'My great-grandchild!' she pronounced, forgetting age, forgetting the pain of arthritic joints. 'May he be cursed to the deepest pit of damnation! The devil! The loathsome swine! I'll see him hang for it! No – hanging's too quick, too easy for him. Ah, for the old days at home! The days of my forebears when a murderer would be torn limb from limb by wild stallions! That is what he deserves!'

Mariana could not stop weeping. It was so good to have found a champion, no matter how aged. She had set out that morning, dreading facing another enemy, never dreaming that before the day was done she would be confiding in a friend. The gnarled hands were clasping hers, an unbelievable gentleness touching the Duchesse's features.

'My poor child, why didn't you tell me when you came here?'

'How could I? You hated me – had hated my mother. I could expect nothing but harsh words from you, and I got them!' Mariana was riven with guilt at her disloyalty to her mother. How could she be feeling such warmth towards the woman who had cut her off, denied her contact, made it plain that she never wanted to see her again? Mamma, dear Mamma, forgive me, she begged silently, her eyes seeking the portrait which still hung in its customary place near the window.

The rain had lifted and the golden, nostalgic glow of autumn filled the chamber. The painting flamed with colour so vivid that it was as if Henrietta breathed within the canvas. Madame followed her granddaughter's gaze, murmuring: 'Yes, she was lovely, wasn't she?'

Mariana's eyes sparked angrily. 'Why did you treat her so badly? My God, d'you know what she suffered living with that brute, Crosby? Have you any conception of how she died? The meanest beast in the field is more compassionate to its young than you!'

A trace of the Duchesse's regality returned, and she stared down her nose, saying loftily: 'You ask me to give an account of myself? I don't see why I should, but I will. Your mother was betrothed to a son of the noblest family in France. She had

341

everything. Money, education, a place in Court, and what did she do? She threw it away. Fell in love with a damned revolutionary and had the audacity to marry him!'

'She was married? Then I'm not a bastard?'

'I should think not! Bastard indeed! Would that you had been – at least you could have been hidden, reared in a convent out of the public eye.' Madame was shaking with an echo of the fury which had once raged within her. 'Your mother couldn't be satisfied to have an affair with Gaston de Loches. Oh, no, she had to go the whole hog and marry the traitor.'

This was proving to be a day of revelations and Mariana was not sure if she could endure many more. 'Why was he a traitor?' she asked, the tears drying on her cheeks.

Madame gave vent to an exclamation of disgust. 'He was a Jacobin – a follower of Robespierre, a cursed intellectual, an agitator who spread discontent among the peasants with his glib talk of freedom and equality. He betrayed the nobility, doubly betrayed them because he was born one of them, a titled man – a Count. The fool gave away his lands, denied his birthright, joined the mob who howled for aristocratic blood. One black day your mother met him and fell madly in love. He was fascinating, even I could see that. There was an irresistible power about him – and handsome! By God, he was handsome! He indoctrinated her, made her into a turncoat like himself; convinced her that the Revolution was a just cause.'

'Oh, love is such a strong force.' Mariana was struggling to form a mental picture of this man who had fathered her but it was impossible. She sank her head in her hands, her bewildered emotions swinging wildly this way and that.

'No excuse!' The Duchesse's voice was hard. 'Don't talk to me of love, you silly girl. There's nothing you can teach me about it. Oh, yes, one loves, given the chance, but one does one's duty, above all. I was married when I was fifteen to a man of forty, an alliance arranged by my parents. It never occurred to me to defy them, and he was a horrible little insect! High-born, of course, but with the manners of the farmyard! He was lank, sallow, squint-eyed and wry-mouthed! We felt an unconquerable repugnance for one another, but we made the best of it. I was refined, dainty in my habits, my flesh steeped in unguents. I had no attraction for him whatsoever. He liked his meat ungarnished! His only interest was hunting, and it made me sick to have to take this sweaty, dusty lout to my embrace. I had to have the sheets changed frequently whenever we spent a night together. This didn't last long, thank God. He was thrown from his horse within a year, making me a widow.'

'Because you made an unhappy marriage, does this mean that you had to make your daughter suffer?' There was deep resentment in Mariana's tone and she could hardly bring herself to look at that cynical face.

Madame shifted restlessly, tired but refusing to admit it, an acid ring to her voice. 'Love! Marriage! That's only gammon and spinach, my girl! I married for a second time. The man who was your grandfather was an amiable fellow. We liked one another, and there's a lot to be said for that.' Her face creased with pain. 'I'd better have my medicine after all.'

Mariana fetched the bottle from the side-table, took up a spoon and administered a dose, muttering: 'I can't think why I'm helping you. You're as ruthless and merciless as Christopher, in your own fashion. Yet, just for a while, I thought we might be of comfort to each other. I'll not come again.'

Madame rested back against the pillows, her eyes faded to a filmy blue shaded by their drooping lids. 'Ah, but you will, Mariana. The slate must be cleared before I die. I want you to know the truth. Imagine, if you can, my life in France at the time of the Revolution. I was extremely wealthy, respected at Court, a friend to the Queen. I had a devoted, if philandering, husband and three children – two fine sons and Henrietta. I paid little heed to the rumours and unrest, secure in my position, totally unprepared for the disaster which swept everything away. My sons were slain by the mob when they stormed our château. My husband went to the guillotine. I escaped by the skin of my teeth, aided by dear, faithful Phineas Cunyngham. And where was Henrietta while all this was happening? Exchanging wedding vows with the enemy!'

'You can't blame her for following the dictates of her heart.' The thought of Radu leapt in Mariana's mind. She would have accompanied him to the ends of the earth, no matter who he was or what he had done.

The Duchesse held up her hand to re-claim her right to continue. Each word fell from her lips as if freshly chilled. 'And what of my heart? My husband dead. My sons dead. And my lover dead.'

'Your what?' Mariana gasped.

'My young, beautiful lover – a boy the age of my eldest son.' The flat statement hung in the air like a sword. Mariana could not look at her, watching her hands. They were nervous and taut, playing games with the fringe of the coverlet. 'You think you've experienced love? How can you know the bitter-sweet love of an older woman for a young man? The agony, the fear, the jealousy. The ecstasy of enjoying a virile body – of being mother and mistress combined. The feverish harvesting of every second, knowing that it can't possibly last.'

'I have seen it.' Mariana was remembering Cora Blake and Howard.

She shivered with sudden cold and went to close the window. The sun was low over the fields, wind buffeted the neglected garden, shafts of weak sunlight glanced and flickered, lengthening and shortening as the breeze shifted the close-growing, half-bare branches.

'Your mother stood by and saw my dear love killed. It was done at the express order of Gaston de Loches. Oh, I know he was defiant, impetuous and arrogant, but de Loches could have saved him.' There was a repetitive sound to the old voice droning across the room, as if she was a clockwork doll slowly running down. How many weary hours and lonely nights had she lain there, year after year, hugging her grief, nurturing her hatred? Mariana wondered.

She pivoted round, struggling with the lump threatening to block the words in her throat, getting them out at last: 'She was your child. How could you have wreaked such revenge upon her?'

'I came to England with Phineas. There was nothing left for me in France. We smuggled out most of my jewels and money. He'd been my financial adviser and had already invested vast sums which the Jacobin Government couldn't touch. In return, I loaned him much and he doubled his own fortune as a result.' Madame struggled up and fumbled with the inlaid panelling which formed the bedhead. As Mariana watched, an aperture appeared just above the pillows. Her grandmother beckoned her nearer. 'Put your hand inside. That's it – bring out those books, and the jewel-case.'

'What is this?' Mariana's fingers encountered leather, and the hard edges of a box.

'No one knows about it, only you and me. These are my journals – read them next time you visit – I've kept them for years. You *must* read them. It's high time we understood one another.' Madame's face was pink with excitement, her eyes gimlet-sharp. She pressed the catch of the casket and the lid sprang back. A riot of colour sparkled from the gems displayed against the black plush lining. 'These will belong to you when I'm dead, and others which lie snug in the vaults of Coutts's bank along with property-deeds and more valuables.'

Mariana was not to be bought. 'I want to hear what happened to my mother,' she said frostily.

'Tsha! The impatience of the wench!' Madame countered.

'You'll learn more when you come to see me tomorrow. I'm tired. I've talked enough.'

Mariana wanted to choke her. It would be so easy. She was old, feeble, a nasty viper! 'I've already told you. I'm not coming.'

Astonishingly, her grandmother's face crumpled like a disappointed baby's. 'Oh, Mariana, don't abandon me!' she cried, and suddenly, behind the mask, the iron will was broken and there was pleading, almost tenderness in her eyes.

'Damn you! Damn you!' Frustration throbbed in Mariana's voice, making her curse sound like a sob of despair. She had to return, she knew that, and that cunning, exasperating creature knew it too. A frail bond was building up between them and each needed the other. There were so many unanswered questions which were driving her mad, and now she voiced one of them. 'All right. Have it your way. But tell me this before I go. How did Christopher find out about my connection with you? Why did he deliberately select me as his bride?'

'If I give you my opinion, will you promise to be here in the morning?' The Duchesse was not so overcome with emotion that she had forgotten how to bargain.

'I promise,' Mariana sighed.

'My medical adviser is Dr Russell. When they thought I was on my last legs some time ago, he brought in a lawyer, no doubt another of your husband's dastardly friends. He knew the contents of my will. I had left everything to you.'

Dusk was creeping across the room. Mariana lit the candles and picked up her cloak, brooding on her grandmother's legacy. 'But why did you do that? You'd never even seen me, and my mother was the object of your detestation.'

'I don't know – a whim maybe. I thought I was dying, and who else was there to inherit? Phineas was gone. I don't like his nephew. I had kept tabs on Henrietta and her miserable life with that drunkard, and on your progress. Reports reached me that you were beautiful but virtuous, hard-working and sensible. I liked that.' Madame was a tiny, lost figure in the vast ostentation of her bed, her voice no longer vitriolic, failing and weary.

Is she play-acting? Mariana wondered, going across and staring down at her, surprised at her sudden reluctance to leave. Mercer and Benedict must be taken to task for their shameful neglect of their mistress. I'll do that in the morning, she thought, saying aloud: 'Is there anything you want before I go?'

The Duchesse's eyes twinkled. 'A new body. A virile stud! Apart from these – nothing.'

345

Mariana's lips curved into a smile. 'There's no doubt about it, Grandam, you've been a very wicked woman in your time.'

'I know. I still am!'

'You incorrigible reprobate!' Mariana scolded, thinking: Radu would get on well with her.

She hated returning to Thornfalcon and Christopher, but was so engrossed in her thoughts, mulling over the startling story of her birth, that the carriage passed between the gates almost before she knew it. Bats circled in the darkness and the watch-dogs gave savage tongue from their kennels.

There were lights in the kitchen, lamps lit in the corridors, but no sign of life. Mariana knew that she must see Christopher. She wanted to get the truth out of him, wearied of his lies and pretences, longing to smash his fantasies, to destroy the insufferable splendour that deluded him. She was not sure whether to be glad or sorry that one of the reasons why he married her was because of the Duchesse's will. In a way, it was a bare-faced insult, yet she recognized that there was far more beneath the surface than mere greed. The biter had been bitten. He had become obsessed with her, perhaps even loving her in as much as a man dabbling with the occult and poisonous brews could be in love. Rather than curing him, the fact that she was no longer infatuated and had given her heart to someone else, had made him even more possessive.

He was not in their bedroom nor in the laboratory, and the platform from which he star-gazed was deserted. The wind was keen up there, moaning eerily around the battlements. The stars performed a spectral dance across the black sky, or hung like bale-fire in the secret universe. Mariana's lantern barely penetrated the gloom, but she was thankful to have it as she left the tower and took the narrow way to the one opposite, where a light flickered.

It was the keep wing of the house. There was stone beneath her feet, stone above her head, stone walls on either side. Apprehension made her scalp crawl. Christopher must have started that inevitable slide from ecstatic heights into the crater of restless misery which always followed his excesses. He had told her that sudden shocks and noises were hateful to him then, everything emphasized beyond all proportion. He shunned society, shutting himself away.

There was a crack of yellow beneath the door. Mariana lifted the latch and walked in. The long low-raftered room was dim. Its barred windows had no shutters or curtains, and the moonlit shadows of the tall trees outside danced like water on the walls.

It was a bare place with no hangings, no pictures, no ornamentation of any kind. Its silence and chill were monastic. Cobwebs festooned the yawning grate. A battered rocking-horse was in one corner, staring at the intruder with its single glass eye. A dusty row of lead soldiers faced an invisible enemy on the broad, ink-stained table. A collection of tattered books leaned drunkenly against one another on a shelf. Two wooden high-chairs held their arms open expectantly. It was an empty nursery, as sad as an empty nest.

Empty? Mariana realized her mistake. Her eyes went to the two single beds. Christopher was sprawled on the patchwork quilt of one, and Agnes on the other. He stirred, throwing an arm over his eyes, muttering: 'That damned light! It's too bright!'

Agnes did not move, her eyes open but blank, a wax-headed doll clasped to her breasts as if it were a living babe. The round baize-topped table between them was loaded with laudanum-vials. The air was sickly-sweet with its odour. There was something peaceful and world-detached in the silent scene, but it hinted at the tranquillity of the tomb. Mariana knew herself to be an interloper, an alien presence in their secret heaven. These opiomanes did not need her. They needed no one, not even each other. There they lay, their disarranged minds soaring into a realm of visions, juggling with past experiences, forming a magic pattern to exclude anxiety, doubts, fears and inhibitions.

Curse them! she thought, losing patience. Nothing worries them, nothing moves them. Their consciences are sedated. They don't care about the fiendish things they've done. Why should they be let off scot-free? Why should they be allowed to float in the warm, milky bath of irresponsibility while others suffer?

She deliberately placed the lamp on the table, knocking over several of the bottles, making sure that its beam shone straight into Christopher's face. 'Stop dreaming!' Her voice was loud and harsh. 'I want to talk to you!'

He propped himself up on his elbow, keeping one hand between his eyes and the torturing light which, to him, held the glare of a thousand candles. His face was a grotesque travesty of the beauty which had once seduced her, his blond hair hanging in greasy twists, his jaw darkened by stubble. A trickle of saliva ran across his chin, and his eyes were narrowed to glittering slits as he stared past her, beyond her, at something which obviously terrified him.

'You think you can trick me?' he muttered, limbs coiling

ready for flight. 'I heard the footsteps of a murderer ascending the stairs. I see him standing at your shoulder with a dagger in his hand.'

'Christopher, you're imagining it. There's no one here but me.' Mariana spoke with slow, clear emphasis, and something horribly revengeful within her rejoiced at his abject fear.

'Ssh! Ssh!' he cried, arms clasped about his body. 'Don't speak so loud! Your voice clangs like a million bells! Someone will hear!'

Communication was hopeless. With a despairing sigh, Mariana stood looking at him helplessly. He would not attack her that night, but tomorrow or the day after when he had crawled back to a vestige of normality, then she had better take care. The withdrawal symptoms were accompanied by fits of black, evil temper. What am I going to do? she thought. Am I condemned to spend the rest of my life imprisoned here with a pair of drug-crazed lunatics? It is no earthly good appealing to Dr Russell, he's their accomplice. Frantic schemes for writing to David or Lancelot flashed through her mind and were instantly discarded. She dared not do it. If Christopher found out – ! Her only hope lay with her grandmother and it was vital that she lull him into a sense of false security in order that he did not suddenly forbid her visits. More laudanum, she decided and she half-filled a glass of wine, laced it with the reddish, heavy stuff, and held it out to him.

He took it with an unsteady hand, drank it down in a gulp and sank back. 'Sleep, sleep,' Mariana murmured soothingly, pulling the quilt over him, wondering how many other wives used their husbands' addictions to free themselves from their insensitive demands. At one time she would have virtuously condemned such tactics, unable to act the hypocrite, but fear had taught her a hard lesson. She thought of her mother. How thankful she must have been when Crosby lay stupefied by drink without the strength to maul her.

She was about to creep away, when Agnes suddenly spoke, addressing empty air, eyes fixed on the ceiling. 'Ah, brother, can't you hear the celestial music? It's beautiful, and I'm flying among the stars. Come with me, Christopher – come! See below us that immense circle of blue waves over which ships are skimming, but beware of that huge black abyss! It's full of the wrecks of universes!'

'You're asleep, Agnes.' Mariana took out her handkerchief, leaning over the wide-eyed woman in the torn, stained ball-gown, clutching her doll, beyond human aid. She wiped the sweat from her face, the same pity welling up which had made her forget herself and help Madame. 'There, my dear, lie still. You're freezing cold. Let me wrap you in this blanket.'

'Cold – yes, it is cold on this dripping iceberg,' Agnes said vaguely. 'The Pole Star's dying, but the planets are gently lowering it into a bottomless grave. The sun has vanished, eaten by that great sea-serpent – everything is being swallowed in a cold, dark void.'

After assuring herself that she could do nothing further, Mariana left them to their dreams. To her intense relief, Christopher did not emerge from the keep. Before going to Kenrick Old Court next day, she went there to check on him, but Mrs Brockwell stood guard at the door, insolently refusing admittance. Silently vowing to dismiss her if ever she had the chance, Mariana did not deign to argue, leaving her to her self-appointed sentry duty.

On arriving at her grandmother's house, she delayed in the garden, filling her arms with a few flowers, and boughs from the evergreens, then entering through the courtyard. It was located in the oldest part. In mediaeval days it had been the inner bailey. The remaining tower precincts had been once used for the peaceful purposes of bakehouses and dairies, but not for many years now. Its mellowness was pleasant in the glowing russets of autumn, faintly warmed by the pale sunshine. The stagnant years had garbed the crumbling walls with a luxuriant green tide of foliage, which had conquered bricks and mortar more efficiently than any armed enemy. Ivy and creepers had stormed the ramparts and, assault unchecked, had occupied the yard, via the roof.

Of course, it's very pretty, but something will have to be done about it when I'm the owner, Mariana caught herself thinking, and was shocked by her acquisitiveness. But a small dream had been forming in her brain – a dream of leaving Christopher and retiring here to live quite alone with her memories of Radu. A recluse, like Grandma? A wry smile touched her mouth. Perhaps this comes to us all, this retreat from a harsh, painful world. Each, in his or her individual way, struggles to achieve it. Christopher and Agnes by a self-consuming introspection; Madame and myself by the desire to erect impenetrable physical walls.

She followed this train of thought as she went under the heavy oak lintel of the kitchen door, then her attention sharpened, angry curses springing to her lips. The place reeked of stale cooking, a patina of dirt and soot lying on every article. A huge fire gobbled up the logs on the wide hearth, and the heaps of rotting bones, the rubbish-strewn floor, the unwashed pots spoke more fluently than words of the slovenly habits of the two people who lounged at the table.

'Mercer! Benedict! How can you contemplate preparing food in this midden?' Mariana demanded furiously, silk skirts swishing as she bore down on them. 'Get this place cleaned at once! D'you hear?' Her voice was so sharp that Benedict nearly dropped his pot of ale, and Mercer became unusually active. Mariana would have given much to see the capable, conscientious Margery come in at that moment.

I'll send for her, she thought with sudden inspiration. She'll show this lazy pair a thing or two and have the house shining in a week. Still giving Mercer the caustic edge of her tongue, she filled a vase with water and arranged the flowers, left the kitchen and went to the Duchesse's bedroom. At least some of her instructions had been followed, she noted. The curtains were pulled back from the huge windows, and in the cold morning light the tremendous room with its massive furniture resembled a mausoleum full of heavily-embossed sarcophagi. Madame should be moved to a smaller apartment, she decided, less cluttered by dust-collecting objects.

The Duchesse was sitting up in bed dipping a roll into a cup of hot chocolate. 'Flowers?' she said with a perky smile. 'How nice. It's years since anyone brought me flowers.'

This set them off on the right footing and they conversed for hours. Mariana heard how her father had been slain when the people rose against the tyrant, Robespierre, slaughtering Jacobins by the score, and how her mother, alone and penniless, had been driven from France. She had had nowhere to go, no home for her daughter, and Madame had taken her revenge. The marriage to Crosby had been negotiated – the rest of the story Mariana already knew.

When the Duchesse dozed after lunch, Mariana sat by the fire and read through her journals. By the time she had finished, she felt that she knew her intimately, all her thoughts, her hopes, her despairs recorded on the crowded pages. A remarkable woman – a survivor. One might not approve of her strong actions and bloody-minded motives, but one could not help admiring her stamina. It was fascinating to see references to herself in those scrawling later entries, the description of how she had arrived out of the storm, and Madame's thoughts on the matter. These had not been flattering or encouraging. Then there was an account of Christopher's visit on his quest for his missing wife. Madame had said of him: 'St Jules is an arrogant upstart! How dared he come tramping in here as if he owned it? He got no help from me, indeed my bowels stirred with pity for the girl, married to such as he. I was interested to meet him. Mercer, that idle wretch, has repeated tales of his actions. I suspect that he's not what he likes to appear on the surface. Wouldn't be at all surprised to find him involved in many dark, unpleasant dealings. Too smooth, too subtle by half! We shall see what we shall see. I think he's after my money!'

'Why did you give me the name "Maria Malton"?' Mariana asked when the old woman woke up, demanding tea and the use of the commode.

Enthroned on its mahogany seat, Madame regarded her from that face criss-crossed with wrinkles. 'First thing that came to mind. "Maria", because it is like Mariana. "Malton"? I had a groom of that name, and when I say "had" him, I mean just that. A fine, strapping boy, rough in his ways, but with skin like velvet.'

Mariana did not know whether to believe her or not. Madame delighted in shocking her, she had discovered. She chose to ignore this, but her grandmother had awakened in an exasperating mood, petulant, childish, finding fault with everything Mariana did for her. It was only the memory of Christopher's far more destructive behaviour which enabled her to keep her temper. Madame quietened and listened attentively when she began to recount her adventures in Vienna, and her meeting with Radu.

It was a joy to be able to speak of his looks, his noble bearing, his personality. It brought him to life, but it also accentuated her loneliness and loss. 'Oh, but I love him!' she burst out at last. 'I long to see him again. I can't bear to be parted from him!'

Madame was looking at her musingly, then she said: 'When you were married to St Jules, was the ceremony performed in my faith, and that of your mother?'

'No.'

'Then you are not his wife, in my book! What of the wedding with Prince Radu?'

'We were married by a priest.' Oh, happy day! Pictures of it filled her memory, forcing the tears to her eyes.

'There you are then. No problem.' Madame spoke confidently. 'You will have to leave St Jules, child. The man's an abomination! A follower of Anti-Christ!'

'It's against the law. Whatever you say, I am his wife.'

'To hell with the law!'

During the following regular daily visits, they continued to test each other, pitting their wits, taking measure. They had spirited discussions and blistering arguments. Sometimes, after very high words had been exchanged, Mariana would sweep out, vowing never to return – but she did. Gradually the bonds were being welded. She had enlisted Margery's aid, and that good woman had come gladly, weeping joyful tears at seeing her again but horrified at her thin, fine-drawn appearance. She took on the task of instilling the rudiments of housewifely skills into Mercer, who welcomed her assistance, a good-natured slattern at heart, prepared to try, once she realized that Margery meant business.

Mariana did not tell Christopher, it fact she saw little enough of him and, on their brief meetings when he roused himself from his lethargy, was able to lie convincingly, pretending that she dreaded going to Kenrick Old Court. This seemed to give him much satisfaction, as did the valuable trinkets which the Duchesse insisted she take home as part of their plot to dupe him. She had spent every night alone, and had begun to hope that he would continue to share the nursery with his sister, but one evening when she went to the Master Chamber to eat a simple supper and retire to rest, she found him there, waiting for her. His velvet dressing-robe was crumpled, stained with wine; he was unwashed and unshaven, on his knees before the statue of Kali. Candles burned at the altar, and the air was rich with incense.

Mariana kept her eyes fixed on him, coming across the room, peeling off her long gloves. 'Christopher?'

He turned his head, her beautiful reality striking through his communion with his goddess. 'Eh? Who's that?' His speech was thick and his eyes, deep in dark hollows, burned as he looked up at her. 'Mariana, is it? So, and where have you been? Off to meet a lover? You're looking very smart. Don't forget who pays your dress-bills.'

Mariana flushed at the slur. She wore a high-crowned bonnet of silver-grey which matched her close-fitting pelisse with its shoulder cape of smoke-blue fox, having taken to dressing-up for grandmother. It entertained the old woman if she arrived in something pretty. She was regaining her self-confidence, becoming aware of her own worth, happy with Margery and, in a strange way, happy with the Duchesse. This inner serenity showed in her face and mien, baffling Christopher.

'You know perfectly well where I've been,' she replied calmly, though her heart was thudding at his unexpected presence.

He left the altar and she shuddered away as he tried to touch her. He gave a crooked smile. 'I've been neglecting you, my love. There's so much to do, planning the temple – the temple for Kali. It will be magnificent, and that damned crone will

352

furnish the money for it. How is she? Dare we hope that she'll die soon?' He had been musing on this for long, unwearied hours, his head filled with floating visions of this stupendous project. His unnaturally bright eyes expressed feverish energy.

'I can't tell you that, Christopher.' She tried to draw away but his hands were gripping hers. 'Why don't you discuss it with Russell?'

'I already have.' The fiery surge was dying down in him, and he was losing the thread of the conversation, adding vaguely: 'We can hurry her along, can't we? You can do it. She already takes opium in her medicine – simple to add a few more drops – enough to ensure that she never wakens.'

'You want me to murder my own grandmother?' She struggled to be cool, warning herself to guard against indiscreet slips.

'Just think, Mariana, when the temple's finished, you'll be its high-priestess! Agnes and you – vestal virgins!' He laughed at this novel idea, repeating it over and over. The fever flared up again, exciting him. 'There's a lot to do. I've my treatise on the planets to complete, and a book on my experiences after taking *Amanita muscaria*. Russell says that it'll be a significant work, of tremendous help to medical science. The world will be ours, Mariana – ours and our son's!'

She was aware of him becoming sexually aroused. It sickened her. The child – always the male child! If what Agnes had said in the chapel was true, he had shed so much blood to achieve this aim, done so many heartless deeds. His hands were on her, shaking as they unbuttoned the long coat, opening it wide, his blue, narrowed eyes watchful above the cheekbones, examining the curve of her breasts under the ruby-red gown. Mariana was rigid, her breath quickening, sick with revulsion. Endure, she told herself, close your eyes, submit to whatever he wishes to do, and pray God that you remain barren.

She gritted her teeth and tried to divorce her mind from her body as he led her to the bed, using her for his pleasure. Endure she did, and for a seemingly endless span of time. Far from increasing his potency as he fondly believed, the drugs impaired it, and he struggled to achieve satisfaction, becoming vicious in his frustration, blaming her for it, hurting her in his efforts to relieve it. Mariana lay there, stifled by his heaving body, gagging at the stale smell of sweat, the taint of wine and opium on his breath. At last, in a final welter of exertion, it seemed he had either reached his goal or thought that he had. Listening to his laboured gasps as he rolled off her, Mariana hoped that he would have a seizure.

Next morning she rose listlessly after passing a sleepless night, too weary and depressed to bother with selecting a charming outfit to please Madame, putting on the first plain dress that came to hand, shrouding herself in a hooded cloak. The sky wept tears for her, and sleet chilled her face when she left the carriage in the wind-torn courtyard. The iron vanes on the chimneys whirled around madly, creaking in complaint, and inside the house tapestries rustled against the walls like dead leaves falling. She avoided the kitchen where normally she stopped to chat with Margery. Today she could not face her, fearing that she would break down. Quietly she sped up the staircase and opened the door of Madame's room. Her first thought was to wonder why her grandmother was looking so pleased, her second to conjecture what had caused her to abandon her bed-cap for a black silk scarf, topped by a lace bonnet with wide frills.

She paused, her hand on the handle, about to make some comment on Madame's unusually stunning head-gear when she was arrested by a movement near the fireplace. Someone was standing there, a tall figure who began to walk towards her. It was Radu.

CHAPTER 4

Everything began to spin. Mariana put out a hand to press back the darkness engulfing her, and Radu caught her as she started to fall. There was a period of star-flecked blackness which netted her and tossed her high. She could not remember who she was or where. The darkness became a red haze and out of it swam her mother's face. I'm dead, thought Mariana, she's come to take me to heaven.

The haze faded. The room gathered itself together and locked into its normal shape. Her mother smiled and stepped back into the gilded picture frame. Mariana was lying on the couch and, sure enough, she *was* in heaven for her head was pillowed against Radu's chest, his arms were holding her tightly and he was murmuring to her, his voice charged with emotion.

'Maria! My darling! Oh, thank God – thank God!' As he spoke, he was anxiously scanning her face.

'Don't waste your breath thanking the Almighty. It's me whom you should praise,' said Madame from the bed, highly pleased with herself. 'Now then, Mariana, never again complain that I do nothing for you.'

Mariana did not hear her, and neither did Radu. She stared up at him with brimming eyes and could hardly breathe for joy. He bent his head and laid his lips upon hers. The Duchess watched them, a broad smile on her lined face, and she blew a deep puffing breath of relief. How she had plotted and planned for this, how cautiously and tortuously she had worked to bring it about ever since a chance remark of Mercer's concerning David Cunyngham's unexpected arrival at Coleshill Abbey had made her put pen to paper and write to him. Her tact and strategy alone had piloted these star-crossed lovers.

It had been hard to keep the secret from Mariana. She had wanted to tell her so badly, but had held her tongue. Last night, Radu had come alone. She had insisted that he remain, silently congratulating her granddaughter on her admirable taste, quite charmed by him. They had talked as if long-standing friends; of Europe, of Napoleon, of Radu's adventures during the war. He had explained his position, thrilled her with the story of his defeat of a conniving bastard brother, made her weep with his passionate declaration of love for Mariana, and his despair of ever making her his own.

It was really so simple. Oh, so simple. No word of reproach, no explanation, only a few happy tears. They had met and clasped hands and kissed, so naturally, so lovingly – the inevitable coming together of people who could not live without each other. Radu was the first to return to reality. He lifted his head and looked at the Duchess. 'Madame, you have my heart-felt thanks, and later we'll talk again, but now I must be alone with Maria.'

The delighted old lady rocked with glee. 'Of course you must! Take her away, back to the room that you insisted on using last night, though you could've slept with me! Oh, yes, my girl, he's faithful! Blast him! Had I been twenty years younger it might've been a different story. Go on! Away with you! Make a cuckold of St Jules – though I don't agree that her marriage to him was legal. Be off!'

The room was further down the corridor, and Mariana could not remember how she got there, hurried along by Radu, pressed close to his side. She was beyond thought, fear or caution, feeding her eyes on his face, her hands on the feel of him. Incredible! Wonderful! Something that she had prayed would happen and, while rationality had insisted that it was impossible, her soul had known that one day she would be with him again.

She was familiar with the guest-room. It was the one she had occupied during those fateful days when she was half mad with sorrow, mourning her lost baby. A place of most dreadful misery, miraculously transformed into a sacred shrine for the happiest moment of her life.

Someone, the ever-caring Margery, she guessed, had lit the fire and tidied up. She must know about Radu, but she would keep their secret. The manor was remote, and the onset of winter would help. People did not meet and gossip when the moors were blasted by northern winds. Mercer and Benedict hardly ever left it anyway, even in the height of summer. This was their haven, their hidden paradise. No matter what the morrow brought, today was theirs.

For a long while they did nothing but sit before the crackling fire, clasped close. Speech was unnecessary as they lapped up the peace, the joy of pressing bruised hearts together, easing the pain. The chamber was small, wainscoted in oak, richly carved and inlaid, accompanied by even more elaborately decorated chimney-piece and door. The crimson glow of the fire warmed the sombre external light falling through the mullioned windows which were plastered with hissing rain.

Empty of emotion, Mariana rested in Radu's arms on the thick fur rug. Her long black lashes lay quietly on her pale cheeks. He held her fast, wanting to absorb her into himself, a part of him so that they might never be torn asunder. If only she would raise her lids, and let him see her eyes – the eyes which darkened to violet in various lights. They must look up at him with the love that had made life so beautiful. How thin she was, even her bones seemed to have shrunk, gone the delightful rounded curves that had contained no hard edges. As he held her, he tried to make the strength pass from his body into hers. The worrying days he had spent without much rest or sleep since arriving in England and dashing up to Yorkshire with David had made little outward impression on his own powerful frame.

He felt that he must rouse her to full consciousness of his presence for she was not yet entirely there, afraid to grasp reality. Once the glorious fact that she was not living a dream penetrated to that inner spark of being, she would recover. So he worked to awaken that consciousness, let the warmth and scent of his body pass into hers, while his mind concentrated into a white-hot point of determination. She was his. He would never let her go.

Her eyelids flickered, and he renewed his efforts, gently caressing her arms and body. He laid his cheek on hers with the old familiar tenderness, and kissed her fingers one by one on the inside, close to the palm. A shiver passed through her. Her arms came up and fastened round his neck. 'Radu, is it really you?' she whispered. 'How has this happened?'

'Through David, and your grandmother,' he answered, his lips near hers. Hunger was in him, desire to possess her, to meld them into one again, physically. This was not the moment for talking, but neither must he force nor frighten her. He slid a careful finger down her cheek, coming to rest beneath her chin, tilting her face up to his, and there was such a look of intense devotion on his lean, swarthy features that she gave a gasp.

Radu had not taken into account her own burning need to purify her flesh from Christopher's touch. 'Kiss me!' she demanded.

With a quick snatch of his breath, he brought his mouth down on hers, running his tongue along her lips which opened in welcome. It was as if he forced out the demons which had been destroying her, and she felt her soul winging its way to freedom. After that, all thought was extinguished. They were lying on the

357

bed, naked, entwined – touching, tasting, conscious of nothing but their oneness. Crimson-spangled clouds against closed lids, then eyes of fire, bright in the darkness of the oaken tester, and Radu delaying the moment of union, rearing above her, saying harshly:

'Look at me as I enter you. I want you to know it is I, your husband who adores you, not some nightmarish vampire-lover!'

Blazing eyes locking with hers, the pupils darkening – steel eyes thrusting into her brain, as his body thrust into her loins. Radu! Radu! He eradicated the memory of Christopher's possession. Her spirit, shining with the hot lightning of desire, shot towards enchanted skies, travelling on bold, forgetful flames. She cried out, drunk with love, then plunged and drowned, the rolling tide pouring out its peace. Cradled in languour, she drifted mindlessly.

Back to earth now – the mattress beneath her, the tumbled quilt above. Her lover lay beside her. She could see his straight handsome profile above the crook of his arm, his tanned cheek rising and falling gently with each deep-drawn breath. She pondered dreamily on the qualities of this man who drew her so powerfully to him and made her ready to take appalling risks for his sake.

With a hand steeped in indolence, she reached out and raked her fingers through his black curls. 'Has there been anyone else?'

'No.' His voice was muffled by the pillow, but his eyes were razor-keen, regarding her over his arm. 'And you?'

'Christopher.'

'You wanted him?'

'He rapes me.'

'The marks on your body? They are fresh weals. You love him?'

She was on her knees, bending above him, her breasts swinging forward to brush his shoulders. 'I hate him, but I pity him.'

Radu rolled over, facing her, drawing her down. 'Love for him lingers in you, despite everything. Evil fascinates. I knew this with Grigore – with Elizabeth. You'll never be free until he is dead.'

'No! No!' Tears ran from her eyes, dripping on to his chest.

He shook her gently, without sorrow, without anger. 'Yes, my dear, recognize it. Hasn't he been in your thoughts every day since first you met him? He's an obsession. Hating him – fearing him – pitying him. He's there, like a cancer in your brain.'

She had denied it, even to herself, but this understanding man opened her eyes to the truth. 'It's you that I love,' she moaned.

'Love wears many guises.' He shifted so that she lay in the curve of his arm, her face against his shoulder. 'I know that you love me, but you've been infected by him. It will take you many years to recover, even when he's no more.'

'Then you abandon me to him?' she whispered, riven with pain.

'Never. I don't know quite how or when, but I'm sure that the crisis is coming very soon. I'll be here to pick up the pieces.' He spoke with heartening conviction.

'You don't have to leave England? What of your country?' Broken, tangled webs of thought bewildered her. 'Oh, Radu, I couldn't bear not to see you again!'

Speaking low, he narrated everything that had happened to him since they last met, assuring her that Alnoch would be able to govern Montezena for some months. 'I'll have to return eventually, of course, but something tells me that you'll be coming with me.' He did not add that it was his intention to make quite certain that she was widowed in the near future, if fate and Christopher's reckless life-style did not do the job for him.

'You do realize that if I conceive a child now, it will be born at Thornfalcon. If it is a girl, he'll not let it live. If a boy, then it will be reared as his heir,' she reminded, feeling him flinch, hating to hurt him, but there must be no secrets between them.

'My daughter murdered, my son brought up by him! Oh, Maria, then it's best if you remain childless,' he groaned, unable to retain his outward composure.

There was such sorrow, such bitterness in his face that she drew his head down to her breasts and kissed away that worried expression, soothing him with the tenderness of a mother. 'I'm convinced that if I become pregnant it will be yours. Christopher has slept with me once since my last monthly flux.'

'When?' he asked, face buried against her breasts.

'Last night.' It would have been so easy to lie, but she resisted the temptation. 'Listen, Radu, the drugs are making him impotent. Oh, he imagines he's virile, that's the strange thing about it. He thinks his physical and mental powers are enhanced, that he can achieve anything, but intentions and performance are no longer distinguishable in his mind. Believe me when I say that he didn't succeed.'

'And tonight, and on every other occasion? What then?' Radu sat up and drove impatient fingers through his hair, eyes savage.

'I'll make quite certain that the opiates are there. He won't be able to resist them. They mean more to him than anything. He may try to take me – oh, don't look so angry, darling.' She put out her hand impulsively, smoothing the hard muscles of his tensed arm. 'What else can I do? He's cruel, vicious – I fear for my life.'

'Maria, my sweet love!' Radu broke down, was taken into her arms and finally went to sleep held tight against her warmth, while she stroked over his hair, aware that she must go soon, imploring a higher power for the strength to stop fighting and allow destiny to carry her along on its flood-tide.

Night and storm-clouds, driven by the screaming gale which rushed across the exposed moorland, making the heavy carriage shudder. They rocked across a high, whalebacked ridge and dropped down into the sheltered valley. The road was a slough of water-filled ruts and trampled mud. The air was full of the noise of the wind's passing, of the roaring with which it shattered itself against the hills. The trees groaned, boughs and hedges creaked and chattered, everything singing of the might of the wind or complaining of its savagery.

Thornfalcon stood like a granite cliff, impervious to nature's turbulent clamour, loftily withstanding it, as it had resisted cannon-fire and battering-rams during bloody wars in times long past. The impenetrable lair of the St Juleses, enfolding them, protecting them from every enemy – except themselves. Mariana stood at the main steps for a moment, holding her flapping cloak tightly around her, face lifted to the sky. Huge clouds, rent and jagged, loaded with moisture, moved ponderously yet swiftly above the towers. No light gleamed at the top of either of them. Where then was Christopher?

Oh, that vast deserted hall! It was too big for three. The whole house was too big. Now that the servants had been dismissed, leaving only Mrs Brockwell, Spyros and an occasional daily woman from the village, the very quietness of it was terrifying. She could hear the coach rumbling round to the stable-yard, a normal, cheering sound, but something else, too, which was far from normal. She turned her head and looked down the dark passage which lay to the right of the huge central fireplace. It was coming from there, and her blood curdled. The ghost of Agnes the Poisoner, perhaps? Or the crazy lord, counting his blood-money?

It was the soft flap-flap of Mrs Brockwell's slippers. In her black dress and snowy cap, she came upon Mariana out of the darkness. She paused with a start of surprise that could not have been anything but false. 'Lady St Jules, we were worried. You're very late.' As she spoke, her eyes moved over Mariana, deliberately measuring every detail: the mud on her hem, the flushed cheeks, the loosened hair.

'How solicitous, and how unusual,' Mariana answered sarcastically, trembling with nervous guilt. 'Generally, no one in this confounded place notices if I'm alive or dead. Where is his Lordship?'

'In the dining-room, madame. Where else, at this hour?'

'Anywhere else, I should imagine.' Mariana swept past her. 'He's not shown himself there for a week.'

Damn! she was thinking. Damn! Damn! Why can't he be in a trance in his tower, or pretending to be a child in the nursery? It would be difficult to face him with any semblance of calm when she had but lately risen from the bed she had shared with Radu throughout the afternoon. In certain moods, Christopher had an uncanny perception. Would he pick up on this?

There was no time to dart up to the bedchamber and change. She was late for dinner as it was, and it would be unwise to aggravate him further. With a defiant tilt to her head, she stalked into the dining-room. The scene that met her eyes was a staggering finale to a most astounding day. There, under the full blaze of the chandeliers, the table was set as exquisitely as for a royal banquet. The service was Meissen china, the crystal glasses made in Waterford, the silver cutlery of Italian design imported two hundred years ago by Roger St Jules. Mariana had not seen these things displayed since her return from Europe. Everything was immaculate, and Spyros and the housekeeper were waiting on table.

'Ah, there you are, my dear,' Christopher called across, rising from the carver at the head, walking over to take her by the hand and lead her to her place on his right. Agnes was seated on the other side. 'It's such a wild night that I confess to being a trifle alarmed on your behalf. Are you well? Not too wearied, I trust?'

'Not at all, thank you.' Mariana was having difficulty in adjusting to his dramatic change of mood and appearance. Piled upon the other confusions of the day was the charming way in which he now treated her, once more the elegant gentleman whom she had married.

He was wearing a beautifully-cut claret velvet jacket, the nipped-in waist of which showed his figure to advantage. Tight beige trousers, a colourful brocade waistcoat, white stock, white shirt-frills, in fact every fashionable accoutrement for which he had once been famous, even earning the title of dandy. Agnes too had excelled herself, in a gown of blue shot-silk chiffon with a matching shawl, its point weighted by a long tassel. Full-length mittens of black lace covered her arms, and on one wrist shone a bracelet of enormous opals. Her hair was dressed high, pale ringlets bunched at her crown. A black ostrich feather nodded from a silver comb. It was only their faces that betrayed them, hollow-eyed, ascetic, like those of martyred saints in a Renaissance fresco. Christopher took up a decanter and poured red wine into Mariana's glass. 'I expect you're wondering why we're so festive,' he said, with a whimsical smile.

'Had I known, I'd have worn something more fitting.' She decided to play his game, having a charade of her own in mind.

Spyros solemnly served the first course and, fork in hand, Christopher explained, his tone light, face expressing a hectic gaiety. 'We're celebrating, my love. Today, Agnes and I completed the architectural drawings of the Temple. You shall see them after we've dined. It will be splendid. Its spire will be the tallest in England, perhaps in the whole of Europe. I shall fill it with treasures in honour of Kali.' He flicked a finger and Spyros stepped out of the background, filled up the glass at his elbow from a different bottle, and retired into the shadows. The liquid glowed on the mahogany-inlaid surface with a deep ruby light.

Mariana pretended to eat, though her appetite had vanished. They were both looking at her expectantly, childishly in need of approval and praise. 'How nice,' she managed to say. 'You're both so talented. I feel quite a dunce when with you. I'm longing to see the drawings.'

'You too have your accomplishments, my dear. Will you play the harpsichord for us later? This will make such a pleasant change.' Christopher's eyes seemed full of genuine affection, and Mariana's head reeled under the thought that perhaps it was she who was insane. Had she imagined that he was evil, that his sister was a lunatic?

When Mrs Brockwell had cleared the table, he sent Spyros to fetch a large folio which contained a number of finely executed plans and elevations. Christopher spread them out proudly, explaining every aspect of his grandiose scheme. Agnes made the occasional comment, but was quiet for the most part, seemingly enthralled by her brother's handsome countenance. Delighted with their new toy, the twins were absolutely lost in it and, to Mariana's intense relief, wanted her only as an admiring audience.

She did choose an appropriate moment to slip in: 'This is going to cost a lot of money, Christopher. D'you really intend to cover the inner walls with beaten gold? How I wish I could be of some assistance, but I'm afraid I may be called upon to undertake sick-nursing at Kenrick Old Court.'

He took the bait, his eyes switching from the drawings to her face. 'Why is this? Could it be that the dear Duchesse is ill?'

'I'm afraid so, Christopher. I've sent a messenger to Dr Russell, requesting that he call there tomorrow.'

'She's really ill? Like to die, d'you suppose? If she does, then you'll be of help indeed.' He was staring down at the plans as if he saw the marble columns already rising.

Mariana's eyes hardened as his callous greed destroyed any pleasant illusion. She was glad that he had taken her carefully baited hook. Grandmother had said he would when they planned the whole thing before she left. With a little luck and a good performance from Madame, she might be able to stay away for a week at least. She wanted to dance with joy. A week! A whole week with Radu!

The evening ended with her playing gigs and gavottes, ballads and lovesongs, as the hour grew late and Agnes insisted on another and yet another, whirling round the room in her brother's arms as they danced the waltz. Mariana complied, glad of anything to amuse, entertain and inspire him, so that he would lose sense of time, space and reality. Her scheme worked and they hardly looked up when she bade them goodnight, smiling into each other's eyes, fingers linked, the drugged wine on the table between them.

When Mariana arrived at Madame's room the following morning, she found Dr Russell already there, standing by the bed, his face grave. She felt like applauding. Grandmother should have been an actress – she's been acting all her life, she thought. Heart-rendingly tragic was the expression on the faint white blur that lay on the pillow. Was this the Duchess's face, this tiny thing that seemed no bigger than the palm of Russell's hand?

'Thank God that you're here,' said Margery in a low, broken voice, at the same time giving Mariana a broad wink behind the doctor's back. Her usually neat hair was a little disordered, and she had managed to arrange her face so that it bore traces of anxiety and want of sleep.

If they can do it, so can I! Mariana resolved, saying in ringing, dramatic tones: 'Is there any hope, Dr Russell?'

'There's always hope, Lady St Jules,' he replied solemnly, 'but precious little, I fear. She has sunk into apathy, lacking the will to live.'

'I will make her try!' Mariana flung herself down on the top of the steps surrounding the bed, seizing Madame's hands. 'Grandma! Speak to me! It is I! Mariana! Your granddaughter!'

'She's unconscious – she won't know you.' Margery seemed on the point of tears.

A slight movement, verging on a shudder, passed through the inanimate form. Madame muttered something, then in a faint, hesitant voice said: 'Is that really you, my dear? Oh, how wonderful! I thought you had left me. I wanted to see you once more before the angels took me to heaven . . .'

The outcome of this piece of well-executed histrionics was as they had hoped. Dr Russell, impressed by Madame's improvement, apparently brought about by her granddaughter's presence, advised that Mariana remain with her for a few days. 'I'll tell Lord St Jules,' he said, as he prepared to leave. 'Keep her quiet. No exertion, no excitement, and make sure that she takes this medicine.'

No sooner had the door closed behind him, than Madame sat up in bed, as lively as a cricket, gleefully triumphant. Mariana uncorked the medicine-bottle, took a sniff and promptly poured it away. Far from saving Madame's life, she strongly suspected that the contents would have hurried her to the grave. In the next moment, she was in Radu's arms – forgetting Christopher – forgetting Thornfalcon.

The next few days were so full of happiness that it became impossible to count them, to notice their going by. Radu was a poet in his wooing, yet had the sure touch and self-confidence that a woman needs in the man to whom she surrenders herself. He swept her powerfully, beautifully, into the net of his passion. There was no hesitation, no doubts of his own ability to please and satisfy. He was certain and direct in everything he did. Mentally and physically Mariana knew herself healed, quickened to a new strength. Yet when she contemplated the empty chasm of life without him, she experienced an actual, bodily crisping of the flesh.

Dr Russell had called in several times, putting them in a flurry, with the Duchess hurriedly assuming the pose of a suffering patient, and Radu hiding, well out of sight. Mariana had watched the doctor closely, but he had given no hint that he was surprised to find Madame slightly improving, though he must have been puzzled. 'Are you quite certain that she has been taking her medicine?' he would ask.

Mariana would look him straight in the eye. 'Yes, doctor. It's that which has wrought the miracle.'

But when he came on the fifth day, she found it almost

impossible to hide her dismay as he said: 'Lord St Jules wishes you to return. The coach will be coming for you tomorrow.'

'But my grandmother?'

Russell gave his coldly controlled smile. ' – Is so much better that I think it safe for you to leave her for a while. You have your duty to your husband, you know.'

To protest would have been foolish, so Mariana endured the agony of pretence whilst he took his time examining the Duchesse, but when he finally picked up his hat and left, she ran to the guest-room on frantic feet. Radu held and comforted her, but: 'What are we going to do?' she cried, beating her fists together in desperation.

'You'll have to go, my love, there's no other way round it,' he replied grimly. 'I'll ride to Coleshill Abbey and talk with David. I expect he'll argue and counsel prudence, but I think the only course is for us to face St Jules and force his hand.'

Her eyes were dilated with fear. 'I can't go back there alone. Don't ask it of me, Radu.' She clung to him for a moment more, then suddenly stiffened as if she could almost hear the rumble of the carriage-wheels which would bear her away in the morning.

'I shall come,' he said, and kissed her.

'Don't delay,' she warned, raising her eyes to him, as if assessing his sincerity. 'Or it will be too late.'

There was a frantic quality about their love-making that night, neither knowing when they would be together again. He slept at last but she found it impossible, rising when the clock struck two, drawing on her dressing-robe and tiptoeing to Madame's room. She too was awake, sitting up in bed, journal open on her lap. Not surprised to see Mariana, she said: 'Well, child, and what are you planning?'

Mariana stood by the hearth, shivering with more than bodily cold. 'Radu thinks we should talk to Christopher, but I know it's no use appealing to his better nature. He doesn't have one. He'll more than likely have Radu killed.'

Madame touched the tip of her quill to her lips thoughtfully. 'I've given the matter deep consideration. Perhaps the time has come to call in the reserves. This is a legal matter. A baby has been murdered, others too. St Jules is a criminal.'

'Ha! Who in these parts is going to believe that?' Mariana cried bitterly. 'Every magistrate, each damned lawyer is in his pay.'

'I'm not speaking of the local numskulls,' Madame replied scornfully. 'Take the case to London. Visit my own man there – Mr Proctor of Messrs Proctor, Elliot and Grace. They've always handled my affairs most efficiently.'

'London?' The impact of her grandmother's suggestion shocked Mariana into alertness. 'You mean, I should go there – alone?'

'Why not? I can provide you with money for the journey, give you the address, arrange for Benedict to drive you to York where you can book a seat on the stage-coach.' Madame was watching her eagerly, crouching forward, face bright.

Her enthusiasm was infectious. Mariana left the fire, coming towards the bed. 'Oh, Grandmother, could I do it?'

'Of course you could. Who needs men? We women are supposed to be the weaker sex, but by God, if that were so we'd never survive childbirth. Get dressed, pack a few things, then come back here to me. Benedict will be waiting below.'

She's right, thought Mariana. If I can find a competent barrister, then I may be able to obtain a divorce at the very least. She made up her mind not to rouse Radu. He should not be involved. When next they met, she would be a free woman – free to love him – free to be his wife. Till that moment, she would not see him. Ah, Radu, he had done her so much good. The surge of health flowed strongly through her veins with recuperative power as she sped back to their room. A stratagem was already taking shape in her mind. She selected a plain black dress and pelisse from the armoire, and a large-brimmed black bonnet over which she flung a black veil. She would be 'Mrs Godwin', newly widowed and visiting her London lawyer. Just for a moment, she hung over the bed bidding Radu a silent goodbye, not even daring to kiss him lest he wake and weaken her resolution.

'You'll not tell him where to find me, Grandam?' she said as she let herself into Madame's room again. 'I'll write to you when I've seen Mr Proctor. If he takes my case, it may be months before the matter's resolved. Christopher will put up a terrible fight.'

'Concern yourself with nothing but shaking off the chains of that wicked man,' Madame said sternly. 'Leave Radu to me. I can see that he's impulsive and will want to kill St Jules or chase after you or both. I'll talk some sense into him.'

She handed Mariana a heavy purse and a letter for Mr Proctor with his address on the envelope. Mariana gripped her hands. 'Thank you, Grandmother. I don't know what I'd do without you.'

Madame flushed and her eyes shone with tears. 'Get on with your nonsense!' she said brusquely. 'You're like me when I was young, tough as old bootlaces! Go out there and fight for the right to be with the man you love.' She reached out a steady, gentle hand and touched Mariana's cheek. 'I approve of the widow's weeds. With a deal of money, a lot of courage and the blessing of that flighty bitch, Lady Luck, you may be wearing them in earnest soon. Look after yourself, and God go with you.'

The lawyer's dwelling was one in a row of houses in the most fashionable, sought-after area of Chancery Row. These were of red brick, two storeys high, with attics on top, plentiful windows and little porches which were scrubbed white. There was a brass plaque on the wall by the front door. A servant answered Mariana's knock and conducted her through a neat entrance hall and into an office on the ground floor. This was a pleasant room with large windows facing the street. The floorboards were highly polished, and bright with splashes of rugs; there were comfortable chairs with carved back panels, a wide table, cupboards and shelves containing bundles of papers, sealed documents, files and similar impressive objects signifying Mr Proctor's profession.

He rose, and bowed Mariana into a chair, then seated himself behind the table, carefully removing his spectacles and wiping them on a spotless handkerchief before replacing them on his short nose and reading the Duchesse's letter. Mariana watched him carefully. He seemed a trustworthy individual, solidly built, dressed in a well-cut dark suit, with greying hair brushed back from a high forehead. When he had finished scanning the missive, he put it down on the veneered surface of his desk and asked her to explain in more detail.

Taking a deep breath, Mariana began at the beginning, until the whole story was out and Mr Proctor in possession of the facts. He listened without interruption, and then studied her thoughtfully, fingers pressed lightly together.

'Well, well, here's a tale straight from a romance,' he smiled at her kindly, and she could not tell by his expression whether he believed her. 'You do realize, Lady St Jules, that your husband is a most influential man. Your accusations will be difficult to prove. Have you witnesses?'

Mariana had to admit that she had not. Each person involved with Christopher was bound to uphold him, none of them would be willing to confess to being party to murder. 'What am I to do?' she burst out. 'I swear that it is true, but he will try to prove that I'm insane.'

'A complicated business, I agree. The battle will be tough,' Proctor warned, rising from his chair and walking over to the marble fireplace. He tapped the glowing coals with the toe of his

367

black shoe and studied the leaping flames for a moment. 'The Duchesse is an old and valued client. We also handled the business transactions of Phineas Cunyngham. You say that his nephew, the present Lord Cunyngham, is a friend of yours? This will be all to the good, but be prepared for a lengthy tussle. Your husband will employ the best barristers in the land, if you bring this charge against him. You could very well end up out of pocket and in danger of being committed to an asylum. You realize this?'

Mariana's heart sank, the courage draining out of her. She had come to him as soon as the stage-coach arrived in London, without pausing to find lodgings. The journey had been uncomfortable and tiring. She had never before used public transport and it left much to be desired. Her first glimpses of the wintry city had not been encouraging. It was dirty, dreary, the air heavy with the smoke from hundreds of factory chimneys, a far cry from the pretty face it had shown her in the spring.

She slumped in her chair, despair beginning to nibble at her mind. 'I must be free, Mr Proctor. As I've explained, I can't live with Christopher. I feel constantly threatened. He killed my child. He will kill me too, eventually. Even had I not met Prince Radu, I should never have returned to him. If you think it impossible to convict him of murder, then can I obtain a divorce?'

'My dear young lady, rest assured that I will do all I can on both counts. If he is a villain, then he must be brought to trial, but I make no promises of success. As for divorce – this is most difficult and extremely unusual. It may take years.' As he talked, he approached a handsome étagère which stood against one wall and fetched a decanter of wine and two glasses. A dapper, dignified figure who would no doubt become a High Court judge. He offered Mariana a drink which she accepted gratefully, much in need of Dutch courage.

'Then what am I to do?' she asked wearily.

'I want you to write a statement, giving the facts, as you have told them to me, also the names of the people involved and dates, if you can. I shall show these to my partners, Mr Elliot and Mr Grace, and obtain their learned opinions. I take it that Lord Cunyngham and Dr Lancelot Gilmour would corroborate your story in as far as they are able? Good. Then I suggest that you start at once.' Proctor drew paper from a drawer, supplied Mariana with a pen, ink and sander, and reseated himself.

By the time she had finished, it was getting so dark that a servant came in to light the oil-lamps. Proctor took the completed draft, read it through, corrected any phrases which he considered erroneous, pushed another blank sheet towards her with instructions to sign both at the bottom, promising to have his clerk make a neat copy of her original on it.

'Good, very good. Most satisfactory, Lady St Jules. Will you call and see me again on – ah, let me see – the day after tomorrow? This will give me time to dwell on the matter.' He twinkled at her through his glasses, certainly not unsympathetic to her cause. 'You do realize that if we decide to go ahead, the authorities will have to be informed? And that if it comes before the Old Bailey, you'll be called upon to appear in Court? Not a pleasant experience for a lady like yourself.'

'I don't care!' Mariana was standing now, slim and proud, very appealing in her distress.

He patted her arm paternally. 'You're a brave woman – very brave. Your ordeal must have been terrible. Rely on me, please do. Is there any further aid you require? You have somewhere to stay in London?'

'No, I haven't,' Mariana faltered, realizing that it was dark outside by now. She felt a little choke of loneliness, suddenly scared of the vastness of this city. 'I'm sure Lady Georgiana Cunyngham would let me reside with her, but I daren't see her.'

'Quite so, it would be most imprudent. Perhaps I can help you,' he said as he walked her to the door. 'Not far from here is a respectable hotel. I know the proprietress. Here's the address.' He handed her a card. 'Mention my name. You'll find Mrs Lovejoy very accommodating and she keeps an excellent table. Better still, allow me to call a hackney-carriage. I'll tell the driver where to take you.'

She paused at the threshold, flicking the veil back over her face. 'I'm travelling incognito. It is safer thus. If you contact me at the hotel, ask for Mrs Godwin.'

He smiled, nodded and bowed, then sent his servant to find a cab. The persistent drizzle which had greeted her in London was falling as if it would go on for ever. The streets were busy though the shopkeepers were putting up their shutters for the night, and pedestrians were hurrying homewards. This part of the town was situated somewhere between the houses of the rich and the hovels of the poor, a middle-class business area. The hackney drew up at a large, well-appointed house in a quiet side-street. There were strictly practical issues besetting Mariana as well as emotional ones. When travelling with the Cunynghams these had been taken care of, but now if she wished to survive in this sprawling, impersonal city, she must fend for herself. Squaring her shoulders, she mounted the steps to the front door of the hotel, bidding the cabby follow with her valise. Admitted by a porter, she managed surprisingly well, and within a short time was being ushered into a large salon by a stately lady who announced that she was Mrs Lovejoy. The lawyer's recommendation smoothed the way and before long Mariana found herself in a small, clean apartment, with a maid-servant setting a match to the coal fire, and telling her that supper would be served in the dining room. Mariana said that she would prefer to eat in her room by herself, and a tray was duly sent up.

To be utterly alone was another fresh experience, and one which she was unsure about. After supper, she found writing materials in a drawer and settled down to pen a letter to the Duchess. Mrs Lovejoy, careful of the comforts of her guests, provided headed note-paper. Mariana cautiously obliterated the address with heavy strokes of black ink. Soon the envelope stood on the mantelshelf, ready to be posted next day. As she rested it against the pretentious marble clock taking pride of place, she noticed that it was only eight in the evening. What was she to do with her time? How to pass the hours, the days, maybe even weeks whilst Messrs Proctor, Elliot and Grace put their clever legal heads together and cogitated on her future?

Boredom proved a greater obstacle to peace of mind than Mariana had anticipated. On the credit side, she had money, was comfortably accommodated, wanting for nothing material, but she was desperately lonely, fearful of the outcome of this rash venture, and heartsick for Radu. What use money if there was no lively companion with whom to shop, attend concerts, while away the hours at museums and art galleries? And always there was the terror of discovery. The widow's veil was an excellent disguise, but even so, whenever she walked the streets it was with that feeling of someone at her shoulder. Her fear of Christopher bordered on that of the supernatural. Would he somehow snuff out her whereabouts and lurk in the darkness of her room at midnight, eavesdropping on her thoughts, a shadowy, brooding phantom?

She kept herself to herself at the Cardiff Hotel. Mrs Lovejoy was obviously bursting with curiosity, but Mariana was not to be lured into confidences. The fact that she had paid a month's rent in advance had immediately put her in that lady's good books and Mrs Lovejoy conveyed her understanding of the delicate feelings of a widow who wished to nurse her grief alone. But after ten days of solitary confinement or hurried calls on Mr Proctor, only enlivened by furtive excursions into the streets, Mariana was beginning to wonder how long her sanity would last under such stress. The lawyers were taking their time discussing her case, frustratingly pedantic and, seated in their office while they hemmed and hawed, she cynically reflected that the more they procrastinated, the higher their fee.

The weather continued to be diabolical, no help whatsoever, and one afternoon, Mariana was returning from a short trip to the nearest public library. Veiled, cloaked, several novels tucked under her arm with which she hoped, though vainly, to amuse herself during the evening, she had reached the corner of Cardiff Street when she became suddenly aware that a man, lounging in a shop doorway, was staring across at her. Keep walking, she told herself, although her legs had turned to jelly, let no movement betray that you suspect him. Thank God for this veil! Lord, but you're getting jumpy! He can't possibly see who it is – don't be so silly.

Without appearing to look in his direction, she studied him as she passed on the opposite pavement. It was no one she recognized; a lean man whose clothing had a kind of spurious elegance, though she guessed that the material was of an inferior weave, his suit knocked up by a second-rate tailor, and there was the same lack of quality in his bearing. He turned and pretended to be absorbed in the contents of the shop-window, but she knew he was studying her reflection in the glass. She almost decided to go straight past the door of the hotel, but the rain was sheeting down and she managed to convince herself that he was harmless, no doubt just a passer-by sheltering from the deluge. She mounted the steps and went inside, avoiding Mrs Lovejoy and escaping upstairs. The windows of her room faced the street. Hiding behind a fold of the curtains, she peered out. He was still there, and he was looking up.

For a moment, she sank on to the bed, mind blank with despair, unable to put two coherent thoughts together. Then a surge of healthy rage galvanized her into action. Very well, maybe she was mistaken and the fellow an innocent bystander but instinct told her that he was working for Christopher, in which case she must leave at once. With quick, angry movements she gathered up her possessions, knowing that she must disappear into the anonymity of the city. It was too risky to take the main staircase, so she slipped out the back way, used only by servants and tradesmen. There was no one about, but she was careful to make her progress casual and unconcerned. This was nearly impossible to achieve and, in the end, she rushed out through the yard gate, taking a turn to the right and dashing headlong through the rain. At last she paused for breath, a stitch clawing at her side. Frantically stabbing around for a solution, she decided to visit Mr Proctor and tell him of this latest development, even at the risk of him thinking her completely insane. But in which direction lay his office? She had always travelled there and back in a hackney, yet she must find it. The winter days were short; it was imperative that she reach Mr Proctor before dark. The idea of having to spend nocturnal hours on those menacing streets made her throat tighten.

Hefting up her valise, she set off but was soon hopelessly lost, traversing dingy alleys, terribly alone in the crowds which jostled her, preoccupied with their own concerns. She masked her confusion, walking as though she too had a purpose and place in the teeming capital and was perfectly at home there. In reality her heart was sinking and fear stalked beside her. The uproar of the dirty streets was so alien. She was accustomed to clear skies and the slower pace of the country. Oh, London was vibrant right enough, pulsing with life, but it was also very alarming. She hurried through the twisting lanes, appalled by the abject poverty of the inmates – the ruffianly men, the coarse women who stared at her as she passed, reading threats into every movement, her ears burning with the rude comments fired at her.

A hackney. She must find one. The driver would take her to Mr Proctor. The cabbies were friendly and obliging, and she knew several by sight, always tipping them handsomely. Surely, if she took this lane she would reach broader streets with tidy houses and shops, private carriages and hackneys bowling along the road? It was a short alley, made even darker by the dusk settling over all. To reach the light at the end of it, she was forced to pass two women dressed in gaudy, shoddy clothes, with heavily painted faces and cloaks flung back to display near-naked breasts. They were leaning against the dripping wall, haggard and disease-ridden, eyes hard as they watched out for possible customers. They stared in open hostility, wondering if she was a rival, someone younger and more wholesome who might usurp their pitch. Mariana continued steadfastly, but they followed her and she heard one of them say: 'Who's the flash bunter, eh? She'd best not be treadin' on our stampin'-ground!'

'Gawd! If she is, not even a leper'll look at 'er by the time I've altered 'er face!' rejoined her partner, and they bore down on her revengefully, raucous voices jarring the echoes: 'Hey! You there! We've a crow to pluck wi' you!'

Mariana could almost feel their nails tearing at her, and tugged at the latch of a door set in the wall. It gave suddenly and she fell inside, slamming it shut and ramming the bolt home. She leaned against it, hearing them muttering threats on the other side of the stout wood, heels battering it in a series of vicious kicks, then their voices fading as they returned to the serious business of earning enough to stop their pimps from beating them.

Mariana's breath rasped in her throat, and she was trembling. She took a swift glance around her. The place was dark, a faint light filtering through a barred window high up. The air was foul, the silence so complete that it hurt her ears. No sound at all but the beating of her heart and the pulsing of her blood, like taking a step back into the past when she had awakened into cold and stillness and terror, following the tracks, searching the moors for Elaine. She gave herself a shake and the strange spell dissipated. No longer the frightened girl she had been then, she looked around her boldly, holding the mental image of Radu before her like a shield. Then she heard something, a tiny crepitus which might have been no more than a rat gnawing somewhere. She thought she saw things moving in the gloom, but it could have been a trick of the greyish light. But no – the stirrings and rustlings multiplied with the certainty of a serpent uncoiling from slumber. Mariana swung round, her back to the door, and could make out several shapes creeping towards her. The smell increased, vile and nauseating. Nearer they came, small, stunted figures with evil little faces. Were they children or drawfs? Misshapen, hideous, clad in filthy rags. Bony hands reached out towards her, fingers touched her gown, tried to wrest away her bag with cold, murderous intent. She had run into the den of creatures forced to live in damp, mouldy corners, theft and brutal killings their only means of livelihood.

With a scream of horror, Mariana struggled with the door, got it open and bolted down the alley, coming out through a turnstile, gasping with relief to find herself in a wide street, away from the slums into which she had inadvertently strayed. It was a matter of minutes to hail a hackney and climb thankfully aboard, directing the driver to Mr Proctor's house. It was full dark now, with bright windows flashing past and the comfort of street-lamps. Blessed light! She shrank into the musty leather of the interior, clutching her valise on her lap, trying to control herself. When the cab rattled to a halt at Proctor's door, she hardly knew what she was doing as she paid the fare, forgetting to ask him to wait. As the vehicle rumbled off, she looked up at the house, realizing that it was in complete darkness. She hammered with the brass lion-headed knocker for some seconds, and at long last a shuffling sound came from within and it was opened a crack by the caretaker.

'Mr Proctor?' he wheezed, an indistinguishable form silhouetted by his lantern. 'Sorry, ma'am, he left early tonight.

Gone to the country for a few days, won't be back till Monday. Mr Elliot and Mr Grace? They'll be here in the morning.' Giving her no time to question, he shut the door in her face.

Damn! thought Mariana. Now what am I going to do? She was tired, her nerves shot to pieces by her street experience, it was still raining and her bag weighed a ton. The Cardiff Hotel seemed a blissful haven just then. There she could change out of her wet things, have a bath, enjoy a meal, dive into bed and pull the covers over her ears, shutting out fear. I'll go back, she resolved, look for different lodgings tomorrow. After all, I can't be sure that the man was spying on me. She stepped on to the shiny wet pavement, impatiently waiting for another hackney. Several passed her, but they were already hired. She was about to give up and trudge to the main street when another idled round the corner, going slowly as if seeking a passenger.

'The Cardiff Hotel,' she shouted to the driver as she climbed in. She felt the sway as they moved off, already anticipating the warmth and security of Mrs Lovejoy's sedate establishment, but in the momentary flare of a street-lamp shining directly in the window, she saw someone else seated in the corner.

Before she could move, a hand was clamped over her mouth and a voice muttered: 'Be a good girl and you won't get hurt.'

Mariana struggled, but he was strong. It was the man who had dogged her earlier. A gag replaced his hand, thrust harshly into her mouth, then ropes were drawn round her flailing wrists. In an instant he had pulled down the blinds and she was enclosed in the stuffy gloom with him. He sat in silence, but the chink of light which sometimes penetrated the blind's edge glinted on a pistol-barrel. This was not the way to Cardiff Street. They had been driving for too long. Mariana held herself still, while her thoughts hammered wildly. This must have been organized by Christopher. She could not begin to guess how he had found her, but the bald fact remained – she was trapped.

Just before the hackney stopped, her assailant leaned across and tied a scarf around her eyes, sealing her into darkness and fear. She felt herself lifted from the vehicle, feet stumbling, supported and guided by hard hands. She could smell wet earth, then the fusty interior of a building. She recognized a nasal, sneering voice – heard Arthur Cartwright say: 'Well done, Hume. Help me carry her upstairs.'

'What about my fee?' Hume replied.

'You'll get it! He'll pay generously, don't worry about that. This little bird'll fetch a high price. Christ, you'll be able to dine on opium for the rest of your natural. Not that you'll last long – not in your dangerous game!'

As they talked, they were dragging Mariana up some stairs. She heard a door open, felt herself falling across a bed. Then the blindfold was whipped from her eyes, the gag from her mouth, the bonds from her hands. She was in a badly-lit dilapidated room, with peeling walls and a sagging iron bedstead on which she lay. Arthur was leering down, Hume beside him, devouring her with equal insolence.

'What's the meaning of this?' she began, sitting up, rubbing her numbed wrists. 'Where am I? How dare you abduct me!'

'Stow it, your Ladyship!' snarled Arthur. 'Won't do you no good. You've been took – clean as a whistle. I'm going to return you to your husband, more's the pity. We could've had a bit of fun with you, couldn't we, Hume?' He was eyeing her closely, but did not dare touch her. Arthur prized his private parts more than anything, and Christopher had threatened that he would sever them from his body if he as much as laid a finger on Mariana. Christopher never made idle threats.

'Christopher is here?' Mariana was living a nightmare.

'Impatient to see him, are you? What a loving wife! Yes, he's here all right.'

Mariana leapt from the bed, straight for the door, but Hume caught her and flung her into Arthur's arms. 'Let me go!' she shouted, fetching him a blow on the cheek. 'I don't want to see him!'

Arthur's face was grim, his grip agonizing. 'Now, now – bloody little hellcat! Naughty girls have to be punished. He's told me to punish you a trifle. There's no one to come to your rescue. Your Prince is in Europe, ain't he? He's forgotten about you by now, I expect – taken some other trollop to bed!'

In the midst of her anger, pain and despair, one thought shone star-bright. They did not know Radu was in England! This gave her strength and she put up a fight, but Hume and Arthur overpowered her, using ungentlemanly tactics, neither averse to hitting a woman. At last, stunned, bleeding and exhausted, she was pinioned on the bed, glaring up at them, spitting defiance.

'Got the brew ready, Hume?' said Arthur, roping her again. Hume brought over a small dark bottle. Mariana twisted her head from side to side but Hume's fingers prised her lips apart while Arthur poured the concoction into her mouth, then clamped her jaw shut so that she was forced to swallow.

It tasted vile, burning its way into her stomach, leaving sickness in its wake. Some poisonous substance, mixed by Christopher, no doubt, she thought, wondering if he intended that she should die of it. Within seconds, it began to take effect, absorbed into her bloodstream. Her eyes refused to function properly, her limbs felt weighted and she was hardly conscious that she was now alone. Where am I? What is this place? How long will they keep me here? So many questions flooded her bemused brain as reality slipped away, only terror remaining like a solid presence. The walls were expanding, or else she was shrinking to doll-size. The ceiling was shooting upwards, dissolving into space. The room became huge, like some sombre, shuttered castle, honeycombed with secret tunnels, crypts and staircases of gargantuan proportions. She wandered among them – the pillars encrusted with twisted faces – reaching the centre of a colossal amphitheatre, bordered by towering ziggurats and cloud-topped minarets. She was lost, dwarfed, alone – so alone. In the far distance she could discern tiny figures toiling up and up the staircases, but no one noticed her, no one answered her cries. The awesome scene was lit by a bloody moon hanging in a green sky. Cascades poured through caves, their waters purple or ghastly crimson. I'm so small, mourned Mariana, no larger than a grain of sand. Up reared some steps, gleaming like burnished gold. She tried to scale them, crawling like an insect across an enormous plateau, hauling herself up by a tangle of blue, thick-fleshed vines which writhed snakelike under her bleeding hands. She lost her grip, felt herself falling – down – down – for aeons – down through icy water . . .

She was on the bed, too weak to move. The dimness gleamed with fluorescent colours – sparks shot from the tips of her fingers – she was so hot. I'm melting, she thought. I'm melting like ice in summer, soon there will be nothing left of me. In her ears, her cries seemed like thunder, but someone answered her feeble whisper.

'Mariana, it is I. Christopher.' Was he real? She looked at him groggily. His face was a terrible hue – white, ghastly – his eyes burning black pits. He held something in his hand. It spun slowly towards her, growing huge. A lake? How could he be holding a fiery silver lake? 'Look, Mariana – look at your face. This is how you are. This is your soul laid bare.'

She was on her knees peering into the water. Reeds rustled in the sighing wind under a bleak sunrise. She saw herself reflected – and screamed. The image flung back was that of a rotting corpse, the flesh hanging in tatters from the skull, the decaying lips drawn back over jagged teeth, the eyes bulging, lidless, maggots squirming from the corners. This was herself. This was what she had become. This was eternity.

CHAPTER 5

Lancelot straightened his aching back and rolled down his shirt-sleeves. 'That's it for tonight, Jim,' he growled at his young, fresh-faced assistant. 'I don't want to see any more torn flesh, boils on people's bums, or pregnant mothers till at least noon tomorrow.'

'Right, sir,' answered Jim cheerfully, busy at the sink, washing up medicine bottles and replacing them on the shelves lining the clinic walls. 'Does that mean I can have the night off, sir?'

'Like hell you can!' Lancelot scowled from under his thick grey brows. 'Just because I'm knocking off early doesn't mean you can do likewise! Someone must man the pumps. Where's Colin? No need for him to assume he can duck out of it now that I'm back.'

'Gone down the pie-shop.' Jim ruffled his gingerish hair, and gave his commander a rueful grin. 'Lord, sir, it's Saturday night, and you know what that means. If we don't snatch a bite before chucking-out time, we'll get no chance.'

Lancelot snorted down his nose as he took his great-coat from a hook. 'Aye, that's right, laddie. Saturday night when the labourer gets his wages and blows them in the nearest tavern. A night for fights and wife-beating. When the drink's in, the wits are out! Stand by the bridge, boatswain, and repel boarders! I'll be in first thing in the morning. You two can have Sunday free,' he added magnanimously as he set his hat on his flowing, grizzled locks, picked up his cane and opened the door.

He had absolute faith in Jim and Colin. They had managed the clinic well whilst he had been away, two most promising medical students, serving their apprenticeship at Guy's Hospital, helping Lancelot in their free time. He thought about this as he walked the length of the well-scrubbed bare passage and let himself out of this small house in the poor quarter which he rented as a dispensary and clinic. He too had served his time in hospitals, before he went in the army, and shared the common view that they left much to be desired. Some people thought them gateways to death, for trainee surgeons needed paupers to practise on. The ignorance and butchery galled Lancelot, his dream to found a hospital where the most modern methods were used. As things stood, it was standard policy not to take in the chronic or highly infectious cases, nothing could usefully be done for them. A surgeon's highest claim to fame was the speed with which he could carry out operations which were simple, quick, agonizing and desperate, performed on patients strapped down on the operating table, anaesthetized only by bumpers of negus and laudanum.

It was a misty, drizzling night and Lancelot was looking forward to his comfortable fireside, there to put his feet up, enjoy a supper lovingly prepared by Fred, and retire to bed early with a book and a bottle of wine. He was feeling his age. Gadding about all over Europe had done him no good whatever and a back-log of work had awaited him on his arrival in London. True, David had generously added to his hospital fund, but there was still a long way to go. His spirits were unusually low, and a day in the company of the most wretched of the city's community had done nothing to alleviate this. He was wondering if it was really worth it, or should he throw in the towel and retire to his charming cottage in Chelsea, there to tend his garden, smoke his pipe, and chat over the gate to passing villagers? Lord, but this is a sorry part of town, he observed to himself, as he stepped out into the muck of the unpaved alley. Fred deplored his habit of walking from the Rookery to his house in the West End, nagging him about it every day, wanting to meet him with a gig.

'You'll get coshed one of these dark nights! Mark my words, sir! Coshed and left to die in the gutter! Then where will we be? What of your precious patients, I'd like to know? How'll they fare without you?' he was fond of predicting gloomily.

'Bosh!' Lancelot would snap, made grumpy by so much fussing. 'They'll not hurt me. I'm too much of an easy touch. They won't bite the hand that gives 'em free food and grog! I know my criminals, Fred. Whilst they can get something out of me, they'll offer me their own kind of protection, rough though it may be.'

Nonetheless he carried his sword-stick at the ready as he picked his way through the rubbish that littered the street, a burly figure, his overcoat with its triple capes making his shoulders look formidable. Whilst appearing unconcerned, his eyes were very watchful and he had spotted the shabby man tailing him long before he felt the touch at his elbow.

'Evenin' gov,' said a guttural voice, and the fumes of gin were a noxious breeze on its owner's breath. 'Remember me?'

Lancelot did not stop, and the man trotted along at his side, wheezing with the effort of that brisk pace. 'Scrabbler, ain't it?' The doctor grunted, recognizing the shambling gait of the broken-nosed ex-pugilist whose brain had been knocked silly by too many prize-fights that had made money for some, but not for him.

Scrabbler grinned, showing broken stumps of decaying teeth. He dragged a bottle from one of the many pockets of his filthy, ragged jacket. 'Want a swig? No? Right-o, all the more fer me!'

Lancelot mused on which petty crime Scrabbler might have committed to be in sufficient funds to purchase liquor. He was an old acquaintance. Lancelot had patched him up after his last big fight, stitching back his right ear which had been nearly bitten off by his opponent. They had almost reached the arch through which even the toughest constable would not enter, unless accompanied by a platoon of soldiers. On the other side of it lay affluence: shops, the houses of wealthy merchants and, further on, the palaces of the great and famous. Lancelot paused, hands resting on his stick, waiting for Scrabbler to say what he had to say, certain that his purpose was not that of a voluntary bodyguard.

Scrabbler took another long pull at the bottle, his adam's apple bobbing, then he wiped his mouth on the back of one huge, hairy fist. 'Well, gov,' he began, squinting at the doctor. 'I done wha'cher ordered like, kep' me eyes skinned. Yer was lookin' fer a certain party, weren't cher? Or noos of a certain party? Now, lookee 'ere, I seen 'im terday – least ways, I reckon it were 'im – young spark – brother ter your pal, Lord Cunyngham.'

Lancelot was not surprised that Edwin had been spotted in a shady area. He had been in bad odour with David since his involvement with Radu's foes in Vienna. Lancelot had rarely seen his genial friend so angry, hardly trusting the boy out of his sight, asking Lancelot to watch him while he went to Yorkshire with Radu. They had returned in a hurry, and matters had not improved. David had cut down Edwin's allowance, refused to pay his debts, and let him know in no uncertain terms that if he did not mend his ways he would find himself out on his ear without further ado.

'Speak more plainly, man.' Lancelot was getting cold, brooding about that tasty supper keeping hot on the kitchen range. 'Don't ramble, for God's sake! Where did you see him?'

'Aw, don't know as I should really tell yer, gov. Yer ain't goin' ter be too 'appy – not if'n 'ees a friend o'yourn.' Scrabbler screwed up his eyes under thick-boned brows in an expression intended to be comradely.

'Spit it out, cully!' Lancelot forgot his supper.

'Well, gov – 'ee were wiv' a feller what I seen round 'ere afore.' The piggy eyes were sly, and he tapped the side of his purple nose significantly. There was an expectant pause and, knowing the rules, Lancelot produced a guinea from an inside pocket. Scrabbler took the coin and continued: 'This cove weren't a gent. Oh, no, not by a mile 'ee weren't. Bloody cocky though – thinks 'isself a toff – wants ter be a toff, but 'ee ain't nor never could be.'

'I think I may know him,' said Lancelot, with a wry smile at Scrabbler's apt description. 'A pup! And an ill-bred pup at that!'

His eyes narrowed thoughtfully. Edwin had started to give them the slip, disappearing for days on end. They suspected that he was up to no good. In a fit of guilty remorse, but chiefly because he wanted to ingratiate himself with his stern brother, Edwin had confessed all that had happened with regard to Grigore, Dimitrie and Cartwright. The sordid story had turned Lancelot's stomach. By all accounts Cartwright was an unscrupulous character, and Lancelot guessed that he was probably still working for St Jules, seeking the vanished Mariana.

The doctor had been watching and waiting, using such spies as this disreputable hulk of whining humanity. There was a lot to be said for rubbing shoulders with down-and-outs. This was not the first time that he had found it profitable. He had been ferreting away behind the scenes, bent on finding Mariana before her enemies did, deploring her foolhardiness.

He kept a wary eye on Scrabbler, suspecting that he might try to escape without imparting further information, maybe hoping to come back tomorrow for another guinea. 'Don't dilly-dally! I'm not squeamish. Tell me where you saw them?'

Scrabbler ran a hand over his jutting, stubbly jaw. 'Down the Ratcliffe 'ighway, doc. Yer knows it?'

'I do,' Lancelot sighed. Many was the time he had been called out to attend some person injured in that seedy district of gin-shops, opium-dens, doss-houses and violent misery. Like St Giles, it was a stony place in which the dispossessed had taken root, brutalized men and depraved women.

'I seen 'em goin' inter the Chink's pad. That's a rum dump if ever I seen one, full o' Malays an' other blackies. I'd rather 'ave me gin, any time, ter that foreign muck what they goes mad arter.'

'There are many different roads to hell,' Lancelot observed, wondering precisely which one Edwin was taking. The drizzle had become a downpour and water was dripping from his hat-brim to the shoulders of his coat. 'And why – oh, inestimable Scrabbler – would Edwin Cunyngham be visiting such a place, think you?'

Scrabbler shrugged and cast a regretful eye at the empty bottle before tossing it into the open sewer which gurgled sluggishly down the side of the alley. 'Stands ter reason, don't it, gov? Must be one o' them opium-eaters. The Chink gits the best the sailors brings in.'

They were interrupted by a rumpus from a nearby tumbledown house. Voices roared in furious argument. A child was howling, a dog barking. Windows banged open, feet clattered over the cobbles and the uproar increased as others joined in what had started as a domestic brawl. Lancelot dragged Scrabbler into the main thoroughfare. The last thing he wanted was to be called upon to perform his office. Let Jim and Colin cope with it. He had more important matters on his mind.

'Don't worry, doc.' Scrabbler assumed a fighter's stance, fists bunched, getting the wrong idea. 'I'll guard yer. I'm yer man. The fust bugger what attacks yer'll 'ave me ter deal wiv'. I'll throttle 'im wiv' 'is own bleedin' tripes! Be damned if I won't!'

'Get me a hackney, double-quick,' Lancelot ordered, and when Scrabbler had obliged by the simple expedient of standing in the middle of the road and whistling shrilly through his fingers, he clambered into the stale-smelling vehicle, leaned from the window and issued further instructions. 'Go to Fu Yuan's at once. Keep Cunyngham there. I don't care how you do it. Knock him out if need be. Wait for me to come. Right?'

'Right, gov.' Scrabbler tugged at his forelock.

A ray of hope ran through Lancelot's thoughts as he watched the infrequent lights flit past, swayed to the rocking of the squeaky springs, and heard the quick trotting of the hairy-heeled nag steaming between the traces. Edwin was still wet behind the ears, for all his swagger and, if he had got himself into deep water with St Jules, it should not be too difficult to make him talk. It was possible that no harm had come to Mariana, yet. Maybe he was unwise to meddle, but he didn't like the situation – didn't like it at all.

The drenched roofs that overhung the wet, pewter-coloured footpaths on either side dripped tearfully down. Pedestrians hurried by with bent heads and collars raised, but he began to feel elated at the thought of action. He rapped smartly on the roof of the hackney when they turned into the street where his house was situated. After striding up the steps and telling the annoyed Fred to forget supper, he gave the driver David's address and got back inside.

Radu was slumped in a leather armchair in the library of the Berkeley Square mansion. He had morosely declined dinner, burying himself in his gloom. When the Duchesse had explained that Mariana had gone to seek justice, he had buoyed up his hopes with a kind of desperate optimism, but nothing she could say prevented him from following his love to London. Over the days it had become increasingly difficult to concede to Mariana's request that he make no attempt to trace her. He burned with frustrated helplessness.

David and Georgiana had proved themselves staunch allies. Radu was travelling incognito, but it was nigh impossible for a man of his looks and bearing to pass unnoticed. Though he stayed indoors much of the time, wearing civilian garb, the Cunynghams entertained a good deal and questions were already being asked about their distinguished guest. They had their answers ready. He was a business colleague from France who was somewhat reserved and would not accept invitations to balls, soirées, card or theatre-parties.

It was hard to keep up the pretence. He wanted to rush from club to club, openly declaring Lord St Jules to be a blackguard, collaring high-court judges and demanding a hearing. David dissuaded him from such impetuous action, and he reluctantly acceded to his common-sense advice, though miserable as sin and sick at heart. Would he ever see Mariana again? He was beginning to doubt it, and despair was sapping the fiery energy which normally burned brightly within him. He called for another bottle, yet was in no better humour after cracking the second. The thoughts seething in his brain remained as dark and heavy as the liquor in his glass. He was prey to passions hard to control – resentment against St Jules, a longing to feel his hand striking that pale cheek, to see blood spreading and running down his cravat.

He was deeply in love with Mariana, as damnably in love as a raw boy. Those precious days in Yorkshire had made him need her more than ever. Now, as he lay back in his chair, staring broodingly at the brandy in his glass, he was in a most dangerous mood. It was thus that David and Lancelot found him, bursting into the library, with the doctor wearing his outdoor garments and David shouting for a footman to bring his coat and hat.

'Lance has a lead!' David shouted excitedly. 'Cartwright's in town and we're going to flush him out! We'll get him to tell us, if he's discovered where Mariana is!'

'How will he know? No one knows, except the Duchesse. Mariana doesn't want me to seek her!' Radu growled.

'There's nothing to prevent your friends looking for her, is there?' put in Lance, splitting hairs. 'I for one don't like to think of her unprotected, with creatures like Cartwright on the prowl.'

'I'll kill him!' This was the first articulate thing out of Radu's fury. The candle-glow emphasized the planes of his face, the high cheekbones and narrow, tilted eyes.

'Not before I've had a go!' David flashed. 'From what Lance has just told me, he's introduced that fool Edwin to an opium-den.' He gave an exasperated snort, pacing the floor, hands knotted behind his coat-tails. 'Heaven forfend! The boy's addled enough as it is!'

'Beat him up later,' advised Lancelot, casting a worried glance at the two large, angry men. 'First we've got to screw information out of him. When we bowl up in full force, it's bound to give him the squitters. I'll stake my life that he's a whoreson coward.'

Radu was on his feet in a single bound, thrusting a pistol into his pocket, eyes blazing. 'Just let me get my hands on him! If he's got hold of her – hurt her – he'll wish he'd never been born!'

Lancelot planted himself firmly in front of the door. 'Not so fast. Sometimes, for an intelligent man, you can be damned stupid. This is England, remember? You can't go round murdering people. No, my friend, we have to box clever.'

David placed a hand on Radu's shoulder, controlling his own desire to hit Edwin for being such an ass and punch Cartwright's head for encouraging him. 'Lance is right. Leave the talking to him. He'll steer us clear of trouble, and make the blighter do what we want.'

Within twenty minutes the three men were journeying to the Ratcliffe Highway. Lancelot had retained the services of the hackney-carriage, deeming it more prudent than arriving there in one of David's crested conveyances. Each was silent, lost in his own reflections on the possible outcome of this night's work. The hackney penetrated deeper into the maw of London's slums. In that vile weather only the homeless roamed the streets. As the wheels squelched through the mud, the yellow beam of its lamps flashed on figures huddled in doorways and beneath bridges. A bonfire of pilfered wood flickered dully on the rubble of a building which had recently collapsed. The tatterdemalions circling it glanced up to watch the hackney's passage. One of them lurched to his feet, rags fluttering as he saluted with a bottle, then fell back amidst screams and laughter.

Lancelot craned from the grimy window, saying as they turned into an even more disreputable lane: 'This is it.'

Two hundred years before, these crumbling tenements had been the mansions of the nobility till the unhealthy stench of the riverside had dictated that those who could afford it migrated west. The upper classes had moved out and the poor moved in. Enterprising landlords had bought them cheaply, and turned them into overcrowded lodging-houses, sitting back complacently and raking in the rents, promising improvements which never happened. As the years rolled by, so they had become ever more rickety and rat-infested, shelters for prostitutes, criminals, dealers in every kind of commodity and vice.

After telling the uneasy cab-driver to wait, Lancelot had gone plunging through the broken gates of the most decrepit-looking of the houses. A flurry of movement from a soggy, half-decayed laurel bush and Scrabbler emerged, his ugly, battered face shining wetly in the light of flares on each side of the large front door.

'I kep' me word, gov,' he whispered huskily. 'They're still in there. I ain't seen 'em leave.'

'Good man.' Lancelot stumped up the steps and pounded for admittance with his cane.

After a tense pause, the door opened an inch. The doctor jammed his foot in the gap and forced it wide. He found himself facing a club-footed cripple, whose emaciated form was shrouded in a dirty coat many sizes too large. His features were those of a youngster, his expression flinty and streetwise.

''old 'ard there, gents,' he remonstrated with a cheeky grin. 'Give us a chance ter git the bleedin' door off the latch. Plenty o' time, my buckos, plenty o' time ter enter Paradise, all the time in the world to join the rest of 'em. Why, in a couple o' jiffs you won't know if it's day or night, or even if the last trump 'as blown.'

'Hello, Clubby.' Lancelot had already attempted to get the lad away from this tainted environment but it was the only place he had ever called 'home'. 'I haven't come to buy. These gentlemen and I are looking for someone.'

Clubby wrinkled his eyes at Lancelot, head to one side. 'The doc, ain't it? Come in, doctor, sir. You looking for a missin' patient? If 'tis a looney, I doubt you'll recognize 'im, there's so many madmen 'ere – difficult to tell one from t'other or which.'

They walked into the hall, a place of clutter and filth, with the overall stench of bad sanitation. Then a most strange figure shuffled from a door on the right. It was a tiny, shrivelled man who looked as if he had seen at least a hundred winters. He wore an embroidered blue silk robe and a round black hat from which dangled a long, stringy pig-tail. His arms were folded across his sunken chest, the hands disappearing into his voluminous sleeves.

'Greetings, Honourable Doctor.' This weird creature, who appeared to have just stepped down from a painted Cantonese screen, bowed low to Lancelot, addressing him in a high, thin voice like the call of a cracked flute.

'Greetings, Fu Yuan.' Lancelot was equally formal, doffing his hat and returning the bow. 'I beg your aid and advice.'

The Chinaman listened gravely, his lips so narrow and bloodless that it was difficult to detect his mouth in that parchment-like face. He stared at them through slanted eyes under wrinkled lids. A hand, corded with veins, each nail encased in a curving gold sheath, crept up to touch the thin white moustache which trailed down to his chest.

'You are free to search my humble house,' he said in that reedy, emotionless voice. 'Names mean nothing here. Men do not give them when they come. By the time they leave, they have forgotten them. He, he, he!' It was as if a corpse had laughed. He bowed again and left them.

Clubby was their guide through the bare apartments, empty of all save rows of rough cots and bales of straw where men lay, dozing and dreaming, their faces earthy, livid, marbled with lines. Some leaned against the festering walls or crouched inert on the stairs – some were well-dressed, others were in the most astonishing rags. They did not speak. The house rang with a peculiar silence, each person there for one purpose only, totally absorbed in the selfish pursuit of a blissful escape from reality.

The lower floor did not yield up their quarry, so they went aloft to the rooms reserved for richer clients – private rooms, each a personal heaven or hell. The occupants were either unaware of their intrusion or merely glanced up from a prone position on bed or couch, before looking away again, completely uninterested. At the furthest end of a dingy corridor they found Edwin.

'Good God!' whispered David, forgetting his anger, for the thing lying on the heap of twisted blankets was deserving of pity. 'Are we too late? Is he dead?'

Lancelot bent over Edwin who was stretched on his back, eyes wide but unseeing. On the floor beside him were empty wine bottles and sticky vessels to which the brown, syrupy tincture still clung.

'He's alive all right.' He gave Edwin a shake, saying loudly: 'Rouse yourself, lad! Here, take a sip if water.' He wedged his brawny shoulder behind and got him into a sitting position.

Edwin's consciousness partially returned. His glazed eyes roamed the room, and his lips moved as he struggled to form words. He focused on David and began to whimper, cringing against the bedhead as his brother, made angry again by relief, started to shout: 'Trust you to mix with louts, muck-worms and addicts! Fine example of the Cunyngham brood you've turned out to be! Thunderation! Only a brainless nincompoop like you would ever set foot in here! Why, Edwin – why, for Christ's sake?'

Edwin held his trembling hands before his face. 'Don't know – can't remember – leave me alone – don't feel well.'

'You bloody will remember! And tell us who brought you!' David stood over him, his face merciless. 'By God, if I ever discover that you've visited this den again, or any place like it, you can starve in the gutter, for you won't get another brass farthing out of me!'

Tears crawled down Edwin's pallid, unshaven cheeks. 'It seemed a *tonish* thing to do. Tried it in Vienna, with Dimitrie, to see what would happen. Lots of people use opium! It stretches the imagination, gives wonderful visions – the poets take it – Byron – Coleridge. I thought it would help me to produce epics.'

'You. A poet? Before one has visions, one must possess inspiration, talent and the discipline to work! You've none of these qualities!' David's sarcasm slashed across the mean room.

Radu, throughout the journey and the subsequent search, had remained absolutely silent, but now he stared at Edwin with such hostility that it stabbed into his fevered brain, terrifying him. 'Where's Cartwright?' the Prince thundered. 'And where is Mariana?'

Edwin was sobbing as he fumbled for traces of opium in the phials, becoming frantic when he discovered that they were drained. 'More – more – get me more,' he begged, falling to the floor and clinging to Lancelot's muddied boots with desperate hands.

'Do as we want, and you'll have it,' the doctor promised. He had judged Edwin's state to a nicety, much experienced with addicts, knowing the various stages. First there was elation, a reckless fever of increased mental and bodily activity, followed by a rainbow-hued dream-world, then stupor and a long, agonizing fall into a pit of depression so deep that suicide was often the only solution.

'I can't tell you anything,' Edwin sobbed, beating his fists, his forehead against the bare planks, grovelling, tortured. 'I don't know what they've done with her.'

Lancelot drew a little bottle from his pocket and held it before the sick boy's eyes. He made a grab for it. The doctor feinted, keeping it just out of his reach. 'So she was here! I suspected as much. Tell me about it.'

'St Jules will kill me! I daren't speak!' Edwin was shaken by long convulsions as if he was freezing, though sweat dewed his face.

'No cooperation, no opium. It's as simple as that.' Lancelot turned towards the door. 'We're wasting our time, it seems.'

'No! Don't go! I'll do anything – just give me a few drops – one drop!' Edwin broke up in panic, horrors afflicting his soul. Lancelot was like a saviour, holding the key to salvation in his great-coat pocket. He tried to assemble his scattered wits, galvanized by fear, by need. In the swinging lantern-light his face was grey, a tic had developed beneath one eye, and he sniffed continually as he talked.

'Where's Cartwright?' Radu's voice was thick with pent-up violence and he fixed Edwin with eyes like steel barbs. 'Is he here, in the same miserable condition as yourself?'

'Arthur a drinker of the honeyed poppy-juice?' Spasms of mirth shook Edwin. 'Oh, no – not Arthur. He doesn't take it. He sells it to others. He's downstairs, doing business with Fu Yuan. Full of plans is Arthur – his only visions are of making vast fortunes.'

Of course, thought Lancelot dourly, I should have realized. Cartwright was not the type to become a victim. His métier was that of the exploiter, not the exploited. He swung into action. 'Scrabbler, look after Mr Edwin,' he commanded, and tossed over the vial. 'Give him a few drops – only a very few, mind. Guard him with your life. David, by your leave, I'll take him home to Fred. He'll give him a good talking-to and nurse him back to health. But first, we're going to have a few words with Arthur Cartwright.'

Fu Yuan rustled from his sanctum with small, mincing steps when he heard them in the hall. 'Have you found your straying bird, doctor?' he asked politely.

'I bloody well have, and not before time by the look of him!' All this bowing and scraping was getting on Lancelot's nerves. If Mariana had been kept captive there, the Chinaman would have been paid for his silence. To threaten him was useless, plus the danger of the thugs in his employ. 'Now I want to see Cartwright.'

'Ah, so. You will not find him amongst the dreamers. Come this way, if you please,' Fu Yuan answered blandly.

They followed him into his private apartment, and it was like walking into the paradise for which his customers craved, a shocking contrast to the squalor outside: light, spacious and serene, with delicately embroidered hangings, carved and gilded furniture, exquisite ornaments and an air of extreme refinement. A wrought-iron stove glowed, throwing out warmth, and near it, seated on a satin-covered stool, was Arthur Cartwright.

'Good God!' he exclaimed, jumping to his feet, thunderstruck. 'What is this? Some trick, you yellow-skinned pimp?'

Without the slightest change of attentive courtesy, Fu Yuan answered: 'Your friends, I understand, Mr Cartwright.'

'Friends be damned! Is this the way you treat business associates, Yuan? I've a bloody good mind to take my custom elsewhere,' Arthur shouted. If he was afraid, he hid it well, taking up a spread-legged stance, as common as ever, in tartan trousers, a yellow waistcoat and puce jacket.

'You bastard! Where is Mariana?' shouted Radu, across the room in a couple of strides, grabbing him by his satin lapels, nearly lifting him off his feet.

'How the devil should I know?' Arthur grated, cockiness wilting.

When he was distraught, Radu's accent became strongly marked. He began to shake Arthur, who lolled bonelessly in his iron grasp. 'Speak! Where is she? Tell me, before I break your goddamn neck!'

'Enough of this!' Lancelot used the tone he employed with the Rookery bullies. 'Let me deal with him. Cartwright, I want some plain answers from you!'

Radu let him go and stood with his eyes fixed on Arthur, who was nervously adjusting his cravat. 'Why d'you think I can tell you anything? I ain't seen her since we got back to England,' he muttered.

'Liar!' snarled David. 'I suppose you're going to say that you also know nothing of the mess my young brother's got himself into!'

Fu Yuan stood with his arms folded, as immovable as one of the porcelain gods smiling benignly from the lacquered cabinet. 'Gentlemen, please be seated. May I offer you some tea?' he said rather reprovingly, as if such uncouth violence was a slight on his hospitality. Without waiting for their reply, he clapped his hands together once, twice, and one of his concubines, a slant-eyed, silk-clad nine-year-old, trotted in on diminutive tightly-bound feet.

'No, thanks,' said Lancelot brusquely. 'Send the girl away. Things're likely to get nasty if Cartwright persists in his attitude.'

'Well, and what have you to say about Edwin?' David's eyes glinted warningly, and Cartwright took a step back.

'It ain't my fault,' he protested, stabbing around for a way to extricate himself. 'I bumped into him in a brothel. He told me you were being hard on him, stopping him from cutting a dash. He seemed rather down in the mouth, so I brought him along here, to cheer him up, you know. Couldn't leave an old mate in the lurch, now could I?'

'Lance, let me hit him!' pleaded David, his hands clenched into white-knuckled fists.

'Patience,' cautioned Lancelot, then he addressed himself to Cartwright. 'Listen to me, and listen well.' He spoke so slowly that every word stood out with separate menace. 'You'll tell the truth, for once in your life. You're toying with a tiger.' He gave a jerk of his head in Radu's direction. 'Any more lies, and I'll loose him on you. If there's anything left of you when he's finished, I'll toss the bits to Lord Cunyngham.'

Arthur's coarse features turned muddy. He thrust his hands in his pockets and meditated flight, darting a look towards the door, towards Fu Yuan, but the Chinaman was watching the proceedings serenely. 'Why're you picking on me?' he blustered, painfully aware of the pistol which Lancelot held. 'You've no right to burst in here, interrupting business.'

'And what is this so-important business?'

Arthur brightened, even strutted a trifle. 'I've got a chemist friend up in the cotton-spinning area. He does a rare trade among the workers. Can't get in his shop on a Saturday night for customers and on market-day he sells at least three pounds of opium and a gallon of laudanum. It's cheaper than gin, you see. For a penny, they can buy enough to see 'em through the week. It keeps the women happy, and the babies quiet. Well, him and me put our heads together and came up with the idea of producing an elixir. Going to call it "Cartwright's Cordial"'!' He pulled a case from beside the stool, undid the straps and displayed the contents.

'Is this it?' Lancelot took out a small vial, reading the label aloud. '"Cartwright's Cordial. The original and only genuine."' It claimed to cure every ailment known to man and a few others not yet discovered.

'Well, doctor?' Arthur watched him eagerly, proud of his brain-child. 'What d'you think? I'm snowed under by orders already – advertised in the newspapers and got a terrific response. Fu Yuan's letting me have the main ingredient, opium, at a low rate for quantity, so I can sell it dirt-cheap and still make a profit.' He suddenly smote himself on the forehead. Believing all men venal, he imagined he could save his neck. 'Tell you what! Why don't you let me cut you in on it? Several gentlemen've invested already, but I'd be more than happy to oblige you. Let's shake on it, eh?'

He held out his hand, smiling in his obnoxious oily manner. Lancelot did not take it. 'I'd rather enter into a pact with the devil,' he declared adamantly. 'The claims you make are wildly exaggerated, as you well know. I'll have nothing to do with your cheap-jack potion. Does it also cure an ache in the anus? Which is what you are, Mr Cartwright!' His pistol swung forward in an arc towards the window. It exploded with a horrifying crash and darting flames. Its muzzle jerked up, acrid smoke poured from it and the bullet hit the wall with a thud. A puff of white plaster drifted like snow to the silken carpet.

Arthur started. His face was ghastly, and his mouth fell open as if he was about to scream. Lancelot had a second weapon trained on him. 'All right! Don't shoot!' he cried, brag and swagger vanished.

'Speak, you dog!' Radu was behind Lancelot, the light sparking on his own weapon. 'Where is my wife?'

Arthur glared back at him, thinking of St Jules and the large sum that he had put into the cordial, not to mention the fee he had paid for the delivery of Mariana. He had a ruthless way of disposing of people who displeased him. 'She's back at Thornfalcon. She never was your wife, never will be – she's someone else's bit o' crackling! The sooner that fact sinks in, the better.'

Radu ignored this gratuitous thrust. 'And?' he prompted.

'St Jules got his hands on a letter she wrote to the Duchesse. Had the postmaster look out for any unusual mail and tip him the wink. She'd scribbled over the address but he's a fly one, knew how to make it clear again.' Arthur ran his tongue over his dry lips, eyeing the guns and the hard faces above them. 'He came straight to London, but didn't let on to her that he'd found her bolt-hole. Oh, no – he likes to bide his time, does St Jules – let the victim sweat a bit. He got me in on it, and some friends of mine. We watched her, and then we got her! Brought her here – he wanted to teach her a lesson, see. Forced drugs into her – not opium – something made of mushrooms – nasty stuff – gave her the screaming horrors!'

'He's driven her out of her mind!' shouted Radu, a powerful bundle of frustrated energy which seemed to fill the room.

'Maybe, maybe not. Who can tell?' Arthur shrilled, his mocking eyes flaring into flame for an instant. 'She's in a right state, or was when he carted her back home to Thornfalcon.'

'When did they leave?' The struggle for control was making Radu sweat. Mariana, in the hands of that man again, deprived of her reason by his poisons.

'This morning.' Arthur was regaining his confidence. These men were gentlemen, with silly notions of honour. They'd not shoot him down in cold blood. In this he was wrong. 'Forget her, Prince. Maybe it's better that she's mad – she'll be happier that way. Look at Agnes. No one could be more barmy, but she's content. She's taken a shine to me, and St Jules don't seem averse to me courting her. That would be a turn-up for the books. Me married into the family!'

Lancelot had a swift mental picture of the haughty Christopher St Jules, and thought the prospect most unlikely. 'He's using you.'

Arthur shrugged. 'He uses everyone. But I know his games. I'm too clever for him. Wouldn't that be cosy – the sister and, who knows, perhaps even the wife?'

'Watch your filthy tongue, lest I tear it out!' Radu snarled.

'They all wanted her. She's a good-looker, ain't she, your Highness? Got a fine body on her,' Arthur jeered. 'She made 'em all horny, but St Jules wouldn't let 'em have her. Funny him being so touchy about that, when it was a free-for-all on the solstice nights.'

'When you say "all", d'you mean the other male members of the coven?' asked Lancelot, pistol held in a rock-steady hand.

In a peculiar way, Arthur was enjoying himself. He liked being the centre of the stage. 'Coven? Oh, so you know about that. Well, yes, you could call our little gatherings covens, I suppose. I joined in for fun, to get along with St Jules, for the sake of business. My father's a bloody old skinflint, won't give me control of the mills, says I'm too young. I'll show him, I thought, I'll get in with the nobs. It was even better when I found out about this black-magic caper, for he's a religious sod, always cramming the bible down my throat. To do something which would shock him into a heart-attack if he found out – well, what a chance!'

'Go on,' urged Lancelot, scowling under his shaggy brows.

'We had a marvellous time – parties, gambling, drinking, and trying different substances which seemed to give the rest of 'em weird and wonderful sensations. Never affected me like that, just made me feel sick.' Arthur was launched, filled with a sense of importance as he recounted the antics of those stupid aristocrats who had believed in supernatural powers. 'They treated me like one of themselves, didn't give a damn that I wasn't titled. And the women! So free and easy. Mrs Wrixon, ill, poor bitch, but always ready for a tumble. Lady Somerville too, a bit of an old tart really. Oh, we had some times at Thornfalcon, I can tell you, but St Jules got nasty if anyone tried to roger his wife. He was dead set on begetting an heir – wanted a son so much that he didn't care what he did to get it.'

'What happened to Howard Blake?' Lancelot asked crisply.

'Fell from the tower.'

'Fell or was pushed?'

Arthur dabbed over his forehead with a red and white spotted handkerchief, visions of police questions, a prison cell, the loss of his money-making cordial imprinting themselves on his brain. 'He was sweet on Mariana. Tired of that old bag, his aunt. They thought he was going to spill the beans.'

'So they killed him?'

'Not exactly. They encouraged him to eat the mushrooms, many more than usual. Told him he could fly up to the universe and bring her back a star. He thought he was a beautiful golden eagle.' Arthur grinned feebly, sly eyes darting from one stern face to the other.

'He ended up with broken wings,' said Radu sardonically, but there was dread within him.

Emboldened by their stillness, Arthur tried to sidle towards the door, but Radu blocked the way. 'Give me a moment.' He did not request it of his friends, he demanded it, then grabbed Cartwright by the collar. 'Come on, you rat!' and he dragged him outside.

He returned alone, and Lancelot said, 'You haven't killed him?'

Radu massaged his bruised knuckles. 'He was spitting out teeth when I left. I think I've broken his nose.'

'Good!' David grinned.

'I must go to Yorkshire. Will you come?' asked Radu.

'Of course,' David replied as they stood at the bottom of the stairs while Lancelot directed Scrabbler in the difficult task of steering Edwin down them. 'They've a head-start, but we'll go faster on horseback.'

'Oh, David, will we be in time to save her?' Radu's eyes were wild as they sought his with hungry questions. David bowed his head, refusing to answer them.

*

A little snow had fallen during the night. Flakes lay like crystallized sugar on the stone steps of Thornfalcon's entrance. It crunched under Mariana's feet as she mounted them. The clouds were heavy with more to come, and a shrill high wind whistled around the house, but to her this was no human landscape. Everything was painfully bright, and she wondered how she had managed to reach the moon. She vaguely remembered an endless, frozen night of travelling, then nothing till she opened her eyes on a lunar view. Scientists had striven to achieve this for centuries, and she had done it. How remarkable! I'm actually walking on the moon! She took a tentative, floating step into a hall which was so enormously high that she could not see the ceiling. Is it inhabited by giants? Creatures of unusual proportions must dwell here.

'Is there anyone there?' Her voice sounded strange, the words jumbled, merging with fragmented notes as of an orchestra tuning up.

No one replied. Gleaming suits of armour stood on guard, mighty weapons grasped in empty mailed fists, empty visors staring. A log collapsed on the hearth with the jar of a pistol shot. Where were the giants? Perhaps she had the moon to herself. She cherished the notion. It became a rose in her hands – a rose gleaming with one pure crystal drop that had once been a tear. This palace – this castle – it was already changing, even as she watched, melting into those fearful majestic realms of dream scenery through which she was pursued by capering, jibbering apelike things, and where even the flowers were carnivorous. Her eyes started with terror. Yes, she could hear them at the door. Oh, why wouldn't her legs behave properly? She was so weak – so dizzy.

The staircase. That was the way. If she went silently, swiftly, perhaps she could hide from them, become minute, slip between a crack in the floorboards. The stairs were moving, a continual upward glide. She only had to stand on the bottom one to be carried smoothly to the top. How clever of the moon-people to invent this. She went through empty rooms, each one larger than the last and, despite her caution, her heels clacked like thunder on the polished boards. The apes were in the hall below, shrieking, indulging in vile antics, pointing up at her. Fear became tangible, a black form growing to horrific size.

She was standing outside the door – knew that she was forbidden to cross its threshold. I can't go in! No matter what! If I open it, I'll be banished from the moon and fall through space! But even as she felt herself already whirling in limitless dark, something grabbed her, the door opened and she was thrust inside.

The light was diffused, but it was brighter than that in the passageway. A circular room, curtains drawn across the windows, candles on an altar, a pentagram painted on the floor, and figures within it, robed and hooded, wearing animal masks. Two people were standing before the statue of a man-goat, its face beautiful, evil, curling hair springing around the horns on its head, at the base of its monstrous phallus.

There was absolute silence. Christopher turned from his adoration of Satan, staring across the circle at her. He too was robed, but in purest white. His face was painted as it had been on their wedding-night. As he moved, so did Agnes, shining like a star in the gloom, flashing with jewels. The person who was holding Mariana flung her to the floor and, wrenching at her hair, forced her face down. She could not move, could see nothing but Christopher's booted foot coming closer. It stopped near her head.

'Oh, woman, you have betrayed my trust and defiled my Master,' he said, in a soft, sad voice. 'You have lied to me. Deceived me. Spurned the greatness which I offered you.'

She felt his hand under her elbow, raising her, making her stand in front of him, staring at her with those lustrous, painted eyes. 'Why are you here?' she demanded, and in her ears her voice was harsh and quacking, the words disjointed, like crazy lines of poetry. 'You shouldn't be on the moon. It's too pure – too clean.'

'Be silent! You stand on sacred ground. None but His faithful worshippers enter here, unless for a special purpose or about to die.' His head was up, his eyes those of a visionary. 'Give glory to Him! Lord of all!'

The voices of his confederates rose, chanting in unison, then whispering meaningless words which bore dire menace. The whispers grew, sibilant, insidious – coiling round her, beating at her senses – a multitude of hideous voices, swamping her with horror. The air began to hum, very low at first, then increasing to a piercing whine. She pressed her fingers into her ears, but could not block it out. The forces of evil were present and her soul cringed in recognition. Great gales of laughter rocked the tower, thundering, echoing – derisive, mocking, lewd – destructive entities summoned from some unexplored dimension.

Christopher raised his jewelled staff. Silence fanned down and Mariana's mind was momentarily lucid. She was back at Thornfalcon! But how? 'You'd better let me go. At once, Christopher! D'you hear me?' It was a relief to storm and shout, to fight, to use scorn, the better to convince herself that this was reality.

She made a dash for the door. He caught her by the cloak, jerking her back. The masks were turned towards them, watching. Agnes stood in a trance, arms straight down at her sides, eyes blank. 'You're being very silly, my dear.' Christopher's voice was almost caressing. 'I shall never let you go. You'll never see Prince Radu again. You thought I was a fool, too drugged to know what you had been doing with him at your grandmother's house. You forget – drugs release my spirit from my mortal flesh. I watched you. Oh, yes – I was there – slipping like a mist beneath the door of the room where you lay, my peerless love, in shameless postures on the bed, your secret parts exposed to his obscene caresses. And then London – and lawyers – such betrayal!'

'You're mad!' She struggled in his grasp.

His grip on her wrists was numbing. He thrust something into her face. 'D'you recognize this, Mariana?'

It was a silver-handled riding crop, a common enough object. 'No! I've never seen it before!'

He threw her from him with such force that she stumbled and would have fallen had not her hands encountered the altar. He was smiling, running the crop between his palms, slowly, lovingly. 'It carries the crest of the House of Varna. How careless of your lover to leave it where it could be found by my good friend, Dr Russell. D'you still deny your sin?'

'Is it a sin to love? I'm glad that you know, Christopher. Perhaps you'll accept that I hate you – detest Thorn-falcon – desire to leave you, for good.' She was becoming disoriented again, the scene flashing with vivid lights. Death looked out of his eyes.

'My dark and lovely one, how I have adored you.' His voice was ineffably sad, his dilated pupils reflecting points of light, like the stars in the depths of infinite night, which he had once shown her. 'But you're a poison in my blood, keeping me from my Master. I think of you when I should be prostrating myself before Him. I was deceived by those wide eyes, so full of faith and love, and by that mouth which stopped my heart. No male child sprang from your womb, and now you run from me. You must be punished.' He beckoned the shrouded man who had brought her there. 'Remove her cloak.'

Mariana struggled, clawed, thrashed out with her legs, but was overpowered, her cloak torn off, the back of her gown pulled open to the waist. The apes had come, slobbering, licking their thick lips.

She was pushed across the altar, face-down, arms spread wide. Christopher leaned over her, his fingers smoothing her naked shoulders. 'Such beautiful white skin, but your lover's whip shall make roses blossom on it – red, red, roses . . .'

The first blow took her by surprise, the smarting agony jerking her against the hands that held her. The second sent a scream tearing from her throat. After that she became a mindless, writhing, tortured animal, aware of nothing but pain, until it seemed that her bleeding back and Radu's crop had become one and the same, blending in a great white searing heat.

'Release her.' Christopher's voice came from a long way off. The hands vanished and she slumped down, sliding to the base of the altar. A touch on her hair, and he was kneeling beside her, wiping the tears and sweat from her face. 'Beloved, I've shared your pain, every flick of the lash has stung me also. There's a bond between us that nothing can sever.'

Banished from the moon. It was true, that forbidden door. She had been taken to a precipice and hurled into the universe, falling through the stars. How pretty they looked floating past. Falling to strike the roaring ocean, the waves parted to let her visit Neptune's kingdom. The haughty mermaids swam by, ignoring her. With a gentle bump, she opened her eyes, expecting to see sand, fishes and swirling sea-weed.

She lay on a bed of leaves. Stretching out an arm she encountered lichenous stone, recognized her surroundings and trembled. It was a cell where gamekeepers flung poachers. A small, confined space, damp and dark, somewhere in the depths of the woods. She could smell the odour of leaf-mould. The warm trickle of blood inched down her back and self-pity swamped her. Poor body, it was so hurt, so broken. Light was filtering through an iron grating. When she dragged herself to her knees, her head touched the mossy roof. There was blood on the hands which gripped the bars. She shook them and, unexpectedly, they were not fastened. But why? For what purpose had they put her there and made freedom possible? What cruel game was Christopher playing? Cautiously Mariana edged her way out. Her dress was torn, her cloak gone. It was cold. She was in a glade, dripping with winter and the creeping shadows of evening. Run, said a voice in her head. 'I can't,' she whimpered. Run – run!

Up and away, each step an agony, the trees spinning, the orange sky too bright. Leaving the shelter of the cell, going upwards, the biting moorland wind tangling her hair, drying the blood and sweat. Up and back into the past – the moors – the gibbet – her baby – all flashed by like images in a child's flicker-lamp. She was there, yet not there. She was dreaming. She was awake. There rose a baying in the distance. The apes were on her track. She could see figures on the skyline, not apes but mastiffs, and riders too. She was a fox, a hind, an escaped slave, being hunted for sport before the slaughter.

The weird song of the hounds spoke of a triumphant gaining on their quarry. Mariana ran into the luminescence of the gory sunset, up to higher ground strewn with boulders, dominated by the Devil's Tor. No! No! the breath rattled in her throat – not that grim rock! But she began to climb the slope, her feet slipping on the sheathing frost. Her hands and knees were bleeding from where she had fallen. Glancing back, she saw savage shapes leaping up towards her. Their eyes shone like burning coals as they gave tongue to a chorus of snarls. She reached the plateau and turned at bay, her back pressed against stone. The sky was livid, shot through with flame, greens and purples radiating from that massive orange ball poised on the horizon. The riders were black silhouettes etched for an instant against it before surrounding her, the growling, blood-hungry dogs whipped into submission.

Mariana was beyond speech, but she flinched as Christopher dismounted and came to her, his cloak tossed by the icy blast. 'My darling, my misguided love,' he said gently. 'Don't be afraid. I'm going to keep you somewhere safe, where no one shall disturb your everlasting slumber. I shall come – only I. Then we'll talk together, embrace one another – you'll be mine for all time.'

At his signal, four of his companions stepped forward, lifting her to the bare granite slab where once her child had lain. With slow, measured tread, the masked figures began to circle. Christopher's voice rang out, strong and serene. 'Mariana, these are your judges. Look at their faces. They would have been your friends had you obeyed and joined us. You were the Chosen One, selected to be my bride and give a son to my House.'

The masks were gone, the hoods flung back. One by one, she saw them, those people who had been her guests and servants. The pieces of the jig-saw were slotting into place. The doctor was smirking down at her, and Grant smiling his placid smile. She gripped him by the sleeve, halting his stately passage. 'You're a churchman! How can you do this?' she accused hoarsely.

He did not reply, freeing himself and drifting onward. Christopher's head was touched with crimson, his pristine robe flecked by sunset and her blood. His face was calm and austere. Both of his hands were clasped around the hilt of a long, shining knife. The worshippers began to circle faster to the quickened beat of their rhythmical chanting.

Mariana stared up at him, marshalling the remnants of thought. 'What of your heir? You won't get one from a corpse.'

His expression was tranquil. 'A new bride has already been nominated. Ah, don't be jealous, jewel of my life. I'll visit you in your tomb. The rich decay of your body will be sweeter to me than attar of roses and sandalwood. Your Lord will rain pearls, rubies, sapphires, upon your winding-sheet. When I take my bride to the marriage-bed, I'll be embracing your putrescent flesh.' The knife swept up, then began its downward plunge towards Mariana's heart.

In that instant, Agnes hurled herself on him with a shriek of fury. 'No more brides!' she cried, her face distorted with jealous rage. 'I am your bride! Your priestess! You shall not have another!' She snatched the blade from him with a surge of lunatic strength and thrust it, hilt-deep, into his chest. His warm blood gushed down on Mariana. She came to her senses, leaping from the altar, running towards the men who now burst upon the sacrificial scene.

'Stand back!' Radu shouted to her, and she froze.

He raised the musket to his shoulder and fired both barrels into the bewildered coven. Noise exploded through the gathering murk, as the golden light faded into dusk. Spyros took one of the bullets, his body tossed back over the slab. Wodehouse was bellowing, blood oozing between his fingers as he crawled, leaving a red trail behind him.

'Hurrah! You've winged two of the bastards!' came a scream of delight from Lancelot, following this up with a cascade of curses and rapid fire from his own gun.

The coven were yelling, falling over one another as they tried to reach their horses. 'Don't let them escape!' shouted David, rushing between the rocks with men at his shoulder, the grooms and farm-workers who formed his makeshift force.

Above the tumult of shots, screams and oaths, Agnes was crying out in exaltation from the top of the crag, her cloak streaming in the gale. 'Christopher! We can fly!' She spread out her arms like the wings of a great bird and stepped into space.

Mariana was seated amidst the jumble of boulders, Christopher's head cradled on her lap. The imprint of death was on his face, his robe stiff with blood. She knew that Agnes had thrown herself from the tor, knew that men were mounting up and chasing the others, was aware of Lancelot stamping around issuing commands, of Radu bending over her, but Christopher was dying and she had to ease his passing.

He opened his eyes which were still ice-blue, and there was confusion in them. 'Mariana – I'm cold,' he whispered. 'Cover me with your hair.' She leaned low, so that her unbound locks streamed over him. He smiled gently, and he was a child again, seeking warmth and comfort, nestling against her. 'I love you, Mariana,' he whispered, and then his lids closed and his head fell to one side.

EPILOGUE

Lancelot bent, scraped a match against the heel of his boot and applied the flame to his pipe. 'That was the best half-hour of my life,' he grunted as he puffed, a cloud of bluish smoke obscuring his features. He and David were sitting by the fire in the library of Kenrick Old Court, going over the fight for the hundredth time.

'Most satisfying, I agree,' David nodded, lounging in a leather armchair, feet cocked up on a stool. 'What a nest of vipers!'

'Pity we couldn't have brought them to justice,' Lancelot reflected. 'Too many important people involved. The magistrate wanted it hushed up. His own son belonged to the coven.'

Lancelot and David had done sterling work during the days following the débâcle. The doctor had gone through Christopher's private papers, after obtaining Mariana's permission to do so. She had been in no fit state to undertake such a task. Astonishing things had been revealed, a network of intrigue involving several statesmen. As Lancelot had suspected, Christopher had relied on blackmail to recruit his followers. The injured Captain Wodehouse had confessed to much, his information supplementing the letters, lists and diaries which Christopher had kept in the cupboard in his laboratory. Wodehouse himself had been indebted to him through some disgraceful card-sharping which Christopher had concealed. Lancelot cornered Dr Russell, and threatened to publish the fact that he was given to ingratiating himself with wealthy patients and then administering poison when they had signed over their fortunes.

Another worthy who made a sudden decision to leave the district after a visit from Lancelot was the Reverend Grant. According to Christopher's records, he had a predilection for sexually assaulting minors. A little girl had been found strangled in the woods, a farmer's child. There had been a hue and cry, but the culprit had never been brought to book. Christopher had seen to that. Ever after, Grant had been his

400

creature. As Lancelot rummaged among the sordid secrets of those supposed to be in charge of the community, his faith in human beings took a downward slide. He wanted to throw the whole scandalous business to the newspapers, but knew very well that those most deeply implicated would somehow escape retribution, whereas Mariana's and Radu's names would be smirched by publicity.

'Ay, 'tis best if the wretched affair is forgotten,' he sighed, speaking his thoughts aloud.

David stretched, and shot him a glance. 'Forgotten? D'you suppose that Mariana will ever forget?'

'The wounds will heal, given time and Radu's loving care.' Lancelot leaned forward to tap out his pipe on the fire-dogs and poke at a log, watching the busy flames. Then he straightened and glanced at the clock whose tick punctuated the fitful rushing sound of the wind round the house. 'You'll be off shortly?'

The library was dim, a warm golden dimness. The scent of the burning wood on the hearth mingled with the spice of old leather, the pungency of yellowing parchment, and of faded print upon ancient paper. It would be a cold journey and David was not looking forward to it. He had grown lazy under the splendid cooking and indulgent attentions of Margery, who had insisted that the three men stay at the manor, instead of roughing it at Coleshill Abbey, with only the caretaker to look after them.

'Must get back to Georgiana,' he said with a grin. 'She'll be wondering what the devil's happened. She was very good about my coming up here again. I've written to her, of course, but it's not exactly the sort of thing one wants to commit to paper. I'm wondering how to tell her about it without frightening her.'

Lancelot stirred restlessly. Margery was late in bringing in the morning coffee and cakes. 'She'll take it in her stride, I shouldn't wonder. Same as she'll take to motherhood, my boy.'

'You'll be returning to London yourself soon?' David wanted him there for Georgiana's confinement.

'Yes. It seems that Mariana has appointed me to settle the complicated legal affairs. You know that she's given me Thornfalcon? Wanted to set fire to the place, said that she couldn't bear to own it!' Lancelot's frugal nature had been shocked by such impetuosity.

David chuckled, rising to his feet, tall and strong, ruddy-cheeked and healthy. Like Lancelot, he had thoroughly enjoyed erupting into action. 'What the deuce are you going to do with such a rambling monstrosity?'

'I'll turn it into a hospice for the sick and homeless. It'll do

401

those poor devils from the slums no end of good. The brisk moorland air will aid the consumptives, and the children can learn about country matters.'

'Oh, Lance, you silly, kindly old fool!' David looked down at him fondly. 'They'll take shameless advantage of your generosity, and get you in terrible trouble with the locals with their thieving ways. You'll be beggared in six months. How the hell are you going to support it?'

Lancelot gave a philosophic shrug. 'Oh, ye of little faith! I'm not as daft as I look! Mariana, bless her heart, has turned over the St Jules fortune to me as well. Couldn't stomach using his money for herself, but she's made ample provision for her brothers and sisters. She'll be rich in her own right, when the old girl dies.'

'Madame was quite tickled to meet her other granddaughters, and makes a great fuss of Ernestine's little lad,' said David and they exchanged a smile at the antics of the eccentric Duchesse. 'Looking forward to a visit from Bob and Tom, when they come home from school for Christmas. Can't help feeling that she favours males.'

There were voices at the library door and Lancelot looked up hopefully, but it was not Margery with the tray. Mariana and Radu came in. Both were dressed for the journey, warmly wrapped against the freezing winter day. She was wearing a black velvet mantle, her face framed by its sable collar, a matching muff covering one arm. A small black bonnet partly hid her shining dark ringlets, but the sombre veil was drawn away from her pale cheeks. The strain still showed, but she had regained her charm and beauty, together with a look of depth and wisdom which suffering had brought.

'My dear,' Lancelot went to take her hand, staring at her under those eyebrows which were like couch-grass. 'Don't get too tired on the journey.' He rounded on Radu with mock severity. 'I charge you to see to this, Highness. Make frequent stops and allow her to rest. She's not fully recovered from those beastly drugs and her savage beating. The wounds to mind and body have yet to heal completely.'

Radu flicked his long riding cloak back with his elbows and put his arm around her protectively. 'I'll follow your instructions, my friend. We'll be delaying in London for a few days before taking ship for home.'

How strange that sounded, and how sweet, Mariana thought, resting her head against his shoulder. She knew a difficult time still faced them. Protocol would demand a delay before they went through another marriage ceremony, people would try to prevent it, but she had absolute faith that they would surmount human obstacles. They were one and nothing would ever part them again, she told herself repeatedly, and yet, despite all she did, the day that Christopher had died continued to be more real to her than the present. She was haunted by his face as he slipped into eternity, by the words of love on his lips, frozen there for ever.

The last two weeks had gone in a flash and yet seemed to drag on interminably. Lancelot had ordered her to bed, not allowing her to rise until after the funeral, then he had insisted that she did nothing of which she did not feel capable. There had been much joy in the reunion with her sisters, and she had hugged Susan and Margaret as if she would never let them go, and smiled through her tears over the downy head of Ernestine's baby boy. She was a self-possessed mother now, anticipating another child. Mariana had been impressed by her neat cottage and contented appearance. Jamie was prospering, a hard worker, Ernestine had assured her, but she had added, with a rueful smile, that he had not lost his roving eye.

Annabelle proved to be more beautiful than ever, though sulky because pregnancy prevented her gadding. She dominated her dull, farmer husband who watched her with adoring eyes. Mariana had found herself conjecturing as to whether he really was the father of the child she carried. Perhaps even Annabelle did not know. Mariana had taken them to be introduced to their grandmother. Knowing that she herself was leaving shortly, Mariana hoped they would be of comfort to her.

Four sisters, two with their lives as yet unshaped. Mariana had provided for each of them, with Lancelot in charge. Susan's and Margaret's portion would be handled by him and the reliable Ernestine until they were eighteen. She made one condition only in every case: no matter what they felt for their husbands or lovers, they must never, never relinquish their wealth. If a woman had money, she was well-armed, able to hold her head high, no man's slave. Ernestine understood, reading her mind. When Mariana presented her with financial independence, she had also given her the whip-hand. If Jamie wanted to end up with a fishing-fleet of his own, then he would have to curb his philandering.

Mariana was sorry not to have seen her brothers, but they were at boarding-school. She made certain that funds were available to ensure that this continued and, as they grew older, it could be drawn on for further education or business investments. So, these matters settled, there should have been nothing stopping her from departing with a peaceful mind, but there was a duty remaining, one she dreaded.

'My darling, are you all right?' Radu was recalling her to the present, the snug library, the anxious faces of her friends.

She smiled up at him. 'Yes, of course.' She saw his dark face, his straight brows and those eyes which held the hauteur, sadness and turbulence of a warrior prince. It gave her courage for the task before her. She had discussed the matter with the doctor and Radu, and Margery had also advised her, dipping into her well of folk-lore.

Lancelot rocked on his heels before the fire, giving her an anxious glance. 'You're going to do it?'

'I must,' she answered simply.

'D'you want me to come with you? It's probably a lot of damned nonsense, all in your mind, m'dear, but if it makes you feel better . . .' He had been saying this or something similar ever since he realized that she was serious. Open-minded, he would have been the last man to try and stop her. He knew that she was convinced evil had existed in that tower room and on the Devil's Tor. Who was he to say that she was wrong? In his opinion, any man who did not consider the possible reality of a supernatural force was a bigoted fool.

Mariana leaned forward and kissed him on the cheek. 'Don't worry about me. I feel strong enough to do it.'

'Time to go, Lance,' Radu interjected. 'We'll see you in London before we sail, I hope. By the by, the Duchesse has been giving us a bad time. Doesn't want Mariana to leave. She's in a black sulk. Wouldn't even bid us God-speed.'

'I'll look after her. She can move to Thornfalcon and queen it there.' Lancelot accompanied them into the hall where David was ensuring that their luggage had been safely stowed in the carriage.

Mariana shuddered, her hand tightening on Radu's arm. 'How can you contemplate spending time there? What of the ghosts?'

'Ghosts!' Lancelot gave a loud guffaw. 'They'll not be able to stand the competition when Madame and my tearaways are in residence. Glad to slink back to their graves, I shouldn't wonder. Margery'll soon have the place filled with wholesome air. Did I tell you that I've invited her to be housekeeper?'

David came stamping in, endearingly normal in his grey overcoat and jauntily cocked top-hat. 'Are you ready?' he shouted.

'One thing more.' Mariana hesitated for a second, and then said tactfully: 'Edwin needs a home of his own. I'm certain that half his trouble is envy of you, David. If Madame is going to Thornfalcon, why don't we let him have Kenrick Old Court?'

'What a singularly shrewd woman you are, Mariana.' Lancelot beamed his approval. 'Get him out of London – do him a power of good. Away from such rogues as Cartwright, who'll try to involve him in their nefarious schemes. Though I've a hunch that he's going to clean up a fortune with his patent medicine. Ah, well, ''The rain falls on the just and unjust alike.'''

'Don't forget that Christopher put money into ''Cartwright's Cordial'','' she reminded. 'The profits will help you to run your hospital.'

Margery was at the front door, and she clasped Mariana in her arms. 'Take care of yourself, my dear. Remember what I've told you. Evil can't harm you if your intentions are pure. You have the things in readiness?'

Mariana nodded, and touched her reticule. 'They're here. I should be afraid but, strangely, I'm not.'

There was so much to be said that words failed them, and then this emotion-charged moment was shattered by the sound of Madame shouting from within the drawing-room. It was not possible to catch the words, but her tone was one of fury. Lancelot grimaced, pressed Radu's hand, slapped David on the shoulder, and blew Mariana a kiss. Then he thrust open the door, ducking neatly as a vase came hurtling towards him, smashing against the frame.

'What's all this?' he demanded sharply as he entered. 'I gather that you've been misbehaving, Madame. A pity, for I was going to allow you to beat me at backgammon. Any more temper-tantrums, and I'll be forced to put you across my knee and whack your backside!' Just as the door shut behind him, the Duchesse's laugh trilled out, as merry and delighted as that of a young girl.

'Have you told David?' Mariana asked Radu as they settled into the coach. Her eyes were huge behind her dusky veil. He nodded, linking his fingers with hers. 'It's something I must do,' she added.

'I know.' His face was grave as he raised her hands to kiss them.

The snow had been sifting thinly down, a soft layer on the road which had become like iron in the merciless grip of the intense frost. Thornfalcon glittered with it, every turret, each pinnacle and chimney sparkling in the cold air, beneath the pallid rays of the sun. The carriage drew up before it, and Mariana walked the little distance to the chapel, letting herself into its solitude. The atmosphere was like an oppressive stone on her heart. With an awed deliberation, she unlatched the portals of her senses, lit one of the altar candles and slid back the heavy iron bolts which secured the door of the crypt.

She prayed aloud as she went down the steps, the candle in one hand, the other held out, fist clenched, thumb between her fingers to ward off evil. It was dank and icy cold. Radu. She kept his face in the forefront of her mind – her sword and buckler. Her calm was astonishing as she went round the chamber, finding further candles, sending light into every gloomy corner, following Margery's instructions, Radu's too. It had been amazing how the legends of his country and the lore of hers coincided. Concentrate, she lectured herself sternly, don't let anything divert you from your purpose. Side by side lay the two coffins of the last of the St Juleses, almost as close in death as they had been before birth, and during life.

Keep that feeling of peace, that state of euphoria which denies fear, she prayed inwardly, putting down the candle and taking the ritual objects from her bag. Each had been duplicated and she laid them reverently on the coffins. Much time and intention had gone into their making. The amulets were metal discs, with an equal cross in the centre, letters scratched on the cross itself, and also round the edges. They seemed to glow, and she repeated their words aloud:

'*Crux Sancta sit mihi lux.* Holy Cross be my light. *Ne daemon sit mini dux.* Let no evil spirit be my guide. *Vade retro Satana, ne suade mihi vana; sunt mala quae libas. Ipse venena bibas.* Get thee behind me Satan, suggest no vain delusions; what thou offerest is evil. Thou thyself drinkest poison.'

The vault echoed her, but she detected no mockery, finishing her work by laying wreaths of specially selected herbs, gathered in the right phase of the moon, at the head of each amulet. Then she sank to her knees beside Christopher's coffin, crying to him: 'Oh, husband! Christopher! Set me free! Don't make my spirit your domain. I can forgive, and so can you. Our child is with you. Listen to her innocent voice of wisdom. What happened between us had to be. Destiny had willed it. Now pass on. Make reparation. Don't cling to me! Let go!'

A deep hush settled and, face buried in her hands, she became conscious that its quality had changed, as if a great grey mass of cloud had dissipated. Her knees were so stiff when she rose, that she guessed she had been kneeling there for some time. Carefully blowing out every candle save the one she had brought with her, she went back to the chapel. It was filled with muted colours as the sun filtered through the stained glass. Somewhere outside, a bird was singing.

In the frosty drive, the great Cunyngham coach stood like a galleon, its four-horse team pawing the icing-sugar coating of snow, smoky breath curling from their nostrils. The driver was in command of this proud vessel, cocked-hatted and many-caped, flourishing his whip, whilst his minions, in the shape of grooms and out-riders, took their orders. There was an air of impatience. They must depart at once if they were to reach the first posting-inn before dusk.

'Thank God! There you are!' Radu's face was alight with relief when Mariana came into view. 'David and I were about to come and rescue you.'

'Shouldn't have gone down there alone!' scolded David from his seat on his tall horse. 'Radu's only just told me what you were up to! Don't know that I approve! The dead are dead, and should be left alone.'

Mariana's face held a tranquil radiance which silenced their fears. Her smile was beautiful. 'It is accomplished,' she said simply, looking at Radu.

He's mine – all mine – dear God! she thought. Mine, all the rich, glad, fearless freedom of his life. Mine, all the rapturous, caressing, priceless passion of his love! It was as if night had been vanquished by a shining dawn, and she laughed, carefree, cured, ready to take part in any adventure he liked to suggest.

With his assistance, Mariana entered the warm, luxurious vehicle, then he was beside her. 'Are you really safe, my love?' he asked, face set with worry. 'What happened in the crypt?'

'I'll tell you later. I don't want to think of it any more.' She clasped his hands, glancing at him teasingly, the black veil flung carelessly aside. 'Aren't you going to ride with David?'

His answering smile was deep and loving. He insinuated an arm around her shoulders. 'I want to be near you, always. Time enough for riding when I'm forced to leave you and lead my soldiers. There's work awaiting me at home. I received a dispatch this morning, telling of an uprising on the Turkish border. But for now, we won't dwell on that, thinking only of each other.'

With a crack of the whip, the horses leaned against the straps, and they were in motion, swinging out through Thornfalcon's massive gates. Mariana did not look back. She turned her face towards London, and Europe, and the distant mountains of Radu's country. The past was already a dream – some unholy nightmare through which she had lived to wake in the peace of his arms. The noontide sun gathered strength, slanting through the window, touching her face as if bestowing a blessing.